THE REALMS OF KALANISI

The Decepter Voyage

THE REALMS OF KALANISI

THE DECEPTER VOYAGE

K D AUSTIN

Copyright © 2024 K D Austin

The moral right of the author has been asserted.

Apart from any fair dealing for the purposes of research or private study, or criticism or review, as permitted under the Copyright, Designs and Patents Act 1988, this publication may only be reproduced, stored or transmitted, in any form or by any means, with the prior permission in writing of the publishers, or in the case of reprographic reproduction in accordance with the terms of licences issued by the Copyright Licensing Agency. Enquiries concerning reproduction outside those terms should be sent to the publishers.

This is a work of fiction. Names, characters, businesses, places, events and incidents are either the products of the author's imagination or used in a fictitious manner. Any resemblance to actual persons, living or dead, or actual events is purely coincidental.

Troubador Publishing Ltd
Unit E2 Airfield Business Park,
Harrison Road, Market Harborough,
Leicestershire LE16 7UL
Tel: 0116 279 2299
Email: books@troubador.co.uk
Web: www.troubador.co.uk

ISBN 978 1836280 071

British Library Cataloguing in Publication Data.
A catalogue record for this book is available from the British Library.

Printed and bound by CPI Group (UK) Ltd, Croydon, CR0 4YY
Typeset in 11pt Minion Pro by Troubador Publishing Ltd, Leicester, UK

Chapter One
The Contract

In the deep, mysterious universe known as Kalanisi, the galactic year is currently 4010. It is thousands of light years away from the old earth's solar system, with that planet decaying 800 years ago. The need to continue human civilisation means exploring uncharted worlds and encountering unknown species.

The progressive scientific technology gives humanity the ability to develop hyperspace travel, which enables them to penetrate a vast expansion of the deepest and darkest corners of the newfound universe, Kalanisi. The Galactic Corporal Union was founded to govern the affairs of the Universe. All governments and elites from the dissolved Sol system have united to establish a governing body for the entire galaxy to promote peace for human civilisation. They enforce most of the law across the galaxy and have previously only acted with integrity. However, a new Director was elected to the Corporal Union's committee two years ago.

Now, this Director, Wilson Volantis, has taken a more authoritarian approach to control since obtaining a mysterious data box. The mastermind politician has stripped away the free will of the citizens of the Kalanisi Universe with the political backing of an intergalactic news network, Mbron Media Limited. The untrustworthy Android Association operates this.

Volantis is propagandising a false picture of united prosperity of the Corporal Union's true motives of power. For citizens of the intergalactic civilisation, opposing the government's decisions poses a grave risk of being lost in the vast voids of space with no trace. This is especially true for those residing in the outskirts of the Suvarna cluster system, where the Corporal Union holds little sway over the governance of the universe. It is an intergalactic trade route shipping-lane meeting place that is out of the Corporal Union's patrolling jurisdiction.

Usually used by small inner-space terraforming businesses, the route attracts roguish smugglers and devours marauders-for-hire who supply the expanding colonisation of inhabited liveable planets around the sector of the Suvarna cluster. The main spaceport haven is an old grey dust ball of a crater moon called Latin-Versa. Most of the deliverables for terraforming equipment are shipped off and stored on the moon. At the same time, the contractors of the planetarium projects self-extract when required for terraforming assignments across new potential worlds.

Approaching the Suvarna cluster is Dan Casey, a successful freelance cargo-runner pilot with a sleek freighter named the *Decepter*. He has a wealth of experience in the space industry, having previously been part of a security space protection group. Following the group's closure due to an unfortunate incident, Dan took ownership of *Decepter* and converted parts of the star-vessel to create a top-of-the-line commercial cargo-running freighter.

Over the last five years, Dan Casey has made a name for himself as a reliable delivery service pilot, quickly taking on interstellar space-flight contracts. With the help of his trusty computerised AI system, Pearl, he is more than equipped to handle any challenge that comes his way.

His contract involves delivering the latest terraforming tech to Sandtex Ltd, an executive company located on the small, gravelled moon of Latin-Versa.

With *Decepter*, Casey travels freely through the hyperspace slipstreams of space and cruises with a whistling drone of high-speed velocity. The slick starship freighter can suddenly submerge with a silent pulsed flash bang, effectively maintaining fluency in the hyper-speed lanes, thus pitching a turning point for the destination of Latin-Versa.

Upon close inspection, the motioning starship, *Decepter*, can be identified as a Machiavellian MK2 Merlin class freighter vessel, a type now considered old-fashioned.

Its shadow silhouette exhibits a streamlined cone-shaped nose and a curved cargo hull, suggesting a ship designed to transport goods efficiently.

The boosters, which appear to be slanted at a three-pinon angle, seem to be the means of propulsion, indicating a reliance on older technology.

The ship's exterior shows signs of wear and tear, including scorch marks and dents, suggesting a long history of use. Despite its age, the starship's design is still striking and evocative, providing a glimpse into the development of spacecraft design over time.

The *Decepter* swiftly closes in on the approaching planetary orbit sequence entry pattern. Inside the interior cabin, Dan Casey comfortably sits in his leather pneumatic pilot's recliner with a black seat. Looking suave and handsome, he wears his brown sleeveless leather waist jacket, basic black t-shirt, matching pilot jeans and supporting finger-cut gloves. He is also stylishly equipped with a half-spacing holster belt containing his silver base, black smoke, and barrelled handgun.

Dan flicks the control pad switches. Adjusting the decorating pitch speed, he asks the starship's AI in his rich, attractive tone, "Hey Pearl, you got us that clearance authentication code. We are approaching the Latin-Versa moon port, plus once we're on schedule, the Sandtex rep will be happy. Hopefully, we'll get the drop-off bonus we deserve, as this isn't the highest-paying credit contract due to all at Mbron Media, cyber service androids! They're taking all the decent cargo contract work and shouldn't be allowed. Damn, tin-headed goons. No offence, Pearl!"

Dan Casey is ahead with the unvalued Sandtex Ltd delivery job as he pilots the *Decepter* through grey moons and orbiting dust particles of Latin-Versa.

The AI computer, Pearl, flashes a crystallised response report to him in a sexy female cyber synthetic voice, "We have clearance to land at port two, hanger bay three. Yet another anti-android quotation of no offence."

The cargo pilot brushes his hands over his thick, black hair. Dan smirks a smiling reply to the starship's AI suite, "Oh, come on, Pearl, don't be like that, sweetheart. You know I'm not keen on tinheads. They're making me unemployed. Plus, you're more of a beautiful crystal to me than a cyber pale-faced tin pot."

His freighter starship swoops in low and steady, rapidly decelerating from the approaching high cruise speed to a more plausible gentle hovering over the moon base facility, easing to a safe touch-down procedure.

A bunching bundle of Mbron Media service cyberbots gather a static grounding hold, and on the moon port, they chug about in forklift-unloader pods. They are now preparing to unload the Sandtex Ltd companies' shipments of terraforming tech equipment.

Inside the starship's flight cabin, a relaxed Dan Casey picks himself out of the pilot's chair, standing to the attention of the job at hand. He takes a casual step to the airlock hatch while hinting at his onboard AI. "Take care of the unloading technique, Pearl. I'll go sign in with the docking port officer, look around, get some supplies, and make sure we can confirm the payment of the credits for the terraforming shipment before launch. As it's more than well known, these deep space manufacturing companies like Sandtex Ltd sometimes try pulling a fast one. I won't be long now. Like I said, easy drop-off."

Pearl flashes a response to Dan Casey's scheduled commands to vacate the vessel. "Engaging cargo hull hatch and extracting slip ramp, linking transaction details to holo secure connection of Sandtex Ltd accounts. Please try to keep out of trouble, Dan. We wouldn't want to anger any service unloader androids again!"

While taking care of the unloading procedures, Dan Casey motions to leave his star-vessel to book the Sandtex Ltd shipment with the Latin-Versa moon's portside officials.

The Machiavellian freighter's armoured hull and cone-angled nose gleam a reflective vinyl matt shine in the dark, mild atmosphere of Latin-Versa's nightly moonlit environment. The starship freighter's airlock hatch shifts open with a short hissing pressure burst of condensation steam that instantly evaporates into a fading mist.

Dan Casey starts to make a move. He swiftly vacates the starship's hatch stairway, casually taking an intriguing glance around docking bay three's port facility while vainly searching for the Latin-Versa's port-bay chief docking officer. Dan's dreamy brown eyes squint over a focused frown. To him, something looks odd.

The gathering cyberbots unload the equipment packages with an army of forklifts, then store them securely in the storage warehouse on the moon base. The portside officials are all busy in the management offices.

Dan Casey asks himself what the galactic security personnel are searching for, as he believes he's witnessing a couple of the Corporal Union's high guard representatives accompanied by an armed batch of ten security troopers. To him, they appear to be doing a scattered search around port one's docking facility.

Instinctively, Dan Casey mutters, "Seems to be a Corporal

Union's scout patrol planetside. That's strange, as the Suvarna cluster is well out of their lawful jurisdiction. There must be something big going down for a federal outfit to be here on a dust ball like this dump. I want no part of being near when it kicks off. Now, where is this docking chief? Lounging about on the job, no doubt."

A bewildered Dan Casey ponders and inspects his bearing. He reaches into his black pilot jeans pockets for his filter smokes and taps a filter out of the scrunched packet, stylishly flicking the filter smoke into his mouth. He pulls his Astro-lighter from his opposite jean cup pockets and sparks a flame. He inhales the green smoke deeply, blowing, gusting smoke cloud.

"Must get some supplies before I launch again!"

Suddenly, he notices an attractive woman with amazingly long pastel green silky hair. Smartly dressed in a tight black jumpsuit. He admires the woman's curvy feminine features, which are shown in a pleasing, high-class display.

Dan Casey is awestruck as the woman clicks her high-heeled leather boots, sexily strutting by, and swings her designer handbag over a short zipper jacket wrapped around her slender waistline. She flirtatiously tilts her gorgeous face and shows off her piercing jade eyes, beaming a seductive sparkling glint of a smile.

Dan Casey stands in an altered state of consciousness, witnessing the wiggling rear view of the sexual green-haired woman casually walking by the Hanger bay. She struts ahead into the mingling mixed bunch of freelance trading smugglers and rogue-type business acquaintances. They are the ones expected at Latin-Versa haven port, veeringly deep in the outer rims of the hazy Suvarna cluster.

Suddenly, he feels a forceful hand tapping on his right broad shoulder. Dan sharply spins, huffing an interrupted response of words, "What the?"

He realises that the moon depot's chief officer is shouting.

"Hey, Mr, hurry up! Get on with it, yeah? Do you want to sign a log for this Sandtex shipment, or are you just going to stand there looking at an Astro-hooker's arse all day?" angrily states a middle-aged skinny, pale-faced male. He is holding a dock-port holo-scanner.

"Let's scan a holo-print of your signature. Then you can look at as many arses as you like, thank you."

Dan Casey tries to keep the tense individual happy and applies the hand holo-scan.

"Move on and wait for the unloading to finish. We're a bit short-staffed today. There are going to be a few delays, Mr Casey. Your holo-scan accepted signature is accepted. We got a few lazy Mbron cyberbots bugged out; they are currently offline, reckoning their cores are lagged out, so you will have to wait out your delay elsewhere. Next!"

But Dan is hungry and asks the cranky officer, "Hey, sorry. I know you're busy, but where can I get a beverage or supplies?"

The hanger bay foreman turns his tired-looking face with a disgruntled glare of pure annoyance. Scruffily dressed in his peaked cap and a uniform that needs a good wash, he huffs a response, "Okay, anything to see the back of you pestering cargo-runner pilots! You've been in the air too long, mate. You have forgotten what hard work is like on your feet all day. Now, follow the track to the end, turn left, and find an old watering saloon. Called the Rhinegold-Goose. Now just go, will you?"

The dashing freighter pilot obligingly remarks, "Thank you kindly."

Dan then heads down the dusty swept track, clearing a trail on the one-way route to the direction of the Latin-Versa saloon.

Dan Casey sees an expanse of beautiful clashing star clusters and colourised nebula gas clouds. It is a blissful sighting of deep space harmony.

Among the hustle and bustle of the Corporal Union's

scout guards, Dan sees the saloon bar, a rundown one-level building. To him, it looks like an old satellite office that has been transitioned into a local cantina for interstellar travellers. He sees a swinging sign outside the saloon-type doorway.

He mumbles out loud to himself. Dan Casey recalls the sign's slogan. 'The Rhinegold-Goose, a haven of happiness.' Dan wonders if it will live up to its happy namesake.

With a nudging push of the swinging doors, he enters.

Instantly, he is met by the pulsing pounding of repetitive ambience bass beats overlayed by thudding and echoing erotic female lyrics. It is accompanied by grinding harmonic rhythms. Surveying his surroundings in the semi-crowded environment, Dan Casey duly clocks the food and drink section of the lounge bar. This circular red neon light fixture glows in the central position of the dome-shaped interior of the Rhinegold-Goose.

Dan takes a steady precursor walk through the hazy, smoke-filled entertainment lobby, catching sight of a sleazy, mixed-looking bunch of pirates and smugglers who are playing a gambling table of cards. Dan notices they all seem to glare at him. He's an unknown new face on the grey dust moon of Latin-Versa.

Dan Casey carries on walking past the fugitive stakes card table. He quickly turns his attention away from the territorial residents, as he doesn't want trouble. He stealthily wanders over to the destined red neon bar and perches on one of the tall neon backless stools.

The charismatic cargo runner leans his bare-skinned elbows on the bright light bar top. While reaching, his slanted holster belt slot pocket hits the bar with a slight knocking of his silver and black-barrelled gun.

Dan slightly flicks his hand up half high. Trying to flag down the attention of the overweight, long-haired barman. His greasy hair and blotchy skin don't elevate his appearance.

Dan Casey raises his charmed voice due to the loud

background noise of the thudding bassline and general mingling chatter around the buzzing environment, "Hey, it's over here, pal. I'd like to order a pint of Kestrel-dew, please,"

The bartender appears to be another abrupt-looking Latin-Versa resident. He just bluntly glares at Dan and ignores him before moving on to another customer who has just arrived. Rudely pushing to the front of the queue, a well-spoken, raised female voice sweeps across the neon light bar.

She places her drink order, "Hi, I'd like to order a Lemon Gin Aston Martini with a touch of ice, please. Thank you, barman."

It is the mysterious, gorgeously well-groomed, silky-haired woman. She is now focusing on the dashing cargo pilot, Dan Casey, from his swept-back jet-black hair and chiselled, handsome face to his fit-muscular build body, casually dressed in his brown leather, sleeveless pilot waist jacket and athletic-shaped legs in tight black formal jeans. There is a high rate of approval, judging by the beautiful woman's piercing sparkle of her fluttering, sexy jade eyes.

Meanwhile, Dan Casey is enchanted by the confident pastel-haired lady from earlier. With a fixated glittering connection with the stunning women's green crystallised gemstone eyes, Dan Casey gives off a handsomely grinning smirk. He soothes his dark, dreamy eyes over her attractive, soft-skinned, blemish-free beauty, all complemented by high-class spectrum-coloured cosmetics.

He witnesses the grungy, ill-faced barman deliver the divine-looking lady her Lemon Gin Aston Martini. Admiringly, Dan glances over her slender feminine figure, capturing the rocking-to-the-beat bombshell's ample curvy charms in the tight-fit clothes.

As she elegantly sips her drink, she sends an acknowledging cheers to the barman and inspecting cargo pilot. With a gracious, sultry, shy smile, she turns away.

Swiftly following suit, Dan Casey turns away from the

glorious lady, self-commenting with smugness, "A haven for happiness. She's a high-class Astro-hooker, hanging around dumps like this place."

Once again, Dan is caught unaware of the blotchy, fat barman. He brashly enquires, "Did you still want a pint of Kestrel-dew, or is the Rhinegold-Goose not up to standard? Make your mind up, as I've not got all day."

Dan Casey sincerely apologises for the misunderstanding. "Sorry, no offence intended there. It's a great little joint, and I'd love a Kestrel-dew, thanks."

While waiting for the scuffed barman to pour his interstellar drink, Dan slants a sly flanking glimpse over his broad left shoulder. He catches the sexy jade-haired lady giggling at his unfortunate antics of upsetting the resident bartender of Latin-Versa moon.

The porky barman returns and serves up the pint of Kestral-dew, slamming the glass down on the neon bar's glazed top. With a slightly sloshed spillage, claiming in a brusk-deep manner, "That will be thirty-two credits, my old squire."

Astonishingly shocked at the cost of a drink, Dan Casey questions the barman's fee, "Hey, come on. Thirty-two credits for a pint of Kestrel-dew. Are you kidding me? Sure you have not made an error? Last I knew, they were around ten credits."

The doughy-faced barman flicks a side-motioned swinging of his long, greasy mane out of his bushy-eyebrowed view. "If I were kidding, squire, I'd be smiling. As you can see, I'm not; I've already said thirty-two credits, lump it, or leave, Flyboy. It's not my problem that the Corporal Union has raised the shipping-lane taxes again; it keeps getting harder to get supplies delivered to dust balls deep in space such as Latin-Versa."

Understandably, Dan accepts the barman's fair terms of explanation. Knowing too well, the galactic government is extorting the cost-of-living payments. Dan scans the payment.

Excitingly, Dan Casey explains to the bartender, "Well, you're in luck, pal. I'm a class-one certificate interstellar cargo pilot. There's no sector in the Kalanisi Universe where I don't know of a quick-fix shortcut. Plus, I'm free and just finished a supply run for Sandtex Ltd, so I'm looking for a new contract. Are you aware of anything? Regarding Corporal Union, why is there a scout swat team combing the spaceport? What's going on?"

The green-haired beauty, sitting just to his left, is taking a keen interest and is eavesdropping on the conversation at hand. Cunningly, Dan Casey breezes a glance over to her.

The bartender replies, "I've no bloody idea of any shipping activity. Do you think I look like an executive galactic contractor? No, me either, squire, or for the Corporal Union being planetside. Well, ask them yourself, as two just walked into the bar. Now, if there's nothing else? I got customers to serve, with the joyful thought of hopefully not seeing you again. No offence, Flyboy. I just can't stand time-wasting smurf-faced pilots like yourself."

Dan swiftly drinks up his galactic pint with the ever-growing intention of wanting to leave the dusty, bad-tempered moon.

He gets up off his tall, backless neon seating stool, clocking the Elite Corporal Union Guards who are snooping around the bass-pumping smuggler's saloon bar. He also notices that the flirtatious, jade-eyed lady has left, leaving her lemon gin drink half full.

As Dan Casey knows, his identification data records are sure-fire clean, with no breaching issues or incidents involving the Corporal Union. So, whatever the reason for the Elite Guards to be scouting Latin-Versa on the grey moon, it certainly isn't going to be him. While quickly leaving the Rhinegold-Goose's haven of rogues, the charming freighter pilot Dan Casey hurriedly returns to his Machiavellian class starship, manoeuvring a swing-shut action of the saloon's doors. He readily steps outside the smoky rundown dive, feeling the mild temperature of the atmospheric Latin-Versa moon, brisk around his bare-skinned biceps.

"What cracking weather temperature for this time of night; let's praise the walk back and make the most of it."

He walks along the dust bowl gritty track, veering back to port two, hanger bay three. But screams are coming from a residential apartment dome.

Dan Casey awkwardly notices and squints his brown eyes. The Corporal Union's scout personnel and Elite Guard raise the tempo of their demeaning sweep around the moon complex with a more decisive, heavy-handed approach and their menacing horror in their black-armoured uniform. They are duly armed and dangerous with semi-sub-pulse blaster rifles. Dan watches as they cruelly push and shove a family to the dusty, gravelled ground.

Dan knows he can't do anything to help the family other than just move on. This has been the theme of proceeding while on Latin-Versa: minding his own business. Even though firearms are permitted in the Kalanisi galactic binding of law, there is no deemed authorisation of use against any Corporal Union employee. That is a prime universal capital offence, resulting in the punishment of off-world Corporal Union prison facilities scattered across the galaxy in scaled sectors of the Kalanisi Universe.

Without the will or desire, Dan Casey boldly ventures a short way ahead further down from the grief of the Latin-Versa family.

Swiftly passing a narrow cut-split alley. Dan hears a well-spoken female voice.

"Pss! Hey, Spacer, over here!"

Dan swiftly reacts, manoeuvring to the low, brokering female voice. He puts his right leather cut-glove hand easily over his slick, black-barrelled weapon and gently caresses the silver stemmed handle with the firm intent of taking precautions, if deemed to be required.

It's the green-haired woman who, only moments before, had just elusively slayed a vanishing act.

Dan replies, removing his prime hand from his holstered firearm. "Hey, there, sweetheart! How are things okay?"

"Averagely well, considering. Thanks for asking. I couldn't help but overhear back at that tavern that you're looking for a contract. I'd say it's your lucky day, darling; I've got a requirement of opportunities right up your alley." She delivers her professional pitch in a high-class voice with a seductive smirk.

"Yeah, I bet I do, lady, but I've got places to be and things to follow up on. I'm quite tied over at present. Sorry, I don't handle conclusion contracts with high-class Astro-hookers. I doubt I could afford you, sweetheart, but thanks. I'm flattered by the offer of interest, but no thanks. Go strut your waddle back to the Goose. Goodbye."

Dan willingly turns to walk away, only to be countered by a more profound intervention of crossed wires by the well-spoken female of suspense.

"I believe you have jumped the wrong hyper-lane, mister. I'm not an Astro-hooker. More of a sinner businesswoman of sport. A cargo pilot is required to deliver a few exquisite class packages, with payment on arrival at the destination. Well, I'm glad that the contract's sorted. Now, we can run through the remaining details of your starship. Shall we get going? No time like the present?"

Dan Casey dumbfoundingly replies, "Hold your heels there, lady. I've not agreed to any seemingly duff-puffed contract. Can't see where your cargo hull is either? With only that dinky winky handbag and luggage sack just quartering your foot, unless you have hidden compartments in that exquisite tight tube top, I'd say you're an Astro-hooker with a very delusional mindset. Goodbye, miss."

At the same time, the jilted green-maned woman smiles. She sighs, "Ah, well, you can't blame a girl for trying. Let's see if phase two changes your mind."

With a sudden flash of an eye, the attractive green-haired lady changes her demeanour. Stealthily, she draws a silver short-scope barrelled pistol from a slant-cut holster belt, cleverly disguised by her wrap-around black waist jacket. Directly pointing the weapon with a two-handed grip at a more-than-bewildered Dan Casey.

While strictly under siege in the dust-pit alleyway quarter of Latin-Versa's moon base, Dan duly confronts his female saboteur with a surprised package.

"Is this meant to be a hold-up by any chance? If so, you should try a better stance, a little less agile and nervous, as if the Corporal Union is more interested in your service of opportunity than me, sweetheart. I'm just hinting so you will look more convincing in the future. Like I've said numerous times, goodbye."

The alluring, beautiful lady teasingly diverts a flipping wave of her long, slick green hair, reorganising her standing approach. While collecting the duffle luggage sack she's dumped close by her designer-labelled black high-leg heeled boots, she projects a false smile of gratitude and then swiftly flicks on the scope switch. This activates the infrared sight. Slowly, a tracer appears over Dan's brown-chested pilot waistcoat jacket.

"Call it a hijacking, hold up, or whatever you choose. I have no time for informal narratives. Now, hand over your weapon. Nice and slow. We wouldn't want you acting out an event of unnecessary proportions because I'm much more capable than you give me credit, but you are correct about the Corporal Union. They are keenly interested in my whereabouts, arriving on this trash ball a few hours ago. That's why you're going to pilot me off this dust-forsaken moon. And if all goes smoothly without any faults, we'll take the third phase from there. Now, time is ticking, and we need to get a move on. You are the newly founded bag man."

Her speech undoubtedly alters his charismatically sullen state of mind to the unjust, temperamental situation unfolding before his widened eyes.

Dan Casey expresses his concerns about her contract plan of escape. "You'll never get away with this, you know! The Corporal Union will compress a full lock of Latin-Versa. What have you done to stir them up? Raided a boutique nail parlour?" sardonically enquires Dan, unhooking his black-barrelled gun cleanly from his swing slant holster. He throws his weapon across to the gun-handling lady of arms.

He catches hold of her duffle luggage sack, which contains her personal effects, with a thudding smack into his handsome face.

"Is there any need for that, miss? Or whatever you Astro-hookers call yourself nowadays?"

Swiftly turning from the grey dusty alleyway and motioning a cautious walk, he heads to his Machiavellian Mk2 class freighter with the enclosing sounds of the Corporal Union Elite Scout Guards.

Aiming the steady hand pistol with a hushing whisper, she says, "Just keep quiet and move. Let's try not to draw unwanted attention and pretend we are a couple on a nightfall stroll, and for your dim-witted gathered view of my appearance, I can assure you, I'm not an Astro-hooker."

He tells the woman two truths. "I never said I disliked your looks. I thought you were beautiful, in fact. It's just the shameful way you behave yourself, sweetheart. Plus, we got two Union guards snooping just around the portside of my starship, and they are damn lazy. Are Mbron Media service bots still not finished unloading? This is not going to work. I have a bad feeling we're going to get arrested."

Approaching sight of the *Decepter*'s rear ram, Dan notes the hatch is still open. Both of his hands are full, carrying the duffle bag. And his silver-black-barrelled weapon is tagged in the waist jacket of his female felon. Dan Casey, by no doubt, fears the worst of scenarios.

The armed, jade-eyed woman presents more of a dashed, confident outlook. She boldly tells Dan, "Just get your old bucket of starship prepped, and let me take care of the guards. There are only two of them, plus they're easily distracted, piece of cake."

Dan Casey slowly takes steps, venturing up the *Decepter*'s hatch stairway. He drops the luggage sack to the floor, landing in a thump near his black knee-slack pilot boots, quickly concentrating on his starship security hatch code.

"Please define a piece of cake, lady. I don't know what's flowing through your mind of a merry-go-round. But any damn hostile action against Union folk is a capital one-level offence. Are you well aware of the consequences? Hmm, lady! Hey, has the cat got your tongue?"

The *Decepter*'s airlock hatch pressures open with a hissing shunt, but there's no response to his question. Dan rapidly spins his dawned attention around, catching no sight of the green-haired woman he presumptuously thought he would find.

Instead, there are two unwanted Corporal Union Elite Guards cloaked in their all-in-one black setting armoured outfit supported with a shadow-cast visor and a face-covering helmet. They are armed and dangerous and possess a clear aim of the caught-in-the-act cargo pilot.

One of the Corporal Union guardians steps forth, demanding answers. "Step away from that starcraft at once, and whatever you're doing up there, all intergalactic transport is grounded, as Latin-Versa is now under immediate martial law of the Corporal Union. A lockdown of all flights has been issued to full effect until further notice or arrest of a female infiltrating fugitive is in our custody. We won't ask again. Move away from the cranked vessel. An identification scan is required. If all your biometrics check out, you have nothing to worry about unless you're aiding an accomplice. If you are, by the Corporal rule of law, you'll be under arrest for a level-one class felony."

The shocked cargo pilot tries to charm his way out of the unforeseen arrival of the Corporal Union Guards.

Dan says. "Hey, officer, I'm sorry I didn't know about the planetarium lockdown. I'm new to Latin-Versa, and what a superb, friendly place it is. One female infiltrating fugitive sounds freaky. You'll be the first to know if I see any green-featured Astro-hooker femininity, and as for my ID card, silly me. I've left it in the cockpit cabin. I spend far too much time in space, which makes me so forgetful nowadays, so I keep being informed! One moment, officer, I'll just get my credentials. So, hang fire, and I won't be a tick."

"Arrest him. We didn't mention any description of the fugitive's appearance. It's not every day you see females with green hair. They are a particularly rare package to find on Latin-Versa. She would stand out by a clear mile, but I gather you already know this, don't you? So you're under arrest for harbouring a dangerous criminal. Cuff him and search his starship. I do believe our target may be hiding close by."

Suddenly, measured, slow-going click-tapping of high heels comes from beneath the landing gear of the Merlin class freighter. The green-haired woman in question stealthily appears and voices in a high-class spoken manner, "Exclusively advocated officer, I'm scarce and very dangerous." She slickly squeezes her pulsed trigger finger of the dainty short-stubbed pistol, stylishly tracing a recoil line of succession shots, professionally taking down both Corporal Union's officers in a slick slingshot manoeuvre.

Now, she yells a warning to Dan Casey, "Come on quickly, fire this tub up. We've got to get off this moon rock. We'll be having scout troops here within seconds." She quickly scarpers up the hatch stairway of the *Decepter*.

"What the fuck are you doing, lady? You just killed two Union guards in a manner of a trained killer. I want no part of this madness, whoever you are!"

The attractive but also intelligently deadly vixen is about to vocalise a defence of her unforeseen actions.

Dan Casey sees a sly cornering scout troop who are manoeuvring a clear-aim avenue of his semi-plus rifle, opening fire directly at the female renegade's left blind side. With a quick thought reaction of natural protective instincts, Dan slickly thrusts his right bare-skinned biceps arm out and, with a lashed connecting grip, grabs the jade-eyed woman's red-sighted pistol. He courageously shields her with a push, turning into the side staircase of the *Decepter*'s hatchway. The stunned woman screams and gasps with a loss of composure.

As Dan Casey wittingly takes command of her dainty slip-trigger finger, interlocking with his own. They perfectly aim a selective traced shot back at the crafty Corporal Union scout trooper, causing an arm-shot wound. He falls into a slump in sheer pain, giving a clear escaping opportunity for chaotically brave Dan Casey and the green-haired woman, thus saving her life from a lapse of concentration.

A suspended shock-absorbing connection of his dazed brown eyes spirals into a deep bond with her beautiful, startled jade pupil eyes, now featuring an unsurprisingly embarrassed expression which portrays her gasping mixed emotions. But the indecision doesn't last, and she aims the silver-scoped gun firmly back at the cargo pilot.

"Come on, move it to the hatch, quick, before there are more guards."

Dan grimly glares back at the conflicting lady. The pilot swiftly turns with a slapdash rush up the stairway to the freighter's entrance hatch. It isn't too long before the militia Corporal Union, scout troops and Elite crack-shot guards arrive. They start to open rapid fire on the Machiavellian MK2 starcraft.

Dan throws down the woman's duffle luggage sack, which he has been carrying. He rushes to the cockpit cabin of the *Decepter*.

"Hey, don't throw my belongings around. Some precious items are in there."

Dan Casey ignores her outburst and, instead, speedily flicks on the flight control pad switches. Instantaneously, this causes a buzzing murmuration of the freighter, and interior cabin lights flash-energise the internal power systems.

Dan Casey mutters, "Come on, you rust bucket of a hatch. Don't let me down today."

Heavily cranking forward on the stationed hatch leverage, the freighter finally engages in a protracted closure of the rear gear loading ramp that causes a manic clashing of directional problems for Mbron Media's service cyberbots.

While inside the cockpit quarter of the pilot's helm, Dan Casey reaches into his black pilot jeans and pulls out his packet of smokes, styling and flicking a filtered cigarette in the temper of the moment, catching it sternly in his mouth. The attractive lady, who is still pointing her silver-barrelled pistol at him, takes her position in the leather cushion co-pilot seat next to Dan Casey.

"You've not got time to smoke one of those, my gosh. Can't you see the Corporal Union's Elite shooting a blast at your starship, and they have now set up a barricade of obstruction? We're trapped! Are you listening to me, or has the cat now got your tongue? Hmm."

"Yes, I'm listening to you; just taking no notice of you, lady."

The astute cargo-runner wingman is well aware of the dangers on the horizon. Dan hits a manoeuvring motion forward with a waltzed jolt of his streamed body, ramming a strike of his black cut-gloved hand, and he presses hard on the sterling ignition throttle lever of the Machiavellian MK2

Merlin freighter. This generates an assertive fusion burst of the *Decepter*'s triple-booster exhausts.

The starship moves forward and moves onwards. Pulling out of the hangar bay area, the engine burners flare. Scraping a ranging silhouette of the freighter starships' slender-plated coned nose along the grey gravel runway track while encountering the gradual confrontation of twitching Corporal Union's scout guards and blasts. But the *Decepter*'s hull survives without any stern stopping effect.

The Machiavellian starship powers a crushing barge through the port barricade barriers. This breaks the blocking chains of situational obstruction hazards, which is instructively demonstrated by smashing a break in Corporal Union's countermeasures to prevent the progression of interstellar space travel.

The seemingly cool under-pressure cargo pilot, Dan Casey, sturdily rocks back in his leather pilot chair. While alternating the vessel's accelerator throttle to full maximum velocity, Dan urges a vast pulling back on the starship's joystick flight controls.

The *Decepter* swiftly accelerates to rise from the barren dust-swirling runway of the Latin-Versa moon compound. Vastly exhilarating to a rhythmic humming roar, pitching a vertical wind thrusting tail of trailing engine boost flares. Surfing a wave storm of high-powered peakiness, rapidly climbing in altitude to a purring venture of the colouring orbital atmospheric skies.

Outstandingly, the Machiavellian class star-freighter swiftly cuts an image through the clustering blissful star patterns of the Suvarna system. Angling a true-line position to slip-jump out of the quadrant, the ship urgently evades the attentive company realms of the Galactic Corporal Union's Elite scout squadron.

Dan Casey brims with confidence in his pilot skills. But he does require some help initialising the jump into the hyper-slip-lanes.

"Hey, Pearl, better scan us a timed trajectory coordination jump to the first slipstream matrix out of the Suvarna cluster system, analyse the subsystem's geography star charts, and make it fast, sweetie. We could be in trouble, as I think we may have a tailing fighter escort on our stern."

He checks over the craft and interfaces radar sensors with his tense eyes.

Meanwhile, the crystalised AI system flashes a response of commands without any vocalised cyber preaching. Sitting in a cross-legged posture next to the freighter pilot, the gorgeous, long, wavy, green-haired woman responsible for hijacking Dan Casey's law-abiding lifestyle enjoys the view of the near-distance sight of Latin-Versa.

"Well done, evading that dump hole of a crater-pitted moon. I really can't believe you pulled that off. I thought you would cave at first sight of the Elite Guards, but no, you impressed me. To be fair, get me out of this star sector, and I'll feel like kissing you, mister. What did you ask me to help with again? I'm no co-pilot, so I hope you know I can't set jump flight navigation coordinates. You called me Pearl; I knew you would warm to me before long. It's a great improvement from being labelled an Astro-hooker, I must say."

The woman innocently smiles with the friendly, pleased nature of shy unawareness. However, she still firmly holds the silver-barrelled pistol in her dainty gloved hands, seemingly aimed with the meaningful purpose of self-protection.

Dan instantly turns while closely checking the projector flight controls and duly informs the mistaken woman of his meaning. He advises the female hijacker, "I wouldn't expect you to be a co-pilot. That's why I wasn't talking to you, missy. More than one lady is on this ship, and the other shows more respect. The systematic AI is called Pearl, and I wouldn't celebrate too soon either, as we got two fast-approaching BX19 Corsair scout fighters tracking us. So, you can save the kiss. I'm not in the mood. The only time I'd want to kiss your type of woman would be when saying goodbye and marooning you on a remote planet before I serve my time in a Corporal Union galactic prison!"

"Well, I can assure you! I was only joking about the kiss, just trying to brighten the mood of things. That's all. Gosh, if I could bring myself to pout for an oil-stricken cargo pilot! And what a horrible thing to think of trashing me on a distant world; that's why I'm holding the guns, mister. And there's me thinking I'd been quite charitable towards you. For the fast-tracking fighter drones, can you slip them, or does this bucket of a starship need winding up?"

Meanwhile, the fast-approaching BX19 Corsair single-based starfighters are stealthy in their swift-offence pursuit coordinate vector run. Unfortunately, on this occasion, as slick as the BX19 Corsair fighter crafts are designed to perform, the *Decepter*, a Machiavellian class starship, is readily preparing to counter by jump-shifting into the hyper-slip-lanes of dark space.

"The answer to whether we can outrun the fighters on this occasion is yeah. We got a bit of a head start from Latin-Versa. Why are they semi-armed, and we are not active? The Corporal Union must have sent those BX19 scout crafts to escort the Elite guard's transporters on the way to apprehend you, sweetheart. So buckle up that handbag. I wouldn't want you to lose your make-up. We're about to hit the hyper-slip-lanes to whereabouts, though, I have no idea."

Instantly, there is the whooshing momentum of the *Decepter*'s engagement into the galactic hyper-speed slip-lanes. It is a timely evasion as the BX19 Corsair fighters are closing in, slipping into the firing range of the vanishing Machiavellian MK2 freighter.

Dan Casey swiftly vacates the Latin-Versa moon sector of the Kalanisi Universe, distancing himself and his uninvited passenger from the grey, dusty venue.

Chapter Two

Attempt to Escape

The *Decepter*, a Machiavellian Merlin class freighter, is cruising gracefully through the energising impulsive paradox of hyperspace slip-lanes with a purring essence of peace and tranquillity.

While in the cockpit cabin of the subsonic speed-travelling starship, there is a sombre mood. The charmed cargo pilot, captive Dan Casey, scrunches his handsome, delicate cheekbones, with a shadowy dark-eyed raised glare, over to the gorgeous female gunslinging passenger.

Dan Casey's usually good-willed patience is wearing thin to the point of asking the starship's AI to down-tool the hyperdrive systems. "Okay, Pearl, enough is enough; I've had it with this turbulence nonsense, drop the interminable subsystems, and knock off the celestial hyperdrive while keeping a vast sensor check on the outer quadrant perimeter, as we may have just become hot property catch of the day."

Pearl instantly decelerates a reverse of the highly energised hyperdrive boosters. Suddenly conjuring with a spark of breaking light in the dark atmospheric circulations of the hyper slip-stream lanes. The starship whooshes a whistling flash-bang appearance of the *Decepter*'s distinctive slick frame, sleekly followed by a near echo-silenced thud of trajectory space gravity. This means that the Machiavellian MK2-type starship is halted in the mid-mass of Kalanisi space.

Meanwhile, Pearl's initial reports are flashing, including instructions for requirements. "Celestial core power dropped to a minimum capacity, scanning search initiating to sub-drive connect. Are we in a cauldron of trouble with the Android unloading organisation again? It's not the first time we have been warned with a delisted cautioning of your behaviours towards the cyber-synthetic worlds of a labour market."

Dan Casey eases off the manually engaged subsystems. He slightly shifts a turn around his upper body from the pilot's leather chair, looking directly into the mysterious woman's lustrous jade eyes, stating the woefulness of this troubling experience on the Latin-Versa moon port, "No, Pearl, it's a lot worse than you think, and unfortunately, sad to say, she's still sitting next to me. Who's about to thoroughly explain her little Astro-tantrums of a galactic handmaid's tale? Aren't you just, little miss, shoot now, think a bit later?"

There is a down-turning of vibrations in the internal systems, purring a droning halt of the triple pylon engines of the stagnant cargo freighter.

"Why have you stopped the vessel here? We need to keep going further out, don't you say? Oh gosh, tell your pet Pearl to restart the flight engines at once."

Dan Casey instantly swings his black pilot's chairs fully around, shaking his head with an eye-rolling bedazzlement. "Why are we stopping? You sure are an unrealistic lady. Well, let me think for a moment. This could spring to mind. We have stopped, lady, so you can be straight and upfront about what happened back there on Latin-Versa, and why you've looped me into your realm of craziness? In the Rhinegold-Goose, there was a stack of rogue-type customers right up your alley, and you could have chosen any of them; why me? I can assure you I'm not what you're after, sweetheart. I'm no smuggler, plus I don't run off world contraband or harbour female criminals from Corporal Union justice. I'm just plain old Dan Casey, a simple interstellar cargo-runner pilot, or I was until an hour ago. Now I'd say I'm prime-time holo-net news, so please do explain your plot for a one-way beckoning of a galactic prison sentence, and is there any need for that damn waving scope gun? Plus, I'd like my smoke back if it's not too much trouble."

The mysterious green-haired woman gives an imperious glare at Dan. She slowly lowers the point-aimed silver-stubbed weapon away from Dan Casey's protruding, handsome-looking facial features. Drawing the infrared barrelled pistol steadily down to her side holster belt, she tucks away the gun. She keeps her pistol at the reachable handy range if required.

"Okay, Mr. Casey, Let's hope there is no need for the gun. I'm a lone woman travelling in the galactic wilderness with an unknown strange man. Now, that could make Mbron Media's holo-net news headlines, and before you tell me to take the airlock exit, call it a woman's intuition. You are not such a bad man; you are probably rude and rough around the edges. Please don't prove me wrong, Mr Casey, or I may find the need to shoot you. I'm not the sleazy woman you have me down for, either."

She explains and introduces herself, "Greetings! It is a pleasure to meet you; I'm Veena Merida, a seasoned remote-based galactic agent for an underground resistance movement. Our primary objective is to challenge the Corporal Union's unethical treatment of Kalanisi citizens. Recently, I've been trusted to acquire a significant item from Kothariya, the capital of the human elites, which is also my place of origin.

"I am pleased to report that I have successfully retrieved the astrological data box from an ancient era and have received new orders to deliver it to a specific location in the deep quadrant of the Isadora system. To ensure the success of this mission, I will be working closely with Tara Harlow, the leader of the United Resistance operation. I'm in the market for a damn good pilot with a pretty fast starship to urgently take me to this secret location of Miss Harlow."

But Dan doesn't know it is just as much of a mystery location in the Isadora system. In a reluctant, hesitant example of not fully grasping the female resistance agent's story, Dan Casey swiftly spins his pilot chair back to a forward helm position, swinging both his legs high, with a sharp manoeuvring of his sturdy black leather boots on the control dash.

"Well, excuse me for sounding cynical and difficult, Miss Merida. Would you like to be referred to as Agent Merida? I'd like to say it has been a pleasure getting to know your acquaintance, but under difficult circumstances, it's not been that great, sweetheart, so the sooner you leave my starship, the better. And for your mixed-up mission of hope and purpose? Where did you come up with that riddled garbage? Let me guess. There is a weekly agent holo-net magazine with all the latest gossip. Come on, you raided the cosmetic make-up store. That's why the Corporal Union's got the hump. At least tell some truth, and I wish you all the best, missy, with your search for that crack-shot pilot.

"Just a quick heads up on your star-charted destination of the Isadora system. You may not know that the starless sector of Kalanisi space is empty. There is nothing in that quadrant but neighbouring plasma gas molecular clouds, and not to forget the twisted maelstrom gravity wells, surrounded by masses of dense-burnout globular clusters. It's a lost venture, and I have no intention of flying there, trust me. Even if you do hold me hostage at gunpoint, I can drop you off at the next service spaceport, agent lady. It's the best I can do, and, missy, can I have my smoke back now, please?"

"Well, for your information, Mr Casey, I don't work on presumptions, only facts and hard evidence of answers. I was sceptical at first myself; I won't lie. I wasn't convinced either until I found answers to be evidence in the question read true. Come on, I can show you proof. Plus, here are the smokes you're craving."

"You should try to practise your willpower more. Here's a good tip for you, Mr Casey, as you would never make an underground agent of universal justice with craving temptations of needing a smoke. Learn a trick or two from me. I quit that habit over two years ago. Now, make haste. Let me show you the data box so you know I'm not spinning you a fantasy yarn," said the upper-class female agent, collecting her zip duffel sack. She places the bag on the side frame of a small, curved sofa table in the dimly lit lounge quarters of the star-vessel's interior rest facility.

Dan Casey twiddles a smoke filter in the tip of his cut-gloved fingers before following her to the lounge. Telling the uninvited, beautiful, blessed female stowaway of a few rules on his spacecraft.

"Hey, it's fine, don't worry about me, sweetheart. I like craving for things; it keeps me sharp. And will you just stop bossing me around on my starship? This old floating bucket is my home. I call the shots okay, not some gunslinging fashion model agent."

Veena Merida is now sitting at the lounge table with the sought-after astrological data box and her agent holo-pad of the desired rendezvous location. She's perched near the round-shaped lounge table. To Dan, she appears to be grinning to herself while witnessing an amusing side to the pilot's ranting grumble of words. Veena politely addresses his mistake of context to her impression of taking charge.

"I wasn't bossing you around. Don't get your holster belt in a twist now, will you, Mr Casey? Please just hear me out, okay? And I love a Star coffee if any is going. Working on that dust ball, Latin-Versa, dehydrates a girl; I take mine with milk and no sugar. I'm watching my figure, thanks. Okay, where was I then? Ah, yes, the data box. This is the item the Corporal Union is after, not me; I've just hurt their pride a little."

Veena grips a dainty hold of the hand-sized cubed box, with

unknown symbol marks imprinted on each cornered side, each representing ancient meanings from another time zone of the Kalanisi Universe.

Standing shortly across from the pillow lounge seating area, Dan Casey prepares two Star coffees. Setting the preferred choices of taste, Dan casually presses the padded scanner on the built-in cafeteria machine and draws his dark-eyed attention to the astrological data box, commenting on the worn-looking prestige item.

"Why make such a fuss about the scratched-up puzzle cube? Doesn't look anything special to me. How sure are you that this agency outfit is not pulling you a fancy yarn without releasing it?"

Dan Casey has reason to be suspicious, as the Resistance works in the shadows of the Kalanisi Galaxy, operating without knowing if they exist for real. This causes Dan to show signs of scepticism about the contract before him.

Meanwhile, Veena Merida, the assigned feminine agent, continues her analysis of the data box riddle. Dan serves up her coffee, and Veena replies with a shining smile.

"Thank you, Mr Casey. The drink smells perfect. I agree with you on this box's appearance. It looks a lot like a puzzle box, but unfortunately, it's a lot more puzzling, to say the least." Veena pauses, taking a sip of her drink. The green-haired agent continues with a gulping swallow and a wipe of her lipstick-red lips.

She says, "According to old galactic folklore hypothesis, there are rumours about an old data box containing a star chart to unknown worlds. It could even be a passage to the Vortex, a black hole leading to the halls of galactic hell before our civilisation time evolved in the Kalanisi realm. However, I don't concern myself with such rumours. I have a request for you. I need you to transport me to the resistance leader's location in the Isadora system. My mission is to extract and exchange, which I intend to do. Can you assist me with this task?

"I will pay you to take me there, call it a contract of affreightment, and make it worthwhile. Even get you a substantial reward credited by the agency. Please, Mr Casey, take a moment to consider you are the only star pilot I saw on that drift ball of a moon Latin-Versa. You were the only one who looked respectable enough to have washed at least once over the last circled week."

Dan takes a swig of his Star coffee, considering the contract, focusing his eyes on the attractive agent.

"And I thought you had selected me on Latin-Versa for my irresistible good looks. Seductively fluttering those jade crystal eyes cross in that haven of happiness, the Rhinegold-Goose." He smirks before continuing.

"I disagree with this galactic run of chance, but if I did have a lapse of concentration, how much would the credit reward be worth? As a handsome, good-willed guy just like myself, I wouldn't want to see a little crush-craving lady get herself lost travelling the frightening galaxy voids with a band of merry rogues."

Veena Merida leans forward and elegantly places the empty Star coffee beaker gently on the table before standing presence in front of Dan Casey. "Twenty thousand credits on the safe arrival of the data box charted at the location on this holo-pad. Tap the primary navigation thread in your systematic assistance, Pearl, and we can start our galaxy-bound journey without further delay. Do we have an agreement, Mr Casey? You claimed back in the Goose that you know many shortcuts through the star lanes of the Kalanisi Universe. You're a perfect candidate for the position, which was not based on your looks, I can rightly assure you. I was working undercover, seeking out the target, not carving out a possible date. I'm far too professional in my qualifications and objectives to interact with such actions or indulge in the emotion of interest. Just bear that in mind, please. Now, I gather I will be here for a few more days to come.

Anywhere a girl can place her personal effects and rest a weary head for a while, Mr Casey."

Dan states, "You seem to have it all planned out, Miss Merida. I'll help you on one condition: no more ruffling the feathers of the Corporal Union. I do not need them dogging my tail. It's hard enough to find a good contract with all the cyberbots working for free electric charges. Your twenty thousand credits sound ideal. I could even fix up the *Decepter* on that kind of currency; I'd be a fool to turn down a genuine offer, which I hope is a true contract, and I don't get shot in the back by your double agent types. And for your comfort while on board, there are two sleeping quarters and a washroom facility on the left, further down the walkway. Oh, and don't stray down the staircase to the second floor. The cargo hold may need cleaning up. Make yourself at home, agent lady. Here, let me oblige with that, please. I will help carry your duffel sack to your quarters, sweetheart."

"Well, I seem to have managed okay so far. Thank you, Mr Casey. And please, for the strutting life of it, try calling me by my name, which is Veena Merida. Surely, it can't be that difficult. Plus, for your impulse response, I don't want to be anybody's damn sweetheart. I'm a bad-arse intergalactic agent of peace. I don't have any time for short-fire flirtatious romances, okay?"

Their arguing is interrupted by a sudden loss of gravitational pull. Veena screams, and she stumbles into Dan, but he protects her from a jolting fall from the Machiavellian freighter's lounge floor walkway. What follows is the deep thundering flash and bang thudding of a massive ripple wave impacting the atmospheric presence of unrest, submerging from the hyper-slip-lanes.

The *Decepter* abruptly sways, shifting and throwing itself into the black depths of space. Suddenly, the reason for the disruption is clear: an Elite brigadier, *Galileo* BX10 class-one type battlecruiser, has entered their hyper-lane. This is seen in the portside windows of the drift-flowing Machiavellian MK2 Merlin star-freighter.

The intimidating *Galileo* BX10 battle cruiser swiftly establishes a clear, aggressive firing range. It activates a protracting of the menacing armed sub-pulse cannons. But Dan is unaware of this situation. He's still in the arms of the attractive agent.

The *Decepter*'s alert systems ring a low-brimmed beeping in the dull, red-zoned emergency lighting.

"What in the world was that? And will you take your oily hands off me, please, Mr Casey!"

"Hey, now, sweetheart, I think you fell on me, remember? Next time, make a note in your dinky agent pad, reminding me to drop you on the damn flooring. Plus, the vibration wave felt like a starship aftermath and a very big one, judging by the ripple diversions of that shockwave. Must have slip-jumped a manoeuvre out the hyper-lanes, directly out on top of us from nowhere."

Assessing a pre-judgement of the unwanted developments, Dan Casey quickly turns his differences of opinion from the defiance of a female resistance agent. The Star coffee beakers roll as Dan urgently motions to Veena to follow him to the flight control cockpit.

"PEARL! Thought you were meant to be keeping a close sector scan of things. This is not what I call an efficiently scanned awareness, sweetie. Who the hell is stalking our trajectory? I need some answers here, Pearl. Fire up the celestial subsystems and optimise the hyper-driven applications quickly. I have a strange feeling we'll need them primed; just call me over-paranoid."

Regrettably, he witnesses the massively daunting *Galileo* BX10 battle cruiser, heaving a diligent shadowing on the port side of his comparatively minimal-sized, light-framed star-freighter.

Flashing a crystalised response to Dan's request for answers.

The starship's computerised AI system, Pearl, duly reports in a subtle cyber tone characterised voice. "We have an incursion of a Corporal Union, class-one advanced battle cruiser, requesting a visual holo link communication immediately."

Veena soon follows a path to the co-pilot's cabin, but along the way, she sees the gigantic starcruiser of the Corporal Union. She stands in a fixed, frozen position but remembers that she is still holding Dan's gun. She raises the weapon with a slick spin of the reverting handle, a peace offering to Dan Casey, the return of his gun with some informal advice.

"Oh shit, I do believe we may be in trouble, Mr Casey. That's the starcruiser that followed me off-world from the human capital, Kothariya, just before I managed to stowaway on a star-bus transporter to the spaceport known as Gyen-Yamion, bordering the outer-rim star reach of Kothariya's hyperlink trade lanes. This was part of my brief visit to the Suvarna cluster system. I suggest we get out of this star sector as quickly as possible."

Dan sarcastically says, "Well, thank you for the expert evaluation, Agent Merida. I'll blast a warning shot out of the cockpit to scare them off. Of course, we're in trouble, little lady. Who is the guy? Ex-boyfriend?

"Hey, Pearl, connect us to the comm-link. Let's just hope it's only a routine patrol zone cruiser. And you, agent lady, just stay out of view. I'll deal with this so-called Corporal Union. Watch and learn now."

The *Decepter* starship's AI systems connect with the communication link exchange with the *Galileo* BX10 battleship. Dan takes a deep, long breath, instantly followed by a delaying calm blow effect, decisively protracting his facial expression to an unwarranted detraction of trying not to look guilty.

Pearl auto activates the *Decepter*'s net-comm router, and immediately, with a flecked hissing haze, the holo screen projects an image of a Corporal Union high-ranking officer.

A masculine, dark-skinned man appears on the rippling holo-net screen. He has a stern face with a distinguishing, red-slashed cut mark beneath a cold, piercing eye. It is particularly noticeable as it stands out courtesy of his metal patch covering the opposite missing eye.

The short-haired Commander wears a black open leather long trench coat, bulging to the seams with his broad demeanour. He is further intimidating as he flexes his right synthetic cybernetic hand, which was installed by the Android Association Society, Mbron Media Ltd. The hand is the result of an assault strike mission of the Corporal Union that had flared unfavourable.

The Corporal Union's star frigate had been attacked by an anti-activist band of political rogues rebelling against the newly elected leader, Wilson Volantis. Now, two years had gone by. This incident angered the captain and contributed to his hatred of any unlawful act of crime against the current rule of law upheld by the ruling Galactic Corporal Union regime, even though much of the dark acts were actually orchestrated by the mysterious mastermind politician, Director Wilson Volantis.

The captain spoke deeply. "Under Corporal Union's interstellar law 2.11.964, your freighter vessel will be boarded and searched. Your ship shows the same signature flares as the starcraft involved in an unprecedented terrorist attack on the moon, Latin-Versa, deep in the realms of the Suvarna cluster system. Any type of resistance formulated against my direct order of demand will feel the full wrath of Commander Calo Tarick. The ionised cannons on this fully armed BX10 battle cruiser are locked on your pathetic starship and will be fired upon, disabling any intended thought of not complying. We have a scan of your record files directly from the Kothariya database. There's no escape from galactic bound law, and for your interest, just to make the outcome clear, I am that law. Do you comprehend my request for your arrest, Mr Casey and that female sleazebucket of a green-haired infiltrating low-grade rat, Merida? Prepare to be boarded now."

The holo screen transmission instantly cuts off with a fizzled static buzz. Meanwhile, swaying in the void blackness of cold atmospheric open space, the threatened Machiavellian freighter starts to whistle a humming ignition of the triple-sectioned pylon boosters. Deep inside the cockpit cabin of the firing up starship, Dan Casey is in an urgent quandary with no time to delay setting the controls of the *Decepter* for a swift exit.

Dan quickly gauges that the belligerent battle cruiser's ion cannons are locking to disable his MK2 Merlin-type freighter power systems with an electrically charged EMP pulse blast. Dan clutches the flight joystick and delivers a slick, sharp check over to the side view of the co-pilot quarters to see the gorgeous agent.

"Well, that didn't go the way I was hoping. I think we might be in big trouble. We need to leave this sector, and pretty damn fast as well. I never even had a moment to get a word in edgeways. How in the world did you meet this guy? He's got my name dead-to-rights; that skinny grunt of a dock-port worker must have blabbed. We're in trouble, missy! Buckle up."

"Well, thank you so much, Mr Casey, for your expert evaluation and enlightenment of an unforgettable lesson in watch and learn. Did I not tell you we are in trouble? Gosh, pilots? Can't you do something? They are going to open fire on us!"

Suddenly, there is a silent blue starlight speaker of a brightening flash, and a spanning twin turbo sound of boom swiftly follows this. The BX10 battle cruiser's weapons open fire, hurling double rounds of the ion plasma bolts.

Luckily, Dan Casey has the vast amount of quick-time reaction reflexes of a crack-shot pilot. He is silent yet alert to the dangerous zone nearing the rear tail of his vessel. With a swift actioning thought of the process, Casey makes a tight hold of the trigger pad joystick. He instinctively slams it to a hard left pitch to suave shot manoeuvre with perfect timing.

The talented cargo-runner pilot courageously performs. Dan bravely pushes his flowing, bare-skinned, toned arm forward, urgently jolting a powered initiating thrust on the sterling booster throttle.

Instantly, the stylish MK2 Machiavellian freighter performs a warping side graviton skid with a syndicate linking burst of the booster exhausts. The *Decepter* surges in a wavery motion of an exhilarating attack vector run, plotting a crude projectile course directly at the *Galileo* BX10 warship.

The politely outspoken pastel-haired agent endures a jolting backlash of her body being thrown around in the co-pilot quarters. She quickly reorganises herself and struggles to lock the ratchet strap buckles. Still, with an urging surge of adrenaline from her manicured, dainty hands, she finally manages to strap herself into the safety harness belt.

"Mr Casey, can you please explain any sane reason why we are going the wrong way? Like a galactic Astro-lamb to the slaughter port. Plus, if we're going to be partners, you could have at least told me about that little jump-shifting stunt. We're going way too fast for my liking!"

She contributes a warning to the cargo pilot. "And just for the future flight track record, you know I have been known to get occasionally woozy during space travel of this turbulent nature."

The *Decepter* swiftly streaks a venture of a collision theory, bridging the gap to the foot of the Corporal Union's battle cruiser stealthily with a rattling, shaking quake. Overseeing the instrumental running of the flight projector sequence at the freighter's control helm, Dan Casey has one hand firmly on the slick swing joystick and the other on the levered thruster throttle. He has self-confidence combined with an element of calculated luck.

"Will you not keep damn quiet for a moment of silence, partner! Where did that come from, lady? If we can skim close enough along his spacious front hull, they won't be able to fire without knocking his systems out. Well, hypothetically speaking. So, I'd hold on tight. We're about to become the interstellar woozy express."

Meanwhile, sitting at the helm of his cruiser bridge controls is the Commander. He is scrunching his scar-shaded dark-skinned face, rippling the distinguished metal-patched eye to a raised demeanour of an angered temperament. He is a frightening sight as he clutches a fist-wrenching of his artificial cybernetic hand.

"Officer One, I do hope for your sake that you have an excuse for why this first-class battlecruiser of the Union Elite fleet missed the target of a rust-shelled outdated freighter. Reload and open fire immediately without compromise or mistake. NOW!"

The first officer stands straight and firm at the head of the control quarters, merely trembling a stuttering defence. The middle-aged Caucasian officer is a clean-shaven man with a presentable statute of requirements for the Corporal Union-ranking Elite. He is smartly dressed in his black, all-in-one sharp uniform and peaked cap.

Clearly, with a deep breath and clearing of the throat, Officer One reports, "Their undersized freighter luckily outmanoeuvred our ion cannon blasts due to the pilot's mastery of adaptiveness of pure chance. But we can't open fire again with the craft coursing an attack run vector. We shall blow our systems with an ion flare blast reflecting a heated pulse wave. It's too close to us, Commander Tarick."

Back on board the *Decepter,* the line of interceptor trajectory sways a rocking jolt of the pressurised cockpit cabin. Bossing the narrative to his own, Dan Casey focuses his charming brown eyes firmly on the tactical flight manoeuvre. He racks the pilot joystick with a hard pressure right-slacking slide, kinking the power-band throttle up a notch.

Tensing with anxiety, Dan raises a command of order, asking Pearl for help. "Pearl, on my mark, boost up the hyperdrive on our right flank; we shall slingshot our way out of this mess. One, two, break. Flash, the son of a bitch, Pearl. Give him a big kiss goodbye."

Exuberantly calm, the hotshot cargo pilot harnesses a daring manoeuvre of evasion. The *Decepter* weaves across the massive armour-plated hull of the *Galileo* BX10, stealthily creeping to a true line of subsonic flight, swiftly slipping in between the middle of the cruisers dual-ion cannons, preventing the opportunity of opening firing.

The MK2 Machiavellian freighter slickly twists, hurling a right-sling cutting manoeuvre with an extradimensional burst of acceleration flare. Waging in close fine-cut brazing of the bulking stand-off tower control bridge of the Corporal Union's Elite brigadier warship. The *Decepter* momentarily shivers with a skimping, disorientating fly past the *Galileo* BX10 cruisers, shooting away and now fully clear of the present danger in the starship's pathway of escape.

Veena Merida gasps with stunned relief from the near-death experience while also praising the efforts of Dan Casey's intergalactic piloting skills.

"Ooh, gosh! Bless the galactic stars. I can't believe you attempted that fly-by of close intention and managed to pull it off, staying in one piece. Not sure whether to be impressed or scared beyond belief."

"Don't applaud me too soon with congratulations, agent lady; we're not out of this conundrum yet by any long chance."

Dan Casey notices the starship instrumental systems' bleeping pulsing alert on the radar dialogue of the Corporal Union's devilish battlecruiser, cunningly manoeuvring an accessible slick slider turn around, engaging in a swift hyper-pursuit of the *Decepter*.

"Okay, Pearl, time to hit the hyper-lanes; set a coordinated entry system to an assessment slip-jump, and anywhere but here, sweetie. We need to shake off this bad vibe I'm having of being clunk, click-locked and jailed for all the wrong damn reasons."

Meanwhile, on board the supermassive *Galileo* BX10 patrol cruiser's bridge control quarters, they are tagging the *Decepter*. The Commander of the war steed battleship, Calo Tarick, is venturing into an angered stage of boiling over due to the defiance and disorganisation of the first officer to follow his orders.

"FIRST OFFICER, if I were in your pathetic boots of a near deceased man, I'd be perturbed indeed by that smart fast-challenged manoeuvre from that cocky scruff-neck of the pilot. Nobody runs a flash game of perception past my battleship. NOW, disable that damn star-freighter. FIRE THE ION CANNONS."

The brigadier class battle cruiser gains a swift pace on the heels of the *Decepter*. They open fire with the full might of the ion cannons, patching a surrounding energising burst of fire plasma orbs. There is a banging and shattering BOOM around the slipstreaming Machiavellian MK2 freighter, which is weaving for a slick evasion, stealthily deflecting the incoming bombardment of hazard artillery directly pounding from the *Galileo* BX10.

Dan Casey notices a red flashing gauge indicator, bleeping repeatedly. He is concerned at the flickering dial readings, vigorously shaking his charmed, stubbled face. He raises a frown of anxiety while asking the freighter's crystalised computer briskly, "Hey, Pearl, what's the damn hold up with hyper-lane slip-jump trajectory? The celestial subsystems show we've got a powertrain fragmentation of the right-infused hyperdrive.

Please tell me that it's not a true statement scan. Of all the days, it can't be broken."

"Celestial hyperdrive subject to seventy per cent blowout if there is an attempt to transcend into the hyperlink lanes, recommended charge of around three hours minimum, or you could purchase a new Caerleon ssd20 hyperdrive upgrade model, as stated numerous times, Dan! You can't say you weren't warned. Now, would you like the results of the body biometric scans?"

"Oh, right! Now you tell me, Pearl, thanks! And stop doing those biology scans, will you? I've told you about that before. Plus, it's putting our woozy female hijacker, oops, my bad, I mean partner of crime, off. As we're just sitting ducks out here in open mass space, with that monster beast of battle cruiser giving a viral chase, I'll have to take a detour to find a shortcut. Hold tight now, Veena."

"Mr Casey, my life's in immediate danger. What berserk idea of a shortcut do you intend to take? We're in the middle of deep, blank space! I see nothing but that partial green cloud leading to a derelict space junkyard full of floating old ship parts! Please tell me you are not considering flying through that hazardous route. Do you not understand the meaning of feeling woozy? It's not very nice, Mr Casey. Let me inform you. It makes you feel lightheaded, and fluttering is not a good sign for an agent girl's image. Plus, has this bucket of a cranked-out starship got any weapons or are they broken as well? I'm surprised that even the Star coffee machine works. Without playing the same holo-track, I wondered if you have any weapons. Have you ever thought this would be a good time to use them? It's safer than blowing up in a derelict space junkyard. Call me a picky passenger if you wish."

"Hey, Lady Merida! Now, you listen to me a moment; I don't want to fly through that dump of floating mesmerised scrap no more than you, but fate has landed us here. We fly a weaving direct route through the starship junkyard, hoping we won't be blown up, and will you stop pinching my damn smoke? Plus, we have a weapon system, but they're offline. Knock yourself out if you feel like breaking a manicured nail and rewiring it together. Otherwise, keep quiet for a minute and hope your Corporal Union Commander doesn't follow our choice of flight pattern."

Dan Casey's Machiavellian MK2 class freighter swiftly takes a vector path through the swirling particle clouds of the hazy green smog, slicing a twisting quarter-looping manoeuvre through deep space trash of old used space transporter vessels, accessories, and hull parts.

The galactic senate of corporate power has been dumping waste in that sector throughout the galactic time frame. They have used the solid storage capacity of a twisting magnesium radius gas cloud venturing around a non-populated space zone in the Kalanisi Universe.

The *Decepter* cruises through the gusting clouds, fortunately just missing an old derelict starship swirling an atmospheric motioning cluster of scrap. While the cool-headed Dan Casey is still alertly on point, mastering the fine fractions, he skilfully avoids the ion blast spectrum from the *Galileo* BX10 battleship. These explosions increase the rippled wave chain effect of the derelict structures, initiating disturbance to an already unbalanced stratosphere mass of the quarantine zone.

Veena Merida sits in the rocked spaceship, screaming out loud in terror of the shape-shifting non-dimensionalised gaps, vanishing to a mere speck of a size to weave a starship through in the murky mists of the barren-green misty smog.

"Ahh no, Mr Casey, you'll get us killed with this maverick madness parade of showing off an impression to me. Can you even see where you are going? This is crazy! I think this is not the normal behaviour of an intergalactic cargo-runner pilot. I feel so dizzy now it's gone beyond words of explanation! Are you even listening to me?"

Dan only half-listens as he does a vital inspection of the radar while professionally using his best navigational expertise not to crash into the large floating pieces of debris embedded in the green gas cloud.

But he feels Veena's terror and says, "Hey, Veena, don't worry; we are nearly through the worst carnage. I agree with you. This isn't the greatest route to take, but it is the only option, and it looks like Commander Calo Tarick's battle cruiser has fallen back to a static halt, according to the *Decepter*'s radar external hard drive systems. I can't feel any additional ion explosions. Their battle vessel is far too big for the Corsair scout fighters to track our location. He must be one daft half-charge hand of a Corporal Union representative, as I would have done that. To be honest, they made it too easy for us to escape their law-enforcing jurisdiction."

"Pearl, please, sweetie, I need you to find us a port of call. Do an analysis depth chart scan of the sector to see where we are currently situated. We can hide for a while, let things cool down a bit, and then give us a fighting chance to recharge this banged-out celestial hyperdrive. Then, we can manage our way back on track to deliver a mysterious data box and drop Veena at her rendezvous point of contact with this resistance boss, Tara Harlow. I'll then collect my twenty thousand credits while hoping our desirable fates aren't unfortunate enough to entwine again. No offence. I have no reason to involve myself in rebelling against the Corporal Union's psychological and political mass control of the Kalanisi Universe."

Dan Casey is smartly aware of the onward dangers of the derelict ships in the grave disposal junkyard, weaving around a swinging chunky batch of old ramshackle turbine boosters and buckled starcraft wings. He's manually piloting the *Decepter* with an enchanted touch of perceptive care, steadily sweeping through the fragments of the star-junkyard domain.

Veena Merida loosens the harness belts of the co-pilot quarter's seat. The ship is now peaceful.

"I think I'm going to be sick. I can't quite believe we flew through that nightmare. I don't think Calo Tarick is going to give up. That's just not in his evil nature. He's a damn menace; I was lucky to escape with my life while on the human capital planet, Kothariya. I had to infiltrate to get the data box and evade his order of execution on sight, dodging his lethal guards. So whatever port of call you have planned, Mr Casey, it needs to fix this crooked craft's hyperdrive swiftly, and by the way, thank you for calling me by my name for once; it shows you can be civil after all."

Veena sighs. "Rest assured, you will get your contract credits, and then I will be out of your hair within a few days, so no personal offence was taken intently, Dan."

The attractive, graceful, young, jade-eyed woman manoeuvres a comfortable twist of her black jumpsuited body. She carefully listens to the flashing crystalised presence of Pearl, beaconing a bright colour flicking glow, directly in the middle of the flight deck control system reporting the location of a possible safe harbour.

"The dimensional analysis formula has tracked a small, marooned moon called Cartonne, the precise destination varying a course vector pitch of 278. The orbital cycle habitat is reportedly damply cold with an extremely muddy origin surface. Per the sonic ranged sensor scan, there is no known implementation of pattern lifeform signs."

Dan Casey instantly releases one of his manly leather finger-cut gloved hands and retrieves his green-dust smoke filter. Only this time, he safely places his filter tip in the top right-hand pocket of his brown leather pilot waist jacket. Dan swiftly revises the information of his starships, AI sub-courses, and strategic intelligence system.

With a charming smile, Dan appropriately alternates the

flick-switch core diameters, stating, "Sounds perfect, Pearl. I'm punching in vector pitch 278 now. Let's hide for a while and have dinner in the slums."

"Oh gosh, that sounds like a bloody wonderful delight. Well, if it's not a dust ball of a moon, it just had to be one made of soggy, mushy mud. Can't an agent girl get a damn break once in a while? It looks like I will have to change to my bigger heels; I shouldn't complain. Sorry, I do apologise, and at least you've offered to cook me a meal. I suppose it's better than being in a Corporal Union prison with Commander Calo Tarick serving up yesterday's leftover pongy rations."

Meanwhile, the brigadier Corporal Union's BX10 battle cruiser suffers from the blockage path of the starship graveyard.

Deep at the helm control bridge tower of the *Galileo* class starship, Commander Calo Tarick expresses his pure frustration by demanding an undertrial report on the double,

"FIRST OFFICER, please tell me you have alternative motivations in place for chasing down these fugitives of intergalactic law. From where I'm sitting, you have given up the ghost. Is there someplace you plan to be? One, we should be cannon blasting our way through this heap of rusting brittle. More importantly, two, why does a flagship of the Corporal Union's Elite fleet not have a pair of BX19 Corsair fighters scouting the criminal's projected path? While I may only have one-working eye, the filthy freighter didn't slip-jump to the hyper-speed lanes when they had the option to. This tells me only one thing. They must be having technical issues of some sort, so what's it telling you, first-class officer of my stationary top-class warship? Please indulge me."

"Commander Tarick, I take full responsibility for my actions, sir. I evaluated the risks to outweigh the gains in pushing this magnificent cruiser through an unnecessary strain and the chance of pointless damage in the chase for just one petite green-haired female thief. At the time, the *Galileo* BX10 was in dry-dock of this request for launching in pursuit of a mere cargo freighter called the *Decepter*. Belonging to a freelance delivery man named Dan Casey, nothing special, just an intergalactic haulage pilot. So, I gave the solo order to leave the BX19 Corsair fighters at the spaceport Diligence while docked in the Corporal Union's fleet headquarters on Kothariya."

The dark-shaven, metal-patched-eyed Commander Tarick crunches a stern frown with an unsettling soul-piercing glare of his red cutlass-scarred eye, not moving a muscle of the heavily built physique or intimidating a flexing of his cybernetic hand. With a double flicking of his fibre fingers, he instantly arms a hidden gun barrel infused into his deformity with an intent to harm. Calo Tarick speaks in response to the first-ranking officer's report, making his words fully aware to be heard by all the fellow crew deck operatives of the BX10 *Galileo* cruiser.

"Thank you, First Officer, for your valuation of the operational task at hand and for informing us that there is no need to worry about a little green-haired woman. Yet, this woman managed to infiltrate the Kothariya ceremony chamber of Director Wilson Volantis. She managed to steal a priceless ancient artefact of tremendous value. Then, she winged her arse on that dust ball of a moon, Latin-Versa. She then linked up with a nothing-special-cargo pilot named Dan Casey, who, for your seemingly dim-shit knowledge of Officer One, has just outsmarted you to the point that your risk assessments may be outweighing the need for your use onboard my battlecraft."

Calo Tarick's cybernet-fibred thumb automatically fires a shuddering close-ranged blast shot that penetrates the first-ranking officer's torso with devastating injuries, blowing a flesh wound trauma of certain death. The skinny first officer falls to the starcruiser's operations deck and, with a grumble of gurgling saliva, moans then is still.

Clicking a revolving reload of his cybernetic gun-barrel fibre-metal antisocial hand of terror, Commander Calo Tarick frowns. Leaning his arching back in the cushioned control helm chair, he heaves his muscular frame, showing off his intimidating rock-ice appearance.

"OFFICER TWO, over here on the double, son, and clean up that fucking sorry mess of a man. Shoot him out of the airlock if you have to! Just get him out of my single-sight view; the pain is too much to endure. I recommend you take his duty badge as you are now the first-ranking officer of this fully armed intergalactic war cruiser. I also suggest, officer, you rig up the dual cannons to conventional ordnance weapons and start blasting a damn pathway through this combustible junkyard. I will report to high command."

Calo Tarick growls, "Don't you dare let me down now, son! Note your predecessor's faults and avoid his lack of poor judgemental foresight. That's if you want to fulfil your promotional position. I expect the highest calibre of order, and nothing less is acceptable. Now, find me that cargo vessel called the *Decepter*."

The newly appointed first officer of the brigadier Elite starcruiser instantly adapts to his new role of honour, taking charge hand of the ship-deck slaughter. He commands orders for a relief crew to dispose of the late officer's bleeding body.

Meanwhile, visually fading from the crew members' presence in the control deck quarters, Commander Calo Tarick inputs a personal key-coded digital combination into the computerised side-arm display of the helm chair. An opening is created beneath the command console with a shifting draw from the panel-plated moving floor.

The chair slowly sinks the seated muscle bulk figure of Commander Calo Tarick's shadowy dark essence to the mid-level communications chamber at the depths of the space cruiser. There is a pounding thud delivery as the chair connects to the chamber-railed floor, smoothly manoeuvring a hiss-pressured rotating position of the leather bedded recliner chair, perfectly linking a directed viewing for the Corporal Union's top-ranked Commander Tarick. He is now in front of a holo-net communication oval plasma screen positioned on the dull-lighted chamber wall.

Calo Tarick looks over the static chair side controls. Activating an eye reconditioning diagnostic detection scan, he engages a wave link transmission between the BX10 *Galileo* cruiser and the human capital home world of Kothariya.

The flat, infused plasma screen flickers a hazy message droning in a repeating cyber-toned male voice, "Mbron Media Ltd, intergalactic quantum datalink is establishing a secure connection; please wait."

There is a connection, and an image of Director Wilson Volantis is projected on the holo-net screen, reflecting the glare of his white, cold, scheming weasel eyes. He speaks forthrightly in a well-spoken Kothariya accent. "Commander Tarick, I gather you're interrupting my rituals of spiritual awakening with the good news you have reclaimed the stolen astrological data box? I assume you have also arrested the resistance agent, Veena Merida. Anything less would be considered disrespectful behaviour."

Meanwhile, the one loyal to the cause, Commander Tarick, explains his reasonable need to interrupt the Director's spiritual meditations, "I'm afraid to report that fugitive bitch, Merida, had escaped the combed sweep of the Latin-Versa moon haven by the time the BX10 *Galileo* slip-jumped upon from Kothariya. The resistance agent of Tara Harlow's rebellion has currently teamed up with a cargo freighter pilot named Dan Casey. He led us into a minor obstruction due to the discordance among the ranks, which has been dealt with in my court of law. Rest assured, Director Volantis, I will have the data box plus the feminine crook dealt with by the end of the day. Do I have full authorisation of apprehensions with any means necessary, even outside the Corporal Union's galactic jurisdiction, sir?"

The air is tense as the politician, Wilson Volantis, stands in silence. His presence emanates a sense of danger and unease, as if he holds a dark secret that no one dares to uncover. Suddenly, his eyes begin to change, dulling and losing colour as if drained of life. Then, in a swift and unsettling metamorphosis, they roll upwards, revealing a burning white light that seems to possess him entirely. His faithful Commander of arms watches in horror as the Director speaks in a deep and otherworldly voice, each word resonating through the room with a haunting intensity.

"Make sure you act on your own accord, Calo Tarick. We don't need delays with the Sulamani project; we have come too far in the shadows to flounder in the light. It has been two years in the making to this point of near-certain victory with the masterful intervention backing of the Core Lord's indoctrination programme. This has deceived the political galactic committee and the useless citizens of the Kothariya into investing in our progressive peacefulness. Where one mind is will be the mind of legions. That ancient data box has the astrological key coordinates to the black hole known as the Vortex, where our conquest of divine power awaits to shape the galaxy as I desire, with no thought of conflicting opinions. Please feel free to use any means required, Tarick. Still, failure is not an option I accept lightly. Retrieve me the data box and bring me the agent woman for a mind-wipe interrogation. Your timed audience has run its due course; do not fail me, Calo."

The transmission from the holo-net abruptly cuts off, leaving Commander Calo Tarick contemplating his next move. He swivels his chair to look out the window, where he sees the new first-rank officer giving orders and directing the ship through the debris-filled junkyard. The green mist swirling around them is thick and gaseous, making it difficult to see, but the cannons clear a path with powerful blasts, leaving a trail of destruction in their wake. Calo Tarick's scarred eye furrows in determination as they barrel through the wreckage, ready to fulfil the Director's commands.

Chapter Three

Dinner in the Slums

The starship sonically zooms across the damp, misty landscape of a seemingly deserted, muddy, rocky surface. A murky, sweeping, foggy grey mist spookily covers the landmass.

Dan Casey is scouting for a safe harbour area to land the *Decepter* and recharge the celestial power-drained hyperdrive. They need to continue to fulfil the contract of the exasperating green-haired female agent, Veena Merida, who is currently hiding from the Corporal Union's law-abiding grip.

While taking a charge hand of the unseen evolving procurements, Dan commences his starship's short-stop landing procedure on the soggy mud-layered moon, calmly seated inside the cockpit cabin, lulling back in his leather cushioned chair, as his brown waist pilot jacket flaps.

Dan carefully looks over the flick-switch navigational systems, checking for the perfect rock-formed spot to take stock of recent events.

"Hey, Pearl, give me what your memory core knows about this barren mud moon. And try to scan for a safe patch to land, preferably not soggy, so that we won't sink in the mist. I don't think little Miss Agent's boots will want to get out and push anytime too soon."

"I think that we both agree on one act of labour! I don't push around starships, but Mr Casey and I can initiate a surveying scan for you, saving poor Pearl the trouble. There's nothing here but horrible mud and gritty rocks. To be honest, I have a major dislike for any dirt. Also, do you have anywhere I can shower and change clothes on this cranky vessel? As it's been an extremely long few days, I'd just love to wash my hair. That dusty gravelled grit from Latin-Versa does nothing for a young woman's image, makes your hair feel like a shabby old pastel rag."

"Yeah, no worries on that requirement, sweetheart; I will give you a tour of the ship when we eventually find solid ground to land on if our cyber, Pearl, is awake. Hey, sweetie, any joy on this muddy moon's habitat information? I'm thinking between the two rocky canyons could treat us well."

Pearl responds, "Miss Merida's analysis of dirty mud and gritty rock seemed quite adequate to report a summary of Cartonne."

A cheeky smile forms on Veena's face. "Ah, see now, Mr Casey, your cyber assistant knows a top-notch analysis when spoken. Aww, thank you, Pearl. Is there any chance of looking at the biometric body scans you performed earlier?" Veena teases the handsome pilot about the analysis provided by his cyber assistant.

Dan Casey duly cuts into the flight cabin conversation, bewildered by Veena's requirements. "Why do you want to check the bio-scans Miss Merida? Are you still fluttering a heartbeat after I held you in my arms for seconds?" he jokes, giving her a sidelong glance as he lands the spacecraft.

"Oh, Mr Casey, I'm more intrigued as to what you were hiding from me! I saw how you flirtatiously looked at me at the Rhinegold-Goose salon bar in Latin-Versa."

Meanwhile, Veena is becoming completely oblivious to the predicament of her problematic galactic agent assignment. Dan shakes his head in amusement.

While closing down the flash-bleeping instrument systems of the cockpit cabin quarters, Dan Casey is intrigued about where they have landed. He rises from his leather reclining pilot seat, politely asking the onboard computer assistance to start the maintenance charge sequence.

"Pearl, start up the emphasis on recharging the hyperdrive, keeping our subsystems running on emergency power only, and can we breathe outside on this mud ball? As I'm going for a look around, I don't want to have any more bogus surprises creeping up on us. Had far too many of them already today."

Veena quickly rises from her co-pilot chair and follows the broad-shouldered cargo pilot down the starship walkway between the flight cabin and the lounge room.

She steps off in her high-heeled black leather boots, asking about the reason for searching the muddy canyon location of Cartonne.

"Do you need to venture outside? As we have all established, it's just mud, nothing more, and nothing less, just sloppy sticky mud! Not good for the designer boots at all, Mr Casey. And you said about cooking dinner for me in the slums; surely that's a better idea than walking around in the pitch blackness of a muddy environment? I disapprove of your actions in inviting danger to our dinner."

Dan Casey isn't taking much notice of Veena's tantrum as he marches into his Machiavellian starship's shadow-set lounge facilities. Pearl has the lighting system set to a low dimmer of a dulling amber glow. Dan, being a gentleman at heart, reaches down and grabs hold of Veena's duffel luggage sack.

In the background, the two travellers hear Pearl's updated reports through the inner comm microphone. These are the requested details regarding the creepy misty moon's atmospheric stability and survivability rate.

Pearl provides the information stored in her databanks about the moon Cartonne. "The oxygen level is breathable, and the weather circle context is a cold, damp, drizzling texture mist with only five recorded hours of sunlight available daily. No lifeforms or natural habitats are detected, but please be careful out there, Dan. I will activate front dual spot-light beams if you are to do a venture walk outside."

Instantly, the two front cone-nosed spotlights of the *Decepter* power up with a buzzing beam of light outside the MK2 freighter's presence. With no time to waste on guesswork, Dan Casey swiftly resumes Agent Merida's luggage to the larger bedroom compartment pod of the two on board the Merlin class freighter.

He presses the soft-touch button pad device, duly activating the fast-shifting traction of the shunting doorway. He takes a couple of steps forth in his black scuffed pilot boots before placing Veena Merida's belongings on the single, cream-coloured duvet air-floating bed mattress. He turns his tall and dark-haired handsome appearance to Veena.

"These can be your rest quarters, Miss Merida, for your short stay onboard my home. The washroom facility is the next room on the right, just down those few steps. Okay, missy, I won't be long. Do what you agents do during downtime, but don't press any flashing buttons. I've got two fleurs de steaks joints; I'll cook when I return. Catch you later."

Dan smiles a kind grin and then leaves the astonished Veena Merida.

"HEY, Mr Casey, are you even listening to me? Gosh! I've already told you once that I don't think it's a smart idea to wander around in the dark; it could be dangerous."

Dan Casey is in no mood to waver as he hurries along through the lounge deck of his starship, soon making his way back to the airlock hatch. Annoyingly, he can hear the scuttling clicking heels on the plated floor behind him. With the cold shoulder treatment, Dan bluntly ignores the distraction while he prepares to key in the airlock hatch authorisation code. But he is soon interrupted by a dainty tapping of long-nailed fingers on the broad right shoulder of his leather jacket.

"Don't worry, yourself, agent-babe; I'm a big boy now with a trusty loaded barrelled gun. So, I don't need any trained-to-kill female chaperone holding my hand or slowing me down unless that trembling is all due to your heart's concern that you will never see me again. Aww, Miss Merida, I didn't know you cared so much as the biometric scans never lie, sweetheart. Why are you putting your jacket on? I thought you were washing your hair, remember?"

Veena aims an unimpressed pouting glare of her pretty eyes directly into Dan's indulging brown pupils with a no-nonsense attitude, carefully zipping up to conceal her black bra top. The young, independent-minded woman confides as he is leaving the depressurised exit hatch of the *Decepter*. "Well, I'm putting my jacket on, Mr Casey, because I'm coming with you, and it is not because I'm concerned about your undying idea of delusional romance either. It's more the fact I can't get stranded on this mudball moon if anything did manage to happen to you. Your words about being stranded without cosmetic perks have slightly influenced my mind. So yes, I'm coming with you, and STOP calling me agent, babe or sweetheart. My name is VEENA. Okay! Now, come on. Try to work with me, Dan. Let us get this mud perimeter searched before I get damn moody."

The personalised authorisation code passes the clearing procedure within a few seconds of Dan Casey's code input. The sealed airlock hatch re-opens with a hissing of evaporating steamed fray. The freighter vessel's flight case stairway leads down the rampway and out of the *Decepter*'s main exit port. Standing in a distilled motion of thought, the handsome-shaped face of Dan Casey blows a stressed breath while biting his tongue, wording an apologetic reply to the flustered-up resistance agent.

"Okay, I won't mention another word apart from I'm sorry, Veena! You must realise I'm not used to working with passengers or getting hijacked daily. So, you may accompany me on our scouting trip; it's not a problem with me. I'm looking forward to it, Miss Merida. We wouldn't want to make you moody, would we now?"

He starts making headway down the stair-ramp of his starship, venturing outside to the atmospheric damp drizzle and the unpleasant conditions of the filthy pit moon.

Dan Casey places a foot on the ground and instantly sinks in the thick surface covering. It consists of mounds of soggy mud and small, undefined jagged rocks. Worse yet, it has the odour of a sewer dump trash pan.

"Hey, you watch your dinky, high-heeled steps. And I'd try not to breathe too deeply. I'm inclined to believe this may not be the freshest or most rewarding place to be in the Kalanisi Universe."

There is the complete silent darkness of a barren-spell moon. The nearing hazy cold mist of nightfall on Cartonne is drawing in extremely fast. This is due to the mud-riddled moon experiencing a minimal time slot of sunlight. With only the *Decepter*'s twin front nose spot-beam lights brightening up the horizon, there are only their shadows.

Not lagging too far behind the inquisitive cargo pilot is the sexy silhouette of Veena Merida, delightfully arriving at the base step of the Machiavellian starship exit side ramp. "Oh, yuk! That's such a horrible surface for any type of footwear, and the pongy damp smell resembles shit, Mr Casey."

Whereas a stride or two ahead, Dan Casey makes his way through the hazy dullness of the rocky canyon path. Veena Merida, now gathering her stride, is now close to reaching him.

"I told you to stay on the *Decepter*. I just knew you would only start to complain. You should have just washed your hair, Veena, as you planned. Let me scout ahead alone. That's always worked well for me before the unfortunate downturns of today."

While he's taking a further inspection around the dampening ghostly mist and the gloomy bottomless presence of Cartonne, he sees nothing more than muddy rock formations entwined with small flowing dirty water streams of lava mud, not fit for drinking purposes.

Veena is shivering in the damp climate and vigorously rubs her dainty gloved hands up and down over her slender, zip-jacketed arms. While checking around the silent brushed moon of mud, she explains to Dan, "I wasn't moaning about your advice of staying on your starship. I was just letting it be known this is a dump, and I'm feeling the cold, stinky air everywhere. Plus, my heels will be ruined in this sticky mud. What the hell have I just stood in? Can't see a clear step forward in this mist without sinking in a pothole of slop."

Dan Casey stops his walking quarry at the edge of the twin rock canyon's shielding light rays. He retrieves the green-dust smoke. With a quick, short, flashy flick, he throws and catches the cigarette in his stubbled mouth before lighting up.

"Pearl warned us it was damp and cold, so you should have brought a bigger jacket, or have you ever tried to wear more suitable clothes for your current place of stay? Just an idea, Agent Merida, for any other short-term hijackings you have planned in your dizzy-minded way."

Dan sparks another flame from his Astro-lighter to the burning tip of his green-dust smoke, simultaneously inhaling the green smoke, reversibly blowing out the smoke with a relieved sigh.

"Did you dare just to call me dizzy-minded! Gosh, Mr Casey, who takes any fashion advice from a cargo-runner pilot? Is that what you say to all the cheap pick-up ladies you truly take to shit-smelling moons? Try to dress more accordingly, sweetheart! I can't believe what I'm hearing from you, mister; it's so rudely shocking. I would have expected more empathy."

The charismatic cargo pilot takes a deep inhaling drag of his smoking filter, squinting his dreamy brown eyes with utter dismay. "Well, I would have thought you must stop moaning by now! But, hey, hell no! The Agent Merida show just keeps on the roll-out of a tune. I don't want to be here either. Let's get that clear for starters, and next time, if fate can be so cruel to strike twice, I'll find you an Elite planet with sunny beach cocktail bars and a damn high-grade woozy shoe shop. Now, will you just button up those sweet, pouting red blossomed lips for a moment?"

Dan Casey raises his voice. "Come on, Veena, let's just get back to the *Decepter* before it gets any darker and we all start to sink in a pool of mud gloom."

Dan was now in a stirring mood himself, while freely too taking another deep drag of his green-dust smoke anguish, only realising the flame had deserted.

"I know I've been warned, but living it for real is two different things, and I certainly don't moan to the extent you're describing! Oh, moody star pilots."

They make their way back aboard Deceptor. Each thinking they have the worst deal. Veena heads off to her pod, but Dan makes his way to the kitchen.

The handsome cargo-runner pilot is busy cooking a meal for two at the dining grill pod just across from the lounge quarters of the vessel. The lights are set at a dim-low spectrum of romantic shading. The *Decepter* is running only on the emergency power resources. The slender-shaped craft's built-in navigation system, Pearl, is taking care of the maintenance procedure by recharging the celestial hyperdrive engines and updating Dan Casey on the intramural synthetic progress report.

Pearl states, "Powered generation energy levels uploaded to forty-five per cent of sublight infuse, advised flight levels admitting to sixty per cent rate minimum. Enjoy your dinner date. I hope it goes well for you, Dan."

The talented chef, Dan Casey, stylishly flicks the fleur du steak over in the sizzling pan on the single grill pod. With a laughing gesture at Pearl's unexpected comments, he brings his self-occupied attention away from the flip-flopping steak.

"NO way is this a damn dinner date! You must be joking, Pearl. She hijacked us into service, and her moaning never ends. It's more like a chance to survive the night without being tempted to lock up Miss Merida in the cargo haul. So, I thought this dish, and a chilled glass of Château Latour 3998, might ease the tension a little bit if we're to work together through this crazy contract; that's if she ever manages to come out of the damn shower. I'm sure that's been running for at least an hour!"

On that outspoken comment by Dan, the bathroom door of the starship shuns open in a hiss as Veena quickly scurries out with only a white towel wrapped around her naked, curvy body, while her wet green hair is dripping a trail along the plated flooring of the *Decepter*'s inner frame.

Veena politely yells out, "Sorry I've taken so long. Hmm, that smells divine, Mr Casey. Give me five ticks, and I'm all yours; pour me a drink, please, Dan."

Dan mutters, "More like agent orders in advance."

He swiftly continues to time the food to perfection. The pilot cook bends, taking the Astro-fries from the steaming oven. He places them fairly on two divided white plates with the help of the kitchen pod's frying shovel.

He quickly completes the same method when taking the fleur du steak joints off the heated grill, veering them to the serving plates, which are also finely balanced on the frying shovel. He finishes the dish off with a mixed mozzarella and pancetta salad with an optional beef dripping sauce for the steak.

With the two prepared meals freshly steaming hot and ready for serving, Dan Casey hurries over to the circular dining table. Gripping the dual warm plates, he places them down on an opposite side seating plan.

Suddenly in the mood to entertain, Dan takes firm hold of the Château Latour 3998 bottled wine, gently coaxing open the corkscrew to pop a nice fizz.

Dan meaningfully starts to tilt a pouring of the sparkling

red wine into the tall-stemmed Taylor glasses. Dan Casey stops his generous pouring of the highly filled wine glasses. He easily manoeuvres a teasing, slow turning around of his brown leather-jacketed, well-built manly body, eventually facing the dinner guest of honour with the bottle of Château Latour 3998 in his black-gloved grip, generating a handsome smile.

"Hey, Veena, wow, you look amazing! I've rustled up a small steak dish to apologise for shouting back at you. It's been a strange day. I apologise. Please, come this way, take a chair. I poured you that glass of wine you require; it's a twelve-year-old 3998 bottle and meant to be a pretty good vintage."

The dashing cargo pilot charmingly takes her tiny feminine velvet-gloved hand and leads the gorgeous jade-eyed agent to the lounge table of the MK2 Machiavellian freighter.

Veena Merida smiles, showing off her glittering white teeth, looking visually stunning in a wrap-around pastel flimsy top, covered by a stylish light suede jacket and skintight charcoal-coloured split jumpsuit leggings, seductively supported by some slimline black strap-heeled boots, and slanted black leather holster belt containing her silver-scoped pistol.

Veena feels reinvigorated after the steaming-hot shower, radiating a beaming jade glow and gleaming cosmetic make-up.

"Wow, Mr Casey, you've gone above and beyond when you hinted at cooking a meal; thank you for your efforts. I'm astonished. Aww, and there I was wondering if dinner would be a pilot's satay curry and some Astro-rice beans."

She continues. "Plus, I'm sorry too for how all this has worked out so far. I truly never meant to hijack you at gunpoint. I was planning to ask for your help in the Rhinegold-Goose until the Corporal Union's shadowy scout officers started poking around. Please accept my sincere apologies, and I dearly accept yours, Mr Casey. Now, shall we forget to talk about work for a while and enjoy this wonderful food? It looks and smells top-class; what do we have on this fine menu? I'm so extravagantly hungry."

Dan, hosting, takes a step back, pulling his lounge table chair forward. As he places a seat down, he explains his chosen evening meal to the beautiful green-pastel-haired lady guest. "Well, I'd planned to get a few supplies at Latin-Versa, but it turned out not to be the most hospitable moon for food grocery shopping. So, I just had to make do with the few onboard supplies that I picked up in between my Sandtex Ltd contract and the Suvarna cluster's drop-off. Featuring on tonight's fugitive runaway menu, Madam Merida, we have grilled fleur du steak joints and Astro-fries, which hopefully are not burnt to an oiled crisp, coupled with a pancetta and mozzarella salad with a homemade beef dripping sauce. And swallow it down with a bottle of Château Latour 3998. Please feel free to start tucking in, Veena, and call me Dan if we'll be cargo partners for a short period."

Veena tilts her cute, pretty face to a leaning, engaged pose, smiling as her long, washed, wavy green hair falls around her wrap-around suede jacket outfit, raising a gentle clash of tingling glasses.

Veena smiles a room-brightening glow, replying to her sophisticated, handsome male host. "To newly found partners and a safe journey of fortune. Cheers, Dan."

The rain outside the *Decepter* starts to pour, slapping a pattering on the starship frame.

As they both eat and drink away the fun, chilled night, Dan smiles a charmed look across the table while taking a small gulp of his Château Latour 3998. He asks with a curious interest, "So what does Veena Merida like to do in her spare time if agents get any relaxation periods?"

Veena looks up from her plate, swiftly engaging her jade eyes with Dan's dark brown ones. "Well! Dan, I don't get asked that question much. I usually get shot at first, and the questions follow later. I do like dancing when I get the chance. Visit the odd universal art gallery. Plus, I adore shopping for new high-class clothes and top-designer shoes, as you have already gathered! What about life as a cargo runner and freighter pilot? How's trade been faring for you lately, Dan?"

Dan Casey quickly finishes his grilled fleur du steak. While full and satisfied, he firmly places the used cutlery on his plate. Calmly leaning his brusk body back in the padded lounge chair, he handsomely smiles.

"It was a simple, boring life until this morning when I met this dangerously armed woman called Miss Merida. Cargo runner duty is ordinarily very quiet."

He smiles and continues, "No, I don't get to see many folks anymore, just contract after contract to keep Pearl and me afloat. So, I suppose, in one way of saying it's been nice to have sidetracked. Thanks!"

The freelancing cargo runner gathers his manly body from the starship lounge setting quarters, taking his plate and the few leftover scraps of streak grille to the trash pod facility. Dan clears off the plates, duly placing the dirty washing on the kitchen pod side, reaching for a fresh packet of smokes stored away in a side compartment.

The outside storm blows over the silhouette-framed starship. Meanwhile, in peaceful harmony, the two are getting merry inside the star-vessel, tipsily starting to ease the levelling tension of the stressful day.

Veena Merida duly swigs back the Château Latour 3998, giggling. "Hmmm, I like indulging in tasty red vintage wine. Dan, can I have some more, please? So, it sounds like this: Veena is a very attractive beauty and a dangerous threat. I think we need {hic} to be very aware. Shoot her! {hic} These are the very words of Commander Calo Tarick on Kothariya when {hic} he found out I wasn't who I should have been. Ha ha. Oh, I do believe this sparkling 3998-year-old red wine {hic} has gone straight to my head."

She grabs her wine glass and wobbles over to the lounge

seating, strutting a swaying tipsy walk in her high-heeled boots, swiftly manoeuvring a sexy wiggle over to the curved three-spaced sofa.

Her drunk, staring jade eyes flutter, and she is having fun teasing him. Dan Casey follows her to the lounge, grabbing his fresh packet of green-dust smokes before topping up Veena's empty glass.

"You sure you want some more of the high-grade wine? It seems to be having a quick effect on you, Miss Merida. I told you it was a good year, 3998, but I don't want to be accused of making you a woozy, dangerous, drunken agent lady and be in stern trouble with your resistance boss, Tara Harlow. Also, do you mind if I smoke? You mentioned you quit the habit, so if it's problematic, Veena. I can easily go outside in the muddy rain; it's not a problem."

She nods that it is okay, so he swiftly flicks his chrome Astro-lighter, indulging in an earned deep inhaling of the smoke vapours, amusingly listening to the waffling wine gulping verbal chatter of Veena, seated a ladylike picture behind him while duly tasking his chores overhearing the tittering centre of her well-spoken tipsy voice.

Veena said with a slight slur. "I'm an agent of intergalactic boundaries! I know myself when I had too much giggle pop {hic}. Haha, plus you seem pretty mysterious and dangerous yourself, Mr Casey. Don't think my skilled training didn't collectively witness how your little manoeuvring stunt on the *Decepter*'s flight step stairs way back at Latin-Versa, {hic} have not gone unnoticed. I saw how you wounded that Corporal Union's Elite snooping guard when you could easily have killed him, or worse, him shooting me! I wasn't even aware of his presence. Aww, you truly saved my life, Dan. So I'm very sorry I've not said it to you before, but thank you."

Dan gracefully makes his way over to Veena from the kitchen.

He decides to explain his thoughts on the Latin-Versa incident to her. "Well, I didn't see any point in why either of you had to die. Plus, your training intuition has come to the fore. You're correct; I wasn't always a cargo runner. I used to work for a space security protection outfit run by a close friend who passed away about five years ago. The space-flight protection unit also shut. After that, I decided to start fresh and become an intergalactic freelance cargo-runner pilot for hire. That's just me, Veena. There isn't much to discuss, especially compared to the exciting life you lead as an agent."

Veena Merida firmly takes a drag of the smoking filter and instantly coughs.

"Ha ha, you are one bad {hic} influence on me. I've not smoked properly for at least two years. My analysis of you is that you're a surprise package, Mr Casey, {hic}. Think I need a little sleep, and pretty damn fast as well. Oh dear, my head feels a bit dizzy. Good night!"

Veena regrettably stands up too fast, clumsily nearly falling over. Dan Casey immediately manoeuvres to catch the fallen, wandering female agent. "Ooh, gosh, Mr Casey, one might think I may be a little bit drunk!"

In her not-so-sober state, she willingly, without thought of consequence, puckers up an appealing red glossy mouth and hovers breathtakingly close to Dan Casey's natural manly lips. But he resists.

"Whoa, steady as you go there, agent lady! You nearly fell head over heels for me there, literally. I'd say you are more than a little drunk, but don't you worry your pretty bonnet as I got a firm hold of you."

Veena Merida nervously mumbles a shying resistance of words, unable to control her feelings. "Oh, Mr Casey, we shouldn't be embracing like galactic students? Mister, you are a naughty cargo pilot."

While the freighter pilot is tempted to kiss the beautiful

woman, he moans a sigh of concern. "Hey, Veena! Are you okay? Come on, Miss Woozy Head, let's get you tucked up in bed."

With a mixture of disappointment and refined judgement of consequence, Dan Casey, gentlemanlike, scoops the unconscious Veena Merida's exotic, shapely figure to her bedroom resting quarters. Outside, there is now an easing of the furious weather to the mere spitting of raindrops freely falling on the hazy dirtball moon, Cartonne.

The early-morning purple-pink sky is a dawning picture of a bland natural habitat. Deep in the resting quarts of the *Decepter*, the asleep, overindulging female agent, Veena Merida, is curled up in a blissful ball in the floating bed duvet of the Machiavellian freighter's restroom facility.

Suddenly, fluttering a flicker of her pretty closed eyelids open, Veena gasps a shell-shocked waking breath; she instantly wakes up groaning due to the previous evening's overenjoyment.

"Oh gosh, my head hurts one spin too many. What in the world happened? Hmm, did I get a little drunk? How embarrassing! I even tried a puckered-up kiss on him, but surely not! I'm on an important intergalactic mission; it must have been the other way around, yeah? I'd say so for certain. Oh, my head is thudding a bang. I need some fresh air and fast if you can find any on this soggy mud moon."

She leaves the snug duvet and springy mattress while yawning and shaking her tangled silk mane. Kicking back the soft, warm duvet covers, the jaded-eyed agent manoeuvres a slick turn of a bed edge perching position, stretching out her long, shapely legs.

Veena notices she isn't wearing any footwear and realises her silver scope barrelled weapon has been removed and placed on the bedroom cabin's side wall rack. Her womanly, sexy, admirable body is still fully dressed in her wrap-around top and jumpsuit leggings. Shockingly, she has a waking vision of thought, mulling her gaze and sparking her eyes to the *Decepter*'s plated flooring with a smile of mixed satisfaction.

"Aww, Dan must put me to bed, removing my personal effects, but left my garments untouched, not even a peek; what a sweet gentleman indeed! Most I've known would have taken advantage of the opportunity or, probably even worse, bless. What am I saying? I don't like him. He's a greasy pilot! Yes, that's all he is, an oily pilot; I'm glad that's all cleared up right then! I'm also going for a short walk before my mind plays more elusive nonsensical tricks of schoolgirl delusions."

Veena slips on her high-heeled slimline boots with a swift gathering of her firearm weapon, readily stepping a light foot out of the bedroom quarters she has acquired while staying on board the *Decepter*. Cunningly tapping the lock device button pad with her dainty gloved fingers, she tiptoes to the across-the-room wash facilities, creeping and scurrying into the bathroom with the hissing clang of the revolving door closing behind her.

Veena presses the water tap, and with an instant trickling flow, it starts to whoosh around the oval sink. She leans forward and performs a reinvigorating wash of her gorgeous face.

"Psst, Pearl, are you in there? If so, can you unlock the airlock hatch? I need to walk a hangover off. I have no authorisation code of note. Plus, I will have a copy of the biometric body scans. Send them to my holo-net address at Merida.V.234@holo.link.mail. Thanks a bunch in advance, Pearl, that's if you're listening to me."

"Hatch authorisation code inputs at 351-974/Casey, dual bio-scan analysation editions of the morning and evening to night results have been delivered accordingly. I hope you enjoyed your fainting date, Miss Merida!"

With a more than cheerful smile of acknowledgement by the starship crystalised flight assistance, Veena giddily replies without thinking about the question provided.

"Yes, the dinner date was a lovely surprise. Hold on one moment now, Pearl. It wasn't any sort of date! What the hell am I thinking? Let's say more of a business arrangement meal. Yes, that's what it felt like a contract dinner. Now, there is no more on the ridiculous matter, okay? Well, you could send me Dan's full bio-scan just for confidentiality identification checks, so we don't need to book in when we get to my chosen location?"

To avoid disrupting Dan's peaceful slumber in his primary bedroom quarters, Veena steadily moves about quietly as she ventures out to explore the rugged and muddy terrain of Cartonne.

Veena Merida elegantly motions her sophisticated pastel-shaded aura to the brimming outside scenery of the *Decepter*. Instantly, in a single breath, the young lady's acute sense of smell is hit with the awful atmospheric-smelling aroma of the remote mud-slushed moon.

"Oh yuck! That disgusting pongy whiff in the misty air circulation did not get fresher overnight. That one could have only wished for! Ah well, carry on, agent girl. Nothing to be afraid about; it's only smelly mud."

Veena Merida, smiling a natural blend of happiness and an unexplained joyful feel, is sidestepping a tender footing over the pocket-sized sinking mud-ridden potholes, with extreme care of her expensive suede boots. But more astonishingly, she is distracted by the body biometric scan results shown on her slim fit holo-pad.

"Wrong! I didn't turn into a jelly blob of love bubbles. No! I wasn't feeling sexually flattered either, and I certainly did not flutter a throbbing heartbeat off the bio-charts. Oh gosh, Pearl needs to recalibrate her biometrics systems. Now let's peek at Mr Cargo Guy's results."

Unknowingly, Veena is overly focused on the holo-pad analysis report to accurately note her bearings, straying away from the *Decepter*'s stationery-viewed landing port of a haven.

Veena duly breezes a reading through Dan Casey's bio-scan analysis while reaching for the borrowed Astro-lighter. She finds the chrome flick-lid gadget and holds the green-dust smoke tip between her velvet-covered fingers.

"Ah, the culprit of crime causing me to faint like a drunken schoolgirl. Oh, dear? I've packed the habit for two years without a glimmer of temptation! Then, one night, with a bottle of wine and cargo-runner pilot, it's all gone into a downward spiral.

"What the hell? At least I had some proper fun instead of an undercover-staged assignment. Plus, it has been a strange few days by anyone's standard of normality. You can't blame a girl for wanting to stray occasionally. Sometimes, I wish I wasn't a mere remote-numbered agent of the underground resistance and had a more normal life to progress and get to know people like Dan. But I'm afraid it's impossible as I must deliver the astrological data box to Tara Harlow, whoever she may be. As a remote operative, I never get to meet the boss lady much, but let's not mention that to Dan, as he may get a little bit flaky at the lack of information."

Veena carries on her slushy walk a bit further, veering a sighting distance of ground right away from the rock canyon trail opening. She stops near a crater pit. Taking the Astro-lighter firmly in hand with a careless flicking wrist twist action, she ignites a burning wind-repellent flame to the ranging tip of the smoke filter's stubbed end.

The purple clustery skies gush a morning breeze that blows Veena Merida's long green hair back in a flowing bundle behind her. She exhales the dust smoke in a practised smoke ring.

"Just one more tiny little drag, then back to my agent work, and damn well, get a grip, woman. How old are you? Twenty-eight, and I'm behaving like I'm eighteen again!"

Veena slickly flickers the used-up green-smoke filter and starts her return journey to *Decepter*. But she suddenly feels a purring tremor followed by a howling behind her.

Veena Merida is profoundly frozen in sheer terror due to the unexpected hideous trembling. Veena is viciously knocked flat in a puddle of soggy, smell-ridden mud.

She yells, aching in pain at the braced impact. "Ah, damn; my back hurts! What in the world is going on in that mud pit?"

Again, she hears a recurring horrible screeching groaning sound bouncing off the canyon walls. Her jade eyes catch the monstrous sight of a massive three-pronged claw that grossly appears in the ghoulish, howling mud-pit crater.

She mumbles in a panic, "Oh shit, you have got to be kidding me? Quick get up off your arse, agent girl, and get out of here fast, or you will be a damn first-class dinner in the slums for that revolting beast!"

Veena is petrified but swiftly manages to roll and leverage a stance, but the mud is making her escape to the starship difficult.

The rest of the beast now appears, and it rises to a towering height. It growls in fang-gleaming rage as the mud-matted phantom monster crawls up from the spiralling dirt-well crater. Organising its curled spike prolonged claws and hideously arching its menacing spiky armoured shell back, it stomps forward on its beastly clawed cumbersome feet.

Veena's expensive black high-heeled boots sadly sink into the muddy ground, hindering her return to safety. With a mumbling, panting breath of conscious, angered panic, Veena frantically screams in bitter frustration,

"Damn blasted heels. I do wish I was just a flat-sole type of girl! But this beast isn't getting the better of me."

But using her combat-trained skills, Venna slips her free hand over the swinging holster belt containing the infrared weapon, swinging hold of the pistol's slick trigger handle stem. She performs a masterful sidestepping manoeuvre and perfectly spins around.

Veena Merida rapidly squeezes her finger along the pulsing sling trigger of the now active weapon, instantly opening fire with a scattershot approach and a daring element of blindsided instinctive luck. The shots penetrate the grizzly phantom mud creature.

Unfortunately for Veena, her efforts cause no harm to the beast's health. The shots only temporarily slow the raging moon phantom of Cartonne. She takes a quick-dashed gaze from her jade eyes and trudges for her life back to the starship.

She loudly screams a pleading cry, "Dan, help me, please. Mr Casey, wake up, help!"

Veena attempts another round of fire while firmly gripping the agent contract data holo-pad. She caresses the indicting silver trigger lever with intent to bodily harm the pursuing grotesque monster. Unfortunately, Veena's boots catch again on the muddy surface, and she falls face down into the smelly slop mud. Her ankle is aching.

"Ahh, no! Dan, help me. Pearl, please wake him up. HELP!"

The crystallised AI system Pearl initiates the emergency alert siren, buzzing a drill around the interior of the MK2 Machiavellian interstellar vessel. Her cyber-toned manner appeals to the hostile trouble of an immense proportion erupting outside in the rocky canyon scenery of the mudball moon.

"Warning! Dan, I advise you to wake up now. I repeat. Be a good time to wake up, warning; our woozy female guest, Miss Merida, may be in slight trouble."

Dan eventually starts to flicker an eyelid open while the alarm sounds.

"Miss Merida is in trouble? What she does is cause a mess of innocent people's lives, like poor mine. I was hoping Veena was just a bad dream and would be gone by now, but by the sounds of the alerting alarms, I guess not. What has she done this time, Pearl? Break a dinky winky nail or worse, by the sounds of that echoing roar! What the hell is growling?"

Dan suddenly feels the unstable mud-ridden ground starting to tremble, a heavily shaking squelch, while simultaneously hearing that dreadful screeching roar. Dan Casey leaps and emerges a swift jump instantly out of the floating mattress bed, swiftly brushing the cream-coloured duvet aside.

He urgently wriggles on his black boots. Quickly he pushes himself up to a firm stance and stretches his hunky body to reach hold of his black-barrelled silver-based gun. Motivated, he leaves his cabin with a sprinting urge through the starship's dullened hazed lights.

He bellows, "FIRE UP the subsystems, and crank up the celestial hyperdrive, readily charged or not. I've got a real bad feeling we need to leave this damn slop-pot moon and pronto, sweetie."

Making his brash, adored presence to the hacked open airlock hatch, Dan tailors a holding slide down the hatchway staircase bannister rail.

He's now outside and is utterly gobsmacked by the giant-in-height, ghoulish spiked monster, smashing a menacing crashing swipe of a three-pronged grotesque spear. Knowing there is little time to think, he furiously breaks through the twin canyon's rocky mud-laced structures.

The beast walks down a raging pathway and heads towards Agent Veena Merida, who is clasping her injured ankle and shouting for immediate help.

Dan quickly shakes off the shock of catching a non-wanted dirt ball phantom monster heading in the same direction as his starship or worse. The interstellar pilot breaks into a sweat to help the fruitful green-haired damsel in distress.

"Where in the world did she manage to find that biological thing? On a barren moon scanned with no known living life force? VEENA! Hang on. I'm coming to get you."

Dan brashly opens a flurry of blast-fire shots shooting spray around the bounding creature's sly yellow evil-toned eyes. The creature's confusion gives Dan Casey a fighting chance to get to

Veena. Dan carefully cups his bare-skinned manly arms around her slender back, slipping a firm grip on her slinky belted waistline.

While heaving a huge sigh of relief, Veena Merida slings her arm around Dan Casey's broad shoulders while clumsily dropping her holo data pad.

Veena yelps, "No, my datapad. I need to go back for it."

But with his energetic arms full and in no mood to backtrack, he hears the howling hideous rock phantom creature regaining ground.

"NO, we're leaving this shit hole of the moon as off right now; you're hurt, so forget the damn holo-pad, and If you want to argue a reason, just take a good look behind us for details."

He makes his way aboard his starship, and while still carrying Veena, he no-nonsense shoulder barges the air hatch touch-pad lock, instantly closing the exit hatch mechanism with a hissed closure.

Outside, the creature continues howling. Dan rushes through the lounge and into the bleeping cockpit-flight cabin. He carefully shifts and places Veena down gently on the cushioned co-pilot flight chair.

"Just buckle up and keep quiet, Agent Merida; I don't want to hear a peeping moan from those sweet, kissable red lips you flaunt about! You never told me your mud-ridden boyfriend was going to join us. If I'd known, I would have cooked dinner for three. Where did you find this beastly thing? It's shockingly massive and heading right for the front port of my starship! Hang on."

Dan quickly flicks the core switch-trip buttons of the vessels and reacts to the humming buzz of the computerised subsystems. Then he ramps up the forward power throttle stick to a high-ranked notch, firmly gripping a palm-sweating hold of the sterling lever-styled pilot joystick activating the starship.

The slanted pylon booster exhausts fire up with the bursting pressure of tripled engine flares steaming, a thrusting surge out the tail of the Machiavellian freighter.

Back inside the cradle-rocking flight cabin quarters, Veena buckles up in the co-pilot's safe harness pull-cord straps. She is in a frightful mood. "Hey, chop, chop, as we need a lot higher altitude than this to claim our safety, Dan. Come on! That ghostly creepy creature charges like a bull, so try to see if you can go a bit faster, as that might help! What are you waiting for, Mr Casey? Do something now, and for your interest, I am officially scared to death!"

The vile, screeching, phantom monstrosity starts swinging towards the hover-motivated *Decepter*. The wild, hungry beast thrusts a vicious attack, luckily falling a few inches short of the MK2 Merlin freighter. Bravely talented as a class-one interstellar pilot, Dan Casey just manages to get the *Decepter* in the atmospheric hazy air, briefly skimming past the hideous phantom monster's furious swinging assaults. He throttles up to an accelerating speed to manoeuvre to an open way away out of the canyon, leaving the beast and Cartonne behind.

Chapter Four

Exchanging Chase

The *Decepter* is thrusting vastly away from Cartonne, capturing a passing glide through the atmospheric orbit at a high cruising speed. They are about to conduct a galactic slip-jump of the hyper-lanes en route to the secret rendezvous location in the Isadora system.

In the cockpit cabin quarters of the *Decepter*, Dan and Veena are still recovering from the mud-slop encounters. Handsomely seated in his leather-padded pilot's chair, Dan Casey sits upright in his mud-splattered brown waist jacket and trenched pilot jeans. He has a stern, gripping hand on the slick-handled joystick, firmly guiding his starship into open space, drifting a pulsing speed away from the moon's orbit.

The cargo runner calmly reassures the jade-eyed agent the worst is over. "Hey, Veena, calm down; it will be okay. It's gone now, whatever that monstrosity was. How's your ankle? You look like you are in pain. Plus, why did the scans fail to identify that mud-sucked beast, Pearl?"

Dan Casey asks multiple questions, while Veena Merida sheepishly replies in an annoyed manner in her classy, feminine voice. "I don't care to know what it was. It smelt horrible, and it cost me my suede jacket. Plus, it ruined my high-heeled boots. They were new as well. And my ankle feels like that hideous beast's face: terribly swollen, sore, and damn cranky. Why take a nice girl like me to a mud moon, Mr Casey? Surely you know it's only asking for trouble?"

Dan Casey's chiselled, mud-splattered face drops to an astonished assessment of being accused. "Hey, don't you blame me for your morning nature trail! If I recall correctly, I was the one scooping you out the shit again, just like the glorious Latin-Versa escapade shenanigans. And, by the looks of the agent issues on the galactic horizon, I might have to save you again as your fan club is back, Veena. What a gracious joy, Commander Him, who hasn't given up this patch-eyed ghost chase. You really must have pissed him off rotten, and I wonder how! Pearl, wake up! We need to get out of this gaff sector now, and I'm still waiting for your cybernetic excuse for not picking up Veena's ex-boyfriend!"

The late responding starship flight analyst confirms, "I must stress the urgency of the situation at hand. The vessel is rapidly closing in and demanding immediate communication. We have received an internal message from the Corporal Union flagship stating that unless the captain of this freighter establishes a direct communication link, the *Decepter* will be apprehended without any consideration for our defence. There's some more bad news. Our bio-scans failed to detect any accurate location of biological phantom presence due to the need for a full upgrade of navigational instruments related to ground scan components. I have warned you numerous times about this issue during our visits to maintenance spaceports." Pearl sarcastically states before reporting, "Activating celestial hyperdrive, setting trajectory sequence as requested; powering up subsystem to hyper-lanes engaged."

The flight cabin flick-switch instruments start to flash a beep intermittently into motivation engagement, and Dan Casey wriggles into a comfy position in his leather-padded pilot's chair.

"No comm-links, Pearl. Keep it hushed. I'm in no mood for talking, and it seems I have two females blaming me now."

Dan jolts a swift ramping forward of the accelerator throttle lever, pushing the *Decepter*'s slick hull-framed silhouette to a slicing weave, pitching to high operating speeds.

While buckling up her pull-strap safety harness belts, Veena sits a muddy sight for sore eyes with a mood to match; she tells the concentrating interstellar pilot, "Great, Commander Tarick, that's all I need, more stress. It's bad enough my favourite jacket was ruined. I just can't get a peaceful moment to get my head around this mission! Can you please outrun him this time, Mr Casey? Remember, I'm prone to getting a little dizzy through hypersonic travel, so there are no sudden shifting manoeuvres like before. Okay?"

Dan Casey smiles and says, "We can outrun them easily. Buckle up and hold tight, sweetheart."

Whirling an invigorated, blue-energised sparkle of the triple-slanted boosters, the *Decepter* shudders a powering surge with a silent flash and thudding bang as the freighter transitions into the next galaxy.

The pursuing BX10 *Galileo* battle cruiser of the Corporal Union's deployed law enforcer unit tracks the Machiavellian freighter slipstream projector into the opening hyper-lanes, thrusting in hot, vile pursuit. By threading a contravene tapestry trace, the Corporal Union's war vessel penetrates the speeding breaking veil of the hyper-slip-lanes, using the full velocity of the Elite sub-warp drive engines with a tremendous grovelling drone. The pursuing spacecraft brutally gains on the *Decepter*. Still, the smaller ship performs a quarter-jump lead to deflect the intended threat of the advanced *Galileo*'s conquesting prevalence for a galactic lawful arrest.

The *Decepter* scorches a pace, cutting a blanket weave of hypersonic trailing flares and stylishly burns a zoomed path through the electrical pulse of the hyper-speed slip-lanes. Yet, it is constantly hounded by a more advanced upgradeable spacecraft like the mighty *Galileo* warship.

Whereas in the emergency-stricken heated cockpit cabin of his old-type Machiavellian freighter vessel, Dan Casey is feeling the g-force factor of the hurling acceleration, rocking a sub-turbulence jolt back in his black leather-padded recliner. Mulling his handsome facial features while double-checking the flight control internal systems, he endearingly cracks the whip and asks the cyber assistant to confirm the tracking battlecruiser range.

"Pearl, why do we have a hot pursuit and gain battle cruiser on our flack? How are they tracking us through the universal slipway? Do you have any ideas, or let me figure out a guess: We're outdated, needing yet another whizz-wonder upgrade? More importantly, sweetie, can we outrun them? The navigation radars are not showing me the desired signs I require for a clean, sharp, exciting escape plot from a Corporal Union prison cell pod sentence."

Pearl swiftly states a calculated response to Dan Casey's urging enquiries. "We are at the maximum speed rate of the celestial hyperdrive capability. Any further tampering strain will explode the *Decepter* into an obliteration of starcraft parts. Commander Calo Tarick repeatedly demands a comm-link exchange of words with you, Dan. Did you want me to connect the external sonar drive link-wave or keep hush?"

Before Dan Casey can make up his mind, a whimpering moan flutters from the co-pilot quarters.

Veena Merida knocks back in her recliner-cushioned seat and buckles up to a tight hold of her divine, sexy presence. "Well, this is going great, Mr Casey, just as planned! Did you say we could outrun the Corporal Union's patrol cruiser? Certainly, it doesn't feel like we are performing to the specification of inspiring hope! This might be a good time to click those damn guns into action, as we're a sitting duck!"

"This is the plan; I can't believe their flashy battle cruiser can track a starship through the hyper-lanes. We may have to link a communication channel with your Commander friend. It isn't meant to happen like this. We should be well clear of any danger by now. And you can't open fire in the hyper-lanes; we'll all blow up, and there would be too much energy entailing flares. Didn't they teach you anything at agent studies? I had hoped your agent skills might have kicked in by now and come to good use, but hell no!"

"Pearl, link up the comm-link transmission and patch us a wire through. I'll have to make a speech to the Commander to get out of this mess, and you stay hidden out of the way, Veena. Let me deal with this, as I don't want you to make things any worse."

Meanwhile, inside the flight control quarters of the MK2 Machiavellian freighter, Veena Merida isn't too pleased with the harsh tone of Dan's words.

"Oh really, Mr Casey, my vocabulary is not up to cargo pilots' standards. You weren't saying that last night when you tried to kiss me, but I don't deny your intentions as I've browsed the biometric body scans while walking adrift on Cartonne. Also, you have no idea how a remote intergalactic agent organisation works, so try not to comment."

"From where I was standing, you wanted to kiss me, sweetheart! Not as it will matter much, as I'm guessing we'll be arrested soon. You will have to blow me a kissing pout through the prison cell bars."

Pearl swiftly connects the communication link to the Corporal Union's Commander Calo Tarick.

The high, small, framed holo-comm screen is directly positioned in the middle of the *Decepter*'s interior front flight control dashboard. A flickering static fuzz appears as the connection prevails, bringing forward the stern, imposing presence of Calo Tarick. The Galactic Corporal Union's high-ranked Commander openly starts to verbally demand the terms of an exchange agreement offer to Dan Casey.

"There is no point in evading a running escape, Mr Casey. As your rust-bucket tub of a ship has no chance against the ultimate power and sheer force of my BX10 *Galileo* bird of destruction. Surrender your vessel's engines now and hand over that vile cheap green-haired bitch and the stolen artefact. Not to me but to our faithful leader, Director Wilson Volantis, and I will turn my one-working eye away from ever-setting sight on you again! Do we have an accord on this exchanging chase of mutual beneficiaries, Mr Casey, or do you want to try my patience by upsetting me? I shall give you the mere count to five to choose your fate wisely. Then, the generous offer of a life worth living won't be valid. ONE."

Dan Casey tries to reason the authenticity terms laid down by the Corporal Union's government lawful treaty. "Hey, Commander Calo Tarick, what a sincere pleasure for letting me get in a word at this time! Thanks, really appreciate it. Plus, I'd love to help! But I have no green-haired nuisance of a very annoying lady on board, and if I did, you would be the first to know. Trust me. This is just one big misunderstanding. I am about as interested in galactic ancient artefacts as your good self, Calo. So, if I'm blocking your way, please feel free to zoom in straight by, and I will stay out of your way forever, Commander."

"TWO! If it was just a misunderstanding of being in the wrong place at the inappropriate time, why did you flee from my warning ion cannon shots? THREE! Times are ticking very fast now, Mr Casey. FOUR."

With the uninspired thought of being arrested, Dan Casey is about to bravely charm a return comment to the commanders with meaningful questions about his rash behaviour. "Well, I can explain all about that, Commander!"

But before the stumbling, handsome pilot can get his words out, the beautiful mud-stricken Veena Merida unwisely takes charge of the matter. "Hey, let me explain in a simpler fragmentation, Calo Tarick. My new partner and I truly agree on saying, screw you, red eye! How dare you to call me a vile cheap bitch. Gosh! You look like a jerk just because I gave you the slip twice on the human capital, Kothariya, and I brushed aside your feeble security systems. By the way, you can please inform Director Wilson Volantis, with a gracious baby smile from me, that I may not fully know what he truly desired to accomplish with the astrological data box. Still, I know enough, in turn, to make sure it won't be happening while I'm breathing. I'll expose you all as a corrupt regime of governmental power wanting to ruin and control innocent civilians' lives."

While feeling the pressure of an incomparable situation rising to heated proportion, Dan swiftly turns his gobsmacked face away from the holo-comm screening vision to Veena. "Didn't I say keep out the way, partner! Let me deal with this now, and you've just pissed off the Commander more than before! If we work together, we must get some ground rules in order."

Veena Merida partly turns her attention towards Dan Casey. "Just kicking in some of my agent training tactics you asked for, darling. Demoralise the enemy into making errors of bad judgement. Now get us out of here; we've got a mission to complete."

Dan Casey was bewildered by Veena's overconfidence.

"You must have hit your pretty little head quite hard, Agent Merida, back there in the sloppy mud as we're going flat out, and your Commander pal can go faster, so outrunning the massive size cruiser right up our arse will not be taking place today. Your little back chat outburst has just angered him, and please don't call me darling, sweetheart."

Veena Merida shakes her face with a deep breath and replies, "Well, honey, you listen to me. I was just trying to make us sound convincing. Plus, I'm the agent in charge of this saga;

you're just the pilot, so follow instructions and get us the hell out of the perimeter!"

Suddenly, they hear the hollering shout from their holo screen. "BE QUIET, the pair of you snarky criminals."

Commander Calo Tarick bellows, "Now you better listen to me, Merida, you thieving green-haired bitch; I told you back on Kothariya there's no escape from me. True to my word, here I am, THE LAW. Yes, you are correct in saying, Mr Casey, I'm extremely pissed off with her bad-mouthing of all who are involved in the outrageous act of defiance against the Corporal Union. I will make sure she pays for her ill-fated defiance. You are just a lowlife, skivvy cargo rat, and my offer no longer stands for your freedom; you are now appraised to be part of a galactic terror attack against my lawful peace and loyal order. Cut off your engines immediately and prepare for your vessel to be boarded. Do you have any pathetic last words, Mr Casey?"

"Yeah, I got some last words, Calo, as my jade-eyed partner said; screw you, arsehole. From where I'm sitting, I will be calling the shots. While you can't open fire on us in the hyper-lanes, or we all go boom, I very much doubt your crusty old politician boss wants his puzzle box in parts. So here are the new terms! Let us skip this bit of space, or we will destroy the data box. Any last words, Commander?"

The Corporal Union Commander woefully replies, "See you soon, Mr Casey. First Officer, FIRE THE HARPOONS!"

Whirling back inside the *Decepter*'s flight cabin in incomprehension, Dan Casey looks over to Veena. She asks, "What does he mean by harpoons? I thought you said he could not open fire in the hyper-lanes! Then again, you said you could outrun the Commander! Look how far we have got with that little adventure! We need a better plan than your on the spot thinking. Gosh, we're going to get arrested, aren't we?"

Dan Casey honestly focuses on the task and answers, "Yeah,

I fully agree with you on that one, Veena; this isn't looking too good at all."

With a sudden whistling double boom, the Corporal Union rapidly closes in. It opens fire, not with conventional weapons, but with two swirling laser harpoons travelling through the electrical pulsing atmosphere.

There's external damage, and thick, dark smoke starts rapidly gushing out at the back of Dan Casey's MK2 freighter starship. Veena lets out a frustrated groan as she is flung back into her seat with the sharp manoeuvres of Dan's piloting skills. She isn't expecting such a rough experience, and it knocks her for a loop. She isn't used to flying, and it shows in her reaction. The pursuing Corporal Union's patrol cruiser is still in hot pursuit, and it doesn't look like they are letting up any time soon. Dan Casey has to make a tough decision.

The massive battleship of Commander Calo Tarick starts to rapidly reel in the *Decepter* by retracing the laser bind harpoons while stalking a shadowy pursuit at subsonic speed velocity, cunningly mowing through the slip-lanes of fast space. While in the panic-stricken cockpit cabin of Dan Casey's rattling Machiavellian vessel, the flight control instrument dials flutter and flash as the emergency sirens ring through the grappled spacecraft.

Taking a knock back in the co-pilot chair, Veena Merida opens her jade gemstone eyes wide in terror, screaming a startled panic, "Oh no! We are being pulled back towards Calo's cruiser. Damn it. We're done for unless you have any shortcuts up your sleeve of pilot tricks. I'm afraid we will lose to the law this time, Dan. I'm sorry. This is all my fault; I should have never involved you."

Dan Casey swiftly turns to the watery-eyed young lady. "Hey, Agent Merida, you're forgetting one thing, sweetheart. You did involve me, and I aim to fulfil my employment contract. So, you close those pretty green eyes and hold on tight, as it seems we can't outrun them or even shoot a shot back, but we can damn well halt! Let the patch-eyed bastard fly right by, in theory, or we could just blow up! What the hell? I have no intention of a mind-wipe, whatever one of those things is. I don't plan on finding out any time soon, either. Pearl, give full power to the front shields if you are still with us, sweetie."

The crystallised heart of Pearl flashes an immediate comprehensive response at the control dash interior, systematically efficient in energising the rear power to the front shields.

Meanwhile, holding on tight for dear life with fear building up, Veena shouts, "What in the world are you planning to do? I do hope you remember I get very dizzy! Will I approve of your actions this time? After the junkyard shortcut, I'm more than a little worried, to be truthful."

"No, your agent's weekly manual will not approve of this stunt. Hold tight, sweetheart; this is gonna hurt."

Dan Casey yanks his right, bare-skinned bicep arm into motion, cranking his fingerless-gloved hand on the power thrust lever throttle, instantly cutting off the triple pylon booster's engines while slam-dunking the silver sterling flight joystick. This brings his left arm down with a pressured gripped shove forward, performing a sudden motioning of the *Decepter*'s hull in the hyper-speed slip-lanes.

This ushers the Machiavellian freighter to dip a wavering dive in the swirling atmospheric speed lanes of galactic space. It breaks the holding laser bind harpoons, leaving the rear frame a smoke-gushing trail of the *Decepter* twisting into a vast spinning vortex.

Dan Casey's freighter launches out of the slipstream electrical flow with a stimulating pulsating effect and rapidly hurls off to any unknown charted sector of the Kalanisi Universe. Luckily, he loses sight of Commander Calo Tarick's straining pursuit.

Coldly seated in the dull lighting of the *Galileo* cruiser

control bridge quarters, Commander Tarick cruelly shouts, "Where has the manky starship got to? Officer One, care to damn well explain your failure to apprehend. Son, don't say I didn't warn you about insubordination onboard my battlecraft, so try to make a good case NOW!"

"We, unfortunately, lost their vessel, sir, due to an unpredictable suicide stunt in hyper-speed by that crazy pilot. He spun a reckless manoeuvre out of our laser harpoon-bound grasp. They could be anywhere if they survived, sir. Orders?"

"You have the benefit of my unwillingly doubted notification this time, son. Don't take it for granted, as it seems we have a live-wire, smug-arsed cargo pilot making a nuisance of himself, which is more of a concern to me than you. Your new orders are to drop the *Galileo* out of fast space and bring us to a static grinding halt, clearly transmitting the word to all starports in the Corporal Union's boundaries and beyond of any sighting regarding these high-grade criminals to inform us at once."

Commander Calo Tarick then has the difficult task of updating the Director of the Corporal Union, the mysterious politician Wilson Volantis.

Chapter Five

The Astrological Data Box

The roguish charmed cargo-runner pilot, Dan Casey, and the attractive ladylike resistance agent, Veena Merida, are now hurtling from the hyper-lanes after a brave performance to escape Calo Tarick's interrogation mind-wipe fate.

The jade-eyed protagonist is vocal with a rash note of screaming lyrics. "Ahh, make it damn stop now, Mr Casey. Ooh! To say I'm feeling a bit woozy is an understatement; I think I will faint!"

The *Decepter*'s cabin lights are on a dull red dimmer mode as the flight control instruments flash, flickering a sequence with the emergency ringtone sirens. Meanwhile, the plated spacecraft veers a horizontal overlapping judder, crafting a floating figure through the masses of star-clustered space. Dan Casey skilfully has his cut-gloved hands firmly around the shuddering, kinked joystick.

"I got no control. We need to ride out the spin, sweetheart. Pearl, if you're still online, hit the equaliser dampers and try to even down our movement a fraction. Gives me something to work on, at least!"

Pearl flashes a crystal-blinkered response to Dan Casey's request, automatically firing up the old-type vessel's slanted triple pylon boosters. Dan cleverly out-rides the soft-hitting shockwaves, weaving the silver-based joystick to the opposite direction of Pearl's short-ranged blast actions. He can generally level off the starship's hull frame to a more acceptable rocking. The atmospheric, panic-churned environment of the *Decepter*'s flight cabin starts to reboot the systematic operation controls. Dan slowly relaxes his grip on the flight joystick, breathing a deep breath of relief, simultaneously turning his concerned face to a shut-eyed, muted Veena Merida.

The galactic pilot slowly brushes his artistic hands through his side-swept jet-black hair, hesitantly asking the green-haired damsel, "Hey, Veena. Are you okay? Wow! I can't believe we made that hyper-looped manoeuvre and survived the hurling fallout, Agent Lady. Are you alright? Talk to me, Veena! Come on, open your pretty eyes; it's over. We're safe now."

Dan Casey, unhooking his pilot chair harness belt, swiftly turns his muscular half-cut waist-jacket-dressed body around in building concern. He witnesses the beautiful woman breathing, but there is no response from her gorgeous mud-splattered face.

Until her jade eyes suddenly open. "Gosh! Mr Casey, I don't know if you have ever been informed about your flying and the word 'safe'! But they do not in any way possibly compare. I'm not okay in the slightest. My head is spinning like a marble on ice; I am covered in mud. I hate mud, especially sloppy mud, and my poor ankle is throbbing like a bad binge hangover. Oh, and let's not forget the psychopath Commander who is on my case. I will lie in my rest quarters for now. Please let me know when I'm about to be arrested for a mind-wipe. It won't be too long before the Corporal Union's patrol cruisers find us in a static drift. What joy! You know how to give a girl a good time, Mr Casey. Many thanks in abundance, and goodnight!"

He watches as Veena leaves the co-pilot's chair.

"Pearl, get the subsystems fired back up. That's if any are still functioning. And find out what sector we're in before Calo Tarick intervenes once more. I have a bad feeling about the Commander. I need to go and see if I can take care of Miss Merida's accusing mud-ridden temper."

Dan quickly follows the clicking trail of the ankle-limping female agent down to the lounge area. The cargo pilot sneakily swoops his toned, bare-skinned arms under Veena Merida's weary, long legs concealed in her shiny jumpsuit bottoms. He grips his opposite arm softly around her quivering, arched back and grips Veena's light, wrap-around velvet jacket. He lifts the feather-light lady off her totty high-heeled boots with a beaming smug grin on his handsome face.

"Right then, Miss Merida! You are coming with me. I'm putting you to bed. There are no arguments!"

"My gosh! Will you put me down at once, please? This is just becoming absurd! Get your grubby, oily, rugged hands off me! Mr Casey! I am arguing the motions of you putting me to bed, and I disagree with your abnormal gung-ho action. Hey! Are you even listening to a word I'm saying, you rough, scoundrel-looking pilot of a man?"

Dan Casey strides to the bedroom area, pounding the floor with his leather flight boots with his brawny arms full of carrying the moaning madam. Swivelling, he arrives at the sliding doorway and presses his bare, broad shoulder, a tabbing knock against the lock device button on the side panel. Instantly, the bedroom door slides open. Dan gently hand drops Veena's bouncing buttocks down onto the floating bed mattress.

Agent Merida sighs and grumbles, "Oh, Mr Casey! You are crossing the line of partnership!"

"Come on, sweetheart, get them off! Let me have a glance now. We haven't got all day!"

Veena Merida swiftly replies with embarrassing defiance. "You have got to be damn joking? I'm certainly not that type of Astro-woman, for your information, Mr Casey. Please try to control your urges. We are on an important mission. My gosh! Was this bizarre scenario not in the briefing spec? Stop this outrageous behaviour at once; pull yourself together, Dan. I'm a nice girl, unlike the galactic alley cats you are used to associating with at those outer-rim scoundrel haven bars."

"Meow! Miss Merida. I was talking about your high-heeled boot so I can check your hurting, swollen ankle. I'm not sure where that agent mind of yours is wandering to again. Here, Veena, let's see if anything is broken. Don't fret. I'm not going to harm you, partner!"

He bends, crouching down on the edge of the floating bed mattress. He holds a caring grip on Veena's black leather slinky boots, carefully unzipping the side seams to slip the high-class footwear off her bruised, dainty ankle gradually.

"Well, yes, erm! Of course, I meant my boots; stop confusing me. You are intolerable. Ouch! That hurts a little, plus your hands are cold as well. I don't think you attend to me as a serious bad-arse agent, do you, Dan? Shouldn't you be taking care of the ship maintenance more than me? We're sitting ducks hovering afloat."

Dan Casey massages her wounded ankle, telling her, "Yeah, I'm taking you seriously, Agent Merida, as we are being chased by a determined demonised man in Calo Tarick, and whatever that ancient puzzle box is. He wants it badly, or his political boss does more. What happened when you were in Kothariya? How did a sweetheart like yourself get mixed up in all this craziness?"

"Seems you should know what we're against. I will explain. One, I'm nobody's sweetheart. I don't have time for attachments, and it's why I got mixed up in this line of work. Well, it has been just over three years since I became a remote agent for peace. My parents were killed by a terrorist bomb the prior year in a galactic restaurant by a petty crook. I was heartbroken and even angrier to find the Corporal Union had done nothing to apprehend the bastard. I reached out to the underground and trained as a renegade. I learned my killer host trade, tracked the murderer down, and eliminated his entire gang. After that, small contract offers became more available close to the heart of Kothariya space sectors, so I was the first choice by Tara Harlow to try and retrieve the astrological data box from Director Wilson Volantis."

Pearl's voice comes through the intercom. "Sorry to interrupt any mutual flirtatious moments again! Dan, due to your required report, we have subsystems back up and running with minimal power. The location we have found ourselves in is the near mists of the Sera sector. The closest known planet to dock for substantial repairs would be advised at Carrageen-Hazen. Also known as Race-World, which is currently the home to many major equine horse racing events, including the 4010 galactic Classic Derby, taking place tomorrow afternoon. I've plotted the *Decepter* a course to the entertainment world of Carrageen-Hazen."

"Sounds like a plan, Pearl. Set the course straight away, and keep the radar on full-scan alert for our deluded new improbable friend in Commander Calo Tarick! As we may be a few star sectors away to our advantage now, but I'm guessing he's a tad pissed off, so I imagine he will signal other Corporal Union patrol vessels about our unlawful exchanging ventures. I think we may have acquired some real, sizzling hot-property cargo on board for once, so keep alert, sweetie."

"Carrageen-Hazen! Two friends I grew up with on Kothariya work around the Sera sector as retail clerk advisers; I'm pretty certain they have accommodation portals on Carrageen-Hazen. I've not seen either of them since my parent's funeral. And since I dropped my holo-pad in that mud, I have no contact numbers to enquire about their location in the sector. Shame. I'm sure they would help us lay low for a while. Ahh, my ankle, ouch! Oh, that's the bit that hurts where your hand is right now. Ah, I'm sorry to bother you, but at the same time, thank you, Dan. It's lovely of you to help me. I duly apologise for my outbursts back at the lounge quarters. This mission is testing me, plus I'm not used to being scooped up off my feet or knowing many nice men."

"Oh, right, so now I'm a nice guy! And here's me thinking I was a smelly, oily cargo pilot. Haha."

Meanwhile, the teasing-eyed vixen duly reminds him of her former insulting words, "You are incorrect with your interpretations. Did I not say you were a scoundrel rough looker? Haha."

"Well, thank you for putting me straight, Your Highness, on my error of self-judgement. You'll need an ice pack, Veena, but you will be fine after a good night. Trust the rough scoundrels. They always know best, and please accept my deepest condolences for the loss of your parents. It must have been a hard time for you. I know what it's like to lose close friends; they can't be replaced, just remembered. And for your miscellaneous slope-sunken holo-pad, don't worry about that; we can fix that as well. What's your friend's name? I'm pretty sure Pearl can track a sneaky comm-link message under the Mbron Media Ltd scans. I will get you another fresh coffee, and then, Miss Merida, you can tell me about your daring agent adventure on Kothariya. Hold fire, sweetheart. I won't be long; I'll go get you an ice pack."

Speaking aloud, Veena says, "You're doing very well. My true interpretation of the lyrics: you're a very charmed-looking man. Oh! No, not again! Slight slip of the tongue, Pearl. Please tell me you didn't hear that silly remark!"

Pearls replies to Veena's pleading, "No daff remarks recorded in data analysis regarding your secret crush, so nothing to report to Dan, for the moment anyhow, Miss Merida!"

"Oh, dear, that's nearly bordering blackmail. Are starship computers allowed to matchmake? My gosh, Pearl. Are you taking the freedom of thought to the very extreme? Woman to cyber woman, mum's the word. Shh!"

At that precise moment, Dan Casey returns to the vessel's

bedroom with his hands full, containing a Star coffee beverage and an ice pack for her swollen ankle.

The handsome pilot asks the bed-stricken beauty, "Hey, everything okay? I heard you talking to Pearl."

"What did you hear? As we were only talking about the weather. Right, Pearl? I was hoping Carrageen-Hazen would be warm so I could dress up in my summer outfit. That's all, so I don't know what you thought you heard. Er, phew. Anyhow, thank you for the coffee. It's wonderful, Mr Casey. I was about to tell you all about the data box saga."

Dan stands back, attempting to leverage himself on the edge of the floating bed mattress while attending the icepack around Veena's dainty, bare-skinned, bruised ankle.

"The weather? I didn't have you down as a fair-weather lady. I thought you might have given Pearl your friends' details so we could send the SOS! Are you sure you are feeling okay, Veena?"

With a sighing breath, Veena replies, "Ah, I am cold. Okay, Dan, my friends' names are Zak Duran and Terri Lace. Suppose you could be so kind as to allow Pearl to send them my holo address, Merida.V.234@holo.link.mail, letting them know I need a favour. In that case, I'm more than positive they will help, as we were inseparable when we were youngsters."

Veena Merida pleasantly slurps her steamed milk Star coffee as Dan Casey listens intently to the pastel-haired agent tell of her daring mission to retrieve the astrological data box on orders from her boss.

Previously spiralling back three days to Veena Merida's undercover covert mission, she tells of arriving at the Corporal Union's main Directorial ceremony office. The climate-set atmosphere in the Elite-owned world of Kothariya is blessed with lush, sizzling sunshine and gleaming blue skies that day.

The futuristic capital is called Isla-Kai and is known throughout the Kalanisi Universe for its thriving enterprises that pay tax hikes to the ever-more-demanding Corporal Union through their corrupt partnership with Mbron Media Ltd. Outside the towering rows of skyscraper buildings, a hover-pod arrives at the green landscape state of Director Wilson Volantis' personal ceremony headquarters.

The passenger door swings vertically in a wheezing shift as Veena Merida, observing her surroundings, steps out of the static taxi-pod, dressed in her all-in-one black sleeveless cling-fit jumpsuit, supporting a holster belt lacing her side-arm-scoped pistol, with a stylish black handbag.

Veena witnesses, with her trained sparkling jade eyes, the security cameras focusing on her presence arriving on the court grounds. Ushering a clicking heel step forward, the green-haired agent turns her gorgeous face to the attention of the Mbron Media cab, brimming a swift wink at the female pale-faced android driver.

Veena tells the pink-haired, coiffed cyber taxi-pod representative, "Thank you, Nayla 1.9.4. Please don't forget to collect me later as planned. I'll be there in around two hours."

The taxi-pod automatically shuts down the open slanted door. The pink-haired cyberbot responds, in a cybernetic-pitched voice, "All is on schedule, Mistress Merida, as per the briefing. Please be careful."

Veena smiles back at Nayla 1.9.4 before the taxi-pod scoots off in a hovering whizz. The feminine undercover resistance agent makes her way from the court grounds to the front reception porch door leading into the main hall of the facility.

The Corporal Union's office guard speaks in a cold, focused manner of no emotion, duly asking the jade-eyed beauty, "Wait there, madam. I require your full name and identification card, which will be followed by an eye authorisation scan."

The undercover operative stands and appears to be a picture of an innocent, attractive woman. Veena politely responds in an assured roll-play manner, "Hi there, officer. Good day, and yes, it is certainly not a problem. I am Sienna Crayton, the newly appointed science grade technician for the Corporal Union's Sulamani project. Our glorious Director, Volantis, expects me for a midday introduction slot. Here's my identification card. Where do I stand for the eye scan?"

The Corporal Union's guard says, "Your ID checks out, Miss Crayton. Please place your face over the recognition eye scanner monitor for the secondary security phase."

She cooperatively steps face-front, silent to the scanning beam. The infrared scan buzzes as it portrays the undercover female's jade irises until the cross-examination cycle ends. The pulse pings a response of authorised access to the centrepiece of Director Volantis' excellence.

With acceptance in abundance, the Corporal Union's guard escorts the so-called feminine science technician to the waiting porch. "Come this way, Miss Crayton. It seems you are a loyal employee of the Corporal Union's science division. Still, your side-arm weapon is prohibited and be warned any hostile actions are dealt with swiftly. Please take a seat, and I shall get an Elite representative to facilitate your meeting with Director Volantis."

Veena delivers a delightful smile to the Corporal Union's young guard and replies in a high-class voice, aka Sienna Crayton, "Thank you so kindly for your professional hospitality. I can guarantee you there is no need for firearms. I am here for a quick pop in and out just for my induction before my real work begins. Thanks again, officer. I shall wait if you don't mind."

Then, the guard returns to his quarters. Veena takes a look around the ceremony hallway arch, gently floating her bare-skinned arm up to her right ear lobe. She takes her manicured green fingernails over to her diamond crystal stud earring and gently presses, whispering to the reprogrammed Mbron Media cybernetic aid, "You copy me, Nayla? How long will the data spike hold out?"

The pink-coiffed hair cyber female android, Nayla 1.9.4,

currently hiding nearby in the taxi-pod-informally advises, "As long as your data-traced earrings are at least in a mid-range velocity of the authorisation scan device, there should be no issues! I'm returning to prep the craft; you are on your own from now on, Mistress Merida. Good luck."

Within the cardia blue marble walls of the ceremony hall, there is the sudden pounding thud of heavy stomping boots, sounding an echoed marching pattern.

Veena Merida, in her alias, awaits the high-profile representative as she witnesses the emerging tall, dark-skinned man dressed in a long black leather trench coat, split open at the seams, showing off his muscular built pecs with his bulging bicep arms in which the left is a cybernetic cloned hand and wrist.

The shadowy man's presence gains ground on the petite pastel-code guest of honour. Veena clocks the sense of an unknown quantity by the squinting expression emanating from her beautiful face. She hears the thumping stomp protract across the marble-tiled flooring until the shaded vision of the hallway shadows is enlightened to the concerns of a stern-faced man.

"I'm Commander Calo Tarick. The loyal first-hand representative to the Corporal Union's Director Volantis. Please follow me this way, Miss Crayton. We have been expecting your arrival, and your early attendance shows your enthused appreciation for your new role as our science technical officer."

"Please, Commander Tarick, call me Sienna. It seems we will be working together in the near-distant future; I'm truly grateful for being chosen for such a high-importance role that links me to the Sulamani project. It's a career-bound privilege. Wow! Look at the size of this ceremony hall. Oh my gosh, amazing, impressive architecture; I bet you could fit thousands of people in here at once. What are those energy containment tanks at each corner of this grand building?"

With no hesitant delay, Commander Calo Tarick walks up

the twisting staircase; he slowly turns his heaving toned chest and ruthless patch-eyed cold face slightly while staring down at the attractive female covert agent.

"I do believe, Miss Crayton, that you were only required here just to inspect an astrological data box, not indulging an interest in our artefactual complexes."

"Oh, pardon me. Here I go again, babbling a yarn about the scientific instruments' structures, bringing out my intrigued vision of how things tick. Isn't science exploration just wonderful, Commander?"

Veena Merida gives off a flirtatious, sexy smile and flutters her eyelashes, teasingly brushing her long green silk mane with a seductive fluster of her dainty, leather-gloved hands. She's purely trying to distract the icily cold officer.

While the pairing bodies advance to the top of the elegant ceremony hall staircase, the dark aura of the Corporal Union's high-ranked Commander sternly replies with an element of warning. "I seem to find flirty science talk particularly uninteresting, and their theories are always hiding something. Which makes me nervous, and I can be very upset, usually bringing out the worst in me, Sienna Crayton. Right here we are at Director Wilson Volantis' office chamber."

The grim-faced man smiles coldly, opening the double-marbled doors for the green-haired saboteur.

Veena whispers in a sarcastic tone. "It's been a charmed walk, Commander Tarick. We must do it again sometime soon. Thank you."

The daring lady of deception makes her solo elegant presentation into the chamber room with a click-heeled step, hearing the doors shut while facing the back of a man sitting at a curved glass office executive table.

The high-backed chair slowly swings around. Veena sees Director Wilson Volantis in his ceremony chamber office, sitting proud and stern upright. The 60-year-old politician's curiosity stands a boundary to the attention of the young woman fulfilling her presentation as the new science modification technician.

The ageing leader of the Corporal Union's domain has a pale-toned face. His beard blends in with his grey honourable ambassador side-parted hairstyle. Director Volantis' soulless eyes set a daunting effect as the well-spoken intergalactic chairman says, "Sienna Crayton, welcome to your new home; I'm more than impressed with your progression through the scientific ranks of Isla-Kai's top-notch academy, my dear."

The leader steps briskly to his female guest, attempting to hold her hand for an inviting congratulatory kiss. Veena Merida, in her disguised personal act, follows along with the greetings of the Corporal Union's mysterious Director, replying about her new position. "You are too kind. Meeting you in person with the directional focus of helping the citizens throughout the Kalanisi Universe is an inspiration to many young scientists, and this project will be an honour to leave my mark on. Where is this data box you found that I will be working on, Director Volantis?"

Veena knows she has only a short window to operate her objective mission before the data spike counterparts fade.

Director Wilson Volantis coldly smiles with a smirk of unease, feeling the air in the chamber office, "Ah, the astrological data box; I know the application briefing you were mailed states it is a star chart from an ancient time, long before our civilisation climbed its way into the Kalanisi Universe. But it's much more elegant than that, Sienna, my dear. Let me show you our only salvation."

Releasing her hand with a grasping presentational flow, the Director of the Corporal Union, dressed in his black-cloaked gown, motions to walk, leading his guest to a side compartment of the chamber office. He slowly places his pale, wrinkled hand palm flat on the stationed wall security scanner. The secret side wall shunts open with a smooth effect. Wilson Volantis swiftly turns his icy presence back to Veena, standing a few steps behind his advancement to his meditation ritual quarters, encouraging her to follow into his private spiritual realm, "Please step this way, Sienna, and don't mind the vapour smoke. It won't cause harm and is only guiding the way to foresee the future of our galaxy. Before you arrived, I had just finished a meditation session."

Wilson Volantis, the grey-haired Director of the Corporal Union, asks Miss Crayton if she participates in any meditation. "Do you enrol in any spiritual rituals?"

His tone is untrusting, and his eyes are soulless as he kneels on a square ritual mat in a secret side room.

Veena observes Wilson Volantis cradling an astrological data box from a small gold altar on a square rug. The Director rises from his kneeling position and adjusts his black gown. He turns towards Veena, the female science technician, who stands before him.

She is eager to inspect the data box and expresses her excitement. "Wow, that object looks priceless. May I hold the prize? And no, I don't intervene in spiritual rituals to your current question. Without overstepping the mark of my curiosity, weren't you banned from performing an afterlife session, which caused controversy when you were surprisingly elected against all odds? I'm so glad you were, or I wouldn't be here now in this spectacular position of employment."

"Mbron Media, the Android Association coverage, put a stop to all that fake scandalous news, my dear."

He hands the data box to Veena, who smiles and thanks him. Wilson looks at her with suspicion but doesn't say anything. She tactfully diverts Director Volantis' suspicions by changing the subject and asking about the device's specifications.

Veena enquires about its functionality and the specific modification. She even mentions the possibility of searching for a new planet.

"So how does this device work, and what are we looking for exactly? Are we searching for a new home world or something beyond my imagination?"

The agent, Veena Merida, posing as Sienna Crayton, questions the Director thoroughly while gently touching the four carved symbols on the data box. This action causes a power surge, which reveals a holographic map. The symbols are also displayed in a star-chart format, providing valuable information about the unknown regions of the Kalanisi Universe.

Deep in conversation with Veena about the purpose of a data box, Wilson Volantis explains, "During a mining expedition in the Isadora system's surrounding atmosphere, a valuable discovery was made on a distant moon, and we found the data dox. As you can see, Sienna, it is a complicated ancient chart of symbols clustering an edge around the outer rim. I have delved into the Kalanisi Universe's mysteries, which exist in a dimension paradox beyond our own. Since acquiring the power of the Galactic Corporal Union's mantelpiece, I have performed rituals and meditated on its ancient lore. Through deciphering the charted symbols, I believe they lead to a hidden black hole known as the Vortex. I require you to find the location of the black hole by modifying the databox and power source of my flagship, the Sulamani, so I can blow the Vortex open."

Wilson Volantis is interrupted by the ringing of his desktop holo-comm in the office chamber.

"Sienna, please excuse me. This annoying, inappropriate call must be answered. I'm a busy man running the galaxy. Return to the chamber room, my charm, and bring the data box. I shall submit Commander Tarick to accommodate your needs while I'm in an audience."

Veena tracks Wilson's path back to the chamber room as the Director strides towards his curved glass desk. She shuts down the data box and observes the grey-haired ambassador hastily departing the office.

With relief, Veena Merida takes hold of the objective and declares, "It's time to leave the party, Miss Sienna Crayton."

She voices her daunting thoughts with composure, "Wilson Volantis is delusional and insane. Incredibly, he intends to detonate a black hole. How could he possibly believe that would benefit a civilised galaxy?"

The pastel-haired female agent finds herself alone in the chamber room when the door suddenly swings open, revealing the imposing figure of the right-hand man, Calo Tarick. Enquiring if there is anything on Miss Crayton's mind per Director Volantis' request, he makes it clear that he is committed to assisting her in any way possible. "At your service, madame. If there is anything I can help you with, Miss Crayton. I thought I heard you muttering in a whisper. This makes me nervous and sceptical about certain people."

Veena Merida quickly responds calmly to Calo Tarick's suspicious comments. "Oh, please don't worry about me, Commander. I was just thinking out loud. I need to freshen up and get straight to work. Could you kindly direct me to the restroom?"

Veena responds with a friendly smile, concealing any hint of insincerity.

Meanwhile, Director Wilson Volantis descends the staircase of the ceremony hall. He is in absolutely no mood for interruptions. His voice is firm and resolute as he declares, "This had better not be a waste of my time, officer. I have an important client waiting for me upstairs."

The guard of the Corporal Union appears nervous as he speaks. He explains his concern apologetically, addressing the Director. "Please excuse me, but it is about your earlier guest; we have another woman at the entrance claiming to be Sienna Crayton, and her authorisation clearance matches positive, just like the previous Miss Crayton."

Wilson Volantis looks displeased, and his wrinkled face

shows a hint of concern as he orders the office clerk, "Retrace the eye recognition scans of Sienna Crayton without using the Mbron Media cyber feeds. I want to know the truth about both their identities. Let us see who the real Sienna Crayton is. I demand a hologram link to Tarick immediately."

Meanwhile, Calo Tarick is in the office chamber room upstairs as the glass desk holo-comm connects with a buzzing flicker. A visual message from Wilson Volantis is shown.

"Please tell me, you still have that green-haired scamp of a woman in your custody. It's been discovered that she is an agent for our absentee Tara Harlow. Her name is Veena Merida. She is here to steal the data box; time is of the essence; STOP HER TARICK."

The Commander has a grim expression as he assures the Director, "Leave her to me, boss."

Commander Tarick promptly swings into action, booting open the marble doors of the chamber offices and slickly drawing his double-barrelled handgun from his holster. He scans the third-floor balcony of the ceremony hall, and his angry gaze finally settles on the green-haired infiltrator, escaping with a strut through the semi-crowds of staff.

Calo Tarick bellows in his deep voice, MERIDA!"

Veena Merida swiftly draws her silver-scoped pistol and deftly manoeuvres through the crowd as a ragged voice cries out her name. The Commander is unleashing a barrage of fire, showing no remorse while fixating on the resistance agent. Veena confidently flicks her infrared site on and returns pinpoint gunfire across at the dark figure of Calo Tarick, who fearlessly tracks her movement on the opposite of the ceremony hall balcony. He evades her blast flares but orders the approaching Elite Guards from the pillar post exit to the stairways, "SHOOT TO KILL THE BITCH."

The marble effect walls of the sacred hall are being shot to shattered pieces of debris as the scampering administration workers flee the erupting scenes of a once peaceful nature. The jade-eyed fugitive is alerted to the oncoming guards, organising their pulse blast rifles; with no time to spare, Veena urgently, with a shivering run, takes a wild chance. The sexy agent mindfully fiddles her dainty hands around the slingshot holster belt, swiftly pulling and hurling a micro-sized scrapping wire hook. She attaches a wrapping grip around the posh exterior railing, taking a leap of faith to swing her body in a twisting drop to the second floor. Quickly heading for the architectural compound's lift facilities, Veena is shocked at the sight of Calo Tarick performing a freefall swing jump from the upper balcony with a thudding booted landing. His focus is on the black jumpsuited charlatan.

On the first floor, watching the unfolding incident, Wilson Volantis instructs the entrance guard with a brash tone, "She's heading for the elevator and must have a contact lurking about the rooftops. Activate the air defences and shield the real Sienna Crayton from harm's way. She is an important cog in my plan. Now, officer."

Veena Merida sees an open glass lift shaft, advertising its escape temptation. Unfortunately, she is confronted by an Elite, black-armoured guard at close range. Using her agent-trained reflexes, the jade-eyed vixen vigorously slices a hand chop sequence, stylishly disarming the Corporal Union's officer, shifting a turning manoeuvre, hearing the pounding boots of Calo Tarick, ranging in close behind.

Veena's body slings around the Elite guard, using him as a sacrificing shield to defend the Commander's rattling rounds, asserting a breathed whisper of guilt. "I'm sorry!"

The bullets find the guard. Veena pushes aside the lifeless guard to obstruct Calo's approach. Scampering into the circular glass lift cage, Veena swiftly and decisively presses the upward active action key and automatically closes the blast-proof enclosure in the nick of time. Commander Tarick lets loose, chaining a rapid burst to no ill effect. With the deflecting shots bouncing a redirection of aim around the second floor, Veena Merida is truly delighted with her handy work, teasingly blowing a puckering kiss, with a sarcastic smile from her red glossy lips, duly to the shocked spectators below including the Director, Wilson Volantis.

The sharp-witted feminine agent raises her gloved hand to her transmitting earring device. Prompting for assistance from the reprogrammed Mbron Media cyber android, "If you copy me, Nayla 1.9.4. Now, be a good time for that pick-up; I'm heading for the rooftop."

Outside the ceremony hall of the Galactic Council, a sleek two-seater aircraft is spotted flying low and fast. The pilot is the stunning android named Nayla 1.9.4, who sports chic pink hair. The entire atmosphere is tense due to the infiltration alert, and the android nods to the now-exposed agent, "Good day, Mistress Merida; I am currently piloting the spacecraft towards your designated collection point. I'd like to inform you that we are facing some challenges en route, as aerial defence cannons are tracking our movement. As your loyal cyber assistant, I assure you I am doing my best to navigate the spacecraft towards our destination safely. Please do not worry; we will arrive at the collection point."

Veena quickly recognises her chance to break for it as the vessel distances itself from the defensive artillery. Despite trying to remain inconspicuous, her remarkable appearance catches the Corporal Union operative's attention. With a sense of urgency, Veena navigates her way across the rooftop of the revered tower, hoping to make her escape without drawing further notice. But no such thing is prevailing for the green-haired beauty.

The Elite guard highlights the position of the female infiltrator within seconds. Reinforcements spiral a flowing path of blast fire. The agent quickly reacts, with a sharp turn of footing, while reaching for a small stud from her slingshot belt. She presses the device and yanks a grenade, which she throws behind in the direction of the Elite unit. There is a whipping bleep until it fully extracts into an area-sized explosion. The Corporal Union's guards scream in vain, meeting their fateful demise at the hands of the engulfing flames.

But that isn't enough to stop the possessed patched-eye Commander Calo Tarick, bursting a leaping charge through the ball of fire, slapping a patting down of his burning black trench coat with his cybernetic metal hand, shouting out in anger to the fleeing perpetrator, "Merida, there's no escaping me. I'm the law, bitch."

But the daring agent extends her advantage to the edge rim of the ceremony rooftop, quickly attaching the micro-wire grappling hook cunningly used inside the hall now to her trusty, silver-scoped pistol. Veena aims fire at the side railing poles, grasping the trigger with a precision shot as the grapple wire binds around with a secure lock. She raises her sighted gun, firing a secondary line cross over to the next featuring building. With no time to waste, her jade eyes collectively catch a clear vision of Nayla 1.9.4 and the sleek-ranged starship.

Veena strides towards her destination with confidence, her high-heeled boots clattering assertively. She remains focused on her mission, determined not to lose her concentration, "You can do this, girl. Just don't go woozy." Suddenly she loudly curses, "Oh shit." She swiftly unclips her leather holster belt, retrieving her pistol. With a powerful swing of her belt, she propels herself towards Nayla 1.9.4, the female cyber pilot of the waiting craft who is keeping a watchful eye.

As they prepare for their escape, Nayla 1.9.4 warns Veena of a potential tracking tail. "Mistress Merida, I fear you're in danger. Behind you!"

But Veena remains unwavering in her determination to complete their mission successfully. Also possessed in following through with his orders to apprehend the green-haired thief is Commander Calo Tarick, who shows no restraint in trying to retrieve the mysterious data box. He performs a running jump, connecting his right cybernetic metal fibre hand and curling a looping hold around the pressuring grapple wire. This causes sparks and a grinding graze as Calo Tarick's extra weight tethers the wire core, resulting in a snap, mid-flight, as the wavering wire slacks off. It causes a free-falling drop to the opposing roof platform.

Veena Merida executes a flawless forward roll, gracefully rising to her feet in her knee-high boots. She swiftly transitions into an offensive turn, her pastel hair flowing behind her like a wave. Calo Tarick crashes to the ground behind her with a resounding thud, but Veena remains unfazed. She expertly brandishes her silver-barrelled scoped shooter, poised and ready for whatever challenges lie ahead. But the fearless, eye-patched Commander Tarick is swift and precise in his heaving attack, swinging his cybernetic hand to disarm the beautiful but equally lethal woman. Slightly knocked off balance while taking the closed ranged shot, Veena's silver pistol fires a mis-flare. She loses hold of the gun's handle, but she decides to taunt her pursuer.

"I'll take you down the old-fashioned way, Commander. Yar!" Veena screams a ragged cry, retaliating with a flourish of punching sliced chops and punishing high kicks.

Calo Tarick duly obliges to the fighting challenge while blocking her hand-to-hand combat swipes. "You chose to die by my hand; that's fine by me, Merida, you thieving bitch."

The growling, muscle-toned Commander pushes back with advancing lethal force, punching out with his cyber-gun barrel hand. He utilises a bout of slick leg-sweeping kicks at the retreating parrying agent. Veena stylishly manoeuvres a sidestepping weave at close quarter, doubling a critical kneeling to Calo Tarick. This is followed by a powerful, stunning roundhouse kick, staggering the trenched-coated figure back a yard, shining a glimmer of hope to escape the scene. Clutching the collection of her silver pistols tightly on the route, Veena Merida quickly enters the vertical flight cabin door of the sleek space vessel. As the elegant lady takes her seat, she can't help but smirk at the thought of successfully infiltrating the human Elite's home world, Kothariya.

Veena finishes the story. She's still on her floating sick bed, being attended to by Dan Casey. "Looking back on our event, I am incredibly proud. The adrenaline rush of the mission still courses through my veins, and I can't help but feel a sense of satisfaction wash over me, getting one over the Corporal Union. Afterwards, I parted ways with Nayla 1.9.4 at the mid-subspace station, Gyen-Yamion, and took a crowded commercial transporter to Latin-Versa, the dust moon. Until I gained your invaluable support, Dan, which was vital, I couldn't have accomplished it this far without your help."

While Dan secures the ice pack around her aching ankle, he can see the young woman has been through a stressful ordeal, commenting on his views of her daring espionage mission. "Well, it sounds like you had a very constructive time in the home world at Kothariya, and that is quite a story, Veena. I'm not sure I dig the part about blowing a black hole up, as politicians are delusional sometimes. But Wilson Volantis' does sound like a crackpot to avoid. You should get some shut-eye, and I'll let you know when we're getting close to Carrageen-Hazen."

Dan swiftly lifts himself from the floating mattress, and with a handsome smile over to Veena, he turns off the bedroom light. The cargo-runner pilot leaves the jade-eyed beauty in peace, heading back to the *Decepter*'s flight control cabin, keeping a close quarter on their trajectory to the lush high-roller sport-orientated planet, the glamorous Race-World.

Chapter Six

Race-World Reunion

A short while later, Dan Casey's starship slowly travels towards Race-World, leaving a trailing cloud on its way to the planet's orbit. The damage inflicted during the conflict with Corporal Union Cruiser has caused black smoke to ooze from the vessel as it passes other crafts.

Dan admires the passing starships from the cockpit controls and asks Pearl, "What was the event you stated, Pearl? It seems very busy."

The AI responds, "Today is the Intergalactic Derby, the biggest race in the galaxy."

The pastel-haired agent is now up from her mid-flight sleep and has come off the holo-net with her contacts. "Some of the wealthiest people in the galaxy will be attending this event. We need to meet with my friends, but we must keep a low profile and avoid drawing attention to ourselves, if possible."

Veena sighs as she gazes out the window, watching the smoke trail from the *Decepter*.

"I'll do my best for you, sweetheart," he says, sparking up a green-dust smoke.

Veena sighs again, "That worries me. Please don't call me sweetheart."

The cargo pilot enquires, "Why not?"

The green-haired beauty embarrassingly replies, "Because I'm a tough intergalactic agent, not someone's sweetheart."

Dan retorts, "You may act tough, but you could pass for a sweetheart or a model. Have you ever considered a safer career change?"

"Are you saying I'm not good at being an agent?"

Dan quickly responds, "No, not at all. I'm just saying that your high credits in modelling could save you from getting shot at."

The well-spoken lady decides not to answer his comment but gives a shy smile, feeling flattered by it nonetheless, as in her line of work, she gets very few compliments.

While piloting the *Decepter*, Dan Casey's companion reminds him that looking the part is crucial for their attendance at the galactic races. Despite the thundering engines making it challenging to hear her, Veena emphasises, "If we're going to the galactic races, we need to look at the importance of fitting in rather than appearing unkempt. Plus, Terri would disapprove of such a mud-slop image. She is a real sweetheart, Mr Casey. I'm sure you'll find her right up your hyper-lane."

Dan flick switches the flight controls while he expresses concern over Veena's friends. "Are these pals of yours to be trusted?"

Veena confidently raises her jade diamond-shaped eyes, sharing that she has known Terri Lace and Zak Duran for many years and that they are trustworthy. "We all grew up together on Kothariya, working and enjoying life. It was great fun, but no violence has been involved."

Veena briefly describes her childhood friends: "Terri is such a dear friend, more like a sister to me, and I doubt that Terri even knows how to handle a firearm, much less use one."

Veena drifts off into a memory daydream and shares details about her male counterpart, "Zak is a kind and true gentleman, quiet and composed in nature, plus a very handsome-looking man."

"Hey there, Agent Merida! You seem lost in thought. Is everything okay? Your mind seems to be wandering off again. Is it because of this Duran guy you keep talking about? He must have caught your attention!"

"Dan, I appreciate your concern. However, I want to clarify that our bond is founded solely on strong affection and nothing more." Veena replies with a touch of annoyance, "I just want to focus on our mission right now. Can we please just prioritise landing soon?"

Dan Casey takes a moment to gather his thoughts as he gazes at Veena's captivating eyes.

"Whatever you say, Veena. I didn't mean to touch a nerve." He glances out the window, noting they will be landing soon.

Veena Merida seems bothered and says, "You have not touched a nerve, okay? Let's just drop this conversation. I'm going to get ready now."

The *Decepter* starship flies through the planet's stunning skyline, showcasing a mesmerising blend of hazy greens and beautiful blues.

As they approach the Race-World Spaceport, Dan admires the impressive view of the lush green grass, glowing futuristic racetracks, towering cities, and sweeping freeways that await them. This world is reserved for the wealthy elites of the Kalanisi universe.

Dan is excited to see what adventures await him at the racecourse on the planet Carrageen-Hazen. After landing at starport, Dan Casey and Veena Merida arrive a short while later, sporting fresh clothes. He looks sharp in his brown leather jacket and sleek black slacks.

Veena is stunning in her light turquoise, form-fitting dress. She looks divine and turns heads wherever she goes. The air is crisp and clean, and the sky is a beautiful shade of blue, adding to their excitement and anticipation. This is the start of their mission to deliver the data box, and they are ready for whatever challenge; as they leave the starship, smoke billows from the back of the *Decepter*.

Dan quickly instructs the craft's auto-repair system to begin fixing the issue. Veena makes her way over to the sleek chrome, Alfa Cupra Gx6 sporty turbo car their friends have provided, eager to get to the Race-World's venue where Terri Lace and Zak Duran are waiting. They receive a message from their personal android driver directing them to meet at the Java Lynx bar.

Veena urges Dan to hurry, and he quickly locks up the *Decepter* before joining her in the red turbo car. The handsome, upbeat cargo pilot can't help but admire the classy Alfa Cupra Gx6.

Dan remarks, impressed by its elegance and contemplating the possibility of test-driving it, "I wish I owned one like this. Your acquaintances must be pretty well-off."

Veena replies, "I haven't seen them in about two years, so I'm unsure. I'm surprised they're still around, honestly. So, let's see."

The handsome cargo runner enquires, "Will they help you after all this time?"

Veena confidently responds, "I see no reason why not. At least they won't send me on a wild goose chase through the hyper-lanes."

Dan asks, "Are you still upset about that?"

Veena asserts in her posh-toned voice, "Absolutely, Mr Casey. I doubt I'll ever forget it. As they say, I'm scarred for life."

Dan reminds her with a smug smile, "Well, at least you made it out alive to tell the tale."

Veena Merida swiftly responds with a sense of assurance, "Barely, but I did, to be fair. This android driver is going too fast as well."

Dan Casey shakes his head in dismay, his face showing signs of wondering how things have gone wrong since meeting Veena Merida. Still, he is going with the flow to see the contract out.

A chauffeur with cyber assistance is driving the stylish Gx6 turbo car. The male android model is called Elton-63, designed by Mbron Media, and is associated with the counterpart Nayla 1.9.4 female version. The car streams into the rush hour highway traffic, and the slick whistling Alfa Cupra turbo car purrs a speeding venture, cruising past the open, flat green landscape space, captivating a stunning view of the towering skyscrapers near the Carrageen-Hazen's Elite racecourse.

Elton-63 reacts, overhearing the whimpering moans about the speed velocity from Veena. The pale-faced copper, coiffed-haired android flashes his red-shaded cybernetic eyes.

Elton-63 announces in his suave cyber voice, "I do apologise, madam, but Master Duran and Mistress Lace have booked an executive suite at the Java Lynx bar, and the tables are booked for seven thirty. I've been commanded not to be late. I must obey the rules set by Master Duran."

While sitting in the stylish back seat of the shifting turbo car, Dan turns his handsome face to Veena, stating with a smug smile, "Leave tin-face to me, sweetheart."

Dan Casey says, leaning forward and stretching his navy leather jacket arm out, firmly tapping the cyber driver on his fibre shoulders. Sternly commenting, "Hey, driver, the lady asked if you could slow down. Try computing that command, thanks."

"Can't do that. I'm in a rush, sir; Master Duran calls the shots, not you, my old human. Just sit back and enjoy the ride; we are not far from the racecourse now."

The turbo car continues to professionally weave around the four-lane freeway's stagnant traffic, with no intention to reduce the current speed. Dan Casey is far from amused by the android's response. Yet, before he can counter Elton-63's verbal sarcasm, Veena places her dainty hands on Dan's shoulders, pulling him back in the passenger leather seating, raising her jade eyes in contempt.

"Hey Dan, let it go; he's only doing his job. If Zak's booked a table slot, we should avoid being late."

Veena leans her elegant presence forward, telling the cybernetic driver, "Carry on, Elton-63. There are no complaints from us. Please ignore Dan; he seems dizzy in fast-motioning vehicles."

Dan replies, "Well, thank you for the information update, Miss Merida. You soon changed your tune, and I can see you made quite an effort yourself. You look very beautiful tonight. Let's hope this Duran appreciates your time dazzling him."

"Can we not just drop this conversation? I don't know why you keep bringing this up. Zak and I are just close friends, okay?"

"Ooh, touchy. Don't mind me. I'm just keeping an eye out for my partner!"

Dan Casey sighs and leans back, heeding Veena's words. As much as he dislikes robots and being told what to do, he sets aside his differences to ensure they don't miss the reservation. The car continues to drive through busy traffic, with Veena again growing queasy. She takes deep breaths and closes her eyes, trying to get rid of her nausea.

Dan notices and asks, "Veena, how are you feeling?"

"I'm fine; the car's just going too fast, making me sick."

The slick chrome Alfa Cupra Gx6 turbo car traces along the open freeway, readily approaching the main racecourse complex of the lush world; the electric-powered dual engine oozes a whistling blurred motioning sound while passing the scenic flat green landscape and glowing draw bridges of the Elite-owned planet. Gradually getting closer to the buzzing entrance of the Race-World facility, they tag onto the queuing rows of civilian transporters and the high-stakes roller's executive sports cars.

Elton-63 eases off the speed, taxing into the jam-packed car park. Veena can see her friends, Terri and Zak, waiting for them just outside the Java Lynx bar.

As the vehicle parks into a slot, Veena can't hide her excitement of being reunited. She quickly flicks open the door and bursts out of the Alfa Cupra. With a gleaming smile, the agent rapidly runs over Java Lynx's foreground with her high heels, tapping a sprinting clutter, greeting her friends with the overjoyed affection of hugs and kisses. She is truly losing herself in the moment as Veena has not seen Zak Duran or Terri Lace in two years since her parents' funeral, and she is surprised they still both work in the Sera sector.

In the meantime, Dan Casey has stepped away from the chauffeur-driven Gx6 turbo car, taking a smoke out of his top pocket; he readily sparks up the green-dust filter using his Astro-lighter. With a deep inhaling and a pursing blow of the vapour smoke, Dan surveys the impressive racecourse, catching sight of the towering glass entrance and the high-class grandstand facility alongside the dog track, even more so at the sexy, lovely ladies dressed to dazzle in their designer summer garments. The women are entering the lush grounds of the Carrageen-Hazen sporting Elite showcase of the famous Intergalactic Derby race for thoroughbred horses.

The cool, collected pilot walks over to the Java Lynx bar, where he witnesses Veena with her friends with a beaming smile. The green-haired beauty introduces the cargo pilot to her best friend, "Dan Casey. I want you to meet the lady I consider my little sister, Terri Lace."

The interstellar cargo pilot replies smoothly. "Hey there, Miss Lace. The pleasure is all mine! You are even more beautiful than imagined."

Dan Casey, with a sparkle in his dark brown eyes, contracts a wandering, admiring glance over the stunning blonde wavy-haired woman.

Terri Lace has a beautiful, blemish-free gorgeous face, enhanced by high-class cosmetic make-up, dressed in a tight-fitting sleeveless, black-coloured outfit, with an open slit revealing front, clearly showing off her curvy perfect sexual figure.

The blond bombshell politely replies in her seductive, well-spoken voice, "Oh, Mr Casey, you are far too kind. I'm sure the pleasure will be all mine, and please call me Terri."

Dan replies, "You don't know how kind I can be. Call me Dan, please. I insist, Terri."

The sexy agent introduces her other companion. "This is Zak; he's a very dear friend, and he's always been a rock of support to me. I'm sure you have much in common, being star pilots."

Dan Casey turns his attention away from the pleasurable company of Miss Lace. "Hey Zak, nice to meet you; Veena speaks so highly of you. It's an honour."

Dan nods his chiselled stubbled face over to Zak Duran, who himself is a good-looking, suave gentleman. He has dark brown hair in a slick swept-back style, a clear complexion and a slight designer stubble, wearing a pair of dark shaded circular glasses, dressed in a high-class two-toned brown leather jacket and slacks to match.

Zak Duran replies, "Likewise, Mr Casey. A friend of Veena's is a friend of mine for sure." But there are no smiles from either.

Zak continues his hosting pitch. "Now, please, let me treat you all to some fine food and cocktails while we celebrate this surprise occasion."

They swiftly make their way into the Java Lynx bar; the music is loud, and the banging bass is thumping with an electrifying pace. All types of high-profile people and alien species are dancing in the crowded venue, from lizard-humanoid creatures to cyborgs drinking away and listening to futuristic beats blasting from the speakers, being played by an alien DJ with four arms, known as a Qaudlin at the front booth. He's mixing his music with all the sexy, hot ladies and gentlemen who are responding to his enduring tunes, dancing on the main stage and in the high-hanging cages above the laser lights, flicking a dazzling effect around the executive saloon bar.

Zak Duran organises the drinks with his Java Lynx waitress as they all sit at one of the round, neon-lighted tables in the executive hub, away from the pounding beats of the Qaudlin DJ.

While the hotshot cargo pilot, Dan Casey, takes a seat opposite Terri Lace, his hijacking agent partner, Veena Merida, angles her sitting position closer to Zak, who, in his calm manner, calculates their drinks order. "Veena would love a Lemon Aston Martini drink with a touch of ice and the usual for Terri, a Pisco Sour cocktail with an umbrella rose," Zak Duran says with a smug smile.

Veena bashfully lowers her jade eyes, replying with a surprised smile, "Oh, Zak, you remembered my favourite drink. How sweet of you. Thanks."

Zak Duran remains the perfect host, pointing to Dan Casey and asking the gifted star pilot, "Well, that's the beautiful ladies dealt with. What do you require, Dan?" enquired Zak Duran, peeking over the top of his shaded glasses.

Dan leans back in his neon seat, instantly ordering his favourite drink. "I will have a Kestrel-dew. Cheers."

Dan turns his handsome face over to the giggle-sniggering Terri Lace with a bewildered look.

Zak Duran also laughs out loud, "Haha. They don't trade Kestrel-dew in clubs like the Java Lynx; they only use it to wash the dishes. Let me advise the Astro-primate beer, my favourite at the races."

Dan looks over to Veena, shaking his alluring face and brushing his hand through his sleek black hair. Knowing the joke is on him, he sarcastically replies, "Well, it seems they don't have strong beverages; I'll take one of the weak ones you recommend!"

At that very moment, Dan Casey suddenly feels a leg under

the neon table rub against his own. He swiftly glances over to Terri, who has a cheeky little grin forming on her charmed face.

Zak Duran asks Veena, "So what's going on, my sweet dear? How can we help? I do hope you are not in trouble?"

Veena replies to his offering of friendship. "Well, our starship had a tangle with the Corporal Union; we could do with a place to lie low for a few days." Veena takes an elegant sip of her Lemon Aston Martini as she continues her plea. "While Dan auto-repairs his spacecraft, we are on an important delivery contract without going into the logistical details."

Veena also notices that Dan isn't taking a blind bit of notice about what they are talking about as he seems to have his mind elsewhere. She raises her posh voice with a hint of irritation. "Isn't that right, partner?"

Dan Casey swiftly turns away from the teasing Terri Lace with no clue of the current conversation, only hearing Veena's phrase. "What? Yeah, sounds like a plan."

Terri seductively slowly moves her bare leg further up between the handsome pilot's groin.

Veena starts to get annoyed and feels embarrassed by Dan's behaviour. Unaware of her best friend's flirting, she firmly asks Dan, "You feeling alright? Seem a bit jittery and dazed. Are the drinks too strong for you?"

The orchestrating culprit, Terri, releases a teasing smile as she sips her Pisco Sour cocktail, telling Veena in her sulky voice, "Veena, you know we will help. No need to ask. Both of you can stay at my accommodation, as there is plenty of room, and you can stay as long as you require. I'm so glad you are here with us again; I've missed you so much over the last two years."

With an emotional sigh, Veena replies, "Aww, Terri, I've missed you too; I can't believe it's been such a long time since my parents' funeral. That was the last time I saw you. Wow! You have blossomed so much; you look like you've hit the intergalactic big time."

Zak Duran stylishly reaches out, placing his arm around Veena's dainty bare-skinned shoulders, with a tender kiss on her soft cheek, gently whispering his condolences, "I'm so sorry about what happened to your parents. You vanished suddenly and never saw Terri and me rise above average paid office clerks."

After a short pause and smug grin, Zak Duran continues, "Now, we run our line of business in consort accommodation, helping our clients with the perfect package deal. Advising the high rollers with credits to burn about high-class apartments to buy or lease while relaxing at Carrageen-Hazen."

Veena compliments their success. "I'm so pleased that you are doing so well, but do you mind if we leave here, as I've got a headache coming on?"

Zak says, "Of course not, my dear. I'll pay the bill and drive you to our shared home."

Veena replies, "Thank you."

While on the opposite side of the club's table. Terri Lace changes the subject, asking Dan with a flirty wave of her long blonde hair, "So what's your fancy for the Intergalactic Derby race in an hour, Mr Casey."

Dan responds with a smile, gazing at Terri's slick-cut black dress showing off her heaving curvy chest while still feeling her leg firmly pressure into his groin, "I've not had the chance to glance at the race card; I was hoping you could point me to the colt or filly with the best chance of hitting all the right spots."

"Oh, I do fancy, Dazzle; he is a colt in great form with a wicked turn of foot. Let me take you for a whirl around the racecourse; it will be fun."

Whereas overhearing the conversation, Veena Merida isn't too happy with her best friend flirting with Dan. She rapidly cuts into the flirtatious chat, commenting, "I don't think that's a good idea, Dan, do you? Let's just go to the accommodation and play safe; we don't want any unwanted attention to remember.

I'd say we need to leave this bar sooner rather than later. Plus, you need to fix your starship so we can fulfil this contract."

Zak Duran agrees with the jade-eyed vixen, "Yes, let's get moving; I have a brand-new starship at the private port for local traders. If you like, I could take you to your desired location. Won't be a problem if Dan's craft is damaged."

The glamorous resistance agent mulls over his proposition with the mission in mind.

But far from impressed is the charismatic Dan Casey, who firmly states, "Thanks for the offer, Mr Duran, but she already has a starship, which will be good to go by the mid-morning."

Zak Duran calmly smiles, asking the irritated pilot with a curious stare, "What do you fly, Dan?"

The dark-haired charmed cargo runner returns the lingering glare. Dan pushes his seat slightly back from the neon table, releasing the caressing leg of Terri Lace, and answers Zak Duran's probing question, "I own a Machiavellian MK2 Merlin freighter; what about you, Zak?"

Zak replies with a shocked demeanour, "You must be courageous, Dan, flying a relic vessel. Guess it's hard getting spare parts! I've just purchased a Panther A1 frigate, a top-class model. Wouldn't you say, Dan, pilot to pilot?"

While not to be undermined, Dan Casey smiles, replying, "I haven't flown that type of craft myself, but I did hear they have tin wings. Is there any truth in that!"

"Veena, surely you don't mind if I borrow Dan for a few hours at the races; I promise I'll make sure he keeps out of harm's way."

With a frowning yawn, Veena Merida says, "Fine, whatever, take him! Zak, we shall consider your helpful offer; thank you."

Terri Lace excitedly replies, "Thanks, sister; we can all meet at my apartment later and have a dinner party."

Terri blows a kiss of appreciation over to Veena with a giggling smile.

They start to make their way to the exit door of the Java Lynx bar. Just as they leave the bass-pounding venue, Zak Duran gets a call on his private comm-link, stating to the reunited group, "I just need to take this business call, so please go ahead. I'll catch up. Give me a moment, thanks."

Outside the high-profiled galactic bar, Terri Lace struts her sexy presence over to the race ground's ticket office, readily purchasing two grandstand entry passes. Veena walks alongside Dan as he escorts her to Zak Duran's stylish Alfa Cupra Gx6 turbo car.

Veena asks him politely with a tone of concern, "So, you're going racing with Terri? I must protest this is a bad idea, but you have your own free will. Just keep out of trouble and look after Terri. Plus, it may be a good choice for us to take up Zak's offer. We can take his Panther starship to the Isadora system and swiftly put this data box contract to bed. What do you say? Sounds like an ideal plan?"

Dan suddenly stops at a standstill, focusing on Veena's observation. He sincerely replies, "Sounds ideal if you're trying to bed Duran, but you count me out. I'm not flying with him either, to be honest; I'm not too keen on him coming across as a cocky snob, and yeah, Terri's going to show me how to make a few credits. So if you want to break our contract agreement, knock yourself out, Agent Merida. I'm sure Mr Duran will accept your eager willingness with open arms."

Veena Merida moodily shakes her head as her wavy, pastel-coloured hair catches the slight breeze in the atmospheric cool evening air across the outskirts of the Carrageen-Hazen racecourse.

In his confident, calm voice, Zak announces, "Sorry about the delay, Veena. Are we ready to go, or have you decided to stay for the derby race?"

Veena responds to Zak's suggestions, "Yes, let's go, as I've no interest in any galactic derby. I just need a private word with Dan; I will meet you in the car."

As the galactic trader waltzes to his Gx6 turbo car, Veena says, "I have an intuition you are not willing to accept Zak's help. Does that mean you won't continue the mission if I take up his offer to fly us to the Isadora system?"

Dan gazes into her beautiful jade eyes, reminding the resistance operative, "It's your mission, Agent Lady, not mine. You hijacked me, remember, and it's probably for the best if we go separate ways, Miss Merida; I am just saying you shouldn't put too much trust in your pal Zak. I've got a bad feeling about him, so be wary."

Veena laughs. "You are jealous of Zak? We are just close friends, plus we're only business partners ourselves! Do you have the same wary feeling about Terri, or is that a different feeling altogether? I saw her flirting with you in the Java Lynx. Look, I've got to go. We can talk later. If I don't see you at their apartment, this could be goodbye, Mr Casey. I will forward any payment owed to you through Pearl; your starship's AI has my contact details."

Veena gives an upset, disgruntled sigh as she starts walking off to Zak Duran's Alfa Cupra Gx6 turbo car, revving a rumbled whistle.

The slanted chrome passenger door vertically springs open. While standing adrift, absorbing her departure, Dan shouts, "Veena, just be careful, okay?"

"I'll be fine, Mr Casey."

She gets into the slick turbo jet car and takes her position in the leather bucket seat. Veena looks sadly back at Dan as the slender vehicle pulls off extremely fast, heading to her friend's private accommodation; her gorgeous face shows signs that her feelings for the rough-and-ready cargo pilot are deepening.

Dan Casey witnesses the car zoom off in the distance as he turns around, catching sight of another beautiful woman, Terri

Lace, waving the Race-World tickets with a dazzling, alluring smile. Dan's face portrays a change of luck after the troublesome few days that have taken place while in the company of the lawfully wanted feminine agent, Veena Merida.

Chapter Seven

The Galactic Derby

A short while later, at the heart of the impressive Carrageen-Hazen racecourse, the grandstand fills up. The crowd is packed into the spectacular venue for the highlight sporting event of the year 4010. The atmosphere brims with anticipation as the top-class stallions start to parade around the Astro-ring before the big derby race. The evening sunset glow shining across the dogleg racetrack, showing the lush green grass in full effect. The racecourse commentator calls out the horses' names and states their chance of winning the classic grade one race.

At the Astro-ring, inspecting the immaculate racehorses, are the handsome cargo pilot Dan Casey and the gorgeous female consort trader Terri Lace. The pair get on well as they walk around the civilian pathway, checking the thoroughbred horses, who are preparing to leave the parade and gallop down to the starting post.

Terri Lace is flicking her delicate hands through the form guide, readily eyeing the race contenders and says to her evening escort, "I'm so glad you came to the races, Dan. Especially with the others going home so early. I would have looked like a right idiot tootling about on my own."

She slips a link of her soft bare arm around Dan Casey's muscular build with a gazing seductive smile.

Dan responds with a smiling glint in his dark eyes, "Thank

you for the invitation, Miss Lace. I can't think of a better way to spend the evening than at a glamorous racecourse with a beautiful woman on my arm."

Terri endorses his compliments with modesty. "Aww, thank you, and you flatter me. So, who do you fancy for the big race?"

The cargo pilot browses, glancing over Terri's revealing black skimpy outfit, insisting with a charmed grin, "What sort of man would I be if I didn't let the stunning lady choose the lucky selection."

"Oh, you're such a gentleman. I can see why Veena fell for you. Okay, for my exclusive tip, I'm still siding with Dazzle."

"Look over there, number five, that's Dazzle. He's a big, strong presenting horse, firmly trained with an excellent turn of foot, which will suit the speedy surface on tonight's track. The odds are fair. Come on, Dan, let's place our bets, as I think he will be a great ride. And I do love a good firm ride, Dan."

Dan Casey's facial expression is crossed with a smile and confusion. "You certainly seem to know about your horses. For the record, Veena and I are not an item; we are more like distant business partners."

They steadily stroll into the betting area. Terri says, "Dan, you may think you're just Veena's work colleague, but I know my older sister twinkles in her loverly jade eyes when she has an interest of the heart."

Dan enquires, "Are you sisters or just close friends? You are both from the capital world, Kothariya, by the well-spoken accents, but you have different surnames."

Terri releases her grip on his bulky arm, gets her payment card out of her stylish handbag and scans the bet with the bookie, stating, "I'd Like 10,000 credits on Dazzle to win, thanks."

The grey-haired, stomached bookie readily takes the bet with a plain face. "You place the same bet as the fine lady here, pal? Another 10,000 credits on Dazzle at three to one?"

Dan quickly reacts with a taken-back, shocked demeanour, relating, "No way, Mr! More like 100 credits only for me."

Terri Lace once again latches her bare-skinned arm around Dan, "Aww, you play safe. Don't you trust my selection? No, Veena is not my real sister. We pretend to be as she looked out for me when I was young and goofy. I'm more intrigued by how she came to meet you, Mr Casey."

Dan Casey grabs a couple of steaming-hot Star coffee beverages en route to the executive grandstand suite. Following Terri's lead, he enquires with a stunned daze of his charmed brown eyes browsing around the reserved suite, "What line of wealth are you and Mr Duran involved in again? Wow! Big horse racing bets and slick sports cars, topped off with high-class accommodation. Makes a small-time interstellar cargo runner feel out of place, sweetheart."

Taking their seat for the big race event to start, Terri reassures the out-of-sorts pilot, "Don't worry about the lifestyle difference. I just want to show you a good time. I do hope you like having me in your company, Dan." She lets her dainty wandering hand roam over Dan Casey's outer leg teasingly, taking an elegant sip of her Star coffee drink and licking her wet glossed lips.

Dan responds to her fleeting touch, "After a strange few days, this evening feels like a dream; I'm having a wonderful time with you, Miss Lace."

Terri laughs with a deep, fluttering gaze of her allured blue eyes, "Your expression and tone suggest Veena's been getting you in all sorts of trouble. So, how did you two link up? What's this important delivery contract that's got her stirred."

Dan Casey purposely answers Terri Lace indirectly, with his attention drawn to the racehorse entering the starting stall, "It sounds like you know Veena well. I'm sure she will tell you all about her woozy misadventures. Now, which one's our lucky horse again? I feel the tension building up, and I've got 100 credits on. I can't imagine what you're feeling like, Terri, with 10,000 credits running on the horse's nose."

"I'm feeling heated and charged up, Mr Casey." Dan is surprised and taken aback by the young consort lady's forward behaviour, covering his indecisiveness with a handsome smile. The grandstand is uprooted as the commentator suddenly announces, "They're off!"

The galactic derby race begins in earnest. Terri and Dan's selection is slow to break away from the gates as the thoroughbred horses assemble into a tight-knit racing pack, jostling for position as they run to the first sweeping bend.

Dan comments to Terri, keeping his eyes on the unfolding race, "He didn't break too well. Let's hope he lives up to his name, Dazzle?"

Terri gazes at Dan and cuddles up to him closer, explaining, "He's a stalker-type runner, so don't worry, Mr Casey; this just makes the race more exciting."

She kisses Dan's stubbled face, teasingly guiding his hand closer up her thigh with a tempting giggle. The furious pace of the race hots up down the back, straight approaching the second bend on the lush Carrageen-Hazen racetrack. Three horses quicken their pace and are clear of the chasing pack. Dazzle stylishly creeps into contention, angling for a late run back and forth. Cruising a few lengths off the race leaders, he attempts to be involved in the finish of the Intergalactic Derby.

Dazzle kicks the fast ground turf as his jockey nudges his mount forward. Readily swinging on the bridle, sweeping stealthy around the impressive undulating track, turning into the home straight two horses wide with a light turn of foot. Their waging thoroughbred colt ranges up to grab the lead of the historic race, hitting the front with a burst of speed, powering clear of the second-placed horse as the spectator crowd roars home the winner.

The ecstatic cargo pilot Dan Casey screams while Terri Lace

jumps up, cheering her winning horse Dazzle, crossing the line first.

With sheer excitement from both parties, Terri's lush blue eyes link a connection with Dan's deep brown eyes. Her hand still firmly pressures his rough gloved palm between her silky thighs; she seductively smiles, asking the cargo pilot, "Do you feel like a winner, Mr Casey? What do you say we skip dinner and go trash some of my 40,000 credits on getting drunk back at the Java Lynx bar."

Terri's red lips hover with a pecking kiss on Dan's cheek, awaiting his response. Dan replies with insight into entrapment, "I was always planning to pass on dinner, sweetheart. The Java Lynx seems just my kind of bar. But won't Zak get a bit twitchy with me keeping you out late?"

Terri sighs, "Dan, I feel you care little about Zak. Don't worry too much. He's, like you said, a distant business partnership."

She takes Dan Casey's eager hand with a flirtatious lead back to the Java Lynx bar, aiming to celebrate their lucrative evening together at the galactic derby races.

Meanwhile, the twilight sky blends in with the dusk of night as sunset fades over Carrageen-Hazen's open-spread freeways. The glowing draw bridges shine, extracting between the jaw-dropping view of the flowing waterfalls below the busy speedway, leading directly into Carrageen-Hazen's impressive capital city, Harvanna. The private spaceport for the local traders is situated just on the outskirts of the stunning shard city, the destination of Zak Duran and Veena Merida. Veena admires the beautiful flat, lush green landscape from the side view of the slick vehicle, whooshing across the light-glow bridge and closing swiftly into Harvanna.

The slender metallic Gx6 sports car is being driven by the sophisticated consort adviser Zak Duran, who enquires with an empathic interest into Veena's sullen mood, "Hey, is everything okay? You have been very quiet since leaving Java Lynx. I'm not going too fast for you, my dear? I'm guessing you still get woozy."

Veena turns her dazed face from the flowing outside view; her long green hair trails across her naked shoulder and sleek, tight-fitting turquoise summer dress. She breaks a smile on her lush red lips, politely answering her pleasant friend, "I'm fine. Thank you, Zak. I'm just feeling a bit tired; it has been an unsteady few days."

"So, how long have you been with Mr Casey? He doesn't seem like the gentleman I would have expected you to be with; I do hope he is taking care of you, Veena. It looks like you had words before we set off, and I feel he's not keen on me either."

"I'm not acquainted with Dan. We're working together on a contract; I've only known him briefly. Let us just call it a hijacked partnership." As she smiles to herself, the green-haired beauty explains, "Don't take it personally, Zak; I'm not even sure Dan will show his face later, win or lose at the races. He doesn't seem to appreciate outside help."

The slick metallic Alfa Romaro Gx6 turbo car steadily slows to an easing static halt. Zak takes his hands off the race-equipped steering wheel, leaning back in the leather chair slightly, turning his handsome face towards Veena.

"Let us not worry about Mr Casey for now; Terri will put a sparkle in his step. She has a knack for bringing the best out in people. I wanted to show you my starship before we settle at our accommodations."

The Alfa Cupra Gx6 doors swing vertically open with a whooshing pulse.

Zak Duran gets swiftly out of the turbo car, followed by Veena Merida. He softly grips her dainty hands with a bragging spring in his step.

"My new pride and joy, the Panther A1 class frigate with a few extra modified designs added to the specs. Come, my dear, let me show you around the interior; I'm sure you will be more than impressed."

Veena Merida's face shows her astonishment as they

approach the Panther; the stealthy black starship oozes class. The craft's long, slick nose is coupled with a slender, sleek, curved hull and short, angled wings supporting two thruster engines. The Panther stands proud in the Harvanna Starport Bay.

Veena smiles at the embarrassment of riches, turning her beautiful presence to Zak, appraising his flourishing career as an Elite consort adviser. "Oh gosh, have you and Terri won the galactic lottery? Your starship is stunning, and you both have identical sporty Gx6 turbo cars; these items must have cost a fortune."

Zak smiles, replying, "No lottery, Veena; I wish. Being rich and famous would be cool, but Terri and I have had some lucky breaks with our financial backers. They trade in high-stake credits and pay back in large dividends. You could have played a part in our business but for your sudden disappearance off the charts."

Zak continues, "You still have not told me what's that important you need to hide from so badly. What have you involved yourself with, Veena? It must be quite serious. If the Corporal Union is hounding a trail. You know you can tell me anything and trust my word of silence."

"Aww, Zak, you are a good friend to have around. I'm sorry I vanished without a trace; there were things I needed to take care of alone. I'm not the same woman you used to know, and I will be honest with you, Zak. I've become an agent of the underground resistance, and I have killed many criminals. Even the ones who murdered my parents, hence my absence."

However, Zak Duran is more than understanding. "Well, I can't say I expected that, but I'll help however I can. I've always seen us as more than just friends, Veena. Please let me know wherever you need to go, and I'll take you there immediately with no delays. Whatever the cargo?"

Zak Duran gives a comforting stroke of his hand over Veena's bare-skinned shoulders.

The crack-shot feminine agent reaches down to her dainty black handbag and retrieves the astrological data box.

Holding the small, ancient, mysterious device in her suede-gloved hands, she deeply explains her mission objectives to Zak, "It's about this data box; my assignment was to steal it from the Corporal Union's vault, disguised as their newfound modifications officer, Sienna Crayton. I believe it is an old astrological chart concerning the Kalanisi Universe. The delusional, corrupt Director, Wilson Volantis, told me they plan to locate a black hole called the Vortex and blow it open by using his new flagship, the Sulamani, hence the project's name. The Corporal Union is losing sight of its purpose under the current regime. It plans to control the galaxy through evil means. How much do you know now about black holes, Zak?"

The charmed advisor glances down into Veena's palm, looking at the data box through his tinted shades, and replies to her questions with a touch of doubt, "Wow, Veena, that is some eventful story, I know nothing about black holes apart from they are dangerous and powerful. I'd advise you not to fly towards them either, my sweetness."

"Look, sorry, I'm not trying to scare you, and having accommodation to stay for a day or two would be more than efficient. I'd never ask you to fly me into uncertainties. Terri will never forgive me if any harm becomes of you, plus Dan and I have an agreement. So, I will kindly pass on your offer, thank you, and I'll try to catch my moody cargo pilot at the commercial spaceport if Terri fails to persuade Dan to attend our dinner engagement."

She slips the data box into her leather handbag and goes to the Panther's airlock hatch.

Zak suddenly pulls her gracefully into his arms, reminding her of past times. "We used to be more than just friends, Veena. I'm sure you remember. I was hoping you would. Seeing you again is so good."

He attempts to kiss Veena's red glossy lips, romantically stroking her charming facial beauty. With shock, Veena Merida shies away from his anticipated kiss, embarrassingly turning her cheek. "Oh, gosh, Zak, that feels like a lifetime ago. Plus, I thought you had formed a relationship with Terri. I'm not here for romance, Zak! I have an assignment to finish. I'm sorry."

"I wouldn't want to see you harmed in any way, Veena. I still care for you greatly, and Terri doesn't always need to know all my business or pleasurable affairs. I will help your rebellion cause. The Corporal Union has gone too far, endangering the innocent with its fantasies. Please, tour my starship and make yourself at home."

Veena sweetly replied, "You're too kind, Zak. Thanks."

The green-haired vixen makes her heel-tapping way up the starship's ramp to the opening airlock. She is instantly met with steamed condensation oozing from the craft's hatch. Suddenly, she stops, and her jade eyes open wide with the unexpected shock of hearing a hideous growl. The galactic agent's instinct is to draw her sliver-scoped pistol in defence. But suddenly, dark shadows of a deadly alien creature appear through the Panther's interior.

Frightfully freezing on the spot and not believing her crystal jade eyes, Veena Merida screams, "Oh! It's a Leecher!" She witnesses the muscular hostile species feared throughout the Kalanisi Universe.

These hideous alien creatures are mainly found on the edges of dark spaces and are known for mutilating their victims with no sense of remorse. In a stunned motion, Veena reaches for her pistol, adjusting for an aimed slingshot. The dark matt, arched body of the vile Leecher bounds in her direction. A weapon belt is crossed over the beast's bulging shoulders.

The Leecher's evil blood-red eyes and drawn face are long-jawed with slobbering fangs, which can manifest into a lethal, face-sucking set of tentacles.

She has no time to raise her gun as the raging creature slaps Veena's shaken face and knocks her out unconscious. She drops her weapon and falls into the awaiting arms of Zak Duran.

Zak Duran calls the alien hound by its name. "Dralon bound her, but I don't want any rough stuff."

Zak takes the data box out of Veena's handbag. Whispering to the sleeping agent, "Sorry, my dear friend. You are very special to me, but the bounty on your head and the retrieval of the Corporal Union's property is just too big an opportunity to pass over. Plus, my sweetheart, for your information, I don't get scared easily; I've always wanted to be extremely rich and famous. Like you correctly said, Veena, we all have our assignments to complete."

He then inspects the data box with intrigue, boarding his starship, the Panther.

The gruesome Leecher, Dralon, slings the unconscious Veena Merida on his beastly shoulders, following his master on board the slick spacecraft.

While leaving no evidence of abduction, the Panther's hatch closes instantly on the brisk night of Harvanna's private starport.

Chapter Eight

Divided Fields

Meanwhile, back at Carrageen-Hazen's racecourse grounds, Dan Casey and Terri Lace are unaware of Zak Duran's alternative agenda while partying the evening away in the Java Lynx bar.

Terri Lace is ordering a tray of Pisco Sour cocktail drinks at the red neon bar. While close by at one of the front row tables, Dan Casey is sparking up his green-dust smoke and getting into the spiralling bass beats. Dan places his Astro-lighter back in his top jacket pocket, inspecting the heaving dancefloor. The laser stage lights of the DJ booth are flickering a strobed beam across the stiletto-wearing crowds.

The futuristic dance music is being mixed by the four-armed resident DJ, dancing a twisting jive in his booth. This friendly alien species is known as a Quadlin. Their faces are similar to humans, but they have purple, shiny skin and slicked-back multicoloured hair, with two arms positioned shoulder high and the others low, nearing their waistline. Making them perfect candidates for night bar work in the club entertainment zones. The pumping bass tunes have the sexy dance girls flirting with a twinkle in the glowing hanging cages. The hazy smoke from the stage technicians fills the dancefloor, creating an underground feeling to the Java Lynx nightclub bar.

Dan Casey stylishly flicks his thick black hair out of his handsome, chiselled face. He takes a massive, inhaled drag of his smoke filter, followed by a gushing blow of green vapour, while admiring the electric pulse setting of the Elite tavern. Dan gives a happy grin, witnessing Terri seductively strutting back from the bar, carefully holding a tray of high-priced cocktails. The glamorous, flirty blonde seductively sits on a perch next to the cargo-runner pilot on the cushioned chairs, placing the Pisco Sour cocktails down on the circular table, crossing her legs in a ladylike fashion with a teasing flap of her open-seam summer garment.

"Okay, Mr Cargo Pilot, let us celebrate our winnings in style."

Dan stubs his grazing smoke out, readily taking hold of an umbrella cocktail. Smiling over to the dreamy blonde, he responds, "Offer thoroughly accepted, Miss Lace. Let's hope you consort-class ladies can keep up with an interstellar class pilot."

Dan Casey swings down his Pisco Sour delight, following his gorgeous hostess suit with a banging of the glass on the tabletop.

Terri screams, "Woo! Dan. Game on."

She giggles a tease, knocking back her second cocktail and fluttering her blue eyes, wiggling her long bare legs to the hypnotic music.

Not to be outdone by the blonde bombshell, Dan swiftly necks his second round, double tapping the empty umbrella glass on the table and commenting, "You want to give up now? It seems you Kothariya ladies get woozy from the slightest thrill!"

Terri Lace charmingly giggles at his teasing comments. Gripping two of the stemmed cocktail glasses, divulging one after another, with a squint and a shake of her wavy blonde hair, duly tapping the glasses similarly on the curved desk, "Oh, Dan, I do believe you're mistaking me for my jade-eyed sister. I'm more than capable of holding my own in any circumstances."

The charismatic cargo pilot lines up three shots of the Pisco Sour cocktails, drinking them one by one in a furious fashion.

Dan also squints with a sour-faced demeanour, commenting, "I'd say that puts me in front; with two to go, I would imagine Duran to have passed out twice by now. I guess this is a new territory, sweetheart."

"I like your style, Mr Casey. It is a rare feat to meet a man in the Sera sector with a rough-edged spirit; I like that in a guy. I like that a lot. It's a refreshing change from the Elite wimps I associate with."

At the same time, the pounding ambience of bass music is being taken up a level by the Quadlin DJ. The mind-bending tracks become more intense with a rise in pace on the dance floor.

Terri Lace is losing herself in the rhythmic beats. Twisting and turning her elegant body, she looks amazingly sexy. Shaking her ample chest through the tight silk fabric outfit, seductively jiggling her curvy rear.

"Dan, dance with me."

While tapping his boots and nodding to the tranquillisation tunes, Dan Casey admires Terri's manoeuvring dance moves. Responding to the teasing temptress, "I can't say that dancing is my forte; I would only cramp your style, sweetheart." Dan says, then finishes off his seventh Pisco Sour cocktail.

But Terri Lace isn't taking no for an answer. She says, "Come on, Mr Casey, I'll teach you a few moves. You can't be any worse than Zak."

She grabs his gloved hands with a persuasive tug and reluctantly leads Dan to the crowded hyper-dancefloor. The hours pass as they both dance the night away. Judging by the stress-free smile on his handsome face, Dan Casey is enjoying this lifestyle.

The night seems to be getting better at the moment. The alien four-armed DJ is rocking the place with his mixed futuristic beats and glittering laser light show. Terri Lace dances closer to the one-stepped cargo runner with her steamy, hot, twisting moves, showing off her perfect charms.

"Do you think I look sexy in this black outfit?"

"Without a doubt, Miss Lace. You are a sparkling standout in any crowd, sweetheart."

Playing to his flattery, Terri moves closer still, erotically rubbing herself up and down him. Trailing her manicure-nailed hands along his brown leather jacket. She starts to kiss his rough, stubbled lips with a sigh and moan. Dan responds without thought and passionately engages in the sexual entanglement.

Terri breaks the heated connection with a sexy whisper, "I'm glad the others never came back, as I need you all to myself, Dan. Do you fancy going out the back alone together? It's becoming hot and steamy here."

Dan Casey smiles to himself, leaving the lively bar in the divine company of Terri Lace. Without a thought, he seems to have forgotten all about Veena Merida's save-the-universe saga.

Terri giggles drunkenly, swaying a walk further away from the bar's back entrance. Her dainty hands wander over his shoulders, mentioning her intentions.

"Fancy a high-class ride in my car, Mr Casey? It's an Alfa Cupra Gx6 turbo, identical to Zak's. We got them both on our business credit accounts; let me just find my key device."

Terri Lace releases her caressing touch, dropping a heeled step back and searching in her tiny black handbag.

Dan Casey strolls a stride to the cornering wired fence, exiting the Java Lynx bar to Race-World's car park facility. The crack-shot, tipsy pilot suddenly stops, hearing a murmured hissing growl in the night atmosphere. He quickly inspects his surroundings, shaking his head and clearing his merry senses. Dan's dark brown eyes widen in shocked astonishment, witnessing dark shadows emerge from the bordering fence of the Java Lynx.

Blocking his intended path are two muscular, horrific alien creatures. Their evil blood-red eyes and monstrous tattered complexion focus intently on Dan Casey, menacingly arching their shoulders in an offensive attack posture. The well-travelled interstellar pilot has had previous encounters with similar types of beasts in his ex-space protection operative days. With an adrenaline rush, Dan quickly draws for his holstered silver and black-barrelled gun. His instinct is to protect Miss Lace.

Dan advisedly shouts out behind in apprehension, "Terri, run back to the Java Lynx and get help. It's a pair of monstrous Leechers!"

Bravely standing his ground, Dan isn't to be intimidated by the growling hostile intruders. Squeezing his glove-cut finger on his killer trigger, ready to suppress their offence, only to have the unexpected feel of a gun barrel shoved firmly in his back.

"What the fuck?" says the shocked cargo pilot, only for his sentence to be cut short by the sultry voice of Terri Lace.

The blonde-haired beauty says in her sultry voice, "I know Mr Casey; they're with me. Let us call them an early-morning chaperone. Now drop the gun and put your hands up."

The deceptive Miss Lace pushes her black, stub-barrelled pistol deep into his side ribcage.

Dan Casey pauses as he reluctantly loops his weapon to a releasing drop to the ground. Expressing his astonishment of surprise to the so-called consort, "You got to be damn well kidding me. I was advised you didn't know how to hold a weapon."

Terri Lace kicks his silver and black gun across the gravel, spinning past the horrific growling duo of Leechers. She slowly licks Dan's brisk, stubbled face and informs him, "I'm afraid your information is outdated, Mr Casey. What can I say apart from being a quick learner? Haha."

Motioning a walk over to the secluded exit, Terri chuckles to herself, situating an elegant posing stand next to the alien beasts. With a tease of her lush blue eyes, she acknowledges, "Please don't take it to heart, Dan. I know it's such a shame, as I wanted to fuck you. But it's just a matter of business before pleasure."

The situation is grim for Dan, and in a tone of annoyance, he seeks answers. "I think your pals here killed the moment, sweetheart. Where's Veena? I thought you were her friend."

"Oh, my bitch of a fake sister is with Zak and our other Leecher associates. She is being prepared to be shipped off to the Corporal Union. The delightful Director Wilson Volantis has placed a significant galactic bounty on her green-haired skull; I can't wait to spend it."

"You and Duran are no more than high-class bounty hunters; I guess loyalty among friends is a rare anomaly. Your type of greed disgusts me, linking up with these sludgy face fucks."

His rant is interrupted by a slick red sports car, that's driven by a third Leecher and swiftly pulls up in the Race-World's parking facility.

Terri Lace comments on hearing the rumbling whistle of the shiny turbo car's powerful engine, "Oh! My new Ferrari Testarossa convertible Gx9000 is top-of-the-range. I'm so excited. I'm a busy girl, and I have to go, Dan. It has been my pleasure; I've had an exhilarating night of fun. Thank you kindly. But unfortunately, the Corporal Union has put you in the category of knowing too much about their Sulamani project, so it's goodbye, Mr Casey."

The gorgeous bounty hunter glares at one of the Leechers, commencing a nod and gives the executive order, "Kill him!"

She strides to her new convertible Gx9000 car accompanied by the other monstrous beast. She is planning to rendezvous with Zak Duran at Harvanna's private spaceport on the other side of the Carrageen-Hazen.

Dan Casey witnesses the beautiful but manipulative Terri Lace swiftly pull off in her new red sports car with a gruesome Leecher for company.

Dan mulls his words under his breath, "What a bitch!" His eyes are drawn to his black-barrelled gun not too far adrift. The weapon is lying just behind the vile creature.

The morning sky starts to break through with a clear sight of the Leecher's blood-red eyes. The grotesque beast growls a snarling roar, showing its slobbering dread fangs. Intimidatingly, it clutches its clawed fist at the cargo pilot. With the pumping bass etching from the Java Lynx bar, Dan glances back with the realisation that he's in trouble, and nobody will hear his demise as the Leecher prepares to creep in his direction.

The charismatic interstellar pilot takes his chance.

"Hey, take it steady there now, pal. We both got dumped off. It's not like I came out on top with her."

Dan Casey attempts a charge for his weapon. But the dubious Leecher is adeptly fast and grabs a clenching grip of his brown leather flight jacket, hurling the defenceless pilot into the corner posts of the Elite bar's yard gate. He falls in a dazed heap.

Dan quickly shakes off the attack; covered in debris, he swiftly jumps to his booted feet, witnessing the Leecher pouncing. With no time to spare, the courageous pilot picks apart the broken gate pole, swerving with a dashed rolling leap of the monster's lunging attack. The grotesque creature manoeuvres a renewed offence.

Boldly with adrenaline, Dan Casey smashes the fence pole across the Leecher's raging face with all his might. The consequence is that the flimsy pole shatters in a breaking snap with no harm to the Leecher's assault.

Dan sarcastically self-comments in a daze of stunned disappointment, "I was hoping that would go better; Ahh, shit!"

Crashing into the mesh wire fence and destroying it in the process of impact, Dan groans in agony, landing directly on his back. He blows his messed-up hair out of his brown eyes, staggering in an effort to get to his feet. The vile Leecher taunts its prey, manifesting its daunting fangs into slimy tentacles.

Swiftly ranging to his booted stance, Dan Casey mumbles, gaining his posture, "That's damn right revolting pal."

He quickly pulls some wire from the damaged fence. The

Leecher lunges, vastly grabbing the ill-stricken pilot by his neck with his menacing sharp claws. Slightly lifted from the gritty ground with a choking sensation, Dan gasps a splutter, struggling to breathe.

The heroic cargo runner manages to wrap the mesh wire around the Leecher's scaly throat. He pulls hard before the vile monster's tentacles get a chance to suck his face off. With a reversed offence, the horrific Leecher growls in manic discomfort, choking from Dan's retaliation. He releases its claw grip, giving the brave pilot a chance to review.

Dan Casey kicks back from the alien beast's hold, swiftly evading its hostile presence with a rolled leap towards his weapon. Gaining the upper hand, Dan craftily scoops up his black-barrelled gun. The disoriented creature frees itself from the mesh, swiftly turning with a pounce.

Dan Casey squeezes on his trigger, blasting two shots into the Leecher's skull, "Suck on that, you damn beast."

The cargo pilot's handsome facial expression shows his amazement that he is still alive. With a pause, though, he mutters, "Veena!" Knowing she is in grave danger, he glances around, mulling for options.

The interstellar pilot notices the Alfa Cupra Gx6 turbo car that chauffeured him from the Carrageen-Hazen's spaceport. He urgently sprints to the slick chrome car and opens the vertical lift doors, but the Mbron Media android, Elton-63, confronts him.

"You are not authorised for a journey, sir."

In no mood to be hassled, Dan Casey grips the copper-coiffed android's pale fibre head with a tugging twist, shorting the Mbron Media cyberbot out with a twitching spark.

Throwing the android out of the stylish car, Dan jumps into the Alfa Cupra, taking the driver's seat. He swiftly starts the whistling ignition, hitting the turbo acceleration and dashes off in pursuit of the fruitful Terri Lace and her other monstrous Leechers.

While back at the private spaceport on the edge of the capital city of Harvanna, Zak Duran's starship, the Panther, is prepping for take-off, awaiting the arrival of Terri Lace. The abducted agent, Veena Merida, is being held in the storage quarters of the craft on the second deck from the cockpit cabin.

She starts to come around after being knocked out cold by the Leecher when entering Zak's starship.

The jade-eyed heroine groans as she finds herself tied up on the deck. Her hands are bound behind and attached to the flight deck chair. Veena's misty focus clears with a scared scream, "Ahh!" She is now realising what has happened to her as she sees the Leecher beast on guard in the dormant cell.

Dralon, the tribal leader of the alien species, catches sight of Veena Merida trying to wriggle and struggle free from her binds. The vile creature instantly pounces, flashing his slimy tentacles in taunted anger.

"Gosh, I'm truly charmed. ZAK!"

Overhearing the commotion on the second deck, Zak Duran approaches from the cockpit. "Ah, good, you're awake. How are you feeling, my dear?"

Veena struggles to break loose, defiantly taunting her betraying ally, "Why don't you release these shackles, and I'll show how I feel first-hand, bastard."

Dralon viciously snaps at her defiant nature, twisting its hideous tentacles in her shocked face.

Zak Duran equally stomps his authority, "Dralon, stand down at once; remember who's in charge of this vessel. You kill when I demand and not before. Otherwise, you will end up back in the slave pit I claimed you from. Now, leave us alone. Give us some privacy. This one is a special friend, or she was!"

The Leecher eases off its menacing harassment, obeying his master's commands.

Veena's diamond eyes track her old friend pacing around the starship's deck. "I can assure you, Zak. You're not doing too well in the special friend's league as it stands by putting me next to these greasy slugs. What in the world has happened to you? Apart from becoming a delusional crackpot, I guess this is about the data box?"

Zak walks over to Veena, stroking her long, wavy green hair. "Please don't take it personally; I do love you, Veena. But the Corporal Union has put the value of a billion credit bounty on your sweet head, and, in truth, I love credits a lot more. I'm sorry."

Veena Merida defiantly flicks her head to the side, evading his touch, firmly stating, "Get your filthy hands off me. I trusted you. Now you hang out with the scum of the galaxy. Have you got Terri mixed up in this shenanigan, or are you just leading her astray while this is your grand scheme to become rich?"

Zak Duran slowly turns away from his captive, removing his circular-shaded glasses. He smiles while explaining his motives to Veena Merida.

"Yes, of course, Terri is involved. She delves into the underground leads, getting us contacts in the rival regimes such as the Galanti's and the Santana sisters. After that business venture, the openings poured in, and we've branched out as independent bounty hunters for the high-class syndicates of the Sera system. Unfortunately, when you left us on a personal vendetta, we were no more than poor, pushed-around office clerks. Now look at us: a galaxy full of opportunities. You could be a part of this extravaganza, Veena, and I could bid with the Corporal Union to claim you as mine. Save you from execution. It seems I have this data box, which Wilson Volantis desires so badly. He believes in the ancient lore of the Vortex, but it is not my concern. I just lust for credits and class reputation. Take your time; we have a short journey to make you carefully think it over."

Veena Merida shakes her long green mane in disgust. She glances down, mumbles, and sighs. "Oh, I should have listened to Dan. I'd sooner die in the hands of the Corporal Union than be your fancy-bit slave."

Zak Duran calmly replaces his shades with a stern tone. "You should have listened to Mr Casey if that's your line of choice, as there won't be another chance. Your friend, the cargo runner, should be lying dead now, I'd imagine, at the back of the Java Lynx bar by the hands of our mutual friend, Terri, who will be arriving very soon in her brand-new turbo car. I'm sure she will tell you about her night at the races."

Veena Merida is left alone as Zak leaves. Her emotions show. She is worried about Dan's fate, and tears form in her jade eyes. "I'm sorry, Dan; it's all my fault."

The starship's engines begin to hum, preparing for a pre-flight launch.

Meanwhile, cruising in her brand-new Testarossa convertible Gx9000 on the long sweeping open straight freeways on the lush glamour world of Carrageen-Hazen, Terri Lace is stylishly seated at the driver's wheel. Her designer-class shoes press firmly on the accelerator pedal, speeding across the smooth surfaces. The blonde beauty is more than impressed with the soaring roar of the electric quad engines culling from the rear of the slender, red vehicle.

She says to herself, beaming a smile, "Oh, I've fallen in love with this fucking car." She asks the Leechers in the back passenger seats, "How're the children back there? Do you have enough room to be so beastly? You are very quiet."

The hideous alien creatures murmur a growl in their response. Terri smiles, weaving her dream car around the stagnant traffic, commenting, "Much better."

Alternatively, she verbally commands the Ferrari's AI systems, "Connect me to a virtual communications link to my favourite clothes shop, Harry & Mckays."

While heading en route to Harvanna's private spaceport, Terri places an order soon after establishing the virtual link, "Hi there, account G621/Lace; I'd like to order five of the newest dresses you have in the Elite range, seven pairs of designer shoes, plus two suede-leather handbags and one of the spacey jumpsuits, Ooh, I do like them, put the items on my credit tab. I will personally collect them tomorrow when I'm extremely minted and rich. Bye."

Disconnecting the comm-link, Terri Lace glances in the turbo car's rear mirror with a frown on her gorgeous face, believing she has seen a ghost.

Meanwhile, closing in vastly behind the red convertible Gx9000 sports car is the bounty hunter Alfa Cupra Gx6 consort car giving chase with Dan Casey at the wheel. Inside the chrome turbo car, seated in the luscious leather driver's pod, Dan witnesses the red Testarossa speeding a few vehicles ahead. He weaves the Cupra out from behind traffic; the engine whistles a cruising purr, quickening a tracking tail. Suddenly, the internal virtual communications dash light flashes. Flicking his finger across the race-style driver's wheel, Dan hits the comm-link soft-pad button connecting a visual link beside the driver's view.

A digital silhouette of Terri Lace's pretty face appears, beckoning questions, "Oh, Mr Casey, I thought I saw my old car giving chase. I know you have a crush on me, but this is a bit extreme, don't you think?"

Dan replies, "Let us just say I'm a persistent guy."

The blonde temptress taunts him through the comm-link, "Aww, I do like that in man; it's such a turn-on dashing to Veena's rescue. That's so sweet; I'm sure she will love the gesture."

"Yeah, thought I'd give it a whirl and fuck you over on the way, sweetheart."

Terri amusingly replies, "Promises, promises! You do know how to make a girl's day, Mr Casey. Like I said before, I'm a busy lady. I've got to dash, and now you have to die!"

The convertible soft top of the sleek Testarossa Gx9000 drops, revealing the two monstrous Leechers armed with laser-blast shot rifles. The passenger seat beasts readily aim and open fire at Dan Casey's Cupra Gx6. The hurling rounds dart and inflict damage, ricocheting along the scooped bonnet of the Alfa Cupra.

Fully aware of the rising issue, Dan Casey asserts the conflictual attack by slickly manoeuvring the luxury turbo car around the Leecher's blast fire, quickly zig-zagging a weaving motion to the purring Testarossa's opposing rear flank. He crouches while ducking inside the under-siege Alfa Cupra. Guiding behind the race-style driver's wheel, Dan swiftly releases his fingerless-gloved right hand from the stubbed controls, readily gauging for his weapons holster with a spinning grip of his silver and black-barrelled gun. The under-pressure cargo pilot keeps one eye on the oncoming traffic speeding from the flat mainland to the glowing light bridges.

Dan Casey seemingly shoots through the side-view window frame of the sleek Cupra Gx6. He is taking his chance while the hideous Leechers reload their pulse rifle. But his attempt is in vain, only pottering damage around his intended targets, causing scorched blast marks to flare at the rear side of the red metallic Ferrari Gx9000.

"Watch the damn car; it is not even paid for yet," says the stressed bounty hunter.

The two high-class sports cars decisively split their alternative offences, swerving around the slow-moving civilian transports. Scorching along the lighted-drawn bridge in the shine of the early-morning skies, cruising at speeds above the flowing waterfall.

The shining Testarossa Gx9000 powers forth to take a slender advantage. The growling alien Leechers renew their renegade assault, blasting rounds at the fast-approaching Alfa Cupra.

Dan Casey draws level in the Chrome Speedster, rapidly opening fire while upside down on his second attempt. Luckily, this time, Dan shoots one of the hideous creature's vile heads straight off, causing the monster's arched body to hurl out the side of the fast-shifting red turbo car.

Terri Lace aims her mini black pistol, readily opening fire over the nippy Testarossa's left flank.

"Now you are just pissing me off. I've got a starship flight to catch. Just die, Mr Casey."

Terri viciously squeezes her dainty fingers over the trigger of her firearm, bombarding the driver-side panels of the Alfa Cupra with the assistance of the remaining Leecher's hazardous blast fire.

Dan Casey hits the brakes hard with a shimmering effect, dropping back behind the cornering Testarossa Gx9000 and evading the blast rounds scattering his battered vehicle. This is quickly followed by a burst of acceleration into the sweeping bend.

With his feet pressed firmly down on the pulsing pedal, Dan's muscular-toned body is thrown back in the leather bucket seat, feeling the pressure of the g-force speed. The Alfa Cupra Gx6 traces a streamlined pace, racing alongside the shifty Ferrari Testarossa Gx9000. The expensive shot-up turbo cars whoosh into the dual freeway en route to the capital city of Harvanna.

Closely with a dared-slamming smash, Dan Caseys slams the Cupra Gx6 into the side rims of Terri Lace's red vixen turbo machine, causing the temptress to swerve, dropping her pistol at the moment. Angrily, the blonde sharply steers, retaliating a nudging scrape as they approach the second array of light-beam bridges. With one of the main beam lanes out of commission, the sleek turbo cars come inches apart, travelling together at a neck-breaking speed.

Tensely comforted in the Ferrari's driver's seat, Terri's blonde hair commands her red-eyed beastly creature, "Go get him and make sure at least one of you lackeys can kill him this time."

The Leecher pounces from the convertible's passenger side, leaping onto the front bonnet of the Alfa Cupra Gx6.

Terri Lace teasingly blows a kiss and a saluting wave. She turns the Testarossa Gx9000 sharply, deviating with wobbling skids veering into the vacant light-beam-bridge lane. Terri Lace powers off in her trashed coupe with a thrusting roar to Harvanna's private spaceport.

Whereas in the slick Alfa Cupra and missing the diverted slip lane, Dan Casey mumbles, "I'm starting to hate Veena's damn friends."

His intelligent dark brown eyes open in awareness of the closed link bridge and the menacing alien Leecher gripping a knife-clawed hold on the forefront of the Cupra Gx6.

The grotesque creature attacks, smashing its slimy horrific tentacles wildly through the driver's tinted screen, trying to suck off Dan Casey's face. The heroic interstellar pilot ducks the enraged slithering tentacles, randomly firing a distracting shot with not a moment to spare.

Dan's shoulder bashes the vertical opening side door, taunting, "Hope you can fly, sludge features."

Dan shoots another blast from his black-barrelled weapon and dares a rolling hurled leap out of the speeding vehicle's door.

Dan Casey smashes to the gravelled ground just seconds before the driverless Alfa Cupra Gx6 skids out of control, toppling over the steep drop of the inactive light-beam bridge with the monstrous Leecher attached to the bonnet, falling to the depths of Race-World's ocean.

Chapter Nine

Galactic Politics

The human-colonised planet at Kothariya is charged with an electric atmosphere as the Corporal Union's headquarters hosted a grand ceremony. Invited galactic citizens who have worked tirelessly for the government are eagerly awaiting their chance to be awarded level-two citizen reputation class by the leader of the Corporal Union, Director Wilson Volantis.

All attendees are required to wear a laser band bracelet on their left wrist to gain entrance to the ceremony, which, once attached, cannot be removed. Families have gathered in their thousands to witness this historic event and to cheer on their loved ones as they receive this prestigious recognition.

The anticipation in the air is palpable as everyone waits for the ceremony to begin, eager to celebrate the hard work that has led to this momentous occasion.

On the second floor of the ceremony hall, in the personal chambers of Wilson Volantis, the galactic Director is debating the universal tax tributes with his First Minister of Logistics. He is positioned at his curved glass table in his dark sequenced cloak.

Director Volantis is in a none-too-pleased mood with the First Minister's performance in public relations across the galaxy. "Minster Osborne, I assigned you one simple task. Have you successfully affiliated our new tax rates among the alien species? We must protect them against hostile pirates or cyborg attacks. Without the correct amount of funding, their well-being could be in jeopardy,"

Wilson, rubbing his pale hands together and giving a cold-hearted glare to the First Minister, ensures there is a hint of threat in the air.

Despite this, the First Minister, Osborne, remains calm and collected, refusing to be intimidated by the Director's aggressive behaviour. This is a high-stakes situation, and there is no room for error. The First Minister of the Corporal Union is an overweight, middle-aged, balding politician, Rav Osborne. He is a knowledgeable man with influence across the galactic committee board. Minister Osborne exudes confidence and expertise as he stands in his black ambassador's suit, arms folded, giving careful advice to the Director on the unfolding settlements.

His measured and authoritative tone conveys a deep understanding of the complex issues, "With all due respect, Wilson, not everyone believes in the Mbron Media broadcasted coverage of the recent terror attacks. The alien species, mainly the quadrans and the reptilians, call them racketeering pirates. These are more highly paid privateers doing the bidding of the Corporal Union, an organised propaganda stunt in an excuse to raise trade route tax fees."

Director Volantis snarkily comments, "No more than speculated conspiracies. Why would a trusted media network relay disinformation?"

Minister Osborne expresses a powerful presence; his piercing gaze surveys the grandeur of the marble walls surrounding him.

He appears to be in deep contemplation, reflecting on his immense responsibilities in responding to the Director's answer. "I will adaptably repose our tax requirements to the alien species with a tolerance of more bite. But I must warn you, Wilson. The committee board is not too happy with the Mbron Media's involvement."

Director Volantis dearly reminds his First Minister of his loyalties, "I recall you get paid a hefty salary to keep the board occupied; I'd try and keep within those guidelines, Rav."

He focuses on the chamber entrance where someone has knocked. "Enter."

The marble doors swing open, projecting a dark, shadowy figure. "Welcome back, Commander Tarick,"

"I have some fortunate news regarding the stolen astrological data box. We will discuss the details privately after graduation."

As the marble door closes with a confirming nod, the shadowy presence of Calo Tarick disappears into the darkness.

The grey-haired Director rises to his feet, brushing the creases in his long black gown, and invites the First Minister. "Rav, you are invited to attend the fourth ceremony gathering. It is the graduation ceremony for the Kothariya citizens who have shown unwavering loyalty and adherence to the rules. They have paid their dues to the Corporal Union, which has elevated their reputation and granted them level-two citizenship. This means they will have access to the golden worlds, a lifetime opportunity. Will you join me?"

Minister Osborne, although dubious, accepts the Director's invitation with a few binding questions pending from the galactic committee. "Thank you, Wilson. I accept as the board has also asked about the integrity of these golden worlds, as they are advertised only on the Mbron Media Limited network. Plus, there have been reports of the ceremony participants acting peculiarly or having gone missing. Can you elaborate on the statements?"

Volantis strolls steadily to the marble entrance, "I fully concur with your sentiments, Minister Osborne." He effortlessly pushes open the doors to the chamber and leads the way towards the ceremony stage.

As they draw closer, Wilson allows himself a small, smirked smile. He exchanges a knowing glance with the other esteemed representative from the Corporal Union, "Opposition in factual rumours, Minister Osborne. Just petty misbeliefs."

As the two men enter the second balcony, the atmosphere in the dome ceremony hall becomes charged with excitement. The thunderous applause from thousands of Kothariya citizens is a testament to the persuasive power of Wilson Volantis's speeches. His vision for the Kalanisi Universe has captured the hearts and minds of people from all walks of life, inspiring them to believe in a future where everyone can thrive and coexist in perfect harmony.

The clapping is dying down, allowing the darkly dressed Wilson Volantis to start his speech proudly at the ceremony podium, "Dear fellow citizens, I am grateful for your warm welcome. It's an honour to stand before you today, united in our shared vision for the future. Let's join hands and work towards creating a universe where everyone can thrive. Your continued support is deeply appreciated. Soon, the new dawn will rewardingly rise, blessing us with a divine sight of freedom."

The Director's words reverberate a droned echo through the vast ceremony dome, leaving an impactful impression on the enthused crowd. The lights gradually dim, and the flickering effect casts an enchanting spell on the throne room. The four-cornered containment tanks exude a hypnotic wavered rhythm that resonates with Director Volantis's message.

The Corporal Union's First Minister, Rav Osborne, stands marginally behind his ranting leader with an uneasy shudder. He witnesses swivelling smoke creeping into the vicinity.

Wilson starts chanting, "Om mani padme hum."

Repeatedly spoken over, the indoctrinated Kothariya citizens follow the chant in a tranced sequencing tone, "Om mani padme hum."

The citizens' wristbands begin to glow a pulsing beat with the hazy spiritual smoke, enhancing a whispering voice along its presence and invigorating the actual ceremony hall.

Director Wilson Volantis proclaims, "The time has come; Om mani padme hum. Let the serpent reign."

Wilson's arms raise high, and his black cloak billows behind him.

The atmosphere in the ceremony dome dramatically shifts, and Wilson's eye's hideously roll, manifesting into white flames. The people below the Director's podium stand in the thousands, raising their left laser-banded hands in an enchanted aura. Sparks of an electrical current transpire over the containment tanks as the smoke twists to a spiralling high around the chamber dome.

The whispering, murmured voices grow intense as the smoky vapours cluster to a silhouette of a female's face. Two burning red eyes emerge with a screeched cry, announcing, "AMELIA!"

Circling with a vicious swoop over the chanting brigade of transfixed civilians, the chastely spiritual demonic female sourly laughs a mocked cackling, "Haha." Repeating her name with cursed effects, "AMELIA demands your souls."

The demoness queen, whose eyes burn bright with an alternating charged flare, culls a blanket of possessed energy over the innocent bystanders.

Civilians of all ages start to scream in terror as static shocks infiltrate their laser band bracelets, connecting all the infused citizens. These bracelets also link them to the drumming containment tanks, absorbing their essence of life, destroying and draining their free will identity into mindless, controlled human drones.

Praising the head of the cult ritual, Director Wilson Volantis continues his raged chant, "Om mani padme hum."

Panicking behind the enthralled cultist, Minister Osborne decisively walks to the dome chambers exit stairway, only to be confronted by Commander Calo Tarick. "Planning on going somewhere, Minister?"

Calo Tarick launches the overweight First Minister with the powerful use of his cybernetic metal right hand into a heap. The embraced containment cylinders are filled with pure human life-force energy. The ritual demoness smoke haze vanishes with a robust whipping whoosh, dispersing into the chamber's atmosphere.

Director Wilson Volantis gazes upon his newly recruited soulless drones with admiration. Slowly lowering his pale hands, Wilson's evil, bland face envisions the tasks they can accomplish at his desire. The Director's gaze shifts from the gathering of human disciples to Minister Osborne, who now stands trembling and frightened.

Wilson strides forward with a stern expression. "Is everything alright here?" he demands, his voice firm and commanding. "Do you require any assistance or support, Minister Osborne? You look like you've just seen a ghost!"

His right-hand guardian, Commander Calo Tarick, comments. "I caught the Minister heading for the exit. Sir, I believe he would blow the whistle on your divine policies to the committee board."

The news sends a chill down Wilson's spine. Still, he remains composed. "Thank you for bringing this to my attention, Commander. We must ensure our policies remain confidential and within our inner circle." The Director knows he can't let anyone jeopardise his divine vision for the future.

The First Minister of the Corporal Union is understandably shocked and appalled by what he has just witnessed. In a dithering state of his pragmatic, conservative nature, Rav Osborne panicky shouts, "Stay away from me, Wilson! What the hell did you do to all those poor people?"

"You've gone too far with this spiritual obsession; what was that demonic monstrosity? The committee board will never stand for this behaviour. You're finished." The Minister shakes as he searches his cloak's pockets for his holo-communicator to call security.

Director Volantis addresses the Minister's fright, "That is a shame, Rav, as I was hoping you had envisioned my euphoria for the Kalanisi Universe."

Wilson slightly turns his disappointed, pale ground face to Calo Tarick, stating his orders in a cold, diluted tone, "Please escort the late Minister off the premises, Commander!"

Without an engaged word of acknowledgement, the silently patched-eye Commander evasively lunges forward, grabbing Rav Osborne's cloak collar with a lifting of the marble-tiled floor. Calo heaves a pounding stomp to the ceremony hall bannister rails, turning his dark-shaven, scarred facial demeanour to the struggling Minister Osborne. "It's time to say farewell to your lovable intergalactic citizens, Rav!"

He throws the valued committee member over the dome chamber's second-floor bannisters. The Minister screams, "Aah, nooo!"

He hits the ceremony floor surrounded by the indoctrinated human drones, who do not twitch an eyelid. Wilson Volantis approaches Commander Tarick at the bannister railing, "I will inform the Core Lord at Mbron Media of today's headline news. Poor Minister Osborne was beaten to a pulp by a group of rebellious thugs, and it was dealt with in a swift, firm manner by the people's Corporal Union."

Wilson Volantis deviously grins, explaining the Sulamani project schedule. "Plus, our culling army of human drones is building up fast. Their life force will be used as the power source to fuel the Sulamani. I will prepare this new batch to be transported to the prison worlds, ready for their combat training. You, Commander, have a rendezvous with a bounty hunter named Zak Duran at the slave-trade station beyond the black moon just off the Sera sector. He possesses the precious data box that holds vital information for finding the Vortex. As for the infiltrating green-haired agent, do with her as you please. However, you must deliver the astrological box to me without fail. Our project's success depends on it. Now go at once."

The loyal Commander Tarick instantly leaves the ceremony hall, knowing his role in implementing the Director's obsessive mind-wipe for all the Kalanisi citizens.

Chapter Ten

Tip from the Java Lynx

Meanwhile, back in the glamorous world of Carrageen-Hazen, sectors away from the dire satanic plan of Director Wilson Volantis, is the Panther-class starship of the esteemed bounty hunter Zak Duran. It takes flight with a tremendous roar through the early-morning skies as it launches from Harvanna's private spaceport.

Dan Casey watches in awe as the sleek vessel soars through the atmosphere and disappears into the darkness of space.

After a steady, staggered walk back along the freeway, he brushes himself off, still recovering from the high-speed turbo car chase that resulted in losing his stolen Alfa Cupra Gx6 transportation. Dan can't believe what he has just been involved in as he re-lives the vigorous tussle with Terri Lace and her vile face-sucking Leecher beasts.

Dan says to himself, "What a gorgeous bitch Terri is, but shame she tried to kill me; the lady is fun for a bounty hunter. But that's no damn excuse. I need to help Veena. Where have they taken her?"

He reaches for the top pocket of his ripped brown leather jacket, searching for his smokes, but there's just a torn patch and no green-dust packet. Dan Casey huffs, "Oh, damn; what else can go wrong today?"

Momentarily, he glances up at the grey skies, hearing a

rumble from a mass of dark grey clouds above, followed by a pattering of sudden raindrops. "Oh, come on! No, you gotta be kidding me. Not a storm. Damn it."

The stressed-out, charismatic cargo pilot quickly shifts his worn flight jacket over his head as the sky bursts with a chilling, heavy downpour.

Dan Casey hurriedly walks along the flat open area, watching for passing civilian cars on the side of the extended highway. He tries to hitchhike back to Carrageen-Hazen's Race-World, but unfortunately, no transport vehicles notice him amid the storm. The interstellar pilot is stuck in the pouring rain, shivering and hoping for a miracle to get him out of the storm. And then, with a sudden stroke of luck, a commercial two-seater taxi-pod hovers to a stammering halt at the side of the freeway.

The vibrating pod's door levers open, revealing a female Mbron Media cyberbot in the shape of Nayla 1.9.4.

"Quick, jump in, fella. You'll catch a death in that weather."

The drenched cargo pilot can't believe his luck. He quickly enters the pod and thanks the pink-haired android for saving him from the downpour. "Hey, perfect timing, 1.9.4. Can you tell me the fare for getting to the Java Lynx?"

With a smooth motion, Nayla 1.9.4 closes the door of the hover-pod. She then turns to Dan Casey and chirps, "No need to worry about the taxi fare. It's on me. I'm not on the clock anymore."

Nayla 1.9.4 enquires about her passenger's whereabouts, "How come a nice, handsome man like yourself is caught wandering in the rain on the edge walk of the highway? What's your name? Are you having woman trouble, dear?"

"I'm Dan Casey. Yeah, I got dumped by some fake companions, and then they took away my friend."

The empathic Mbron Media steers the taxi-pod around the sweeping bends, "Aww, fella, that's awful news! So, what are you going to do about it, Dan?"

The cyberbot displays unparalleled precision and expertise while navigating the hover-pod controls, effortlessly activating the window wipers with her nimble synthetic fingers.

Dan Casey replies with an unsure look of honesty creasing across his dashing face, "I thought I'd start by getting a strong drink, followed by another a lot stronger."

Nayla 1.9.4 strongly advises against his option in her high-pitched feminine voice, "No! Dan, please don't go down that spiralling route, trust me. I've been there. A few months back, I was let down by an Elton-63 model. You know, the latest cocky edition from my core makers at Mbron Media."

Dan acknowledges, "Yeah, I've seen the 63 models. Can't say I'm a fan either; they keep stealing all the high-paid contracts for no fee, just a quick-fix electrical charge. I much prefer your cybernetic version."

Nayla continues conversing, "Aww, thanks, fella; that's kind of you, as I say. That Elton-63 broke my core in two, telling me he wanted a totty-bot with curves. I ended up computing everywhere, shooting up nightly on high-voltage electric bolts. Then, one day, I re-booted and computed: Hell no! To the core deactivation bin with him! I'm going to make something of my cyber-self. You need to do the same, Dan. Throw caution into the cosmo wind. Get your beloved girl."

The sleek taxi rapidly approaches Carrageen-Hazen's main equine sports complex and whooshes through the rain-soaked environment. The extravagant Java Lynx bar is in sight, and it is Dan Casey's best option for tracing a lead on the Elite-based bounty hunters Terri Lace and Zak Duran.

The hover-pod slows down, pulling into the Java Lynx's parking facility. Behind the pulsing driver's wheel of the taxi-pod, the ultra-friendly Nayla 1.9.4 notices some activity near the back end of the exotic night tavern with a fluttering blink of her cybernetic eyes, "Oh, gee, there's another murder! An Elton-63's head has been completely twisted off."

Turning the hover-pods ignite off, Nayla 1.9.4 speculates on the events witnessing the Java Lynx bar staff carrying a broken android and the Leecher's dead carcass to the disposal dump.

"I'm computing an anti-android activist group that hires an alien monster to take out 63! The Core Lord has been preaching on the holo-net that this would happen and that the Android Association Committee will rise and take Arthurian power in vengeance. Soon, all human life will become extinct to mere dust. What do you think happened here, Mr Casey?"

Nayla 1.9.4 expresses her interest in Dan's opinion, not knowing he is marginally to blame while undoubtedly defending himself against the Leecher attack orchestrated by Terri Lace.

The collective cargo pilot glances at the inquisitive cyberbot, vaguely answering about the crime, "I have no idea! Who's this Core Lord you mentioned?"

Smoothly coy, Dan Casey changes the subject back to Nayla-1.9.4's manufacturers.

The colourful, coiffed, hair-styled android replies, "Don't worry about that insane psychopath; I'm hoping he blows a fused core. I don't believe in his programming rants. More importantly, you need to find your woman."

The hover-pod's side door swiftly lifts open. Before Dan attempts to leave the taxi, he puzzlingly enquires with the smiling android. "Hey, Nayla, how did you know my friend is a female? I've never mentioned a name?"

"Aww, that's easy, fella. It's written all over your handsome face. You miss her, but if you're ever free. Sorry, I'm on the rebound." Nayla 194 jokes. "I'm going to configure into sleep mode. If you need a journey, give me a nudge."

The whizzy female cyberbot instantly closes her robotic eyes with a falling nod of her pink quiffed hair into her synthetic chest.

Dan Casey quickly vacates the stationary hover-pod, shielding his jacket over his head from the driving rain. He motions a brisk walk to the Java Lynx entrance with a sneaky glance over his shoulder at the bar staff disposal team clearing away the damaged wire fence and deceased bodies. Directing himself away from the crime scene, Dan momentarily enters the Java Lynx bar. He gently pushes open the door, and he's instantly met with a low, chilled ambient beat. The atmosphere at the electric jive bar has shifted to a more subdued setting, with just a handful of late-morning dancers and some dozing patrons relaxing in the booths. As the cargo pilot strides towards the red neon-lit bar, he absorbs the vibrant energy of the winding-down venue. His dark brown eyes are drawn to the four-armed Quadlin bartenders, who are vigorously cleaning glasses with broad smiles.

Dan returns the charmed smile, feeling completely comfortable in the dreamscape ambience of the Elite bar. Sitting on the neon bar stools, Dan Casey orders a drink to suit his mood. "Give me your strongest tonic, pal."

The alien, purple-skinned barman chuckles a deep, bubbly laugh. "Haha, you look like you've had one rough night, man!"

"There you go, son. Drink that beauty instead, one of the house specials, a Mimosa-Sun Breeze cocktail. That will be sixty-two credits. I'm Leroy Nivea. It's nice to make your acquaintance, man. What's your name?"

Dan takes hold of the Mimosa cocktail's stemmed glass, readily exchanging credits for his drink. He replies to the upbeat Quadlin. "Thanks, Leroy. I can see drinks are getting very expensive across the Kalanisi Galaxy, though I suppose it is value compared to the Rhinehold-Goose."

"I'm Dan Duran, visiting from off-world. I came in here earlier this evening with my brother, Zak. But we separated in the exhilarating night of unforgettable entertainment he had planned for me!"

Folding two of his arms and rubbing his chin with the third, Leroy Nivea laughs and comments, "Haha, Dan Duran. My purple arse! More like you, the sucker who got lured in by his mistress, Terri Lace. Before being thrown about my wired fence, resulting in one dead Leecher and a headless android."

With the truth exposed by the Quadlin, the barman pulls a wire particle from Dan's torn brown flight jacket with his bottom arm as evidence.

Dan Casey embarrassingly smiles with a change of content, "Okay then, I'll have another Mimosa-Sun Breeze. Have one yourself, Leroy. I sincerely insist on me. Cheers, pal!"

The Quadlin jigs a dancing step, twisting around the neon bar to the light ambient music, composing another Mimosa cocktail. Leroy stylishly swivels around to Dan, handing him the selective drink, formally stating,

"Three hundred and fifty credits to the man with no name. That includes two high-spec cocktails and a replacement wired fence; I'll tab mine for later as we close. Plus, a sizzling tip for the Java Lynx."

Dan Casey silently nods his acknowledgement to the Quadlin, handing over the credits with a sense of relief.

The alien leans in closely and whispers, "Zak Duran and his tantalising woman, Terri Lace, operate on the outskirts of the Sera system, mainly on a slave trader's space station. Orbiting near the back of that nasty dark Dread Moon. You seem like a nice guy. I'd keep away unless you're looking for trouble. Those bounty hunters and beastly Leechers are bad news, man! Don't say you ain't been warned."

Dan's facial expression portrays the making of a mental note to stay cautious and keep his guard up while in that sector.

Edging his toned muscular body off the neon-slotted bar stall, Dan Casey salutes the Quadlin bar staff member, "Thanks for the productive talk, Leroy. You keep well."

The weather outside shows no let-up as the storm continues to downpour. Dan quickly motions a jog over to the commercially parked taxi-pod. The hotshot pilot urgently taps on the driver's side window, instantly reactivating the sleep mode of the cyberbot, Nayla 1.9.4. With a flutter of her robotic eyes, the female android raises her synthetic head with a tilting smile. She readily opens the hover-pod passenger door.

Brimming with suspense and intrigue, she buzzingly asks in her high-pitched cybernetic voice, "You found your woman yet, Mr Casey?"

"Not quite, but I do have a vague lead," cheerfully confirms Dan, sweeping his fingerless gloves through his dampened, slick black hair, divulging the valuable information by the Quadlin.

The charmed pilot continues, "Veena may be captive on a slave-trade station, lurking behind a Dread Moon. I require a ride to Carrageen-Hazen's main spaceport, where I have my starship docked. Throwing caution into the cosmo winds, I'm going to get her back, Nayla."

The hover-pod's powered motor hums a whistling vibe, and Nayla 194 swiftly gets her mini-taxi in motion with a slick reversed spin, exuberantly expressing her delight, "Way to go, Mr Casey. I will get you to the starport on time; hold tight."

She slams her fibre-heeled boots on the accelerator pedal and hits the throttle hard. Taken back in their seats by the thrusting force of the taxi-pod, Nayla 1.9.4 determinedly guides her two-passenger vehicle through the heavy rain, swiftly turning away from the Java Lynx's grounds, and heads for Carrageen-Hazen's freeway. After a short journey, they arrive at the spaceport where the *Decepter* is stationed.

The taxi-pod stops to a braking, hovering halt in the starship hangar bay. Inside the shiny mobile, Nayla 1.9.4 tilts a turn of her elegant oval face with an emotional farewell. "There you go, Mr Casey. One first-class ticket ride to save your woman, Veena. Aww, it's been a real joy meeting you, and thanks for calling me by my name and not the Mbron Media service code, 1.9.4. I will miss you, fella. Now would be a good time if I could cry a tear."

Dan Casey presses the button on the side panel as the pod's door shifts open; he turns his handsome, stubbled face towards the female cyberbot, acknowledging her fine assistance with an invitation, "Why don't you come with me? You have been more than helpful, Nayla. I will probably need a hand to pull this off."

The rain splatters down over the pod's frame as Nayla declines his offer with her objectives, "Wow, that sounds so exciting, but I must refuse, as I've nearly got enough credits to be an independent taxi-pod owner in the lush galactic shopping world, Xanadu. You should bring Veena. Visit me. And every woman loves shopping, even cyber ones like me!"

Before he leaves the taxi-pod, Dan leans over to the cute female android and kisses her on her pale, synthetic cheek.

He advises her, "You take care, Nayla, and if I'm ever on the planet Xanadu, I will look you up and surely book a ride. Keep safe, sweetheart."

Nayla verbally reacts with blushing on her pale, cheeky face, "Oh, gee, I got a kiss! Keep breathing. See you around the galaxy, Mr Casey."

Dan Casey urgently makes haste to his Machiavellian MK2 Merlin class freighter. Slouching through the puddles of the hanger bay, veering to his starship hatch. He quickly punches in the authorisation code, assessing the entrance of the *Decepter*. Entering his vessel, Dan takes off his torn, damp brown leather jacket with a hurling toss in the lounge compartment.

"Another damn good jacket ruined." Flicking on the starship's subsystem control instruments, the charmed pilot checks in with the ship's computerised flight companion. "Hey, Pearl, you miss me, sweety? Please tell me we're flight-worthy."

Pearl flashes a response confirming in a sultry cyber voice, "Auto-repair sequence has been successful, the damaged hull from the harpoon assault is patched up, and the celestial hyperdrive is energised."

"That's great news, Pearl. We need to set a course for the

outer rim of the Sera system, in search of a slave-ring space station orbiting behind a big shady moon."

An authentic warning is heeded from Pearl. "Galactic data files in that area are deemed classified by the Corporal Union."

In defiance of the rules, Dan Casey replies, "Well, that's our next stop, so hack their database. We've got a green-haired damsel to rescue."

The *Decepter*'s triple-slant rocket engines fire up with an instant power thrust. Emerging steadily out of Carrageen-Hazen's spaceport hangar bay, the sleek hull-framed Machiavellian MK2 class freighter gradually picks up speed, launching off the lush Elite Racing-World. With a sudden flash and a bang, the *Decepter* zooms into orbit and jumps to hyperspace, disappearing into the slip-lanes on its way to the darkest realms of the Kalanisi Universe.

Ahead of Dan Casey in a tumultuous expanse of space, the Panther immediately drops out of the slip-lanes with a pulsating flash. The sleek and stylish bounty hunter vessel of Zak Duran has entered the outer rim of the Sera system, containing the notorious black moon and perilous slave traders' station. The moon is a formidable presence, massive in size and ominous in appearance, shrouded in a dark, hazy atmosphere and assaulted by violent hailstorms and lightning within its asteroid belt and beyond. A foreboding location that requires the utmost caution in approach.

The Panther cruises a cantering route through the dread and unease, encountering a black, corroded space station spinning amid the ghastly region. The station serves as a trade hub for many slave ships. It is an exchange ring for the universe's criminals, who lack law and respect for life and instead prioritise monetary gain for the less reputable species of the galaxy.

The Panther frigate's sub-drive engines cut out to a droning whistle, echoing around the interior crew decks, including in the starship's brig quarters where Veena Merida is being held captive.

The young feminine agent is gazing at the vessel's deck in despair. Then suddenly, she hears the shifting sound of the brig door open, and her jade eyes are drawn to a womanly figure dressed in a silver outfit.

"Hello, Veena," says the sultry voice escaping from the luscious red lips of Terri Lace, elegantly posing in the brig entrance, donning a tight, clinging silver catsuit and knee-high black boots.

Terri holds a similar black garment in her dainty hands, placing it on the side cabinet as she casually walks into the brig and closes the door behind her.

Meanwhile, sitting a captive and shaking her head in disbelief, Veena replies with a shocked tone in her well-spoken voice, "Terri, some best friend you turn out to be! I trusted you like the little sister I never had."

"Have I hurt your feelings, sister? You have only yourself to blame for this messy situation. You chose to be a fugitive on the run from the Galactic Corporal Union. I'm just doing my job as a law-abiding bounty hunter."

"Is that what they call dealing with scum slavers in this day and age? What's happened to you both? Bounty hunters? I damn well believed you and Zak were like a family to me!" Tears well up in her jade eyes, threatening to spill over at any moment.

Terri Lace raises her voice and shouts in an emotional clash, "Well, you're a fine one to talk to when it comes to family. Suppose you had stayed around instead of joining an outmatched resistance organisation? You might have known what changed our lives from being pushed-around office grunts to high rollers of the Kalanisi Galaxy."

"I had to take care of personal matters. Dealing with dangerous individuals who had murdered my family. I had to take action to avenge my loved ones. I'm not ashamed of my motives, and that's no excuse why you turned out to be a backstabbing greedy bitch."

Terri responds to the bitter words, retaliating with a vicious backhanded slap around Veena's face, "Shut the fuck up; don't you dare slander me about dangerous individuals. I will never class you as my sister. When you vanished, I was raped twice! Left in the gutter alone. I wondered where my big sister was to keep an eye on me. After that episode of shame and abuse, I said to myself it was time to turn the tables. I will be the bitch calling the shots from now on. That's when I convinced my darling Zak that the underground route was the best link to prosperous careers. You should have a proper line of work, as trusting in people doesn't pay. I found that out the hard way."

With tears in her jade eyes, Veena Merida says, "I'm truly sorry, Terri. I had no idea. I can only imagine how challenging it must've been for you to handle that situation."

Terri Lace slowly paces around the brig compartment of the Panther; her booted high heels tap lightly against the metal floor. She surveys her green-haired bounty. "I appreciate your concern, but I don't require your sympathy. I am proud of who I have become, and maybe I should thank you for pushing me to achieve my goals.

"However, poor Mr Casey is another story, and you should regret how you treated him. Dan is a nice man; he wanted to fuck me; I could tell by the way he kissed me. A true gentleman to the end. He was on his way to rescue you; such a sweet sentiment. It's just a shame he died driving off the edge of an awful light-beam bridge."

Veena Merida gasps a stomach-churned sigh, "Ah, no! You bitch."

Mocking her pain, Terri laughs. "You liked him. Even better, I love watching you cry and suffer, Veena."

The blonde-haired mistress, with a tone of venom,

temporarily releases Veena's ties. "Now, put these garments on; we don't want our Corporal Union prize looking like a washed-up troll."

Veena quickly regains her composure and says, "I promise I'll end your misery, sister."

Terri Lace laughs, "You can dearly try, but don't make petty promises you can't keep, Veena. Remember that no one knows or cares about you here. So don't count on a happy ending, SISTER!"

With that, Terri leaves the brig as the sleek black starship echoes a decline in flight speed, approaching the dock at the slave-ring trade space station.

Chapter Eleven

Hotel from Galactic Hell

A short while later, Dan Casey is in hot pursuit of the Elite bounty hunters' antagonising trail.

The *Decepter* cruises effortlessly past the fading suns and stars, transcending with a flash and bang out of the hyper-speed slip-lanes, bursting into the out-rim of the Sera system. The once bright and vibrant space around the Machiavellian MK2 class freighter gives way to a gloomy darkness that seems to swallow all light. The stormy atmosphere that creeps over the starship only adds to the horrific atmosphere while approaching the dreaded black moon's orbit. Inside the *Decepter*'s cockpit cabin, Dan Casey is preparing himself for a daring rescue attempt of Veena Merida.

The hotshot cargo runner is gearing up in disguise as a galactic trader. Dan is wearing his beige quarter-padded jacket and leather weapons belt containing his black-barrelled gun. He attaches a pack of lock breakers to his slanted holster while commenting to the ship's AI, "I'm ready to hit this slave trader's station, Pearl. We have got to make this run quick and quiet. You know the drill, just like the old days when being a part of the space protection security group."

Dan adjusts his disguise in the mirror, placing an old-style worn cowboy hat on his head, ensuring his identity is completely concealed. He can't afford to be recognised for this raid; the galactic underworld crime network would condemn him if they knew his name. Pearl has the *Decepter* piloting on an auto cruise in the unstable atmospheric weather.

As Dan equips himself with preparedness, the cyber-based navigation assistant flashes a crystallised response report. "Coordinating flight Directory path 291 to the moon's orbit, we now have a visualised projection."

"That's one big, damn ugly moon; I can see how it got its name, Dread." Dan whispers, "Let's make this collection of Miss Merida fast and get out of there. Keep scanning for the trader station; I was told it orbits close behind this crackpot moon."

Pearl complies in her sexy, cyber-toned voice, "Navigation specifications confirmed and executed successfully. We are on course to reach the space station as planned. Are there any other tasks you would like me to perform?"

"Yeah, take the liberty to reactivate the weapon systems. I have a bad feeling we may need them."

The hailstorms are viciously unrelenting in the atmospheric depths of the Sera system. Still, the steadfast Machiavellian freighter steadily slices through the dense smog, leaving a vaporising mist trail in its wake. Lurking ahead of the *Decepter*, spinning in the distance, is the slave-trade station. Massive in size and scope, the rusty old station is designed in a wheel-shaped cog and contains numerous docking bays, some armed with laser cannons.

The main deck is a circular tube with slit-caged windows and a control tower in the middle of the creaky slave station. A drone hums as the floating prison orbits in the horrific atmosphere. It is the space station from galactic hell. Visualising the imposing trader's hub from the *Decepter*'s front view, Dan Casey inhales a gust of his green-dust cigarette with a slightly chuckled cough.

"Well, what an inviting place to stay! No wonder a dump like this is not stated on the commercial star charts."

Pearl interprets his inspection of the space station with some informal facts, "The Corporal Union turns a blind eye to the merchant trade of biological enslaved people in return for substantial credits and public backing for their silence. Their partnership is linked to the Mbron Media broadcasters who cover up unwanted attention. This gives the crime lord syndicate family, the Galantis, a free region to do as they wish on this repulsive station.

"It appears to be a large-scale racketeering cabal, where only corrupt individuals benefit at the expense of the honest, hard-working people."

Dan expresses frustration at the discouraging reality; he is determined to stand up for what is right, even if it means challenging those in power.

"Take us in nice and slow, Pearl. We don't want any unwanted attention ourselves. Judging by the size of the cannons, we are well outnumbered in the firepower department. Try to slip in and follow the slave transporters to one of the docking bays. Our delivery contract with Veena has become an extract and rescue mission."

The starship AI replies, "This will be the first operation the *Decepter* has taken part in since the space security protection team fell."

Stubbing his smoking filter out on the side-panelled ashtray, Dan reminisces about the sentiments made by Pearl. "Yeah, I know it has been a while, and this time, we're missing the main man, Von Rye. Your boss and my best friend; I'm sure he's watching over us with a smile. Keep it simple, nothing too heroic. Go get her, kiddo," says Dan Casey with a shallow fade of sorrowful expression across his face, mourning his dear friend.

Pearl responds positively, "I'm calculating we won't let Von Rye down. We are approaching the stardock, and the landing sequence is activated."

Numerous unfamiliar-style starships and potential

slave traders are gradually approaching the station port. Accompanying them is the significant Corporal Union Cruiser of Commander Calo Tarick, the *Galileo* BX10 that has just arrived from hyperspace approaching the spinning trader's station. Dan Casey and Pearl are about to embark on a risky mission.

The *Decepter* freighter has just landed in the docking bay of a dilapidated old space station. Moments before Dan Casey leaves his spacecraft, he quickly checks the equipment and warns Pearl of the potential risks. "I'm stepping into the heart of a criminal cabal operations base. If this goes pear-shaped, it's been nice knowing your acquaintance, sweety."

Pearl ensures the ship's defence systems are in place and wishes Dan the best of luck. "Bring Miss Merida back safely; her bio-scans perfectly match yours."

Dan Casey chuckles with an honest answer to his feelings, "I already know. I promise I'll return Veena; just keep frosty, Pearl."

Dan takes in the surroundings of the trader's station, motioning an eye-wandering walk down the *Decepter*'s ramp. The place appears gloomy, with conveyor belt tracks transporting cargo and purchased enslaved people up and down and around the station hub. There is a powered tower positioned along the top level of the station, supplying the energy to the cages.

The bustling marketplace is a sour sight; shady traders lurk around every corner, eagerly anticipating the chance to make a fast profit, with merchants hawking their wares and sleazy customers haggling for the best slavery deals. Dan Casey makes his way forward, walking through this crowd of horrors. He expects the station to be full of thug bounty hunters and alien species; looking around, he is not disappointed.

Dan Casey says to himself in a low-key mumble, "These look like a fun bunch of crooks; what am I doing!"

The disguised interstellar pilot also notices from his alert dark brown eyes peeking from beneath his cowboy-style hat. The powerful Galanti crime lord family has personal trader guards at most corners not to keep the peace but to prevent any enslaved people from escaping once purchased. The cargo-runner pilot carefully tries to blend in with the ruffian traders.

Dan glances up and notices a main trade office about two levels up. He spots a lift leading to a corridor just before the office's front entrance. As he approaches, Dan sees a batch of Corporal Union Elite security guards in the dome-shaped lift, including a cloaked and heavily built Commander with a noticeable metal eye patch and opposing scar on his face.

Dan Casey says to himself, "Calo Tarick. Well, now I know I'm in the right place; it's time to make a personal appearance."

However, he decides to take the stairs instead of the lift to avoid any potential encounters with the guards. As he walks past some sleazy traders, Dan Casey knows he has made the better choice, catching sight of the curved stairway with only one trader guard at the entrance.

The trader's space station is chaotic, with many voices and constant announcements blaring through the speakers. Not letting the atmosphere faze him, Dan Casey makes his way swiftly towards the staircase only to notice a young girl with bright red-bobbed hair locked up in a cage.

She can't be older than a teenager. Seeing someone so young in such a terrible situation is heart-wrenching for Dan. He stops his progress with an empathic look on his handsome, chiselled face.

The young girl readily notices his presence and duly calls out to him. The sweet girl is afraid and nervous, dressed in a ragged, stained white top, sleeveless jacket and torn leggings.

She timidly whispers from her laser-bound cage, "Hey, Mister, help me! Please, buy me; I don't want to be hurt by an alien trader. I'm scared. Buy me, please!"

Dan Casey is shocked at how such cruelty could happen

in the galaxy without anyone stopping it. As he walks past the cages, his heart aches for the little girl locked up inside. Without hesitation, he approaches and crouches down to ask, "Hey, what's your name?"

She replies timidly, "Charlena Jones."

Dan kindly smiles at her. "That's a nice name; I'm Dan Casey."

In comparison, Dan is rumbling his right fingerless-gloved hand around his weapons belt under his quartered padded badge jacket. He then quietly hands her one of his lock breakers and whispers, "Charlena, in a few moments, it's going to get a little noisy here. I need you to put this little device on the cage's laser lock and press the button. Once it's activated, stay back, as it will unlock the lock and free you. From there, you must run to the starship in the bottom docking bay as quickly as possible. Can you see it?"

Charlena Jones nods in agreement and grips the device tightly in her hand.

Dan praises Charlena and tells her, "Good girl, run fast and don't look back." He stands up and walks towards the stairs.

He looks back at Charlena and encourages her to move swiftly,

"As fast as possible towards the starship. Okay!"

The disguised cargo pilot catches sight of a formidable figure. The man has dark skin and a thick head of dreadlocks, and he wears dark shades that conceal his eyes. Although Dan can't see his gaze, he feels the man watching him. In his late thirties, the shady man is large and imposing, dressed in a black coat with rounds of ammo in his pocket. He carries twin silver shooters, making it clear that he is well-prepared. Dan knows the dreadlocked man has noticed him and keeps his composure as he walks away, even though the situation is tense.

Dan Casey stealthily goes to the staircase entrance leading to the higher-level floors. Luckily, the Galanti trader guard wanders on his rounds away from his post, allowing Dan to slip and avoid the guard while sneaking up the stairs, heading for the dingy corridor on the second floor in search of the back entrance to the central control room. The daring cargo runner carefully strolls down the curving corridor; the lights flicker intermittently, casting intriguing shadows on the rusted walls. The need for maintenance is evident in the space station.

Despite the dimness of the surroundings, Dan Casey makes progress, sneaking around in the dimly lit passageway and finding the back route entrance to the main chamber office. Vanishing from the sight of the patrolling slaver guards, Dan motions a light-footed walk through the room dressed in his trader's disguise in vain search of his contract partner, Veena Merida.

Meanwhile, deep inside the control chamber of the slaver's station, the awe-inspiring circular-shaped room has four posts and a middle room boulder. The cured glass window is breathtaking, providing a panoramic view of the expanding conveyor belts. This is the control hub for all the unfortunate caged enslaved people being exchanged and transferred between the sleazy client's starships. Veena Merida has the world taken away from her against her will. Her closest friends have cruelly deceived her and unceremoniously betrayed her to the Corporal Union's high command for a monetary bounty.

Her wrists are bound together by laser-locked handcuffs, which are attached around a tall sealing pole connected to the vented floor. With her limbs yanked behind her body and pushed to the ground, Veena is left in an exposed and powerless state. Tears stream down from her tinted jade eyes as she helplessly contemplates what dangers and uncertainties await her.

The sultry bounty hunter, Terri Lace, is in the chamber room with the vile pet Leecher, Dralon, keeping guard of the green-haired resistance agent. Her devilish, charmed counterpart, Zak Duran, is waiting to greet Corporal Union Commander Tarick, coming out of the dome lift with his four Elite Guards.

Zak approaches, saying in his excellent, calm manner, "Welcome, Commander Tarick. We have obtained the item Director Volantis required. It's been an honour to offer our collection services."

Zak Duran hands over the astrological data box to the dark presence of Calo Tarick. He eagerly grips the mysterious data box in his cybernetic hand and replies with a grin, "Well done to you, Mr Duran. Bounty hunters are never my first port of call when seeking assistants, but you and your companion have done the Corporal Union a grand honour."

Both men walk from the lobby into the main chamber, where Veena Merida is bound on the floor. Terri Lace sexually struts a walk across to Zak Duran and the broad-built Commander and provocatively introduces herself. "Oh my, what a pleasure to meet you, Commander Tarick. You're so handsome."

The scar-faced Commander replies, "The pleasure is all mine, Miss Lace, in meeting such a stunning woman. Now, I can see why this operation runs so smoothly."

Terri replies, smiling and fluttering her eyes, heaving her bust forward teasingly in a tight silver jumpsuit. "You are too kind, Commander. And please call me Terri. I hope the Corporal Union will call upon our services in future projects."

In the background, behind the trio of the mingling unlawful representatives, Veena Merida breathily mumbles a tone of sarcasm, "Oh, really."

She shakes her long, wavy pastel mane, and although despair has slowly consumed her soul, Veena's beautiful, tear-ridden face still expresses her determination to fight for her freedom. She catches sight of her handbag effects, including her silver-barrelled pistol.

Observing from a short distance at the back entrance of the chamber office, Dan Casey is advancing swiftly and without making a sound towards the bounty hunters and the Corporal Union Commander. He makes an effort to remain concealed in the shadows. He does not want to be detected, prompting himself to question his intentions and feeling curious about his next move.

Dan knows he can not face them by himself, but he is more than relieved Veena is still alive, witnessing the jade-eyed resistance operative on her knees, bound by laser lock handcuffs around the sealing post. With a cheeky smirk forming on his chiselled stubbled face, he peers from underneath his old-style cowboy hat. Dan Casey whispers, "Hang in there, agent lady; don't go woozy on me now, sweetheart."

The handsome cargo pilot's expression is contemplative as he ponders his following action. Dan knows he needs to execute the extraction and rescue operation precisely without causing undue harm. It is a complex and delicate mission, but he feels assured in his capabilities. He repositions his grip on his weapon holster, caressing the handle of his silver and black-barrelled gun and removes his worn hat disguise, preparing to make his move.

Upon departure from Zak Duran's office meeting, Commander Tarick informs the smug hunters, "Your bounty payment will be credited to your starship's encryption link account.

"I will advise Director Volantis that you are perfect for the Corporal Union's high-ranked Elite personal division."

Before exiting the dome chamber, Commander Tarick thoughtfully instructs the armoured guards to ensure that Zak Duran and Terri Lace are safely returned to their starship, the Panther. Accompanied by the four-armed guards, they navigate their way out of the chamber.

Commander Calo Tarick turns with a menacing, slow walk over the chamber room's vented floor. His black boots stomp a shudder. The bulky-bodied dark presence of Calo's metal-patched eye approaches Veena with the ancient data box and an evil glint in his other scarred eye.

Veena Merida knows she is in deep trouble, her watery jade eyes open wide in frightful anticipation as the dark-shaven-haired Commander stands firmly in her view, meaningfully glaring a stare down at the helpless green-haired heroine.

Calo Tarick tells of Director Wilson Volantis's strict instructions, "Miss Merida, or is it Miss Sienna Crayton? I get confused?"

The Commander humbly mocks her about the Kothariya infiltration undercover disguise she obtained when stealing the data box from the Corporal Union's vault.

"I've been granted to do whatever I please with you, and for all the trouble you have dealt me, I've been flushed with several ideas!"

Veena Merida gulps in agonising fear, knowing she will not get off quickly.

"Great, go knock yourself out, Commander."

Calo Tarick responds, "I don't like your evasive attitude to Galactic Law, bitch."

Commander Tarick viciously slaps her across the face, pushing his temper to the brim.

Veena screams, feeling the blunt sting of the Commander's cybernetic backhand across her exotically beautiful but terrified face. "Aah! You demonic bastard."

But Veena is not to be intimidated by Calo Tarick's physical threats of torture. She takes a deep breath of courage, boldly raising her stinging, slapped face and quickly regains crucial eye contact with the Corporal Union Commander. She reminds him of a few home truths. "Law! Gosh, don't make me laugh; you took an oath of loyalty and devotion to protect the citizens of the Kalanisi Universe. Are you aiding and abetting the delusions of a spiritually warped Director?"

Calo Tarick cackles a deep barrelled laugh, "Nice try, Merida. I feel touched by your moral concerns; I shall contemplate the thoughts after I have disposed of your miserable existence. But first, tell me something. Why risk your life for a resistance group led by Tara Harlow just for this little ageing data box? Do you even know what it's for?"

Restricted and bound on her knees, Veena Merida holds her vocal ground, maintaining her sparkling jade-eye contact with her foe. In a calm and determined voice, she growls back, "You know the damn reason too well, Tarick. Your boss, Wilson Volantis, wants to blow a dent through a mythical black hole; he boasted about his hellish desires to me. It will only destroy everything we know and love. Even yourself, Tarick, when you're no use to him anymore. I must do whatever it takes to stop him; should I fail, another one of Tara's agents will follow."

At this ignorance, Commander Calo Tarick flies into a steamed rage. He bellows, "No! Director Volantis is a great leader! He wouldn't do that to me. I've seen his vision for the galaxy, and it's beautiful. It's a shame you won't attend to witness our divine saviour. I believe in Wilson's inventiveness of powerful foresight; the galaxy needs his order to eradicate wasteful scum like yourself and misdirection chaos within the Kalanisi Universe."

Commander Tarick quickly raises his right cybernetic arm from his black-cloaked, long leather mack and points his gun-barrelled hand straight towards her startled face. As the Commander steps closer, Veena Merida sees his cybernetic hand, which is far more menacing than she had ever expected. It resembles a solid metal gun barrel rather than the fingers of a man. She can't take her eyes off it. Veena has heard rumours about these advanced cybernetic hands in her agent portfolios, and now there is one aimed right in front of her with the consequences of destroying her life.

Veena Merida takes one last, desperate, gulping breath, pleading desperately with Calo Tarick, "Kill me if you need to, but please destroy the data box; I beg of you. Wilson intends to unleash destruction of a mass nature we have never experienced."

However, Calo is unwilling to listen to her words no matter what comes out of Veena's mouth, and he seems adamant about trusting Director Volantis.

Commander Tarick just laughs, informing the pleading resistance agent, "I plan to fulfil my honour to the chain of command and deliver the data box to Wilson Volantis, giving him the key to the Vortex. There is nothing you can do to stop me, Agent Merida."

A horrific feeling of dread and terror begins to creep up around her as the Commander holds the fixed gun barrel placed in his cybernetic metal arm directly towards her. Veena Merida closes her jade eyes in a silent farewell prayer, expecting the inevitable to approach her like a black wave. She is resigned to her fate, unable to scream, willing time to stand still and stop at any cost before her fate seals itself. It is as if everyone and everything around her on the trader's station is frozen in time, just her and Commander Tarick standing alone as death lurks closer.

Suddenly, a perfectly executed laser bolt strikes Calo Tarick's cybernetic right hand from nowhere, knocking it astray from the line of fire and causing him to drop the databox in the surprise attack. The high-ranked Corporal Union Commander groans in agonising pain, being knocked off his ranged stance and quickly witnesses the perpetrating figure appear at the doorway, revealing himself to be Dan Casey.

Whereas bound as a prisoner to the facility structure, Veena Merida's head swiftly turns, and her heart skips a beat at the unforeseen sight before her. "Dan!"

Meanwhile, the daring hotshot cargo pilot takes a deep breath and moves a motioned walk towards the data box with the utmost care. His movements are slow and measured, still pointing a fixed aim of his black long-barrel gun directly at Calo

Tarick's shocked and unamused scrunched-up face. Dan Casey has overheard their conversation hiding in the smoggy back layer of the trader's office chamber. He quickly realises what the ancient lore data box contains.

Dan Casey throws the lock-breaker device to the back of Veena's bound hands. She catches it with a gracious smile and starts fumbling a connection to the shackles. Her soul takes a relief sigh before she takes the first step to freedom by burning the lock.

Dan glances in concern and asks the green-haired damsel, "Hey, sweetheart, you okay? I'm sorry I've taken so long. Your friends had some late-night entertainment arranged, and I had to take care of it first; I didn't want to disappoint their deflated egos. Hope I've not missed the Commander's party. Hands in the air now, Tarick. The show's over, pal."

Outside the heated tension chamber office, the dark side activity of the space station full of rogue traders and slave hagglers carry out their sleazy business in secrecy. Nobody knows their true purpose here; they carry out trades that would be illegal elsewhere, usually dealing in exotic and lawless goods and slave-bound creatures.

A few sly glances are exchanged amongst the criminal traders and slave bargainers who congregate outside the commotion of the market. They swear they hear a blast shot go off, sending vibrations through the metal structure of the hell-bound space station. Still, with all the noise of the exchange and the loudspeakers, they decide to continue with their business. But alert to the ricocheting echo is Charlena Jones, the young red-haired slave girl trapped in the cage beneath. She hears the blaster shots from above while holding the device Dan had given her.

Charlena whispers, "It's going get noisy; oh boy! It's going to be noisy!"

Edging to the front of her constricted cage, Charlena bravely attaches the lock-breaker to the laser bounds and presses the button as Dan Casey instructed. A buzzing hum grows louder, and Charlena shockingly watches as the laser bounds slowly light up. She gasps in amazement; it is finally happening, and the freedom she has long dreamed of is in sight. But the young imprisoned red-haired slave girl isn't the only delicate ear to hear the sound of the blast tremor.

Upon hearing the sudden gunshot, the sophisticated consort-class bounty hunters, Zak Duran and Terri Lace, exchange a startled dubious glance at each other as they lead the way down the curved corridors, motioning a swift walk towards the space station's second-floor elevator back to the main floor of the floating slave cabal hub.

Zak Duran immediately takes control and orders the Corporal Union Guards to investigate the source of the sound. Terri Lace's elegant presence follows closely at his side, ready to assist in any way possible.

Zak instructs his blonde-haired darling, "Take the armoured guards and check it out, but don't be too long; the window of opportunity is a revolving maze, my sweetness."

In contrast, Terri Lace and the four elite-trained guards swiftly engage in their return to the slave trader's chamber office to investigate the disturbance. Zak Duran quickly turns his slick presence and walks to the elevator shaft, commanding the alien Leecher beast at his disposal, "You are with me, Dralon. We shall prepare the Panther for take-off; I have a strange feeling things are not what they seem."

Dralon growls in response to its master's demands while waiting for the lift pod to arrive from the elevator shaft.

Meanwhile, as the tension inside the slave trader's office continues to escalate, Dan Casey exerts his influence of conditional negotiating with the under-siege official, Commander Calo Tarick. With years of experience in hostage situations, he was a valid member of a space protection racket before turning his trade into an interstellar cargo pilot. Dan calmly argues for safe extraction from the space station without seeming aggressive or confrontational.

"You can surrender, Tarick. Let's make this easy, pal; nobody needs to get hurt. I'm taking Veena and the data box off this floating piece of junk. I have no qualms with you, Calo or the Corporal Union, but you can inform that crusty old politician, Wilson Volantis. His shit is not happening on my watch. Do we have an accord, Commander!"

The scar-faced Commander has an evil grin rising on his dark demeanour. He says to the advancing cargo runner in his deep voice without repetition, "I'm so glad you cared to join us, Mr Casey. I mean, as if your view matters. I can assure you that you will be the only one surrendering today. It will be my priority, and I promise you, Casey, that I will always follow my lawful objectives down to the core."

Veena Merida quickly intervenes in the debated conversation; her dainty gloved hands are still bound in a stretch behind the chamber office pole. She waits for the lock-breaker to perform the cutting circle, happily smiling at Dan.

Veena intriguingly asks her brave rescuer, "How did you manage to find me? They told me you were dead!"

With good grace, Dan Casey smiles at the entrapped damsel, slowly reaching down to retrieve the astrological data box.

While glancing over to Veena, he swaggers and replies, "Your lame brain friends lack practice."

Just as the charismatic cargo pilot utters the smug words, a metallic gun-barrelled arm swings in Dan Casey's direction. Enraged by the formidable insult of his infiltration, Commander Tarick viciously shouts out across the trader's chamber office, "I'll make amends for their costly mistake and make it fucking take this time, Casey."

Calo Tarick activates his trigger-linked cybernetic hand, flicking his metal thumb, readily opening fire from his cyber-gun barrel, and blasting a veered shot with an intent to kill the charmed cargo pilot.

Dan leaps and boldly dives away from the cybernetic blaster fire, rolling over the steam-jagged vent floor. He quickly jumps up and bravely charges back at Commander Tarick, both locked in a duelling battle as Dan Casey slingshots an aim and attempts to shoot, racking out a flurry of shots. But wise to the offensive move, Calo Tarick easily deflects the bounding shots with his deadly metal arm.

Raising his rough, deep voice and aggressively shouting a sneered roar to Dan, the Commander says, "You should never have come here, Casey. Now, you have got involved in a nightmare beyond your league of belief. But luckily for me, I will make sure you pay for your crimes against Corporal Law, putting you out of your misery."

Dan Casey has no other option but to fight Calo Tarick if he wants to survive and save Veena, and his old skills come alive with his determination to fight back despite the odds. The two of them fight fiercely, weapons sparking against each other in a clash of wills, trading punched blows.

Whereas helpless to assist, Veena Merida waits anxiously for the lock-breaker device to free the laser bind. Knowing security will soon hear the echoed shots, Veena desperately fights against her bonds. Amidst the fray, Dan Casey and Calo Tarick are locked in an intense escalating battle, being catapulted around the chamber and crashing all that is in their way. Suddenly, the laser lock defaults and snaps, breaking Veena free.

"Yes!" As she rubs her sore wrist, her jade eyes immediately fall onto her infrared-scoped pistol. In a split second, the long green-haired crack-shot agent quickly grabs her silver stubby barrel weapon and turns on the infrared sight.

But she couldn't get a precise angle without the risk of hitting Dan. This obstacle infuriates her; Veena angrily says, "Damn it!"

The astute Calo Tarick immediately notices Veena's black jumpsuited presence. As Dan and Tarick continue their close-ranged fight, the leather-cloaked figure of the Corporal Union Commander lunges forward and headbutts Dan, kicking him hard down on the chamber's floor in a dazed heap. Calo rapidly turns to face the emerging threat from the galactic agent, Veena Merida. As adrenaline courses through her athletic body, Veena stylishly bursts into evasive action. Firing her silver-scoped site pistol wildly at the imposing Commander Tarick, he speedily evades the veering blasts and, using his cyber hand, again equally draws on his opposing side-arm weapon.

In contrast, Veena's short-stubbed pistol soon becomes overheated, and the trigger jams. Screaming in frustration, she says, "Oh, shit!"

Commander Calo Tarick pleasurably aims his long-barrelled gun with a sinister smirk protracting from his dark, disfigured face. "My turn, you green-haired bitch." There's a fraction of time before the deadly Commander pulls the pulsing trigger and shoots on his sworn promise.

Whereas back on his booted feet, Dan Casey sees his only chance, and without a moment's hesitation, he swiftly runs up to the self-occupied Calo Tarick from behind, jabbing him with a diving elbow that sends him flying into the panoramic curved window of the trader's office, misfiring the shot through the tinted glass. With a manoeuvring clash of entangled bodies, Dan Casey and Calo Tarick take a free-falling plunge out of the shattered glass opening, luckily crashing on the first-level running conveyor track. Dan and Tarick glare at one another without seeming fazed by the hurling fall.

They instantly rise to a fighting stand-off covered in trade office debris as the data box falls from Dan Casey's coat pocket and rolls onto the dust-panelled conveyor belt. Commander Tarick was a decorated military leader before having his arm replaced with a cybernetic model courtesy of an intergalactic battle injury. The patch-faced menace grunts in sheer anger, trying to hit the resilient cargo pilot, furiously swinging his mechanical metal arm and missing. Dan Casey is an agile man. He easily avoids the cybernetic attack, ducking beneath it and delivering a blow of his own, which rocks the Commander's mechanised frame.

The cargo runner taunts Calo, "You want to fight me? You can still surrender, Commander?"

"I'm going to fucking tear you apart, Casey!"

While continuing their brutal feud, the conveyor belt track flows its intended course around the trader ring station. Meanwhile, still bound in captivity, Charlena Jones watches in awe and horror as Dan and the Commander duelled in midair above the trade office. As they fly towards the first level conveyor, they are surrounded by a mass of rugged traders and slave handlers, all with their eyes fixed upwards, transfixed on the two men.

Until a few weeks back, Charlena Jones was a happy galactic student. The young girl never expected that she would be illegally sold into slavery after being tricked by the false promise of investigating the disappearance of her friends. The red-haired slave girl witnesses the lock-breaker melting her laser bounds with a single blast, freeing her with ease.

Charlena readily kicks the door of her cage open, but she is panicked and confused. The female student knows once she is seen, it will be dangerous.

She sweetly mumbles in a soft whimper, "It's going to be noisy. Oh boy, it is noisy." Unfortunately, it isn't long before her fear is realised.

Four of the Galanti slave trader guards approach, and their mission is clear: obtain her. Charlena Jones is startled to see a bulky-shouldered dark-skinned man with stylish dreadlocks dressed in a long open jacket and tinted shades suddenly whip out two silver guns. The blades are attached to the sleek firearms, and the mystery male figure shoots them at two of the slave guards, hitting them right between the eyes. He spins his weapons, crossing his muscular arms and shooting the other two approaching Galanti contracted slave guards, sending them flying back before hitting the ground, certifying them dead. Charlena is shocked and awed at the gunslinger moves he has just pulled off.

The dreadlock saviour offers her his hand and calmly says, "I'm Jay Haines. I'm here to help you, girl; your mother hired me to free you."

Despite her fear, Charlena Jones grabs his hand in faith as they move through the space station prison. The young girl tugs his arm in a pleading explanation, "We need to help the other slaves; we cannot abandon them. Please, Jay!"

Little did Charlena Jones know this would become the beginning of her journey for justice and survival. She is in it for the long haul, and she has Jay Haines by her side, who agonisingly comments on her madness of an idea. "Oh kid, we gotta be quick; your mother warned me you were trouble, so come on. If we're going to do this before the guards catch on, oh man!"

"How is Mum? I've missed her?"

"Your mother is damn worried about you, kid. Come on, keep up."

Still present in the high-view slave trader's office, Veena Merida glances out of the shattered panoramic window and sees Dan Casey and Commander Tarick still locked in vile combat, firing blaster shots back and forth. The conveyor belt track is taking them closer to the power towers, and Veena can't help but feel a sense of unease.

She softly mumbles in awe, "You are not behaving like a typical cargo runner, Dan."

Suddenly, she hears footsteps outside the chamber and spins around just in time to see two Corporal Union Elite Guards enter the trashed room.

Veena leaps and rolls, firing her silver-scoped weapon and hitting both guards precisely. They fall to the ground, and before she knows it, two more black-dressed armoured guards have entered the chamber office. Veena wastes no time and quickly runs towards them. Her long, green, silky hair wavers while she performs a flying kick that strikes one of the enforcing guards with incredible force.

The other Elite officer is caught off guard and stumbles backwards, allowing Veena Merida to strike again by shooting him through his armoured-tinted chest and roll-blasting the other stunned Corporal High Guard. Her agent-trained skills have paid off, and she can easily fend off the Corporal Union attackers.

Momentarily, following the armoured guards into the chamber office, bounty hunter Terri Lace swiftly enters, taking in the seemingly chaotic scene around her. She takes a deep breath and surveys the trashed room. Several of the dead Corporal Union Guards have their weapons still drawn, their blood staining the station's metal floor. She sees Veena getting up and back to her feet. Veena and Terri have been best friends since childhood, but their reunion is anything but friendly.

Terri Lace watches and panics, uttering, "Oh fuck." She starts running away from the battered chamber room facility.

Veena Merida is close on her heels, openly shouting, "Hey bitch, I got you that promise!" She adjusts her infrared-scoped pistol and starts shooting warning blasts around her.

Terri Lace turns her elegant body, swivels, and rapidly shoots back at Veena as they run along the bending corridors of the rusty old space station. The gunfire echoes off the walls as the two feminine ladies close the distance. Veena can see Terri slowing down and getting ready to aim more precisely.

But Veena doesn't stop. She just dodges the attack. She keeps sprinting with her loyal pistol in her suede-gloved hand. Terri Lace refuses to submit to Veena. She has been promised famed retribution and prepares to fulfil it. On the other hand, Veena Merida is determined to try to save her old friend if possible. She knows that Terri has been through a lot, and maybe what she is doing now is driving her to desperation more than pure evil.

Veena says, "Look, Terri, this doesn't have to be a fight to the death. We can still work this out. Please talk to me."

But Terri Lace just jeers and mockingly replies, "You require a new fucking fellow sister."

And with that veered spat comment, Terri dodges Veena's offer of a truce and disappears around the corner. Veena Merida swiftly follows as the shoot-out continues in vain.

In the meantime, still fighting a duel for the ownership of the ancient, prized data box on the manoeuvring twisting dust-ridden conveyor track, Dan Casey bravely evades the persistent blaster fire, weaving and diving his rip-jacketed body away from the ongoing assault from Commander Calo Tarick. The charmed but capable pilot jumps up and spins midair, shooting an energy beam from his silver and black handgun. It strikes Calo Tarick in his muscular leg, where the Commander's armour is weakest due to the fall from the trader's office.

Commander Calo Tarick painfully shouts, "You scummy bastard, Casey. Now I'm going to take pleasure in fucking destroying you."

Dan Casey intentionally tumbles to the plated conveyor belt and rolls away from the raging Commander Tarick. The heroic interstellar pilot has to think of something and fast. Looking up, he sees space station pylon cables and takes a random potshot. The blast deflects, hitting the power towers. At that moment, the power towers began to explode, boom, one by one, in a chain reaction of fire. The force of the blasts causes the old space station to creak and groan, and it starts to become unstable.

The pylons roar, and sparks fly as the energy is released in a massive wave. The strain of the overload begins to shudder and shake the slave-trade ring prison. This gives Dan Casey the chance to escape. He quickly gets to his stance and collectively picks up the mystery data box. The daring pilot starts to sprint away from Calo Tarick, who is still focusing on blasting him. The echoes of blaster fire still reverberate off the walls of the old space station as Dan looks back to see the Commander follow his route along the conveyor belt track, with the power towers still glowing bright red in the background. A single blast isn't stopping Tarick. Calo Tarick is more than just blast-proof. At this moment, Dan Casey's handsome face realises the gravity of the situation. He is a little over his head. The commercial cargo runner has stumbled on to a mission he had no business getting involved with, and the consequences can be dire.

The young galactic student, Charlena Jones, and the gunslinger for hire, Jay Haines, have set out on a secondary mission to free all the caged slaves from the sleazy traders on the space station. Their purpose is made easier by the power towers draining off the electrical current that feeds the laser cages. Most devious hagglers and rogue buyers are in an overreacted flurry, trying to escape by running, screaming and finding a way off the doomed station.

Brave to the bone, Charlena tells the freed slave prisoners in her sweet, innocent voice, "Go hurry, run and find a starship."

Some of the freed slaves run in sheer panic, but most want revenge on the sleazy traders. This causes chaos and mayhem to break loose on the defaulting space station. This is followed by a massive explosion, suddenly due to one of the main reactors going critical. Everything starts to sway.

Jay grabs Charlena and tells her, "We need to get a moving kid and get to my ship; this bucket of a station is going to blow!"

Charlena Jones replies, "Hell yeah, run fast; oh boy, I'm getting scared now."

The dreadlocked gunslinging chaperone Jay Haines replies to the frightened young student, "Just stay close, kid! And don't look back. I promised your mother I'd take care of you, and I don't go back on my word. Come on, girl."

As Jay and Charlena prepare a rushed sprint to the station's docking bay amid the turbulent crowds, the fiery young student informs her saviour of a few facts, "Thank you, Jay, whoever you are. But stop calling me a kid; I'm seventeen, and it's my birthday in a few months, so do the maths, hotshot."

The situation at the trader's station is a dire shambles. The infrastructure is bending and deteriorating completely due to the impact of the main reactor explosion. It's becoming a hazardous, unstable environment to navigate around as the crippled station sways, making the main floor contents inside shift from side to side. This causes a challenging predicament for Jay Haines and Charlena Jones, who are just approaching the docking bay where his scout starship is.

They stop only to witness it being damaged by the expanding explosions. Jay Haines comments on his disappointed venture, "Oh shit, that's bad, girl. Now we are in trouble! We need another starship and fast."

The station's tenor speakers are blasting out a protocol warning, "PLEASE EVACUATE THE STATION. THIS IS NOT A DRILL; CRITICAL."

The astute Charlena Jones gazes around and sees the Machiavellian MK2 *Decepter* in the bottom hanger bay. With a veering tug of Jay's wandering attention, the inspiring student points and informs Jay, "Quick, this way. We shall take that starship, the one that Dan Casey advised me to board."

"Who is the man that helped you? He didn't look like a slave trader to me."

"I have no idea; he just told me it would get noisy!" says Charlena, stretching a sprint as Jay Haines matches her running pace, his dreadlocked hair flicking a bouncing bob.

The slick gunslinger replies, "Well, he made it noisy, kid!" Amusingly, Jay Haines suddenly gets a glimpse of the oncoming privateer slave guards owned by the powerful crime lord family of Mach Galanti.

With moments to spare, Jay Haines stylishly spins Charlena Jones behind him in a dashing, skilled manner and strictly tells her, "Quick! Run. I will keep you covered; I've got this, kid."

Jay Haines stylishly spins his dual silver shooters, readily crossing his lighting-fast arms, opening fire and blasting the Galanti-trained guards in a cunning crossfire display, presenting himself as one of the best gunslingers in the whole Kalanisi Galaxy.

Meanwhile, back on the second level of the creaking station, Terri Lace is swaying into the rusting walls of the bending corridor, running as fast as she can to the lift elevator. Turning back, she sees Veena Merida still chasing her, pistol shots blaring.

Terri had a moment of curse words, "Ah, shit! The lift's fucked, and the controls are damn well damaged!"

She quickly decides to pursue the stairs instead but is dismayed when she finds Veena still on her tail. Terri Lace raises her gun to aim, yet Veena is quicksilver and anticipates her moves in executing a high kick and knocking the pistol from Terri's hand.

Terri, reacting quickly, retaliates with a sweeping hand chop and a spinning high kick, with a mischievous giggle.

Terri Lace says, "Game on, sister! Come on then, bitch. You want a fight? Let's see how good that agent training is!"

To which Veena Merida also readies herself for combat and replies with a focused demeanour, "Well, let me show you, sister!"

And with that taunt, the two galactic jumpsuit beauties start to exchange fierce jabs, lethal punches and swinging slick kicks, demonstrating their martial arts skills and showing off their fighting prowess.

Veena is getting the better of her opponent, Terri, as she

blocks her attacks while spinning and kicking her right in the ample chest, knocking the blonde-haired bounty hunter to the ground.

Terri Lace shouts, "You damn bitch!"

Veena Merida swiftly approaches and leans down to end the fight, but as she does, Terri Lace has another trick lurking. She cunningly twists her diamond ring, and smoke gushes from the opening. This allows Terri to kick viciously back at Veena, pushing her hard in her chest and launching her back next to the broken lift doors. Veena is slightly shocked and somewhat dazed, attempting to comprehend what had just happened as Terri Lace sprints away to the stairs.

Veena sighs, "Gosh! I must get one of those rings."

While the sexual blonde bombshell is surging a high-heeled dash through to the staircase, Terri urgently connects her comm line to her daring partner in crime, Zak Duran, who is safe in his starship, the Panther A1 class frigate.

She yells into the communications device, "It's all gone to shit, my darling!"

Zak replies in his relaxed, cool, calm voice, watching out the Panther's front view, "I thought you said you had taken care of the cargo pilot. He looks alive and kicking to me, my sweetness."

Zak sees Dan Casey fight and battle Calo Tarick, going around the damaged conveyor belt track and the sparking chain reaction of the power towers, causing the station's imminent destruction and total mayhem of the enslaved and trader guards brawling all over the station.

Terri Lace says in a pissed-off manner, "Well, come and fucking assist me, darling! And we can comb through any faults at a more appropriate time."

As Terri brashly arrives at the top of the winding staircase, she glances vaguely behind and sees Veena vastly recovered and performing a determined chase, firing blaster shots from her silver-stubbed pistol.

Zak Duran apprehensively can hear the shooting echoing out of the Panther's comm-link and urgently advises his consort mistress, "I'd get your pretty sexy arse back to the ship quickly; you have a tiny window!"

Terri curses her cold-hearted lover's reception, "Fuck you, Zak!" She venomously moans while swiftly tapping a heel-clicking run, veering down the stairway and briskly reaching the first-floor level of the doomed slaver's trade station. Veena Merida is closing on her again, tapping her heel boots down the twisting steps. The scarpering blonde temptress, Terri Lace, is making haste on the main floor of the decrepit space station when she sees two Galanti trader guards.

She bitterly orders them to go apprehend Veena, "The culprit for this disaster is up the nearby staircase; go get her and make sure you shoot to kill."

Veena Merida darts down the curving stairs until her sparkling jade eyes spot the Galanti security guards rapidly approaching her. She quickly shoots one in his chest while sliding down the staircase railing and then proceeds to kick the other in the head, sending him flying, displaying that her training as an agent is a force to be reckoned with. Then, she continues her pursuit of Terri Lace through the crowd in the midst of the fighting mayhem.

However, with the space station beginning to collapse, it is difficult to make any headway. As both females sway to and fro, Veena has an opportunity arise. With no time to think, she decides to take aim and fire a shot that hits her old friend, Terri Lace, right on her bare-skinned arm.

Terri screams out in sheer unbearable pain, "Aah!"

Unfortunately, this is only the start of the destruction as a shockwave explosion sweeps through the station, bringing down a storm of debris that impacts both Veena and Terri, leaving them stricken amid falling rubble.

Close by and adrift in the docking bay, Zak Duran stands

with concern posing from his handsome, roguish, stubbled face as he witnesses from the Panther's cockpit his affectionate partner Terri Lace getting shot and slightly covered in rusting panel debris.

Zak turns his cunningly deceptive presence to the lead alien tribal Leecher beast with a tense, smirked grin and commands his pet creature, "Dralon, go now and retrieve Mistress Lace at once." He then gives the second hideous Leecher permission to excel. "Take your time to entertain the crowd, and please, show no mercy."

The Leechers growl in loyal obedience to their master, and their hunger for destruction seems unstoppable. Zak Duran craftily activates the Panther's subsystems, and with a humbling whistle, the sleek black vessel's entrance hatch opens to expose two monstrous figures. The eerie and bone-chilling Leechers have an evil, hideous glint in their reddish eyes. Their deathly fanged ploughed faces underscore their dark, muscular, arched bodies and long, razor-sharp claws protruding from their intimidating menace as if ready to kill anything or anyone.

Veena Merida is recovering from the tumbling fragments, quickly sweeping the dusty grit away, only to be deeply shocked by the sight of the two grotesque Leechers appearing on the Panther's extruding hatch. She watches as they gruesomely transform their drooling fangs into face-sucking slimed tentacles.

Veena knows she has to act fast; seeing the threat of the alien monsters, the green-haired heroine thinks out loud, diving for cover behind some fallen structured debris. "Oh shit! These beasts will kill everyone in a raged frenzy."

The brave female galactic agent swiftly starts shooting blasts at one Leecher.

Dralon is on his way to collect his mistress, Terri Lace, who is covered in trash, sprawled out on the panelled floor, hurt, mumbling a deep breath of a groan for aid. "Aah, help, Zak!"

The loyal alien menace Dralon viciously growls in thunderous anger while striding clear with meaningful intent, evading Veena's open offence.

Suddenly protecting his devoted interests of heart, the cool, calm presence of Zak Duran appears from the shadows. He stands at the steaming hatchway of the Panther as his renegade starship engines begin to roar to life. He draws his black handgun from his slant holster with a stylish gripped spin of the trigger. Zak Duran aims his weapon and opens fire, trying to provide cover for Dralon to overwhelm the offensive attack from Veena Merida.

The jade-eyed bombshell swiftly adjusts her attention to the handsome man she once considered a potential lover. "Zak!" Putting her feelings aside, knowing he isn't the man she used to know, Veena readily returns and opens fire, blasting around the Panther entrance hatch. Zak Duran equally dodges her shots and lets his sheer luck overwhelm his foe's accuracy. He grins at her missing as he deftly shoots the silver-scoped pistol from her dainty hand. The gun flies across the station. Veena Meirda screams a yelp at the stung attack, self-criticising her performance.

She groans out loud, "Gosh, girl, agent rule one, never drop your damn gun."

Meanwhile, with a confident and smug demeanour, Zak Duran shouts, "I've always loved you, Veena." He boldly announces in his attractive smooth voice, ranging across the crippled station's bay area before blowing her a one-handed kiss, half mischievous and half genuine.

Dralon has meanwhile recuperated Terri Lace quickly to the safety of the sleek starship. The hatchway closes as the Panther makes ready to take off. The engines roar a pulsating purr as the frigate smoothly glides out of the deteriorating space station and leaves behind the chaos and destruction of the trader's ring station into the vast expanse of Kalanisi space.

Veena Merida stands in the degrading hanger bay. Her mood is bleak and speechless as she furiously slaps her arms down and pats her curved thighs through her dark catsuit, truly disappointed by witnessing her deceitful friends elude her gallant efforts. Without letting up for the young pastel-haired agent, a new fear arises when she sees the cruel Leecher that Zak Duran left behind, sucking on the sleazy trader's face with its horrible tentacles. Instantly, he throws the poor man's carcass onto the space station's damaged flooring.

The horrific alien Leecher now turns and bounds forward with its evil red-blooded eyes fixed on Veena. Trapped in a corner without her silver infrared pistol, Veena unwittingly panics and screams at the top of her well-spoken posh accent, "NO! NO! AH!" The vile beastly creature then grotesquely roars and wraps its slithering tentacles around her elegant carved neckline, choking the stunned agent and moving upwards towards her face. Struggling to match the Leecher's strength in vain to break free of the alien's clutches, Veena closes her eyes in distress as her efforts weakly tamper.

Suddenly, with a gushing whoosh past her troubled face, two piercing blades slosh into the slimy tentacles entangled around Veena's delicate throat, cutting the slithering fangs in half. The arched-back alien yelps, growling in angered pain. The stunned beauty's jade eyes flutter as she swiftly catches sight of the dreadlocked gunslinger Jay Haines, imposingly spinning his dual silver shooters, cunningly taunting the hideous, rough-skinned Leecher.

"Hey, you mother fucker, don't you know it is rude to bully ladies. Why not pick a damn fight with me? Come on, you greasy-looking piece of chicken shit."

He skilfully spins his class-designed weapons, witnessing the growling Leecher divert its attention from Veena, who is just getting back up to her booted heel stance. Jay Haines tilts his pleasantly charming face and glances over his trendsetting shades.

"Go, lady, do what you gotta achieve, but leave this hideous fanged freak show to me; I've got this creepy dude nailed."

There is an acknowledging nod from Veena Merida as she hurryingly collects her scoped weapon and sprints off in the direction of the conveyor belt tracking to assist Dan Casey in his conflict with Commander Calo Tarick.

The monstrous blood-eyed alien engagingly pounces with a powerful lunge towards the black-jacketed gunslinger, landing with a swooped swiping clawed offensive.

Jay Haines stylishly manoeuvres his muscular body from harm's way while taking a random blast shot at the vile beast. The Leecher roars fearlessly, instantly retaliating with the surging ram of its arched black body, knocking Jay Haines off guard with an unfortunate mishandling of his dual silver guns.

Jay quickly rolls away and jumps up, regaining his composure, raising his clenched fist with a vigorous taunt to the beastly hound, "Hey, shit features, is that all you got in the locker? Come on, you ugly mother fucker. Let us do it the old-fashioned way. Care to dance?"

The grotesque Leecher growingly obliges as the wilding beast renounces its attack. A clash of forceful punches and mortal kicks fly as man and beast lock in a gruesome battle.

While tearing ahead of the intense brawling nightmare, the free-bound galactic student, Charlena Jones, is following instructions to run fast from the chaos and not look back. She closes in swiftly to the damage-stricken hangar bay area where the *Decepter* MK2 freighter vessel is docked. But the young red-haired teenage girl has a renegade streak running through her veins, and it is one of the reasons she was captured and enslaved while investigating the several disappearances of her student friends, who have cruelly fallen into the clutches of the mighty crime syndicate family of Mach Galanti. With astute awareness, she instantly stops to a braking halt and quickly turns around, witnessing Jay Haines fist-fighting the alien Leecher from toe-to-toe.

Blowing her red-bobbed silky fringe out of view, Charlena mutters, "No, Jay! I need to help him. Now it is going to get damn noisy."

Jay Haines is still in brawling combat with the vile Leecher and has to focus all his strength and courage to dig deep and defeat the Leecher. As the creature roars, it charges towards him with its big claw-edged fist swinging.

The slick gunslinger is ready, sidestepping the monstrous creature, "Whoosh, bada bing."

The gruesome black monster falls, but the Leecher is far from down. The alien terror quickly gets back to its massive, webbed feet. The fight is starting to become difficult for Jay, who is already exhausted but is not giving up. The brave gun-for-hire must do whatever it takes to survive this fight. So, he closes his eyes and focuses as the Leecher charges at him again.

Jay Haines is winded on the rubble-littered floor of the shuddering old space station. He quickly catches sight of the galvanising Leecher growling with its blood-red eyes glowing, wiggling its still active, hungry tentacle hounding and stalking the galactic gunslinger moving in for the kill to suck his face off.

The attractive red-haired student stares at the hideously arched Leecher approaching Jay Haines as he is still sprawled out on the interior creaking station, stunned by the alien's deadly strike.

Charlena Jones says in a panicked tizz of confusion, "Oh shit, No! What can I do?"

The observant young girl sweeps her bright blue eyes around the mayhem of the slave station for options. Until she commits to locating the dual silver shooters with the detachable blades scattered ahead of her position. Charlena takes a deep breath and dashes at the shining handguns; she quickly bends down and grips one of the legendary shooters, her soft palm hands caressing the weapon handle stem as her finger squeezes around the trigger. Charlena has never fired a side-arm in her seventeen-year-old life. Being a galactic student in the human home world of Kothariya, she is used to studying mass-energy equations, not the trained, skilled art of a crack-shot gunslinger.

Charlena Jones bravely holds out the double-barrelled weapon and aims straight and true as the Leecher's grotesque tentacles prepare to smooth out Jay Haines's dark, handsome face.

"Hey, monster, back off." Boldly screams the daring teenage student, instantly pulling the silver gun's trigger and opening fire, shooting the attachable spinning blade with a hurling effective pace, cutting through the smoke-filled hazy air and hitting the browbeat Leecher's muscular-bound shoulder. The hideous alien creature howls and filters around the doomed station with its vile black matte body quivering from the slicing impact. Raging from the wounding shot, the Leecher reaches with its long knife-edge claws, swiftly yanking out the pieced blade covered in green-coloured blood and throwing the blade a yard away.

Then, with no fear, the monstrous horror sharply spins around, powerfully kicking Jay Haines with its razor-sharp webbed feet aside in the traumatised rage, smashing the dazed gunslinger and veering into the side interior of the decrepit station. With a terrifying growl, the Leecher's red drooling eyes fixate on the frozen-to-the-spot galactic student, arching his hideous frame, ready to leap for a pounced kill. Charlena Jones opens her blue eyes wide, stunned in shock that the alien beast is not gone and is preparing to maul her to death.

The hysterical young girl screams, "No! Why didn't the weapon fire a blast? Oh, boy! Help?"

"Pull the other trigger, kid! There's a second trigger. Quick, girl."

The nightmarish creature maliciously pounces a bounding leap as Charlena Jones embraces her fears, looping her dainty finger onto the second trigger, with no time to think about the consequences of fate. The red-bobbed hairstyle of the galactic student flows as she instinctively squeezes the other trigger, rapidly opening fire.

The impact knocks Charlena off her agile stance and hurls her across the station area. But, the gun sounds out a flurry of blast rounds, which tear shreds into the alien Leecher until it collapses in a slumped heap on the floor, defeated.

Quickly getting back on her scuffed-shoed feet, Charlena moves cautiously closer to the dead alien creature; she gazes at the beast with shock in her blue eyes.

"What a damn shot, kid; you saved the day, girl." Jay Haines sprints over to the young student, hugging her tightly, relieved to be alive.

Charlena Jones is happy, though shaken by the attack. Stunned at her performance, she says dazedly, "Oh boy! I've just shot a Leecher; I can't wait to inform Mum."

They both laugh, and Haines collects his silver shooters and the weapons with a stylish looped spin holster.

He advises his young sidekick, "There are a few details your mother doesn't need to know about, kid! Now we gotta move and board that starship, as this place will boom!" says Jay in his deep voice, grabbing hold of Charlena's hand.

The young galactic student robustly replies, "I wish you would stop calling me a kid!"

The pair of renegade misfits march a stern sprint towards the hanger bay of the *Decepter* starship.

Meanwhile, the heroic Dan Casey and the distorted Commander Calo Tarick are still swinging punches and performing hard-hitting manoeuvring kicks on the damaged conveyor track belt.

The exploding power towers have smashed onto the twisting track, causing the dusty belts to form cavities and electrical fires to hinder the smooth running of the conveyor belt system.

Commander Tarick violently swings his cybernetic hand at the ducking cargo pilot, shouting his demands in his deep husky voice, "Give me that damn databox, Casey!"

But with a slick weaving and agile manoeuvring turn, Dan Casey's leg sweeps a tense roundhouse kick into Calo Tarick's wounded thigh, knocking the well-built dark menace back on the slave cages rolling freely.

"Fuck you, Tarick, I fulfil my contracts whatever the cargo, pal."

Instantly retaliating, the fearless Commander Tarick heavily kicks back with a powerful lunge of his Corporal Union editioned black steel toe-capped boots while cunningly activating his weaponised killer metal hand with a flicking click of his trigger thumb. The Commander aims his lethal induced mobilised gun to open fire at Dan Casey.

Still, the attack is short as the main core reactor of the slavering station produces another massive explosion, causing Dan Casey and Calo Tarick to lose their footing stance, and both parties fall over on the shifting, withered conveyor belt. The rickety old floating prison facility structures start to peel apart.

Boom! Another explosion sweeps over the shattering conveyor track as the power towers and rusty steel beams start to fall and crash onto the twisting maze, causing a massive pile-up of infused components and torn sheeted panels, inflicting devastating carnage.

Dan Casey is knocked flat down on his princely chiselled face, though swiftly looking up, he sees the track coming to a dead end, severely damaged by one of the towers that smashed, jamming the track belt and building to an explosive climax. The charmed cargo runner attempts to push himself back up. He suddenly feels Commander Tarick's metal-fibred hand sweepingly flip-tripping his legs from beneath his muscular, toned body.

Unfortunately, this causes Dan to scupper his efforts, and

the astrological data box again rolls out of his quarter badge coat onto the conveyor track. Commander Tarick decisively gets to his heavy-booted footing and lunges for the data box.

Dan Casey gives the enraged scar-faced adversary, Calo Tarick, a treat of his own medicine, reaching out with his fingerless-gloved hand and grabbing the Commander's black boots with a cunning swooped trip, bringing the bulky imposing foe to fall as Calo's long leather-cloaked coat sprawls over his presence.

This gives the undaunted cargo runner a chance to grab the ancient lore box, and his finger touches the edges of the historical cubed device, but suddenly, it rolls back, and Calo Tarick grabs the prize with his left human-formed hand. They stare at one another in a test of sheer will, and both counterparts rise to their stance. The trader's space station is critically imploding to pieces around the depleted duelling arena.

Commander Calo Tarick's commentary states his true feelings, "You've been a pain since I met you, Casey. Making me chase you across the galaxy, damaging Corporal Union property without moral respect. Whatcha think you are, apart from being just some dirty scum? You have forfeited the chance to surrender. Now it's time to die finally, Mr Casey, and be remembered as nothing more than a mere petty criminal."

Despite getting hard knocks, Dan Casey recovers quickly and yells, "Enough! It's time for this to end. I'm glad I could accommodate your personal ranking chart of crooks, but I'd never surrender to someone like you, Tarick!"

Relaying his feelings, Dan desperately lunges forward with a sharp elbow to the Commander's rib cage, stunning him with a transpose blow, recasting a drop of the pretentious databox. Dan Casey bravely swerves and rolls away from Calo Tarick's opposing presence, trying to slip away, snatching up the data box and the black-barrelled weapon he dropped in the conflictual saga, preparing to jump a leaping dive off the doomed sizzling conveyor belt.

But before Dan can perform the escaping feature. Almost simultaneously, Commander Tarick grabs the interstellar pilot by the collar of his trader's disguised jacket and, in a fit of manic rage, headbutts him as he unloads a barrage of verbal insults, "Give me that fucking data box, Mr Casey! You scoundrel lowlife piece of shit." But Calo Tarick is not going to stop at verbal intimidation.

He aggressively reaches back with his right foot and savagely swings a forceful kick with his big black boots, impacting Dan unsuspectingly hard in his stubbled face and sending him flying. In an instant, Dan Casey is sent staggering, crumpling backwards in the sheer force of the unexpected outburst. He vaguely tries to scramble away in a dizzy, desperate attempt to get away from his metal-patched eye aggressor, gripping the databox with a shocked, intense glare of his handsome dark brown eyes at the suddenness of the Commander's violent attack.

Meanwhile, a short distance from the hazardous conflict affair of honour, Veena Merida is running as fast as her legs can carry her, slightly travelling below the conveyor tracks. She has drawn the silver-scoped pistol in hand, ready to assist.

Veena's heart sinks a skipping beat as she witnesses Calo Tarick beating Dan Casey down to a pulp, laying on the churned-up unstable conveyor belt.

Veena screams out loud in a shocked panic, "No! Dan!"

The realisation that Dan is in danger sends waves through her mind; her chest tightens as she is desperate to figure out a plan to save him.

The pastel-haired galactic agent sees where they are quickly heading towards the damaged power towers with electrical sparks flowing across the crumbling station as it starts to break up in the atmosphere, sending shockwaves across the tracks, which are critically damaged and on blazing fire.

Amid certain danger, Dan Casey locates his silver and

black-barrelled weapon lying astray on the burning track, too far away to reach as the Corporal Union Commander stands firm; heaving his muscular chest out in vain confidence he has overcome the gallant effort of the unlawful resistance by the heroic cargo pilot.

Calo Tarick steps forth, grinning with an evil demeanour and spells out the future of the Kalanisi, "I'm going to enjoy blowing your head off, Mr Casey. It's a shame you won't see how the rest of the galaxy fares. It will be beautiful when Director Volantis releases his mythical lore policies.

"It will be a pleasure to hunt down any type of resistance I've classed as endangering galactic peace, and first on my list will be that cheap, green-haired bitch that dragged your sorry-scuffed arse into this mess."

The Commander mocks a teasing laugh of a goodwill gesture, "Any final words, Mr Casey? What do I need to inform your next of kin? You were a disreputable fugitive of Corporal Law and died by my very cybernetic hand."

With fate bearing down on him, Dan glances to the side of the conveyor track, wielding a charismatic smirk advising the Commander, "You should never call a lady names behind her back, Tarick; it always ends up biting you on the arse!"

Dan Casey boldly says as he witnesses an infrared dot appear on Calo's metal gunshot hand.

Before the upbeat Commander Tarick could take the allured avenging shot, Veena Merida's determination beats him to it from the side of the crumbling conveyor track as the green-haired heroine runs in from behind. The blaster bursts hit Calo Tarick twice, hitting and grazing just below his cyber-gun barrelled arm.

Veena shouts, "Who are you calling cheap, Red Eye!"

The blasts force Tarick's arm back and send him flying. He lands hard but quickly rises to his solid booted feet. His cybernetic arm has been damaged, but he is still alive and ready to battle to the death. However, the persuasive Dan Casey has other ideas, gaining his chance from Veena Merida's discretional offensive.

Quickly gathering his trusted black-barrelled gun, Dan blasts the Commander's already injured leg, vastly lunging his entire body weight at the shaken Calo Tarick, followed by an uppercut punch firmly placed on the Commander's grunting face. He quickly grabs his fragmented metal arm and forces it carelessly into the jamming-up conveyor track.

"Aah, Casey!" screams out Commander Tarick in agonising pain as his defining cyber arm is trapped, and as the tarnished belt moves, it viciously rips the limb from out his socket and tears his arm straight off.

Calo Tarick screams in dramatic shock and traumatising pain as he falls to a twisting heap on the jolting conveyor track, groaning from his intense injury. Ahead of Tarick is a charge of electricity power towers stacking up at the end of the disintegrating track, ready to explode.

Realising what is happening, Dan Casey sees Veena running towards him. She shouts at the top of her voice, "Come on, jump quickly. This place is going blow!"

Dan pushes himself and starts running faster towards Veena Merida, skipping over the flaring bursts of the damaged track surface, sprinting for his life.

The jade-eyed galactic rose screams and shouts desperately, "JUMP DAN!"

Veena's divine face shows her fear that he won't make it in time. Suddenly, there is an almighty BOOM of a massive backlash explosion.

Dan Casey leaps over the crumbling track, narrowly escaping the energised blast. The impact throws him into a piled heap on the ground next to the burning rubble and scattered parts of the conveyor track. Commander Calo Tarick is also hurled in the smoggy smoked air by the invigorating impact, clashing a fall on the upper side as a reinforced batch of Corporal Union Guards comes to his aid.

Veena Merida drops her red-lipsticked mouth in shock and horror, screaming, "Oh no, Dan!"

Veena is apprehensive and scared about what has just happened. Needing to pull herself together, she gasps, "Praise the galactic heavens; please be okay!"

She makes her way swiftly through the fire and smoke-filled area to where Dan Casey is lying on the smouldering floor, covered in rubble from the explosion and not moving a muscle. Veena takes a deep breath and urgently pushes the cremated components of the conveyor belt off Dan Casey's battered body. Using all her strength, she rolls him onto his back with a tearful, pleading check of his health, "Dan, come on! Wake up, please."

But with no immediate response from the cargo runner, Veena's face gasps as tears flow from her jade crystal eyes, "Don't you dare die on me, Mr Casey. There are so many things I must tell you; wake up!"

Veena bows to her knees, whispering close to Dan's blank, bruised face, "Like I've fallen in love with you, so I beg you, please wake up for your sweetheart?"

Veena Merida's trickling tears turn to watery drops of hopeful joy as suddenly Dan Casey coughs a groggy splutter, "Ah, huh, what the!"

He starts to realise his bearings, witnessing the sheer beautiful horizon of Veena Merida, gazing upon him with a gracious smile beaming like a bright shooting star.

"Oh! Dan, you're alive, thanks to the heavens. I was so worried."

She quickly helps her heart's fondness to his feet with an entangling cuddle of affection. Dan Casey smiles while blowing his messed-up black hair out of his dark brown, alluring eyes, connecting with Veena's colourful, dazzling gems. Cupping one hand around her tender sexual waist, his other cut-gloved hand fumbles in his pocket of torn quarter badge jacket, producing the astrological data box.

Veena passionately sweeps his slick hairstyle back as Dan hands over the problematic historical data box.

"I believe this belongs to you, Miss Merida."

Veena's heart is beating fast. "I'm pretty sure that's mine too, Mr Casey," she says emotionally, puckering up her red-glossed lips in a trancing urge to kiss him.

With the trader's space station falling apart around them, it is as if time stands still for their connected, loving bond. Neither would have expected the hijacked meeting in the back-alley lane of the dust ball moon, Latin-Versa would materialise into a mutual feeling of love.

Dan strokes his hand over her soft cheeks, attempting an embracing kiss as their lips hover a tingling tease.

An armoured Elite guard surprisingly blasts a wielding shot, just vaguely missing the affectionate couple. With a revised spring in their step, Dan and Veena dive a manoeuvring roll, simultaneously drawing the firearms in a maverick fashion and opening fire in their defence, cunningly blasting the pestering Corporal Union trooper to his demise, dropping him in his tracks.

Dan Casey swiftly takes hold of Veena's petite hand with a tucking pull; he tells her, "We gotta get off this cracking contraption before it blows to smithereens."

"Can't argue with that one, partner. Let us get out of here and quickly get to the *Decepter*."

The cargo pilot and galactic resistance agent hurriedly sprint to the docking bay, locked by hand.

Dan and Veena make haste, motioning a calculated time-dashed run to the smoke-riddled Hanger bay of the freighter. The cargo pilot catches sight of the red-haired slave girl he gave the lock-breaker to being helped to escape by the dreadlocked dark stranger he also clocked before the mayhem kicked off.

The remaining loyal Galanti slave guards are intently hounding both participants.

Dan shouts to the potential fellow allies, drawing his silver and black weapon, "Hey, Charlena! Quickly, this way, run fast."

Dan Casey ranges an offensive stance of cover fire, associated with the inspired Veena Merida, rearranging her infrared site with some high-glass precision shots. The enslaving trader guards fall aside one by one from Dan and Veena's crack-shot marksmanship.

This gives the gunslinger Jay Haines and the galactic student Charlena Jones the perfect opportunity to sprint aboard the *Decepter*'s entrance hatch, opened by the starship's loyal cyber navigation system Pearl. Without orders, she fires up the triple-slanted engines which produce a purring whistled hum.

Cunningly, two blaster cannons emerge from the slick coned nose of the spacecraft as Pearl activates the freighter vessel's weapon systems and readily assists cover for Dan and Veena to board for a daring escape from the doomed station.

Chapter Twelve

Trip Around the Dread Moon

The rusting space station owned by notorious crime lord Kingpin Mach Galanti spins vastly out of control. It is in immediate danger of impacting as the main reactor output core exceeds critical mass levels, erupting with clustered chained explosions. Its ageing, diameter-designed hull fractures and outdated control systems are no match for the developing and intensifying nucleonic wave projections coming from the detonator fusion core. System alarms go off as flared sparks light the primary chamber room. Emergency automated protocols are initiated, but it is too late to prevent a horrific disaster. The duteous Galanti-trained security trade operatives are frantically trying to evacuate onto any vacant starship possible to escape the powerful energy shockwaves that reverberate throughout the sleazoid hub. Its containment walls shatter, and large pieces of jagged debris scatter wildly into the hailstorm-bound atmosphere.

The sleazy space station is going down with a spiralling subsonic bang, and the remnants of the feared Galanti family's criminal empire and its loyal rogue supporters are facing their ultimate demise. While the heroic cargo-runner pilot Dan Casey and his newfound crew of misfits gather themselves inside the cockpit cabin of the *Decepter*, they are far from safe.

The robust Machiavellian MK2 Merlin class freighter tilts,

and using reverse thrust, the slick vessel makes its way through the frenetic carnage of the precarious hanger bay.

The crew's tensions are at a knife edge as Dan Casey takes his familiar upright position in his leather air-cushioned pneumatic pilot chair. The interstellar pilot concentrates on the task of getting everyone out alive. Still dressed in his quarter-torn jacket and ripped black pilot slacks, the sleeves of the rugged coat fold firmly as his cuffed finger-cut gloves grip the craft joystick, taking control of the flight helm.

The black-hair styled charismatic pilot asks the starship's built-in crystalised AI companion, "Hey Pearl, how long have we got till a certain impact, sweetie? We could do with a bit of a hurrying upon vacating the premises. I believe we may have outstayed our welcomed hospitality."

"Bio-scans completed, the station will implode in one minute five seconds and counting; welcome back on board, Miss Merida."

"You must stop those bio-scans and get your priorities in order. It is not the first time we had this debate. I'm guessing a minute warning is a fair time, considering the sort of week it has turned out to be."

"Hold on, everyone. This is going get scary; I'd buckle up tight if you are prone to getting woozy in life-threatening interstellar flight situations!"

Whereas, yet to seat her curvaceous, sexy figure, elegantly wearing a clinging black catsuit, the daring feminine shadow agent, Veena Merida, sways on her knee-high, booted heels, kindly attending to the buckle straps cords of the frightened Charlena Jones and politely obliges in turn to Pearl's hospitality, smoothly in her enticing posh-toned voice.

"Thank you so much, Pearl. I'm pleased to be able to make a personal reappearance in gratitude for Dan's bravery; now we need your combined efforts to get us out of the hellfire space station."

Turning to Charlena, she continues, "Hi. It's a pleasure to be an acquaintance. I'm Veena Merida. Don't worry, young girl, we shall get through this traumatic ordeal. I promise."

As the cute, soft-spoken, but renegade mindset teenager wittingly replies, "Hey, thank you! I'm Charlena Jones. It's nice to meet you, Veena. You're a beautiful woman, but to be blunt, I'm not a kid. I've just killed a monster, and I will be turning eighteen soon, and Jay looks a lot more scared than me!"

The dark, handsomely toned, dreadlocked gunslinger-for-intergalactic hire nervously tilts his shaded glasses at the tension-smirking females.

"Oh man, we're not going to make it. This rusty old dump bucket is going to blow, and we only got a small window to float out of; things are looking very dicey to me. Damn, girl! Your sweet mother told me you are too enthusiastic for your good."

Jays straps himself in the back cockpit seat accommodation and holds tight to the safety harness pull-cords.

"I'm Jay Haines, ma'am, technically a private help for hire at your humble service if needed, that's if your hotshot pilot, Dan Casey, can get us out of this foreseen danger zone in time!"

"Rest assured, Mr Haines, if any interstellar pilot can evade us from this burning place, it's my partner!"

Veena turns around and straps herself in. "Don't worry. Hey! Have faith. Dan and Pearl get into impossible dire situations like this all the time, don't you, darling!"

The spinning wretched station is falling apart as the charismatic, charmed pilot momentarily pauses at the flight helm controls with a bewildered glance.

"Okay, Pearl. Let's show this new crew how we cargo runners get paid for a living. Swing us out a hell of here, sweetie. It's time to go home. Punch it, Pearl!"

And with Dan's inspired motivational words, the *Decepter* Machiavellian starship slickly manoeuvres a spinning drone thrust. The ship smashes its slender frame coned nose through the station's wrecked Hanger bay fragmentations with a screeched roaring burst of accelerated speed, and their timely race against the engulfed flaring explosions fiercely coincides with a swept tracking of the *Decepter*. The vigorous freighter starship engines scintillate a glistening blur with a widening margin of fate.

They whoosh out of the exploding doomed trade ring space station without a moment to spare. Suddenly, within an instant of the *Decepter*'s exuberant departure follows a bright yellow blinding flash-bang with swirling red flames and a silent delay engaged by a deafening sonic boom.

A massive explosion roars, ripping the wheel-cogged space station into two, sending burning shattered debris in all scattered directions. The impact blast wave hurls around the dark expanse of the Sera system illuminated by lightning-crackled flashes. One of the rouge scout patrol ships in the vicinity gets caught in the massive blast, causing it to instantly lose orbit as the craft attempts to set a fleeing course away from the explosion.

The sleazy marauder's vessel spins evidently out of control, twisting a veered dive, crashing into the exploding space station with an earth-shattering boom, causing further destruction. Meanwhile, the other weasel-owned starships who attended the Galanti families' slave-trade event, including the mighty Galileo Cruiser of the Corporal Union, thrust into highly evasive action. It is desperately trying to evade the danger. It prepares to scatter a forging passage through the hailstorm environment, chaining up the quad-powered afterburners in an attempt to escape the blast wave impact.

The *Decepter* Merlin class freighter is soaring through the unsettled turbulence atmosphere of the untamed electrical cosmic storms that fiercely curse the perilous outer-rim sector of the Sera system. Courageously inside the cockpit cabin are the dashing cargo pilot, Dan Casey and the intelligent cyber-AI navigation assistant, Pearl.

The sleek Machiavellian MK2 vessel galvanises a coordinated course in a straight fashion of its silhouette haul frame. They are trying to outrun the shock wave blast from the ill-omened trader's slave station, which vigorously washed an expanding octane solar flare deviating across the already dark thunderous environment. This is a troubling feature for any class interstellar pilot to overcome.

The swirling energy blaze dangerously starts to caress the rear end of the *Decepter*, causing the starship to skid. Anxiousness is deeply evolving from within the tense cockpit as Veena Merida confesses her fear concerns from the co-pilot quarter,

"You got this dead-to-rights, Dan, yeah! I'm not saying I'm faltering in trust and your piloting abilities, but it's starting to feel extremely dizzy in here, or is it just me?"

"Ain't just you, lady. We are pushing this to the limit. Oh, man! Hope you can get us out of here, Casey, or we will all be galactic-fired toast." Jay Haines' attractive voice bellows over the pulsating vibrations of the gurgling triple-powered booster engines.

Jay's hunky, dark-allured figure tremors while shaking in the passenger row seat as the brave gunslinger readily offers his supporting hand across to the trembling Charlena Jones. The young galactic student, still in her white-wrapped slave outfit, reaches over from the coinciding flight seat, accepting Jay's kindness once more in the face of danger, with a tight squeeze grip and a silent, endearing smile.

The starship's emergency siren blares through the flight cabin with a serious effect, mulling a red-shaded flashing echo around the craft's interior, stating the sense of urgency. At the pilot helm crafting his skilled fortunes of the profession, Dan Casey has his masterful hands firmly gripped around the joystick controls, weaving the siding vibrations and trying to ride out the stormy grooves from the exasperating solar flare. With tensions rising high and the sweat dripping from his strenuous brow, the daring, under-pressure cargo pilot shouts out complex instructions to the cyber assistant,

"Pearl, we need to get out of the range of this impact wave, switch and divert all power to the boosters; it's now or never, sweetie."

Pearl confirms, "Engaging full maximum power to sublight boosters."

The slanted engines of the *Decepter* starship emit a brilliant blue glow as they accelerate rapidly, thrusting at the critical moment, leaving a trail of danger in their wake. Dan Casey and Pearl successfully navigate through the hazardous blast wave threat with whooshing, deft rolls, and evasive manoeuvres. They press on boldly towards the foreboding destination of the dreaded black moon's asteroid belt, poised to enter the jump to the hyper-speed lanes.

Inside the starship cockpit, the atmosphere is filled with jubilant celebrations and joy as the *Decepter*'s crew is overwhelmed by the near-miss escape. Dan Casey shouts out in appraisal and relieved laughter while easing off the throttle lever and setting the flight controls to auto-cruise. "Woo! Way to go, Pearl. I never doubted you for a moment, sweetie." He swings his leather reclining pilot chair around to check on the others, "Is everyone okay?"

Veena Merida quickly releases her harness cords and flings them to one side, expressing her gratitude, leaning across the co-pilot chair for a hug. Without the need for words, their starry eyes lock together with a tranced effect.

Dan caresses Veena's enchanted face, anticipating her desire for a kiss. But their actions are interrupted by a joyful slap on their compressed shoulders followed by a deep laugh.

"Wow! Man, nice flying back there; I'm in awe. I must confess that I thought we would get fried."

Dan and Veena smile towards each other with a sigh. Simultaneously, they turn their flustered attention to the dreadlocked passenger.

"I'm Jay Haines, a private gunslinger for hire. I never had time to introduce myself properly! We had one lucky escape! The way you two dismantled that Galanti deathtrap of a space station will be broadcasting across the Mbron Media for an eternity. I was hired by this young girl's mother to free her from the enslaving grip of Mach Galanti. Your help back there was invaluable, so thank you, both."

Jay Haines suddenly swings his jubilant attention around, feeling a tap on his broad shoulders. He tilts his circular shades, witnessing Charlena Jones unstrap the safety belts, shaking her head with a wave of her red-bobbed hair.

Bewildered by her actions, Jay asked the young student, "Hey, what's the matter with you, kid!"

"Well, for instance, you don't interrupt a kiss. I can tell you've been single for a long time. Two, STOP calling me a kid. I will have words with Mum about who she sends to rescue me next time." Now, turning to the pilot, she says, "Thanks for saving me, Mr Casey; you warned it would be noisy. Oh, boy! It went boom. Where are we going now?"

Dan Casey welcomes both new acquaintances aboard.

"Glad to oblige, Jay, and I'm more than pleased you got free, Charlena, but I can honestly admit that blowing up a space station wasn't the initial plan; it was meant to be more of a snatch and grab operation. Our next destination is the Isadora system. It could bring up more danger on the way, so it might be best to drop you off at a haven port."

Merida agrees with Dan Casey's decision for a commercial starport. In her posh tones, she explains the importance and repercussions of their mission while revealing the data box to Jay and Charlena.

"We have to deliver this star-chart device to an unknown location and prevent it from falling into the hands of the Corporal Union to save Kalanisi Universe from a sinister force. I'm unsure what to expect, and I'm a part of the galactic resistance agency, so I wouldn't want you both involved or to endanger your lives."

Charlena Jones's eyes nearly pop out of her sweet head, witnessing the mystical object in Veena's palm hand.

"Whoa! It's an astrological databox from lore gone by? Gee, where did you get that from? It's so exciting I'm in; let's go to the Isadora system."

"No, girl. You're going home to your dear mother in Kothariya. I gave her my promise that I'd bring you back safely, not going around the galaxy and chasing mythical ancient lores. Plus, talking about things like that scares the damn shit out of me."

Dan replies, "I can accommodate getting you to safety once we pass this Dread Moon's asteroid belt, but the human capital world, Kothariya, has become a no-go zone for me and Veena. After the little stunt we just pulled, we will be listed as galactic fugitives against the human governmental state."

Dan then swings his leather pilot chair back around to the flashing subsystems and presets the *Decepter*'s flight controls to the trajectory coordination for the jump to hyperspace.

The gorgeous green-haired agent backs up the cargo runner's theory of legal containment. "Dan's correct in what he mentioned; if either of us steps foot on the planet of Kothariya, there will be an automatic arrest followed by public execution for the crimes we have committed. Director Wilson Volantis has no interest in public relations or even a fair play trial. Our best option would be to find you a safe starport en route to the Isadora system. Otherwise, you might be classed as an accessory to our cause."

She whispers with an annoyed sigh, "You better come good, Tara!"

The *Decepter* MK2 freighter is being piloted on a digital auto cruise with the assistance of Pearl as the sleek hauled craft readily approaches the spooky moon's asteroid ring belt perimeter, cutting a fine sweeping trail through the misty storm haze with crackles of lightning scarring across the starship.

While firmly seated in the cockpit, Dan Casey reaches over for his packet of smokes. He squarely flicks a filter, catching it in his appealing mouth with a glance over to Veena, teasingly commenting on her past actions, "Hey, I half expected you to snatch my smoke. What's the matter, Veena?"

With a deep breath, Veena turns her perched elegance towards Dan and explains what has been dwelling on her mind, "Well, it is about Tara Harlow's planned destination in the Isadora sector and how remote shadow agents operate across the Kalanisi Galaxy."

Dan Casey takes the green-dust filter away from his puzzled face, asking the bashful female agent, "How well do you know Tara Harlow? And what are we looking for in the Isadora system exactly, an agent base or a resistance armada fleet? Don't tell me you're not an agent, Veena."

"Haha! Of course I'm an agent. Gosh!" says the fluttering jade-eyed beauty. "But as a remote agent, I've never met the boss and have no idea what to expect. We work on signal communications. I'm sure it will all be fine, though. Phew! Now I feel much better for getting that off my chest. Shall we hit the hyper-lanes, partner!"

Before a gobsmacked Dan Casey can reply to the green-haired madam, suddenly, there is a thunderous roar in the Sera system, veering a short distance behind the *Decepter*. A ship emerges from the blast flare clouds of the doomed trader's station.

The rebellious gunslinger Jay Haines shouts, "Hey, you guys, that sounded and felt bad!"

Alert to the imposing threat, Dan Casey quickly attends to the flick switches controls, turning on the starship's hydraulic systems and firmly grabbing hold of the joystick lever.

He answers Jay's query, "It's the *Galileo* BX10 battle cruiser, which can only mean one definition of worse than bad!"

Veena Merida shouts out, "TARICK!"

Dan Casey warns his newfound crew, "Buckle up tight, everyone, as I doubt Commander Him is going to give up the ghost without a fight; it's just not in his nature. Pearl, activate evasive manoeuvres and forward deflector shields to our rear guard."

"Defective systems initiated, advance weapons are online. We have a holo-communication demand pending from the *Galileo* BX10."

Veena Merida enquires, "Can't we jump to hyperspace and try to run him into the slipstream matrix?"

"The only problem with that escape option is that the oversized *Galileo* BX10 will track our trajectory through the hyper-lanes. Like before, I will have to spin out your cute bootie again, sweetheart!"

"Gosh! Dan, behave. We have a young child on board; concentrate on the matter."

A sweet voice floats over the starship's interior, buzzing flight instruments, "Carry on. Don't worry about the minor, Jay! He's got his eyes shut again anyhow!" says the young renegade student, quickly leaning forward in her padded passenger seat.

Charlena is eager as ever and duly enquires about the tracing danger of the *Galileo* BX10 battleship,

"Who gave us chase, Mr Casey? That nasty man with the metal patch you were fighting on the conveyor belt back at the slave station? I guess they are after the mythical lore data box?"

Dan Casey responds to the young girl's enthused intuition while swiftly pushing his hand on the starship's throttle lever to initiate more subspeed velocity, "Yeah, that's the menacing man, Charlena. But we aren't going to let him get the data box now, are we?"

Veena squats on the edge of the co-pilot quarters and alertly browses the *Decepter*'s radar navigation display while asking the handsome cargo pilot what he has planned. "I don't know what you got in mind, but you better perform it sprightly. Tarick's onto us, closing the deficit extremely fast."

The beautiful feminine agent's view of upstanding concern is equally backed up by Jay Haines, "No way! Can we take on that damn mother of a cruiser in a fair fight and expect to be victoriously on top!"

"That's why you always try to negotiate first, Jay. Or at least buy yourself some time. Pearl, connect to the comms!" says Dan Casey, using the diplomacy skills from his space protection training days.

The *Decepter* quickens with a slicing whoosh through the electrified storms of the Dread Moon's asteroids.

The fearful *Galileo* BX10 battle cruiser is fully ranging in close behind, executing a driven pursuit of the Machiavellian freighter. Calo Tarick's patrol flagship has taken immense damage, travelling an escape route through the sonic blast wave. The quad-purported engines purr a roaring rumble of the fire-stricken *Galileo* BX10. The outer armoured shield plates break away from the vessel's haul, performing to their limits while barging their presence forth under the guidance of Commander Tarick. Seated inside the towering bridge control helm of the Corporal Union's Imposing flagship, the disgruntled metal-patched face of Calo Tarick glares intensely from his scarred eye at the forward view, cunningly enduring the inflicted pain from his torn-away cybernetic arm. The first officer on deck informs the focused Commander with a progress report in a positive tone.

"The fugitive freighter vessel is now in range of our blast cannons, and the villainess scum has accepted our holo-communication demands, sir!" says the first-rank officer standing firm in his black slack uniform, awaiting his orders.

The dark-bulked figure of Calo Tarick doesn't move a muscle. "Connect me to the holo-comm transmission, lock in a range of our triple shot scatter guns and prepare two batches of BX19 Corsair fighters. There will be no escaping the law this time, Mr Casey."

Meanwhile, at the head of affairs on board, the Machiavellian Merlin MK2 class freighter is cruising into the Dread Moon's atmosphere. Dan Casey and his mixed crew brace themselves for trouble as the holo communications exchange connects a link. With a firm caressing grip over the joystick, the brave cargo pilot sits upright in his reclining flight chair, exuding confidence.

Dan takes charge of the tense interchange, "Commander Tarick, you seem to be tracking the rear stern of my starship. We duly appreciate the Corporal Union's escort out of the Sera system. Still, I can assure you it's unnecessary as I now have civilians on board who have no part in our field, so shelve your obsession. I suggest you lower your energised weapons and let us go peacefully! If you are a true man of honour, do we have an accordance, Calo?"

"I decline your offer of acceptance bullshit, Mr Casey! In serving your last rights as an intergalactic terrorist of the Corporal Union state, any member of the public coinciding with such actions will be intently included in your punishment of execution by the arm of my abidance to the law. I shall carve that damn data box out of the remains of your rust-bucket vessel once destroyed and in pieces. Do we have accordance, scum!"

Dan maintains a steady gaze at the metal-patched menace that dares to challenge his peace offer. "I expected much better from you, Commander! So which arm of the law are you planning on pulling these threats off with as you look a bit unbalanced and flaky like your battle cruiser."

The immediate response from the fuming, insulted Commander Tarick results in angered words of an offensive, driven, sinister nature, "Officer One, commence the nucleation of Mr Casey's outdated starship and his worthless crew. Open fire!"

With unwavering shelled confidence from Commander Calo Tarick, the holographic transmissions cease abruptly, disrupted by terminated interference from the *Galileo* BX10 patrol ship that silences the echoing verbalisation in the *Decepter*'s flight cabin.

Dan Casey warns the novice crew, "Hold tight, everyone. Brace yourselves. This is going to get a little rough."

The *Decepter* Machiavellian class freighter assertively twists an agile swoop, navigating the hazardous asteroid field surrounding the ominous Dread Moon, evading the penetrable strikes from the *Galileo* BX10 warship's triple scatter blast cannons. Commander Tarick's horrific scoped cruiser is angling a steadfast pursuit for the *Decepter*, swiftly reloading the triple mechanised turrets and readily opening fire with the supporting aid of duel batched BX19 Corsair fighters. Stretching a weathering lead into the hailstorm haze of the asteroid ring, the *Decepter* cradles a rocking ride, sleekly levelling off into the turbulence-lightning-struck grooves of the orbital atmosphere creeping around the hideous Dread Moon.

Panic has set in the exhilarated cockpit of the fleeing freighter as the dreadedlocked gunslinger points out, "We got Corsair fighters on our tail, four approaching fast."

While intensely seated at the pilot quarters with more than enough on his plate, Dan Casey asks for help, "Jay, I could do with you upfront. I need a co-pilot if we're going to get out of this predicament."

Quickly responding to the cargo runner's urge, Jay Haines laughs off the suggestion, "You gotta be joking, man. I only fly in straight lines, and that's mainly on autopilot, but I can manage these rear gun turrets if Pearl has got the front cannons covered."

Dan Casey momentarily slants his engrossed attention aside to Veena Merida, witnessing her grabbing onto the safety harness cords for dear life with her jade eyes tightly closed.

The dashing pilot asks with a serious plea and sweeping flick of his dark, messy hair out of his face, "How do you feel about your first flying lesson, sweetheart!" With a paused, hesitant reply, Veena opens her petrified eyes, "Gosh! You must be desperate if you need me to fly. I haven't a clue. I can try, but one hoped the negotiations would have turned out better. I told you Tarick wanted to kill us all; you should have blown him a kiss as you did to Terri!"

Surprised by Veena's speculation of the night at the races with her childhood friend, Dan Casey enquires with a depth of interest to her verbal statement, "Where did that ridiculous comment come from, Veena? And flick the top hydraulic switch."

"Well, that ridiculous quote is straight from Miss Lace's kissable lips. We had a right old girl talk on the way to that floating space prison. What switch? They all look the same!"

Suddenly, a shadow and youthful arm leans in from behind the co-pilot quarters, flicking on the hydraulic power switch. Dan and Veena, not for the first time, line up mutual eye contact with a turn of heads, bringing their shocked attention to galactic student Charlena Jones, who is breathing heavily and eager to help.

"You know how to pilot a starship?" Bewildered, Dan responds with a smile over to the young red-haired girl.

Charlena replies with a host of encouragement, "Not quite in real-time pursuit, but I had the top score on an intergalactic wingman holo-net space-fighter competition for two years running. That's before I started investigating the Galanti family."

Veena quickly releases the harness straps and removes her curved elegance from the co-pilot seat, swapping her position immediately with the red-bobbed renegade student with a highly praised proposal, "You're a resourceful young girl. Ever thought of becoming a galactic resistance agent?"

"Don't give her crazy ideas, lady; she's already a fired-up wildcard and I hope you all are shuffled and settled as we got company!" says the skilled marksman scanning the vector approach of the BX19 Corsair fighters, readily gripping hold of the trigger-style operating system.

At the front helm of the *Decepter*, Dan Casey spritely takes control of the levered joystick and thrashes forward the throttle, tensely muttering, "Okay, here we go, kiddo. Nothing too cocky now; just keep it simple; everything will be fine!"

As the newfound co-pilot Charlena Jones replies with a brief reminder to the cargo runner's words of wisdom, "I've got your lead, but I ain't no kid!"

Dan, amused in the face of danger, informs the young student, "I was momentarily talking about myself, Charlena. Stay with me now and keep it tight, sweetheart."

The sleek MK2 freighter swoops into action with a diverted swivelling dive to the Dread Moon's rock-formed surface. The *Decepter*'s dual rear artillery opens fire with the raw intelligence guidance of Jay Haines, judging the aim of the swift stealth fighters. They remain followed by the awe-inspiring *Galileo* BX10 starcruiser ranging in with a droned manoeuvring offensive pitch repetitively opening fire on the triple scatter cannons. This causes destruction and atmospheric chaos as the veering blast rounds collide with the twisting orbital asteroids. The sweeping BX19 Corsair fighters slip into pairs, opening fire on their short-range laser chain cannons simultaneously. The *Decepter* starship constantly drops in altitude, skimming the boundaries of the lightning-struck Dread Moon. But not without taking some rear-blast haul damage hits from the crafty BX19 Corsair starfighters.

Feeling the impact inside the Machiavellian class freighter, Dan Casey seemingly has trust in the reputational private hire gunslinger. "Get those jackals off our rear tail, Jay. Pearl transfers all sub-power to rear deflector shields," shouts out the slick cargo pilot amid the galactic battle while fully engaged in piloting to safety.

Jay Haines reassures the wavering crew of his sharp hawkeye abilities, "I've got these hounds locked and fired. There's no need for concern. It's child-play, dudes." The dark-shot gunslinger redeems the quick-fire trigger and readily blasts the rear turret cannons with a stylish crossfire display trailing from the back of the *Decepter*. Instinctively with purpose, he catches the attacking BX19 Corsair stealth fighter with a devastating fireball-flashed explosion.

"Oh, man! That's what I'm talking about, you fried starfighter. I dare these Corporal Union duped goons to bring it on."

While tensely perched in the buckled-up flight seat next to the Elite crack-shot gunman, Veena Merida congratulates him. "Nice shooting, Mr Haines. There are three more fighters to go and one monstrous battle cruiser, and we're home free. Ha! Piece of cake, right?"

Dan Casey indicates to the red-fringed female co-pilot, "We got one BX19 Corsair fighter that's manoeuvred a slipstream and gone by Jay's zone range of scaling blast fire. It's tracking our six with intent to harm. Okay, Charlena, I require a stern starboard jolt on my mark. Two, three, break!"

Simultaneously, the cool-headed Dan Casey and eager-to-please Charlena Jones harmonise their dual performance and quickly crank the levered joysticks to execute a sharp right slam. The *Decepter*'s triple-slanted boosters screech a whistling vroom, evasively shimmering a quarter-looped roll, avoiding an oncoming asteroid cluster. The fast-stalking BX19 Corsair scout fighter alternately copies the same manoeuvre without successful time to evade the orbital mass danger. Inevitably, the fragile amour-plated BX19 stealth drone clips its stubbed angled wings and spins off, veeringly into a fatal explosion. Their counterpart Corsair squadron soon prolongs the attack chase, swarming low on either side around the *Decepter* as they close into the vicinity of the Dread Moon mountaintop canyon.

Lightning bolts materialise deadly electrical strikes on the dark crater moon's unnatural surface. Rock-pounding eruptions turn into a haze-mist atmosphere, thus ensuring a difficult navigation passage around the forbidding Dread Moon. The *Decepter* MK2 freighter swiftly swoops in on a low-set projection with a swivelling rocketry sweep of the deteriorated conditions. The Machiavellian Merlin class vessel is being devilishly tracked and heavily bombarded with intense offensive laser blasts, galivanting from the persisting BX19 Corsair fighters.

While inside the functioning cockpit at the pilot's helm, Dan announces with a pool of tension escaping his smooth, attractive voice, "They are trying to flank us into submission and cut off our course of evacuation. Be ready on the rear guns, Jay. I need you to read the forthcoming script."

Jay Haines replies while calibrating a turret reload, "I'm adaptable to any hostile narrative which involves shooting, man!"

The stunning galactic feminine agent feels slightly left out of the preparation procedure. Witnessing the crew working as a revolving team, Veena Merida bravely perks up her courage with a frantic facial expression as she spoke out in a fading posh voice, "Anything you require me to perform at hand, apart from being exceptionally woozy and potentially faint!"

"Shut your pretty eyes and keep smiling, sweetheart! We shall get through this problem. I promise."

He grips the accelerator throttle with his anxious dark brown eyes peeling over the radar dials, witnessing the bleeping dots indicating the Corsair fighters are closing on their arrest.

Pearl flashes a crystalised warning in her cyber voice, "Corporal Union BX19 scout crafts flanking forefront and posterior tail haul. Anterior Gatling weapons activated."

"I know, sweetie, they're trying to box us into the crater canyons. Let us show them how we handle uninvited Dread Moon traffic. Okay! Miss Jones, now. SWITCH IT," says Dan Casey, constantly pushing forth on the portside power throttle.

Meanwhile, Charlena Jones nervously pulls back intently on the decelerating starboard side boosters. The *Decepter* weaves a fluctuating skid manoeuvre, flying only with the portside turbine burners to maximise operation. The freighter's silhouette sequences a drift of the rock-gravelled belt along the Dread Moon. Skimming the canyon venture with a side-shifting quaver, Pearl rapidly lets loose and opens fire on the front array of the Gatling guns, thus tactically taking advantage as the BX19 Corsair speedily flies by with a withering run, becoming the ranged exterminated target of the *Decepter*'s weapons. The rear dual laser turrets coordinate a coinciding assault on the tracking Corsair fighter with mutual devastating effect as both Corporal Union stealth enforcer's spacecraft impact into a flash-sparking of flames.

Casey and Charlena Jones swiftly alternate the turbine throttles to a stabilised conduct, levelling off the starship to a balanced vector. They defeat the slingshot manoeuvre with exceeding relief and overwhelming joy and delight.

Dan executes a high-five slap of impressed congratulations over to Charlena, who returns with a gasping cute smile responding to the kind gesture. "Oh boy, I can't fathom we just performed that equation and survived to tell the tale."

Jay Haines leans a reaching arm forward from his leather gunslinger ammo-belted jacket with a back-patting bundle of praise, "Way to go, man! That is some damn skilled flying if I've ever seen it before, and you, kid! Wait till I tell your mother her daughter is a little gem genius!"

"Who are you and Pearl? I don't know much about your background, Dan. That piloting is exemplary second to none, and Charlena, I believe you have seriously outranked your holo-net wingman top score. My gosh! I'm impressed with you both, but we still have the daunting, troubled matter of Commander Tarick."

His *Galileo* BX10 battle cruiser submerges from the hailstorm asteroid ring in a tilted diving procession, disrespectfully ploughing into peak mountain canyon tops as the hazardous lightning bolts score over the starship's front haul. The fearsome triple cannons open fire, scattering a mortified pattern of imploding crater holes over the moon.

The *Decepter* urgently weaves accelerating low, skimming through the rock-strewn valley, masterfully evading the dust cloud explosions the driven-for-order Corporal Union Commander sets upon them. The option of dodging for cover soon starts to look bleak as the *Decepter* crew mulls over their escaping possibility.

Jay Haines is the first to raise the concern, "We can't keep up this running saga. Our tiny guns are no match for that mother of a starship, man! We wouldn't even dent their armour. Any ideas for a new plan are needed and fast, brother."

Charlena Jones sits fixated at the co-pilot helm. Her fiery red hair blows around her shapely face as she navigates the twisting, rocky maze with raw bravery. She steals a quick, confused glance as her blue eyes meet the handsome cargo pilot's, awaiting instructions.

Veena Merida tries to exhibit her inspirational thoughts during challenging circumstances, providing a genuine source of motivation without the intention of being taken seriously. She comfortably says in her attractive posh voice, "Why don't we just turn around and fly the other way? Let Commander Tarick ransack his battle cruiser into one of the mountains. Use the obstacles as an advisable weapon. It seems we are the more agile starship!"

"Yeah, brilliant idea, Veena! We shall take Commander Him out of the equation."

He swiftly looks behind at the love-smitten female agent, who is backtracking on her advice, "It is just a figure of foolish speech, trust me. I haven't a clue about interstellar starship tactics. Please don't follow anything I suggest in such an unsteady frame of mind. GOSH! We shall all crash!"

Dan Casey gives Veena the respect she deserves. "Don't sell yourself short, partner! I like the plan. It's nice and simple, and the blotchy, scarred eye of Calo Tarick will never see it coming."

Dan says, "Pearl, I need you to deactivate the deflector shields and transfer all power to the turbines. I'm sure Jay can cover guard for us a tab and create a smokescreen distraction."

The starship's onboard AI system flashes a crystallised response, activating the power exchange. In his deep, husky voice, Jay Haines replies, "I'm on it, man!" He instantly opens fire on the pursuing *Galileo* BX10 warcraft.

Veena Merida leans forward in the turbulence conditions from the rear passenger seat as her green frazzled hair invades her cosmetic-infused face, and with a puffing blow, she asks, "What have I advised we're to do again?"

Dan Casey replies, "We're going to slingshot around that mountain canyon top and give Commander Calo Tarick a flashing kiss goodbye, just as you proposed. Very cunning."

"I may have converted my idea into a slightly different context. Gosh! Sounds amazing, let's do it, honey!" says the sexy resistance agent, reissuing her harness belt tight and secure in preparation for Dan Casey's escaping venture of the Dread Moon.

Commander Calo Tarick bellows his orders to the crew deck, "Launch another squadron of BX19s and close in on our perimeter range of cannon fire. This mess needs cleaning up now; it's our top priority, and failure is not an option."

"Sir, I duly regret to acknowledge that our remaining Corsair fighters were damaged during the escape of the sonar blast wave explosion. The *Galileo* BX10 has taken immense damage. Our perimeter cannons are offline. Plus, Dan Casey demands a communication link. He says it's your last chance to surrender," the first officer nervously relays, standing proudly dressed in his black slated peaked cap uniform.

Calo Tarick laughs, a deep, bewildered response to the first officer's development. "So Casey's calling the shots now, is he? Haha. I dither in not being sure to admire his damn boldness or his sheer stupidity in taking me on.

"First Officer, connect me the comm-link and give the fantasising fugitive pilot his final audience before I truly disintegrate his beloved *Decepter*."

The fearfulness of *Galileo* vessel's holo link communication screen mobilises to prevail a buzz-flicking digital image of Dan Casey saluting with a holding swipe and warning message, "Give up the ghost, Tarick! Surrender this insane pursuit, and I might let you go with your life!"

"Ha, I'm more inclined to witness how you will achieve your objectives. Then, I will surrender myself to the cargo-runner vermin. Have you not noticed that my classy starcruiser is much bigger than your discoloured bucket freighter, and your toy single-shot guns only tickle my fanciable ego? What are you planning on doing, Mr Casey? Getting the crew to shout boo out the rear cargo hold?" mocked Calo Tarick, imposingly standing on the bridge deck of the *Galileo* BX10 with a cunningly evil and dry smile pervading his scar-cut dark-skinned face, and his missing cybernetic limb sparking a traced fuse in the mighty vessel's dimmed lights.

Dan Casey quickly responds smugly and bluntly, "RIP, pal." He cuts the transmission off, leaving a static ripple stench of defiance in the air.

"Enough of this damn nonsense, first officer. I demand you to destroy that fool and blow up his rugged starship to oblivion." Commander Calo Tarick orders in a trifle-raged temperament, agitated by Dan's free-willed spirit.

The supreme *Galileo* BX10 battleship moves in for the lethal assault, advancing low altitudes with the quickness of thrusting speed and blazing triple cannons at their mere disposal, severely smashing into the ghastly foundations of the rock-formed valley pursuing the *Decepter* MK2 freighter through the electrical low mist storms.

Seated at the pilot control helm, Dan Casey focuses on the navigation radar dials with his fingerless-cut gloved hands, pulsing on the joystick lever and throttle. The daring crew's emotional tension is at a silent knife edge as they travel at high velocity towards a head-on collision with the spooky Dread Moon's largest canyon peak mountain.

Suddenly, the interstellar pilot says, "Pearl, flash our unruly Commander Tarick a welcoming goodbye."

Dan Casey breaks the vocal silence and slams forth on the throttle control. The *Decepters*' booster flares up with a captivating roar, tactically releasing a batch of four EMP floating mines from the craft's exterior. Sparks began to form around the *Galileo* BX10 patrol cruiser.

The Corporal Union's deck crew notices a shower of electric flashes emanating from the front hull and quad engines. They quickly realise that something is wrong and try to assess the situation. In moments, all power to the hyperdrive and subsystems goes offline, rendering the BX10 Brigadier Cruiser helpless. The imposing battleship starts spiralling into an uncontrollable nosedive, with a howling eerie whistle protruding from the stuttering engines. The first-ranked officer frantically tries to regain control and stabilise the vessel. However, the battle cruiser's altitude is too low to recover, and the situation quickly turns dire as the droning vessel hurtles towards the jagged crater's mountaintop, with Commander Calo Tarick and his obedient crew bracing themselves for the inevitable fatal crash. The *Galileo* warship crashes into the musky rock terrain of the Dread Moon, slamming down with a thunderous explosion. Boom! Skidding an unstoppable scuttering into the enormous mountain canyon top.

The armoured plates of the *Galileo* dreadnaught's slanted haul fold upon impact, followed by more intensified explosions tearing the stricken vessel into shattering parts inside the doomed cruiser. Commander Calo Tarick and his loyal first officer are slung across the disintegrating bridge, screaming in terror for their lives, colliding into the burning interior with no chance of escaping their fateful demise. As the black mountain crumbles, fragmentations of sliding debris rock over onto the BX10 *Galileo* cruiser's ghostly defeated image. The Machiavellian MK2 *Decepter* swiftly manoeuvres a slingshot hook around the falling canyon peak, vastly gaining speed and higher altitude while escaping the dark Dreaded Moon.

Chapter Thirteen

Duel in the Stars

The stylish *Decepter* MK2 freighter carves a safe passage through the daunting asteroid belt, pulling vastly away from the Dread Moon's horrific atmospheric orbit, confidently manoeuvring with a whooshing sweep of authority. Inside the starship's cockpit, the crew's feelings are filled with prosperous hope and emotional joy at the success of defeating Commander Tarick and his menacing *Galileo* BX10 battle cruiser.

Dan Casey is the first to praise his new crew for their heroic efforts while seated in his pneumatic pilot's chair, guiding his starship through the last strains of the hazardous asteroid ring,

"Top marks everybody on that springboard performance! Charlena, your co-piloting skills are excellent, and Jay, your marksmanship is as outstanding as any gunslinger I've ever met.

"Phew! I'd say more nervous luck than skill on my behalf; thank you for your piloting guidance, Mr Casey. It is so much more exciting than galactic college studies," replies the young student.

Veena Merida comments on their combined bravery, "You were all amazing. Without your countless acts of heroism, I'd be in a Corporal Union prison or worse! Thank you all kindly; I wish I could have been more helpful than the dizzy, embarrassed mascot."

Meanwhile, seated next to the jade-eyed beauty at the weapons quarter, Jay Haines gently pats the blushing Veena Merida on her elegant, defined shoulder, still dressed in her catsuit, congratulating her in his deep, husky, allured voice.

"Hey! Ma'am, without your crazy idea, we would still be scouting the belle of that nasty mother of a rock crater moon, so stand up and take a bow. Don't be a shy lady."

"Yeah, Jay's correct, sweetheart! Your intervention was priceless at a crucial point, and without Calo Tarick dogging our tail, we should at least get a clear slip-jump to the Isadora system. Once we drop off our exclusive guests, then we can find out if this astrological data box and the mythical Tara Harlow were worth the damn trouble."

"Don't worry, Dan, you will get your contract payment as promised, and Tara Harlow is not a myth! She is just a very elusive woman. And for the ancient lore data box: true or not? I can only confirm what Director Wilson Volantis remarked; he seemed very intent and sincere in finding an uncharted black hole called the Vortex at all costs."

Charlena Jones turns her recliner co-pilot seat around, facing her colleagues, commenting on the subject with awe and enthusiasm, "The ancient lore myths suggest the mysterious data box is from a time ago, long before we colonised the Kalanisi Universe."

With intrigued interest, Dan Casey asks the sweet minor, "What else do you know about this puzzle cube myth?"

Veena politely says to the young red-haired girl, "Yes, please, carry on. It could be meaningful knowledge for the mission."

With an adventurous smile, Charlena explains, "The rumours tell us the data box is a gift from the divine prophets and was awarded to the galactic royal family called Dela. The two princesses had the choice to find a golden world in which to live happily after. Still, after unforeseen circumstances, one of the princesses chose the Vortex, opening the black hole and releasing all demonic hell on the Kalanisi Universe until the extinction of all life."

Suddenly, deep laughter fills the starship cockpit, "Haha! Oh, come on, kid. You don't believe in all that hocus-pocus nonsense of historic galactic folklore? They are just made-up silly bedtime stories," says Jay Haines, leaning back in the weapon division seating with his muscular flexed arms resting behind his head and a dubious sceptical smile.

Politely retaliating, Charlena informs the amused gunslinger, "If they are just bedtime stories, why do we have an astrological data box on the starship? Hey! Bright eyes?"

Veena unzips her black scuffed handbag and fumbles around for the data box. "The clever girl has some valid points. So, fractions of the myth lore must tell the truth. I have the ancient star chart to prove it."

Jay Haines says, "Oh, ma'am! Put that thing away just in case it is real and goes off."

Dan Casey also has mixed thoughts on the ancient myth.

"I sort of side with you, Jay. But the Corporal Union's Director seems hellbent on retrieving the device, so there must be some realism."

Before Dan can speak another word about the rustic data box or the Director's intentions of potential domination, Pearl issues an alert on the starship's tenor speakers,

"We have an unidentified spacecraft approaching on the radar, intentionally blocking our trajectory. Evasive action is required immediately."

Dan Casey swiftly turns his attractive body around with his full attention back to the flight helm controls, yanking back on the accelerator throttle while activating the whistling reverse thrusters. The *Decepter* Machiavellian MK2 freighter soars to the edge of the Dread Moon's asteroid ring. The vessel's reverse thruster engines fire up with sectional blasts, gradually slowing the *Decepter* to a static hovering halt. They see a sleek black starship amid their intended flight path. Inside Dan Casey's cargo-runner craft, the crew jolts forward in their seats at the sudden braking momentum.

Rising back to his seat with a shaking of his dreadlocks, Jay Haines comments on the arrival of the intruding starship, "Oh, man! That's the slick mother who let loose those two Leecher beasts to damn feed on the trade ring space station."

Dan confirms Jay's suspicions with a tense glint in his dark eyes, "It's Duran!"

"It's Zak and his Panther starship. They have come for the data box to fulfil their bounty contract with Wilson Volantis," says the beautiful female resistance agent.

Charlena Jones swifty spins back around in the co-pilot's chairs. She readily grips the levered joystick while forming a nervous gaze over to Dan Casey, stating, "Oh, boy! Here we go again!"

Dan agrees. "Yeah, it's going to get noisy. Keep frosty as we have Veena's jealous ex-boyfriend looming on our case."

Zak Duran's vessel lurks a menace ahead of the gruelling asteroid field, presenting an impeccably chic silhouette stealth-shaped haul. The ship has advanced pulsating Anancio-designed hyper-dual-booster engines attached to the stubbed angled wings, swaggering a powerful aura amidst the shadows of the Sera system awaiting an exchange.

Inside the *Decepter*'s flight cabin. Pearl duly reports in her cyber tone, "The Panther is hailing our communication hub for a response to negotiations."

Dan Casey brushes his gloved hands through his slick black hair while reaching to the side dash for his green-dust smoke, "Connect us a link, Pearl, and keep the celestial hyperdrive ticking over, as I don't want to be messing around with this weird, puffed-up guy too long."

Swiftly rising from the passenger seat quarters, Veena stands on her booted heels and quickly steps in Dan's direction.

"I just like to protest my innocence. Zak Duran is not an ex or present boyfriend in any such terms. We used to be very close acquaintances. But that was before Zak became obsessed with high riches and a glamorous reputation. He handed me over to Corporal Union and left me for dead. Gosh! That's not a blooming recipe for a budding loving relationship!"

Turning around his pneumatic pilot's chair, Dan Casey pauses and responds to the now-seated feminine agent. "Are we quite finished, Miss Merida? You didn't have to get all hysterical. I am just mentioning that Duran seems to have the hots for you. Touchy! And I thought you Kothariya ladies liked it adventurous. Seems you hijacked me at gunpoint and haven't stopped trying to kiss me since!?"

"If you didn't originate from the human capital world of Kothariya, where did you come from, Mr Casey?" asks Charlena.

Dan relays some insight into his past as the holo-comm screen buzzes. "I was born on one of the colony planets called Lilandra-Coste."

Pouting a whisper behind the mingling pilots, Veena mutters, "You can have your smoke back when we land, and Lilandra-Coste is a world with a mindset full of men who think everyone wants to kiss them. Gosh!"

Sitting opposite the bashful Miss Merida, gunslinger Jay Haines politely enquires with a smirked smile, "Is that true what he mentioned, ma'am?"

The galactic resistance agent quickly whispers back with a shocked demeanour, "No! I have never tried to kiss him; he's delusional, been in the air too long."

Jay Haines quickly corrects the young woman's mistaken answer. "I am talking about the gunpoint hijacking, ma'am, not the kissing!"

"Oh! It's partly literal, with a lot of exaggerations. Phew!" sighs an embarrassed Veena Merida, slumping back into her cushioned flight seat.

The communications link transmits between the two static starships, connecting an image of Zak Duran on the holo screen. Zak's slick, swept brown hairstyle and handsome looks gleam through the holo trajectory screen as he greets the *Decepter* crew in his cocky manner, "Hey, Dan! How are things going, my old friend? It's been quite an eventful day, wouldn't you say? Your contribution to the trader's space station's demise is broadcasting all over the Mbron Media network. Makes quite the spectacular holo-net viewing. I'm unsure the crime lord Mach Galanti will see it in the same context."

Dan Casey stoutly connects eye contact with Zak Duran, piercing through the holo-comm transmission and returning his welcomed greeting, "It's good to see you, Duran! But the truth is you annoy me quite a lot, and you are in my flight path. Any reason for that, my old friend? Plus, I've never been one to tune into Mbron Media. So, I'd advise this crime syndicate kingpin, Mach Galanti, not to believe all the hyped-up flaky news from mindless tin-headed cyberbots."

Zak Duran smirks with a devilish grin at the cargo runner's defiant response as he glances over the holo-comm screen, choosing to pick out his old flame, "Veena, I expected much better from you, my dear! Embroiling yourself with this motley crew? A childish student chaperoned by a thuggish gunslinger and a scuffed-up interstellar pilot. Hmm, the life of a cargo runner! Sounds exhilarating!"

Veena Merida shrugs the unstrapped safety harness to one side, ranging from her passenger flight position to her heel-booted stance.

"What do you want, Zak, apart from causing trouble? This has nothing to do with you. Can't you just let this go and get another payday elsewhere, please, for me?"

Zak Duran teasingly responds to Veena's urges for a peaceful truce in his extraordinary, calm way. "I'm afraid things aren't that simple, and you know what I require, Veena. Hand over the astrological data box and exterminate the *Decepter* crew as we agreed, and I shall get you a pardon for your crimes from Wilson Volantis. I promise you can live a normal life, Veena. Do we have an agreement, my sweet beloved?"

Veena Merida expresses her strong disapproval and disdain at the suggestions put forth by the bounty hunter. She is astonished and responds with integrity, "Damn you, Zak! We did not agree to such terms; I would never stoop to the despicable depths of existence by engaging in the reprehensible behaviour you seem to find agreeable. Liar."

"I second every word, sweetheart; you want me to blow the cocky snob up?" says the charmed pilot, looking behind his broad shoulders and dishing a wink to Veena Merida.

The female agent smiles back, smitten, as another voice starts behind her.

"I'm with her too, and I'm no child, mister! Whoever may you think you are?" said Charlena Jones.

The safety harness belt buckles tinge a clanging from the weapons division. Jay Haines uncuffs his imposing body, stands beside Veena, and places his arm around her elegant shoulders.

The stylish dreadlock gunslinger peers through his designer shades at the holo-comm screen with a warning message for the taunting bounty hunter, "I got this; please take your seat, ma'am. Hey, Duran, name your remote planet; that's if you got the damn balls to a duel, man. I will teach you a few tough tricks about thuggery behaviour."

While on board the sleek Panther, Zak Duran seems uncompromised by the challenging offer of a duelling shoot-out, smirking in an amused fashion as Terri Lace makes her glamorous presence from the lower deck of the Panther frigate. She elegantly takes the co-pilot's position dressed in a revealing black trousers outfit, red bra and a white blood-stained bandage where she had been shot in the arm.

Terri teases her blonde-styled hair as she sexually perches

on the black leather flight chair, "Have I missed anything while I had to dress my wounds, darling?"

"Only a few idle threats of no importance from Dan Casey's miscellaneous crew."

Terri seductively turns forward to the holo screen showing her heaving cleavage, commenting on the *Decepter*'s personnel. "Aww, Dan! You found a little toy crew; how sweet! You have been a busy cargo pilot since your lucky escape off that inactive light-beam bridge on Race-World, ruining my new Ferrari Testarossa red convertible Gx9000 sports car and blowing up my favourite slave space station. Charming as you are, Mr Casey, that sexual kiss we had in the Java Lynx bar is turning out to be a stroke of bad luck omen. Be a gentleman, hand over the sought data box, and settle your debt so we can destroy your starship and all go home."

The *Decepter* MK2 freighter and the A1 class Panther frigate hover over a drifting stand-off in the atmospheric outskirts of the Dread Moon's asteroid belt. As the compelling conversation ensues, Dan Casey responds to Terri Lace's annoyance, while having a soft spot for the blonde consort beauty, "Hey, sweetie! Nice to see you up and about with that nasty-looking arm wound; how did you achieve that? I guess Mr Duran cannot look after you properly, Miss Lace. You need to find yourself a real man."

Zak Duran readily reaches forth and grabs the Panther vessel's slick double-based joystick, endorsing a wicked hostile glare.

Terri Lace responds to Dan's teasing concerns through the holo screen video with a nasty sarcastic bite of her ever-changing nature, "Thank you kindly for your empathy and considerate words, Mr Casey. But the applause must be awarded to your green-haired bitch of a girlfriend and the gullible cheek to assume she's an agent with her half-hearted threatening promises and misfired shooting. You deserve to find yourself an intelligent and sexy woman, Mr Casey! Not an unfathomable rigid piece of unattractive trollop."

Miss Merida is still reeling from the betrayal of her former best friends.

Composing herself, Veena takes a deep breath and kindly smiles, shimmering a glimmer of her naturally white teeth, commenting, "Please, Mr Haines. Take your seat! I've got this toad-faced tart covered."

Veena says, "How can you call me a trollop? The way you dress and flounce around you disgust me; the next time I draw my pistol and aim, I promise to deliver a shot between those cold-hearted eyes, sister!"

The sultry, provocative feminine bounty hunter is unfazed by Veena's threatening remarks as Terri Lace replies with a sharp, acidic tongue. "Well, judging by your first attempt, I won't be losing any sleep over your unfearful despatch of unachievable threats. Are you the best agent of trash that this pathetic resistance movement has to offer? I'd say the Corporal Union has nothing to worry about. Darling, please immobilise Mr Casey's cranked-out vessel. I shall promptly board with Dralon. The Leecher can feed on the worthless crew, while I will professionally exterminate the green-haired bitch with immense pleasure and retrieve the valuable databox. She can long fester with her murdered parents! Good riddance."

With a chilling cold silence invading the cockpit, Veena freezes on the spot with a shivering down her spine as she pauses, followed by a deepened sigh of saddened emotion; tears start to form in her jade eyes from the spiteful verbal assault. Dan Casey quickly emerges from his pilot quarters, standing in his scuffed, tarnished flight boots as a reminder of all the unforeseen challenges he has faced and overcome on this *Decepter* voyage contract.

Radiating warmth, the handsome black-haired cargo pilot motions a vast step to Veena Merida with open arms, offering affectionate custody. Dan holds her close to his broad chest. He wipes the sorrowful tears away from her pretty pastel eyes. He smoothly whispers, "I'm going to get you through this intertwined affair, sweetheart! Don't worry. I will take care of you. Promise."

While back on board the daunting stalking Panther-class frigate, Terri Lace can't help but trifle a sarcastic comment, "Aww, don't they just look like the most adorable couple? Zak, we should take a holo visual and place it on their graves with their humble words carved in their tomb."

Zak Duran cunningly smirks regarding Terri Lace's unprincipled, hurtful antics. The suave bounty hunter presses a selection of soft-padded buttons flashing on his sleek frigate's control dash with a warning, "Time's up, Dan! You have intruded and dismantled my kind hospitably without a variable invitation, causing ripples on a major level. The Director's contracts must be finalised, and royalties paid in order with the cost of your pathetic life."

Zak Duran's hostile intentions to fulfil his bounty contract are revealed as the Panther's dual-side weapons reveal themselves from the opening slots positioned along the black slender haul of the deluxe A1 frigate.

Meanwhile, on board the *Decepter* MK2 class freighter, the crew is appalled by the bounty hunters. Dan Casey is the first to mention his disgust while cuddling with Veena Merida, "Who the hell does this snubbed-up prick think he is? We need to get out of his deranged reach."

Now truly stressed, Dan releases his entangled body away from Veena's delightful womanly figure. The sorrowful green-haired agent reclaims her flight seat, recomposing herself.

Jay Haines echoes his concerns over the humming cabin control instruments. "These types of people need to be taken down a few pegs and be shown a taste of Haine's reality! Though I warn you now, man! That imposing Panther starship has activated its multi-advanced weapon systems." alertly observes the brave streetwise gunslinger, readily piercing a glance through his designer-shaded glasses as he eyes over the division scanners.

Before Dan Casey can act on the heads-up warning from his newfound gunslinger colleague, seated ahead at the co-pilot helm, Charlena Jones takes matters into her delicate hands with an angered frown on her attractive, sweet face.

Confessing a mere resemblance to her galactic high-school experiences, she rambles, "He's a spitting double for Zain Mathers from my mass equation studies, class 343. As a rule, I never did like him. Zain's always belittling people and trying to bring them down. Snubbed-up prick!"

She masterly flicks the control switches on and re-roots the *Decepter*'s weapons to manual. Bewildered by Charlena's fiery temperament and motioning actions, Jay Haines worriedly asks the young red-haired student, "Hey, kid! What the hell are you doing now? Our weapon systems are flashing up like a stack of overcharged fairy lights. Oh, man!"

But Charlena Jones has come to her conclusion without taking notice of her chaperone. She continues reminiscing in her well-spoken voice, "The ugly blonde bitch, Toady Lace! Reminds me of Penny Grafton from maths, class 355. Horrible on the inside and out, disgusting tramp of a girl."

Charlena continues with her determined mindset to prove a point and adjusts her grip on the levered joystick, caressing her fingers over the firearm trigger.

Veena Merida alarmingly notes, "She has activated the weapons!"

While Dan Casey quickly moves to the pilot's helm, his dark eyes open wide with feared anticipation as he shouts, "NO, Charlena!!"

Dan ranges in close quantity behind the co-pilot's hub. But not in enough time.

"Be damned with them all," she bellows, squeezing the trigger and rapidly opening fire to the crew's shock.

The *Decepter*'s front-ranged dual Gatling guns unleash a barrage of scattering laser bolts aimed at the impressive Panther frigate's portside haul with the offensive intention of neutralising its defences. Regrettably, the *Decepter*'s unauthorised gunfire is no match for the Panther's advanced deflector shield capability, resulting in a detrimental backlash effect.

While seated inside the *Decepter*'s cockpit, squirming in the co-pilot quarter, Charlena Jones looks out the starship's front view in astonishment as she witnesses the Panther's advanced shield abilities absorb her calculated attack. With a profoundly embarrassed, puzzled frown, she nervously murmurs, "Oh boy!"

Dan Casey swiftly regains his pilot position in the pneumatic recliner chair.

Not before the steadfast Panther A1 Frigate retaliates with its armed side cannons opening fire directly aimed at the *Decepter*'s slick front fuselage with disastrous consequences, indisputably penetrating the Machiavellian MK2 freighter deflector shields with scatter bursts of small explosions. Also, streaming undesired effects in the cockpit cabin with buzzed sparks and electrical flares form, affecting the flight controls.

Charlena Jones shouts out in pain, seated at the co-pilot hub. "Ahh, my hand!" She's received electrical burns while gripping the chrome joystick lever.

The smoke and fumes enter the cabin air, making the visuals blur. This provokes Dan Casey as he springs into action, adjusting his body postage in the pilot's helm and swiftly grabbing the joystick. He looks up, hearing the taunted laughter echoing from the holo comm-link, with a verbal review escaping the lush red lips of Terri Lace, "The cheeky little red-haired brat deserved that for calling me a toad!"

This is directly followed by Zak Duran boasting about his Panther starship's upgraded specifications. "You like my shields, Dan? They are Anancio-designed and top-of-the-range. The same manufacturers as the dual-booster engines. Your deflectors didn't fare too well, my old friend! Perhaps you should have researched better weapons to counteract advanced shield technologies."

"Thanks for the heads up, Duran. I'll bear it in mind, and you probably should have done your research about tiny wings."

Dan Casey sarcastically tones it with an alternative plan in motion, "Pearl! Cut this weird goofed-out guy and his darling wench off and give them a courtesy farewell nudge on me, reminding him of the name Casey."

The focused cargo pilot thrashes his right hand forward on the accelerator throttle with his other hand masterly guiding the jagged chrome joystick. Pearl confirms a crystalised flash response, bringing the subsystems and the celestial hyperdrive capabilities promptly online. The staunch *Decepter* springboards into action with a rumbling whistle of the triple set boosters. With a sheer burst of initial speed and vast manoeuvring, the starship nudges past the Panther's portside stealth-shaped wing.

The Machiavellian freighter performs a slingshot twist, whooshing to an escaping vector pitch through the voids of the Sera system.

The Panther frigate suffers a weaving orbital fluctuation by the surprising impact of being knocked out of its territory path. While recovering inside the sleek deluxe vessel's cockpit, Zak Duran quickly stabilises the Panther's flight controls, readily gripping the double-triggered joystick with an annoyed, dubious glance over to his sexy counterpart.

Terri Lace angrily comments in shock and horror after being tossed about in her leather-padded co-pilot seat, "Why, I believe Mr Casey dared to ram us, darling?"

"I think our mutual friend, Casey, as he likes to be referred to, is hinting he wants to play rough. Let's not disappoint our cargo-runner guests."

With utmost confidence, the skilled entrepreneur demonstrates his expertise and mastery of the situation by swiftly pushing the Panther's throttle forward and deftly manipulating the double-actioned joystick hard to starboard. The precise movements and decisiveness of Zak Duran signal his superb piloting efforts, leaving no doubt as to his capabilities. The Panther's Anancio-designed boosters engage with a pulsating purr accompanied by a slick manoeuvred turn, rapidly launching in pursuit of the *Decepter*.

While the Machiavellian MK2 freighter is slightly ahead of the chasing Panther vessel with a dwindling advantage zipping through the galactic stars, Dan Casey raises his concerns about his co-pilot's burnt hand from within the cockpit,

"Veena, see if you can attend to Charlena's injuries and take her to the back bedroom, where I left the med kit when treating your twisted ankle on that mudball of a moon, Cartonne."

"Come on, young lady, let us get you patched up! Everything is going to be fine; I promise."

The renegade student accepts the help with an apology for her actions, "I'm sorry, everyone; I just wanted to help; please forgive my misjudgement."

Praising Charlena's bravery, Dan Casey states while concentrating on piloting the spacecraft, "Hey, Wingman! Jones, you can assist me in being my co-pilot anytime."

This is followed by Jay Haine's deep, husky voice relaying his knowledgeable applause, "You did great, kid. Our weapon systems are ineffective against this scoundrel due to your fiery insight tactics."

"Hey, Jay, I've got an idea; it might be a long shot. But they have been coinciding well of late. Can you recalibrate the rear dual weapons to fire a single shot?"

"Got it, man! But I'm going to need time to re-root the

circuit bypass. So, can you provide me with the luxurious opportunity of a free galactic dance? I've got this cookie wired and fired. Haha!"

Seated at the helm, Dan Casey cunningly smiles at hearing the dreadlocked hotshot confirming his talents, "Great, Jay. I can take care of that daunting matter with the help of Pearl by giving them a duelling lesson around the stars and seeing how advanced his touted A1 Panther-class frigate proclaims to perform."

The daring interstellar pilot forcefully slams his expert hand on the speed accelerator. With his other masterful touch, Dan kinks the chrome-levered joystick to execute a skilled dog-legged manoeuvre, slickly weaving the *Decepter* into a twisting freefall diving pitch. The slender image of the Panther frigate's deluxe silhouette looms largely behind, with a slipstreamed display of aeronautical prowess half-looping an unparalleled wavering manoeuvre in chase of the Machiavellian MK2 freighter.

The dual starships cruise the grooves of galactic space with a spiralling dogfight-style flare as the Panther vessel's front cannons open fire with trailing patched explosions around the *Decepter*'s escaping hull.

Meanwhile, Veena Merida has safely escorted Charlena Jones to the secondary bedroom. She gets the young, red-bobbed hairstyled girl onto the floating mattress, and the attractive, jade-eyed resistance agent starts to treat the student's burn wound.

Veena goes to apply some medical gel to Charlena's sore hand, and she is kindly advised, "This will sting a little now! Try and think of nice things."

"Ouch!" yelps Charlena, willingly holding her hand out for medical attention, explaining her actions back in the cockpit, "I'm sorry! I just wanted to stop those people from being horrible to you, Veena. Terri is only jealous because you are real and pretty. Whereas she is not."

"Aww, thank you so much!"

"What's that for? I don't like needles!"

"It's not going to hurt you; just take away the throbbing pain and make you sleep for a while," the green-haired beauty professional says, administering the anaesthetic injection.

"How long have you and Dan...?" muttered the young teenage student, unable to finish her inquisitive insight and quickly falling asleep.

Veena smiles to herself while strapping the brave girl onto the floating mattress for safety. Whispering a soft response to her inquisitive suggestion, "I shall advise you on that wondrous outcome in due course. Let us take a raincheck on that answer for now."

Only to be rudely interrupted by a small explosion around the lounge area of the *Decepter*.

"That's if we don't all get blown up first."

She vacates the bedroom and makes a click-heeled dash sprint to the diner lounge deck of the starship, only to witness some smouldering fires and fallen structure beams damaging the dinner area where Dan cooked her that fabulous meal. Quick in hand to assist with the onboard hazard, Veena briskly looks around the smoggy lounge quarters for the fire extinguishers.

She amusingly notices straggly pastel strands of hair flicking in her close-range vision. The vain agent sighs in the tense situation. "Gosh! I'm a fuzzed-up mess! I must treat myself to a new, up-to-date hairstyle."

Veena Merida finds the fire extinguisher she urgently requires to tame the relentless lounge fire. While concerned about her appearance, she operates the vessel's fire hose canister accordingly to ease off the flames.

Ahead in the cockpit, utilising his maverick piloting skills with paramount confidence, Dan Casey slickly manoeuvres the chrome joystick with the subsystems rammed to maximise capacities and accurately weaves his starship through the hounding interception blasts from Zak Duran's prowling Panther stealth craft. "How's the weaponised recalibrations coming on, Jay? I Don't want to rush your expertise, pal. But we can't take any more pounding hits from the Panther's calibre cannons."

Jay Haines responds to the pilot's urging call while crouching under the weapons quarters, performing his skill mastery, intensely rewiring the circuitry bypass. "Nearly there, man! Just a few minor adjustments before it's boom time, baby!"

While aboard the sleek flight cabin of the pursuing frigate, Zak Duran has his finger on the pulsating trigger, stylishly seated at the pilot's helm with a calm demeanour and his handsome features shining through the bleak cockpit lights. "You can't keep running away, Dan! You must be delivered for your fugitive galactic crimes.

"Activate the photonic ionised seeker missiles, darling! We shall disable the *Decepter*'s booster engines. The monstrous Leecher can board the vessel and execute all personnel while we collect the prize and wrap up this troublesome bounty."

"Ah, splendid choice of weaponry. The seekers are now armed, my love. No escaping the net this time, Mr Casey! The show is over, I'm afraid, and I can't delay spending the Corporal Union's extravagant bounty purse on a brand-new red metallic deluxe turbo car."

The Panther's stealth undercharge shifts open instantly, revealing the imperil missile launchers. Within seconds of exposure, the launcher executes two blue neon flash-ionised rockets hurling fast in a locked-on vector of the *Decepter* MK2 freighter. Aware of the homing ionised missile dangers, Pearl flashes a corresponding response to the imposing threat.

"Warning! Ionised seeker rockets are tracking our posterity and closing. Six seconds to impact."

With no time to ponder the inbound threat, Dan Casey instinctively yanks back on the levered joystick with a sheer test of his piloting reflexes. He insists on the required help from Pearl, "Initiate our decoy defences now!"

He pilots the *Decepter* with a skilled twisting quarter loop accompanied by the defence decoy shafts, luckily fielding a shield barrier and misguiding the ionised seeker rockets off their intended target.

Back on board, the perpetrating Panther A1 class frigate reloads a stock of ion missiles. Terri Lace is entirely impressed by the decoy tactics, "You have to hand it to Dan. He knows how to pilot a starship with his slam dunk manoeuvres."

Zak Duran snaps back with a stern glare from over the top of his designer glasses, enquiring with venomous spite, "It sounds like you are impressed by him, my dear. Please don't let a cheap, thrill cargo rat impede your intelligence or judgement and lower yourself to Veena's living level. Now activate the stealth systems, and we shall see how good Casey is! Can he pilot the stars while being blinded by the superior opposition?"

"Predictive stealth camouflage commencing. Now you see us!" says Ms Lace.

The wilful Zak Duran finishes her toying sentence with a smug smirk. "Now you don't, Casey!" he ominously announces, caressing the killer trigger.

The *Decepter* levels off speedily from the sweltering swooped evasion of the seeker rocket's first striking attack. The Panther deluxe class frigate springs another surprise tactic. The stealth drive activates with a sudden vanishing from the stalking realms of galactic space.

"Where's he gone, Pearl? The radar's showing nothing on the scope?" Says a stunned Dan Casey, sweeping a perspective side to side glare around the cockpit view of the slender black starship.

Pearl responds with another timely notice alert, "Warning! Second wave of seeker missiles launched. Seven seconds to impact."

The Panther sneakily hunts and opens fire on its menacing rockets while performing under cloaked conditions. Immediately, it becomes a problem for Dan Casey and the plan he aims to achieve. The *Decepter* trails a flair of decoy shafts, ushering the ionised rockets adrift with no precise time to spare.

Pearl flashes an update to the under-fire cargo pilot with the dire news he doesn't want to hear, "Decoy shaft's malfunctioned, celestial hyperdrive power reserves gauge below fifty per cent."

With a disgruntled brown eye-rolled expression, Dan Casey stressfully brushes his fingerless-cut gloved hand through his dark black hairstyle with a deep sigh of annoyed inconvenience, "Oh great! Music to my ears! Ready the slip-jump trajectory to the hyper-speed lane, Pearl!"

Veena Merida quickly makes her presence from the squashed lounge fires, producing a heel-tapped echo as she holds on to the side-panelled interior to balance her progress back to the flight cabin. The green-haired agent witnesses the sight of Jay Haines getting himself organised with a bunch of cut wires in his talented hands, retaking his position at the weapons division of the *Decepter*, "How's the kid doing, Merida?"

"She is going to be fine, just shaken up."

"Why do you have a thread of circuit wires loose, Jay? Has our situation veered that bad!"

Jay intensely shakes his colourful beaded dreadlocks, replying deeply, "Things don't look too bright, ma'am. I believe we require a lucky shot to open the path to freedom. Look at that cosmic storm!"

Jay starts to compute the bypass to activate the rear weapons with intense concentration.

Dan Casey backs up Jay Haine's sentiments by slightly altering the original plan, "We are going clip Duran's tinny stealth wings with a heavenly single blast shot and make a slip-jump run through one of many storms in the Sera sector!

Hopefully, we will survive and make your agent-related date in the Isadora system."

"Hopefully? Gosh! Things are bad, I'm gathering."

With astonishment in his charmed dark eyes, Jay Haine flicks up his fashion designer glasses, "I can't recall the invention of flying into any crazy storms! But we're good to go on trying to take this sleek stealth bird out."

Dan Casey explains the derailment while manoeuvring the *Decepter* on course for metamorphosing cosmo storms, "I'm sorry, Jay, for the slight deviations in alterations. But since Duran wants to play hide and seek around the galaxy, we'll have to take you and Charlena to the Isadora system. We only have enough power in the spanked-out celestial hyperdrive to make one jump through the galactic slip-lanes."

The adaptable hotshot gunslinger acknowledges the cargo-runner's agreement terms, "I read you loud and clear, man! Some things can't be helped; I'm sure the kid will be overjoyed; just don't tell her mother. Haha."

Veena Merida asks about the possibilities of survival, "Can you jump-slip through the eye of a storm and expect to speak about the saga? Surely, going around the gruelling weather hazard would have the same effects and the prospects of living a bit longer!"

Opposite the panicking jade-eyed beauty, Dan Casey sits focused and composed in his leather pneumatic pilot's hub. He intensely adjusts the lever flight controls and timely cranks up the Machiavellian MK2 freighter hydraulic subsystems, bravely setting course for an atmospheric solar storm bleaching on the navigation radar.

Dan laughs to himself, then advises the starship cyber assistant in his smooth, fetching voice, "Pearl, Lock in our trajectory entry at 619 and offset a deviation exit of 601."

"What can you find so funny at a time of complete madness? Please disclose the humour. Look ahead at that electrified monstrosity of a solar cloud and try to produce a smile, which is virtually impossible. Are you certain about this, Dan?"

With a hesitant vibe in her well-spoken tone, Veena Merida witnesses the storm out of the front cockpit view of the *Decepter*. The imposed galactic solar storm is a formidable manifestation of phenomenal spent energy, characterised by a tumultuous cloud that swirls and collides with great force. This produces intense electric lightning bursts, specifically illuminating the whirlwind spiral and penetrating the very core of the cosmic storm.

Dan Casey and his late friend, Von Rye, had modified the Machiavellian Merlin spacecraft when they were both members of a privately funded space protection group. The steadfast starship glides superbly through the treacherous galactic cosmic storm with exceptional accuracy and slick precision. However, the Panther A1 frigate of Zak Duran and Terri Lace lurks unseen in the hazy shadows.

The stealth-cloaked, highly advanced pirate vessel relentlessly pursues the freelance MK2 freighter with unyielding vigilance and determination to collect their Corporal Union contractor's bounty purse. The situation is agitated, and the stakes are high-risk as the *Decepter* freighter must stay one step ahead to emerge into the hyper-slip-lanes and avoid being captured by the Panther frigate.

"Hey, don't worry! It's not as bad as it first sounds. I was advised of this trick by a small-time smuggler called Gary Payton. He used to slip-jump governmental blockages like this all the time before he was rumoured to be dead!"

"Gosh! Are we relying upon suicide tactics from a rumoured ghost smuggler? That hardly seems inspiring. Is there anything I can help with? While I'm feeling flush with the hopeful prospects of Mr Payton's last wishes?"

With a playful tone of teasing authority, Dan Casey quickly answers, "Thought you would never ask, partner! Grab that joystick and give it a good yank left when I ask you to, okay? And don't forget about that hot kiss for good luck, sweetheart!"

The handsome pilot swiftly leans his fine-toned muscular body over to the co-pilot quarters and invades Veena's personal space with a surprised manoeuvre, gently caressing her face. Caught off guard by the slick enlightenment, Veena Merida stutters her sentence in a stunned clinch, "Oh, Mr Casey!"

Dan takes matters to the fore while gazing into Veena's sparkling jade eyes with their lips hovering adrift, "The kiss, Agent Merida!"

The smitten couple entwines in a twisting, passionate kiss and the penetration of erotic tongues amidst danger. In dire need to break up the propounded loving moment, Jay Haines embarrassingly interrupts again in his manly, husky voice,

"I am sorry, folks. But, dudes, do a nasty armoured stealth spaceship and big bad storm ring any bells?"

Jay then turns his broad-smirked attention back to the *Decepter*'s weapon systems.

Dan Casey whispers to Veena, pulling back from the lingering kiss with an allured princely smile, "I'd declare that I've got something worth taking the chance to live for, Miss Merida! Okay! Veena, Let's do this. Are you on board with us, Jay?

"As soon as the Panther gives chase in this electrical storm and goes to launch them daunting seeker missiles, they should deflect into the fierce current and expose his position in theory. Otherwise, we all go bang and end up merry-drinking with Gary Payton in some heavenly sleazy nightclub bar. Mr Haines, please aim for the tin wing we nudged earlier, and we should be home free."

Jay Haines pauses with a deep breath. He replies with a serious demeanour about his sharpshooting skills, "I got this bounty-hunting bird covered. You just do your stuff and get us outta here, man!"

Casey takes a brief moment with proud admiration engulfing his handsome stubbled face, reflecting on his newly formed gunman and witnessing Veena also nod her blessings from the co-pilot hub with hands at the ready.

Dan Casey readily gives them both a holding honoured salute with a dashing flick. "Fire up the hyperdrive, Pearl! Produce with the kinked trajectory plot. Just like the good old times! The bad guy's chasing our tail with the odds against us, sweetie! Let us show the weird guy, Duran, how we styled interstellar cargo runners deal with goofed-out materialised snobs!"

Pearl activates the triple-booster engines with a flashed buzz, applauding the crew's achievements in her cyber voice, "My databanks are inclined to calculate our former chief Von Rye would have been proud of the new crew's performance. Fifty-five seconds till impacting hyper-speed lane entry and counting trajectory."

The Machiavellian MK2 freighter quickens up in lightning fashion and zooms into the cosmic maelstrom with a purred roar. The Panther looms a stealth venture, whooshing at speeds into the hectic storm.

While inside at the advanced flight helm, Terri Lace confirms in her posh voice, "Ionised seeker rockets reloaded, wave three ready to fire at your will. Surely Mr Casey isn't going to slip-jump a hyper-route through a galactic storm? That's pure madness by any nature of sanity."

Zak Duran is concentrating on his target with a quick, smug, slanted glance over to his partner, and he brags, "Casey! Just bluffing; he's trying to test my resolve!"

This is confidently presumed by the hunter, who is squeezing the trigger and opening fire. The stalking Panther instantly launches the ionised missiles while in a cloaked figure statue, only for the deadly seeker rockets to veer off their intended target and explode in the ferocious electrical maelstrom. Backlashing, a plasma discharge of lightning bursts to score fiercely over the

Panther's invisible sleek haul frame and to expose the deluxe starship's flight orientation.

Terri Lace screams in a vile rage as the flight controls spark a fusion reaction.

"Ahh, fuck! Does not look like he's damn bluffing to me, Zak!"

Zak Duran smirks a sly grin with slight admiration for the cargo pilot's persistence. "Clever, Mr Casey! Very adept. I retract my previous comment sincerely. You did do your research on taking down advanced technology shields. We shall range in close; I'll take him out using the conventional trace cannons. Flying directly into a cosmic maelstrom is not one of my favourable achievements, darling."

Meanwhile, on board the *Decepter* freighter, Dan has his sequence crew working in angelic harmony, witnessing the Panther's vessel suddenly decloak. The charmed pilot precisely orders with a creative zest, "There's Duran's Panther. Now open fire!"

Jay Haines wastes no time in his essential role and naturally takes the shot decisively. The *Decepter*'s rear cannons discharge a singular, protruding projectile that homes in on the stealth craft's tedious wingspan. The blast shot accurately impacts and successfully inflicts damage upon the menacing Panther's wing. This causes the deluxe frigate to waver in an unbalanced dimension. Zak Duran, unfortunately, loses control of the starship's hydraulic systems, and the Anancio-designed booster engines stall.

Zak groans a promising taunt, "A little insurance; catch you soon, Mr Casey!" He then fires a tracking device attached to the rear of the *Decepter* as Dan Casey's starship launches by the horrific storm's eye.

Dan glances over at Veena, telling her, "Now, sweetheart!"

In unison, the smitten couple quickly slams the craft's dual joystick's hard portside.

The *Decepter* vastly manoeuvres a full looped roll with a straight burst of speed, shooting off safely with an impressive flash bang into the galactic hyper-lanes on route to the Isadora system, avoiding the storm altogether with a deviation tactical flight path pulled off in style by Dan Casey.

Chapter Fourteen

Cosmic Love

The *Decepter*'s voyage has been plagued by constant stalking and harassment at every known corner of the Kalanisi Universe. However, things are simmering to a relaxing regiment as the Machiavellian freighter cruises through the misty blue parallels of the hyper-speed lanes in silence. They are destined for the Isadora system in search of a secret location allotted to the beautiful resistance agent, Veena Merida, to deliver the valuable astrological data box and relay any known information to the shadowy agency leader, Tara Harlow. They are trying to scupper Director Wilson Volantis's plans for the data box in his delusional spiritual obsession with galactic dominance.

The adorable crew kicks back, chilling in the *Decepter*'s cockpit, having experienced an overwhelming sense of triumph and inspiration, having escaped from the clutches of Commander Calo Tarick and his heavily armed battlecruiser while evading the Panther stealth craft. They are filled with renewed hope and determination to continue their journey, no matter the challenges ahead.

Dan Casey is the first to start the celebrations with a recommended amount of gratitude for his misfit crew's sheer bravery in performing under pressure, "Wow, guys, you were amazing. I couldn't have pulled that off without you trusting me and Pearl. So, thanks a lot, appreciate it! I believe we all have earned and deserve a victory drink."

The modest cargo pilot praises as he pre-settles the vessel's flight controls to an automatic sequence. The *Decepter* glides peacefully through the secluded hyper-lanes. As Dan Casey rises from his pneumatic recliner, he feels the soft suede fabric of a glove caressing his stubbled, sweaty face. He looks up to see Veena Merida standing in front of him with a smile on her face. She leans in and surprises him with a tender kiss, the warmth of her lips sending shivers down his spine. Dan can't help but show gratitude on his charmed face for the small but meaningful time they have shared, reminding him of the joy and love that can be found in even the simplest moments.

Veena teasingly breaks away from the kiss and seductively whispers in her allured posh spoken voice, stroking his dark black hair, "I'll pass on the cabin drink and have my mine brought to me as a nightcap in the captain's quarters where I can thank you properly!"

Dan Casey stands on the flight deck mesmerised by Veena Merida's appealing rear presence dressed in the tight-fitting black outfit until a voice disturbs Dan's daydreaming thoughts.

"I'll have an Astro-beer with you, man! That is one different transporter trip across the galaxy to what I'm used to travelling, dude. You are one hotshot interstellar pilot for sure, damn! We showed them mothers who's the boss in the fine champion style of any Corporal Union Elite unit."

Dan makes his way to the recreation quarters of his battered freighter vessel, noticing the damage inflicted. The fallen loose wires spark in the dimming lights over the lush curved padded sofa ripped and burnt in the smoke-filled atmosphere.

He mutters a self-conscious moan while heading for the swing door of the refrigerator. "We'll need some serious home renovations and credits to cover."

He returns two cans of his favourite beverage to the cockpit and hands one over to Jay Haines with an amused-riddled toast, "To galactic fugitives and for those scoundrels who dare to fly with them, Cheers!"

"Speak for yourself. As far as I know, the Corporal Union and the Mbron Media cybernetic broadcasters don't know my or the kid's name. So, it's only you and the pretty lady who have wanted identities on this craft and are listed for the gallows. Cheers!"

With a raised eyebrow, Dan Casey agrees. "So, what's the whole story saga with you and Charlena? How did you both end up on that crime lord's space station?"

Jay replies, brushing his manly hands through his dreaded bead hairstyle as he explains his reasons, "The kid went missing a few weeks back; she was investigating why some of her student friends had disappeared without a trace and got too close to the truth, linking leads back to Mach Galanti."

Jay takes a swig of his drink and carries on.

"As her dear mother told me, Charlena is too curious for her own good. She sneaked into a slave recruitment hub in the human capital planet of Kothariya. And got snatched up by some of the Galanti goons, and the poor kid was enslaved as saleable trade trafficking property. Her worried mother hired me to save and return the young girl. I'm a galactic gunslinger, man! Private investigator and lovable chaperone all-in-one mean bad-arsed package. I just wanted to make a difference for the people who can't and show them some of us do care. So, what's you and the chick's story?"

Dan replies with no ghosts hiding in his closet, truthfully telling the gunslinger of his recent involvement in unpredictable activities since being acquainted with the female agent.

"I was just a simple cargo runner until a week ago; I struggled for a delivery contract until Veena hijacked me on a smuggler moon called Latin-Versa. After hearing her agent's fantasy story, we came to the agreement I would help for a credit fee, but that was before her so-called friends abducted her. I felt the same way just mentioned; I could probably make a slight difference to someone in need and show them that someone cares with accountability to prove it. So, I took to the hyperlanes and found the slave trader's station and sprung the damsel in distress, leading me to have a Kestrel-dew with you now, pal."

Jay Haines finished his drink, placing the empty can on the starship's side panel. While raising his legs and straightening his booted feet to rest, Jay enquires with a degree of scepticism about their destination rendezvous in the Isadora system, "Any idea what to expect at this secret location and the chilling reason for that spooky data box? Do you believe in folklore stories? They seem too far-fetched to be real; just made up bedtime tales!"

Dan Casey turns his head around to the flight controls and checks over the trajectory plot dials. He finishes his last drops of Kestrel-dew, commenting on Jay's theories about the mystical databox and the rumoured stories of the galactic dead rising from a mysterious black hole called the Vortex and wiping out all life in the Kalanisi Universe.

"In six and a half hours, all will be revealed. I couldn't say, to be honest, but in retrospect, these myths might be more than just delusional fabrications. The Corporal Union has put enough effort into claiming the astrological star chart, which worries me."

Dan pauses his sentence while placing the empty Astro-beer can down on the side recess.

"What do you know about this, Wilson Volantis?"

Jay replies, "I was in Kothariya at the Director's election ceremony. Mbron Media rigged the voting ballot system, and Wilson Volantis was elected against the citizens' will. The rumours are that he is spiritually based and the wrong man for the government position. The dissident people rebelled fiercely, only to be labelled as galactic terrorists and convicted with no league trial in court. Since that old grey-haired dude rose to power, the galaxy has been a weaponised shit hole against the normal people who have been going missing in the thousands. Still, it's not reported by the corrupt Mbron Media Ltd, which means nobody knows or dares speak the truth for fear of life-threatening repercussions. Worrying times, man!"

"It sounds like whoever operates Mbron Media has coincided with the Corporal Union and is covering all crime across the Kalanisi Galaxy."

Dan's mind wanders as he recalls a recent memory.

"I got a ride in a taxi-pod with a cyber android called Nayla back in the glamour world of Carrageen-Hazen. She proclaimed there is an android called the Core Lord, who preaches to all Mbron Media cyberbots that one day all human lives will be extinguished."

Jay Haines repeats his earlier phrase of language, "Worrying times, man! Feels like all the warped-out bad guys are conspiring behind the scenes with an evil strategic plan. What about Miss Merida? Has she got any insight into the bewildering matter, being an agent of the resistance movement?"

Dan replies, "Veena is in the dark as much as the rest of us; she is only given vague instructions on this assignment by her elusive boss. I believe it's all getting on top of her not knowing the outcome, and it's hard with the cruel betrayal of her friends. I should go and check on Veena and Charlena. It's been great to make your acquaintance. Now you get some well-earned sleep."

Dan Casey notices that Jay Haines has already fallen asleep in the weapon quarters.

Dan gives the AI navigation cyber suite some general orders while leaving the flight cabin, "Keep frosty, Pearl, and dim the lights for Jay."

The cargo pilot quietly walks back through to the trashed diner lounge compartment. Pearl instantly flashes a crystallised beckon, quavering the cockpit to a sedate light tone. Jay Haines is blissfully snoring away in his sleeping crunched-up position in the weapons division. Dan Casey makes a heist, gathering the last can of Kestrel-dew and holding it in his finger-cut gloved hands. He pauses and raises his dubious head to one side, intently listening to the *Decepter*'s triple-booster engine's whistle, with an offset vibrating deviation as they travel at speed through the hyper-speed lanes.

"Damn, no way! You have got to be kidding me; that sounds like both the hydrostatic bypass buffers are knackered. They will need replacing, or or the starship will blow up!"

To his surprise, the annoyed but charming interstellar pilot opens the kitchen cupboard. All the drink glasses are smashed and shattered as they fall onto the lounge deck, creating a more derelict mess. Dan sarcastically whispers, "Going to need some new kitchen cutlery as well."

He steadily walks from the crippled smoggy lounge area down the stairway steps to the bedrooms to check on the relaxing ladies of the vessel's crew. Only for the bannister rail to snap off in his free hand.

"Ah, fuck! At this rate, I will need a new starship for more than just renovation repairs. At least we're all still alive; that's what counts."

The secondary bedroom door is also broken, swinging on its hinges, and Dan kicks it open with a gentle tap of his black leather flight boots and thoughtfully checks on Charlena Jones.

With a grand smile, he whispers, "Sleep tight now, Wingman Jones! You will wake up to a pleasant surprise in the morning."

Dan Casey knows that the young student wants to travel to the Isadora system. He swiftly turns around and hears a soft trickle of dreamy ambient music from his master quarters. Dan smiles to himself.

He lightly taps on the closed door, which is quickly acknowledged by a faint feminine voice. "Please, come in."

The cabin door automatically opens from the inside

operating mechanism by Veena Merdia, who is seductively lying semi-naked on the floating mattress.

Standing at the master room entrance, Dan Casey experiences excitement and nervousness. Being the perfect gentleman, the charismatic cargo pilot raises his muscular arms to mid-waist. He presents his hand-cluttering items with a playful introduction remark: "Room service! One nightcap for the lady and one broken rail bannister, an exclusive part of the starship as a souvenir gift to remember your time as my gorgeous partner!"

He takes in the delicious sight of Veena Merida, dressed only in a skimpy black lace bra and matching g-string with her knee-high-heeled boots left on to tease.

In return for his valiant efforts, Veena replies with an erotic measure of flirting empathy, "Aww, Dan! I'm feeling responsible for breaking your starship; probably we could patch things up together if you cargo pilots ever get free time."

Veena Merida smiles, fluttering her piercing jade eyes and flouncing her long green wavy hair around her appealing neckline with a seductive stroking of her manicured hands. She shows no signs of her usual defence shyness.

"Please take that ruined jacket off and come sit next to me; let me apologise sincerely for being such a woozy agent. Hmm, partner!"

Veena slowly runs the other wandering hand down over her black lace bra and ample breasts with a dominant, teased glare. Veena reveals the smoke filter she had stolen on the flight deck and places it between her creamy chest accordingly,

"Oh, I may have something you desire, Mr Casey!"

She says with a gasping sexual smile, witnessing him remove his torn-up quarter jacket and placing the rail bannister down. Dan Casey approaches the floating mattress dressed in his black t-shirt and pilot slacks, mesmerised by Veena's kinky enticements.

"You have many qualities I crave, Miss Merida!"

He attempts to place his knee on the bed, but he is halted in his tracks.

"Remove the gun holster, please! We wouldn't want any unfair advantage play; I'm technically disarmed, or I might have to perform one of my agent-trained combat moves with thrusting gravitation."

Veena sexually torments the pilot by stroking over her curved silky thighs and parting open her luscious long legs.

Dan swiftly unclips his slanted holster belt and silver-based black-barrelled gun, throwing both effects on the vented floor.

"It's well rumoured that those capable, sexy female agents can get rough in close-quarter physical situations."

He hands Veena the Kestrel-dew and caressingly removes the green-dust smoke filter seductively from between her heaving buxom cleavage.

"Think I shall save this smoke for when we land?"

Veena laughs out loud in response. "Oh no! You heard me moaning back in the cabin?"

Embarrassedly blushing, the giggling female agent places the Kestrel-dew on the bedside cabinet.

Dan Casey amusedly comments with a revealing answer. "Yeah! We kissable men from the Lilandra-Coste also have very astute hearing."

He quickly pulls off his rough, fingerless-cut gloves. She moves her semi-naked body close.

Veena caresses her wandering hands on his broad chest, tugging the seams of his black t-shirt. In her posh, sultry voice, she proclaims, "I should never trust rumours about handsome kissable men from Lilandra-Coste, not without gaining first-hand experience."

She pulls his black t-shirt over his head and messes up his swept-back hairstyle. Dan Casey moves in close to kiss her luscious red lips. His manly hands caress her kinky thighs and shapely long legs. Veena places her dainty finger on his lips before they entangle in a passionate kiss. Her lace bra rubs over his naked chest with effect. She kindly says in a severe tone, opening her heart to him, "You came for me, Dan! Saved me from a certain fate like the fairy stories my parents would read to me as a little girl."

Veena deeply sighs, and a cluster of shallow tears form in her jade eyes, "When Terri told me I was worthless and to fade away with my late parents, it did make me wonder if she might be right. I've just been running and kidding myself from hidden grief."

Veena Merida stops in her sentence again, swallowing the painful memories she had encountered. Dan Casey carefully wipes the trickling tears away from her cheeks. He tells her in his attractive voice, "Hey, take your time. And you are not worthless."

The starship's triple engines drop to a smooth decibel as they emerge at cruising speed for the later part of the journey to the Isadora sector.

Veena carries on, revealing her heartwarming moment with shadows of despair, "I have no family left or even friends who don't want to kill me or trade me in for credits. Then you came along. A mystery cargo man who is not meant to be a part of my mission but has been there for me at every corner. Oh, gosh!

"What I'm trying to say… What I've never felt the need to say before is that I've fallen madly in love with you, Dan Casey, and it scares me."

"I know; it scares me, too." Dan Casey goes in for a passionate French kiss, and his eager hands fondle Veena's breasts, slipping down the black lace bra straps. Panting and obliging moaned sighs of pleasure, Veena Merida runs her eager hands over his developed thigh leg and quickly starts unzipping his pilot slacks.

Dan Casey flings the skimpy bra and kisses her neckline, teasingly down to her naked breasts and stroking up her inside thighs. "Aah, oh!" she groans, easing open her trembling legs and scratching her manicured jade nails down his naked sternum in a sexual frenzy of manifesting lust. Dan Casey and Veena Merida finally make heated, sexual, cosmic love during the romantic night flight cruise with a pleasurable penetrating embroidery of passionate craving bodies. They glide mildly through the hyper-speed lanes of the Kalanisi Universe and are ever closer to the mysterious destination in the Isadora system.

Back in the unsettled Sera system, far from the blissful harmonic mood embracing the *Decepter* freighter, the temperament isn't at the same equal balance on the Panther frigate of the high-profiled bounty hunters. The sleek image of the starship floats amid a swirling mist in the depths of open space, bearing the signs of system damage sustained in the pursuing conflict with Dan Casey's Machiavellian vessel and the hazards inflicted by the galactic maelstrom. Inside the Panther's redlight cockpit, Zak Duran is on his hands and knees under the flight control panels, repairing the internal subsystems after the power shortage.

While the beautiful lady of leisure, Terri Lace, relaxes at the co-pilot's hub with her shapely legs crossed and filing her manicured purple nails with tension growing in her boredom. "How much longer, darling? Surly, only so many wires need to be rewired."

Zak Duran raises his voice and demands with a flared-toned temper, "Ignite the damn subsystems again and try being useful instead of tarting around like an Astro-hooker. I believe Veena will be showing a lot more class to Casey than just sitting around flashing her tits!" Coldly mocked the handsome, selfish entrepreneur who swiftly edges himself from beneath the circuitry panel with the intent to irritate his beloved.

"Fuck you, Zak. Just because Dan managed to outsmart your tactics! Don't take it out on me, degrading me to a level of trash. Probably, Mr Casey is correct in saying I need a real man!"

In a spiteful row of venomous words, she is retrying the starship flight controls. She keys in the flight codes, and to her surprise, the deluxe frigate's power restarts with a vibrated pulse.

"Okay, smart arse, give yourself a round of applause; you fixed the ship. We now have sublime power and are back in business to a degree, but with no intended bounty target or purse to collect. Our green-haired bitchiness of value has slipped the net, remember?"

Meanwhile, the scheming of Zak Duran's mastermind criminology comes to the forefront. He smirks, brushing the dust fragmentations off his light brown leather and suede designer jacket. Zak casually sits down in his pilot's position and takes his place at the control helm.

The bounty hunter craftily keys in a security code with a hidden side compartment shifting open on the recess. Delightfully revealing a bottle of expensive red wine and two cysteine stem glasses. Zak Duran pops the cork and pours out the bubbly red velvet. "Care for a vintage glass of Château La Clarière to resolve our tiff?"

The sultry, stressed blonde counterpart duly responds by stopping her nail maintenance and readily accepts Zak's offer of redemption.

"What's running through your divulging mind, darling? I know that fruitful smirk, the one that makes me all tingly and moist!"

With the utmost confidence in his thinking, Zak Duran explains his methods,

"Casey and Veena might think they're home free. But I don't play a game of chance without insurance policies of convenience. You should know me better than that by now, darling." He casually activates the Panther's navigation screen display.

Terri Lace smiles in the sheer delight of witnessing a

beeping dot on the frigate's radar scoop, "Aww! Dan's been so kind to leave us a galactic breadcrumb trail. Bless him! It's so thoughtful of him to invite us along. Don't you share my views, dear?" Terri says.

She swiftly sloshes back the remaining quarter glass of expensive red wine and quickly uncrosses her long legs. Rising from the co-pilot's hub to her Gucci designer-heeled shoes, she seductively motions a walk over to Zak Duran, who is seated at the pilot's helm admiring her beautiful sexual composure and ever-changing mood swing. She teasingly stands in front of Zak, dressed in her skimpy tight black boob tube and black leather catsuit bottoms with a lusting glint in her sparkling blue eyes.

Terri slowly manoeuvres her voluptuous figure over his posture and straddles him with a lusting want of heated passion, evading her sultry facial expression. "Can I flash my tits now!"

Zak Duran finishes off his Château La Clarière and places the empty glass beside him. The contemplating bounty hunter answers Terri's adventurous proposals in a smug, delayed fashion of his self-assured demeanour,

"I do agree with your views intently, my lovely. We shall scout out Casey's and Agent Merida's secret location and retrieve the astrological data box for the good Director. With an added element of an uncharted destination in the Isadora realm!"

He raises his manly hands to Terri's heaving chest and caresses her charms with a firm squeezing touch of self-appraisal, "Nice breasts; it's a shame to keep them covered!"

She sighs a pleasurable, taunting, flirtatious moan, "Ooh, mmm!" Wiggling her curvy body on his manly lap while undoing his brown designer Prada trousers. Zak Duran laps up the attention, explaining his future foresight. "I'm sure that Wilson Volantis will be pleased to elevate us to the high-profile Elite positions we deserve to occupy for such a thoughtful gift. Do you agree with my views, dear?"

Zak leans forward, and kinking his body to the automatic flight controls, he presents the Panther frigate's hyper-lane course route to the Isadora system.

"Oh, I agree, darling! That's why I love you so much and desire to screw you in the hyper-speed lanes; the vibrations are such a favourable sensation."

The high-rolling, esteemed bounty hunter couple divulges into a steamy night of hot, passionate, and rough sexual encounters. The Panther frigate's Anancio-designed booster engines blaze up with a purring drone. Quickening to speed with a silent flash, they bang into the hyper-lanes, pursuing their alluding bounty purse reward.

The morning soon dawns after the lustful night of passionate intimacy on board the *Decepter* freighter between Dan Casey and Veena Merida. They've shared a soulful unison, finally making love while cruising through the galactic hyper-speed lanes. The Machiavellian starship travels on auto-control with Pearl's valid assistance as they venture close to the decent Isadora system with a steady purring of the triple boosters. Inside the depleted battle-stricken interior of the steadfast MK2 vessel, Dan Casey is still asleep on the floating mattress bed. He gets a slight tender nudged tap on his broad naked shoulder from Veena Merida, with a whispering kiss on his stubbled, rough cheek, "Wake up, Dan."

The sexy female agent rises to a straight stance and places a hot-steamed mug of Star coffee on the nightstand. "Dan, wake up; the navigation radar is rapidly beeping, and I got you a black Star coffee!"

The interstellar pilot opens his dark brown eyes with a faint flicker and a shake of his head, slowly edging up on the mattress. Dan rubs his eyes. "Are we there? Or did we crash!"

He sees the black coffee and Veena Merida, standing in front of his mesmerised expression, dressed in a short revealing wrap-around shoulder top and matching skintight leggings, finished off with her knee-high boots and slack holster belt.

"No, we're not crashed yet, but we must be getting in range of the location."

Dan Casey slightly turns his naked muscular body with a groan, reaching for his coffee mug, "Ah, my damn back hurts!"

He grumbles as he goes to rub the wound. With affectionate concern for his well-being, Veena Merida motions her presence forward, kneeling on the floating bed. She quickly attends to his aching pain with a massaging feminine touch and a warning caution of words.

Her nailed hands dig into his back as she asks, "Aww! Are you okay, Dan? That is what you get when fighting and diving through panoramic screens. You should be more careful; what were you thinking about then? You're lucky it's only an aching back muscle. You could have been killed."

Dan Casey reaches over to grab his coffee and takes a welcome gulp.

"I acted that way because Calo Tarick was going to shoot you, and I didn't want him to, Miss Merida! And I'm suffering after our late-night encounter with agent-trained moves."

"You call that a valid excuse!" teasingly smirks Veena. "Then you nearly got blown up on that beaten-up conveyor track when brawling a punch-up with that deluded Commander Tarick! My heart dropped an anchor when I saw you lying still in the smog with that smouldering rubble scattered all over your body. Promise me you will be more careful. You are acting more like an agent than me."

"I'm fine, honestly, Veena. I guess you just woke up my old reflexes being my new adventurous partner." Dan pushes himself up off the floating mattress bed and gets dressed to attend to the navigation radar systems.

Veena Merida watches her charmed manly lover pull up his black pilot slack jeans with a delighted erotic glint in her jade eyes. She probes into his past task force career revolving around the performances she had witnessed with modest intrigue, "So what is this space protection racket group you worked in before becoming a cargo runner?

"I've got to admit you have impressed me. According to the galactic agent training manual, you have been adaptable in high-risk situations and fared above average. You must have been a credible part of some special Elite operations team. So, what happened? Pearl mentioned why the outfit was disbanded. The chief would have been proud of the crew. You can confide in me, Dan. That's without me intruding on your privacy, of course," she said while kindly fitting his leather-slanted holster belt and weapon to his waist.

Dan Casey's dark brown eyes connect with Veena's sparkling gems. He scruffily tucks his black t-shirt into his creased flight jeans. Bearing a sorrowful expression of loss and reminiscing, Dan speaks about his past security career. "We were a privately owned shadow outfit that operated on the outer rim of the Suvarna cluster. We aimed to keep all the space pirates and marauders at bay and make interspace travel safe for the more honest intergalactic traders. That's how I came to meet Gary Payton. We apprehended him once trading contraband; I never believed in a word he said or the hazy rumours of his sudden death. He is or was a galactic con artist of the highest order. I knew never to lend him any credits or let him buy the first drink when he struck his con. But he was also a good man in general. He tried to help us out that troublesome night when he could have easily escaped."

Veena interprets, "That's why we didn't crazily slip-jump to the hyper-speed lanes through that unsettled maelstrom. You never trusted that he performed the stunt himself, creating a distraction with an alternative motive to flee the scene of his criminal con. This Gary Payton rogue sounds like a very sneaky individual, indeed! Please carry on, darling."

"Straight after we had obtained Gary, we had an emergency alert from headquarters that a commercial fuel vessel had been hijacked by a criminal android calling himself Henderson. The report said he had already killed the crew and commodore of the craft with threats to blow it up over a civilian moon base that was close by called Delapre-four. The sparked-out cyber-terrorist had it all planned. Henderson demanded a fully six-figure credit ransom from Delapre-four's counsel committee, or he would detonate the fuel vessel over the civilian populated base without fear of any life being extinguished.

"Our team consisted of three members, four if you include Pearl." Chuckles Dan Casey in amusement to Veena Merida as she readily passed him another flight boot. He lays out their operative roles and friendship values.

"I was the main pilot of the *Decepter* and was handed the responsibility of taking out the fuel-tanker engines with the assistance of our rookie wingman, Kira Savannah. She hadn't been in the squad too long and was about the same age as you, twenty-eight, and also very beautiful. You have a lot in common. Kira was a great friend and crack-shot co-pilot in every manner, one of the best I'd ever seen. But I never let it go to her head, which kept the job flirtatious and fun. Kira Savannah was very rash in her decisions and eagerly wanted to help. Reminds me a bit of Wingman Jones."

"Charlena does take Galactic Wingman to another gaming level. Bless her! So, were you and this, Miss Savannah, in a relationship?"

"No, nothing in such terms. Can't say we didn't flirt with each other, and I cared about her a lot. But I caught Kira and the squad chief kissing on more than one occasion. Check in with Pearl and the starship's database for bio-scan evidence. Ah, my damn back!"

He groans and bends down, retrieving his green-dust smoke flicked on the floor before their night of passion. Veena stands with her hands around her hips, shaking her head and witnessing his actions.

"Gosh! You don't learn? I gather the squad chief was your best friend, and Henderson caused problems."

"Yeah, Von Rye was a great friend, the best. I knew him for years growing up on Lilandra-Coste. He was loyal and always had your back. Von was a master at his trade. But that night, to his better judgement, he took Kira along for the extraction as he wanted me to guard the *Decepter* and to keep an eye on Gary Payton. He had already tried to steal the ship once, and another con could have been in the make-up."

The handsome pilot speaks in detail about the infiltration of the fuel vessel as the memories flood back, "Von and Kira boarded the ship only to find out there were about twenty civilian hostages imprisoned in the cargo haul, changing the complexity of the operation. I stressed to Von Rye that I'd come aboard and swap over roles with Kira. But they refused, and to prove me wrong at first, they utilised Henderson. They started to free the hostages, and all looked well until Kira heard a sudden noise in the vessel's cockpit.

"She investigated alone and was attacked by a Leecher! We all froze apart from Von Rye, who bravely fought off the boundless beast and saved Kira from certain death, even though she was badly hurt. The next thing I witnessed on the onboard holo screen was the cybernetic android Henderson getting back up and giving a speech. I will never forget the words he computed. 'My core is for eternity; one day, all humans will be extinct!' He laughed then exploded, taking half the starship out with him."

Stressed, Dan Casey pauses in his reminiscing sentence as the pain of recalling the ghastly night shows on his serious, toned face.

"The cybernetic psycho committed digital suicide, and everybody was injured or worse. I panicked as the detonation blast was causing the fuel vessel to lose orbit over the Delaprefour moon base. The *Decepter* was also being dragged down with the blazing fuel craft. I had to act fast with little time, and that's when Gary Payton told me to trust him and have faith and claimed one day he would be legendary."

Dan Casey smiles as he recalls his true respect and admiration for the slippery rogue pirate.

Dan places his rough hands gently around Veena Merida's slim, naked waistline and whispers in a sorrowful, conflicted voice, "I was too slow in saving them, and I only managed to get a few of the hostage passengers out of the burning fuel rigg. Von Rye insisted I left him till last to save Kira Savannah against her screaming protest. I did as my friend asked and saved Kira. He saluted me as I carried her to the *Decepter*'s airlock. Von Rye knew there wasn't enough time to return for him. The fuel vessel exploded and hit the Delapre-four moon base, killing hundreds."

Dan Casey and Veena Merida clinch in a hugging, loving kiss after opening their hearts up over the calm period aboard the Machiavellian freighter. Oozing sympathy and empathy, Veena slowly pulls away from the passionate embrace and tells him, "You were courageous and did all you could. Your friend saw that quality, and you saved Kira Savannah for him. I'm sure he looks down on you proud to this day and doesn't ever presume otherwise."

Before either of them can say another emotional word, there is a tiny, faint female voice shouting an echo from the secondary bedroom of the starship.

"Hey! Don't forget me. Can someone quickly undo these harness straps? Oh, boy, adults!" yelps Charlena Jones, in distress, who remains safely strapped in on the floating mattress after receiving medical attention.

"Gosh! I forgot I'd left Charlena strapped to the secondary bed for her safety during the rough flight. Bless her! The young girl must have woken up thinking she was in a student asylum. I better attend to her aid quickly before Wingman Jones gets trigger-happy again."

Dan Casey kisses his stunning and empathetic blessed woman. "Okay, Veena. Meet you back up in the cockpit and break the news to Charlena. She got her wish that there were no galactic studies today. We are now in the Isadora system. Thank you for everything."

The darling feminine agent sexually blows her lover a radiant kiss as she leaves the master bedroom. The enthralled interstellar pilot again bends down and picks up his fingerless-cut gloves with a spring in his step. Dan Casey quickly washes his stubbled face and grooms his swept dark hairstyle using the master room facilities. Stylishly, he spins his silver and black-barrelled gun around his hand and slickly slots the firearm into the weapon holster. Dan collects his mug of black Star coffee and heads for the cockpit. He witnesses Jay Haines waking up with a groan and yawning stretch after spending the night asleep in the weapon quarters.

Dan Casey amusingly taps his free hand on the gunslinger's padded ammo belt jacket and broad shoulders, "Good morning, pal. Rise and shine. Did you sleep well?"

Taking a comfy seat in his leather pneumatic pilot chair, Dan Casey regains control of the *Decepter*'s flight systems. "Switching over to manual navigation control, and, Pearl, knock off the hyperdrive and sequence the trajectory flow. Let's see what joy of wonders await us in the Isadora system."

Meanwhile, Veena Merida has made a milky coffee and is approaching the secondary bedroom. She opens the broken swing door, witnessing and hearing a huff and puff mumble from the young red-haired galactic student lying vertically and trying to wriggle free of the harness straps.

Charlena Jones sighs, "Oh boy! If only Foxy-D were here, I'd be free!"

"Boo! Let's get you unshackled, young lady," kindly teased Veena Merida, quickly placing the freshly brewed Aroma Red milky Star coffee on the sideboard and assisting with unbuckling the leather straps. Charlena Jones's cute face is filled with an overjoyed, beamed expression while she blows hair out of her dreamy blue eyes.

She happily screams out, "Veena! What happened? Did we make it? I thought you had all forgotten me, and have you snogged Dan?"

"That's a lot of early-morning questions for an injured teenage girl. Why don't you wake up first with a coffee, and how is that frizzled hand feeling?" asked Veena, showing naturally concerned behaviour patterns of caring for the young student like an older sister. Charlena edges up the hovering mattress, taking the milky coffee mug from Veena Merida's kind offer and responding to her empathy, "My hand is still a little sore but feels a bit better and thank you for the hot milky drink."

Gratefully Charlena Jones says, "Wow! You look so beautiful dressed in that shoulder garment. I've always wanted a wrap-around lace top outfit to make me look pretty like you instead of looking unpretty like me. Call me Scraggy Jones. I feel like a tramp in my dingy slave dress and smelly trader coat."

"Aww, you don't seem scraggy, and we shall get you a new dress so you are presentable to your mother when we return from the Isadora system."

Charlena Jones's freckled face beams with delight. "Oh, boy! Thank you, Veena! Wait till I tell my buddies at galactic studies that I've ventured into an uncharted zone of the Kalanisi Universe. Wow! This is so exciting. What happened to your nasty friends? Did we blow them up?"

Veena replies with vague details of the Panther's stalking pursuit and demise concerning her old companions. "Dan had a few manoeuvrable tricks in his locker, and Jay managed to damage their stealth spacecraft, so don't worry; they are long gone now, and good riddance too, as they are no longer friends of mine."

Charlena Jones can see the sorrowful expression invade Veena's pleasant and well-presented manner and tries to help her new companion with some thought. "My mum always told me if people set out to make you unhappy, they are not your real friends and don't deserve your time, so close your eyes and count to three, then blow all the badness away to where the stars don't shine. Now, changing the subject, I'm ready to conquer the Isadora system. Let's go!"

Veena kindly responds with a laughing smile as she gently brushes aside Charlena's sweeping auburn fringe from her blue eyes, "Oh, Charlena, thank you for the advice. What's your mother's name?"

The young female student replies with details about her siblings. "My mum's called Lena Jones, and I don't know my father. He left before I was even born."

"I shall take Lena's wise advice on board, and don't you want to go home? The Isadora system could be dangerous, so don't let your eagerness get the better of you. Let us clean you up and check the proceedings in the cockpit cabin."

Veena offers her dainty velvet-gloved hand out as a kind gesture. Charlena Jones places her empty coffee mug on the nightstand.

"I miss my mum and Foxy-D. But I'm ahead in my galactic studies, so a few days playing truant won't hurt."

The two bonding ladies leave the secondary bedroom and swiftly walk to the stairway before the restroom. The *Decepter* freighter shivers a waver in the hyper-speed turbulence as the slick starship prepares to drop out of the galactic hyper-lanes.

Veena duly warns, "Be careful of the stair rails; they have been prone to snap off. And who's Foxy-D? You mentioned that name when I sneaked into the bedroom with your morning Star beverage."

Charlena says, "Foxy-D! He's my pet cube-bot. He is so cute and naughty. I've modified him to a surveillance combat bot, but don't tell my mum. Foxy-D helped me get in and infiltrate Mach Galanti's Laire on Kothariya. That evil crook has secret plans for where my missing student friends are being held captive. Foxy-D downloaded the relevant data, but I got snatched on my escape and enslaved. My pet cube-bot must have informed Mum what happened to me, and she privately hired the gunslinger, Jay Haines, to come and rescue me."

Veena Merida smiles and responds to the young teenage girl's enthusiasm while closing the restroom door using the press-pad button on the side panel. The female galactic agent praises Charlena's digital companion's bravery. Still, with a warning of past advice, "Foxy-D sounds like a very useful pet cube-bot to have on your side, and you must be very careful indeed, Charlena. Deluded kingpin crime lords are not to be messed with lightly. They are dangerous individuals, and getting involved in that pattern of scenarios leads to a troubled path of no return. Believe me! It's not worth the misery and strife of witnessing pain. So, you leave the gangster crooks to agents trained for such villains so you can live a happy life and spend time with Lena and Foxy-D."

Charlena Jones's youthful spirit shows no such fearful barriers of restriction, and she asks a few more probing questions, "Can you train me to be an agent, and then I can save my school friends from the horrible fate of a lifetime in slavery and be like you? Bad arse and beautifully presented with a cute-arsed boyfriend to snog as I'm saving the galaxy?"

Veena laughs as she fills the sink basin with hot water. "You make life as a galactic agent sound so glamorous, Charlena Jones! But I very much doubt Lena Jones would see it on the same spectrum, and I wouldn't call Dan my boyfriend! We have a warm romantic spark, which I find very elegant to my heart after our rocky first appearances!"

"Oh, boy! You are in love, Agent Merida. So, did you snog him, and what else did you do?"

Veena shyly avoids the teenager's questions.

The *Decepter* Machiavellian starship prepares to slip-jump out of the hyper-lanes and into the Isadora system with an unknown, secret location and meeting with the agent leader, Tara Harlow. They need to safely deliver the astrological data box away from the Corporal Union's grip.

Chapter Fifteen

The Isadora Alter

As the silhouette of the *Decepter* MK2 freighter navigates through the hyper-speed lanes, it employs a slip-jump manoeuvre that creates an electrical flash wave and a stealth-contained bang. The starship flares with an emerging presence into a steady cruising velocity, effortlessly gliding with purpose through the outer blue mist of the Isadora sector. The mass expansion of space surrounding the Isadora system is regarded as a dangerous and uncertain region, as deemed by the prevailing galactic star charts. However, upon closer inspection, it becomes apparent that the reality of the Isadora system is far more remarkable than expected. Its orbit is surprisingly serene and unwavering, defying all prior assumptions and projections.

This soon becomes obvious to Dan Casey, who is seated in the cockpit cabin and is viewing the touted atmospheric environment. The charmed pilot wriggles forward from his pneumatic recliner chair and quickly double-checks the flight coordinates, telling the cyber navigation suite in a puzzled tone of dismay, "Well, the coordinates are correct. But this is not the solar system we are after; there are no hard storms or even a ripple of turbulence. Pearl, double-check the trajectory sequence core. I think our navigation hardware RAM is on the brink again. Unless you miscalculated the slip-jump coordinates, performing too many bio-health files. Those scans do have to stop, sweetie."

Jay Haines is seated behind the baffled pilot in the weapons division of the craft, leaning back in his padded seat and drinking his black Star coffee. He enquires, not having the best knowledge of space travel, "What were you expecting to find in this bleak system, man? I'd have thought no turbulence was a good thing. Call me naive, but I only travel galactic trips in straight lines as a rule, dude!"

He removes his designer tint glasses and places the expensive lenses on the weapon control keyboard. He continues to explain his means of transport as an intergalactic gunslinger, "That cheap two-seater planet-hopper starship that got wrecked on Mach Galanti's trade slave station is only on a week's rent, which now needs accommodating. I like to keep my sharpshooter boots firm to the ground."

Pearl flashes a crystalised response to the navigation system's recalibration scan, "Our GPS confirms this to be the Isadora system with no hardware fault detected. The navigation corruption spike is in the Corporal Union's star-chart data banks. Computing the galactic government's files on this uncharted spectre of the Kalanisi Universe are redeemed as misguided data!"

The handsome pilot leans back in his leather flight chair, conveying a silent expression of mystified thought prevailing on his face.

Jay Haines has his interpretations of the relayed solar chart information, "Another fabricated lie from the trusted Corporal Union and Mbron Media collaboration. No surprise to me, man! I lay a hefty wager they are hiding a dirty, profitable secret. The hard-working Kalanisi citizens are paying for the extortion of credits to fund the self-interested project. I keep telling folk that something big in the making is going down, and it will be bad. Worrying times for us all, man! Now, have you got more of that black coffee on offer?"

"Feel free to help yourself, Jay. Watch out for the broken

glasses on the floor and the percolator coffee machines in the smashed-up lounge. I also agree with you. There's a possibility that the Corporal Union has been informing the Kalanisi Galaxy that the Isadora system is unsafe. Are they broadcasting propaganda indoctrination through the Mbron Media's network while they run mining exhibitions on the outskirt moons? This can only mean that the Union wants something out here or further beyond with immense value, and who knows what their purpose of intent will be under that grey-haired lunatic, Director Volantis?"

Jay Haines nods in agreement with the cargo runner's threading together the Corporal Union's plans with an element of guesswork.

Pearl flashes a responsive data trace of positive energy ahead. The crystalised nav-suite states, "We have accrued a mass ecosystem on the navigational radar scope. There is too much static interference to identify the object at the present course and closing in for investigation."

Dan Casey pushes himself back up from leaning in his pneumatic pilot's chair and gazes his brown eyes intently out at the front view of the *Decepter* at the stunning fluoresce mist before him.

"An ecosystem can only mean one thing. Take us in nice and steady, Pearl."

The gunslinger asks, "Ecosystem at the edge of deep space not heard of before? Where the hell are we, man?"

The *Decepter* navigates gracefully through the misty atmospheric smog of the Isadora system, leaving behind a trail of light as it approaches the enigmatic energy source. The prospect of uncovering the secrets of this mystery data box is likely to captivate the imagination of any individual daring enough to embark on this journey. The galactic information regarding the nature of this mass-energy source is currently unavailable, adding to the mysterious intrigue surrounding this undertaking of the Isadora sector. The Machiavellian starship steadily cruises through the static atmosphere into clearer space.

Dan connects the internal tenor speaker, "Ten seconds till visual of the mystery location. Please, can all woozy female agents come to the cockpit."

Jay Haines quickly stands, laughing at Dan's arrival announcement. "So, what do you expect to find out here, man? Floating Astro-junk and wasted dust moons surrounded by dying star clusters?"

"All will be revealed soon, my dear friend; we have visual contact in three, two! What the?"

Dan Casey is shocked at what he witnesses and is taken aback by the ecosystem's interaction on the *Decepter*'s navigation radar entrustment. However, the charmed cargo pilot proceeds with a composed focus, trying to make sense of an adaptable approach to analysing the unforeseen situation. His primary objective is to comprehend the observed phenomenon thoroughly. He evaluates the flight control data with his meticulous dark brown eye and makes astute observations.

"It's a vibrant world, not showing on the intergalactic charts with a fully operational ecosystem."

Dan explains as he swiftly re-issues the use of the vessel's flight internal speakers with excitement and anticipation in his alluring voice. "Veena! Hurry up to the flight cabin; I believe we found your rendezvous and much more."

Dan Casey smiles, turns off the microphone and witnesses the presence of Jay Haines sitting in the co-pilot's chair with a stunned expression. The lion-hearted gunslinger places his empty coffee mug down on the dash controls.

Jay Haines comments on the uncharted world. "Wow! Man, the ecosystem is an actual planet. Can you believe this shit?"

Dan Casey replies with a grin, ascending his well-proportioned face and asking the AI navigation suite to perform her beloved advanced cyber scanning process.

"You're up, Pearl. It's time to initiate what you do best, sweetie. I need a rundown of the planet's core liveable stability and try to scan for the location of the data coordinates from Veena's holo-pad before she lost it on Cartonne."

"Confirmed planetary scans are now in process."

Dan slants his attention over to Jay Haines with an honest foresight of events, "I wasn't sure what to expect. But it wasn't a new flourishing world, for certain!"

He concentrates on the trajectory of the flight path towards the planet's blue glowing atmosphere. Not to miss out on the exciting discovery of an unknown quantity, the galactic agent, Veena Merida, and the young galactic student, Charlena Jones, quickly run to the cockpit. With the tapping echo sounds of their clicking high heels on the starship-vented panel deck, they both stop to gasp in awe.

Veena is the first to comment on the spectacular sight; her glistening jade eyes beam a spark, witnessing the fresh planet orbiting out the front view of the cockpit cabin. The gorgeous green-haired resistance fighter expresses her thoughts with the apprehension of the fear lying ahead, "Gosh! It's an uncharted planet; the agent briefing never said anything about a new world! If I had my holo-pad, I could have tried contacting the agent leader, Tara Harlow. Without the holo communications device, it will make things challenging to find anybody in a world of that size and scope."

The young, adorable, red-haired female rushes to the front view of the starship. Charlena comments on the prevailing ecosystem, "Wait till I tell my student friends about this unexpected adventure of a lifetime. Wo! A mysterious new world and one small step for Scraggy Jones."

Dan Casey charmingly smiles at the eager student, asking her, "How's the frazzled hand faring, Wingman Jones? I'm guessing this will beat a school nature trail around Kothariya's countryside."

"Oh, yeah! Mr Casey, thank you for letting me accompany you and co-pilot your starship. This is truly amazing."

Jay Haines says, "Hold it down now, kid! Stay away from those weapon triggers. I don't want to take you back to your mother, all battered and bruised; she'll be deducting my contract fee for your rescue, and I already owe for that leased starship."

She quickly replies in a teenage back-chatting manner, "When will it sink into your bullet brain? I'm not a kid. I will be eighteen soon, and for the starship debt, you can take that up with Mach Galanti when we rescue my friends from his palace on Dolore?" She cheekily says, "I've got a contact's name stored in the memory banks of Foxy-D. She's an undercover female spy who can help us get in and free my friends."

"Who the hell is Foxy-D? And no, we'll not be raiding any crime lord kingpin palace! You are going home to your mother, Lena. As soon as we finish this explorer's field trip and return to reality, kid."

Veena Merida intervenes with an amused smile and informs Jay, "Foxy-D is Charlena's pet cube-bot. I was informed everything about him while dressing her wounded hand. He sounds quite a useful chaperone companion to be by her side."

The gunslinger cringes. "Oh, man! I hate them, damn, freaky cube-bots. Those square and bleepy things are always pissing around, moving and hiding your belongings, being a pain. They're only good for target practice if you ask me."

"Dream on, bullet guy! You would never be able to get shot on my Foxy-D. He has been fully modified to a combat cube-bot and would be far too fast and adept for an old-timer gunslinger like yourself."

Pearl interrupts the light-hearted bickering between Jay and Charlena with a piece of information regarding the vague mystery planet they were swiftly approaching. The planet's atmosphere is deemed suitable for breathing, and sub-scans indicate no toxic levels of pollution. Due to surface interference, no life forms are showing, and the secondary scan continues. It is safe to presume I have successfully found the location on Miss Merida's holo-pad link."

Casey replies, "Great work, Pearl. Lock in the pinpointed location of the holo-pad directions. We shall take a swoop in close range and try to go unnoticed as much as possible.

"Hey, don't look so worried, sweetheart. I've never failed an interstellar delivery contract yet, and I'm not planning on making a career out of it now. So, gear up, people; we are going into an uncharted world and will be holding our heads high."

Says Dan Casey, with a determined face brimming with self-confidence, to the rest of the misfit crew as they prepared to descend fully into the planet's atmosphere.

The *Decepter* accelerates at an exceptional lightning-fast velocity, performing full-tilt navigation through the turbulent, flushing ecosystem of the newfound world with remarkable slick precision, covering vast distances in mere seconds. The Machiavellian starship gracefully emerges through the cerulean skies and lilac-tinted colliding clouds with minimal effort and maximum stability, oozing with the rumbling roar of the triple-slanted booster engines.

The sleek spacecraft soars through the vast expanse of the tranquil blue ocean, with its wings slicing through the air and the tail leaving a trail of spraying fray mist as it heads towards the lush tropical jungle island. The serenity of the ocean waves below is breathtaking, and the flight is made even more beautiful by the sight of the verdant greenery of the island looming ahead. The *Decepter* freighter maintains a sustainable cruising altitude, leaving a minimal environmental footprint to track if any inhabitants are keeping an eye on the skies. Inside the cockpit cabin of the slender, lightweight vessel, Dan is adjusting the flick-switch flight controls and activating the angled land gears while coinciding with the starship cyber suite. He is comfortably seated in his pneumatic pilot's chair, his fingerless-gloved hands firmly in charge of the levered joystick.

"Pearl, have you got the results of the secondary sub-scans digitised yet? I'm witnessing a tropical jungle island with a beachfront and a rising peak mountain covered by a tangled green, steamy jungle. I'm betting with my last cargo credits that our location with the agent resistance leader is the one that's always the most difficult to find!"

After the secondary bio-geography scans, Pearl responds with information about the rising peak jungle, "You are correct, Dan, in your insightful predictions and judgement of the island. The signal indicates the mass landscape rise is the rendezvous location of choice."

"Great! For once, Pearl. I was hoping you would lecture and inform me I was wrong. Pearl, have you got any updates on lifeforms down there on that tropical island? I doubt that we are the only living species in such a vibrant world, so keep frosty. And keep me advised on any current upturns."

He continues, "We shall stage a landing near the beachfront to set up camp and get a clear spectrum of that treacherous jungle trail."

"Reducing sonic power to the celestial hyperdrive and composing subsystems to engage auto-brake flaps. Please be careful down there, Dan, as I worry about you! We have only sketched blueprint data concerning the jungle map, with no real data to explain the natural habitat or mystery revolving around this tropical island."

"Hey, Pearl! Sounds like you're getting a touch sentimental in your old digital cyber cycle, and I'll be fine. Don't worry, sweetie. And remember. I've got a new adopted crew to watch my back."

Dan hears the other members of the crew congregating around the damaged lounge area of the *Decepter* freighter, talking and joking as they get organised with weapons and supplies for the landing party's expedition to the mysterious island.

The stylish Machiavellian MK2 Merlin class freighter traverses gracefully over the picturesque turquoise waters and beautiful tropical green landscape. The sonorous whistling rumbles from the easing down triple-booster engines and the reverberating from the sleek vessel are almost therapeutic. The gentle summer breeze carries the sound away across the ocean bed. The sleek starship hovers over the astounding tropical island's oceanfront then descends with a gently steamed whoosh onto the golden sand as the steadfast starship touches down to land. A cloud of sparkling glistering sand encircles its unmistakable shape, adding to the otherworldliness surrounding its unique silhouette.

Meanwhile, inside the stationary craft, Dan Casey finishes the systems checks in the cockpit cabin. In the stricken lounge quarters, the galactic agent, Veena Merida, is equipped with her faithful silver scope pistol and looks deadly in her tight black catsuit with knee-high-heeled black leather boots. The green-haired beauty checks the astrological data box.

The inquisitive-natured agent slowly levers her dainty suede-gloved hands over the unrecognisable symbols. Veena instantly activates the mystical folklore cube with a dire-droned ring scampering around the starship's lounge. The data box portrays an arrayed globe image of the Kalanisi Universe.

Jay Haines, dressed in his long navy leather jacket and ammo cross-body belt, stands firmly beside the voluptuous female agent while preparing himself for the tropical jungle trek. The stylish gunslinger wears his designer-tinted shades, checking and reloading his dual silver shooter with the attainable firing knife blades. Jay momentarily pauses his action of preparedness and gazes at the data box's projector of the galaxy.

He flicks his damper shades back upon his beaded dreadlock hairstyle, commenting on the mystic star chart, "I don't like it when you turn that strange, patterned cube on, Miss Merida. It makes me feel like I'm starting to believe in rumoured folklore with unfathomable comprehension of my good-natured sense. Do you know how the damn thing works, ma'am? I recognise the universe, but none of the symbol's markings make any recognition to my knowledge."

Veena turns off the statistical data box device and readily places the item in her small, black, shiny handbag. She responds positively, agreeing with his theories about the ancient rumours.

"Can't say I've indulged in supernatural beliefs. But this data box does feel it's got an abnormal presence surrounding its very existence, and Director Volantis is more than adamant about its purpose and capabilities in a sinister aspect of evil delusions.

"I'm keeping my mind open to any possibilities as I'm trained to expect the unexpected! Without good reason or explanation, Tara Harlow would not have summoned us halfway across the galaxy to a tropical island in the middle of the ocean on an unfound world."

Meanwhile, while Veena and Jay exchange views concerning the data box and the rumoured stories, Charlena Jones is preparing the luggage bag with any supplies she can find in the damaged interior of the beaten-up star-freighter. The seventeen-year-old galactic student is checking over the survival items, mumbling in a soft, excited voice.

"Astro-binoculars and medical bandages check, food and water supplies check and my blast weapon. Oh, that's not been checked off yet!"

"Excuse me. I'm sorry for interrupting, but I will require one of your silver blaster guns, Jay! And an adjustable holster belt and spare ammo. I can't venture into a wild jungle unprepared, and you can rest assured that Scraggy Jones will be more than ready to conquer this tropical oasis world."

"No way, kid! You gotta be joking with me, girl? What would your mother think if she knew you were in a strange world, shooting blaster weapons in a tropical jungle? You just stay close to me, Charlena. I'm all the protection you need; trust me, kid."

Charlena Jones smiles back with a tearing bundle of gratitude towards her chaperone.

"Aww, Jay! Thank you so much for your kindness, but who will protect you? That's why I need a weapon to help if trouble arises, and without Foxy-D here to cover our backs, things could get noisy."

Charlena pleads for a firearm as she picks up the field trip supplies and motions a walk with a sulking facial expression to near the exit hatch. She remains dressed in her white wrap-around dress and white lace-up boots with her jewelled cuffs.

The drop-dead gorgeous galactic agent graciously smiles with embarrassment, "Don't you give me that sweet, sorrowful pout, Miss Jones! I've got to agree with Jay. He will keep you safe in the jungle. And if it goes south, you can share my agent-issued scope pistol. I promise you."

The craft's lounge area lights dim to a lower-shaded spectrum as the bonding crew mingles. As Dan Casey enters the recreation quarters from the cockpit cabin, he flicks the power switches down to preserve the vessel's energy. He is preparing for their journey to the rendezvous point with Tara Harlow and the exploration ahead. Dan is dressed in his brown pilot jacket and plain black t-shirt, with his slanted holster belt containing his black-barrelled gun placed around his waist over his navy jeans with black leather boots.

Dan has a bunch of wired communication earpieces in his hands and gives one to each crew member as he explains the plan in due course, "Is everyone ready to go jungle-bound and dare face the unknown? Pearl wants us to wear these wired comm-links devices so she can keep track of our position in the jungle and monitor for any signal links with the illusive resistance leader. We checked over the tropical landscape grid, and Pearl has calculated a two to three-hour trek into this safari island with a drop in terrain and a sharp rise to a peak cavern surrounded by jungle bushes. They seem to have some sort of signal blocking. Are there any further details I can provide? If anyone has questions or suggestions, speak now. We may only have half a dozen hours of light to our aid, and I don't fancy spending the night in a mysterious tropical bush."

"I'm good to go; let's do this, man!" says Jay Haines, taking the supply rucksack from Charlena Jones and heading for the vessel's airlock hatch.

Veena Merida approaches her heart's desire and gives Dan Casey a peck on his stubbled cheek. The glamorous, jade-eyed agent confirms with spoken affection, "I'm ready as I'll ever be for a trip in the jungle, and thank you for everything, Dan. Especially for a wonderful time throughout last night!"

Dan Casey stands in the lounge quarters of the *Decepter*, with his thoughts wandering in distraction as he admires the feminine agent's sexy posture. Until he is kindly confronted by Charlena Jones, who is standing cutely in front of the courageous intergalactic pilot and swiftly attaching her wire communication link. She innocently waves a blown flick of her red-fringed hairstyle and relays an issue with the rendezvous plan.

Charlena speaks softly, "They won't give me a handgun or a weapon, and I know it's going to get noisy out there in the hazardous jungle. I wondered if you got a spare gun for me, Mr Casey. Please!"

He goes to the smashed-up diner's table and bends down, picking up some silver cutlery. Dan regains his composure and returns to the interested teenage girl, handing over a buckled silver fork, "There you go, Miss Jones! You are now weaponised and ready to tackle any obstacle that stands in your way."

Charlena tugs the pull cord of his brown leather pilot jacket. Asking him with a cute, bewildered expression of sheer confusion, "It's a fork? What am I supposed to do with a cutlery fork!"

"Improvise, young lady. You never know that silver fork may end up saving us all. Now, come on, people, we estimate about six hours of sunlight left. Let's not waste time and deliver our precious cargo before it gets too dark and nightfall draws in."

The *Decepter*'s exit hatch quickly opens with a shunting spur followed by a steamed whistle sound. The sloped ramp connects with the breezy sand pockets below the Machiavellian lightweight freighter. That causes shallow frictions of sandy dust clouds below the landing gears around the starship. The tropical mystery island is beaming with warm sunshine and a slight breeze. Dan Casey, the leader of the jungle-bound field party, is the first to step down the exit ramp, followed closely by Veena Merida.

Dan takes a deep breath of the fresh air. "The clean oxygen is too good to be true; it's near enough pure," he says in amazement, continuing to venture onto the ocean beachfront.

Veena echoes his sentiment as they exit on the sandy beach, "The golden lush green scenery is just such a beautiful ocean paradise; I've never experienced anywhere like this before. It's truly spectacular."

The positive, joyful outlook and enthusiasm inspire Jay Haines and the enthusiastic renegade student, Charlena Jones, who follow their new companions promptly to the sandy beachfront paradise. Jay Haines wastes no time operating his survival skills, having the Astro-binoculars in place and scanning for the safest route into the tropical jungle bush. Dan Casey also searches around and becomes familiar with the tropical sunshine environment.

After a few moments, he swiftly approaches Jay Haines. Dan asks for recommendations and thoughts on what track to pursue through the daunting jungle, "What do you see out there, Jay? Any gifted shortcuts through this safari expedition! If such thing exists in a mass tangle of tropical jungle weed."

Dan Casey is in good spirits, considering recent events which have turned his life upside down. He casually reaches up with his right hand to the top left corner pocket of his leather pilot's jacket for his last green-dust smoke. Dan stylishly flicks the smoke filter into his luscious manly lips and readily lights the smoke using his Astro-lighter, waiting for a bearing response from Jay Haines.

Meanwhile, behind the surveying gunslinger and pilot, Veena Merida walks over to Charlena Jones with a squinted facial expression. She witnesses the red-haired student on her hands and knees, collecting sand samples.

Veena bewilderingly stands to a halt as her high-heeled boots sink onto the beach and dubiously asks Charlena, "What are you doing down there with that mysterious glowing sand?"

The student swiftly gets up from her knees, brushing the sand off her legs and white dress. Charlena Jones smiles, dangling three test tubes full of glowing beach sand in front of Veena's frowning face, and explains her reasons with a mischievous giggle. "They are samples for my galactic exploration studies. When I pop these babies into Foxy-D's memory core, I will have the best samples in galactic high school and pass my exams with top triple grades."

Seeing Veena's gun, she asks, "Let me hold your scoped stub pistol. Please! I've only got a crooked cutlery fork. I won't pull the trigger. I promise you, Veena. I want to train and be a galactic agent like you, and then I will save my missing school friends from Mach Galanti."

Veena Merida sighs deeply and gives in to the pleading, as she recognises a familiar look. She draws her sliver scope pistol from the holster belt and gently tosses it over to Charlena Jones.

Veena advises, "Okay, be quick, or you will get me into trouble, Miss Jones. And I had the same face you are portraying now when my dear parents were killed! I know how you feel inside, Charlena, and that nothing will stop you, whatever anyone tries to advise. Once you get involved in this agent lifestyle, it's tough to get out and live a normal, pleasant life again. Being an intergalactic agent may look and sound glamorous, but it can be a very lonely swansong filled with sorrowful tears at times. I warn you now in advance, Charlena Jones. Please take it as sisterly advice."

Charlena holds the silver-scoped weapon and tries to stylishly loop-spin the hand pistol around in her dainty fingers like Jay Haines. But she fails to perfect his skilled art with a cute, sniggering, embarrassed smile. The attractive, humorous, fun-loving student quickly hands the scope pistol back to Veena Merida before the others even notice and thanks Veena for her kind words of support, "Thank you so much for understanding, and I take your experienced advice as a galactic agent and, more importantly, as a new big sister! But for the meantime, the beautiful, glamorous wonder-agent, Scraggy Jones, has a dangerous, uncharted tropical jungle to conquer, and I'm ready for galactic agent business, ma'am!"

The two smiling females link their hands together and swiftly make their way forward to get on point with the other members of the *Decepter* crew. As the breezing light wind sweeps through the masses of green tropical bush, producing eerie noises and rustling echoes around the forefront of the steamy tropical jungle entrance, Dan Casey stands while talking over their plausible options with the gunslinger, Jay Haines. He shifts his leather-jacketed body to a quarter-angled posture. Dan flicks away the green-dust smoke, noticing the two galactic ladies rejoining the group with giggling laughter and high spirits between them.

Dan Casey greets them with a friendly smile as his female colleagues walk across the golden beach with the blue ocean waves splashing in the background. The secluded island provides beautiful, picturesque scenery with a charming atmosphere.

With amusement and humour, Dan asks about their cheerful and giggling moods. "Why do you two look so happy? What have you sweethearts been chatting about and doing over there? Let me guess, making glowing sandcastles!" says Dan Casey with a joking touch of kind-hearted sarcasm. He smirks, looking down at the medical test tubes filled with sand samples held in Charlena's youthful hands.

"Well, Dan. This young genius has just given me my first lessons in sand technology studies, and now I have a new feather in my agent's book of tricks. I would tell you all the secrets, but it is only female agent talk!"

The gushing wind catches a flow of her long, wavy, pastel-coloured hair. She hugs him tight and closer to his muscular body, seemingly forgetting her mission with a deep, happy sigh of peaceful contentment.

"Oh, I see it's like that now, the glamorous woozy agent and the trigger-happy wingman teaming up against the interstellar cargo pilot? I better be careful that you don't try to steal my starship and leave me stranded on an alien world with no cosmetic perks?"

Charlena Jones is astute and alert in answering the cargo pilot's humoured banter, "Agent business, Mr Casey, and you are not meeting the correct specifications."

Charlena Jones waltzes over the sandy beach to Jay Haines and asks him, "So what's the plan? I'm ready to go!"

He advises the young student about his scouting plan, "Come on now, kid! We shall track ahead and give them two some space."

He bounds into the steamy jungle bush with his bravery in a highly positive order. Charlena nods in agreement and readily ventures into the unknown wilderness alongside Jay

Haines. While a short distance behind on the golden ocean beachfront, Dan Casey is in an entangled, loving embrace with Veena Merida. The handsome pilot's dark eyes gaze deep into her bright jade eyes, with his manly hands caressing her slender waist.

Dan smiles with a teased verbal note, "You will be a bad influence on Charlena! What will her dear mother say? Training her to be an intergalactic agent. I saw you showing her how to enable the infrared pistol. It is charitable that you are looking out for her, Veena."

The interstellar pilot smiles, "It must have been daunting for Charlena, being alone on that slave-trade space station of Mach Galanti."

He swiftly turns and starts walking towards the creepy jungle-vine entrance. The charmed cargo pilot releases his grip on his beloved female agent's slim waistline and readily leads the way deeper into the steamy tropics without reluctance or anticipated fear.

Veena graciously raises her beautiful jade eyes with a flirty flutter. The sexy feminine agent counters his teasing words. She amusingly utters in a well-spoken fashion, "Gosh! You're a fine one to talk about improper adult responsibilities, Mr Casey! Did you start her crusade off with the crooked cutlery fork? I believe the young student will influence me badly!"

Veena Merida continues, at ease about her feelings, "It's nice to have the role of big sister to play after I supposedly let Terri down in her unfortunate time of need. Against all knowledge of my prejudged guilt."

Dan Casey asks her, while chopping restricted jungle vine bushes off his path, "Is that why Terri Lace tipped the friendship scale with you? She holds you responsible for something you weren't aware of."

"Yes, Terri is hurting badly." Veena pauses again. "I can't help but wonder if she spoke some truths. As I would have been there to help her if it wasn't for the personal vendetta, I cursed myself to avenge my dear parents. So I feel I'm the mechanism that set Terri on this merry path of self-destruction."

"You can't bear the weight of Duran and Terri's burden. Whatever happened to them is not your fault. Don't think it is, sweetheart. They became damn cruel bounty hunters, the sort of people who catch little girls like Charlena and then willingly sell them off to crime lords for credit. While celebrating over a three-course meal and endless bottles of champagne. So don't ever let your guard down on that bitch, Terri Lace.

"Promise me. Okay! Terri won't hesitate to pull the trigger on you, Veena. I've seen her turbo car driving. She is damn ruthless and puts herself first, so just remember that the friends you had before are now gone and have become predators."

Veena Merida nods in stern agreement with the wise words spoken by the cargo-runner pilot. They continue to flirt and talk as they swiftly follow the indented footstep trail left in the golden sands made by the front-running pair of the field parties, Jay Haines and Charlena Jones. The daylight slowly fades as the massive shadowy vine-laden trees shade the overgrown jungle vegetation.

Trickling streams of crystal-clear water contribute to the steady flow of the river as it meanders through the uneven contours and terrain of the mysterious jungle island. After an hour of traversing and struggling through the tropical jungle paradise, the deeper they venture, the more it feels like something is watching or preying on their positions.

Jay Haines is confident in his instinct abilities and has become alert to this prodigious sentiment.

The adept gunslinger warns Charlena Jones, "Stay put for a moment, girl. I'm just going to check through those rustling vine bushes."

Jay Haines whispers as he becomes increasingly aware of a potential threat. Jay takes a cautious step forward and connects the microphone earpiece, reporting to Dan Casey and Veena Merida. The dreadlocked gunman's hands slip over his dual holster belt, and he caresses the spur handles of his twin silver blasters.

He informs of his suspicions, "Hey man, I think something is moving out here. I've got a sense of unease and would advise you to maintain a closer distance."

A short interspace behind the investigating shaded gunslinger, Dan Casey, confirms his warning through the earpiece communication device; he responds by telling his colleague, "Jay, maintain and hold your position until we make up ground. We are en route and will arrive shortly."

The pilot also asks the starship's AI navigation systems, "Pearl, keep a fixed location on them and their surroundings. Pearl? Where are you, sweetie?"

Dan looks at Veena, hearing just static interference. He says with a tense strain, "Looks like we've lost Pearl! We're on our own from here. Come on, Veena. Let us proceed expeditiously and join the others."

Ahead, the young galactic student Charlena Jones stands her ground as Jay Haines has advised. She hears rustling to her side. With a tense frown on her cute face, she blows her red-coloured fringe hairstyle quickly out her blue eyes. The pretty student clutches her silver cutlery fork and whispers a mutter to herself, "Oh boy, what is that crackling noise?" Being a curious teenager, Charlena decides to investigate with caution.

Charlena Jones quickly scatters the tropical vine bush to reveal her anticipation and initial fear. Which promptly turns to blissful awe when she uncovers a purring, baby black fang-tooth tiger. Charlena can't help but relax as she sees it, "Aww, oh! You're so cute."

She then turns her whimpering attention to Jay Haines, who is a bit further ahead of her, and lets him know what is causing the rustling in the steamy bushes,

"Hey Jay, it's okay. It is just a baby black fang-tooth tiger, nothing to be afraid of, Mr Haines."

The daring gunslinger quickly advances through the constricting vines, backtracking a few yards and standing on the verged bank before the cute, wandering student. "Charlena, step away now! It's not the cub I'm worried about, it's the damn mother!" Before Jay Haines can finish his sentence of warning, a massive, black-fanged tiger pounces at the off-guard gunslinger.

Jay Haines swiftly finds himself entangled with the large cat. The gunslinger is knocked flat and stunned as the menacing wild beast quickly leaps up. Jay looks up at the circling wild predatory animal, and he also notices his dual silver guns have fallen adrift in the tangled jungle bush during the attack, causing him to become incapacitated and vulnerable to further harm from the black raging tiger.

The gallant intergalactic gunman glares over his designer-tinted glasses and mutters, "Oh, man! Troubling times." Jay Haines gradually pushes up to his heavy boot stance, quickly composing himself, eyeing the growling, slobbering fanged-tooth tiger.

There are terrified screams of his name coming from Charlena Jones. "No! Jay, are you okay?"

Given the scarcity of time, Charlena Jones hastily connects her communication earpiece device and urgently voices, "Dan, we require your assistance urgently. Please help me, Veena!"

Amid her plea, the youthful girl is abruptly interrupted by a low, menacing growl from behind. Charlena Jones gulps in fear. She spins around, drawing her silver cutlery fork to defend the lurking threat, catching sight of the growling black fanged-tooth tiger cub, looking more menacing than before.

Charlena frowns and mutters in shock, "Oh, boy! You are not looking so cute anymore." The scene is chaotic as the fanged-tooth tiger cub arches its back legs and swiftly pounces forward with a bounding leap. Charlena quickly turns around and runs, screaming in fear, "Help me, help Dan!"

Dan Casey is apprised of the distress emanating from his wired communication earpiece. In a swift response, he vocalises his intention to help Charlena, "I am en route, Wingman Jones. Hold on."

Dan and Veena, in stylish unison, draw their weapons and swiftly navigate through the densely grown jungle terrain with slick alacrity, boldly leaping over obstructions and vines of entangled vegetation along their energetic path. Dan's heart races as he sprints up the jungle terrain embankment. The heroic cargo pilot arrives just in time to see Charlena Jones frantically running with her crooked silver cutlery fork, pursued by a black fang-tooth cub.

Without hesitation, Dan Casey stylishly spins his silver and black-barrelled gun and aims. He steadies his breathing, and his dark brown eyes fix on the black-fanged cub, and he pulls the lever trigger. Veena Merida readily backs him up. Their blast shots echo through the tropical jungle haze, and the black fang-tooth cub pauses for a split second before darting away into the safety of the vine-laden bushes. Dan and Veena breathe a sigh of relief, witnessing Charlena is now out of harm's way for the time being. They quickly sprint to the young, shaken-up female student.

Dan Casey asks Charlena, "Where is Jay?"

She points to the right side of the jungle bed environment, "He... was... catapulted off the jungle verge as the massive black fanged-tooth tiger beast pounced on him!"

Dan Casey turns to Veena Merida, who is daringly covering their rear guard. He speaks with purpose and faith in her abilities. "Stay with Charlena and keep her safe. I know you can. I'm going to get Jay."

The green-haired galactic agent nods, her muscles tensing in anticipation. Veena tensely replies, "Don't take too long." She warns, aiming her silver-scoped pistol and recoiling a rapid shot at the approaching beastly foe. As she craftily shields Charlena,

Veena stresses, "They're now coming from every angle. The blast flares must have alerted the whole damn fang-tooth tiger pack."

Dan Casey acknowledges her warning with a flicked salute before exiting the entangled jungle-vine bush. He knows that time is of the essence, and he has to find Jay Haines before it is too late.

Jay faces challenging hand-to-hand combat against a mother-fang-tooth tiger in a deep jungle crevice. Despite the formidable opponent, he relies on his quick wit and resourcefulness to gain an advantage. In a moment of strategic observation, Jay notices a nearby bush laden with vines, which he promptly dashes for as the fearsome, black-toothed tiger lunges towards him. He skilfully manages to catch hold of a vine, using it to swing himself out of harm's way. With remarkable agility, he readily grabs one of his silver shooters, which had detachable blades, to defend himself against further aggression from the ferocious creature. Jay firmly grasps his sleek blaster weapon, carefully aiming as the menacing black fang-tooth tiger launches itself in a formidable pouncing leap. With a sense of dread, the gunslinger pulls the pulsating trigger, only to discover that the weapon has jammed, "Oh man, give me a damn break," Jay sternly mutters in shocked disbelief.

Reacting quickly, the adaptable gunslinger executes a nimble leaping roll to evade the tiger's razor-sharp claws, which rake against his jacket. The brave, dread-beaded gunslinger stands his ground and can see his other dual shooter weapon buried in the jungle embankment between him and the whipping-around grizzling black fang-tooth creature.

Dan Casey charges towards the heart of the jungle with unwavering determination as he witnesses Jay Haines confidently calculating his attempted odds of survival. Dan Casey takes a deep breath, composing himself swiftly and skilfully aiming his trusty, black-barrelled firearm with fierce determination in his piercing eyes.

He shouts at the top of his lungs, "Hey, you fanged beast! Come get some!"

The daring cargo runner rapidly opens fire, expertly chaining out blast rounds at the aggressive fanged-tooth tiger. Despite the danger, Dan is fully focused on taking down the ferocious feline predator and helping Jay Haines escape. The massive, black-fanged tiger is wildly raging a roaring growl due to the blasts of shots and distractions fired by a cargo-runner pilot. The fanged tiger gracefully turns its muscle-bound physique and fiercely leaps towards the jungle bush embankment. The mother tiger rages and is prepared to attack Dan Casey. The cargo pilot has cunningly distracted the raging animal by using himself as bait.

Jay Haines uses this opportunity to escape, and he quickly acts with a dive roll. He stylishly grabs his other silver gun, which is lying buried in the jungle bush. As a skilled gunslinger, he activates the secondary trigger without a flinch. The collective gunslinger accurately fires the knife blades at the offensive black fang-tooth as the wilderness creature pounces for his cargo-runner companion. The razor-sharp knife blades swirl through the hazy jungle mist with a whooshing silence, slicing through the vine-laden green bushes and penetrating the arched, muscular back of the black-fanged tiger. The gigantic creature roars in pain, trying to escape the knife wounds as it falls down the embankment.

Dan Casey lets out a sigh of relief and quickly motions to the verge edge, offering his hand to assist Jay Haines up the steep jungle embankment, "Come on, Jay. We must return to the others before that wild-fanged beast gets its second wind."

The darkly handsome slingshot gunman thanks Dan Casey for his mastery help, "Hey man, I owe you big time. I thought I was a damn goner back there."

The sense of danger is palpable as Veena Merida's agent-trained skills shine, and she urgently grabs hold of Charlena Jone's delicate hand. The green-haired galactic agent feels the adrenaline coursing through her veins. Vicious, black-toothed tigers surround them, their razor-sharp teeth bare as they prepare to attack.

Veena doesn't waste a second. She knows they had to get out of there fast. With a swift motion and rapid array of scattering shots, she pulls Charlena towards her and starts running, her heart pounding in her chest vigorously in her black catsuit as she hears the ravaging tigers' growls closing in behind them. Despite the fear and chaos, Veena remains focused and determined to get them both to safety.

Veena Merida's amazing long, wavy pastel hair flows as she swiftly sprints through the opposing vine bush, urgently trying to escape the fanged, menacing, packed black-tiger predators. With utmost confidence, Charlena Jones strides alongside Veena Merida, her red, bobbed fringe hair swaying around her cute face. She is determined to keep up with the beautiful galactic agent, and nothing can stop her. As they approach the jungle bank's running river stream, the ground becomes unstable in the shifting tropical maze.

Veena and Charlena, unfortunately, lose their traction as their heeled footwear causes them to stumble and fall over with no control of their bodies. The running river takes them quickly, rushing down the bending stream, gaining speed, spinning and whooshing them around in a troublesome frenzy.

They both yell, "Ahh!" They swiftly come to the end of the steaming jungle ridge, which has a small free-falling drop over the waterfall's edge. With an unstoppable, powerful force, Veena Merida and Charlena Jones are rapidly swept over the riverbed edge with a hurling, twisting fall. "Aaahh!" Their screams intensify, dunking a bombed splash into the below river's cornerback.

Dan Casey's dark brown eyes narrow with shocked anger as he rapidly turns his stunned gaze towards Jay Haines. Both are transfixed by the sight of the two ladies being washed over the steaming ridge. Dan's face contorts with a grunting expression, a mix of frustration and helplessness as he watches the scene unfold before him. The merciless river is unforgiving; the sound of the water and the roaring pack of black-fanged-tooth tigers litter the area, making it extremely difficult for Dan and Jay to communicate. Despite their efforts to intervene, they are no match for the raging river, and all they can do is watch in horror as the two ladies are swept away.

The mastery ace pilot, Dan Casey and courageous crackshot, Jay Haines, make a swift dash towards the jungle ridge of the fast-flowing river. Their relationship is strong and adaptable, as they duly fire warning shots to scare off the pack of black-fanged tooth tigers. Tensely sprinting to the end of the river's ridge, Dan quickly comes to a staggering halt with a sigh of relief shading his stressed facial expression. Peering over the edge of the verge, he sees Veena and Charlena safely surfacing the river bend, gasping for breath.

Dan Casey turns his scratched leather-jacketed body towards Jay Haines and says, "They look okay. Thank the galactic heavens."

But before he can finish his sentence, he is interrupted by something that widens his dark eyes. With a fierce roar, the massive, black-fanged tiger reappears through the jungle-vine bush with a vengeance, arching its muscular, wounded back and pouncing with a projecting leap over the matting jungle terrain. Its drooling fangs and viciously yellow-scorned eyes are focused directly on its stalked prey near the riverbed ridge's end.

Jay Haines draws his active silver shooter weapon and takes an aimed offensive stance, "Oh! Damn, Mamma is back with that second wind, and she looks pissed!"

In the heat of the moment, with the bounding, black-fanged

tiger looming large, Dan tugs Jay's shoulders and says, "Come on. Let's not hang around and find out. Let's go this way!"

Jay Haines quickly manoeuvres a quarter turn and follows the cargo-runner pilot. The dapper-dressed gunslinger stresses the choice of Dan Casey's direction. With a deep breath, the gunslinger mutters, "I was hoping it isn't this way, troubling times!"

Dan and Jay exchange a knowing glance before running towards the riverbank edge without uttering a single word. As they approach the edge, they both take a deep breath and jump into the air with all their might, as if they were taking a leap of faith. The waterfalls down below are roaring with immense power, and the water crashing against the rocks echoes through the jungle. The two friends descend with lightning speed, their hair whipping around them as they fall towards the water crevices below. And then, with a loud splash, they hit the water hard, sending waves in every direction and disappearing beneath the swampy surface.

After a daring descent down the rapid-flow waterfall, Veena Merida manages to swim her way over to the swampy jungle shore. Despite the treacherous waters, she has shown remarkable skill and courage, quickly navigating the currents. Charlena Jones has been watching her every move and is doing her best to copy Veena's adept and skilful manoeuvres. The sexy female galactic agent emerges from the water, dripping wet. The renegade student appears in the same damp condition and follows closely behind. Charlena's eyes are fixed on Veena's every move.

Veena scans the area to get her bearings and figure out the best way forward. Charlena watches her intently, trying to learn from Veena and apply it to unforeseen situations. Together, the two friends stand at the edge of the swampy jungle shore. They are determined to conquer whatever obstacles come their way with Veena's guidance and Charlena's tenacity.

After experiencing the sudden impact of swampy water, Dan Casey and Jay Haines emerge from it while coughing and gasping for air. They subsequently swim to the shore, where Veena and Charlena hasten to their aid with emotional hugs and gracious expressions of relief. The four adventurers have narrowly escaped the threat posed by the black-fanged-tooth tigers.

Dan expresses concern for everyone's safety and reminds them of the urgency, "Is everyone okay? That is a close call with those feline-fanged beasts, but we must keep moving before nightfall. Following a wild guess, this data box has a link to the sculptural architectural archway directly ahead."

The interstellar pilot sees an elegant marble-stoned arch in the misty haze of the deep tropical jungle. Veena Merida observes the architectural discovery with great interest. She admires the intricately sculptured archway as the field team advances through the shallow, swampy waters towards the imposing structure.

Puzzled by its presence amid a steamy jungle, Veena asks, "What could have motivated someone to construct such an exquisitely designed edifice in this location?"

Jay Haines holds Charlena Jone's hand tightly, keeping her close for protection as he comments on the discovery, "What's more worrying is where the archway leads to, ma'am!"

Charlena Jones remarks, "Whoever built it must have had a good reason to advocate so much time and effort."

As they trudge through the jungle swamp and past the intriguing archway sculpture, Dan Casey suddenly stops and looks up, taking in the unexpected view. He turns to the rest of the *Decepter* crew and says with a confident feel to his allured voice, "I believe all the answers we seek lie up there in that temple!"

The handsome cargo pilot's words fill the group with renewed determination to reach their destination and uncover the astrological data box's mysteries.

Veena Merida reaches her arm right to her wet, tangled green-pastel hair and shrugs behind her dainty neckline. She gazes up at the temple, and her jade eyes open wide with anticipation and bewilderment,

"I think we've found out where the archway leads. Why would Tara Harlow want to meet in a lost temple in a jungle?" says the mystified female resistance agent.

Dan Casey places his fingerless-cut gloved hand on her shoulder in a comforting gesture, telling her, "Let's go and find out why this Miss Harlow keeps putting us in harm's way?"

Veena nods back with a quarter smile on her luscious red gloss lips and kindly strokes his caressing hand in return, appreciating his moral support and bravery.

Charlena Jones is also gazing up to the temple buried in the overgrown jungle bush above and says in awe and disbelief, "No one's ever going to believe me back at galactic studies about all this being real. Oh, boy! I wish Foxy-D were here too; my pet cube-bot could have taken a live holo visual of us exploring the ancient folklore temple."

"Good old-fashioned target practice is all those annoying chunky cube-bots are any good for!"

During their field trip through the tropical jungle, the group engage in casual conversation as they reach the base of the winding jungle trail.

Dan Casey proposes, "We can follow the bush-laden path up to the buckled bridge gap and improvise a way across from up there."

Despite repeated attempts to contact Pearl via the earpiece communication device, Dan is unsuccessful, likely due to damage sustained by the equipment from the swampy water. Dan Casey leads the misfit group up the tropical bush trail, ascending with an adventurous smile on the final stretch of the misty path. He is followed by the glamorous Veena Merida, whom he assists in reaching the top, while Charlena Jones trails slightly behind. Jay Haines hangs back, providing rear guard coverage.

As Dan Casey looks ahead, he spots a silhouette of vine trees arranged in an arched shadowy pattern, leading to a buckled and damaged ropey bridge. Bravely, he moves closer to the bridge with Veena Merida by his side as they investigate. In contrast, Charlena Jones waits for Jay Haines to join them at the top of the temple peak. A small distance ahead, Dan Casey turns his head slightly towards Veena as they cautiously move through the hazy, vine bush-tunnelled maze.

He takes a few delicate monitoring steps towards her and says with a glimmer of astonishment belaying over him, "Did you hear them, the whispering voices in the mist? Keep frosty, Veena. Something feels wrong about being close to these mysterious temple grounds."

With a serious facial expression, Dan Casey relays a perspicuous feeling as his leather-gloved hands slip intensely over his slanted holster belt. He draws his black and silver-barrelled gun with steady observation.

Veena Merida has complete trust in her fanciable partner's institution and abilities without doubt or any hesitation. The capable, glamorous, feminine agent with striking jade eyes listens carefully to his cautious insights. Veena quickly draws her silver-stubbed agent-issued weapon with her dainty gloved fingers and swiftly activates the switch for the infrared-scope site, her sharp eyes scanning every inch of the surrounding ghastly vine tree environment with a watchful gaze.

Dan's astute hearing picks up whispers, and Veena declares, "I can hear them as well, but it's not making sense with their hushed vocals."

Dan Casey aims his short-barrelled weapon as the whispers grow louder while they explore the temple's vicinity. The cautious cargo pilot turns back with an eye and ear signal as a warning to Jay Haines and Charlena Jones, indicating they should stay wary and alert.

Jay Haines soon picks up the coded scent and acknowledges the warning with a solemn nod of his dark, dreadlocked head. Jay quickly reaches for his holster belt and draws the stylish dual blaster with detachable weaponised razor knives. The collected gunman keeps a calm, slick, wandering eye out for the whispering dangers as he starts to hear echoing around the arch vine-laden passage. Charlena Jones stays close to her chaperoned gunslinger's side and follows suited code with a nodding head notion over to the other members of the *Decepter* crew. The red-haired teenager draws her crooked cutlery fork from her white wrap-around dress sash belt with a scared look around the haunted presentation on the temple's outer grounds.

Dan Casey and Veena Merida navigate through the thick, misty jungle trail with great care. They walk shoulder to shoulder, their weapons drawn and at the ready, as they move through the dense foliage. Within the humid atmosphere, there is palpable tension, and the faint sound of whispering voices seems to echo through the vine-laden trees, coming from all around them, making it difficult to pinpoint its source. As they make their way deeper into the temple vicinity, the mist grows thicker, making it difficult to see more than a few feet in front of them. The damp earth muffles the sound of their footsteps beneath their feet, and the only other sounds are the rustling of the leaves and the distant call of birds.

Despite the difficulty of the terrain, Dan and Veena move with practised ease, their steps silent and their senses alert. They are in this dangerous environment, and their weapons are a testament to the dangers lurking in the shadows. As they continue their way, the tension in the air grows thicker, and the whispering voices seem to be getting louder. Dan and Veena don't speak, but the unspoken understanding between them is clear, and they would do whatever it takes to make it out alive together. Suddenly, out of nowhere, strange figures emerge from underneath the jungle floor. Dan and Veena are taken aback by the ghostly figures. Dressed in long black hooded cloaks with red piercing eyes and mummified face masks, they are intimidating and unnatural. Each holds an ancient spear weapon. Dan Casey is stunned and doesn't know what to do. He turns to Veena Merida, who is also frightened and confused by the surreal events unfolding before their eyes. The charismatic cargo pilot says in gobsmacked confusion, "What the fuck!!"

The cloaked ghosts begin to converge on their position with their twisted, jewelled spears, posing a menacing threat. They speak in a deep, ominous voice that sends shivers down the spine.

The dark, shadowy figures intone in unison, "You do not belong here. We are the Zealot Templars of the forbidden Temple of Delas. And we will not allow outsiders to defile our sacred space."

Their eyes glow with an otherworldly energy, and they begin to attack, hurling their jagged, pointed spears.

Reacting swiftly to the hostile intentions of the Zealot Templars, Dan and Veena inadvertently split up. They perform a stylish diving roll to evade the chanting Templar's deadly sharp spears. Dan wastes no time gaining composure and retaliating against the shadowy masked Templars, tactically opening fire on his sleek silver-black gun while keeping an eye out for Veena. He soon spots her in full swing, taking aim with her infrared-scoped beam and blasting the chanting Templars to smithereens. The Zealots explode into powdery black dust clouds upon impact.

Dan feels the sinister Zealots closing in on his position. He daringly manoeuvres from the vine tree cover and opens fire, chaining an array of blast bolts and hitting the shadowy Templars. Amid the conflict, Dan shouts to Veena Merida, who is holding her own in the terrifying encounter. "Veena! Retreat to the rope bridge and try to get across to the temple. I'll try to hold them off and return to help the others."

Veena confirms in a hesitant response while preoccupied with the Zealot Templars darting around the misty jungle environment, "Okay, I'll try to do my best. You be damn careful, Dan."

The interstellar pilot masterfully surges his body forward with determination through the whispering jungle, deftly manoeuvring with precision, quarter turns with his black-barrelled weapon in hand, expertly firing at the stalking Zealot Templars with high accuracy. Dan Casey urgently dashes a weaving, energetic run through the jungle-arched vines ahead of his companions, Jay Haines and Charlena Jones.

They are facing the same issues as the chanting Zealot Templars, who keep repeating their message in a droning and wary voice, "We are the Zealot Templars for the forbidden Temple of Delas, and you don't belong here on our sacred grounds."

The mysterious mummified Templars are wielding their jewelled spears in a menacing form, making the troubling situation more daunting for Jay and Charlena.

The jungle island has transformed from a tropical sunshine paradise to an unnatural nightmare in moments. The gallant gunslinger, Jay Haines, keeps his main thoughts on protecting Charlena Jones. He grabs her feminine hand, stylishly showcasing his undeniably talented skills as a hotshot marksman, professionally taking out the Zealot Guardians with some cunning sharpshooting.

Jay Haines and Charlena Jones are instinctively aware of the dangers surrounding them. Luckily, they witness Dan Casey battling his way through the Zealot Templars towards them to help.

"Come on, girl! We need to damn move and fast. We're getting overrun," Jay says urgently.

Charlena Jones screams in fear and panic, her cute, frightened face showing the stress of the situation. Two menacing, masked Zealots emerge from the jungle-laden floor, flanking their position. Jay Haines acts quickly, springing into action and kicking simultaneously, blasting the mummified ghost while hurling Charlena with a lifting lunge, swinging her towards the approaching Templar. The young renegade student adapts to his countering move, bravely lashing out with a kicking attack at the black-cloaked Zealot, knocking him back. With the rising advantage on his side, Jay Haines opens fire, and with the unbalanced Zealot Templar caught off guard, Jay launches the shining razor blade knives with speed and precision. The chaperone gunslinger turns the mummified Templar into an evaporating cloud of metamorphosing dust.

Jay Haines is a storied gunslinger, the man everyone throughout the galaxy knows and respects. Looking upon his dark, rugged, and courageous face, the frightened seventeen-year-old Charlena Jones knows she is in capable hands despite her fear.

Jay looks into Charlena's fearful blue gemstone eyes, and without hesitation, he speaks earnestly, "I promised your mother, Lena, I'd keep you safe. Now, you run, kid, and don't look back."

Charlena refuses to leave. In a panicked plea, she exclaims, "No! I can't leave you, I can't!"

But Jay Haines isn't to be denied. He firmly pushes the galactic student forward and shouts in his deep, allured voice, "Run, Charlena. I've got this, so go now!"

He is to be her guide, protector, and assurance in the dark times ahead. Though her heart is heavy, Charlena does as commanded and quickly approaches Dan Casey, slowly edging closer to the pair, motioning a battle with the hostile Zealot Templars.

Charlena Jones knows Jay is right. Standing amidst the

untamed battle, he looks out for her well-being, unselfishly putting her needs before his own. With an aching heart, she runs with all her might, not looking back, holding the cranky cutlery fork in her defence and never forgetting the powerful words of the dreadlocked gunslinger who has been promised to keep her safe.

Dan Casey sees the galactic student running towards him and knows they are in trouble. He fires covering shots, distracting the rampaging Zealot Templars, giving her time to sprint through the vine-laden archway. Charlena Jones grits her white teeth fiercely as she runs, determined to make it through. The ghostly Templars Guards viciously throw their jewelled speared arrows at the young red-haired teenage girl with intent. The determined cargo pilot Dan Casey tactically blasts the ghostly foe and shouts words of encouragement to her, "Come on, Jonesy, show me that sprint!"

He swiftly turns, bending slightly, and Charlena springs onto his broad back.

"I've got you," Dan says, and the pair surge forward. "Let's go! Catch up to Veena!"

The two of them work as one, dodging every Zealot Templar attack along the way through the misty jungle arch. With barely a moment to spare, they make it to the safety of the rope bridge courtyard entrance. Dan Casey allows himself a moment of proud relief for a lucky escape.

The charmed pilot still has Charlena Jones clinging to his back as he watches Jay Haines back up to their position, and he wastes no time firing off more rounds to buy them time.

Dan Casey looks ahead and sees that Veena Merida has made it unscathed to the rope bridge but looks distressed. She relays back with her silver-scoped weapon still drawn in an offensive stance, "The bridge is tattered and hanging in pieces. We shall never get across. Gosh! I believe we're trapped."

Dan knows they have to cross that rope bridge before the

ghoulish Templars catch up with them. It is the only way to the mysterious sacred temple, and he has to get Charlena and Veena there as soon as possible. He scans the jungle-stricken area, rapidly searching for a quick-fire solution. The shadowy Zealot Templars angrily grumble in response with their jewelled spears drawn and shout for the pilot and student to turn away. Charlena clings to Dan's neck in fear. But the interstellar cargo haulier is determined to get into the temple. Suddenly, glancing up, he notices something that sparks a wild idea. Thick tropical vines are hanging from the trees on either side of the worn bridge.

Taking a deep breath, Dan Casey turns to Charlena Jones and says, "Shut your pretty eyes and hold on tight. Please don't tell, Veena!"

The handsome under-fire star pilot daringly smirks a devilish grin, and Charlena knows he is trying to reassure her. Dan Casey is always brave and chivalrous, so it is no surprise to him or anyone else when he springs into action with hardly a moment's notice at the ruins of the broken, trap-filled bridge. Veena Merida is there, acting as a guard, and when she spots the Zealot Templars attempting to make a break for it through the fog-shrouded jungle, she acts quickly, yelling and popping off shots to scare them away. Dan can't help but take a moment to admire her elegant beauty as she has her black catsuit back turned to him. Courageous and strong, Veena is an incredibly dedicated and skilful intergalactic agent. Without warning, her attention is suddenly on him, and the surprise on her face is unmistakable. Looking up, Dan spots a vine-laden swing suspended above, and he dashes towards it, grabbing Veena and hoisting her into his grip in one swift movement. Once securely attached, he leaps into the air. Reaching up with one arm, he grasps the swing's rope and swings it across the void.

Trying to secure Veena and Charlena, he soothes them gently, calmingly, "We'll make it, trust me!"

The jungle-vine rope surges them higher and higher. Eventually, bravery and luck deliver them safely to the Temple of Dela's courtyard. Dan lands in a heap next to Veena and Charlena. Despite the difficult journey, Dan Casey can't help but feel a sense of pride for being able to help his friends in such a way. The ventured plan isn't to everyone's liking, though, as Veena Merida is mildly fuming. Dan has just caught Veena off guard with his usual shenanigans.

She quickly brushes herself off to regain her composure but glares at Dan with piercing jade eyes, "Don't ever do that to me again," Veena says, her voice dripping with warning. "Gosh, pilots!"

Veena exhales slowly, trying to keep her composure, and proceeds to take aim and provide cover fire for the gunslinger. Jay has just reached the damaged bridge, and the mummified Zealot Templar guardians are overrunning.

Veena Merida quickly assesses the situation and determines that it will be because of her expertise that anyone will survive this ordeal. She readies her silvered scoped weapon and begins to fire at the guardians. Veena's beautiful face shows the feeling of her heart racing with adrenaline. Dan Casey glances over his shoulder and smiles reassuringly at Charlena Jones, who stands behind him, her white wrap-over dress streaked with mud and dirt. He has a momentary flash of guilt shadowing his chiselled face that she is here because of him. But this is no time to linger on guilt; there is a job to do. As the Templar Guards continue to swarm from the jungle foliage, Dan and Veena unleash a flurry of blaster fire in defence of Jay Haines, who teeters precariously on a thin rope bridge suspended between two cliff faces.

Jay glances back at Dan and Veena and shouts, "Oh, dudes, troubling times!"

Dan, tensely and with a frown, waves him on, shouting encouraging words with each burst of his black-barrelled blaster, "Keep going, Jay! We've got you covered; you can do it!"

Still somewhat dazed by her ordeal, Charlena Jones blows her red fringe from her face and finds her footing quickly, joining the defensive companions. The young student has nothing but a battered fork but takes up a position, desperately wanting to help in any way she can. Dan Casey smirks to himself as he witnesses the bad-boy gunman making his daring run.

The mummified Zealots are gaining on him, but the cool-under-fire dreadlocked gunslinger has seen a chance and gone for it. Dan is filled with admiration and fires away with renewed vigour. Veena keeps up the barrage; finally with one final lunge, Jay Haines leaps for the hanging vine, and, with a mighty push, he swings to the courtyard. The trio of heroes let out a cheer, and then, suddenly, just as quickly as they have come, the Zealot Templar guards disappear back into the jungle along with their whispering chants. Dan, Veena, and Charlena watch until Jay is out of harm's way.

Veena turns to Dan and realises he has been watching her out of the corner of his alluring brown eyes. She blushes, giving a teased smirk and shrugs off her temperamental behaviour.

Dan looks at his bewildered crew tensely as he rubs his fingerless gloves over his stubble-shaven chin. He hasn't a clue as to who or what the Zealot Templars are, but one thing is certain. Their dark, ghostly form isn't from this galaxy. The astute cargo pilot turns to his recovering crew and asks them with concern after the encounter, "Is everyone okay? What the hell are those blabbering mummified things? They appear from underneath the surface!"

No one can explain what they have just fought off and undoubtedly witnessed. Veena Merida has been an intergalactic shadow agent for over the last two years, but nothing could have prepared her for this mission to deliver the astrological data box. She still has her weapon drawn as she moves through the sweeping vine bush courtyards. Veena is calm but ready for any oncoming attack. She analyses the accounts of her information source. But the Zealot Protectors of the Temple of Delas don't make much sense to her from their droned verbal chanting.

"Who are these mysterious, daunting Zealot figures, and why did Tara Harlow think it was important to meet her here without any warning communications of such absurd dangers?"

Veena Merida strolls through the deserted jungle-stricken courtyard and its hidden nooks. An annoyed tone fills her voice as she continues the debate, muttering her worries about Tara's decision, "This is not a practical mission of following strategic rules; I have a bad feeling there is a lot more to this data box than an old, out-of-date star chart!"

Her inquisitive jade eyes search her surroundings for any sign of danger. At the same time, her right arm holds her sliver-scoped pistol steadily. This place is peculiar, and Veena knows she is on the right path, but she has to be careful. There may be a secret that the Zealot Protectors are desperately trying to remain hidden, and Veena is determined to find out what it is.

Dan Casey sees that Veena is feeling stressed by this agent assignment. He advises her in his kind, charismatic manner. "Hey, sweetheart, don't let the uncertainties consume your focus and worry too much about this Tara Harlow and her warped-out meeting location. It won't help you out here, trust me, and I'm with you till the end of this mystery, and I'll be having stern words with this agent leader."

Dan Casey and Veena Merida have been on the path of the data box rendezvous since their meeting. They have finally come close to finding the answers as they approach the domed temple hidden in the tropical jungle. It has been a complicated and often treacherous journey from the start, filled with dangers they could never have imagined. Veena can't help but let out a relieved breath, and the built tension seems to melt from her enticing, curvy body. With Dan's affectionate assurance, she can focus and determinedly presses forward through the courtyard to the hidden temple entrance.

Jay Haines is just behind Dan and Veena, his muscular arm casually draped around Charlena Jones as he speaks loudly in his distinctive deep accent, "Oh, man! Those ghoulish Zealot Templar freaks evaporated into supernatural dust particles when I was blasting them away, which was unexpected.

"What kind of joke is this? Are we being set up?" Jay's voice suddenly gets louder, and his bulky arm grips firmer around Charlena Jones. A sense of dread starts to crawl up his spine.

The brave gunslinger has never thought these tales might have some truth. To him, they are all made-up stories for kids to have a good scare; how could it be any different? Charlena Jones has faced a terrifying ordeal. Zealot guards have threatened them and followed their every move along the misty, arched jungle route to the temple grounds. Feeling vulnerable and too scared to speak, she clings to the safety of Jay Haine's side, trying not to let fear consume her.

Charlena finds her enthusiastic voice. She begins to tell the battle-hardened gunman about the ancient myth revelation she has heard. Her voice is timid and sweet, but passionate about her story.

"The old folk tales say that there is a mystery temple of vision. Its loyal prophets guard a Crystal Serpent Altar, and eventually, it is discovered by one of the galactic princesses. They say that when she opens it, a black hole is revealed, known as the Vortex, and all horrors are set loose until all biological life in the Kalanisi Galaxy has been made extinct."

Jay listens intently to her ancient mythical story. His wandering facial expressions show his thoughts about how intense their experience with the Zealot Guards has been, and he responds, "Let's hope you are wrong, kid. I've seen enough beastly monsters with those hideous alien Leechers in the universe. Let's not add supernatural ancient ghouls to contend with from any mythical Vortex."

The vibrations of nightfall slowly awaken, and a sense of

foreboding settles in the humid tropical air as the sun dips in the horizon on the mysterious island. The ancient temple looks daunting to venture into. The stillness seems to convulse at the bottom of the spiral stone staircase and vibrate from every vine tree, and weeping jungle bush is seen blending inside the temple cracks. The level-headed Dan Casey and his partner Veena Merida are curious about what may lie beyond the sealed entrance; the dimming of the light entices the individuals to ascend the stone stairs up to the closed imposing door despite the warning signals echoing and announcing danger.

Upon arrival, the hazy air seems electric with anticipation. Yet, shallow breaths are taken as Dan and Veena cross the threshold to the temple-paved staircase, closely followed by the gunslinger Jay Haines and the renegade student Charlena Jones.

Dan Casey stands in the archway of the mysterious temple with his black-barrelled weapon still drawn; he keeps alert as his dark brown eyes search around the mossy stonework to open the sealed door, moving his free left hand over the rough, dusty textures to no prevail.

Dan turns his scuffed brown leather-jacketed body from the granite door and asks the others for their take on the situation, "Any ideas how we open this tomb? There's got to be a way to elevate it."

Veena Merida is looking high and low around the overgrown jungle bush. She responds to Dan's invitation to ideas and replies, "Must be a secret lock or key to gain entrance; the Zealots says we didn't belong here. Maybe they hold the key or telepathically open the door?"

"Somehow, sweetheart, I don't think they seem the type of Templars to hand out exploration keys to whatever in here is sacred."

As Dan and Veena continue searching the temple's archway, Jay Haines hangs back and purposely guards the temple stairs, his silver dual shooter drawn, surveying each corner of the jungle court grounds. Meanwhile, the galactic student is eager to find the mysterious key. Charlena Jones is on her hands and knees, pressing the gritty paved slabs.

She mutters, "Oh! I've said it once and will repeat it, if only Foxy-D were here to help; looks like it's up to the intergalactic explorer, Scraggy Jones."

Suddenly, upon her spoken words, Charlena notices with a brow-raised frown a gargoyle-faced shape imprinted on the paving stone in front of her dazzling blue eyes; without hesitation, the young female student presses her dainty hands firmly over the gargoyle sketching. The ground beneath the temple starts to rumble with a slight vibration as the sealed stone case doorway gradually opens.

Charlena Jones swiftly looks up with astonishment and expresses joy at witnessing the parting of the massive stone door. She comments on her elementary finding, "Oh boy, it looks like we are going into the lost Temple of Delas. They will never believe me at galactic studies."

Dan Casey stands a few paces back while the carved-stone door fully opens. He steadily brushes his finger-cut gloves through his swept-back black hairstyle as he turns and proudly smiles at Charlena.

"Well done, Jonesy; come on, let's go see who's home."

Confidently, Dan Casey leads the way through the temple entrance and embraces the sacred place, his trusty weapon drawn and ranging high as he steadily motions along the candlelight-moss-ridden hallway.

"Keep close and touch nothing. We don't know what artefactual secrets are hidden in this mystical pit or why they are here."

Veena Merida is pacing a high-heeled step close behind him, inspecting the mural carvings on the jagged stone walls with her pistol still handy.

She responds to his warning with added texture, "Or the

unforeseen motivation they are hiding in the first place is what worries me."

Charlena Jones makes haste to join the capable female agent's side. "The murals seem to be imagery of what happened in the Kalanisi Universe long ago."

Scouting in behind the trio covering the rear guard, Jay Haines duly points out the scenario of the primitive sketches, "It doesn't look like it ended well for the people in the wall carvings. As blazing fires and shadowy ghouls are coming out from that big black hole and destroying them all without mercy."

Dan Casey continues to lead the daring *Decepter* crew further into the enclosed temple, descending the winding, rickety wooden staircase that echoes with the dripping of mossy water and the hushed murmurs of voices.

These ethereal warnings seem to grow ever louder as Dan passes, repeating the droning phrase, "You trespassers don't belong here; turn back before it's too late!"

Undeterred, Dan Casey says confidently to the others, "Ignore the cult whispers! We've come this far, and they won't intimidate us now."

His adventurous team pushes on, determined to reach the sacred dome. As they emerge into a lavish ritual room, their eyes widen upon the sight of a grand sculptured altar of a serpent coiled around itself at the centre of the room. Apprehensive glances are exchanged as the misfit crew pauses at the edge of the temple ritual chamber.

Dan comments in astonishment at what he is witnessing, "What the? It's the Crystal Serpent Altar spoken about in the ancient myths, and I thought the crazy stories were all hocus-pocus!"

Shockingly, he looks over to Veena, who is just as amazed and bound in silent awe. She quickly reaches for her dainty scrubbed-up leather handbag, unzips the fashion accessory and fumbles around for the astrological databox. Charlena Jone's stunning blue eyes are transfixed on the Crystal Serpent Altar; she takes a few steps forward, leaving Jay Haines's chaperoned custody, being an inquisitive-natured student.

The young feminine teenager enthusiastically says, "Wow! Oh, boy, the cursed folklore tales must be true, and the Black Vortex exists!"

As the red-haired student speaks about the ancient rumours, the whispering voices whoosh around the sacred ritual engravement, "You do not belong here; turn back before it's too late."

Swiftly getting the bad vibe, Jay Haines checks their quarter flank conspicuously with a weaving search of his designer-shade-covered eyes sternly around the spiritual room, his stylish sliver blaster drawn and poised. The gunslinger states with a tense glow to his voice, "I ain't one that believes ancient ghost tales, man! But I'm starting to get the feeling we are in one! That Templar's muttering sounds like a spiritual threat to me, dudes?"

Calmly, the sharpshooter Jay Haines composes himself and continues his rearguard duty. The menacing whispers seem to resound in the mossy air, giving them more reason to believe they are treading intrepidly around the ancient serpent altar. Dan Casey is in total agreement with his fellow gunslinger. The hotshot pilot raises his black-barrel weapon to the fore, anticipating something lurking ahead, warning the others, "Jay's right; stay alert. Don't let your guard down. Charlena, get back behind us now."

He pulls the young girl back and gently pushes her into Veena's care. Dan feels it is his responsibility to ensure the safety of his crew.

The brave pilot claims, "No one can predict what may be around the corner, so stay close and ready for anything."

The eerie feeling seems to intensify as they approach the serpent altar. Dan Casey braces himself for what is ahead. With a silent prayer that his courage will see them through, he boldly steps forward into the unknown.

The Zealot Templar whispers suddenly stop with a cold silence tingling through the cold atmospheric air. Dan Casey slowly progresses to the crystallised altar. Veena Merida hangs back a little, the data box tucked under her arms with the gun-scoped weapon primed. Jay Haines is next in a broad-armed stance to the female galactic agent with Charlena Jones, dropping to the group's rear.

Dan takes another bold step forward, his weapon aimed with great caution, only to stagger back to a stunned halt as a Zealot Templar guardian metamorphosises directly in his pathway to the mystical Crystal Serpent Altar. The frightening, mummified protector stands firm and tall in his mounted black jewelled cloak and menacing masked face with his soulless, daunting eyes squaring up to the static cargo pilot; the ghostly mummified figure chants in a haunting, deep droning voice, "You do not belong here and heed our warning with no respect for the sacred ground. Now you must die, trespassers!" grimly says the threatening Zealot Templar, wielding his imposing jewel spear staff weapon in an alternating weaving offence at Dan Casey.

The surrounding edges of the dome temple fill with a low mist fog as the enchanted whispers lower to a humming muffle. Veena Merida and Jay Haines quickly scout the enclosing mist, their weapons drawn and ready to defend themselves with a dubious glance across from each other. Charlena Jones quickly moves between her protective companions, preparing to draw her cutlery fork.

The Zealot Templar guardian begins chanting in a ghostly voice, "You do not heed our warning and respect the sacred ground; surrender and leave or die!"

Dan Casey swiftly checks his surroundings and hears the whispering shadows, knowing that he and his crew are in grave danger if he fails to comply. He reluctantly steps backwards and bows in reverence. Dan lowers his handgun to the dusty paved stone ground and urgently yells to the others, "Stand down!" The daringly charmed interstellar pilot slowly levers his muscular body to his scuffed leather-booted stance.

Dan slowly backs away, his heart racing a beat, never taking his dark eyes from the eerie masked figure until he bravely speaks to the Zealot Templar guard, "Hey, we're not here for any trouble; whatever you beings are. Please understand that we did not know about the Temple of Delas." Dan Casey explains their valid reasons for stepping on the Templar's sacred ground.

Dan keeps his calm and composure as the angry Zealot Templar guardian slightly retreats on his offensive stance, lowering his jewel-pointed diamond blade spear and bellowing his inquisition, "Why do you infiltrate the peace? What is your purpose here, trespassers? Tell me, NOW!"

Veena Merida swiftly steps forth to Dan Casey's side in defence. She holsters her silver-stubbed agent-issued pistol and holds out her womanly hand, showing the Zealot Templar guardian the astrological data box.

She advises the supernatural being, with intense adrenaline flowing through her posh voice, "We mean you no harm and have come here on a secret mission to deliver this ancient star-chart device to an agency woman called Tara Harlow. Do you have knowledge of her or information about this mysterious data box?"

The Zealot Guard responds to the female agent's questions in brief. The Templar Ghost deems these brash words to be their plea, "I know of no woman, but I recall the astrological data box. It is mastered for good but used for evil and should not be here so close to the Crystal Serpent Altar."

Stressed, the cloaked Zealot raises his inquisition to a higher degree of concern, "Why do you bring that cursed trinket here to the ritual tomb? Do you trespassers not heed the dangers of the past times?" says the bewildering Zealot Protector, lowering his armoured gloved hands. The whispering voices in the hazy mist instantly vanish into the wilderness of the tropical jungle's hidden temple. The room's temperament eases to a more tranquil level of communication.

Dan Casey witnesses the falling tension in the Zealot Templar guard's presence and the clearing of the smoky, muffled voices. He glances over at the cloaked, imperious figure. He asks for some clarification about his heeded warnings of past times in the Kalanisi Universe,

"We've only heard about the folklore tales of past times as mythical rumours and no evidence to back them up. Who are you? What's the purpose of the astrological data box," says the cargo pilot, waiting for a response from the Zealot. Dan glances over to Veena and checks in behind Jay and Charlena with a reassuring smile and a winking eye.

The Zealot Templar guard replies in a shallow voice, "I will make you wise of the past times. But the data box must be destroyed, and you leave and never return to the Temple of Delas or your mortal lives will be forfeited to the eternal voids forever. Do we have an accord, trespassers?"

Dan Casey and the *Decepter* crew agree in earnest with swift head-shaking nods for the sake of escaping with their lives. The mysterious Zealot Templar is about to explain the folklore myth and grim destruction of the Kalanisi Galaxy before the colonisation of humanity made their terraforming presence from earth's decaying solar system.

Chapter Sixteen

The Cursed Temple of Delas

Deep in the far reigns of Isadora's system on a newfound world not stated on intergalactic star charts are the courageous interstellar pilot Dan Casey and daring feminine intergalactic agent, Veena Merida, with the assistance of gunslinger for hire, Jay Haines, and the enthusiastic renegade student, Charlena Jones. They find themselves in the middle of a mysterious tropical jungle island and have discovered the lost ancient Temple of Delas, which they believe is the rendezvous location chosen by the shadowy agency leader, Tara Harlow. The *Decepter* crew have also come across the unwelcoming presence of the Zealot Templar Guards and their daunting warnings to leave the sacred temple and destroy the astrological databox or die with consequent ignorance. After coming to a truce of understanding, the heroic cargo-runner pilot, Dan Casey, stands before the mummified Templar, waiting for the spiritual being to reveal the secret revelations of past times in the Kalanisi Galaxy.

The atmosphere around the Crystal Serpent Altar is filled with anticipation as the imposing hooded Zealot Templar guard approaches Veena Merida. He holds out his black-armoured hand for the data box. Veena's jade eyes are fixed on the ghostly Templar's masked face and lifeless eyes. The beautiful galactic agent hands the mystical databox over without showing any signs of her inner hesitation or trembling nerves at being in the presence of a supernatural entity. The masterful Zealot Guard takes the data box from her presence with his jewelled gloved hands clutching around the preternatural device.

He looks vaguely down at the ancient star chart. He announces, "I am Sirius Ramo, the figurehead Zealot Templar Master and first loyal protector to Princess Delas, the sister of the possessed and ruler of the Kalanisi Galaxy."

The mummified ghost introduces his previous status and continues to explain the dangers. Sirius Ramo speaks out. "The astrological data box was crafted by a genius alchemist known as Talross. He made the specially praised trinket to locate hidden golden worlds not shown on conventional star charts."

Sirius Ramo pauses, moving his hands around the ancient data box and hesitantly pressing the symbolic icons patterned on the magical device.

The data box starts to glow and emit a buzzing hum, instantly portraying global imagery of the Kalanisi Universe. Dan Casey remains silent, witnessing the astrological star chart form before his presence. He holds his fingerless-cut gloved hand out in assurance and kindly grips Veena Merida's willing hand in unison. Close behind, Jay Haines glances at Charlena Jones with his weapon semi-drawn to his quarters.

Jay whispers in his deep manly voice to the young girl, "It freaks the living shit me out when they turn that damn cursed thing on; just stay close, kid. I've got a bad feeling!"

His dark, handsome, stubbled face reacts as if he hears several motioning noises outside the Temple of Delas. Charlena Jones distractingly breaks his concentration into the investigation as she caringly grips his hand.

She whispers back, "Shh, Jay! This is getting fascinating. Let Sirius Ramo speak about the truthful version of ancient folklore myth. I will be up for the annual galactic student of the year award after mentally absorbing these mystical gems of knowledge."

Sirius Ramo continues the ancient legacy, "The data box was a celebrational gift to the two princesses when they forged to power after their mother, Queen Lucinda Delas, passed over to the eternal void. The royal sisters were granted divine rights to the golden world and were privileged to award their loyal followers and loved ones the chance to live in peace and harmony in paradise. Talross later found out his creation had an Achilles heel that would cause terror across the Kalanisi Galaxy."

The Zealot Templar Master turns the astrological data box off with a twisting of its structure.

Dan Casey stands mesmerised by the unfolding story and asks with intrigue, "So what happened, Sirius Ramo? How does everything get wiped out in this galaxy?"

"Talross first produced the Crystal Serpent Altar to channel the data box's scope to go beyond the boundaries of known space. He performed an alchemist ritual of supernatural magic only to acquire it, leading to a sinister black hole beyond his worst imagination. Talross named his genesis the Black Vortex and banished the Crystal Serpent Altar to this hidden tropical temple before sealing the tomb. The mighty alchemist corrected his unheavenly mistakes and utilised a less intensified spiritual ritual, recreating the Altar of Vision, which led only to the golden worlds."

Veena interrupts his speech, advising the whereabouts of the second altar. "I saw the Altar of Vision you speak about at the Corporal Union headquarters, hidden in a secret wall cavity vault inside the office of Director Wilson Volantis."

Veena Merida exuberantly turns her alluring presence to Dan Casey. Her expression is calming yet seems to send a deeper, hidden message of affection to her lover. The sexy green-haired agent holds his hand and continues in her well-spoken voice, "Wilson Volantis holds the wrong altarpiece in his unlawful possession. It is like a starship without thrusters.

The delusional madman can prepare his Sulamani project in whatever way he likes, but it will lead him nowhere for what he seeks. We should destroy the data box and the Crystal Serpent Altar to make certain, and to hell with Tara Harlow's agency mission."

Veena's gaze is determined, and her posh voice rings with patience and understanding. She knows the dangers and backlash they will face and the opportunity ahead of them in this unusual mission. Dan Casey is taken aback by Veena's words and is impressed by her sharp intellect and focus. He smiles back at her and kisses her cheek. His facial expression reassures confidence that together, they can conquer this mission and emerge victorious. Veena smiles, relieved that Dan is just as determined as she is. They have come a long way together on this spiralling journey that has potentially changed their lives. She feels excited and optimistic, something that has been missing from her life for a long time.

The Zealot Templar Master, Sirius Ramo, is alerted to Veena's context, and he sternly enquires as to who wants to use the astrological data box and seek the mythical black hole. "Who is this Director Wilson Volantis, and what's his purpose in finding the Black Vortex? Does he not heed the sinister dangers of Amelia Delas and her soulless nature."

Veena Merida swiftly responds to his raised-voiced warnings and tells him about the current galactic power structure. "Director Wilson Volantis is the surprisingly elected charge hand of the Galactic Corporal Union, an organisation once with integrity that has been weaponised against its citizens to gain complete power over the Kalanisi Galaxy.

"The galactic government has become obsessed with finding the mythical Black Vortex, which is foreseen to grant the holder unparalleled strength and knowledge. Wilson Volantis believes he can control the universe with this unnatural divine power. All the other alien species would scutter to his demands, and no one could defy his orders or profitable abrasions. Wilson practises spiritual rituals in the mastery of dark arts to find this black hole. Unknown to him of the Crystal Serpent Altar's whereabouts and the loss of the databox, he had been foiled by his ignorance."

"You must destroy this Director Volantis and his tainted hostile structure before the balance is beyond reach. If this man connects spiritually with Amelia Delas, she will conflict and indoctrinate his thoughts to wield her will's desire. Amelia is very seductive and persuasive in her movements, and no one controls her lust for dominance and power. You must destroy this Wilson Volantis and end his contaminated life to save the future of the Kalanisi Galaxy."

Casey turns his muscular body to the temple floor, retrieves the black-barrelled gun, and re-holsters his weapon as a sign of peace, relieved that the terrifying threat of the Zealot Templars no longer seems so immediate. Dan responds to Sirius Ramo's call for them to seize galactic power.

"The Corporal Union is a hugely powerful force and has a backhander in many affairs, including Mbron Media, an arrogant android-rigged news broadcaster outlet. The Corporal Union has corrupted the cyberbots of Mbron Media to transmit false propaganda that Wilson Volantis is the galaxy's saviour. They ensure these messages are heard, seen, and followed without question."

He quarter turns his attention away from the Zealot Templar and asks Veena and Jay, "Have you two heard starships fly over in the last few moments?"

But before he could get a response from his miscellaneous crew, the ancient Templar Master, Sirius Ramo, demands answers. "Why do your people not stand against this Wilson Volantis? Have they no fighting spirit in this circle?"

Veena Merida gives the curious Templar an insight into present times. "At first, many citizens hesitated to accept the news. It seemed far-fetched that this small-time figure would be the one to save them all. But, as time passed and people were exposed to more and more messages from Wilson Volantis, they began to accept them.

"They bought into the Corporal Union's propaganda, and soon, the unforeseen Director Volantis had a devoted following. Wilson knew he could easily manipulate the Elite Galactic board and Android Association Committee. As long as nobody questions him or his decisions, the Corporal Union has a solid grip on the Kalanisi Galaxy."

The Zealot Protector gravely responds to Veena's in-depth animation, "By the indication of your troubling words, there are echoes that indicate that Amelia Delas may have already made her presence felt in the environment of this Director's life. The man must be destroyed, or she will find a way to re-emerge, and all will perish."

The renegade student, Charlena Jones, can hardly curb her enthusiasm and has a few questions she wants to ask the Zealot Templar Ghost. She steps forward and asks, "So why did Princess Amelia Delas become a woman to fear? She is blessed with everything you could dream of belonging. What did she do to everybody? What happened to her soul?"

Sirius Ramo slowly turns his unnatural bodily presence away from Dan Casey's crew and glances from within his hooded cloak at the Crystal Serpent's Alter, hinting at an expressed tone of sadness in his suppressed voice. "Amelia Delas is a beautiful, intelligent woman and is an inspired empress to the galactic crown. She is cherished by many a man who wants to claim her hand in a proposal of union. Amelia's heart is drawn to the same bond as her older sister, but the princess experienced rejection for the first time in her exquisite life, and she is torn by anger and jealousy.

"Amelia is an old-fashioned traditional woman deep within herself. She claimed the astrological data box and took it to the high seas in her beloved sailing ship, an old relic named the Bonny-Rigg Wench. She searched in vain for a place of happiness to cure her scorned heart, but the data box gave her no joy, and she sought further knowledge of the trinket's secrets."

Dan Casey intervenes and asks the Zealot Ambassador with intrigue about the adaptiveness of Amelia's sailing vessel. "I can't imagine that old-type of ship could have helped her much, constricted to the ocean and unable to leave the planet's atmosphere; what is Princess Amelia Delas looking for to heal her broken heart? Is it the Crystal Serpent Altar?"

"Yes, trespasser! You are correct," says Sirius Ramo. "Amelia cunningly seduced the alchemist Talross so that he could reveal the hidden secrets of the astrological databox. Talcross did this in his moment of weakness, showing her the way to this tropical jungle island and willingly opening the temple-sealed tomb, exposing Amelia Delas's lust to entwine with the Crystal Serpent Altar. Together, they performed a black magic ritual to open the Black Vortex. Once Amelia had the location of her desire, she cruelly killed Talross to cover her tracks, sailed the Bonny-Rigg Wench into the mists of this luscious world, and vanished without a trace."

Dan Casey's handsome, chiselled face is bewildered by the enchanted tale. He asks with a sworn conviction of trying to understand the outcome, "So where did Amelia Delas and her crew of the Bonny-Rigg Wench end up going? They couldn't have just vanished off the surface of the planet!"

The Templar Master responds by bowing his cloaked mummified facial disfigurement to the temple's stone-paved floor. He finishes the ancient myth in his secluded ghostly voice, "The next time the Bonny-Rigg Wench was sighted, it emerged from the Black Vortex, bringing a hellish trail of horrors in its wake. The relic ship and loyal crew have become possessed, tainted by an evil darkness. Amelia Delas now declares herself as

Queen of the Kalanisi Universe, demanding the souls of galactic citizens to feed her lust for dominant power and destruction of the realm."

Dan releases his assuring grip on Veena's hand with a dubious glare, stating his intentions, "I'm not too swayed to believe all that hocus-pocus, but Sirius did appear from the ground, which does hold certain credentials. We'll destroy the ancient artefacts and then get off this tropical island just to be safe, as you said, sweetheart."

Veena Merida nods in agreement with Dan Casey, followed by a question for the Zealot Templar. "So, what did Amelia Delas's sister do to counter her sibling's actions? You have never mentioned her name in this saga. Is there a reason behind that?"

Jay Haines adds to the dissection of Sirius Ramo's delivery. The bead-hair-styled gunslinger asks in his deep, manly voice, "You pointed out this circle has not had any fight, but what did you do to retaliate against Amelia Delas and her possessed force of tainted ghouls?"

Charlena Jones's head swiftly turns. Her sweet facial expression says she may have heard a creaking sound near the temple entrance a few yards behind them. The red-haired student readily runs her hands over her sash belt, containing her cutlery fork, and tiptoes away to investigate the rustling aggravation.

The ghostly, imposing hooded presence of Sirius Ramo talks about the enduring conflict between the two royal sisters and the devastating effects on the galaxy. A gust of wind seeps through the temple's crevices as the Zealot Templar stands ahead of the Crystal Serpent Altar.

"Amelia Delas raged terror across core worlds. She imposed the might of the Bonny-Rigg Wench to destroy the defence of the populated planets before invading with her unnatural crew. The demoness took the souls of the weak and enslaved the worlds to her tainted realm, indoctrinating our people against us and tearing the royal alliance apart from within. The royal sister and the loyal Templar Guards combated the threat to the best of their abilities. Still, our starships were no match for the Bonny-Rigg Wench and the defending ground force was incubated to deal with such beautiful evil."

Dan Casey has been piloting starships since adolescence and is bewildered by one vessel causing them so many issues. He asks in a sceptical matter of interest, "What happened to the Bonny-Rigg Wench after it came out of the black hole? It would be an old-type sailing ship made of fragile materials compared to a battle-hardened class starship. Your fleets should have disposed of Amelia Dela's relic vessel with minimum fuss."

Sirius Ramo explains the vintage ship's raw capabilities, "The Bonny-Rigg Wench is no longer a normal ship of the untamed blue oceans. It's possessed beyond return with immense firepower and speeds that should never be underestimated. And neither should Amelia Dela's evolving black heart. If she can't find happiness in her desires, then no one else in her demonic realm will experience that pleasure."

Jay Haines points out some facts to the dark-cloaked supernatural figure, "You must have had some sort of sustainable victory, or we wouldn't be standing here now. The Kalanisi Galaxy is thriving, so how did you defeat Amelia's hostile blitz of ghouls?"

The Zealot Templar lord swiftly responds to the gunslinger's question. "After a year and a half of intense, conflicted battles to no prevail, our resources had constantly been bleeding, fighting for freedom. The royal sister bravely collaborated on a last stand, ordering the remaining starships to assemble near the Black Vortex. Without the vast knowledge of Talross, the royal sister and her lover performed a scientific experiment to bind Amelia Delas and banish her to the black hole for an eternity, but not without repercussions of the blinding love ritual, exposing vast amounts of untamed energy across the galaxy causing dismissal of our very existence."

Veena Merida asks, "So, what is the name of the royal sister you protect so fondly? Were you her lover, Sirius?"

Sirius Ramo turns his sole attention to Veena Merida and bows his masked presence with the words, "Your heart yearns to love, young woman, just like Amelia once sought; I can feel the vibes within you. But remember, it's a powerful essence of joy that can be very fragile and easily scorned to inflicting pain if overwhelmed by jealousy."

Veena listens to Sirius Ramo's philosophy with a blank frown of confusion. Dan Casey bluntly asks the mummified ghost, "Drop the damn riddles; what is Amelia's sister's name, and how did she bind her to the mythical black hole?"

Sirius quickly responds to Dan's tempered tone, "The royal sister's name is aah…!"

Before the Zealot Templar can reveal the name of Amelia Delas's sister, he is suddenly vaporised by a laser-blast flare, hurling in from behind the mystical temple's entrance. The astrological data box falls with a spinning topple from Sirius Ramo's handling presence as he evaporates into black, smoky dust. Without warning, the hidden temple of Delas's entrance is occupied, and familiar figures appear. Swiftly engaging the sudden turn of shock events, Dan Casey slickly turns his muscular body physique, quarter-drawing his black-barrelled gun from his slated holster belt, ready for the unforeseen intruder. Veena Merida follows his sharp actions of offence. She instinctively draws her silver-scoped barrelled pistol, swirling her elegant figure to the temple entrance. Meanwhile, Jay Haines swiftly turns his presence and drops to one knee, drawing the spinning sling handle of his dual shooter to an aimed halt. Dan Casey aims his black-barrelled weapon and says in shock, "Duran!"

Craftily standing with a smug smile at the temple's doorway, Zak Duran stands bold with his stylish black hand blaster drawn and pointed firmly at Dan Casey. The handsome bounty hunter readily poses with his tinted designer shades and slick dark swept-back hair, smartly dressed in his quarter-length brown leather jacket and sleek grey slacks with a leather cross belt holster.

Zak Duran cunningly says with a smirk, "Enough of the bragging about the gloomy past times. We should be talking about the present and prospects, Dan!

"Oh, I forgot, you like to refer to yourself as Casey, either way, drop your damn guns. All of you or the kid gets it and becomes artefactual history!" says the entrepreneur-style bounty hunter, referring to his teenage red-haired hostage being bound by his counterpart in crime, Terri Lace.

The long blonde-haired mistress grins, following his comments. Terri is sexually dressed in her black diamond bra top and wrap-around red slit mini skirt with a slender holster belt. The beautiful, long, leggy woman stands elegant in her knee-high designer boots, her left bare arm tightly gripping Charlena Jone's neck with her other hand digging a black calibre pistol into her side.

Terri Lace teases the young girl with a tortured tongue, "Oh Zak, I'd say one less mouthy little brat in the galaxy won't go amiss."

Terri cruelly pushes her gun deeper into the teenager's side and continues the threatening pitch, "Who will lose any sleep over this ugly red-haired thing? If you dare to call me Toady Lace again, I will make you an artefactual myth, little girl, and you will be spat all around this lost temple."

The intergalactic feminine agent and the gunslinger Jay Haines have their weapons aimed and focused on the gorgeous consort bounty hunter.

Veena shouts across the temple to her old friend, "Let Charlena go now; the young girl has nothing to do with your feud towards me. Don't you dare lay a hand on her. I'm warning you I will shoot you without hesitation, Terri."

Sweat perspires down her shapely, tense face; she quickly flicks on the pistol's infrared-scope site. Veena's agency training has taught her to refuse to back down in any hostage situation, no matter how high the personal stakes may be. Jay Haines is on one knee in the same frame of mind as the green-haired agent, aiming his silver dual shooter.

He confidently reassures the galactic student, "I made you that promise, kid; I intend to keep it, So don't worry, nobody can pull the trigger and shoot in this temple quicker than me. We've got this, Dan! Let's take them out; there's only two!"

Zak Duran instinctively takes charge of the stake-out predicament. He yells out with an authoritative voice echo surrounding the Temple of the Crystal Serpent Altar's cold, crisp atmosphere, "Get your crew in order and drop your fucking weapons, Casey. Including yourself, cargo runner, I won't be warning you again, and Veena, I thought you would have shown more compassion for the kid's welfare; guess the agent lifestyle has changed you for the worse, darling."

"Mr Haines, I recognised your distinguished face when you offered me a duel, so I checked your ID records on the Panther's database systems; it's a pretty impressive record that you ranked up in the gunslinger arenas. Dralon, it's a shame you can't count out the number of your opponents as well."

The vile, hideous alien Leecher emerges from the temple's shadowy entrance. Growling with its horrific red eyes drooling and slithering tentacles masquerading, the beast's muscular, rough-matted body is arched and ready to pounce at Zak Duran's summoning.

Dan Casey has a fixed aim on Zak Duran; the daring pilot's fingerless-cut gloves caress the pulsating trigger of his black-barrelled gun, but he glances over to Charlena Jones, grimly being held hostage. Dan isn't prepared to risk the female galactic student's life. He sternly says with annoyance at compliance with the bounty hunter's demands, "Veena and Jay, drop your weapons; let's hear Duran out. I'm sure he's a big enough man not to hurt Charlena."

He slowly places his hand weapon on the temple's flooring while keeping direct eye contact with Zak Duran. Quick to follow suit is Jay Haines, reluctantly tossing his chrome dual shooter ahead of him, the gunslinger cunningly eyeing the lurking alien Leecher beast's taunting antics.

Meanwhile, Veena Merida still has her old blonde-haired friend in the sights of her silver-stubbed pistol. She takes a deep breath and repeats the warning, "I've got a clear shot on you, Terri. Now let Charlena go free; she is just a teenage girl, damn it!"

Terri Lace reacts with a tempered gesture. She quickly ranges her calibre pistol under Charlena's shaking chin and stares at the young girl with an angered frown.

"Aww, has Veena been playing big sister? She's good at that until she decides to run out and leave you lying in the gutter. I warn you now! But then again, your life expectancy doesn't look too sweet, brat. Haha!"

Zak Duran snaps, smirking, "Ladies, please! I'm trying to have a civilised conversation with Dan on how he values his future and the safety of the crew. So, drop the gun, Veena. Nobody needs to get hurt; you, of all people, should know I'm not a cruel man."

The smug entrepreneur pauses with a mischievous smirk before stating, "I'm just a greedy and vain man seeking recognition!"

Veena Merida pauses with a deep sigh, looping her dainty finger around the trigger frame and gently throws the agent-issued pistol across the stoned floor of the temple. Dan Casey takes the initiative and asks the bounty hunter about his intentions.

He says with intrigue, "How did you track us here, and how's this going to work out for the best of us, Duran?"

Zak Duran casually takes a motioned step forward and reveals the need for a satisfactory conclusion. "Well, it depends on you, Casey. I have got to hand it to you. Those are some neat flying tricks you performed back in the Sera system. It's too bad you didn't account for a tracking device attaching to your clunky starship's fuselage," Zak says with a radiant spring in his step as he rounds Dan, Veena, and Jay to the forefront of the Crystal Serpent Altar.

Dan Casey sarcastically responds to the bounty hunter's smug taunts, "So I outflew you, Duran. What do you want, a signed autograph? State your terms and let Charlena go."

Zak quickly reacts to Dan's humour while swiftly kneeling and picking up the astrological data box with his sleek black gun pointed at the trio gathering around the Crystal Serpent Altar. Zak Duran admires the data box held in his hand.

He comments with an exuberant tone to the interstellar cargo pilot, "It's all about fulfilling this data box contract; we must make credits, Dan. I'm sure Director Wilson Volantis will be more than impressed with our efforts to retrieve his property, plus a lot of added extras. And, by the way, don't for one moment think you outflew me, Casey. You just got lucky, delivery man. The Panther A1 class frigate can take down your hunk of junk freighter any time of the galactic circle."

Jay Haines smirks at the bounty hunter's high-class ego. "You got outflown and outgunned, Duran. No doubt that will happen again if I have any say in the matter. Now, release the girl," says the muscular, toned, dreadlocked gunman, bravely squaring up to the glamour world bounty hunter. Jay shows no fear and is more concerned about Charlena Jones's safety. The daunting Leecher lurks menacingly at his master's side with an evil gargling grunt and whipping taunt of its hideous tentacles.

Zak Duran slowly approaches Jay and asks, "I can't remember you being part of the bargaining campaign, Mr Haines, but I recall your pathetic invitation to a duel. Is that offer still open? I'm sure the Leecher, Dralon, would like to advocate my position of acceptance, Mr Haines; it seems the creature's tribal brother got killed on Mach Galanti's slave-trade station; the beast has taken it to heart."

The mischievous bounty hunter casually approaches his old lover, Veena Merida. He smiles, placing the ancient data box in her suede-gloved hands, "Have you been informing Casey of all the good times we used to have together, Veena?"

He slowly runs his left hand over her skin and asks, "I imagine it's hard for a lowlife second-rate pilot to live up to my level of expectations. I always thought you had more class, sweetheart; this is your last chance to accept my forgiveness and get you that galactic pardon. Don't lie to yourself, Veena! You know you still have feelings for me. Join my crew. I'm sure you and Terri can amend your differences, and it will be like the old days."

Terri Lace angrily yells, "You got to be fucking kidding me, darling. I'll never forgive the unloyal bitch, don't tell me you've still got feelings for her; let me kill the jade-eyed trollop and cure my lustful urge."

The blonde-haired mistress quickly withdraws her calibre pistol from Charlena Jones' stomach and slickly repositions her adaptable, sleek weapon's aim to Veena's face. Honourable to her defence, Dan Casey quickly puts himself in the line of fire, surging his body forward and shielding Veena Merida from harm's way.

Dan shouts across to the tempered consort madam with urgency in his voice, "Let this go, Terri. You know that Veena's not the reason you got hurt. You're just making her take the blame."

Zak Duran promptly waves his gun at the cargo pilot and warns, "Get back in line, Casey and don't push your luck. If not for my past with Veena, you would already be a dead cargo man."

The fired-up bounty hunter slowly steps back and glances at Terri Lace, "Withdraw your weapon and remember who the fuck's in charge, sweetheart!"

Veena Merida places her arm around Dan Casey and speaks with piercing jade eyes fixated on her old companions, "I have no feelings for either of you. The friends I previously knew are gone. You both disgust me deeply. I'm standing with the man I love; nothing can break my resolve. I'd sooner perish than bow to the Corporal Union for a pardon of convenience."

Terri Lace instantly eases her offensive stance, lowers her weapon, and cunningly shoves it sharply back into her teenage hostage's side. The temperamental blonde bombshell says in a sullen-tempered tone, "This is not over, Veena, by a long way, I promise you and Dan! As much of a gentleman you are, please don't try to understand my feelings. I have no time for moral sympathy. Zak! My darling, shall we get things rolling and wrap up this data box contract? Hiking through that steamy tropical jungle is bad enough, and this bloody hidden temple is becoming stuffy and sour. I'm starting to get impatient and moody!"

Charlena Jones finds the courage to speak out, "You're both horrible people and deserve nothing. Veena's too good a friend for you. I hope you end up sad and lonely."

Terri swiftly responds to the feminine teenager's backchat, "Who the fuck asked for your pointless opinion? Shut it up, you annoying, ugly little creep!"

"Okay, Veena, Let's see how that data box performs when attached to that mythical altar. No point in being in an ancient ritual temple without playing a ritual, and government contracts always work best when you know the specifications you are about to trade.

"I imagine the Director of the Corporal Union will be very pleased when I hand over his lost data box and everything else this glorious golden world has to offer. Thank you for sweetening the bounty purse; I'll be in the galactic boardroom soon once Wilson Volantis finds out what I've discovered. Now, move it; there is no time to waste."

"You are crazy, Duran! Suppose there are any truths in the Templar Master's words before you unnecessarily vaporised him. In that case, the Crystal Serpent Altar is cursed; it's best to be destroyed and forgotten, not to be handed over to a spiritual lunatic, and no way is Veena performing any ritual. If anyone has to do a damn ritual, I will."

Standing a little further back from the Crystal Serpent Altar, Terri Lace comments to the charmed cargo pilots about his honourable antics. She purrs in a sultry voice, "But you're not calling the shots here, Mr Casey. We are! So, the pastel-haired trollop performs the mythical ritual; it's her assigned mission to complete. It seems only fair to me if it kills her!"

"Zak, please stop; this is ridiculous nonsense; the last time the databox connected with the altar, the galaxy suffered immensely. A high purse and a valued galactic reputation are not worth the risk!

"What do you plan to do with us after the ritual? Kill us all?"

The bounty hunter responds to her pleads, "No, Veena, I'm going blow up Casey's starship and leave you all stranded on this tropical jungle island, giving you a head start before the Corporal Union arrive in legions; call it a one-off goodwill gesture, attached with an Achilles heel, Veena."

Zak Duran readily commands his alien Leecher beast, "Dralon, keep that temple entrance guarded. We don't want any of those interfering Zealot Templars ruining things with their ancient chanting dribble. Now, Veena, please! If you would be kind, place the data box on the Crystal Serpent Altar."

Dan Casey glances over to Jay Haines with a hesitant frown, portraying his worried face and witnessing Veena Merida reluctantly stepping into the Crystal Serpent Altar.

Jay glances back at Dan Casey through his stylish tinted shades, his dark eyes lingering on their weapons on the temple's dusty stone floor. The dreadlocked gunslinger turns his attention to Charlena Jones. The red-haired female student is still under siege and in the captive stranglehold of Terri Lace's dominance. Veena Merida is approaching the Crystal Serpent Altar with reverence, fully aware of the gravity of the task. Taking a deep breath, she carefully places the data box on the smooth surface, ensuring it is secure. As she runs her hands over the quilted symbols that adorn the altar, she can't help but show a sense of fascination at the intricate design. Each shape has been carefully crafted and imbued with meaning.

Veena wonders at the ancient mythical stories they hold and the secrets they guard, even with the heeded warnings from the Templar Master. The astrological data box emits a mesmerising hum during the dome temple ritual ceremony. With the activation of the mystical trinkets, a stunning blue atmospheric globe of the galaxy is created, leaving everyone in shock and awe. The unforgettable experience leaves a lasting impression on everyone who witnesses it. But not everyone is impressed with the active databox.

Terri Lace comments on the projection of the universal globe, "Well, that is disappointing to think we trekked through a steamy tropical jungle for a glowing trinket. Wow, a few stars and symbols of no meaning; there must be more to it than that. I thought it would make my day brighter and make us filthy rich."

Zak Duran agrees with his devious sexual lover and brashly shouts out, "Veena, there must be a trigger switch to activate the damn thing. I'd have thought Wilson Volantis was after a weapon of sorts to persuade his policies. Have a look at the Crystal Serpent Altar. It seems to have some ritual words engraved. I can't make them out from back here, but I know you can; read them out, Veena, now!"

Veena's jade eyes wander over the engraved words. She says them out loud without any conscious, knowledgeable meaning, "Om mani padme hum." Veena Merida suddenly jolts her body a staggering, high-heeled step back from the Crystal Serpent Altar. The ancient cube device starts to react to the chanted ritual words and vastly changes its coloured spectrum.

The mysterious data box and ceremony Crystal Serpent Altar transfuse and seem to display symbols of a dramatic shift in the appearance of the Kalanisi Universe. The planetary display vastly alternates from the previously luscious blue globe to an uninviting burning fireball, motioning a weaving spin in a patterned sequence, indicating a potential pattern or order to the presented information.

Zak Duran steps backwards, his expression a mix of surprise and satisfaction. He feels torn between conflicting emotions as he speaks, "That is more in line with our high expectations. Please repeat the engraved chant, Veena. Let us not be half-hearted in our approach."

Dan Casey makes a valiant effort to surge ahead and halt the ritual, urging Zak Duran with a measured tone and flared temper. "I must intervene and prevent this madness from escalating any further. Veena, please remove the Crystal Serpent Altar and refrain from reciting the ritual chant!"

Zak Duran aims his high-calibre weapon at the advancing interstellar pilot with a warning shot, skimming the sandy paved stone just before Dan. "Next time, I won't miss the target. I'm warning you, Casey."

Veena Merida turns her view sharply from the altar on hearing the blast shot. Her green, frazzled hair breezes along her naked shoulders. The female agent's jade pupil eyes open wide with shock as she witnesses her lover cruelly under gunpoint.

"Say the damn ritual inscription. Don't stall procedures now; this is just getting interesting," smirks the smug bounty hunter.

Veena gathers her courage and takes a deep breath, preparing to confront the Crystal Serpent Altar. Despite knowing that the challenge she is about to face is unwinnable, the sexy agent steels herself for the challenge, against her will and in defence of her friends.

Veena Merida reluctantly repeats the ritual ceremony chant, "Om mani padme hum." She says in a withering, unsure voice.

A sudden burst of energy illuminates the Crystal Serpent Altar, emanating from the astrological data box. The result is a mesmerising display of a revolving star chart map projecting onto the elegant ceiling of the Temple of Delas, courtesy of the weaving orange planetary globe. Veena seems to fall into a hypnotic trance as she chants the inscribed ancient words,

"Om mani padme hum." She utters with sweat rapidly, perspiring from her brow as the mystical chant starts to have an unnatural effect on the glamorous resistance agent.

The stone-curved imperial pillars within the hidden jungle temple's interior begin to surge with high and low electrical currents; the fiery orange globe quickens its rotation while emitting a vivid and resonant humming and droning sound that reverberates throughout the ancient surroundings. This is accompanied by a creeping, low-lying, glowing, foggy mist forming in the air and an indistinct voice whispering faintly in the background.

Upon observing the Temple of Delas, Dan Casey becomes concerned about the presence of shimmering beams of light and billowing whispering shrouds of smoke that appear to surround the ancient tower in a manner that defies natural explanation. The occurrence is seemingly supernatural, evoking an air of mystique and intrigue.

Dan slowly raises his bewildered facial expression of disbelief and vertically looks at the ritual temple ceiling. He witnesses the universal stars and mysterious symbols projections all come together and manoeuvre into an alignment of a single pinpointed location in the Kalanisi Galaxy. The shifting transformations have revealed the folklore myths and Sirius Ramo's warning about a black hole beyond the Galactic Veil to be true.

In confusion and disbelief, Dan Casey mutters, "The Vortex is real; the myths are true!" Dan glances across at Jay Haines and whispers, "We got to stop this and save Veena before she becomes possessed. Be ready!"

The chaperoned gunslinger replies in a deep whisper, "I am always prepared, man! What is flowing through your mind?"

Dan addresses Jay Haines discretely with a remote glance to ascertain the location of the alien Leecher creature, "I am uncertain of the plan but cannot stand idly by."

The young female student acknowledges him with a frightened look. She, too, has become aware that the bounty hunters are preoccupied and subtly signals to her male companions by running her hand over the cutlery fork wedged in her white dress's sash belt and bravely nodding her cute head with intentions to help.

Zak Duran, a highly skilled and accomplished bounty hunter, has his weapon trained on Dan and Jay, who are both in his line of sight. He looks up at the temple's ceiling, where he witnesses the mystical appearance of the Black Vortex, even as he remains focused on his intended targets. He says to the erotic, beautiful mistress, "Looks like Director Wilson Volantis isn't chasing wet dream fantasies after all; we're going hit the big time, Terri, after I'm finished bartering with the Corporal Union's financial purse."

"Wonderful, the ancient trinkets performed as required. Wilson Volantis will be happy! Can we leave this daunting tropical island of a mythical proportion and return to a more normal life of glamour formalities? I'm so excited to be leaving, darling! This dreadful smoke and electrical bursts are becoming too unnatural for my acquired taste. Let's wrap this deal up and get back to the Panther."

The smoke, characterised by its creeping and hazy nature, gradually swells around the temple's vicinity. Its speed rapidly increases with the electrical flashes as it spirals around the Crystal Serpent Altar, and the galactic agent, Veena Merida, continues to chant the ritual inscriptions in an unstoppable motion of her well-spoken voice, "Om mani padme hum." Veena witnesses the revolving Black Vortex, accompanied by the frightening appearance of two emerging red eyes. A female voice projects her name, "Amelia Delas wants your soul!"

Veena Merida stands at the forefront of the Crystal Serpent Altar, shouting a piercing scream of terror. Despite her innocence, she manages to snap out of the ritual chant while visualising the ghostly presence of Amelia Delas. As she does so, enchanted supernatural smoke vapours begin to twirl around the Crystal Serpent Altar and mystical data box, with a whispering echo of the demoness' name reverberating around the temple, "Amelia!"

Suddenly, the grey smoke grossly metamorphosises into a female goddess with burning red eyes, and an evil shadowy laugh echoes through the temple. A sense of all-around shock fills the ceremony chambers.

Even the orchestrating Zak Duran is taken aback when he witnesses Amelia Delas transform into a demonic goddess before his eyes. He can't believe what he is seeing. Despite the shock, he knows he has to act fast.

Zak turns to Veena Merida and yells, "Okay, pull the plug on the damn thing. Shut the databox down. I've learned everything I need to know about this unnatural situation."

Dan Casey's main objective is to ensure the safety of Veena Merida. The heroic pilot observes the ghostly, smoky serpent figurehead hovering over her while she appears dazed. Without hesitation, Dan makes a quick decision and signals a nod to Charlena Jones, indicating that he will dash sprint towards the Crystal Serpent Altar.

The astute red-haired student, Charlena Jones, quickly grips her cutlery fork, and with a slick swipe, she yanks it from her outfit sash belt and offensively stabs it in Terri Lace's bare thigh with a vengeance. The sudden attack catches Terri off balance, and she screams out in agonising pain, "Aah, little bitch!"

The red-bobbed-hairstyled renegade student follows up her assault with a pressured hooking elbow to the feminine bounty hunter's rib cage. Charlena manages to break free of Terri Lace's hostage grip and deftly runs to her companions, surrounded by weapons on the temple's stone floor. In a swift motion, the young, feminine seventeen-year-old teenager grasps the agent-issued silver-scoped pistol from the dusty stone-paved floor and swiftly fires at Terri Lace.

Despite fumbling momentarily with her weapon, the brave young female readily adjusts her stance and shoots at her target. As Charlena's torn white dress flaps in motion, she pivots her agile feminine body and cleverly flicks on the infrared-scope site, aiming with precision.

Terri Lace uses her skills of adaptive wellness and tactically leaps a quick dive for cover around the temple's stoned pillar, stylishly evading the trigger-happy teenager's blast shots. The fuming blonde temptress rejuvenates her composure and grips her high-calibre weapon, ready to retaliate. Zak Duran becomes annoyingly aware of the unruly galactic student's vigilantes. He swings his pulsating gun from the sprinting Dan Casey, diverting his crack-shot aim towards the young girl, and coldly advises Charlena Jones of the consequences of her actions.

Zak taunts in his tense, attractive voice, "So you want to play the hard way, kid? Don't say I didn't warn you. I won't be showing no mercy, sweetie!"

Zak attempts to squeeze his killer finger on the calibre trigger with Charlena Jones in his line of fire. But before the lethal male bounty hunter can carry out this poised threat of execution, his weapon is knocked out of his hand by a lunging swept kick from the dreadlocked gunslinger, Jay Haines, catching the dark-haired bounty hunter off his balanced stance.

Jay aggressively grabs Zak's designer flapped collars of his brown leather jacket. The dark-shouldered gunman taunts, "So you wanna play the Haines way? I definitely won't be showing mercy, dude!"

The sly male bounty hunter is thrown backwards, and his body collides with the hard, paved stones of the temple, causing him to land in a dazed heap while his high-class weapon spins out of his grasp. Desperate to defend himself, the cunning entrepreneur shouts, "Dralon!"

In an immediate response to its master's call, the Leecher beast emerges from the shadowy entrance of the temple with a bounding leap.

Jay Haines knows he has to perform to the best of his abilities and urgently dashes for his dual silver weapons in the middle of the ritual ceremony grounds. Jay swiftly lowers himself to one knee, his long leather jacket brushing against the coarse gravel floor. With agility, he tightly grasps his dual shooter, equipped with detachable blades, poised for action with a skilled gunslinger. Jay Haine's meticulous attention to detail allows him to retrieve the cargo-runner's black-barrelled gun successfully.

As he quickly looks up, Jay observes his audacious companion, Dan Casey, approaching the Crystal Serpent Altar. The adept marksman urgently shouts in a deep, stressed voice, "Dan!"

He deftly wields his weapon and launches the interstellar pilot's silver and black-barrelled gun towards him. Jay Haines has no time to spare as the monstrous Leecher, Dralon, launches his beastly arched body towards him with a bloodthirsty, slobbering roar. The hideous alien Leecher attacks the gunslinger's position. It weaves its menacing, slithering tentacles in a taunting, vile manner, striking fear into Jay's heart with its grotesque appearance.

With his characteristic dreadlocked hair and tinted designer shades, Jay Haines confronts the formidable alien creature with unwavering bravery. Jay attacks through deft and calculated movements despite the monster's ferocity, avoiding the alien Leechers' pouncing offensive strike with remarkable agility. With a fluid motion, he regains his footing and draws his dual shooter weapon, activating its razor-sharp blades with a display of masterful precision. His skilful manoeuvres and unflinching determination exemplify his exceptional expertise in stylishly displaying his brave prowess.

Dan Casey dashes to the ceremony ritual Crystal Serpent Altar with a sense of urgency. His dark hair sweeps back in motion as he sets his sights on retrieving his black-barrelled gun. In a swift motion, he scoops up his trusty weapon and adjusts his grip, and his gloveless fingers firmly wrap around the primed trigger.

Dan pauses and takes a hesitant slanted glance back, witnessing Jay Haines in combat with the monstrous Leecher, Dralon, in the spiralling temple and Charlena Jones, duelling in a fearsome shoot-out with Terri Lace, around the circular pillared posts.

Dan's handsome, chiselled facial expression shows the strain of wanting to help his colleagues. He notices Zak Duran slowly lumbering to his feet. But he has to eliminate the threat of the demoness to save Veena Merida's soul from being possessed by the ancient spirit queen. The hotshot cargo pilot quickly shifts his focus upon hearing Veena's scream. He immediately notices Amelia Delas approaching Veena in a tranquil, flowing hover across the ceremony chamber, leaving a lingering trail of creeping smoke in her wake.

Dan Casey spins his sleek, black-barrelled weapon and firmly grips it with both hands, aiming at the advancing Amelia Delas. He dramatically opens fire, but his efforts prove futile as the demoness absorbs the shots with a cackling laugh, seemingly unfazed by his attack.

In a valiant attempt to break Veena Merida out of her trance, Dan shouts, "Veena, snap out of it!" But the feminine galactic agent is numb to his urgings.

Amelia Delas observes Dan Casey's valiant efforts with a spiritual smokiness enveloping her presence. The seductive demoness queen smiles alluringly in a skimpy black sequin gown. Her pale, immaculate skin glistens and her possessed erotic eyes glow with a bright red hue.

Amelia seems amused by Dan's intervention and licks her luscious lips in an irresistible, sexy gesture; she speaks out in a sultry Greek-accented voice, "You two share the same bond of love; I will soon break that atrocious curse and set you free of your pain."

Amelia Delas laughs, switching her ghostly attention back to Veena Merida and teasingly warning of her cruel demands with a wave of her long, wavy black hair. "Your man is handsomely curious. I shall make him mine for my pleasurable entertainment!"

Amelia then says in an evil hissing taunt at Veena, "After I've devoured your innocent, pure soul, beautiful lady. Haha." Cruelly teases Amelia Delas, slowly raising her right hand with her diamond-encrusted gold rings and pointing her elegant, pale, manicured fingers sternly at the feminine green-haired beauty.

As Dan Casey stands poised for action, he looks on in alarm, witnessing Amelia Delas deftly flick her elegant fingers, unleashing a thick plume of hypnotic smoke vapours from her well-manicured fingertips. The spiritual smoke envelops Veena and engulfs her, causing her to waver and lose her balance.

She screams out, "Dan! Help! I can't move!"

Despite her desperate plea for assistance, Veena Merida is filled with emotional despair, feeling paralysed and helpless by the ancient possessive soul ritual that the demoness goddess is performing on her against Veena's will.

The dashing cargo pilot directs his attention to the Crystal Serpent Altar, which features a rotating firebrand globe and astrological databox. With Veena's welfare foremost in his thoughts, Dan Casey quickly takes selfless action, sprinting forward and making a bold, leaping catch of Veena before performing a graceful fall and roll on the temple grounds.

Dan takes a deep breath and looks into Veena's emerald eyes, holding her shivering body close in his muscular arms. With relief softening his chiselled features, he asks, "Are you alright, Veena? You had me worried there for a moment."

Still catching her breath, Veena Merida nods in response to her lover. The two individuals promptly rise to their feet, with Dan carefully shielding Veena from harm. The cool-headed pilot quickly brandishes his silver and black-barrelled gun, aiming for the demon queen as she nears them. Much to her devilish amusement, Dan Casey rapidly opens fire on Amelia Delas.

The stunning serpent goddess absorbs the barrage of shots with a playful, mischievous smile on her lush red pouting lips, teasingly responding to Dan's vain efforts, "How romantic and chivalrous of you, my dearest hero. Your gallantry has won my heart!"

She elegantly approaches Dan and Veena, her eyes emitting a fiery red hue, signifying her evil presence. Dan Casey diverts his aim from Amelia Delas and aims his faithful gun at the Crystal Serpent Altar.

With a characteristic smirk, he says, "You aren't my type, sweetheart. I've always preferred jade eyes to red! Now, go back to the damn hell hole you came from, bitch."

He courageously blasts the Crystal Serpent Altar to smithereens, causing an aftermath explosion that shatters the rotating globe. This action cuts off the spiritual connection with the mystical databox, and Amelia Delas is viciously sucked back into the Black Vortex dimension with a swirling whooshed vacuum and into the jungle temple's ceiling.

She screams in her authentic Greek sultry accent, "Nooo!! Aah, I will return and rule your universe!"

Dan Casey instinctively shields his body around Veena as the energy vapours suddenly flare up, causing the precious astrological data box to fly around the ceremony chamber. After successfully exorcising Amelia Delas, the cargo pilot and galactic agent share a gracious hug, their relief evident in their eyes. However, their moment of peace is short-lived as they still have to contend with the roughish bounty hunters and help their companions, who were duelling fiercely. Dan Casey swiftly adjusts his weapon's aim and targets Zak Duran, who is making a hasty beeline for the ancient data box.

Zak is purely driven by the allure of profit and personal gains. Dan is determined to prevent him from claiming the coveted prize and save his crew. The situation is intense, and the outcome has significant implications for all involved parties. The interstellar pilot rapidly opens fire on his cunningly capable foe. Zak Duran is known for his adaptability and proficiency in handling firearms, and he quickly seeks cover around the temple's stone pillars before retaliating with a series of blasting shots aimed at Dan and Veena.

Despite the dangerous shoot-out, the exquisite male bounty hunter remains composed and focused, leveraging his skills to gain a tactical advantage in the gunfight. His luscious feminine partner in crime, Terri Lace, the seasoned consort bounty hunter, demonstrates her expert skills, giving her a superb edge in positioning and adaptiveness over Charlena Jones, effectively cornering the young student within pinpointed range.

Meanwhile, across the ceremony's grounds, Jay Haines is engaged with the alien Leecher, Dralon, contributing significantly to the ongoing conflict. Despite the odds against the dreadlocked gunslinger's gallant fight against the slithering tentacle beast, Jay remains focused on his survival and fights valiantly to overcome his monstrous adversary. Amidst the chaos of the intense gunfight raging between the *Decepter* crew and the Panther's bounty hunter pack, significant damage to the ancient temple's ornamental elements is caused, leaving them in shambles. A sudden power shift in the atmosphere occurs when a commanding female voice is heard through a set of sonar speakers outside the hidden temple's entrance, issuing a critical order, "SHADOW AGENTS NOW!"

Within seconds of receiving the commanding vice, a squad of highly trained agency personnel swarm the Temple of Delas. They are brandishing formidable infrared-scope plasma rifles, trained meticulously on all parties involved in the destructive conflict.

Chapter Seventeen

Shadow Siege

The enigmatic tropical island's once calm blue sky becomes engulfed in a nightly storm as the dark clouds interact with the planet's moonlight, causing lightning and rumbling thunder bursts to echo across the glowing sandy coastline. The dramatic scene intensifies as half a dozen resistance agency drop-ship transporters swiftly descend from the skies, drowning out the jungle island's natural sounds.

The heavily armoured type of spacecraft, equipped with formidable front and side artillery cannons, floats above the beachfront and shallow waters, causing the waves to crash violently against the rocks. The bulky oval hull is deep and wide, creating an imposing presence in the twilight sky. The vessel's rumbling quad-booster engines roar with a vibration pulse that can be felt throughout the area, and more squads of resistance agents free-drop from the imposing vessel's armoured side vents. The shadow agency's siege becomes even more intense with a military-style campaign.

Within the Temple of Delas, an atmosphere of intense stillness permeates the air. The swarming agent operatives navigate the chambers of the relic temple with the utmost caution, their plasma rifles at the ready. The beams of infrared light emanating from the weapons scour every nook and cranny of the ritual room. Veena Merida remains tightly clinched to

Dan Casey's broad shoulders. The infrared scans contract around their static bodies.

In a calm, professional tone, Dan whispers to Veena, "We must hope that this shadow squad is on our side, or we find ourselves in a precarious situation."

Before Veena can answer his reasonable plea, she turns to the attention of the temple entrance.

The woman's stern voice bellows, "Drop your weapons, now!"

The female in charge and armed personal guards cautiously enter the ceremony chambers. The well-spoken woman is dressed in an agent's navy-blue uniform with an armoured, peaked electronic helmet. Her piercing blue eyes wander around the individuals one by one, waiting for her orders to be carried out immediately.

In the tense situation near the circular pillars of the temple, Charlena Jones makes the first move to surrender her weapon. The brave and attractive red-haired student throws her scoped pistol to the dusty stone floor and raises her hands in compliance without saying a word. Jay Haines follows suit and discards his silver dual shooter.

The daring intergalactic gunman taunts the alien Leecher, saying in his profound verbal manner, "You're lucky they showed up; I was about to take you!"

The hideous creature withers its menacing tentacles. Dralon is a wild, raging alien but also intelligent enough to realise the infrared beams from the agent's plasma rifles threaten its life. He is holding back his lust for blood with a growling taunt.

Dan Casey is next in line to surrender his weapon. He throws his handgun to one side and raises his free finger-cut gloved hand while still entangled with Veena Merida. The pilot defends his crew member's actions, addressing the official, "We comply with your terms, Miss Harlow! Our objective here was to deliver the astrological data box without the intention of causing any trouble until these rogue bounty hunters showed up."

The scene is tense as the agency woman marches forward in her clicking boots and fixes her piercing gaze on the cargo pilot.

She asks, unamused and intrigued, "You have the liberty of knowing my identity; I don't recall I have your information. And why do you have your arms wrapped around my field agent?

"Agent Merida, please compose yourself and give me a quick update on what the hell has been happening here." She commands with authority, "Wasn't the briefing clear? Come alone. Yet here we are, with a delegated temple full of misfits and an off-the-charts energy source."

Tara Harlow's awkwardness is palpable as she witnesses the sophisticated bounty hunter's reluctance to be disarmed. Sarcastically, the resistance official declares, "Oh, I see you two are not fully comprehending the meaning of 'drop your weapons'. Well, I can certainly offer an alternative solution."

She bluntly snaps at the hard-of-hearing individuals and turns to the SWAT team agent on her right, issuing orders, "Agent Barnes, please disarm these individuals using any means necessary."

Prompted by Tara Harlow's orders, a young dark-skinned agent removes his electronically armoured helmet, revealing a dark, handsome and smart-looking man with neatly styled black hair and designer stubble.

He respectfully responds, "Agent Mason Barnes, reading you loud and clear, ma'am."

Agent Barnes approaches with total confidence in his abilities. His short-stocked plasma scope rifle activates, and he is ready to apprehend Zak Duran. The agent says, "You heard the lady; disarm now. I won't be asking twice."

Zak Duran smiles and drops his high-calibre weapon down to the agent's black boots. He remarks, "Do I know you from somewhere? Your face looks familiar to me."

"You don't know me for shit. Now tell your pretty woman to drop her weapon."

The gorgeous blonde temptress, annoyed, surrenders her black deluxe single-barrelled pistol with a teasing looped gesture around her manicured fingers. "Are we going to listen to this old woman rant on? She has no lawful jurisdiction over us; we are innocent citizens of the Galactic Corporal Union!"

The advancing Agent Mason Barnes marches across the temple's curled pillar stones and crouches down, apprehending Terri Lace's disposed calibre weapon. He swipes back in defence of his superior officer. "You're far from the glamour worlds you belong to, lady, so follow the supreme commands without the mouth!"

Terri sexually flutters her beautiful, dreamy eyes, alarming Agent Barnes. "Oh, Agent Barnes, you must be the old woman's little pet trooper. Has she promised you a high ranking? I wonder if you will have the same confident approach when Director Wilson Volantis and the might of his Corporal Union's Armada discovers this lost golden world."

Taking charge of the shadow agent siege, Tara Harlow confronts the female consort and informs her in a no-nonsense manner, "You have a high opinion of yourself, but it has no value here. Director Volantis will never know of this world from your vulgar lips. You will be in a high-security detention cell for interrogation, like the rest of you."

"Agents, round them up. It's time to blow this battered temple as there's not much left to study. Please, Agent Merida, let go of that man and bring me the data box and a damn good explanation of events!"

Veena refuses to follow protocol and stands in defiance of the given order. The green-haired galactic operative speaks out, "No, ma'am, I protest and demand that the weapons be withdrawn from my friends immediately. If not, then consider me a fugitive. I stand alongside this man, Dan Casey. He's the bravest interstellar pilot I've ever known, and without his help, I doubt we would be standing here now. Charlena Jones and Jay

Haines are innocent bystanders who require a safe passage back to Kothariya. Your precise astrological data box is in the corner of this ceremony chamber, as your mission briefing required, ma'am!"

Veena's body is still interlocked with Dan Casey, and she speaks confidently with a determined look. Tara Harlow sternly glances at the gloomy field agent and waves her hands in a gesture to the surrounding agents.

The resistance SWAT operatives immediately diminish the infrared tracing beams from their plasma rifles away from Dan Casey and his colleagues. Jay Haines and Charlena Jones quickly show their respect to the strict female agent official with a thankful nod as they slowly go and stand with Dan and Veena. The resistance forces comb through the sacred ritual temple, leaving no stone unturned before setting the explosive charges.

Agent Barnes retrieves the scuffed data box and hands the mythical star-chart device to Tara Harlow. He then asks her with curiosity drawn on his serious face, "What about the bounty hunters and alien Leecher, ma'am?"

Tara replied with her objectives at the forefront of her strategic mindset, "Bring in the star-carrier and collect their vessels from the coastline. And contain the bounty hunters and their vile creature in the Brigg detention area. We shall assemble at headquarters and then unravel this tangled mess. Veena and her collateral baggage can accompany me on my shuttle, hovering outside this dreadful place."

Agent Barnes has protocol concerns about the procedure and says, "I don't believe it's proper practical guidelines for remote agents or unidentified personnel to travel with the leading officer; you can't be sure Agent Merida hasn't been compromised, ma'am. I would feel much more at ease if they were detained on the fleet carrier until we reach headquarters for a full security check."

Tara Harlow is inflexible in her reply, "Noted, Agent Barnes, but we shall roll with my given orders and make sure you keep that Leecher confined. The last thing we need is an alien beast running free aboard my fleet carrier."

Mason replies with a dissatisfied demeanour and royal salute, "Yes, ma'am!" He starts to organise his fellow resistance agents and quickly asserts to the bounty hunters, "Move it now. There is a holding cell with all your names on it. Let's not delay."

Zak Duran is a suave entrepreneur, the type of person who earns high credits for taking risks. He finds himself in a temple surrounded by Tara Harlow and other agents. Zak protests his innocence, but no one is listening. He isn't about to go peacefully.

The bounty hunter sneers at Tara's authority and the other agent's intimidating threats, "You don't have the galactic legal rights for these actions. I'm warning you: I never play any game of chance without an insurance policy. You think you can push me out of here, but think again, Harlow!"

Tara Harlow is getting cross and urges him to leave the temple under arrest. Tara sighs in frustration. She has hoped the arrest would be smooth, but Zak is complicating it. She can tell he isn't about to give in, "Let's not make this any harder than it has to be, Mr? I don't believe you have submitted your name!"

"Just remember the name, Zak Duran!" says the handsome, dark, slick-haired bounty hunter with a glint from his devious brown eyes, tilting from behind his designer shades.

Tara responds to his smarmy threats, "Zak Duran, you're under galactic arrest for hindering an operation of the most importance to secure universal peace; anything you do say, maybe take in a statement of evidence while you await trial. Agent Barnes! Please take this mockery of a man and his two beasts to their cells."

Terri Lace is displeased by the taunting remarks and responds with a bitter tongue, "You will regret using those words, old lady! I promise you."

The alien Leecher, Dralon, has a batch of resistance

personnel covering his every move, their infrared sights tracing the vicious creature's muscular body and slithering tentacles. With the tension still at a high gauge in the presence of the resistance agency, Dan Casey and Veena, accompanied by Jay and Charlena, quickly make their way outside the Temple of Delas and follow the path of Tara Harlow and her duel-armed response guards to her private shuttle.

The agent shuttle is a lightweight craft with a slender hull and twin engines equipped with two front and side guns. The craft hovers low over the planet's surface with its landing ramp down. Tara Harlow boards the sleek white shuttle with the company of Dan Casey and the *Decepter* crew. The wind whispers around them as the craft leaves the tropical island below, the ramp and hatch closing with a shuddering thud. The ship's propulsion engines whir into life, and the craft shoots off with a short burst of speed.

Inside the cockpit of the slender vessel is an agency pilot setting the coordinates to the agent headquarters. The pilot updates Tara Harlow on their journey, noting that the electrical storms mean they'll have to take a longer route that will add delays to the total charter flight, "Estimated flight duration one hour and forty-five minutes, we shall fly above the planet's atmosphere to avoid the electrical storms, ma'am."

Tara Harlow adjusts her seat and fastens her seatbelt. She is the lead agent official, known among her peers for being daring and ambitious. During her years of service to the Corporal Union government, she was a key political figure in Director Wilson Volantis's early election campaign. There, she earned the nickname "Fearless Harlow", and she now aspires to be living up to that title.

While in the rear passenger quarters of the Ariel starship, after a long silence, Dan Casey asks his crew members how they are feeling after the supernatural ordeal of witnessing the ghostly image of Amelia Delas. And if their story will be believed.

The experience they have just gone through has been unprecedented and difficult to fathom. The handsome black-haired pilot casually sits in his brown leather jacket and dark blue slacks. He says in an easy tone, "Is everyone okay? That is quite an experience; I'm still trying to wrap my head around it. Amelia Delas, a supernatural apparition? I don't know if anyone outside of this crew is going to believe it, and now these military-style agents apprehending us and my freighter?"

Veena and Jay nod in agreement. Charlena gazes out the starship windows, admiring the view with a listening ear on the conversation.

Dan Casey inhales a deep breath sharply and looks around the shuttlecraft. Witnessing the dual, armed agents escort guards he whispers in close quarters to the others, "We all have different stories to tell about what we saw. Some of us may be able to describe Amelia Delas better than the rest. But regardless of what we say, I doubt anyone will believe our story."

He runs a hand through his wavy black hair as he looks around at the exhausted faces of his crew members. "All I can tell you is to hold on tight and tell our story. We have to trust that in the end."

Veena Merida leans in next to him and strokes his slick, black hair. She smiles and says with anticipated reassurance, "Don't worry, Dan. Once I've had a chance to brief Tara of events, I'm sure it will be okay, and I will arrange a safe passage back to the human capital world of Kothariya for Jay and Charlena. I promise."

The personalised, sleek shuttlecraft quickly climbs above the atmospheric turbulence from the thundering electric storms with a vast levelling-off altitude as the engines shift to a patterned cruising.

Jay Haines is relaxing, seated in the cream leather flight seats facing opposite Dan Casey and Veena. He comments on the temple's expeditions. "I don't know about you guys! But I saw horrors in that ancient temple I never believed possible. I didn't get a close-up view of the demon bitch first-hand, with that damn alien Leecher hounding me, but I saw enough to scare the living shit out of me. Troubling times!"

The craft internal communications link pings with a static buzz and echoes a bland message, "Agent Merida, immediately come to the flight cabin for debriefing and alone!"

Veena Merida sighs. She has been expecting this, but not so soon. Veena quickly prepares herself with a slick brushed wave of her frazzled pastel hair. She stands up, straightening the folds in her tight black catsuit, and approaches the flight cabin for the mission debriefing. When Veena reaches the flight cabin, she sees Tara Harlow standing with arms crossed and a serious look on her face.

Veena knows that this means that Tara expects her to give a detailed and accurate debrief. The sexy, jade-eyed agent explains what went wrong on the mission. She describes how Sienna Clayton blew her cover when stealing the databox. She explains how she hijacked Dan Casey into helping to get to the Isadora system while being hounded by Commander Calo Tarick, with events leading up to how they had got lost in the tropical jungle and had been attacked by mystical Zealots and the ghostly spiritual presence of Amelia Delas.

The two female agents discuss the assignment briefing in the private flight cabin with the echo of raised voices from the enclosed confinement.

Lounging in the high-grade passenger section of the lightweight starship, Dan Casey hears the murmured shouting of the agent briefing. He attempts to get up and help explain the chain of events in Veena's defence.

But Jay Haines stops him and places a hand on his shoulders, advising him, "Supreme Commander Harlow says, alone, man! I'd sit tight and try not to make it worse than it sounds if you want your starship freighter back."

"Agent Harlow's got more stuck-up backbone than Miss Reynolds in geographic studies; oh boy! I didn't think that feat of being an Astro-gorilla was possible. I would not go in there without crying for help, and I doubt Tara will believe how the cool galactic student, Scraggy Jones, saved the day!"

Dan Casey laughs with the young female student in a fun-loving manner with congratulations due. The charmed pilot says, "Did I not predict that crooked cutlery fork would be useful? You were courageous back there, Charlena, and showed Terri Lace how to shoot straight. I'm proud of you, Miss Jones, and you can be my wingman anytime!"

"You did good, kid! Be proud of yourself. You'll make a gunslinger chick one day. Haha!"

Charlena Jones, cheeks blushing, says, "Aww, guys, Thanks. Honestly, I was petrified but wanted to help. I don't like those bounty hunters."

Dan Casey is in unison with the galactic student's view. In his smooth, manly voice, he explains how the high-rolling bounty hunters got drawn into the mission, "I don't get on too well with them either. Unfortunately, we had to make an emergency stop in the Sera sector. When we attended the galactic derby in the entertainment world of Carrageen-Hazen, we fell into their bounty purse, being none the wiser that they were compromised. Veena believed they would help us find refuge until the Corporal Union's trail eased off.

"Still, Zak and Terri have sold out their long-term friendship for a high-stakes credit funded by Wilson Volantis. I'm afraid they have shown their typical bounty hunter's loyalty traits of not being trusted. Let's hope we have seen the last of them."

Jay Haines agrees with his opinions and enquires about their forthcoming accommodations. "Where do you think they will be taking us for the night? Some top-notch agent facility with a five-star restaurant. I'm hoping they have plenty of food on offer. I'm starving, man!"

"A warm, comfy bed and heated blanket with a mug of steamed coco-choc would be nice. It would be so cool and a big upgrade from Mach Galanti's dumped-out slave station!"

They endure the rest of the flight in the secret agent headquarters. Dan Casey and his two companions relax and sit chatting merrily, enjoying the downtime in the lush passenger quarters of the sleek, lightweight escort craft.

Veena Merida holds the debriefing meeting with Tara Harlow in the front cabin. While en route to the resistance secret headquarters complex, the agency transporter glides at a steady cruising speed, gently pitches a quarter turn, skimming across the swirling atmosphere crust of the luscious world.

Meanwhile, the cleaning-up operation is complete on the tropical jungle island. Agent Mason Barnes stands on the glowing sandy beach with a grin of satisfaction as he watches the hulking transport vessel descend. The *Decepter* freighter and Panther frigate are winched up into the lower haul landing ports of the fleet carrier.

Mason Barnes leads this final phase of the operation himself, and the success of its completion is proof of his skills and eagerness to be respected.

The resistance flagship carrier has a deep hull with three-level flight decks. The starship is slow and cumbersome but heavily armoured with triple gun turrets lining the back and front of the space carrier attached with dual quad boosters for deep interstellar flights.

The pulsating engines roar with a deafening vibration awaiting departure. Agent Barnes rounds up the last squad of the agent operatives and the artefact collections from the Temple of Delas.

He shouts, "Come on, move it, troopers, move it. We need to wrap up this garage band and be gone before that brewing electrical storm hits these shores."

A squad member of the ground team approaches Agent

Barnes with an update on the evacuation. He reports with a salute, "The explosive charges are set around the temple, and we have cleared out anything that may be useful to the science division; we even have this smashed-up altar. Did you want it loaded on board, sir!"

Mason steps forward and inspects the damaged parts of the altar. "Just some shattered parts of a serpent ornament, yeah! Load it on, private. I've not got time to look through the ancient junk; the science division dudes get paid enough to sort their crap out. Right, we fall out. ETA two minutes. Move it, private; let's get this sluggish transporter in the air."

He removes his electronic armoured helmet and stands on the loading ramp being winched up to the vessel's haul. The fleet carrier's cargo hatch closes with a clamping seal as the boosters flare up with a hovering motion from the tropical mainland to the blue oceanfront. The night sky is dark and stormy as the massive carrier gains speed and height, rising like a wave into the stars. Clusters and moonlight combine in a gloomy view as the heavy vessel's boosters kick in faster and louder, steadily pushing the starship carrier into the sky. After a few moments, the lights from the shoreline fade, replaced by an ever-increasing darkness that seems to envelop the carrier and its cargo as it flies ever higher into the atmosphere.

While inside the pitching vessel on the first deck port, Agent Barnes gives his orders to the craft's security squad, "Make sure nobody goes near these artefacts, and two of you go and check on our prisoners and report to me; I'll be on the control bridge, detonating that temple's foundations before we are out of range."

The security team returns a salute and goes to their assigned tasks. As Mason Barnes reaches the second deck, he clears his circuit code access to the control bridge on the sliding shutter door. Agent Barnes enters the flight cockpit and asks the pilot and navigation crew with a tone of authority, "I need an ETA on flight time arrival. Give me a rear holo visual on that temple and activate the detonation procedure on my mark."

The female navigation officer responds professionally, "Scanner detectors are locked in range, and primarily visuals are now online. Destination arrival to headquarters is one hour and thirty minutes, and systems are all green and five by five. Explosive charges are now activated on your command, sir!"

Agent Barnes smiles and leans back in the leather recliner command chair. "Good, flight officer, blow the joint and take us home!" He orders, watching the detonation of the hidden jungle temple live on the holo scanners. The temple explodes with an illuminated aftermath, projecting a flicking of static on the holo screen.

"Boom! There goes ancient history and good riddance. Now, where is that security team? I need a report on the prisoner logs. Officer, get me an internal communications link."

Meanwhile, on the first deck of the carrier starship under armed custody are the bounty hunter Zak Duran and his Mistress Terri Lace, along with their loyal alien Leecher, Dralon. They are ushered down a network of narrow corridors to the brig confinement section, which resides on the first deck of the vessel. The appearance of the brig does not bode well. Grime and rust coat the walls while the air, thick with moisture, hangs like a veil between them and a bulky steel bar door. The agent officers who have arrested Zak Duran and his entourage seem to believe that they are dangerous criminals and have handled the trio with a great deal of disdain. A single overhead light in the brig casts a sullen glow over the cramped, dismal quarters. Cold metal beds are lined up along the walls where worn blankets and pillows have been provided, with few chances of escaping their captivity and being surrounded by the unchanging hum of the ship's engines.

Despite the grim circumstances, Zak Duran smirks with a smug, sarcastic comment to the armed agent guards, "I'm guessing the resistance agency is low on private funding. This palace could do with a ten-credit touch-up. It doesn't speak much in volume for your career prospects. Well, at least I won't be overstaying my welcome, agents!"

The beautiful Terri Lace sniggers at his remarks mockingly, relaying her take on the galactic agency. "What do you expect, darling, with that old woman coordinating affairs? I doubt her galactic pension stretches far enough to build a proper fleet."

The officer responds by pointing his plasma rifle at Zak, stating through his microphone helmet, "Move and less of the chatter from you both."

Terri Lace witnesses the other security personnel attending their duties, and with an elusive sighing cry for help, she screams, "Officer, help me, please. I feel so faint; the high atmospheric turbulence makes me dizzy."

The officer is concerned and immediately goes to her aid, swiftly holstering his scoped pistol. "Hey, you okay, madam?"

Terri Lace quickly swipes her hand from her gorgeous face and gazes at the gentleman agent with a seductive, cruel smile. The devious blonde mistress responds, "Yes, I'm fine. I just wanted your weapon, stupid!"

She then runs her long-nailed fingers over her expensive diamond ring, releasing a gushing cloud of stun gas, followed by a slick hand-stealing manoeuvre, drawing his infrared pistol from his holster. Terri coldly shoots the stunned agent in his stomach without a thought of mercy before she activates the gun's scope-sight.

The cold-hearted bounty hunter's feminine face is full of tempered anger. She readily traces the pistol infrared beam across the remaining trio of agents and opens fire with accuracy in the manner of a trained and deadly professional killer. The security agents groan fatally, holding their blood-riddled bodies and dropping their weapons as they fall, slumbering to the containment cell's floor of the Fleet Carrier in a spiralled dead heap.

Terri Lace seductively opens her long, shapely legs as her mini skirt etches up her thighs in a sexual posing stance. She aims her scoped-barrelled weapon at the containment cell's locks and readily blasts them off the brig cages.

Zak Duran casually swings the barred steel door open with a devilish, handsome smirk evading his charming, slick looks. He claps his hands impressively, applauding his beautiful feminine lover's efforts, "Outstanding performance there, sweetheart. You nearly convinced me. Let's leave this floating hulk of a carrier and return to the Panther. I'd say it's time to cash in on that insurance policy!"

Keeping his eyes peeled for any signs of the enemy, he grabs the fallen agency personnel's plasma rifle. Zak knows he has to act quickly and warns of advancing dangers.

While reloading the plasma rifle, he advises Terri, "The blast flares will have appeared on their internal sensors, so keep alert, sweetheart. If they have not already become aware of our escape, they soon will be."

The glamorous blonde purrs her intentions, "I'm in no mood for that old woman's agents, and I will blow them away one by one. This bounty purse is becoming more hindering than rewarding. I knew Veena and that damn data box falling into our laps on Carrageen-Hazen was too good a venture to be true, and now we have nothing to show for our persistence."

Suddenly, a loud bang comes as two backup security guards burst into the containment section. They see the bodies of their fellow agents on the floor, lifeless and bloodied. Without a moment of hesitation, the guards draw their plasma weapons and aim them at the two bounty hunters who are now free from their containment cells. Terri sees the shock on their faces, and her instincts take over. In a split second, Terri raises her infrared pistol and fires two single shots at the heads of the guards. Their bodies slump to the floor, lifeless.

The blast shots echo through the containment section, setting off the fleet carrier's security alarms.

Zak Duran says, "Now they will be on to us, but not all is lost, my love. I thought I saw some of those agents collecting parts of the Crystal Serpent Altar as we boarded this craft, meaning if we get them on the Panther, along with the location of this planet logged, we will have more than enough high-order bargaining chips for Director Wilson Volantis, to give us an audience."

Terri Lace deviously smiles with an erotic impression, kissing his manly stubbled cheek and adding with a sultry whisper, "I think we need a distraction to even the odds in our favour, darling!"

Zak Duran strokes his wandering hand over her revealing flimsy red skirt and mindfully caresses her curvy butt with a smug smile.

The adept entrepreneur barks his unruly orders to the beastly Leecher, "Dralon, please check down the agent numbers and don't hold back. Give them a body count souvenir to remember us by."

Laughing, Zak Duran swiftly makes his way out of the confinement section in a confident-seeking stride with his plasma weapon activated, closely followed by the strutting Terri Lace in her black leather high-heel boots with her smoking pistol's infrared beam surveying every quarter of the vessel's narrow corridors.

The Leecher growls in compliance with Zak Duran's spoken command, and its tentacles scratch against the carrier vessel's walls as it bounds forth, ready to disturb any who dares to challenge its master and mistress. A batch of four agents approach the containment section and halt as they see the alien Leecher, their eyes widening in fear and disgust. But they quickly regain their composure and draw their plasma weapons, preparing for a fight. The Leecher, Dralon, is fearless and charges towards them; its massive arched body moves with unnatural speed and agility. Its tentacles lash out, grabbing onto the agents and pulling them towards its gaping mouth, eager to feast on their flesh.

As the capable bounty hunters attempt their escape, they trigger the security sensors on the fleet carrier's bridge control. Mason Barnes, a skilled agent of the Resistance Agency, sits in the command chair of the fleet carrier's bridge control. He keeps a vigilant eye on the craft's internal sensors, ensuring everything runs smoothly. However, his focus is quickly interrupted by the blaring alarms and flashing lights from the security sensors.

"Sir, we have a security breach on the level. It seems the bounty hunters we captured are attempting to escape," says the female navigation flight assistant with her voice laced with concern.

Mason Barnes immediately stands up, and his muscles tense as he processes the information. The bounty hunters are notorious for their cunning and skills in evading capture. He knows they won't go down without a fearsome fight. "Get the security team to the lower level immediately. I want those bounty hunters secured."

As the navigation assistant relays his orders, Agent Barnes frowns, and his mind races with possible scenarios. The lower level of the fleet carrier is a maze of corridors and compartments, making it the perfect place for someone to hide. The bounty hunters are most likely armed and dangerous, with the alien Leecher causing havoc. Just as he is about to give more orders, the alarms suddenly stop. Mason frowns, a sense of unease settling in his stomach. It is too silent, especially after the chaos of the alarms. He quickly checks the internal sensors, but they show no signs of the fugitives.

"Sir, the security team has reached the lower level, but there's no sign of the bounty hunters."

Mason's frown deepens. How can they disappear just like that? He knows they are skilled, but this is too quick even for them. The under-pressure agent says, "Check the external sensors. They must have found a way to escape without triggering the alarms; check the Hanger bay."

As the external sensors are checked, it becomes clear that the devious bounty hunters have found a way to escape undetected. Barnes guesses that they have used a hidden compartment in the cargo bay to sneak out of the fleet carrier's narrow corridors.

"Sir, we found them in port section two; they've managed to tap into the core system and are disrupting engine capacity. We are losing power on compensators boosters one and two."

Mason Barnes heaves with his shoulders slumping in defeat.

"We need to apprehend them before they disable the ship. I want all agents to be on high alert. These bounty hunters are dangerous and must not be allowed to roam freely. We also have a damn monstrous Leecher on board."

Mason can't shake off the feeling of disappointment and frustration. The mission had been going smoothly until this very moment.

Mason's voice rings through the flight cabin, "Drop the ship's altitude ten degrees and skim through the orbital crust but maintain on course for headquarters. And get an SOS message to Supreme Commander Harlow advising her of our situation. We have a code red."

The agent, a seasoned male pilot, immediately follows orders. He punches in the coordinates and directs the craft down ten degrees, keeping a steady hand on the vessel's controls. The female navigation officers quickly work together to send an SOS to Supreme Commander Harlow at headquarters. Mason Barnes promptly springs into action, adjusting his plasma pulse rifle from his shoulders and checking the weapon. He has been trained to handle any situation, and this is no exception. He has to act fast before the mayhem spreads any further.

Mason turns to the flight crew members. "I want this flight cabin on lockdown; don't open it no matter what. I'm going down with a squad team to end this breakout." The navigation crew members nod in understanding and immediately begin securing the cabin.

Meanwhile, Agent Barnes patiently waits on the control bridge until he has gathered a SWAT squad to join him on his bold mission. Mason takes a deep breath and checks the internal camera sensors, and his heart sinks as he witnesses the aftermath of the bounty hunters' attack.

Bodies of his crew members are scattered everywhere, their lifeless eyes staring back at him. The once pristine decks of the starship are now covered in blood and debris. Blast-fire burns mark the walls, and smoke engulfs the lower decks. The Agent team sent to handle the unrest is under siege.

Chapter Eighteen

Code Red

The sleek, personalised craft of the supreme leader, Tara Harlow, approaches the vicinity of the resistance agency's headquarters. The shuttle pitches and descends, signalling their arrival at the highly guarded facility. Tara's shuttle, the *Aurora* LX, is one of the fastest and most advanced in the Kalanisi Galaxy, designed for escorting high-profile individuals to safety. Its sleek, stealthy exterior blends with the dark space expanse, making it nearly undetectable to most surveillance systems.

Tara Harlow sits in the plush, leather cushioned seat of the private agent escort shuttle, watching the stars whiz by outside. She has been tasked with obtaining the ancient data box and is currently in a debriefing with her remote galactic field agent, Veena Merida. The tension in the shuttle is palpable. Tara Harlow releases the strap from her armoured helmet and places it on the side shelf, letting out a sigh of relief. The helmet's weight has been pressing down on her head for hours, and she is finally grateful to be free of it. She shakes her head to loosen her hair, revealing a black tied-back bun hairstyle with slight streaks of grey.

Tara frowns, relaying her submission, "Apart from involving yourself with the outside company and provoking a potential security risk, you have done extremely well, Agent Merida, under a very testing assignment. I will arrange accommodations and transport for your friends and get their sworn secrecy regarding this world's location. By the way, this is called Nova Conti, according to the old databank records we found, so welcome your colleagues on my behalf. If you have any questions, speak now. If not, you can go back to your colleagues."

Veena Merida sits nervously in her cushioned seat, her back straight and her hands folded neatly in her lap. She tries to maintain a calm expression but can't hide the disappointment and frustration that are stirring inside her. Veena takes note of the supreme leader's analysis of her extract and retrieve mission with a despondent shallow response, "Thank you, ma'am! I have no further questions. You have made yourself more than clear, and all the details will be in my assignment report, whether believed or not by the administration board."

Tara Harlow keeps her lips sealed with a disapproving glare at her remote agent's discontent until the shuttle pilot requires her attention. As they fly towards their destination, the helmsman's voice crackles through his microphoned flight visor.

"Sorry to interrupt, ma'am, but we are getting a serious report from the fleet carrier. Agent Barnes has issued a code red emergency. The renegade bounty hunters and their alien beast are on a killing spree around the ship."

Tara's heart drops at the mention of the code red. It means that a hazardous situation is unfolding, requiring urgent action. She quickly turns to her remote agent, "Looks like your unwanted friends, Duran and Lace, are going to be a problem after all; this is what I meant by security hazard, Agent Merida!

"Turn this craft around and get us back into that aerospace immediately. Relay this message to the fleet carrier and activate the Delta 629 code red response. Let's hope Agent Barnes can prove his worth!"

Veena quickly sits back down and straps herself in. The

shuttle pilot instantly engages the flight controls, and with an increase in throttle, he starts to manoeuvre the *Aurora* LX starship around, setting a course for the fleet carrier's distress call.

While unaware of the unfolding commotion, Dan Casey is relaxing back in the passenger quarter, talking to Jay Haines, who has Charlena Jone's head resting on his shoulders as she has dosed off during the journey from the jungle island. They are surprised by the *Aurora* LX's sudden shift in flight pattern and change of course. Dan reacts with a swaying jolt in the leather seat, his shocked brown eyes link with the dreadlocked gunslinger.

The handsome interstellar pilot says, "What's going on? We seem to be turning around in an evasive manoeuvre." He continues to speak in a low voice of discretion, "I'm going to the flight cabin and check on Veena to see if she knows what's happening. So, Jay, I need you to keep the escorting guards off me kindly. If they tend to make a preventive move, nothing too rough, though. Just a friendly diversion, okay?"

Jay Haines responds with a cunning smile, "Yeah, I got your back. And don't worry about the agency personnel; I'll only tap and trip the escort guards up a fraction!"

Charlena wakes up, rubbing her sleepy eyes. "Huh! What's going on with you guys? Are we at the agent base yet?"

Jay Haines responds with a kind cuddle, telling her, "Not yet, kid, you just sit tight. Everything's going to be alright. I think we just hit a bit of turbulence."

Dan Casey is profusely sweating as he makes his way down the narrow walkway towards the flight cabin of the spacecraft. The move is risky. He has no time to waste, and the guards are hot on his trail. He takes a sneaking glance behind his shoulder and sees the escort guards shouting, "Hey, stop! You're not allowed in there!"

His heart races as he quickens his pace. He can't afford

to get caught now. As he reaches the flight cabin, he hears a loud commotion from the direction behind. He knows it is Jay Haines, who is always up for a good joke.

Jay stands up and obstructs the approaching guards without missing a beat with a pleading motive. "Can any of you two show me the restroom?" He asks in a mocking tone, "I'm not good with sharp aerial manoeuvres and feel a bit woozy, man!"

The agent guards look confused before Jay's words sink in. They quickly realise he is trying to distract them, and they scowl at him. But Jay just stands there with a cheeky smirk on his face. Dan seizes the opportunity, quickly presses the latch device, and opens the stutter door to the *Aurora* LX flight cabin. He slips inside, closing the door behind him.

Tara Harlow swiftly turns her shocked face to the shutter door and witnesses the cargo pilot enter the shuttle's flight cabin. "Who do you think you are, barging into my office with no invitation warranted? Get out now!"

The charmed interstellar pilot knows something is wrong by Tara's blank face, and he responds to her abrupt inquisition, "I'm Dan Casey. I want to know why the craft is turning around so evasively. Have we got some sort of trouble?"

Dan turns his handsome face, and his dark brown eyes are drawn to Veena Merida, "Are you okay, sweetheart? What's going on? I heard raised voices from outside the flight cabin?"

Veena dearly replies, "It's Zak and Terri trying to storm the fleet carrier en route to their miraculous escape from trial." Dan picks up her hand and gently squeezes it.

"I wish you would take your hands off my field agent, Mr Casey! I've been informed of your bravery, and your ten thousand credit reward will be arranged in due course; now, if you will please leave the flight cabin, this is agent business, not a public gathering."

Dan quickly responds with aggression, "You made it my

damn business when you conversed with my freighter on your marooned vessel. Also, refrain from talking to my crew members like that, ma'am!"

The authoritarian female leader of the agent organisation duly reminds the interstellar pilot of a few facts, "I think you've made a mistake about Agent Merida's place. Veena is a remote galactic agent, not a pick-up girl, and your starship is the last of my concerns; I have a brigade of agents on board with an alien Leecher running riot."

"Please, ma'am, I'm sure Dan can give us some technical insight if he stays. He used to be a member of a space protection outfit; his knowledge of this type of affair is valid, and I'm more than confident he will keep reticent."

There is a silent pause of numbness on the flight deck with propulsion engines whistling from the *Aurora* LXs. Tara Harlow takes a deep breath and shakes her head, looking at the inseparable pair, relaying her thoughts, "Against my better judgement, Mr Casey, you can stay and advise us, if required! But I'm more than confident that Agent Barnes and his advanced SWAT squad will take care of matters promptly. This is what they have been trained for: unprecedented situations.

"What is ETA with the carrier, and have I got a damn update from Agent Barnes yet!"

The shuttle pilot checks the navigation radar and responds through his microphone, "ETA, thirty minutes plus. We must account for the electrical storms in this climate, and we've had no further contact with the fleet carrier, ma'am."

Tara Harlow sits back in her command chair with minimal words to help the situation, "Thank you, pilot. Keep on course and let me know if any changes are averted." Her facial expression is bland and lost in thoughts of concern.

Dan Casey intervenes with his interpretations. He asks, "Can't this shuttle go any faster? By the time we get there,

Duran will have slipped the net, and his Leecher creature will have dismantled your SWAT squads."

The shuttle pilot replies through his crackling microphone, "We can launch off the spare energy reserve pods, which will help with duration but also reduce our flight time in the air."

Dan pointed at the pilot, stating, "Do it helmsman."

The *Aurora*'s pilot activates the controls and relieves the craft's weight by ejecting the energy pods.

Tara Harlow feels the chain of command slipping from her grip as she states, "I'm sure my pilot is qualified to make his adjustments, Mr Casey. Plus, I'm well aware of the dangers onboard that star carrier, and when did we hand off the reigns to civilians? Remember, this is an agency operation; don't overstep your mark."

Tara swiftly unbuckles her seat belt and stands up on the flight deck next to Dan Casey with a stirring glance of disapproval. Before the personality clash expands to a full-blown row, Veena Merida quickly intervenes, asking, "What rank and skill does Agent Barnes have? Has he ever come up against aliens before, ma'am?"

Tara replies to her female field agent inquisition, "Mason is a good agent; his heart is in the right place, and he tries to impress. He's only been with us for six months. He once ran with a street gang back in the human home world but has grown through the academy ranks at an exceptional rate of improvement. I'm pinning my hopes that his hot-headed rashness will not get the better of him in a tense situation, and he will be more than a trained match for your bounty hunter friends."

Casey says, "Duran and Terri are not our friends; both have tried to kill us more than once and don't underestimate either of them. If they escape, they will bring the full might of the Corporal Union fleet, knocking on your doorstep, so you want to hope Agents Barnes is more than just efficient."

The atmosphere in the flight cabin of the *Aurora* LX is

tense as they make their way through the thick layer of clouds. The pods are quickly ejected from the ship's rear, releasing a blinding burst of energy trailing in the night, swiftly followed by an acceleration of speed venturing to the carrier.

As the fleet carrier descends through the atmosphere of Nova Conti, the sound of alarms blares throughout the ship. The SWAT teams scramble to their designated positions, bracing themselves for the imminent battle.

Meanwhile, in the ship's cargo bay, the bounty hunters and their ghastly alien Leecher are causing more than their share of problems for the agency personnel. Terri Lace is no stranger to high-stakes gun fights. As a seasoned assassin, she has trained for years to hold her own amid chaotic battles. And the current situation is no different. She is crouched behind a stack of crates, her blonde hair falling in front of her face as she focuses on her targets. The sound of gunshots fills the air as she exchanges fire with the enforcing agents, who are determined to stop her and Zak from completing their escape.

Terri's blue eyes narrow as she aims her pistol, her finger barely twitching as she fires a chained flurry of blast shots. The agents are caught off guard, and before they can even react, Terri has taken down three of them in quick succession. But more are still coming, and they are getting closer every second. Terri knows they can't hold out for much longer. She glances over at her male counterpart, Zak Duran, who is frantically working on a security lock device to grant them access to the cargo bay.

"Hurry the fuck up, darling," Terri shouts over the sound of blast-fire flares. "They're coming at us like swarms. What's taking so long with that damn lock devise?"

Zak's dark eyes briefly meet hers before he focuses on his task. "The system is encrypted," he yells back, frustration evident in his voice, "I need a few more minutes."

Terri Lace curses under her breath. "Ah fuck!"

They don't have a few more minutes. Ms Lace can feel the

agents getting closer, their footsteps growing louder as they approach. She needs to buy Zak more time. Scrambling to her feet, Terri takes cover behind a different set of crates and continues to fire her pistol at the oncoming agents. With her sharp reflexes and precise aim, she takes down a few more of them, earning herself a momentary respite. But it isn't enough. The agents are now just a few feet away, and Terri can see the determination in their eyes. She knows they will stop at nothing to take her and Zak down.

Just as Terri is about to fire again, a loud beep echoes through the corridor. Zak Duran has finally cracked the encryption, and the locking device is now operational. Without wasting a moment, Terri runs towards Zak and grabs his hand. Together, they rush towards the cargo bay, the sound of blast shots following closely behind them.

Quick on their heels is Agent Mason Barnes. He arrives at the cargo bay doors with three other Elite agents, his weapon drawn and ready for anything. Mason Barnes quickly takes charge of the apprehension and presses the cargo bay's lock device controls, only to discover a malfunction.

He shouts, "Damn, they've burnt the system out from the other side. I need some explosive charges on these shutter doors, now, private."

The private quickly gets to work, reaching into his backpack to retrieve two small charges. He has been trained extensively in explosives and knows these charges are powerful enough to destroy the cargo bay shutter. He carefully places the charges strategically, covering all exits and entry points. Mason suddenly turns his attention from the cargo bay area. His face freezes in a state of shock, hearing screams and growling along the vessel's shot-up and battered corridor.

The alien Leecher, Dralon, is making his hideous presence felt, cruelly devouring the agents en route to link with his master and mistress in the cargo bay.

"Okay, private, keep on that shutter door and you two agents with me. Let's take out this slimy mother fucker."

Agent Barnes and his colleagues are trained to handle the most dangerous and unpredictable of missions, but even Mason isn't prepared for what he is facing now. Standing in front of him is a Leecher alien, a creature known for its deadly tentacles that can suck the flesh off its victim's face in a matter of seconds. Mason desperately tries to devise a plan as the alien easily tears through the defences. But the slimy tentacles are too quick and strong, and they seem to anticipate his every move. The agents have to act fast before it is too late. Dralon roars a growling cry as the alien creature lunges and attacks them, ripping their bodies apart with its razor-clawed fists. Dodging and weaving, Mason Barnes manages to avoid the first few strikes, but he knows it is only a matter of time before one of the tentacles will reach him. Unfortunately, he drops the plasma weapon in the brawl.

Agent Barnes has to find a way to fight back. Thinking quickly, he grabs an emergency flare from his belt and sets it off, blinding the alien momentarily. Taking advantage of the distraction, Mason bolts down the narrow corridors of the stricken fleet carrier, hoping to find something to use as a weapon. But as he turns a corner, he can hear the hissing and slithering of the alien approaching. Agent Barnes has to act fast. Spotting a metal pipe lying on the ground, he picks it up and braces himself for the creature's attack.

The Leecher alien comes at Mason with a force that shakes the ground. Its tentacles lash out, hoping to latch onto him and suck his flesh dry.

But Mason Barnes is ready, he shouts, taunting the grotesque beast, "Come on, you slippery alien fucker is that all you got? I was taking shit like you down on the backstreets for joy!"

He swings the pipe with all his might, landing a solid blow on one of the Dralon's tentacles. It lets out a shrill screech and recoils, allowing Mason to catch his breath. But the adept Agent

Barnes knows he can't let his guard down. The alien Leecher is still a formidable opponent, and it is only a matter of time before it will come at him again. Taking a deep breath, Mason lunges forward and swings the pipe again, aiming for the creature's head. The impact knocks the alien off balance, but it quickly recovers and retaliates with a swift strike from one of its tentacles.

Agent Barnes feels a sharp sting on his right arm as the slimy appendage latches onto his flesh. But he refuses to let it take him down. With all his strength, Mason pulls the tentacle off and swings the pipe again, this time aiming for the alien's gruesome body. The Leecher lets out a guttural moan as it stumbles back, its slimy tentacles thrashing wildly. Seeing an opportunity, Agent Barnes takes a deep breath and rapidly charges at the alien, swinging the pipe with all his might. The impact sends the alien creature tumbling to the ground, its body writhing in pain.

Mason believes he is bravely getting the upper hand and range to kill the alien Leecher, only for the expert charges to detonate around the vessel's cargo door, causing a shattered rocking of the first deck. Agent Barnes loses his footing as the Leecher's tentacles wrap around, slapping him to the wall before throwing him adrift. His colleague comes to help.

"Hang on, sir, I got the beast!" The explosive SWAT member shouts as he comes to Mason's aid. But his bravery is short-lived as the Leecher quickly turns its attention to him. The agent raises his plasma weapon to open fire, but before he can shoot, he is shot in the back by Zak Duran.

The handsome, roguish bounty hunter stands at the cargo hold entrance with a sarcastic smirk as he looks down at the fallen security personnel. The cargo deck of the spaceship is chaotic, with crates overturned and alarms blaring. But Zak Duran seems completely at ease, as if this is just another day at the office. Zak is one of the best bounty hunters in the galaxy, with a reputation for being ruthless and unflappable. And from the looks of it, he is living up to that reputation.

Zak's attention then turns to Mason Barnes, the hotshot agent sprawled on the floor, barely conscious. He can't help but chuckle as he remembers how cocky Barnes had been when they first met in the hidden jungle temple. The guy thought he was unstoppable, but Zak has proved him wrong,

"Watch your mouth, agent; it will only get you into trouble," Zak says, his voice laced with taunting amusement as he whacks Mason around the head with his plasma rifle. Agent Barnes groans as he struggles to sit up, clearly disoriented and in pain. Zak knows he has hit him hard enough to leave a lasting impression.

Dralon is creeping closer to finish him off. The Leecher's blood-red eyes roll with lust to kill the wounded prey. Zak stops the alien Leecher from fulfilling its torment.

"No, Dralon, you had your fun. Help Terri prep the Panther and load up the remaining parts of the Crystal Serpent Alter artefacts. We shall leave this mess for his Supreme Commander to see. I always follow through with my threats, so remind Harlow to smile for the Mbron Media cameras!"

Agent Barnes courageously murmurs a defiant sentence with blood dripping from his mouth, "We shall stop you. I'll make sure of it, Duran."

"How do you plan to stop me, Agent Barnes? You are nothing but my lapdog, crawling at my feet. Plus, I am already getting away with it," laughs the bounty hunter.

Zak pauses, taking a moment to think before he speaks. "I do remember your face, Barnes. You used to run with Rans Palmer when he was still a member of Dystart Blades. You should have stuck with him. But now, Rans is in the pocket of the Corporal Union. They control everything in the city, including the gangs. Life has never been better for them, but what about you?"

Zak Duran's voice holds a hint of pity as he looks at the beaten and bruised agent. Mason Barnes groans as he tries to get up from the ground, but Zak swiftly smacks him with the handle of his plasma rifle, knocking him out cold, "Choose a side, Barnes. Make it one worth fighting for. This ten-credit agency of prosperity will be a distant memory by sunset," Zak says, his voice firm and unwavering. The sleek entrepreneur bounty hunter stands over a beaten Mason Barnes with determination and urgency to vacate the fleet carrier.

Agent Barnes, on the other hand, is confused and disoriented. The hit from Zak Duran's rifle handle has knocked him out cold, and as he slowly regains consciousness, Mason tries to piece together the events that have led to this encounter. He remembers his past as a member of the Dystart Blades gang, run by the notorious Rans Palmer. They are a small but fierce gang, and Mason had been loyal to them for years. But when Rans struck a deal with the Corporal Union, Mason turned his back on the street gang and left the violent lifestyle behind to join the resistance.

Agent Barnes slowly regains his consciousness. He can feel himself sprawled out on the deck of the fleet carrier's cargo bay. His head spins, and he can barely make out anything around him. But one thing is for sure. He can hear the low hum of the starship engines and the sound of steam hissing from the Panther's sleek undercarriage filling the air.

Mason tries to sit up but is stopped by a sharp pain in his head. As he reaches up to touch his temple, he can feel the warmth of blood trickling down his face. He must have hit his head when he blacked out. Mason Barnes can only lay there in unbearable pain and witness the Elite bounty hunters escaping his authority. Zak Duran is a notorious high-class bounty hunter known for his black amour stealth ship that can slip past any surveillance and destroy its targets undetected. But Zak's reputation isn't just limited to his advanced technology. He is also known for his charm and quick wit, which often lands him in and out of sticky situations.

As he heads towards his sleek starship, Zak Duran can't help but turn his body on the craft's rampway with a mischievous smug salute towards Agent Barnes. Zak's dark brown, alluring eyes fall upon Terri Lace as she approaches the Panther cockpit. She sits in her leather co-pilot's seat, her long bare legs crossed as she focuses on setting up the flight systems and booting up the Anancio-designed dual hyperdrive and weapons.

Despite the dire situation, she looks stunning, dressed in a revealing bra and a skimpy red silk skirt. Terri's long blonde hair flares across her naked, dainty shoulders and elegant neckline. Her manicured fingers fly across the control panel, and her gorgeous blue eyes scan the blinking lights and screens. She is in her element, calm and composed under heated pressure.

Zak Duran can't help but appreciate her beauty but quickly snaps out of it. There is no time for distractions. They are in a fierce battle, and the agent reinforcements are closing in on them near the cargo bay entrance with highly advanced plasma cannons.

Zak says, his smooth voice urgent, "We must get out of here; activate the override on the carrier hanger doors, now!"

Terri Lace nods with a delightful smirk, her fingers frantically keying in the bypass on the Panther's control panel. She is a skilled co-pilot and knows what needs to be done in this grave situation. As the Panther's systems activate, Terri Lace seductively turns her glamorous face towards Zak Duran.

"Override commencing; weapon systems are now online."

Zak gives her a nod before focusing on the control screens. They are outnumbered, but he isn't about to give up without a fight.

The Panther stealth class frigate is highly equipped with state-of-the-art weapons, and Zak Duran is confident they can take down their resistance attackers.

"Here comes the old woman's little agent force; blow them to smithereens, darling."

Zak braces himself without any hesitation, activating

the lower cannons. He grips the joystick, opening fire on the weapons and sending powerful blasts towards the gathering heavy artillery SWAT squad.

Agent Barnes is slowly regaining consciousness. He can hear the sounds of their starship's weapons firing and knows they are still in danger, witnessing the agents diving for cover as explosions erupt inside the cargo hanger as the battle rages on. The Panther frigate shakes with the impact, but Zak and Terri continue to fight, their eyes never leaving the cockpit's interior screens.

Terri checks the Panther's flight controls and reports, "Thirty seconds left for override spike to break their encryption code. Amancio hyperdrive is charged and locked into the automated subsystem. We're ready to vacate this floating cesspit and good riddance."

"Don't fret, sweetheart. We shall soon be dining in the high-class company of Director Volantis."

Zak flicks the control switches and engages the dual thrusters, feeling the powerful engines roar to life. The Panther's sleek design makes it easy to handle. Taking a deep breath, Zak pulls back on the joystick, raising the Panther's landing gears to a static hover. The starship starts lifting off from the cargo hanger deck, and the dual boosters work perfectly in synchronisation.

Terri Lace says, "Ten seconds and counting until hanger bay's security cache is decrypted."

As the cool-headed bounty hunter reaches the desired altitude, Zak leans forward, pushing the joystick forward and tilting the stealth craft towards the hanger door. The Panther responds effortlessly, gliding through the hanger with grace and precision. Zak Duran can't wipe the smile off his dashing face. He witnesses the cargo bay secure shutter begin to prise open; he manoeuvres the ship around to a launching vector and kicks in the thrusters with an instant speed acceleration. The Panther frigate, a sleek and deadly vessel, flies out of the side hanger bay doors of the fleet carrier in a whooshing blur. Its engines roar as it manoeuvres through the vastness of space, evading any obstacles. Weapons are armed and ready, primed for their next target.

In this case, this is the Elite Agency Shuttle of the Supreme Leader, Tara Harlow. The *Aurora* LX cruises into the vicinity of the fleet carrier with a high velocity and pitching manoeuvre, gradually adapting to a level altitude. Inside the sleek craft's flight cabin, Dan Casey is trying to advise the agent pilot to combat the threat of the Panther. He warns with tension flowing through his manly voice, "There's Duran's stealth craft, bursting out the carrier's flight side hanger deck. He's manoeuvring and heading straight for us, pilot. Evade now, damn it; you can't take him head-on; that's suicide. Their starship has highly advanced shield capabilities!"

Tara Harlow is tense and seated behind in the command quarters, conducting her overruling orders. She demands with pure authority ringing through her focused voice, "Pilot, if you have the selective target in range with a clear shot, then take him down; that's a high-priority order!"

Veena Merida also protests the daring aerial offensive. She warns in a raised tone of her well-presented voice, "Ma'am, with all due respect, Dan's right; the Panther is a highly sophisticated assault stealth craft. Its shields are nearly impossible to penetrate by any conventional weaponry."

Tara Harlow is in no compromising mood. She blandly responds with a slight glance to her remote agent, "Point noted. Agent Merida." She quickly turns to *Aurora*'s helmsman, "Now, pilot, open fire at will. I don't get dictated to by bounty hunters."

Cursing, the authoritarian female supreme leader brushes her hand through her tied-up hairstyle, holding her nerve in an awkward situation. As the trained agency pilot adjusts his flight helmet and prepares for battle, his heart races with excitement and nerves. He has been through countless simulations and training exercises, but nothing can fully prepare him for the real thing.

The pilot officer's voice crackles through his helmet, "Yes, ma'am, battle computers are online and front weapons are activated. We're now engaging an attack vector run at maximum speed. Hold tight, everyone."

Meanwhile, in the rear passenger section of the *Aurora* LXs, Charlena Jones sits nervously, her heart racing as she watches the alarm and warning lights on the control panel start to flicker. Being on an agency spacecraft is a nerve-wracking experience, but this is different. This time, the danger is real. Looking out of the side view, she notices something that makes her heart drop. A sleek, dark spacecraft is cruising towards them at a rapid pace.

Charlena recognises it immediately. The Panther is the notorious stealth ship causing chaos in the galaxy.

"Oh boy!" Charlena exclaims, her blue eyes widening with worry. "This is more than your definition of just turbulence, Jay. What's going on? We're in trouble, aren't we?"

Jay Haine's brow furrows as he tries to make sense of the situation. In his deep, tense voice, he replies, "I don't know how they escaped custody. But seems like we have our unwelcome bounty hunter visitors back."

Charlena Jone's heart races as she watches the Panther get closer and closer. She quickly hugs Jay Haines, knowing they are no match for the powerful frigate.

As the sleek, black silhouette of the Panther spacecraft emerges from the cover of the night sky, its engine purrs as it swoops in close on a direct course for the *Aurora* LX. Inside the stealth craft's cockpit, Terri Lace sits calmly in the co-pilot's quarters. She keeps a check on the navigation and weapon instruments.

The dazzling blonde tells her deadly male counterpart, "I recognise that shuttle, Zak. That's the old woman's ship I saw at that hideous temple. Dan and Veena will be on board, thinking they can stop us. Let's blow them all up, darling and show them who's boss."

Zak Duran is in his element, dictating affairs from his pilot seat. He sits upright and focused, firmly gripping the advanced controls. He responds to his sexy lover's flaunting torments with a cheeky grin, and Zak steadies his hand over the Panther's weapon systems.

He says in his cunning fashion, "We shall leave them a lasting souvenir to show our appreciation for their hospitality."

Zak opens fire with a devious smirk. The agent shuttle weaves and swerves desperately to avoid the Panther's scattered blast fire. Explosions erupt in the lower atmosphere of Nova Conti. The *Aurora*'s front lasers return fire, the punishing blasts hitting the Panther's advanced shields but doing little damage.

Zak Duran smiles with smug comments, "Amateurs. They think their little guns can take us. I would have thought by now they'd know I don't play a game of chance. When the stakes are down!"

Zak flicks his fingers over the joystick and selects the neutron laser cannons. He sets the target tracer, waits until he hears an indicating bleep, and opens fire, locking onto the *Aurora* LX flight cabin. The sleek black Panthers painted on the sides of the stealth spacecraft seem to come to life as they fly by with incredible velocity. The *Aurora* shuttle, known for its smooth and efficient design, is no match for the ruthless Panther-class assault frigate with its rapid speed rush.

As the Panthers tilt and weave in a looped roll, the pilot of the *Aurora* shuttle can only watch in terror as the fierce predator unleashes a barrage of neutron laser bolts. With a loud sound, the bolts impact the sleek shuttle, causing damaging explosions on its slender frame. The once graceful and efficient *Aurora* LXs shuttle is now a crippled and wounded vessel, its exterior riddled with gaping holes and its internal systems in disarray. The *Aurora* LXs soars through the vast expanse of the lower atmosphere; the agent pilot suddenly slumps over the flashing flight controls, his body going limp and falling unconscious.

Dan Casey immediately springs into action, his instincts taking over, trying to revive the agent pilot. The cargo runner checks his pulse and, unfortunately, states the fatality to the others, "He's dead! Veena, quick, help me move his body. I'll try to take control of the shuttle."

Dan lugs the pilot's body from the helm against the elements in the depressurising cabin. Veena Merida composes herself and quickly unbuckles her flight belt to assist him. Meanwhile, the supreme leader, Tara Harlow, having been knocked back, is dazed in her command chair by the pressure of the impact.

The *Aurora* LX begins to dip and dive, hurtling towards the nearby ground of the planet, Nova Conti. The adrenaline-fuelled screams can be heard from Jay Haines and Charlena Jones as they hug in the passenger section of the damaged shuttle.

Charlena's screams are filled with terror as she looks at her companion, the red-haired teenager's freckled face twisted in fear, "We've been struck! We're going to crash! I'm scared, Jay!"

Jay Haines holds Charlena close with his strong, muscular arm and reassures her. "Hold on tight to me, kid. Don't let go. If anyone can get us out of this mess and back to a stable flight, it's my man, Casey. Trust me."

By now, Dan Casey is gripping the control panel tightly, his heart racing as he frantically inputs commands into the *Aurora* LX. The cockpit is chaos, wires dangling, screens flickering, and the previous pilot's lifeless body lies against a console. With the help of Veena Merida, they manage to remove the body and make room for Dan to take the pilot seat. But as they work, the pressure inside the cabin begins to build, knocking Veena off her feet. Despite the struggle, she continues to assist Dan, her booted heels digging into the floor for stability.

As the ship jolts, Dan can feel Veena's presence beside him, and her determination and strength give him the courage to take control. But his thoughts are interrupted when he hears a soft whimper behind him. Turning to look, Dan sees Tara Harlow, the supreme agent leader, holding her seat with one hand and clutching her head with the other. She has taken a heavy blow to the head during the impact and is shaken up.

Without hesitation, Veena rushes to Tara's side, checking on her and offering reassurance. "You okay, ma'am? You took a heavy, quick knock. Let me strap you in and ensure you're secure."

Tara weakly nods as Veena helps her into her seat and straps her in securely. She then returns to the control panel, taking over co-pilot duties and helping Dan.

"What do you want me to do? I need guidance. I've no idea about flight controls."

"Come on, damn it, where is Pearl when you need her!" Dan groans in frustration.

Dan quickly turns to the assisting green-haired agent and says urgently, "Veena, get on the emergency communication channel and contact the fleet carrier. Let them know we need immediate assistance and an emergency landing if possible."

Veena Merida acts without a moment to spare, connecting the microphone headset, "Mayday! Mayday, I repeat."

"Keep trying, sweetheart. I've got an idea; we can reboot the main drive core and glide on one engine in theory!"

He bravely turns the craft's power off.

Veena asks in a shocked tone, "Oh gosh, will this work?"

"Let's hope so, or there will be no dinner for two this evening. I'm rebooting the drive now."

Chancing his luck, he rapidly presses his hand on the shuttle ignition touch button with no response from the stuttering propulsion booster.

The *Aurora* LX scores from the cloudy night sky, losing altitude in a fierce draping nosedive; black smoke oozes from the rear fuselage with a gashing trail as the sleek shuttle loses control, wildly spinning as it descends towards the rough seas below.

Despite the odds, Dan Casey remains determined and presses the ignition controls, "Come on, start up already," he exclaims angrily.

His emotions get the better of him, and he slams his fist on the flight dash. Suddenly, a bleeping sound starts on the controls, and the systems reboot.

Dan looks at Veena with shock and hope, "It's working! Come on, baby, you can do it; ease up now."

He pulls back on the *Aurora*'s joystick controls. With renewed optimism, Dan is determined to turn the situation around and get the shuttle back on track. As the starship begins to respond to the central drive core rebooting and stabilising to a safe level of altitude on a single booster engine, Veena Merida breathes a sigh of relief inside the cabin.

The *Aurora* LXs has successfully averted the imminent danger, and Veena can't help but smile in admiration of Dan Casey. "Looks like it's dinner for two."

Despite the close call, Veena is grateful for Dan's dedication and expertise, which has helped them overcome the crisis and ensure their safe journey ahead. After skilfully manoeuvring the craft to a stable level of altitude and reducing speed, Dan Casey takes a moment to catch his breath at the pilot's helm.

As he assesses the damage to the flight cabin, he asks Veena, "Have you received any communications from the carrier? And where did Duran go?"

He quickly checks the navigation systems to ensure they are still operational and searches for the Panther frigate. Despite the tense situation, Dan remains focused and determined to protect the crew. Veena Merida stands at her station on the bridge of the small spacecraft *Aurora*, her long wavy hair falling in front of her face; she focuses intently on the microphone in her hand. Her jade eyes are wide with hope and anticipation as she waits for a response from the fleet carrier. Veena has sent out an SOS after the Panther's neutron lasers hit their ship.

Suddenly, she establishes a communication wave link with the cabin's speaker system and is relieved when she hears the static hiss of a response from the other end. The carrier's captain is on the line, and Veena's heart races as she waits for his message,

"We copy you loud and clear, *Aurora*. Commence emergency ETA four minutes." The captain's voice clearly says, "Flight bay three will be on standby, over."

Veena feels relief wash over her as she relays the message to Dan: "Four minutes." She says with a sparkle of hope. That's all they have to hold on for, and help will arrive. She quickly adapts the communication wave link to the speaker system in the flight bay, knowing that her fellow crewmates also need to hear the good news back in the passenger section of the *Aurora*.

Jay Haines hears the message with deep gratitude and relays his faith to the young galactic student, "See, nothing to worry about, kid. I told you that Casey would iron things out; he's the best damn pilot about to have on your side."

She smiles sweetly and playfully tugs on his beaded, dreadlocked hairstyle, "I'm not a kid, you know." The attractive teenager teases. "You are screaming louder than me!"

Despite the scary situation they have just encountered, there is a sense of camaraderie and light-heartedness between the *Decepter* crew.

Even the shaken-up supreme leader is impressed with his efforts, "I owe you my thanks, Mr Casey. Without your adept response, we would all be dead. Veena, has the fleet carrier performed an analysed surveillance report of casualties, and has anyone heard from Agent Mason Barnes?"

Veena replied, "Not yet, ma'am. You just conserve your energy until we dock. I'm sure Agent Barnes will be fine."

Dan firmly has control of the *Aurora* LXs, even in its damaged state, and informs the others with some personal gratitude, "My pleasure saving you, Miss Harlow. I'm sorry I can't help your pilot, and unfortunately, Duran got away. His Panther frigate is not showing on the radar scopes. He must have cloaked and scarpered. We dock in sixty seconds. Hold tight, everyone. I'm taking you home."

It is a peaceful night in the outer bound atmosphere of Nova Conti, with the moons shining brightly, the stars twinkling, and the planets slowly rotating in the vast expanse of space.

But amidst this tranquillity, a deadly game of cat and mouse is unfolding. The advanced Panther-class frigate, one of the most technologically advanced spaceships in the galaxy, is lurking undetectable to radar with the predictive stealth camouflage activated. On board are two bounty hunters, Zak Duran and Terri Lace.

Zak checks the surveillance screen inside the sleek flight cabin, analysing the latest navigation detector readings, "Looks like they survived, darling,"

He says with a hint of disappointment. "Still, it won't affect our long-term plans. We need to set a course to the human home world of Kothariya. I believe we have a dinner arrangement to attend with the Director of the Corporal Union."

Terri raises an eyebrow in response. "Shame they didn't explode," she says with a slight pout. "I was looking forward to that part. They had a lucky escape. Must have been Casey flying the shuttle, as no doubt the old woman has proper training, judging by her agent's shooting skills."

Terri plays with her perfectly manicured nails, showing her disinterest in the outcome. Zak and Terri are known to be ruthless bounty hunters in the Sera system, taking on any job that pays well and eliminating any obstacles in their way. They are both highly skilled and are known for always getting their target. But this assignment, with its supernatural twists, is proving more challenging than they initially thought. Zak Duran adjusts the Panther's flight pattern coordinates, preparing to jump into hyperspace. Terri Lace can't help but give a sexy smile. This assignment may be taxing, but the rewards will be worth it. With the dinner arrangement with the Director of the Corporal Union, they will have an opportunity to expand their network and earn more lucrative missions and an even higher reputation.

Chapter Nineteen

Forecasts and Rewards

The early-morning sun rises over the breathtaking world of Nova Conti, and a gentle breeze sweeps over the planet's surface. The fleet carrier has safely touched down at the headquarters of the resistance agents. They are on high alert due to the recent controversy surrounding the bounty hunter's escape while in high guard custody. The agency personnel are reminded of the situation as they disembark from the carrier, ready to tackle the challenge and ensure their home planet's safety and security.

The agent complex stands tall, with its massive, high-towered dome building visible from afar. The facility boasts an enormous runway and a cut-off link to the planet's dual freeway, providing easy access to the central city. The impressive agent base is strategically located near the oceanfront, nestled between the wilderness and mountain canyons, adding to its charm and beauty.

As the agents and hospital personnel work tirelessly to evacuate the injured, Dan Casey stands at the pier before the complex. The gusts of wind blow back his black hair as he leans his elbows on the side bannisters of the base, watching as his Machiavellian MK2 freighter is towed out of the transporter's cargo bay. Dan manages to persuade one of the ground marshals to give him a smoke, and he takes a few moments to reflect on everything that has happened. He knows that it will be difficult to return to his old life as a cargo drop supplies pilot, given his involvement with the resistance agency and the death of Commander Calo Tarick. Despite the challenges, Dan is resolved to continue his cargo contracts and support the agency in any way he can while he stays on Nova Conti.

After the medical staff assesses his colleagues, Dan Casey waits for his crew to be released. He finishes off his smoke and disposes of the compostable filter in the blue ocean waves as he admires the morning skies breaking through.

Jay Haines is the first to emerge, and he makes his way over to Dan. Laughing, he says, "Apparently, I'm certified with a clean bill of health, thanks to you, man. You saved our arses up there. I've said it before, but I owe you, Casey."

Jay expresses his gratitude to Dan, who stands there with a humble smile, appreciating the kind words. The camaraderie between the two colleagues becomes palpable as they discuss their daring mission and next steps.

Dan asks, "So I guess you are heading back to Kothariya and collecting the welcome awards for returning Charlena to her mother. You deserve it for your bravery. Just watch your back when you're in the home world, Jay. The Corporal Union may have your ID flagged up on their central database for collaborating with us on that trade station! Zak Duran recognised you in that Temple of Delas."

Jay Haines leans his broad shoulders and back on the railing, readily slipping his jewelled ringed hands in his navy quarter jacket with a shrugging gesture of feeling the early-morning coldness brushing over him.

"The thought has already crossed my mind; I just need to get Charlena home safe, and I'll take my chances with the Corporal Union. In my work, you're always watching over your shoulder. It unfortunately comes with the underground territory."

Jay enquires about his friend's prospects. He asks, "What about you, Dan? Are you planning to stay in this newfound world to help their cause or protect your beautiful lady from harm's way? You are a sharp, intelligent fighter and a crack-shot pilot; I'm sure the resistance agency can do with a talented man like you assisting them."

Dan Casey responds with a humorous smile, his brown eyes twinkling in the brisk sunlight, "I don't think I'll be fitting in with the agency life anytime soon. I doubt the supreme leader will put up with my attitude, and I haven't had a chance to review my options yet, given the recent chaos and unforeseen changes."

Jay nods, understanding his friend's sentiment. They have been through so much danger and uncertainty in their mission to deliver the astrological data box to the agent authority. As they stand there, watching the waves crash against the shore, Dan speaks again from his heart's desire, "But one thing's for sure, I'd like to get to know Veena better without all the shooting. Take her away from this dangerous play against the Corporal Union."

Jay Haines laughs heartily at Dan's comment, knowing his friend has a soft spot for Veena Merida, the resistance agency's top remote agent. "I feel you don't think this agent base of operations will last out. What's going through your mind, man?"

"Well, if a couple of bounty hunters and a monster can rip through a transport carrier, causing the damage they did, with at least fifty agents aboard and still get away, just think what a quarter of the Corporal Union's fleet can do?" Dan says to the private gunslinger for hire. He glances at the agent base facilities and notices Veena Merida and Charlena Jones getting checked out at the medical booth entrance.

Dan Casey's words hang heavy in the air as he and the private gunslinger contemplate the gravity of the situation. The recent attack has shaken the agency to its core, and they know they need to be better prepared for future threats. Dan Casey's eyes dart back to Veena and Charlena, emerging from the agency's medical booths, looking none the worse for wear. He breathes a sigh of relief, knowing they have survived another close call.

As the two women make their way towards them, Dan and Jay exchange a few more words, "Let us keep this conversation between us for tonight; I think our ladies have been through enough drama and a hot meal followed by a good night's sleep will be more to their liking."

Jay Haines replies with a joking gesture, "I won't say a word, but just remember, I need the same kind of pampering as the ladies, dude. I've been complaining about hunger since we left that haunted temple."

Dan Casey greets his two female crew members with a kind smile, relieved to see they are both okay after their medical check-up. He asks, "So how are you two gorgeous heroines faring up? Ready for more action? We can infiltrate another space station or find a mysterious island?"

Veena looks at Charlena with a smile. "Shall I slap him, or will you like the honour, Miss Jones? We can say it's your first training lesson as an agent. Never let the enemy lead you astray."

Charlena Jones is amused at their exchange and responds, "I am inclined to let him off the hook this time, Agent Merida, given his favourable appearance. However, I would like to redirect my frustration towards the security agent who confiscated my test tubes containing the glowing sand particles from the mystery jungle island. He deemed them hazardous, yet they are essential to my geographical studies."

As they stand there, bantering back and forth, Dan laughs at Veena's and Charlena's quick responses, knowing that both have a sharp wit and a fierce determination to succeed.

"May I enquire about the high-class meals that are available for agents? Additionally, do we have access to a five-star apartment as a reward for our heroic efforts?"

Veena responds with a gracious yet misleading smile,

stating, "The cantina will be open at 9am. Unfortunately, our arrival is short notice, so Tara can only manage to provide agent personnel pods, which she assures me are quite comfortable."

Jay stands there, stunned by the response. He rubs his stomach and laments, "No food? It's only 3am. These are indeed troubling times."

The *Decepter* crew goes through the bustling building, filled with agents rushing about and the constant blaring of loudspeakers issuing orders and shift changes. Veena is guided to the elevator by two security agents. Charlena follows close behind, amazed by the sight of it all and secretly wishing for the opportunity to become a recruit if her mother, Lena Jones, will allow it. Dan Casey trails a few yards behind Jay Haines, inspecting the headquarters with keen interest. The cargo pilot and his companions reach the escalator pod and enter alongside the security officers.

Dan observes his surroundings as they ascend the agent tower and whispers to Veena, "I can't shake off the feeling that we're under house arrest. Are we going to be questioned about the temple artefact discovery?"

In her posh tone, Veena reassures him, "It's just protocol with civilians around, and Tara has decided not to ask any further questions. She only requested my field report. She believes we might have come across a visual defiance weapon in the hidden temple, not the mythical artefact of Amelia Delas!"

Dan Casey gives Veena an eye-rolling glare and retorts, "Visual defiance weapon! Are you saying that the supreme leader doesn't believe us? It's a shame she wasn't in that temple a few moments earlier. It seems highly believable to me, as did the Zealot Templar, Sirius Ramo."

Charlena's sweet voice comes to their defence, "I know what I saw, and it is not a visual weapon."

Jay Haines quips, "Typical answers from those in power. They never want to know the truth or provide us with food."

Veena shares her thoughts on Tara Harlow's decision to discard the truth. "I'm with you guys all the way. I was at the forefront and felt Amelia's cold presence touch my soul. Whatever the officials deem true, what happened in that temple was no illusion."

The security agents open the elevators once they arrive at the accommodation level. Agent Merida steps out of the elevator and into the bright, sterile hallway of the agency's headquarters. Dan Casey is by her side, followed by Jay and Charlena. The attractive green-haired agent is greeted by two more security agents who have come to escort them to their pods. They each have earpieces and stern expressions, clearly taking their job of protecting the headquarters seriously.

"Agent Merida, we've been expecting you," one of them says as he hands her a couple of visitor's passes.

Veena flashes a smile in recognition and follows them down the hallway, her high-heeled footsteps echoing against the sleek floors. They swiftly arrive at the personal pod section of the complex, a series of individual sleeping compartments for the agents to rest in between missions. Veena follows the escorts to show her the designated pods. She nods her thanks and watches them leave before turning to face the others.

Charlena Jones is standing nearby, looking tired and worn out. Veena can understand. It has been a long day for them both. She approaches Charlena and hands her the pass card, "Pod 249, here's your pass key."

Veena says with a gracious smile. "I do hope you sleep well. I'm sure I will. It's been a testing day."

Charlena's tired expression turns into a grateful smile, "Thank you, you are a lifesaver, Veena. And you sleep well, too."

Veena Merida nods and turns to the rest of the team, "Okay, well, I'm in pod 251 if anyone needs me. So good night, and see you all later."

With a quick, mischievous wave, Veena turns and heads towards her pod. As she walks, she can't help but notice the vivid colour of her hair contrasting against her sleek black jumpsuit. She runs a hand through her long green hair, taking a deep breath as she reaches her pod.

Dan's bewildered frown deepens as he glances at Jay. "Did you feel Veena is acting a bit strange?"

Jay, the dreadlocked gunslinger, nods in agreement, "Yeah, man, this whole place is. I thought we were getting a pod each and food, but it looks like I'm sharing with the kid."

Charlena tells Jay Haines, "You better not snore in your sleep."

While Dan and Jay spend a few moments in the corridor talking, Veena inserts the pass key and steps inside, feeling the door slide shut behind her. She lets out a sigh of relief as the familiar comfort of her pod welcomes her. It feels like a home away from home, where she can finally let her guard down. She quickly changes from her jumpsuit into a comfortable pair of sweatpants and a t-shirt before collapsing onto her bed. She closes her eyes and lets out a content sigh, feeling the mission's exhaustion finally catching up with her.

Dan Casey shakes hands with Jay Haines, wishing him well, and goes to Pod 251, but he has no pass key. He gently knocks on the door and whispers, "Veena, open up. I'm locked out of the pod."

Dan waits for her to unlatch the slider door. With a brief look at the agents guarding the corridor, he says slightly louder, "Hey Veena, why are you asleep? You can't be sleeping already."

Suddenly, the pneumatic door slid open. The handsome pilot witnesses Veena standing casually at the entrance in just her nightwear garments and with a tired expression.

"About time!" he says, preparing to enter the room. "I thought you had forgotten me!"

He suddenly feels Veena's dainty hand halting his progress. The jade-eyed vixen stops the interstellar pilot at the entrance and reminds him, "You can't come in, Dan. Agent Rule 49 has been imposed, which states that no active agent on call can interact with outsiders. It's not my call, but you're a civilian member. And I'm on duty right now."

Dan laughs, thinking it is a joke, "Who says you are on duty?"

"Tara!"

Dan decides to push the boundaries set by the supreme leader. "Well, you can inform Miss Harlow that I don't abide by Rule 49."

Veena responds just as confidently. "Tara said you would say that. And if you choose to defy Rule 49, I was to let you know that every pod has surveillance cameras. So, don't try to sneak in, or she will have you removed from the building, and you'll have to sleep in your starship in the cold hanger bay," Veena says, with pouting red lips.

Dan's expression shifts from a smile to a serious demeanour as he realises Veena is not joking about Tara Harlow's rules enforcement.

"What about our romantic dinner for two?"

Veena informs him that they will have to reschedule due to Tara's strict adherence to protocol. She twiddles her long, wavy green hair and says, "We'll have to take a rain check. Sorry, but do you know how impulsive and proper Tara can be? Goodnight, Mr Casey!"

Veena closes the pod shutter door. She can't help but burst into hysterical laughter, knowing that they will overcome this minor obstacle and eventually enjoy their romantic dinner together. Dan can discern Veena's amusement on the other side of the slider door.

He calls out to her with a polite tone, "Miss Merida, will you please open up?"

Veena responds with a giggle and cites Tara's rules as the reason for not opening the door, "No! Rule 49."

Despite Dan's amusement, he finds the inflexible nature of

the rules established by the supreme leader unacceptable. "Rule 49 is merely a guideline, not a hard and fast rule. Where am I expected to reside?"

"Pod 249 with the other civilians," she relays, which prompts her to burst into laughter again.

Dan Casey expresses disbelief. "Are you kidding me? Pod 249 is fully occupied; I should have let the *Aurora* crash," he chuckles.

Veena purrs in response, "Good night, Dan. Try and get some sleep. Love you!" She follows this with a mocking kissing gesture and laughter, "Mwah!"

Dan is bewildered and amused by Veena's unexpected gesture.

The guarding agents in the corridors cast a curious glance at him, but he says, "Agent Merida wanted a good night kiss, but I said NO. I'm not breaking Agent Rule 49!" Dan Casey turns and lumbers towards pod 249 with a smile.

The cargo pilot mumbles to himself as he taps on the door, which automatically opens. Dan Casey enters the pod, still grumbling. He exclaims, "Can you believe that they made up this rule? It's ridiculous!"

He stops and pauses as he witnesses Charlena Jones, with her hand on the pod room controls, sprawled out comfortably on the bed while Jay Haines is on the floor, shaking his dreadlocks in disgust as he prepares to make his bed with his jacket. Dan continues, "And can you believe there is only one bed in each pod?"

Charlena giggles upon witnessing Dan and Jay's reaction to the lack of beds.

Jay exclaims, "We've been done over, man! No food or bed; it's horrible." He begrudgingly beds down on the floor.

Dan acknowledges the grim situation, "Now I know what you meant by troubling times. Jay's right. It seems like everything is against us. Even little Miss Jones is mocking us."

Charlena continues to laugh and reassures them, "I'm sure you'll be fine down there together."

Jay Haines quickly responds, "That's easy for you to say, kid. You got the bed. Oh man, I'm so hungry,"

"I'm going to complain to Harlow in the morning. One bed?" huffs the handsome pilot, wrapping himself up in his leather jacket.

Jay adds, "And no food until 9am? That's shocking."

Charlena Jones uses the remote device to dim the lights. She smiles sweetly and remarks, "I wish you would refrain from discussing your appetite, as it makes me hungry."

Jay responds as he tucks himself in his long quarter jacket, "One fizzy sweet, kid, and you are sated. I require at least a three-course meal, being a grown gunslinger."

Charlena tuts and focuses on the bleeping video screen affixed to the wall. She activates the remote for curiosity, and a visual image of Veena appears on the monitor.

The young student waves to Veena through the flickering video and greets her, saying, "Hey, Veena!"

Charlena shares, "The bed is wonderful, but I wish I had a steamy hot cocoa. Though I'm not complaining."

Lying on the floor, Dan Casey calls in the conversation between the ladies, "I am not settling in too well. Rule 49 is ridiculous!"

Jay Haines adds, "The floor seems colder when you are hungry."

Veena laughs through the video screen and asks Charlena, "Are the tough men comfortable enough!"

Charlena Jones replies, "I think they will be trouble."

Veena bids her farewell and disconnects the link to the video screen.

Charlena gently yawns, expressing her gratitude for an unforgettable adventure, "Thanks for an amazing time, guys. I'll always remember it."

Meanwhile, Jay assures her he will safely escort her home to her mother. As Dan lies on the floor next to the gunslinger, he can't help but praise the teenager for her bravery, "Thank you, Wingman Jones, for keeping us all safe with your cutlery fork. Sleep well, my dear."

Charlena dims the lights, the room's atmosphere relaxes, and she soon falls asleep, exhausted from the entwining adventure. However, Jay Haines remains awake and asks, "Casey, are you still with me, man?"

The charismatic pilot responds sarcastically, "I'm still with you, Jay. Just here on the floor, sucking up Rule 49!"

Jay then asks Dan if he knows his plans for the next day. Dan guesses, "Cantina?"

Jay nods, saying, "Yeah, man! At 8:55 sharp. Like a gunslinger on heat, that full-fried Astro-breakfast is mine, dude!"

Dan can't help but smile at Jay's morning plan. As he looks around the room, he notices a set of navy blue agent uniforms hanging up neatly. In a sly move, he removes the brown leather jacket he's wearing as a night blanket and quickly changes into the uniform's coat and peaked cap-style hat.

Jay, trying not to wake up Charlena, whispers in disbelief, "What the hell are you doing?"

Looking sharp in the navy uniform, Dan replies with a confident smirk, "I'm about to enrol in Tara Harlow's agency."

With a swift motion, he sneaks out of pod 249, keeping a check on the guards along the corridor.

Dan Casey walks through the bustling agent base, his head down and the cap of his peak pulled low over his features. He fixes his gaze on the ground as he approaches pod 251, trying not to draw attention to himself. Taking a deep breath, he taps on the slider door, disguising his voice to sound more profound and more authoritative. "Urgent hologram for Agent Merida," he says, his heart racing, checking on the escort guards.

The door to the pod slides open, and Dan steps inside. He

is immediately greeted by a dimly lit room with a single figure sitting on the corner of her bed. Agent Merida, with her long pastel green hair and piercing jade eyes, looks up at him with curiosity, "Who's the hologram from, control?" she asks, raising an eyebrow at the cargo pilot's disguise.

"I cannot disclose the identity of the high-profile recipients." Dan Casey replies, facing the floor, his voice still disguised, "But this message is of utmost importance. It concerns the safety of our entire organisation and the abolishment of Rule 49." He can't resist the urge to reveal his identity. As he quickly glances up and takes off his peaked cap, Veena's eyes widen in shock and amusement.

Before she can say anything, Dan flings his cap over the surveillance camera, ensuring they won't be overheard or caught on camera.

She chuckles at his impulsive move but can't help but remind him, "Oh, Dan, you're breaching Rule 49."

He grins mischievously and shrugs, "Rules are meant to be broken, and Rule 49 is no exception."

With that, he lifts her slender waist, causing a twirling sensation in her stomach. They land on the nearby bed, her back pressed against the soft mattress. Their gazes lock, and Dan can't resist the temptation any longer. He leans in, his lips dangerously close to hers. "I've been dying to do this," he whispers before locking his lips with hers in a seductive French kiss.

Veena can't believe her luck. She has secretly been crushing on Dan since they started working together, but she never thought he felt the same way. But then, as his lips move against hers and his fingers tangle in her hair, she knows she is falling for him even harder.

As they break the kiss, gasping for air, Veena can't help but let out a sweet moan, "I think we just compromised Rule 49," she sighs, her eyes sparkling with desire.

Dan chuckles and brushes a strand of hair from her face, "I think it is worth it."

Their lips collide once again, this time with more passion and hunger. Veena eagerly responds to his kiss, her hands wandering over his back and hair. She has never felt such a strong connection with anyone before, and it only makes her want him more.

As they finally break the kiss, they are both out of breath, but their eyes fill with pure desire. "I don't think I want to go back to following rules anymore," Veena whispers, her cheeks flushed.

Dan grins and pulls her closer, "I know. Especially when breaking them brings me to you."

With that, he leans in for another kiss, sealing their loving bond with a promise of more. The lights dim in pod 251 as the passion rises with moans of pleasure as they make love in the night.

The Kalanisi Galaxy is vast and mysterious, spanning dozens of star systems and housing countless worlds. It is a place of wonder and danger, where advanced technologies meet ancient civilisations and blur lines between reality and fantasy. In one corner of this spectacular galaxy is the human capital world of Kothariya. As one of the most populated and influential planets in the galaxy, it is constantly buzzing with activity.

The skies are filled with ships of all shapes and sizes, from massive industrial starships to small personal shuttles. The atmosphere is hazy and unsettled, causing a constant fog to hang over the entire planet. But amidst all the hustle and bustle of this bustling world, one spacecraft stands out. It is a sleek and powerful vessel adorned with the emblem of the Corporal Union, the governing body of Kothariya.

As it glides through the dense clouds, the starship's name, *The Dantius*, is written in bold letters on its hull. Inside the craft, sitting confidently in the lounge seat, is Director Wilson Volantis, one of the most powerful and influential members of the Corporal Union. He is known for his sharp mind and cunning tactics, and his private spacecraft is a testament to his wealth and influence.

Wilson's spacecraft cruises over the bustling city of Kothariya. He can't help but show pride and accomplishment. For years, he has worked tirelessly to bring change and reform within the Corporal Union and his visions of a singular power to govern the Kalanisi Universe.

The Director of the Corporal Union is amid a high-class business lunch with a potential associate when he receives a notification on his holo-phone from the flight cabin of the *Dantius*. Wilson is dressed in a stunning black sequenced cloak with padded shoulders, giving him an air of royalty. He has paired it with a pristine silk shirt and a patterned tie, adding to his impressive aura. His pale, worn skin and grey hair are neatly styled, while his trimmed beard gives him a sophisticated look. However, his dark, intimidating eyes truly catch one's attention. They are piercing and exude confidence, making it clear that Wilson Volantis is not someone to be trifled with.

Wilson Volantis politely excuses himself from his dinner guest upon receiving the urgent notification.

"Please pardon the intrusions," he says in his well-spoken, sinister-toned voice as he elegantly rises from his lounge seat. "We can continue our affairs once I've taken this call of utmost urgency."

Wilson's guest nods as he watches the Director stride purposefully towards the cabin. As the Director disappears, the guest can't help but be impressed by the man's commanding presence and sense of responsibility. It is clear that Director Volantis takes his work seriously and is always ready to deal with any situation. Wilson makes his way through to the back quarters of the starship. Finally, he reaches his office cabin, a sleek and modern space far from most personal crafts' dark and dingy offices. As he settles into his curved leather chair, the fabric of his black cloak falls behind. Wilson knows that the law of the galaxy rests on his shoulders.

He opens his secure computer terminal, pulling up files and data on the recent activities of Commander Calo Tarick's mission to retrieve the databox. The Director's face is etched with pure annoyance as he reads through the analysis report of the events unfolding at the slave-trade station. It is a constant headache for him to deal with this resistance force led by his former minister, Tara Harlow. But what makes his blood boil is the destruction of his flagship battle cruiser, the *Galileo* BX10, and the loss of its commanding officer, Calo Tarick.

The mission to retrieve the highly coveted astrological data box has failed miserably, and now it is in the hands of the people he is trying to suppress. The Director's ageing skin lines are stonily disgruntled, reflecting his growing frustration and anger. He has spent countless resources and manpower to acquire the data box, which is key to his domination over the galaxy. And now it is slipping away from his grasp because of one woman. Tara Harlow was once his most trusted ally, his minister of defence. But she became disillusioned with his authoritarian regime and turned against him, forming the resistance force, now causing him so much trouble. But the Director refuses to accept defeat. Wilson cannot back down easily, especially concerning his power and control. He will do whatever it takes to crush the rebellion and regain the data box.

Wilson Volantis sits at his desk with his eyes fixed on the data screen. He furrows his brow as he scrolls through the reports, his mind racing with calculations and strategies. But suddenly, his focus is broken by a beeping sound from his desk. Wilson's pale fingers swiftly type in a personal code, connecting the desk's holo projector to his communication system.

A figure appears on the visual display.

Wilson recognises the face and coldly greets the officer, "Space Marshall Viper. I hope this interruption brings me the desired news about the salvaging operation of the *Galileo* BX10."

The Director continues, "Is the mission a success? Have you found Commander Tarick's body, dead or alive?"

Viper's masked face appears on the holo projector. The space marshall apologises. "Sorry for the interruption, Director Volantis."

His voice sounds grim through his visored helmet, and Wilson's heart sinks at his tone. He has waited for this update for hours and fears the worst. The retrieval mission on Dread Moon has been a challenge.

Viper begins, his muffled voice is full of urgency, "But we have managed to retrieve the *Galileo* BX10 advanced database and drivecore successfully. However, we have not found Commander Tarick's body."

The space marshall of the Dread Moon's salvage team reports in through the static holo-comm, awaiting his next orders. His face flickers in and out of view as the transmission struggles to establish a clear connection.

The Director looks blankly at Space Marshall Viper as he stands before him. Wilson Volantis can feel Viper's silent, sinister aura as he rubs his hands together,

"Please continue with your perimeter search for the commander," Director Volantis declares. "And stop whining about testing conditions, Space Marshall Viper. I have no concern for your atmospheric obstructions. You are trained and paid highly. I expect you to perform to that standard without complaint."

Viper knows better than to argue with the Director, especially when he is in one of his moods. But he can't help but feel frustrated with the difficult conditions he has to work in.

Director Volantis carries on with his demands, his voice dripping with malice, "I want all the footage of the *Galileo* star cruiser's fatal crash and the floating debris and toxic gas clouds sent to Mbron Media's headquarters. I want it to be smoke-screened across the galaxy as a terrorist attack by Tara Harlow's resistance agents. This is why all world organisations and even alien species need to fall under the banner of the Corporal Union, for their protection, of course."

Viper pauses in shock. He can't believe what he is hearing. The Corporal Union, which is supposed to be a force for good, is responsible for orchestrating a false flag attack to gain control over other worlds and species. And they are using Tara Harlow and her resistance as their scapegoat. But Viper knows better than to voice his thoughts. He has seen first-hand the consequences of going against the Corporal Union. Their power and influence are unmatched, and anyone who dares to oppose them will face severe consequences. Wilson Volantis has an evil, smug smirk on his face. Viper realises that they are both in on this plan and are willing to do anything to maintain the power and wealth of the galactic government.

The space marshal, known as Viper, responds with a crisp salute, his expression serious and focused, "All your commands will be carried out to the distinct detail, sir."

The Corporal Union's Director, Wilson Volantis, awkwardly grins as he stands up, reminding Viper not to falter. "Don't fail me, Viper," Wilson says, his tone on edge. "I'm not very forgiving when it comes to failure."

Wilson Volantis flicks the holo projector, cutting off the transmission to Viper, and returns to his dinner guest through the starship's walkway. As he walks, he can't help but feel a sense of satisfaction. He knows that Viper is one of the best in the business, and with him on board, he is confident that their deceitful mission will succeed.

The Director makes haste back to the lounge section of the *Dantius* and apologises to his guest for his absence. He stands and says, "Sorry about that, Mr Duran! So where were we before being rudely interrupted?"

Zak Duran sits up straight, savouring the exquisite taste of his high-class sirloin steak cuisine, with glazed potatoes and mixed salad. He sips champagne and fixes his gaze on Wilson Volantis, who has just returned to their table.

"I think we are just getting to the part about the weapon you desire," Zak says, his voice ringing with confidence. He knows he is a formidable negotiator and isn't afraid to push for what he wants. Wilson smirks and witnesses Zak produce a fragment of the Crystal Serpent Altar from his pocket. "This is all I have at the moment," he says, placing it on the table. "I know it's broken, but my business partner, Miss Lace, is trying to piece it together."

Wilson's eyes gleam with excitement as he examines the damaged fragment. He knows the ancient altar is a powerful weapon capable of unleashing untold destruction. "And where exactly is the data box?"

Zak Duran leans in with a serious expression. "It's in the possession of a rival agent resistance bandwagon."

The bounty hunter's voice is low, "But I have a plan to get it back. And with the data box in our hands, we'll be unstoppable."

Zak knows working with someone like Wilson is risky, but he has no doubts about his abilities. He takes another sip of champagne, feeling energised and ready for whatever challenges lay ahead.

Wilson Volantis savours every bite of his luxurious lobster dinner, feeling much better after his intriguing conversation with the confident entrepreneur.

The pale-faced senior can't help but ask, "I will assume someone as skilled as you won't give up such a valuable treasure without proper compensation, Mr Duran?"

Zak Duran confidently responds, "My partner Terri and I only want what's best for the galaxy's well-being. You can say we're a loving couple for the people, a symbol of hope."

Wilson replies, "Well, presenting gifts like this is a rare

delight, Mr Duran. You will be highly regarded for available positions within the Corporal Union."

Zak Duran, the renowned bounty hunter, sits in the luxurious lounge of the *Dantius* spacecraft. As they soar through the galaxy towards their next destination, the ship's engines purr with a hum. Zak is a man of style and sophistication, which is evident in his suit and perfectly groomed appearance. He sips his champagne, enjoying the crisp bubbles as they tickle his tongue. This is a lucrative deal, and Zak is determined to finish the job.

"I must say, Director Volantis, your hospitality is impeccable. This champagne is exquisite," Zak states smoothly.

Wilson Volantis nods, a sly smirk playing on his lips, "We spare no expense for our valued partners. And I must say, your reputation precedes you, Mr Duran. Your skills as a bounty hunter are highly regarded in the underworld."

Zak smiles, knowing that his reputation is well-deserved. He has only been in the business for a few years and has never failed to complete a mission. "I do believe our services will coincide with mutually beneficial results," Zak replies.

The Director raises an eyebrow, intrigued by Zak's confidence, "I can't agree more. The data box we seek is of great importance to the Corporal Union, and we are willing to pay handsomely for its retrieval."

Zak leans back in his seat, surveying the Director with a calculating gaze, "I assure you, Director Volantis, that my team and I will secure the artefact coordinates for you. But I must ask, what makes this supernatural weapon so valuable? I witnessed the presence of Amelia Delas. She isn't graceful enough to cooperate?"

Director Volantis leans in closer, his voice calm, "It's said she possesses powers beyond imagination. With it, we can dominate the entire galaxy and expand our corporation's reach to new heights."

Zak Duran's interest is piqued, "As I say, our goals align perfectly. Consider it done."

The two toast their partnership, sealing the deal with a clink of their champagne glasses. The rest of the time is spent discussing the details of the mission, with both parties agreeing on the terms and conditions. As Zak Duran, the smooth-talking leader of a notorious bounty-hunting crew, sits comfortably in the luxurious private craft, the *Dantius*, he can't help but smirk at the thought of his next big score. Across from him sits Wilson Volantis, a wealthy and powerful Director who tends to collect rare and valuable artefacts from across the galaxy. The bounty Zak has brought to the table is no exception: the elusive Crystal Serpent Altar. But while Zak Duran works his charm and negotiates the terms with Director Volantis, his ruthless counterpart, Terri Lace, oversees the ground preparations for the artefact's collection.

Terri is known for her beauty and prowess in the field, and she is dressed in her signature revealing outfit, a black leather bra top and a red mini skirt that shows off her long legs, paired with knee-high black heeled boots. As Terri receives an update from Zak through their secured comm system, she wastes no time giving orders to her loyal companion, a fearsome alien known as a Leecher.

"Get the crate with the artefacts and bring it to the meeting spot. I believe one of Director Volantis' sweepers will be there to collect the goods in exchange for the bounty purse."

The alien, Dralon, nods obediently and retrieves the crate from their Panther stealth ship, currently docked at the Kothariya spaceport on the outskirts of Isla-Kai, the capital city. Terri Lace watches as Dralon effortlessly lifts the heavy crate and carries it to the designated spot, where Wilson Volantis' sweeper is waiting.

Terri approaches the two men, her hips seductively swaying as she walks, "Ran Palmer, I trust you'll find the Serpent Altar to your satisfaction?"

Wilson Volantis' sweeper, a burly dark-skinned man named Ran Palmer with bleached white punk-style hair, grunts as he inspects the crate. "Looks like everything is in order," he says, eyeing Terri. "And who might this lovely lady be?"

Terri leans closer to Ran, her sly smile never faltering, "Just a humble bounty hunter here to ensure our client is happy."

Ran chuckles and hands the bounty purse to Terri, who quickly counts the credits and nods in approval, "Thank you for your professionalism, Mr Palmer. We hope to do business with Director Volantis again."

As the two men are about to leave with the crate, Terri Lace smiles and informs the sweeper about his old friend. "Mr Palmer, before you go about your recreation day, I wanted to mention I saw one of your old Dystart Blades gang members littering the Isadora system."

Ran Palmer has always been a man to be reckoned with in the underground world when in the Dystart Blades. He had risen through the ranks with ruthless determination and became the boss, feared by many and respected by few. But his rise to power wasn't without its dirty secrets. Ran made a deal with the Corporal Union, the corrupt government that controls criminal activities in the city. He pays them a cut of his illegal proceedings in exchange for immunity and protection. And so far, it has worked out well for him.

However, Ran is always looking for new opportunities to expand his empire. That's why he is more than interested when Terri, a beautiful and cunning member of the Director's criminal network, approaches him with some interesting information.

Ran stands dressed in his signature black studded leather jacket, with jewels sparkling around his bare chest and neck. His bleached punk hair whips around in the blowing wind as he asks Terri to divulge her findings. "Terri, my dear." Ran Palmer flirts with a sly smile, "What do you have for me today?"

"Well, Mr Palmer, I've found some interesting information about a former gang member."

Ran's interest is piqued. "Do tell."

Terri leans in closer, her breath grazing his ear as she whispers, "Mason. Remember him?"

Ran Palmer's expression turns cold at the mention of the name. Mason had been his right-hand man, but he had betrayed him and ended up on the wrong side of Ran's wrath. "Oh, I remember him," Ran growls. "What about him?"

Terri's lips turn into a seductive smile, "Well, the last time we spoke, Mason was spitting out teeth and bleeding his guts, all thanks to a little game he was playing with a delusional old woman."

Ran's eyes narrow in confusion and annoyance. "What game?"

Terri chuckles, enjoying her effect on Palmer. "Oh, just some agent game. But I'm sure you can figure it out, being the clever man that you are."

Ran's mind races as he tries to piece everything together. Mason was playing agent games with someone and ended up injured. And this game involved an old woman, who could it be?

Terri continues, "It's quite sad that someone who was once your right-hand man has now stooped to such low levels. Maybe you should give him a call, Ran. Brighten up his day."

Terri's seductive posing and suggestive words are not lost on Ran. He knows what she is doing, trying to play on his emotions and get him to make a move on Mason. But Ran isn't one to be swayed by a beautiful woman. He is a leader and a boss, making decisions based on logic and strategy, not emotions. Still, he can't deny that Terri's words have struck a chord within him. Mason had been a valuable member of his gang until he betrayed him. Maybe it is time to see if he is willing to redeem himself. With a nod towards Terri, Ran watches as she struts back to her sleek Panther, enticingly swinging her short mini skirt.

As he returns to his car, Ran can't help but think about the possibilities and consequences of calling Mason. But one thing is sure: Ran Palmer is not a man to be taken lightly, especially regarding business matters. And he will make the best move for himself and his empire, no matter what anybody has in their store.

Meanwhile, on the other side of the galaxy. Deep within the agent control tower on the resistance home world of Nova Conti, Nayla 1.9.4, a rewired Mbron Media cyber android, stands vigilant in her cyber-body armour and cute, pink-coiffed hair that glows in the office lights. She monitors the internal affairs of the tower and converses with other agent personnel on duty when their supreme leader, Tara Harlow, enters the bustling reception area.

Nayla 1.9.4 immediately recognises her and approaches her superior with a robotic salute of respect.

She says, "Ma'am, I have computed that due to the trauma you and Agent Barnes received during the incidents on the *Aurora* LX and the flagship carrier, I have taken you both off the rota duty for 48 hours. I can confirm that all operations are running smoothly, with no signs of any issues. Please go and rest; there is no reason for you to be here, with all due respect."

Her cybernetic voice is clear and precise as she speaks, a testament to her loyal, advanced, rewired programming.

Tara Harlow acknowledges Nayla 1.9.4's kind calculations, but as the supreme leader, she prefers to be in control and insists on following orders, "Thanks, 1.9.4, but I'm fine. Can't say the same for the *Aurora*. What's the damage report? Will my craft fly again? Keep Agent Barnes on the trauma support and off duty, with a full medical evaluation. It must have been a hectic time for him. Also, did you follow my other instructions?"

Nayla 1.9.4 processes Tara's requests and replies in her

precise cybernetic voice, "Yes, ma'am, I have submitted the damage report for the *Aurora*, which is currently being repaired. Agent Barnes is receiving the necessary trauma support and is off duty. I have also arranged for a full medical evaluation. As for your other instructions, I have followed them to the letter and can confirm that all objectives have been achieved. The agents reported that Veena's civilian friends have been shipped off to Kothariya but are not happy humans. The dreadlocked man complains about a lack of food and respect, and the young girl wants to say farewell. She has left an encrypted message."

Tara nods in approval, satisfied with Nayla 1.9.4's efficiency. She knows she can rely on the rewired Mbron Media cyber android to handle the complexities of the agent control tower and its operations. Tara Harlow walks over to her command desk and pauses momentarily, her face dropping, asking the cyber assailant, "And the cargo pilot, Dan Casey. Has he vacated the planet yet? Have you checked in on Agent Merida?"

Nayla 1.9.4's cybernetic face contorts into a twitching frown as she reports, "Mr Casey isn't with his colleagues. The agents presumed he was on board his starship in the hanger bay due to the activation of Rule 49!"

Tara Harlow's eyebrows furrow in concern as she asks, "Can you check the flight logs and see if he left?"

Nayla 1.9.4 quickly keys in the input data and states, "No, ma'am. The *Decepter* MK2 freighter is still in hanger bay four, which means Mr Casey is still on the premises. However, I'm not sure where he can be."

Tara Harlow considers this information briefly before saying, "I have a pretty good guess. Check Agent Merida's surveillance pod, 251."

Nayla 1.9.4 nods and immediately begins to check the surveillance footage. After a few moments of analysing the data, she tells Tara, "You are right, ma'am. Mr Casey is currently in Agent Merida's surveillance pod 251; they both seem to be lying on the bed, naked! It appears he's been there for the last few hours."

Tara Harlow nods, satisfied with Nayla 1.9.4's quick thinking and efficient work. She knows that the rewired Mbron Media cyber android is an invaluable asset to the resistance, and she is grateful to have her on their side.

Tara Harlow walks across to the control desk with authority and checks the internal camera feed in pod 251. As she watches the footage, she sighs deeply and says, "1.9.4, can you find Agent Merida a new, less revealing uniform? It seems she has trouble keeping her clothes on and is constantly being touched by Mr Casey. I think we shall keep her on active base duties for a while so she can clear her head."

Nayla 1.9.4 quickly processes Tara's request and replies, "Yes, ma'am. I will find Agent Merida a new uniform and ensure it meets the appropriate dress code standards. I will also ensure that she is reassigned to base duties until further notice."

Tara Harlow nods in approval, satisfied with Nayla 1.9.4's response. She knows that it is essential to maintain a professional and respectful environment within the resistance, and she is determined to ensure that all agents act accordingly.

Tara Harlow settles into her operations booth at the front of the command tower, overlooking the ocean waves and the base complex. She relaxes back in her recliner chair and adjusts her bun hairstyle before ordering the rewired android, "1.9.4, can you please go get Agent Merida to report in? I think sending a familiar face like yourself might jog her memory that she's an agent and not an Astro-hooker. And while you're there, tell Mr Casey to attend with his uniformed cap. I can explain the meaning of Rule 49 to him in person."

Nayla, 1.9.4, responds with a smile, "Yes, ma'am. It will be good to see Mistress Merida again. Do you think Mr Casey will be a problem?"

"I believe he has already become a problem. Charming men

like him can make agents lose their way, and Veena's too good to lose. But don't tell her that," Tara adds with a wink.

Nayla 1.9.4 nods in understanding and leaves to carry out Tara's orders. Nayla 1.9.4 knows it is essential to maintain protocol within the resistance and that sometimes, a little reminder is necessary to keep everyone in line.

As she walks towards Agent Merida's location, she prepares to handle the situation tactfully and diplomatically, befitting a helpful, fair, and safe AI-powered assistant.

Tara Harlow is closely watching Nova Conti's defence systems when the radar shows an unidentified energy source on their long-range scope scanner. She immediately orders one of the control crew to investigate the intrusion, "Agent, I want a full scanned report on that power source that's emerged. Grid reference Delta 233 lateral 559. Is it a weather storm or an asteroid? They're clustered together."

The agent gets to work and analyses the navigation systems but has to wait for the results.

Tara is getting impatient and asks, "Have we identified the perimeter breach?"

The agent responds, "Sorry, ma'am. Our main scanners are getting interference from the atmosphere of Isadora's system. I'm working on the secondary backup sonar scanner now, ma'am."

Tara Harlow nods in understanding, knowing that sometimes unexpected circumstances can cause delays. She continues to monitor the situation closely, waiting for the agent to complete his analysis. She knows any breach in their defence system can have dire consequences, and she is determined to take all necessary measures to protect the resistance and their home world of Nova Conti.

Chapter Twenty

Media Interference

The lush world of Nova Conti, located in the Isadora system, boarding the outer rim of the Kalanisi Galaxy, has been hit by an unexpected energy source that is breaching its atmosphere. The incident catches the attention of the resistance agency, which launches its long-range satellite probes to collect data. The initial readings show that a meteorite storm is passing through the area, which is not entirely unusual. However, upon closer inspection, the probes have detected the presence of unidentified star cruisers scattered in the asteroid field, which seem to be shielding their approach to the secret world.

The resistance agency is now trying to gather as much information as possible about the situation, but it is a complex and dangerous task. The star cruisers appear to be hiding their presence by blending in with the asteroids and using a cloaking device. The probes detect some unusual energy signatures coming from the cruisers, but they cannot identify their origin or purpose. The situation is causing concern among the inhabitants of Nova Conti, who fear that the energy source might be a prelude to an invasion. The resistance agency is working around the clock to analyse the data and devise a plan to protect the world from any potential threat. The fate of Nova Conti hangs in the balance, and the resistance agency's success or failure can determine the fate of the entire galaxy.

Nayla 1.9.4, the rewired cyber female android, is designated to escort Agent Veena Merida, the primary galactic agent responsible for the top-secret mission of retrieving the astrological data box. As the female cyberbot approaches the complex's accommodation section, her primary objective is to locate personnel pod 251, where Agent Merida is located, and escort her to tower control while ensuring her safety. Nayla 1.9.4 quickly turns her pale fibre face, her cybernetic eyes narrowing in disbelief at the sight before her. She is here to collect her former operative, Agent Merida, but instead, she is met with a shock at the door of pod 251.

"Oh, naked man!" Nayla 1.9.4 yells out in surprise, her voice filled with embarrassment. She has not been programmed to handle this situation, as her primary function is to carry out missions for the agent organisation.

Dan Casey, the cargo pilot who is unauthorised to be in pod 251, stands just as shocked as the android. He quickly realises he isn't appropriately dressed and sheepishly smiles at Nayla 1.9.4. "Veena! I believe you have company," Dan says with a hint of amusement in his voice.

Veena Merida has just come from the pod's wash area, fully refreshed and dressed in her customary black jumpsuit. She scrunches her damp green hair and approaches the door, instantly recognising the cyber android and that Dan is completely naked.

"Whoa, Nayla 1.9.4! It's so good to reunite. I didn't know you were on base. And Dan, please put some clothes on. You're making her uncomfortable."

Nayla 1.9.4 turns away and tries to compose herself. She can't believe she has been sent on this mission and has ended up in such an uncomfortable situation. As an android, she isn't programmed to feel emotions, but for a moment, she feels a twinge of awkwardness and humiliation. "Sorry for the interruption, Mistress Merida. I was sent to collect you for the mission report."

Veena nods, understanding that the organisation never wastes time and always has a new mission. She bids farewell to Dan and follows Nayla 1.9.4 out of the pod, giving Dan a stern look before the door slides shut behind them. Upon exiting the pod, the android experiences a momentary lapse in computational function. However, she regains her composure, "Supreme Leader Harlow has expressed a desire for Mr Casey's attendance at the meeting to familiarise himself with specific regulations."

Remote agent Merida enquires, "Am I facing any repercussions, 1.9.4? I am eager to inform you that you're my loyal field assistant."

Despite Veena's question remaining unanswered, she proceeds to open the shutter door of pod 251, awaiting further instructions. As they step back into pod 251, they are greeted by Dan, who is now fully dressed and prepared.

Nayla's robotic demeanour momentarily falters as she witnesses the friendly atmosphere. She has never experienced anything like it before, "Hello, ladies. That was a quick mission briefing?" Dan says, smiling at them both.

Veena can't help but smile back. "Tara wants to run you through the rule book. You are beckoned to attend the briefing on Rule 49."

Nayla 1.9.4 stands silently, unsure of how to respond. She observes the humans interacting and wonders if she can understand their emotions and actions.

Dan Casey responds with amusement, "I have a few matters that I would like to discuss with Miss Harlow, and I am confident that Jay will want to put forth his opinions regarding the opening schedule for the cantina."

The cargo runner's words elicit a chuckle from Veena. But not so from Nayla 1.9.4, who cannot resist informing him and Veena of the latest development.

"I regret to inform you that Mr Haines will be unable to

file any further complaints, as he and the young lady have been transported to Kothariya under Tara's directive. The red-haired girl left you an encrypted farewell message, which I have processed."

Dan and Veena exchange glances, visibly disappointed with the outcome. Before they can voice their concerns, however, the agent base is suddenly put on red alert.

Dan enquires of the female cyber unit, "What is happening?"

Clad in a black jumpsuit, Veena stands out among the other agents as they hurry to their designated positions. "Nayla, can you please check in with control?"

Nayla 1.9.4 tilts her pink-coiffed head to the side as she relays, "Mistress Merida, I am already on it. We appear to have nine undefined cruisers that have breached our safe zone. Supreme Leader Harlow is taking no chances and has ordered the fleet to be on high alert as a precautionary measure."

Veena looks at Dan with concern, realising the gravity of the situation.

Dan attempts to comprehend the situation and suggests, "Do you think it's the Corporal Union?"

Nayla 1.9.4 responds to his enquiry, "No, Mr Casey. We have all the details of their starships on our database, and they do not match any known origin."

Veena takes charge and says, "We must get to the control tower immediately to assess the identity of the visitors to Nova Conti."

The three of them swiftly make their way through the agency headquarters. Dan and Nayla 1.9.4 follow Veena as she leads the way to the elevators. Her confident demeanour and sharp jade eyes give off an air of authority. Despite the urgency of the situation, Veena remains composed and focused.

As they enter the operations room, Tara Harlow's staff hands her and Dan a warm cup of black coffee. They take a sip before turning their attention to the supreme leader.

Tara swiftly revises an update from her navigation officer, a young agent who stands tall and proud in his crisp navy uniform. He reports, "We have a clear visual of the cruisers on our long-range detector scanner. But still no recognition of who they are. Do you want an on-screen visual, ma'am?"

Tara nods, her eyes drawn to scanning screens before her. "Yes, put them on screen. But I want no attempt at communication until we can be sure they are not hostile. And activate the planetary defence shield."

However, their hopes are dashed when the agency's navigation officer says, "I have bad news, ma'am. The global defence shield is down. We suffered an energy drain due to the last weather storm yesterday. It's currently undergoing maintenance."

Tara's face hardens in determination, "Damn! Well, tell them to get a move on. We need that shield operational before it's too late."

The navigation officer nods, inputting the keyboard controls to get a close-range visual of the unidentified starship cruisers. As the image comes into focus, Dan and Veena's hearts sink. The situation is worse than they have anticipated. The enemy ships are heavily armed and outnumber them. Tara's mind races as she analyses the data, trying to devise a plan. The unidentified starships are getting closer by the minute, and they need to act fast. She knows their only chance is to turn off the imposing ships' weapons before they can reach their defence borders. She relays her plan to her team, and they scramble to their stations, working quickly and efficiently.

Nayla 1.9.4 responds to the space cruisers' visuals, "We're in trouble, ma'am. They are Mbron Media Buccaneer G16 battle class cruisers. It's the pirate fleet making way for the satellite ship, the *Excalibur*. Which can only compute one meaning: Supreme 63!"

Tara Harlow glances at the navigation radar screen, then

says quickly to her android, "Who the hell is Supreme 63? I thought that Mbron Media is a propaganda broadcaster organisation, judged by their latest false news report, coinciding with exploding space stations." She glances at Dan and Veena and rants, "Not an intergalactic platooned battle fleet; tell me more 1.9.4."

Nayla 1.9.4 immediately responds to Tara Harlow's request for more information, "Supreme 63 is the right hand to the Core Lord and leader of the pirate media fleet, known for their vicious tactics and disregard for innocent lives."

The cute female AI assistant explains, "The Mbron Media Buccaneer G16 battle class cruisers are heavily armoured with grid force shields and neutron ranged cannons, making them a formidable opponent."

Tara Harlow nods, taking in the information, "Alright, we need to devise a plan." She turns to her galactic operative and the interstellar pilot, "Dan, Veena, any ideas? Now is a perfect time?"

Dan Casey enquires, "Who's this Core Lord? It's not the first time his name has been mentioned. And how can his charge hand 63 and a media pirate fleet find Nova Conti without the help of Duran?"

Before Nayla 1.9.4 can respond, they hear a commotion in the control room. Tara's vocals burst into their conversation, her face red with anger, "Damn it!" she exclaims, her voice filled with curses. "Looks like Mr Duran isn't bluffing about his insurance policies. I didn't think Wilson would have the authority to send his Corporal Union fleet so soon after the destruction of the *Galileo* BX10 flagship."

Tara glances at Dan and Veena, who are standing near her desk. They have been discussing something in hushed tones before Tara Harlow's sudden, unapproving glance, "So, our mastermind Director has sent his armament in the disguise of the Mbron Media broadcasters. Wilson is quite clever." Tara

Harlow continues, mockingly, "Avoiding his decisions and getting some other party to do his bidding. It's Volantis all over again."

Nayla 1.9.4 provides a detailed report of her knowledge before her reprogramming. According to the pink-haired cyberbot, she says, "No androids or individuals are aware of the identity concerning the master. The Core Lord established Mbron Media approximately five years ago and maintains a close relationship with the current Director of the Corporal Union. The only individual granted an audience with the Core Lord is Supreme 63. The pirate fleet is responsible for causing chaos in the galaxy. At the same time, the *Excalibur* satellite ship disseminates misinformation throughout the Kalanisi Galaxy, asserting that the Corporal Union is the sole entity capable of ensuring safety in deep space."

Veena's brow furrows in concentration as she scans the radar monitor before her. Her jade pupils are intently focused on the screen as she tries to make sense of the blips and dots representing the approaching enemy fleet. "I can only see nine cruisers on the detectors. So where is the *Excalibur*? And will our fleet be a match for their type of spacecraft?"

Nayla 1.9.4 walks over to the screen, her silver cybernetic jumpsuit shimmering in the low lighting of the control room. She points to a specific area under the clock symbol on the screen, "I would think the satellite ship is positioned here."

Veena's eyes follow Nayla 1.9.4's finger, and she nods in agreement. Nayla 1.9.4 is an expert in all things related to space navigation and technology, and her cybernetic enhancements make her a formidable agent.

"But will our agency fleet be a match for their ships?" Veena presses, a hint of worry creeping into her posh voice. Starships are not her primary forte, and she feels a pang of unease at the thought of going up against such advanced crafts.

Nayla 1.9.4 studies the radar momentarily before turning

to Veena. "Once the Buccaneer G16 Cruisers divide their flight formation and enter the atmosphere, the Supreme 63's *Excalibur* will orbit the planet for data and send the footage back to the Mbron Merida headquarters. We may have the advantage of surprise, but there is no firm data on whether our vessels can match the pirate fleet."

With Nayla 1.9.4's expertise and the element of surprise on their side, maybe they did stand a chance against the enemy fleet.

Tara Harlow takes a deep breath and tries to push aside her doubts. "Alright then," she says, regaining her composure, "Let's get ready. The *Excalibur* won't stay hidden for long. We shall position our starships and take them on a head frontal assault. I know we will have to play our hand one day, but I wasn't planning so soon."

Dan Casey confidently proposes a different strategy to the supreme leader, "You may not have to, ma'am! Let the *Excalibur* satellite ship de-cloak and start its media run."

Dan turns to Nayla 1.9.4 and asks with a theory, "Will the Isadora atmosphere interfere with the Mbron Media footage systems and prevent them from sending the signal until they are out of the sector?"

The cyberbot analyses the data on the control keyboard and provides a blueprint of *Excalibur* from her internal memory. She acknowledges the uncertainty but suggests they can activate the recording, which will only delay the sending to the main transmitter hub.

Nayla 1.9.4 confidently asks Dan Casey about his plan, "What do you have in your human mind, Mr Casey?"

Tara Harlow echoes similar concerns with a sarcastic tone, asking, "That's a good question 1.9.4. Why give the *Excalibur* free rein? You planning on throwing your cap on the camera lens, Mr Casey?"

"Technically, sweetheart!" he says with a wink to Tara.

"Can't you see? They only want the footage to trigger a message and showcase Nova Conti to the entire galaxy. This, in turn, will enable Wilson Volantis to obtain clearance to mobilise the Corporal Union's armada and secure the new world for the people opposing."

Dan's explanation clarifies the reasoning behind their strategy.

Tara Harlow reflects on Dan's suggestion and reorients his perspective, "It appears that Director Wilson Volantis intends to lure us into combat with the Mbron Media pirate fleet, with the expectation of achieving a victory before the arrival of the Corporal Union legions. This will render our fleet vulnerable and easily defeated, allowing the Director to claim a triumph over the galactic resistance. Mr Casey has made a valid point. I concur with his assessment. What measures do you propose? And I would appreciate it if we can avoid using informal terms such as "sweetheart" by adhering to Rule 48."

Dan asks with bewilderment at the agency's structure, "How many rules does your agency manual contain?"

Tara replies, "Keep breaking them, Mr Casey, and you will find out! More importantly, how does your plan unfold?"

Dan proceeds towards the digital radar monitor, "I recommend that you hold your fleet near the blind side of Nova Conti. The asteroid weather storm should conceal your vessels from their scopes. This will enable you to play them at their own game and wait for my signal. Meanwhile, I will get a SWAT team aboard the *Excalibur*, remove their signal capabilities, and shield defence systems. Otherwise, regardless of the circumstances, Mbron Media will send the message to the Director to order his armada in, and you will be defeated."

Tara Harlow responds with intuition, "Okay, but how are you going to get aboard?"

Dan replies, "I need 1.9.4 to help with that."

The pink-coiffed android responds with a robotic salute, "Agent 1.9.4 ready to assist, sir."

Veena listens in on the plan and turns from the radar screen. The beautiful remote agent states, "I'm going with them. I will prepare myself right away."

The supreme leader raises her eyebrows with amusement. She says, "I always planned for you to take the lead, and I've got a new uniform for you, Agent Merida."

"Thank you, ma'am!" replies Veena with a curious expression on her face.

Another voice echoes across the control tower's operation room, "I'm going too, Agent Barnes reporting for duty, ma'am."

Mason Barnes is in his navy SWAT uniform with his plasma weapon strapped over his broad shoulders, standing proud with a salute at the complex entrance. Mason has just woken up and is still groggy when he sees the supreme leader of his agency seated in front of him.

Tara is pleased to see him up and about. But she has bad news for him. "I want you to sit this one out," she says. "I've got my SWAT team organised, and you can accompany me on the fleet carrier."

This takes Mason aback. He is a trained field agent and doesn't want to be left out of an important mission.

He says, "With all due respect, ma'am, I'm a trained field agent, not the coffee maker! And Mr Casey is only a civilian; that's against agency protocol."

The stylish, dark-skinned agent with a handsome face is determined to prove his worth.

Tara Harlow, the supreme leader of the agency, swiftly replies with leadership authority, "Noted, Agent Barnes. But this is for your welfare, so act like the agent I trained you to be."

Tara shifts her attention to Dan, the civilian cargo pilot, causing tension in the room. She looks at him straight and speaks loudly enough for everyone in the control room to hear, "I've checked Mr Casey's records. He was formerly a member of a privately funded space protection unit, and that's the skill we require in this mess. So, I've decided to make him our temporary space deputy. Please respect this chain of command!"

Her words seem to have the desired effect as everyone falls silent and returns to their duties. Tara doesn't waste any more time on pleasantries. "Now come on, people. To your posts! We have a planet to defend."

As the other agents attend to their duties, Mason Barnes looks dejected. That's when Nayla 1.9.4, the cute pink cyberbot, greets him, "Good to see you back in action, Mason."

Mason sarcastically replies, "But I'm not in action, 1.9.4. The supreme leader's new favourite agent, Merida, and her damn civilian pilot are top of the bill. What a joke this place is becoming. The protocol only fits when it suits Harlow."

Nayla 1.9.4 tries to cheer him up, "I have received an encrypted message for you from Ran Palmer. Did you want me to process it now?"

Mason is shocked to hear that name again in such a short time. Agent Barnes replies, "Palmer, you say? No, send it to my quarters. And 1.9.4, you need to get me on this mission!"

Nayla 1.9.4 says, "Mason, that's against protocol. I'm programmed to obey. Sorry! I will see you after the mission. Keep well." The female cyberbot goes to join Dan and Veena, ready for the cargo runner's plan to infiltrate the Mbron Media's satellite starship.

Meanwhile, out in the deep space atmospheric borders of Nova Conti, the Buccaneer G16 battle cruisers have penetrated the safe zone and are forming their approach vector.

The round-shaped armoured cruisers are slow-moving starships with a humming drone from their dual thrusters in their menacing wake. The Buccaneer's neutron cannons are armed and ready on the front of the craft, securing the vicinity for the *Excalibur*.

The atmosphere is tense as the enemy forces close in, and the agents on the ground know that they have to act quickly to defend their planet. Inside the Buccaneer's G16 cruisers' flight deck is a batch of Elton-63 enforcer androids. They stand motionless, with their ginger-coiffed hairstyles and pale, gaunt faces, armed with rapid-fire lasers. They are the male counterpart to Mbron Media's other android on the galactic trade market, the 1.9.4 model. The Buccaneer's G16 cruisers are piloted by an inferior version called Zero, a cybernetic-based android with no human resemblance, just a round metallic face with a flight visor and built-in helmet designed for flying starships across the galaxy.

Zero sits at the flight helm and sets the controls for the Buccaneer battleship to hover above the close-ranged perimeter of Nova Conti; the cyber pilot reports in with the other cybernetic flight captains across on a Mbron Media encrypted communications link.

Zero transmitted, "We are in position, and all systems are engaged. The grid force field has been activated and is ready for the *Excalibur*. Confirm."

The Buccaneer G16 star captains are on high alert as they confirmed the presence of an atmospheric spectre. Their battleships are equipped with state-of-the-art technology, including an active, advanced grid beam that paved a safe way for the satellite vessel Supreme 63. The grid beam is a crucial part of their defence system, extracting a pulsating vibe undetectable by typical radar systems. This unique feature gives the Buccaneer star captains an upper hand in battles, making their ships almost invincible. As the captains survey their surroundings, they know they are safe within the force grid.

But suddenly, with a flash and thundering bang, the *Excalibur* emerges from its cloaked status. The juddering ripple and vast noise it produces shakes the atmosphere of Nova Conti, leaving the Buccaneer captains in awe of the *Excalibur* in action, mesmerised by its power. The command ship of Supreme 63 is a massive and imposing vessel with a size and scope that surpasses all other starships in the galaxy. Its hull is deep with a selection of landing bays, indicating its ability to carry out various missions. However, what makes the ship truly unique isn't its weapons.

Excalibur is not designed for attacking but rather for surveillance and reporting. It is equipped with a cluster of turning satellite dishes that allow it to gather information from all corners of the galaxy. In place of weapons, the ship has a support brigade of drones that weave around it in case of any attacks.

The Buccaneer star captains watched in amazement as the *Excalibur* moves gracefully through the force grid, easily evading its invisible barriers. They know the flagship is in safe hands with Supreme 63 at the helm. The captain of *Excalibur* is a legendary figure in the cybernetic sphere and right hand to the mysterious Core Lord, known for his strategic thinking and quick reflexes. As the *Excalibur* makes its way to the front of the fleet, the Buccaneer star captains can't help but show a sense of computerised pride. They are honoured to work alongside such a prestigious vessel and its crew. With the *Excalibur* leading the way, they are confident they will emerge victorious in any battle.

On board the *Excalibur*'s bridge control stands Supreme 63, an imposing android that is an upgraded version of Elton-63. He has a pneumatic exoskeleton chassis, dark shades covering his blue fibrotic eyes, and pale, gaunt fibre skin.

The cyber boss is partially dressed in his Mbron Media charcoal uniform. Supreme 63 glances at his flight captain and orders, "Zero, take us in for a global scanner before we perform the satellite broadcast at quarter speed. Break off from Buccaneer escort."

Zero responds. "Media run confirmed, sir. We are about to surf the shield beam, speed set at nought point two," says the more miniature-framed star captain.

Supreme 63 responds with his gaunt posture, "Tremendous! We have a new golden world ahead. Looks like the information relayed is more than authentic. Generate the satellite propulsions. We shall scan some live footage before the invasion."

Zero responds in a blandness of its programming, "As you command, Supreme 63."

The *Excalibur*'s engines thrum as the starship enters the heart of Nova Conti. The vessel's powerful quad engines engage as it approaches its destination, propelling it forward with a mighty roar. The satellite camera system is activated, its lights flickering on with a vibrating hum as it begins to scan the area. The defence drones, programmed to follow the satellite ships, quickly spring into action, weaving a complex pattern as they form to provide additional protection.

The scene is a spectacular display of technology, with the sleek vessel and advanced drones working together seamlessly to accomplish their mission. The Buccaneer G16 battle cruisers are on high alert, watching the galactic perimeter with their powerful neutron cannons. They scan the vicinity for any signs of disturbance, ready to take action immediately.

Meanwhile, the *Excalibur* begins to perform its first global orbit, moving gracefully through space as it scans the planet below. The starship's advanced technology allows it to gather data quickly and efficiently, while the Buccaneer battlecruisers provide additional security. The scene is a testament to the power of Mbron Media's superior technology and another armament of Director Wilson Volantis.

The *Excalibur* is currently in full motion orbit with a projection of Nova Conti's surface. The starship's bridge is bustling with high activity. Supreme 63 takes his seat at the controls. His appearance is stoic, almost unfeeling, as he oversees the vital data recording process. In a cold and calculated voice, Supreme 63 addresses the metallic flight captain, "Zero, I want a full energy spike scan to detect and eliminate any potential lifeforms on the planet before we proceed with the first contact brigade. Also, ensure that two batches of elite-trained Elton-63s are put on standby and activate the armed and dangerous mode immediately."

There is a sinister smirk on Supreme 63's pale face, indicating that he is pleased with his direct orders. The situation seems tense and potentially dangerous, with the possibility of an imminent threat.

Zero replies without remorse, "Confirmed; any lifeform found will be disintegrated upon contact."

After receiving Supreme 63's orders, the metallic flight captain quickly relays them through the starship's internal communication system. With an instant response, the Elton-63 cyber-SWAT team springs to life, their movements organised and precise. They immediately fall into their ordered positions, ready to carry out their assigned tasks. The Elton-63s are a formidable force equipped with cutting-edge technology and weapons. Their presence on the spacecraft serves as a warning to anyone who might threaten the crew's safety. They are prepared to respond to any situation with the armed and dangerous mode activated.

As the *Excalibur* spacecraft continues its descent towards the planet's surface, the crew remain alert and ready for whatever lies ahead. The tension in the air is calculated. Supreme 63 sits back in his command seat with a devilish smirk at the smooth procession of events.

While back on the surface of Nova Conti at the agent headquarters, the strike team prepares to board the cargo runner's Machiavellian MK2 freighter.

The *Decepter* starship has been through a rough battle with the Corporal Union's *Galileo* BX10 battle cruiser and the bounty hunters' stealth Panther craft. Despite taking some damage, the old-style starship has proven its toughness and never let its pilot, Dan Casey, down. Dan stands at the loading ramp with Agent

Veena Merida, surveying the damage to the starship and the conflicts. The handsome cargo pilot appears calm despite the danger ahead. He knows the mission they are about to embark on is crucial, and he is determined to see it through.

Meanwhile, the cyberbot Nayla oversees the equipment Agent Merida requires for the mission. The bot's advanced technology makes it an indispensable team member, capable of efficiently managing complex tasks. As Nayla 1.9.4 works, Dan Casey and Agent Merida make final preparations before setting out.

The bright sun and refreshing wind illuminate the agent base platform. Outside of hanger bay four, Dan gazes at Veena with a bemused smile as he notes the stringent dress code for their intended mission.

The dark-haired and handsome pilot amusingly comments on their appearance. "I assume Harlow, your boss, is attempting to make an example of me for violating Rule 49 and making me wear this uniform and peaked cap. It will be removed as soon as I board the *Decepter*, and I can assist you in removing yours as well," he says teasingly, shaking his head in disbelief.

Veena has also been issued a navy-coloured agent SWAT uniform with a helmet and tactical combat visor. She responds to Dan's comment with an admiring gesture. "You look quite the part in uniform, Space Deputy Casey!" She laughs, walking up to the *Decepter*'s entrance hatch. "Perhaps I'll be the one to help you take it off," Veena says with a playful expression. "Additionally, I have informed Nayla 1.9.4 to pack a spare jumpsuit in the equipment box."

After gathering their technical tools on board, the MK2 freighter, with the assistance of some ground staff, Nayla 1.9.4, the rewired female cyber android, approaches Dan and Veena as they close the cargo hatch of the Machiavellian vessel.

She salutes them and declares, "All the necessary items are on board and secure. Agent 1.9.4 is ready for combat."

Dan Casey replies, "Very well, 1.9.4. You can join me in the cockpit while Veena sets up the tech. Are we all set?"

The cargo pilot walks through the lounge to the *Decepter*'s cockpit, with Nayla 1.9.4 following him to the flight helm.

Veena smiles and astonishes the cyberbot, "What's in that large, armoured case, Nayla?"

The pink-haired android looks at them, puzzled, and replies, "It's a tool that can be converted into a massive weapon. We may need it."

Dan smirks and remarks, "She has a point. The *Excalibur* will be full of tinheads; the bigger the gun, the more cyber scrap."

Not a fan of Mbron Media cyber androids, Dan Casey finds himself thoroughly amused. On the other hand, Veena is not, and she gives him a stern glare from her piercing jade eyes, gesturing towards Nayla 1.9.4.

The cargo pilot realises his tongue-tie of words and backtracks his statement. "None of the tinhead comments is directed at yourself 1.9.4," says Dan Casey with an apologetic face to the cute android. "Pearl and I joke about tinheads taking the cargo contracts. Don't we, Pearl!"

He glances at the crystallised core in the flight cabin, "Pearl!"

Amused, Dan takes his place in the leather recliner chair at the pilot quarters, as Pearl keeps silent and takes no part in his defence.

Nayla 1.9.4 moves through the flight cabin and sits herself into the co-pilot position. The pink-quiffed cyberbot responds, "No offence taken, Space Deputy Casey, and who is Pearl?"

As Dan Casey sets the flight control entrustments, he responds to the rewired cyberbot's inquisition, "Pearl is usually an accommodating flight navigation assistant, but I believe Miss Harlow, your boss, has reactivated Rule 49 everywhere! Come on, Pearl, introduce yourself to our guest 1.9.4. Don't be shy, and fire up hyperdrive. We have an interview scheduled with the Media!"

The charming cargo pilot takes off his uniformed cap and flings it across the flight cockpit, revealing his dark hair. Nayla 1.9.4 sits in the co-pilot seat, strapping herself in, but can't help feeling flustered by Dan's actions.

She warns him, "Oh no, Space Deputy Casey, I must advise you that you have just broken Rule 37. You showed no regard for agent equipment while on active duty. The supreme leader will reduce your wages for that."

Overall, Dan Casey appears charming and confident with the cyber individual, while Nayla 1.9.4 displays a mix of admiration for his demeanour and concern for the rules.

Veena Merida, who has been issued a navy-coloured agent SWAT uniform, plans to change into her black jumpsuit. The sexy feminine agent takes a moment and appears to be observing the amusing interaction between Dan Casey and Nayla 1.9.4 with a pleased expression. She suddenly hears a clanging noise come from the lower level in the cargo section of the *Decepter*. Veena investigates as the freighter's triple-slanted engines purr into life.

At the front cabin of the Machiavellian vessel, Pearl announces that the subsystems are operating at the maximum core and the celestial hyperdrive is engaged. Her sultry, crystallised voice echoes through the cabin, affirming that the vessel is ready to launch and venture into space,

"Dan, we're ready when you are."

With a dynamic and self-assured tone, Pearl greets Agent 1.9.4, expressing her eagerness to meet any of her requirements.

Dan Casey is fully ready to take on the satellite mission. He puts on his leather finger-cut gloves and holds the joystick tightly as he levers the throttle, "Okay, let's gatecrash this satellite party and shut it down. Pearl, can you please connect with Nayla 1.9.4 and play Charlena and Jay's encrypted message they left us before Tara shipped them back to Kothariya?"

Pearl flashes a confirmation response, and Nayla 1.9.4.

appears in front of Dan, her pink presence shining brightly, "I'm sorry you never had the chance to say goodbye to your friends. The supreme leader is rigorous regarding protocol, and Tara is just trying her best for the planet's safety. Despite her tough exterior, she has a big heart, Space Deputy Casey!"

Dan Casey sits poised in the pilot quarters, ready to take on the mission. He quickly reminds Agent 1.9.4, "You don't have to call me by Tara's given title of Space Deputy. Dan will do just fine. And what about your name? Do you prefer 1.9.4 or Nayla? I met a taxi-pod driver on Race-World who looked just like you but had a different hairstyle. She dropped the serial number and wanted to be called Nayla. She was trying to rewire herself from the Mbron Media update feeds."

Nayla 1.9.4 pauses, calculating her response, "That's an interesting concept, Dan. We may all look the same, but we don't have the same core. I would love to meet Nayla. And as for my name, 1.9.4 will suffice."

Dan knows that Nayla is a sophisticated cyberbot with advanced capabilities. He trusts her to help him take on this mission; even though it will be difficult, he appreciates her willingness to engage in conversation. Dan pushes forward on the joystick and slams the throttle to thrust, causing him and Agent 1.9.4 to be knocked back into their flight seats.

The *Decepter* responds instantly and speeds across the landing strip of the agent tower complex, its velocity quickening with each passing moment. As the Machiavellian MK2 freighter launches into the open skies above Nova Conti, Dan expertly weaves and turns, navigating through the clouds and across the vast expanse of the ocean below. Nayla 1.9.4 watches as Dan Casey manoeuvres the starship with precision and skill, admiring his bravery and determination. She knows they have a difficult task ahead of them, but she is confident they can overcome any obstacle together. As they fly towards their destination, Nayla 1.9.4 efficiently plays the message they received from Jay Haines and Charlena Jones, her advanced algorithms working to unravel the complex code. Dan and Agent 1.9.4 are a formidable team, each bringing unique skills and strengths to the mission.

They know that the fate of their planet rests on their shoulders. Dan requests the starship's navigation suite to replay a message to the Resistance Agent Tower, "Pearl, please inform Commander Harlow to keep her fleet back until further notice. We have two hours tops before the *Excalibur* exits orbit and has enough data to send the signal, per 1.9.4's instructions. Pearl, please tell her not to break cargo rule one."

With her sweet cyber tone, Nayla asks the interstellar cargo pilot with mesmerising intrigue, "What does that rule consist of, Dan?"

He takes a deep breath before responding, "Cargo rule one is crucial to our mission. It states that under no circumstances should they jettison and jump the gun. They should stick to the plan and wait for my word, no matter how dire the situation may be. Where's Veena got to? We shall be cutting into the atmosphere anytime."

Nayla 1.9.4 nods in understanding and responds to his wanting question, "I deem that Veena wanted to change her issued SWAT uniform, stating the supreme leader's choice of clothing is irrelevant for success."

Says Nayla 1.9.4 as she transmits the encrypted message to Pearl, and the cyber unit responds as a flashing sequence.

"Due to my overextension with bio-scans, I have successfully located Miss Merida in the cargo bay. Furthermore, the message from Miss Jones and Mr Haines has been decrypted and is now available for viewing."

Dan Casey and Agent Nayla 1.9.4 are deeply engaged in analysing the visual decryption recording.

Meanwhile, Veena investigates an unexpected noise emanating from the cargo section of the *Decepter*. Dressed in her SWAT uniform and visor helmet, Veena carefully ventures into the dark and ominous cargo bay, with only the celestial hyperdrive and energy flowing through the subsystems audible in the background. Her heart races as she meticulously navigates the compartment.

Despite the limited visibility, Veena activates her digital visor, giving her a thermal image of the cargo bay. Upon closer examination, she observes that the crate previously placed on the starship by Nayla 1.9.4 is open.

A highly trained agent, Veena is on high alert as she detects a possible intruder. She quickly reaches for her leather holster belt and attempts to draw her silver-scoped pistol. However, an infrared beam skims her chest before she can do so, and a shadowy voice declares, "Too slow, Agent Merida. I've marked you since you stepped into this cargo haul."

Veena freezes with a shocked gasp as the voice is revealed to her. "Agent Barnes? What are you doing? Please lower your weapon; we're on the same side!"

Barnes explains that, despite his orders, "I'm doing my job, regardless of Tara's selective protocol, and I'd appreciate it if you don't stand in my way. Now, where's 1.9.4? I need to run through the plan."

Agent Barnes withdraws his infixed plasma rifle away from Veena with lingering eye contact. Following suit, Veena turns off her visor helmet and readily takes it off, revealing her long, wavy green mane.

She keeps things simple as Barnes seems to show a negative attitude towards her, "Come, follow me to the flight cabin; you can meet Tara's chosen SWAT squad."

Veena tries to reason with him, but Agent Barnes seems determined to stick to his agenda. Despite this, she remains professional and cordial, inviting Barnes to follow her to the flight cockpit.

The *Decepter* MK2 Machiavellian class freighter enters the

lower strata of Nova Conti's atmosphere, undetected by the Mbron Media's pirate fleet detectors. Within the confines of the starship's cabin, Dan Casey and Agent 1.9.4, a female android, have just concluded their analysis of Jay and Charlena's decrypted transmission and are deliberating its implications.

"Do you believe this plan will be effective?" Dan asks.

Nayla 1.9.4 responds with a measured perspective, stating, "It is worth attempting if all other options have been exhausted. May I send an authorisation response?"

Dan chuckles in amusement, "Why not? It may infringe upon all of Tara's guidelines, but she did bestow upon me the title of Space Deputy Casey!"

Agent 1.9.4 laughs and transmits an encrypted message to the gunslinger and galactic scholar. With no invitation, Veena arrives on the starship's vented walkway, wearing her clicking high heels, accompanied by an uninvited guest. In her refined voice, she states, "I have found the large tool that can be transformed into a weapon."

Seated in the pilot's chair, Dan Casey swivels around and exclaims, "Agent Barnes! Welcome aboard."

The cargo pilot looks at Veena in confusion before turning to Nayla 1.9.4 and enquiring, "Are you aware of this addition to the team?"

The pink cyberbot responds in a neutral tone, "Oh, you found him. As I mentioned, he may prove useful."

Mason Barnes removes his plasma rifle from his shoulder and places it to the side before sitting in the passenger quarters. He speaks confidently, providing his reason for being a stowaway. "I have no intention of causing any trouble. I don't care about Tara's assumptions. She was not on the fleet carrier when the bounty hunters and their monstrous accomplice killed well-trained agents for the sake of some serpent's alter junk. It is time for payback. I hope you understand that I am not here to make friends. It is simply a matter of duty."

Mason's voice is sincere, and he speaks with a stern expression.

Dan Casey and Veena Merida exchange a worried glance, both asking in unison, "Serpent Alter?"

Mason's tone is bitter as he replies, "Yes, they took some broken pieces of ancient relics and caused many innocent lives to be lost."

Agent Barnes lounges back in the passenger seat, clearly shaken by the events.

Nayla 1.9.4, the helpful AI-powered assistant, picks up on their emotions and asks in her sweet cyber tone, "Is the Serpent Altar causing trouble?"

Veena responds with a heavy sigh, "High command claims that the altar is nothing more than a visual weapon. It's shattered into pieces and hopefully useless without the data box."

Dan, who has witnessed the power of the Crystal Serpent Altar first-hand in the Temple of Delas, expresses his concern, "Let's hope that the fragments of the relic do not cause any further trouble beyond what we have already witnessed."

The cargo pilot's words hang heavy in the air, a poignant reminder of the devastation that has been wrought.

Nayla 1.9.4 says, "I have received intel that the supreme leader has custody of the data box. It has been stored in a highly secure vault, and only Tara has been authorised to access that section of the tower complex."

The dark-toned agent, Mason Barnes, expresses his lack of interest in ancient folklore, "I have no interest in past relics. My focus is on stopping these media people from invading our planet. It seems that Zak Duran may have tipped them off. He gave me a message to pass on, telling Tara to smile for the cameras. I am determined to put an end to this. Period!"

He adjusts the buckled belt cords and straps himself into the flight seat; his neatly shaved hairstyle and designer-trimmed beard add to his sharp appearance. The crew know that Mason means business and that they can count on him to do whatever it takes to protect their planet.

Dan Casey sets the trajectory for the starship to align with the media pirate fleet, "Pearl, take us in on auto-cruise slowly while we prepare to board."

The cyber navigation suite of the starship flashes a confirmation response, and the vessel smoothly accelerates to a steady pace. Dan rises from his reclining pilot's chair and tells Agent Barnes, "Back on the *Aurora*, Tara spoke highly of you. I don't mind having you on board, but please follow my lead. I don't want any lone heroes trying to prove a point. Check in with Nayla 1.9.4; she will inform you about the cargo rules. Stick to that, and we shall be fine, Mason."

Agent Barnes takes a deep breath and replies, "Yes, sir. You have nothing to worry about with me. Let's just get the job done," with a sarcastic flicked salute.

Dan doesn't react to his comment and turns away, saying to Veena, "I'm going to change out of this uniform. It's just not my style. Keep an eye on things, and Pearl will coordinate the flight plan. Catch you soon, Veena."

The cargo runner kisses her as he leaves the *Decepter*'s cockpit to prepare for the infiltration strike of the Mbron Media satellite dreadnaught.

Meanwhile, back safely in the human capital, Kothariya, away from the media troubles on Nova Conti, the galactic gunslinger and the renegade student have been home. They quickly change their garments and collect equipment before visiting the capital city's private spaceport at Isla-Kai.

The weather is bright and sunny, with a low gush of wind sweeping across the busy spaceport complex. Standing at the entrance to the hanger bay is Charlena Jones, who has changed from her ripped, tatty wrap-around slave outfit to a new, gleaming white summer dress.

The short-styled garment looks elegant with her white-sleeved gloves and jewelled neck chocker. Her red-bobbed hair waves in the wind as she glances behind at Jay Haines, who is paying for the taxi-pod.

"Come on, hurry up. We're on a tight schedule, so be careful with my box. It's got precious equipment inside."

She says, bossing her stylish chaperone with instructions to get a move on.

As the taxi hover-pod departs with a smooth whooshing sound, Jay Haines turns his well-groomed demeanour towards the hanger bay entrance to inform Charlena Jones of his punctuality, "Please wait a moment, Charlena. I am on my way, and this package is quite heavy."

He is sporting a pair of dark sunglasses and has his dreadlocks arranged neatly. He is attired in a navy quarter jacket and matching waistcoat, with his dual silver revolvers securely fastened in a slanted brown leather holster belt. Jay Haines and Charlena Jones are preparing to undertake a daring mission after receiving the encrypted response from Agent 1.9.4.

Charlena sweeps her crimson fringe away from her sparkling blue eyes and confidently addresses her trusted aide, "Are you prepared, big guy?"

Jay replies solemnly, "I am as ready as possible, but you must understand that there can be serious repercussions if our mission fails."

Charlena Jones proceeds towards the hanger bay, with Jay Haines following closely behind her. She whispers to him, "Let us not fail and try to avoid looking suspicious. We can complete our mission without being detected if we operate swiftly and skilfully. Trust me."

The confident young student walks with a swagger while Jay, the experienced gunslinger, watches their surroundings.

Jay amusingly replies, "I look suspicious, as we're about to perform suspicious activity."

Charlena then asks Jay if he has left a message for her mother before they depart.

"Did you leave a holo note for my mum, and what did you say?"

Jay calmly replies, "Don't worry, I left her a holo-pad recording. I informed Lena that we'll pick up some Mac Moon Burgers."

Charlena stops in her tracks, shaking her red-bobbed hair in dismay, "Oh, boy, my mother knows I detest Mac Moon's. She will be suspicious of our actions. We will have to deal with her later. Let's proceed."

Jay can't believe that Charlena doesn't like Mac Moons, and he can't help but voice his surprise, "How can you not like Mac Moons, kid?"

Charlena, however, is more focused on her mission and walks up to a middle-aged private star pilot who is prepping his fighter. She gets his attention by complimenting his ship, "Wow, that's a Vulpine X24 slip jump fighter with a 2.4 hyperdrive and equipped with quick-fire retro blasters. Nice ship!"

The ageing star pilot, bald and with a podgy belly, is impressed and compliments her knowledge of starfighters. "You sure know your starfighters, kid!"

Charlena Jones replies. "I collect visuals and specification details on my holo-pad. One day, I'd like to pilot a Vulpine X24. Please, can I sit in the cockpit?"

The starship owner sternly looks at the young girl and says, "I'm sorry, but I don't let anyone else inside my ship."

Charlena's face falls, and she looks disappointed. "I just wanted to sit in the pilot seat and tell my friends about it."

Before the pilot can say anything else, Jay Haines appears and puts his arm around the pilot's shoulders, "Hey man, this is my sweet niece. Why don't you let her sit in your starfighter? It'll make her day."

The pilot explains that he can't risk damaging his ship, but

Jay understands. "Yeah, I get it. But she's just a kid," he says, winking at Charlena Jones.

As Jay distracts the starship owner with his conversation, the renegade student signals back with a sly nod and quickly climbs up the cockpit ladder. She opens the canopy and sits in the pilot seat, placing the headset around her face. Her heart races as she flicks on the control switches, and the Vulpine X24 engine starts to engage with a pulsating whistle.

The overweight pilot hears the commotion and is shocked that the girl has turned on all the flight systems. "What the hell is she doing?" he exclaims in anger.

Jay smiles and tries to excuse her actions, "Oh man, she's just playing around. Let her have some fun."

The bald civilian is not impressed and says he will call spaceport security. Jay asks for the pilot's name, but the pilot is angry when he answers, "I don't care if she's just messing around, and why do you want my name?"

Jay's good-naturedness shifts to something more in line with Charlena's plan. He advises the pilot, "I always like to know the name of the person I'm about to knock out."

With a devious smile, he swings his arm back and punches the pilot in the face, sending him flying onto the tarmac. Charlena sees their chance to steal the ship and swiftly inputs the deactivated sequence for the Vulpine X24 brake pads to release.

She is buzzing with adrenaline and knows her way around starfighters. "Quick Jay, get in and don't forget my box; we're about to make flight."

Jay Haines swiftly drags the knocked-out pilot's body from the sleek ship's thrusters for safekeeping. The gunslinger apologises for his abruptness, "I'm sorry, man. It's nothing personal, but we must borrow your fighter."

"It appears there is limited space for my legs and room for me to turn my head. I am curious, Charlena, why did you choose a starship with such a constrained interior?"

The student's equipment box is wedged between them, adding to Jay's discomfort. Charlena, who has a firm grip on the flight joystick, responds confidently, "I'm sorry to hear that, Jay. But we require a high-speed starfighter, not a larger vessel. The Vulpine X24 is the most suitable option for our mission. Despite its size, it is highly manoeuvrable and fast. This vessel is an excellent choice. I will demonstrate our capabilities and prove that we are not to be underestimated."

Determination is evident in Charlena's expression as she activates the turbo on the Vulpine X24 thrusters, producing a breathtaking effect. As the stolen starfighter rapidly gains speed, it quickly exits the spaceport hangar bay and soars through the blue skies of Kothariya. Upon reaching the outer atmosphere, the starfighter slip-jumps into the hyper-speed lanes with a flash and a bang. As the galactic gunslinger and his sidekick student commit the heinous crime of spacecraft theft on the human home world of Kothariya, chaos erupts across the planet's spaceport.

Meanwhile, on Nova Conti, the atmosphere is charged with tension and apprehension as the Mbron Media pirate fleet's coverage of the mysterious hidden world nears completion.

The fleet's orbit around the globe is a spectacle as their ships gleam in the nearby star's light.

The supreme leader of the resistance organisation, Tara Harlow, knows they cannot let the Mbron Media fleet continue their coverage unchallenged. She launches their older and less advanced fleet, positioning it strategically on the blind side of the planet.

Tara Harlow, the supreme leader of the resistance organisation, is seated at bridge control on her flagship fleet carrier. She proudly wears her navy high command pleated uniform as she checks on their ETA with the carrier's pilot, "What is our grid reference, and are we still off the Mbron Media radar scopes? I don't want conflict with their Buccaneer G16s battleships while they have the force field up. We need to give the strike team enough time to infiltrate their sanction. Have we detected the *Decepter* on the radar, and what is their current vector? And does anyone know where Mason Barnes has gone? Check the flight attendance log and make sure he boarded."

The agency pilot responds, "Grid 229 latitude 446. We are on target, and the *Decepter* is approaching the *Excalibur* satellite ship. Mason Barnes is logged on board by Agent 1.9.4, ma'am!"

Tara feels a sense of confusion and disbelief, "That's impossible. I put him with the strike team. Do you have any idea where Mason might be? What are they doing?"

The weight of the mission is bearing down on her. Despite their outdated technology, the Resistance Fleet is determined to execute a strategic plan of attack with precision and skill. The anticipation of the impending battle is palpable, and the planet's fate hangs in the balance.

Chapter Twenty-One

The Battle for Nova Conti

The *Decepter* MK2 Machiavellian freighter appears as a slender and elegant silhouette against the thick, hazy atmosphere of Nova Conti. Its sleek and durable design indicates the robust technology that powers it. The cyber navigation suite is expertly programmed to pilot the vessel to avoid detection from the pirate media fleet. This is crucial, as the mission is to infiltrate the *Excalibur*, a satellite dreadnaught that the enemy heavily guards. The *Decepter*'s strike team needs to disable the transmitting and shield capabilities of the *Excalibur* before the Resistance Fleet can commence its attack pattern. The stakes are highly tense, and the success of this mission depends on the crew's precision and skill onboard the *Decepter* MK2 freighter.

Pearl quickly flashes a crystallised report inside the flight cabin to the rest of the crew, "We're getting close to the contracting force-feed beam, currently approaching at a speed of 2.1 with shields at maximum velocity."

Dan Casey, the cargo pilot, has a plan up his sleeve. "Drop our shields and deactivate the weapons systems, but keep at the current speed. Okay, 1.9.4, this is when you come in. Open the communication link and send the SOS."

The pink-haired cyberbot activates the Mbron Media secured connection built into her programming without hesitation.

"I've sent the link, Dan. We are now awaiting confirmation," she says calmly.

The tension in the cabin is palpable as the crew waits to see if their SOS signal has been successfully sent.

Agent Barnes doubts the plan and voices his concerns by leaning forward from the passenger quarters, "What happens if they don't take the bait, Space Deputy Casey?"

Dan glares at the questioning agent, but before he can say anything, Veena from the weapons division speaks up, "If all else fails, we send Mason Barnes, the lone solo act. But until that point, you should try to act like the agent Tara has you down for. If you're as good as she rates you, we can you on our side!"

Mason gives a slow salute regarding Veena's praising words and expresses his pledge of loyalty to a certain extent, "When the going gets tough, Agent Merida, I've got your back. The same goes for you, Casey. But don't expect me to buy the drinks later, okay? If you had hidden your tracks properly, Merida, those damn bounty hunters would never have killed half of my crew and given away the planet's location. That's why I'm here, to fix the mess you created with all due respect."

Veena wisely ignores his remarks, knowing she has exceeded her training and contractual obligations. "I will bear that in mind, Agent Barnes. Now, shall we get to work?"

The team's determination to continue their mission remains steadfast despite the tension in the *Decepter*'s flight cockpit. Dan Casey takes charge of the situation and speaks of the mission at hand, calming the tension in the cabin.

"Alright, people, this is it. The success of our mission means the lives of many depend on us down there on Nova Conti. We can't allow this Media pirate fleet to report back to the Corporal Union. Otherwise, Nova Conti will suffer the same fate as Kothariya under the grip of Wilson Volantis. We'll split into two groups: one will take out the shields while the other disables the satellite core. Once we call in Harlow's fleet, we run like hell.

We need to put our quarrels aside for now, and who knows, Tara might buy the celebration drinks. Are you all with me?"

The speech moves Agent 1.9.4, who admires the humans' passion. The cute pink cyberbot proudly salutes, "I'm with you, Dan Casey."

This is followed by a pat on the back from Mason Barnes. The team is united and ready to face whatever challenges lie ahead.

Veena smiles with a sense of fond admiration towards her lover, "I'm always with you and proud to be so, darling."

Dan Casey's inspiring words have brought them together, and she feels proud of each member's unwavering commitment to the mission. They are ready to face the daring challenge ahead to protect Nova Conti.

The cyber captain reports inside the dreadnaught's bridge control, "Supreme 63, we have an unidentified star-freighter approaching from the far side of the planet. They are transmitting a Mbron Media signal code and requesting immediate assistance. Orders, sir!"

Supreme 63, the commanding android overseeing the expeditions of the Media run, sits with a stern and upright posture in his command helm. His copper-coiffed hair and pale, sinister face convey an aura of authority that demands unwavering obedience from his subordinates. He scrutinises the cyber pilot's findings keenly and commands, "Zero, retrace the signal code and match it against the current Mbron Media authorisation directive. If it appears expired, destroy the freighter."

Zero, the inferior cyberbot, responds with a report, "After a thorough reassessment, the code has been confirmed as authentic. They are requesting visual contact orders, sir."

Conveying a sense of deference to the supreme android's authority, "Put them on screen, Zero, with no delay. I'm intrigued to see our visitors."

Supreme 63 is clearly fascinated by the situation. Reports of resistance habitats on the planet have been circulating. The supreme android is eager to see what these newcomers have to offer.

"I calculate with certainty that they have no link to Mbron Media's database, so this makes the code all the more fascinating."

He continues, rising from his command helm. His robotic joints hiss and gasp as he moves towards the visual screen, adding to the menacing aura of the dangerous android.

The *Excalibur*'s small light-framed Zero series pilot responds efficiently, "Confirmed, Supreme 63. Visual link now transmitting."

The screen flickers with static interference caused by Isadora's atmosphere, obscuring the image of the incoming transmission. Zero quickly adapts to a more secure transmission, and soon, the monitor displays a clear picture of Nayla 1.9.4 seated in the pilot seat of the *Decepter*.

She has one fibre hand on the joystick controls and uses the other to wave a greeting, saying through the communications link, "Hey guys! It's only me."

On the receiving end of the link, Supreme 63 is firm and directs in his response, "Why is a Nayla 1.9.4 series so deep in space? You should be working in the commercial glamour world. Explain yourself at once, you inferior model."

Agent 1.9.4 responds to Supreme 63's writhing tone with a giddy demeanour, "Well, what can I compute, guys? Gee! I got sucked into a space vacuum and lost control of my craft. The hyper-lanes dispelled me near this pretty blue and green world. Are we going to live here? I must say, I dig your hair, 63! Oops, delete. I need a rewire, guys!"

Nayla plays her disguised role through the visual communication link, trying to deflect attention from her true intentions. Supreme 63, however, is not amused, "Your systems are all over the place, 1.9.4. Come aboard for a full memory-wipe and be resigned to a glamour world. Any problems or misbehaviours will result in termination. Do I make myself a clear, inferior tool?"

"Zero, dismantle the force beam and have a batch of security Eltons at Port Bay Two."

The cyber captain immediately combines the order and deactivates the *Excalibur*'s force shield. Supreme 63 returns to the visual screen and informs the pink-haired cyber female, "Port Bay Two, you have clearance to dock. But be swift 1.9.4. The force shield beam is only down for a minor fraction."

"Oh, thanks, you're so cool, 63. I've always been a top fan! Oops, delete. Bye, guys!" Agent 1.9.4 says cheekily before Zero abruptly cuts off the communication.

As they gather on board the *Decepter*, Agent 1.9.4 shares the good news with a smirk on her pale face, "We're in! They fell for it. Not bad for an inferior tool!" Nayla exclaims, proud of completing her first mission task.

Dan Casey commends the female cyberbot's efforts and gives further orders to Pearl. "Well done, 1.9.4. You make him look like a dork, and his appearance backs that up. And Pearl, take us in swift before the force beams reactivate and keep blocking out their bio-scans so they only see one female android on board."

Veena is impressed with the pink cyberbot's acting. She applauds Nayla's performance, "Supreme 63 thinks he's superior and can never imagine the 1.9.4 model will ever get rewired and have a unique edge. They believe you are a faulty model."

Meanwhile, Mason Barnes warns the team to be careful with the Elton-63s. "We need to be alert when tackling these 63s, and this little action bot has all the skills and tricks hidden up her sleeve, but don't go overboard 1.9.4. We have lost too many good agents lately."

Dan Casey stands up from the flight quarters and says,

"Okay, let's do it. No turning back now. It's time to go make the Mbron Media headlines!"

On the cargo runner's brave words, they start to make their way from the cockpit to the exit hatch of the freighter.

Pearl expertly navigates the *Decepter* through the inactive defiance grid of the *Excalibur* dreadnaught with complete control of the vessel's flight trajectory. Though the satellite ship is massive compared to the *Decepter*'s haul frame, Pearl remains unfazed, flashing from the cyber suite.

Suddenly, Port Bay Two's hatches open with a pressurised clang, and the MK2 freighter, proceeding with its land gear unfolding from the lower haul, enters the hanger bay of Mbron Media's renaissance flagship.

The atmosphere is tense, with the terrifying android, Supreme 63, at the helm of the dreadnaught. As the *Decepter* enters Port Bay Two, the interior lighting is dimmed, creating a gleaming and immaculate platform. The shuttle crafts hanging around are registered as escape pods, providing a quick exit in an emergency. Suddenly, an electrical buzzing sound echoes through the starship's circuitry panels, announcing the vessel's arrival.

The starship is preceded by a security batch of Elton-63 cyber androids, each dressed in black circuitry uniforms and visor helmets that conceal their faces. The helmets make them appear similar to Supreme 63 but are smaller serial versions with less ability. The cyber androids are menacing, each armed with neutron blaster rifles. They are highly trained elite bots, ready to follow the orders of Mbron Media's sociopathic right-hand android, the Supreme 63. The squad comprises four of these androids, and they approach the *Decepter* with an air of authority and precision. Although they are there to provide security, their presence sends a chill down the spine of anyone who witnesses them.

As the *Decepter*'s hatch opens, steam hisses out from the

pressure, followed by silence until a clicking sound of high-heeled pink boots can be heard.

Nayla 1.9.4 goes down the freighter's exit ramp with a joyful skipping motion, arriving in front of the Elton-63 security unit. The cheerful pink fuzzy android greets her male counterpart production model with a warm smile, "Howdy, guys, how's it going? Whoa, nice helmets! I think they will squash my hair. I require a core rewire. I keep acting strange. Where's the control hub, sweet cheeks?"

However, the Elton-63 security unit is not impressed and replies in an authorised robotic manner, "Your behaviour and vocal programming are not up to Mbron Media standards. You will have a complete memory-wipe and upgrade to standard functions."

The security androids are sinister as they escort her to the mind-wipe hub, down the corridors from Port Bay Two. Nayla 1.9.4 responds with a beaming expression as they enter the control hub.

The Elton-63 cyber units gather around her with a daunting presence. She smiles at the pale enforcers and states, "Cool, I can't wait to get a rewire. It makes my earlobes tingle. You know, guys, I've picked up so many bad habits mouldering with the humans; I've started smoking, and I drink a lot and been performing a load of random sex. It has been great, but there is one downside."

The Elton-63 cyberbots pause in the confusion of her manner and enquires in an intrigued fashion, "What's the worst fault you have developed, Inferior Tool."

Nayla replies, "Oh, gee, the worst habit is I don't care about you guys."

She mocks and swiftly springs into action with a masterful move of her delicate body. Agent 1.9.4 turns in a lightning fashion, gripping and twisting each Elton-63 head in a 180-degree offence. The armoured cybernetic enforcers quickly malfunction with a gush of sparks cultivating from their flimsy mechanical necks and fall to the floor of the hub room in a piled heap of scrap.

Agent 1.9.4 is a highly skilled, trained, and rewired professional. She is a key member of the resistance organisation led by the powerful and cunning supreme leader, Tara Harlow.

Nayla's mission on this occasion is crucial: infiltrating the enemy's satellite ship and destroying their control hub. It is a dangerous task that Nayla 1.9.4 is more than willing to undertake. As she makes her way through the enemy's territory, Nayla's cybernetic core races with adrenaline. The darkness of the hub provides her with some cover, but she knows she has to be quick and precise in her actions.

Agent 1.9.4 can't afford to be caught by the other Elton-63s that patrol the area. Nayla reaches the controls and immediately takes action. With no time to waste, she steps over the dysfunctional Elton-63s and readily activates the hub's system. Using her expert hacking skills, she inserts her index finger into the power socket and briefly twists it.

The core spike immediately knocks out cameras and security systems. It is a temporary solution but will buy the resistance some time. She quickly connects to the *Decepter* infiltration team, giving them the go-ahead,

"I have disabled the alarms and cameras, but only for a limited time. We must be quick before more Elton-63s arrive to investigate the core system downtime. And if we do get company, aim for their heads. It's always been a fault of the Elton-63 enforcer series."

Dan Casey says, "Well done, 1.9.4, we're on route, keep us covered."

As they make their way towards the control hub, Nayla 1.9.4 monitors their progress through the hacked security cameras, ensuring they remain undetected. She knows that time is of the essence, and any delay can jeopardise their mission. Dan Casey's team is about to reach the control hub when Nayla 1.9.4 hears a loud thud from outside. The enemy has caught onto their plan and has sent in a group of Elton-63s to investigate.

Agent 1.9.4 quickly transmits a link to the team, "Hurry, we have company. I'll hold them off."

The cyberbot immediately approaches the entrance and takes out her agent-issued weapon. Her fibre hands are steady as she aims for the heads of the approaching Elton-63s. They are caught unaware, and there is no match for her expertly placed shots.

"I guess our window of opportunity has just shortened. Are they on to us? Or is that just a routine scout patrol?" Dan asks as he approaches the control hub, his black and silver gun drawn. He scans the area for any further unwanted cybernetic guests, noticing the destroyed Elton-63 androids in the hexagon corridor.

Nayla 1.9.4 advises the strike team, "They can have just been a patrol unit, but I'm not sure. Either way, we don't have long; the core spikes will expire soon."

The pink-haired cyberbot is focused on the schematics of the Mbron Media hub, trying to ensure a smooth operation. Veena is close behind, dressed in a black jumpsuit and holding a silver infrared-scoped pistol, her long green hair flowing behind her.

She speaks urgently. "We need to split into two groups to confuse them. Nayla, how many Security 63 batches will be on board a vessel this size?" The glamorous agent is trying to understand the enforcer android count.

Agent 1.9.4 responds with a calculation of the satellite ship's personnel, "This is Supreme 63's ship, the right-hand android to the Core Lord. It's going to be well-guarded with at least 100 Elton units. The first contact invasion squads will be on the Buccaneer G16 battle cruisers and will commence their landing once the *Excalibur*'s surveillance has cauterised its data."

Nayla's explanation adds to the sense of urgency among the strike team.

Mason Barnes is covering the rear entrance and corridor, holding his plasma rifle sternly aimed to keep guard, "We are outnumbered big time. You two get going and disable the signal transmitter. Me and 1.9.4 will keep this area secure and remove the shield core."

Dan Casey responds, "We shall meet back here in thirty minutes. Good luck!" The heroic pilot salutes as he rushes off with Veena to stop the Mbron Media coverage from going live.

In the control bridge of the *Excalibur*, Cyber Captain Zero reports a disturbance in the starship's internal systems, "We have detected a bug in the system core. Cameras and alarms have been turned off, but the broadcaster and energy beams are enabled. What are your orders, sir?"

Supreme 63 stands motionless on the vessel's deck and responds to the cyber pilot with urgency, "Organise the elite enforcer to generate a patrol sweep. Activate the bridge force beam barrier. I may have made an error in letting the inferior 1.9.4 on board. How fascinating. Arm security and impose the order to shoot to destroy on sight!"

Cyber Captain Zero immediately follows the orders of Supreme 63 and deploys cyber patrols on all decks of the vessel. The Elton-63 enforcers march along the perimeter of the hexagons in batches of six, ready and armed to shoot on sight with no hesitation.

Dan Casey, now outfitted in a distinctive brown leather sleeveless pilot jacket, black t-shirt, and matching slacks, brandishes his silver and black firearm and is poised and prepared for potential hostiles. Leading the daring assault on the signal generator, he is accompanied by Veena Merida.

Agent Merida methodically covers each corner of the hexagonal corridor with her infrared-scope pistol. Dan's voice is tense as he relays the information, "Based on the schematic provided by 1.9.4, the portable elevator will take us to the transmitter on the second deck. Veena, stay close. We should expect resistance if they're aware of our presence."

He holds Veena's soft hand with one hand while the other remains firmly engaged with his gun, tracking any movement approaching the pod elevator.

Veena gracefully takes hold of his empathetic hand as they increase their pace, her long hair blowing behind her.

With a heaving breath, she says, "Let's hope they believe it's only Nayla on board, and we'll have time to deactivate the transmitter. We must also pray that the others can hold out."

A group of six heavily armed Elton-63 patrol enforcers gather near the elevator walkway beside Dan and Veena. The two quickly unlink their hands and spring into action, expertly opening fire with precise aim and slick reflexes, obliterating the cyberbot unit, "They may outnumber us, but these tinheads are slow. We have a slight advantage. Let's go," Dan quips as he watches the hexagonal aisles while Veena Merida steps into the elevator pod. Her movements are quick as she keys in the level two options on the elevator controls. The pod shuts instantly and begins ascending the escalator.

The pressure mounts and Veena's jade eyes sparkle mischievously as she teasingly asks, "You look like you're enjoying yourself, Space Deputy Casey!"

"Tara must hate me with all the rules and nicknames!" He keeps his weapon at hand, ready for any sudden stops.

Veena moves close and wraps her bare arms around him, saying, "I think Tara is impressed with your quick thinking on the *Aurora*. You saved her life. I don't think she recognises what an asset you will be to her. The agency always needs a good man, as do I, Space Deputy."

As time is short and their fate of surviving is uncertain, they embrace at that moment with a passionate kiss, showing the affection they have built upon this voyage.

Their intimate moment is interrupted by a flashing indication that alerts them to their imminent arrival.

Dan breaks off the kiss with a smile and whispers to Veena, "You ready, sweetheart?"

Veena responds confidently, flicking on her infrared site and saying, "Always, darling!"

As the escalator door shimmers open, they step out and immediately spring into action. The room contains a patrol batch of Elton-63 enforcer bots.

Dan and Veena's guns blaze as they exchange fire with the enforcer bots. Gunfire echoes through the transmitter room as they move forward, taking cover behind hexagon pillars. Despite the odds against them, they remain calm and focused, their training and experience evident in their movements.

Veena's infrared site allows her to see the Elton-63s' heat signatures, giving an advantage in identifying their targets.

Meanwhile, Dan's quick reflexes and precise aim take out bot after bot. The air is thick with the smell of smoke and the sound of metal hitting metal, but they press forward, determined to complete their mission. Finally, after an eternity, the last Elton-63 android falls to the panel-vented floor.

Dan and Veena exchange a quick nod of acknowledgement, their breathing heavy with exertion. They know there will be more obstacles ahead, but they are ready for whatever comes their way. Dan Casey's heart is still pounding after the intense shoot-out with the cyber enforcers from Mbron Media. He turns to his attractive but deadly partner and says, "There's the transmission control hub, but we must turn off the power barrier around it before we can get close!"

Dan quickly contacts the other strike team through his earpiece, "1.9.4, do you copy? We've got a problem. We're at the signal transmitters, and there's an energy field protecting it. Is there anything you can do from the control hub?"

Veena sees more patrol units approaching and knows they need to act fast.

She takes charge, telling Dan, "I'll keep guard at the escalator entrance and block them off at the corridor while you work with Nayla to shut the barrier down. We can't let them get to us."

Dan nods, acknowledging Veena's plan as he sprints towards the control hub. Nayla 1.9.4 advises in his earpiece, "Okay, I will switch the format; this will take a while!"

They know that time is of the essence, and they need to act quickly to turn off the power barrier. Dan's experience as an interstellar pilot and Nayla's technical expertise make them the perfect team to tackle this challenge.

Meanwhile, Veena positions herself at the escalator entrance, ready to defend against any incoming threat. She takes cover behind a nearby pillar, her pistol at the ready. Her training comes to the forefront as she surveys the area, watching for any signs of movement or danger.

Dan quickly arrives at the control hub for the transmitter generator, his adrenaline pumping as he brashly places his black-barrelled weapon on the side recess. He follows the instructions of an input code from Agent 1.9.4, who talks to him through the headset.

Within seconds, the force barrier starts to disassemble, and Dan is overjoyed. He praises the rewired android, "Great work, Nayla! I've now got access to the signal transmitter. I'm setting the EMP charges for three minutes. It should create a power surge and break down the core system. How's it going on your end? As soon as you have the shields down, get back to the *Decepter*."

Dan places the EMP charges on each corner of the buzzing signal generator and shouts, "We've got under three minutes, Veena. Get back to the elevator!"

He quickly picks up his barrelled weapon and motions to sprint back to the elevator as the EMP charge timers begin to bleep a countdown.

Veena is backtracking to the entrance, blasting the Elton-63 security enforcers in a wielding shoot-out.

She shouts urgently, covering his run, "Come on, Dan! Move it! We're getting overrun!"

Patrol batch after patrol is heading their way, and they need to get out of there fast. Dan Casey can hear the sound of gunfire behind him as he sprints towards the elevator, his heart racing with excitement and fear. He knows they are running out of time and needs to escape before it is too late. As he reaches the elevator, he sees Veena holding off the enforcers, her gun blazing as she fights to defend their escape.

He quickly joins her, firing his weapon at the enforcers as they make their way to the elevator. Together, they fight their way onto the elevator and hit the button to descend. As they ride down, Dan can feel the tension in the air. Dan carefully places his arms around Veena, relieved they have made it out alive.

He says, "Whoa, that was a close call. Are you alright, Veena?"

Agent Merida is still catching her breath, feeling the pace of the Elton-63s pestering them.

She replies, "I'm fine, thanks. Are you? These damn androids are relentless and dangerous. Gosh! Mbron Media is out of control. They need to be closed down."

Dan Casey is in a serious mood. "Both Nayla units I've spoken to have said that this Core Lord calls the shots. It coincides with the rise of the Corporal Union's Director. They seem programmed to be against humans. And both came to power around the same time, a few years after the space protection group broke down."

Veena is confused and asks, "I'm not following you. We all know Wilson Volantis is using Media for his purpose, so what's bugging you?"

Dan speaks with conviction in his voice, "Wilson only

manipulates Mbron Media to gain political backing. He does not own the company. That's why no one finds any links between them. I believe the Director doesn't even know the location of the broadcasting headquarters. The Core Lord's preaching reminds me of an android. It hides in the shadows, preys on the weak, and vanishes without a trace or trail. It can't be, surely?"

Dan's words hang in the air as they both contemplate the implications of what he has said. They know they have a lot of work ahead of them and need to remain vigilant if they want to bring down Mbron Media and its dangerous android enforcers.

Dan and Veena exchange a determined look as Agent Barnes calls in on the secure channel transmitting in their earpieces. The tense atmosphere is palpable as Mason's voice, thick with stress, comes through the comm system.

The sound of blast fire in the background only heightens the sense of danger. "Casey, I'm expecting an electrical boom from the upper floor. Tell me you've got the ordinances activated. We're getting overrun down here and need your help. Do you copy?"

Dan Casey responds quickly, his fingerless-gloved hand rising to his earpiece as he shouts back, "The EMP is set to detonate any time. Hold on, Barnes, we're on our way."

His voice is laced with concern but also determination to aid his comrades.

Agent Barnes, ever the cool-headed elite agent, responds with a bit of humour amidst the chaos, "I'll hold you to that, Casey. If you come through, I might be tempted to buy you that drink!"

Veena, a critical team member, chimes in with a crucial question, "Mason, have you got the shields down? Can we call in the fleet?"

Unfortunately, the EMP detonations interrupt Veena's communication, which causes a static pulse on level two.

The signal transmitter and the patrolling cyber enforcers are knocked out, faulting to a shut mode. Despite the success of the sabotage strike, there is a bitter twist.

The EMP energy pulse fragments on the elevator drive cause the lift pod to jolt to a stop. It's a precarious situation. Dan and Veena stumble around the pod as it falters in favour of holding on to each other; they quickly compose themselves and try to rewire the elevator's digital control panel.

As the chaos and danger unfold on the upper levels of the *Excalibur* satellite dreadnaught, Mason Barnes and Agent 1.9.4 face their challenges on the first deck at the shield core section. They are battling against the relentless assault of the Elton-63s.

The streaming hordes of these dangerous enemies are proving to be more than a match for the two agents struggling to hold their ground. Despite the odds stacked against them, Mason and Agent 1.9.4 are determined to protect the shield core section and deactivate the force beam.

They fight with all their might, using their skills and training to fend off the enemy attack. The atmosphere in the shield core section is tense and fraught with danger.

The sounds of weapons firing and explosions reverberate through the air. Mason and Agent 1.9.4 exchange quick, urgent commands to each other as they work together to stay alive and protect their mission. As they continue to battle against the Elton-63s, Mason and Agent 1.9.4 can only hope that their comrades on the upper levels will be able to join them soon and that, together, they can turn the tide of this intense and dangerous situation.

Mason's voice crackles through the comm system, his concern evident as he asks Nayla, "How are you doing on the deactivation sequence?"

It's clear that time is of the essence, and the success of their mission depends on Nayla's ability to hack into the shield core and deactivate it.

Agent 1.9.4 is multi-tasking, trying to focus on hacking the shield core and blasting the cyber enforcers approaching from every corner.

She's feeling the pressure, as evidenced by her response to Mason. "There are too many interruptions from these tinheads."

It's a difficult situation, but Agent 1.9.4 is determined to succeed. As Nayla continues to work on the deactivation sequence, the cyber enforcers are closing in on her position.

The sound of their weapons firing can be heard in the background, adding to the moment's tension. Despite the odds stacked against her, Nayla remains focused on her task, determined to see it through. Mason watches and listens intently, hoping and praying that Agent 1.9.4 will be able to succeed. The success of their mission depends on it.

Agent Barnes is stationed a little way out from the control hub room, bravely defending Nayla 1.9.4 as he takes cover near the hexagon corridor. He rapidly opens fire with his infrared plasma rifle, determined to keep the Elton-63 enforcers at bay. Mason also keeps a close eye on the situation, taking shots with deadly accuracy to destroy any Elton-63 enforcers approaching their position.

Agent 1.9.4 is in the final phase of shutting down the shield core sequence, her whimsical pink hair contrasting the danger and chaos around her. She drops her guard momentarily to exterminate a nearby enemy, only to be ambushed by a half-damaged Elton-63.

The enemy takes a random shot, hitting Nayla's left side and blowing off her fibre arm with a sparking fuse. The cute pink android yelps in pain as she is hurled across the shield core control hub, crashing in a heap as her digital eyes deactivate.

The situation is dire, as Nayla's injury threatens to derail the mission.

Mason Barnes remains focused on the task despite the

danger and chaos around him. He bellows out at the top of his voice, "NAYLA!"

He watches his squad member being blasted with devastating effect. Agent Barnes fights with all his might, taking down enemy after enemy to protect Nayla 1.9.4 and complete their mission. The sound of weapons firing and explosions echoes through the control hub room, adding to the sense of danger and urgency.

The fate of the *Excalibur* satellite dreadnaught mission hangs in the balance as the elite agents fight to protect it from the dangerous Elton-63s.

Agent Barnes is a force to be reckoned with as he charges forward, blasting his plasma rifle at will. His rage is mounting, and he shows no mercy to the Elton-63 enforcers, "You want a piece of me? Come get your cybernetic freaks!"

He shouts, the sweat dripping down his dark skin as he weaves and dodges through the androids, "Too slow, you electrical mother fuckers."

Mason, using all his combat skills to smash the fragile heads of the Elton-63 enforcer series with the handle stock of his weapon, says, "Hang in there, 1.9.4. I'm coming for you!"

He bursts into the control hub room with a smashing roll from the hexagon corridors. He manoeuvres into a slick, low crouch and readily opens fire on the Elton-63s, inspecting the pink female's damaged body.

The sound of weapons firing and the hiss of plasma rifles echo through the control hub room as Agent Barnes fights with all his might to protect Nayla 1.9.4 from any further harm. His movements are swift and fluid as he takes down Elton-63 after Elton-63 with deadly accuracy.

Despite the danger, Agent Barnes remains focused on the task at hand. He knows that the success of their mission depends on his ability to protect Nayla 1.9.4 and shut down the shield core sequence.

Agent Barnes finds himself in a tense situation as he enters the control section. He quickly takes action by shooting out the door device on the entrance panel, causing the shutter to slide down with a loud slamming bang.

As he swiftly connects his earpiece to try to communicate with the others, he also checks over the smoking body of a female cyberbot.

In a raised voice, Mason says, "Casey, Veena, you copy me; 1.9.4 has been damaged. I've no idea how to deactivate the shield core!"

But there is no response except for a hissing buzz in his ear. Panic begins to set in as he realises that 1.9.4 has been removed, and he has no idea how to deactivate the shield core.

He mutters, "Damn it? Is there anyone left?"

But only the sound of his voice echoes in the control section. Mason brushes his hand over his short, shaven-styled hair, trying to calm himself down, and takes a deep breath to recollect his thoughts. He can see the Elton-63 enforcers moving in on his position, and he knows the sealed-down door won't hold out for long.

Despite the dire situation, Mason refuses to go down without a fight.

He taunts the enforcers, saying, "We all know this can be a one-way mission, but I'm not going down without taking you tin fuckers with me. It's time to bring in the big guns."

He quickly moves to the keyboard console in the control hub, inputs an emergency agent code, and transmits the signal, hoping for the best. Mason then bends down and picks up Nayla 1.9.4, holding her tight in his muscular arms as he readies his plasma weapon for the oncoming slaughter. The tension in the control section is palpable as he awaits the inevitable confrontation with the Elton-63s.

In the command bridge of the *Excalibur*, Supreme 63 is pacing around with a mechanic hiss, inspecting the assault on his satellite dreadnaught. The cyber technicians boot up the backup systems, and the sinister android orders the metallic cyber captain, "Zero, inform the Buccaneer G16 Cruisers to prepare for their ground invasion. We have completed our orbital scanning coverage, even with the slight disturbance on the lower decks."

The cybernetic captain responds obediently, acknowledging the order, "Invasion orders being relayed to Buccaneer captains as you redeem, oh, mighty sir."

The tension in the command bridge is emotionless as the Mbron Media android crew awaits the outcome of the impending invasion.

Supreme 63 is known for his ruthless tactics and cunning strategies.

Following his daunting commands, the android boss instructs his crew, "We have enough data for live coverage of this golden world. With the signal transmitter damaged, Zero will move the *Excalibur* out of the Isadora system and prepare the jump to hyper-lanes with a destination set for Kothariya. I will personally deliver the data to Director Wilson Volantis so he can commence the Corporal Union's armada."

Zero responds by engaging the battleship's main thrusters and setting the course for the human capital world. Supreme 63 remains cold-faced and bland in his expression as he informs the cyber captain, "I will interlink with Core Lord directly and send him a progress report. With the infiltrators trapped in various sections, I deem them an inferior threat. Keep them contained, and we can add them to the prison list. I do not wish to be disturbed. You have command of the vessel, Zero."

With these commands, Supreme 63 automatically closes down on the spot, his cybernetic eyes shut, and an electrical buzzing emanates from his inner core.

The *Excalibur* starship starts to break off its orbit of Nova Conti in its slow, sluggish vector as the Buccaneer G16 battler cruisers break their formation and begin to prepare their given invasion run of the civilian home world.

The android crew of the *Excalibur* compute quickly and efficiently to carry out Supreme 63's orders, knowing they have to act fast to deliver the data to Director Wilson Volantis and commence the Corporal Union's armada.

As the dreadnaught ship makes its way towards Kothariya, the Resistance Fleet, under the command of Tara Harlow, is assembled on the blind side of Nova Conti.

The agency's starships mass into a brigaded formation on the outer atmosphere of the golden world, ready for battle. At the spearhead of the fleet is the flagship fleet carrier, its massive hull armed with multi-cannons and seeker missiles, while the quad booster's engines at the back end of the vessel roar with a rumbling presence. Near the flagship are the four frigate destroyers and six armoured-plated transport ships, hovering adrift in space, preparing for the battle of Nova Conti.

The starships are manned by the bravest and most skilled pilots and crews, all determined to protect their home world at any cost.

As the starships mass into formation, the tension in the air is nerve-wracking. The brave agency pilots and crew members check and recheck their equipment, ensuring everything works. The engine's sound and the weapons system's hum fill the air, creating an ominous atmosphere. The fleet carrier takes its position at the front of the formation, leading the charge towards the enemy fleet. As the starships advance, the crews remain focused and determined, ready to engage in battle and defend their home world from the impending invasion.

The fight of Nova Conti is about to begin, and the galaxy's fate hangs in the balance. The agency's starships are the last line of defence against the enemy fleet, and the pilots and crew members prepare to give their all to protect their home world and the people they love.

The supreme leader, Tara Harlow, is seated at the command helm of the fleet carrier. She is focused on the ship's scanners, witnessing the Buccaneer G16 Cruisers moving into position to invade.

She turns to the navigation officer and asks, "Any response from the strike team? We can't sit and wait much longer."

The young male officer replies, "We are getting a faint signal from the *Excalibur*. I think it might be Agent Barnes?"

The officer's face shows shock as he relays the information to Tara.

She stands up from her flight chair and declares, "Get Mason online now, officer."

As the navigation officer works to establish contact with Agent Barnes, Tara takes a deep breath, trying to remain calm and focused. She knows the battle ahead will be intense and gruelling, but she is determined to lead her people to victory.

Finally, the navigation officer gets through to Agent Barnes, and Tara brashly takes the communications, "Mason, it's Tara. What the hell's happening over there? We need the strike team to turn off the force beam now. The Buccaneer G16 Cruisers are closing in, and we can't hold them off for long with that type of defence in place. We're counting on Deputy Casey's team to save our home world, Mason."

Agent Barnes responds with a muffled microphone, "I've lost contact with Casey and Veena. I'm pinned down in the control hub, and Nayla's been shot up. I can't operate the shield core console. I'd advise you to concentrate all firepower on the *Excalibur*. Ma'am, it's your only hope. Target the satellite ship," bellows Agent Barnes, stating that the infiltration mission had failed. The message keeps breaking up, causing Tara to order the navigation crew to secure the connection.

With a buzzing hiss, Dan Casey's voice fills the bridge of the fleet carrier, "Delay that order, Tara! We're not finished. The signal transmitter is disabled for now. But the *Excalibur*'s boosters have kicked in, meaning they're headed for the hyperlanes. We'll get the shield down; give us time. Backup is on its way!"

Tara Harlow responds with a deep sigh, "I'm putting my faith in you, Mr Casey. Get that defence system down, and my agents out of there."

Veena replies to the supreme leader's plea, her posh voice breaking up, "Trust us, ma'am. We won't let you down. Agent Merida over and out."

Tara knows that she has to trust Dan Casey and his team. The future of their home world rests in their hands, and they have to work together to repel the enemy invasion.

She takes a deep breath, trying to remain calm and focused as she waits for news from the strike team. As the fleet carrier and the other starships move into position, ready to engage in battle, Tara prays they will emerge victorious and protect their home world from harm. The struggle for Nova Conti is far from over, and the fate of the victory hangs in the balance.

While back on the Mbron Media satellite ship, Veena is frantically trying to reboot the control device of the elevator lift shaft. The elevator remains jammed between two decks, and the team is trapped inside it. Veena's body is tense with nerves as she fiddles with the fused circuits.

She connects her earpiece and tries to establish communication with her team members, "Barnes, if you hear me, we are coming; hold out. Two minutes. The lift pod's starting to reboot!"

However, just as she finishes speaking, there is a sudden interruption in the communication, leaving Veena worried and anxious. She knows time is running out, and they must get out of the elevator shaft before it's too late.

Meanwhile, Dan Casey's expertise is vital, as he was once part of a seasoned space infiltration group. He is deep in thought, his mind racing with ideas on how to save the team.

He knows they are in over their heads, but he is not one to give up hope. He has a plan and is determined to see it through. It's a do-or-die situation, and the strike team's survival depends on Veena Merida's ability to reboot the control device and Dan Casey's quick thinking of a backup plan.

As the lift pod slowly starts to move, Veena has her silver-suited pistol drawn, ready for any danger that may come their way. She is determined to help Barnes and Nayla, their other teammates, to safety. Dan Casey agrees with Veena's plan and takes out his silver and black-barrelled weapon, ready to face any challenge that comes their way.

He connects his earpiece to an alert line and speaks with tension in his smooth voice, "How are you doing for time? Are you close? We need you!"

Veena looks at Dan Casey in astonishment, "Who are you calling?"

Dan smiles and replies, "I have a few friends in high places. They owe me a favour or two. I've called in some reinforcements to help us escape this mess."

The action suddenly shifts to the far side of Nova Conti, where a sleek starfighter emerges from the hyper-speed lanes, thriving at a high cruising vector. The fighter pilot, Charlena Jones, transmits a message to the strike team on the *Excalibur* dreadnaught. "I just got into the Isadora system now. It looks like the fleets are on high standby," she says, her voice calm and collected. Charlena's voice is accompanied by another familiar person in the two-seater cockpit, Jay Haines, the gunslinger.

His voice is a mixture of amusement and panic as he exclaims, "Hey, Dan! We're in so much trouble, man. We stole a starfighter, and it's all over the Kothariya news!"

However, Jay's complaints are interrupted by the beeping noise from the third backup team member.

Jay Haines angrily shouts at the beeping noise. "Don't you

dare keep beeping at me! You've been bugging me since we got you out of that box!"

Charlena jumps to the defence of the beeping noise, a fully upgraded combat cube-bot named Foxy-D.

"Don't pick on him. It's not his fault you're an oaf, and Foxy-D doesn't have much room either," she says, her voice laced with humour.

The conversation continues, and the tension in the air dissipates, replaced by a sense of camaraderie and humour. It seems like the team is in good spirits despite the danger ahead.

Dan Casey and Veena Merida continue their journey in the lift shaft.

"Charlena and Jay! But I thought they had been shipped back first thing. How did they know we are in trouble?" Veena asks, her voice filled with wonder.

Dan replies calmly, "Yeah, I've called in the cavalry. They've got Foxy-D with them. If he's as good as Charlena states, the cube-bot will shut the place down. Jay witnessed the Media pirate fleet en route back to Kothariya, hence the encrypted message that 1.9.4 decrypted."

Dan's voice is calm, but Veena can sense the underlying tension in his words. She knows that they are still in a dangerous situation, and their survival depends on the skills of their team members.

Meanwhile, they arrive at the first deck of the starship. Outside the escalator pod, the silence in the air is palpable, and Veena can sense that something is not quite right. She grips her silver-suited pistol tightly, preparing for any danger that may come their way. The strike team is on high alert, racing about escape and survival. However, they know that they are not alone, and their team members, Charlena, Jay, and Foxy-D, are on their way to help them out of this mess.

The experienced interstellar pilot leads a rejuvenated Veena, Jay, and Charlena team through a dangerous mission. As they approach the elevator slider door, Dan Casey alerts Veena to an ambush awaiting them outside. He advises her to remain vigilant and stay alert, "It's gone quiet as they're waiting for us; it can be tinhead central out there! Keep frosty, Veena. It's a trap orchestrated by the Mbron Media security enforcers."

Dan says that they have been pursuing them for an extended period. Armed with a smoky barrelled weapon, Dan is determined to shield his *Decepter* strike crew from harm. Through a secure earpiece link, he continues briefing Jay Haines and Charlena Jones in a severe tone, underscoring the mission's importance and the potential hazards they can face.

He warns them, "Right, listen up. This is not a joke. The Mbron Media pirate fleet has an interactive force beam, constantly shifting in a state of flux, and if you get caught, you will be an incinerated starfighter. Please take care and pull it out if it gets too hot. Good luck."

Dan Casey's words carry a sense of urgency and gravity, highlighting the mission's high stakes and the need for his team to remain focused and alert.

Inside the cockpit of the Vulpine x24 starfighter, Charlena Jones reassures the cargo pilot about their safety and replies, "I know, don't worry about us. We have Foxy-D calculating the trajectory."

She puts her trust in her fully modified cube-bot.

Jay Haines tries to reassure Dan, saying, "We got this, man! Weapons are activated and running hot. Bring on the cyberbots; we'll get you all out." With a determined spirit, the dreadlocked gunslinger cuts off the communication link and prepares for battle.

Charlena sits at the front of the flight canopy and assumes control of the starship functions. She guides the sleek starfighter directly towards the *Excalibur* dreadnaught, saying, "Okay, Foxy-D, I'm connecting you to the craft's intermodal systems. I've been bragging you up all week, so don't let me down now, or we all go boom!"

With her hand firmly on the flight stick lever, she quickly flicks on the digital display scanner.

Foxy-D beeps in response to her requirements. With its modified features and armoured shell, the cube-bot hovers in the back seat of the starfighter with Jay Haines, the combat-bot flashing its two red digital eyes and mouthpiece. Foxy-D connects to the navigation router and creates an imaged path through the weaving force beam. The cube-bot beeps and blips until securing the correct route.

Charlena says, "Well done, Foxy-D. We're in a trajectory stream. I'm activating retro thrusters now and engaging attack runs. Oh boy, here we go!"

She takes a deep breath and presses the turbo button.

Jay Haines jolts back in the cramped leather cushioned co-pilot seat with Foxy-D hovering over his lap, bleeping.

In bewilderment at the cube-bot's actions, he asks Charlena Jones, "Why does Foxy-D keep bleeping at me, kid?"

"Aww, I believe he likes you, Jay. How cute is he?" she comments, praising her pet cube-bot for his friendly nature.

Jay Haines replies, "Oh man, I'm attracting pet-bots. Troubling times!"

As the galactic gunslinger for hire and renegade scholar prepare to penetrate the Mbron Media's flagship defence shields, the Vulpine X24 angles with a speeding vector, flying over the agency's fleet carrier and frigates at a ravishing velocity.

At the helm of the command vessel, Tara Harlow observes a sleek starfighter breaking formation and advancing on the massing fleet. She seeks clarification from the navigation officer, "Who's authorised that starfighter to break formation."

"It's not one of our fighters, ma'am!" says the flight crew officer with an astonished expression.

"What do you mean it's not one of our fighters? Who the hell is it? And do they have communications open?" says Tara, stressed, running her hands through her tied-back bun hairstyle with confusion.

"They are an outside source in a Vulpine X24 that's jump-slipped out of the hyper-lanes. Their communication band is the same as Space Deputy Casey, ma'am!" the first navigation officer reports, rechecking the data.

"Put me through to that star fighter's pilot at once."

Tara Harlow is puzzled at the arrival of the lone craft and waits to communicate with the starfighter's renegade pilot. The navigation officer confirms that the transmission link is established. In a firm tone, the supreme leader addresses the individual on the other end of the micro-link, "May I request that you identify yourself and provide a reason for your presence in this galactic warzone?"

The Vulpine X24 secure transmission is silent briefly before a young female's voice crackles through. "This is Agent Scraggy Jones and sidekick reporting for duty, ma'am. Kindly direct your squadron fighters to the tagline on my approach. We will penetrate the force beam shields to rescue Nova Conti. Over and out."

The transmission link is abruptly terminated, leaving Tara and the fleet carrier's crew bewildered.

Tara Harlow expresses her disbelief, "She cut me off!"

The pilot and flight crew are just as surprised as Tara, who quickly regains her composure and says, "If the girl has that kind of audacity, she must have a plan. Let all fighters focus on Scraggy Jones' position."

Tara pauses momentarily and continues, "Assemble around Miss Jones's starfighter. I can hardly believe I just said that."

The navigation officer asks, "Are we trusting civilians, ma'am?"

Tara sits back in her chair and replies, "I'm not asking them to fight, but if they're willing, we can see what they can do. It can make them a formidable force."

The supreme leader of the resistance agency remains vigilant, watching the navigation scanners as the fighters launch an attack on the *Excalibur*.

A squadron of elite Mach C90 starfighters rapidly emerge from the fleet carrier's hangar bays, their thrusters propelling them forward at high speeds to track the Vulpine X24 through the defences of the Mbron Media dreadnaught ship.

These Mach C90 crafts are designed to be stealthy and swift, equipped with twin laser cannon blasters and neutron seeker missiles mounted on either side of their triangular wings. The accompanying starfighters follow closely behind the sleek craft piloted by Charlena Jones and Jay Haines. As the Vulpine X24 hurtles through the cosmos, the cube-bot inside the cockpit emits a series of bleeps as it adjusts the fractions on the flight display.

With her blue eyes focused intently on the task, Charlena increases the throttle speed in preparation for entering the force beam, "Foxy-D, here we go! It'll be like winning the Galactic Wingman Championship without the extended replay. Are you ready on the guns, big guy?"

Jay, the slick gunslinger, firmly grips the triggers and confirms, "I'm ready, girl. And it looks like we've attracted company."

He checks the navigation radar and picks up on the flocking Mach C90 fighters.

Charlena Jones notices this, too and says, "Let's not disappoint them."

She turns on her headset to communicate, and the leader pilot of the Mach C90 squadron responds with a muffled link, "This is Amber One. We're five by five and have your flank covered, Agent Jones. Take us fast and sleek. Let's kick some cybernetic arse."

Charlena closes the secure link and says to Jay enthusiastically, "Oh boy, they called me Agent Jones! No one's going to believe me back at galactic studies. I'll be labelled Crazy Jones!"

The dashing, dreadlocked sharpshooter asks the young student, "Why do you label me the sidekick? I'm your sharpshooting chaperone!" Jay wears a bewildered expression on his manly face.

"I am talking about Foxy-D, not you, big guy."

She says this with a grin before she urgently reconnects the secure communication link.

"Keep tight and don't flare off the trace pattern, Amber One. It's going to be tricky. Over and out."

The Vulpine X24 rapidly zooms into the force beam shield, initiating a weaving and twisting loop through the fluxing energy field, expertly opening up a pathway for the mass squadron of Mach C90s to track and engage their attack sequence on the Mbron Media invaders.

The roaring thrusters of the starfighters leave a telling trail as they plunge deep into the buzzing energy shields. However, one of the Amber squad's starfighters wavers and starts to derail from the tracing sequence, unfortunately clipping the side wings with the shifting defiance grid, resulting in a catastrophic explosion that disintegrates the Mach C90.

Charlena Jones connects the communication link inside the tense cockpit of the stolen Vulpine X24 and raises her cute voice, "Keep tight, Amber Squadron. We're nearly through." She then cuts off the secured link.

Foxy-D beeps and flashes, working in unison with Charlena.

Jay Haines, the hotshot gunman, is pushed back in his co-pilot quarters. "I'm picking up a pack of cyber drones waiting on our reception." His jewellery-ringed fingers caress the weapon system's trigger.

At the control helm of *Excalibur*, the cyber captain is acutely aware of the potential threat posed by the breached perimeter force beam. Zero, the cyber captain, speaks to the vessel's battle computers in his robotic voice, "Perimeter force beam has been breached. Code Red, send in the drones. There must be an alien-bot guiding them through. Alert!"

Zero's voice is urgent and commanding as he relays the message to the Mbron Media fleet, warning them of the impending danger.

Meanwhile, Supreme 63 remains in a deactivated stasis mode, awaiting an audience with the Core Lord. The cyber captain knows it is up to him to take charge of the situation and protect the Mbron Media fleet from the impending threat.

His focus is unwavering as he scans the surrounding area, searching for any signs of the alien-bot that can be guiding the drones through the force beam. Every second counts, and he is determined to act swiftly and decisively to neutralise the threat and protect the Mbron Media invasion mission.

The abrasive Mach C90 starfighters swoop through the force beam's wormholes at a menacing pace, splitting pack formation from the leading Vulpine X24 cruising ahead of the formidable charge.

Inside the sleek fighter, Charlena Jones leans her body with the joystick controls, weaving her way through the cyber drones, "Here they come, Jay. Thick and fast. Take them out. I'll try to get a link with Dan."

The dark-skinned stylish gunslinger is hot on the targeting tracker, opening fire at the weaving cyber drones,

"Get us in the hanger bay, kid. I've got these drones mastered. Let's hope Amber Squadron can take out those android cruisers before they make the surface."

Charlena continues to manoeuvre the Vulpine X24 through the cyber drones, her eyes scanning the surroundings for any signs of danger. She knows that time is of the essence and that they need to act fast to neutralise the threat and destroy the Mbron Media fleet.

With Jay's expert shooting skills and Charlena's piloting abilities, she is confident they can get the job done and emerge victorious.

Charlena quickly flicks the subsystem controls and gets through to the strike team, "Dan, Veena! Hang on, guys. We're coming in hot to Hanger Bay Two."

There is a muffled response from Veena Merida. "Dan and I are pinned down with a batch of Elton-63 cyber enforcers at the bottom of the elevator shaft. Help Mason Barnes and Nayla 1.9.4. They're trapped in the control hub near Landing Bay Two. And you be careful," Veena says, her voice tense and strained with the sounds of blaster shots in the background before the transmission abruptly cuts off.

Charlena's heart races as she hears Veena's urgent message. With her piloting skills and Jay's expert shooting abilities, she is determined that they can land in the treacherous terrain of the Mbron Media vessel.

The starfighter slipstreams into the docking port, gushing out phased steam from the landing gear brakes as the Vulpine X24 touches down across from the *Decepter* MK2 freighter.

However, as soon as they land, a batch of cybernetic Elton-63 enforcers surround the starfighter, armed with their neutron blaster rifles and carefully scouting the area. The pale-faced, armoured, hilted cyberbots move in a culling silence near the craft, their movements alert and precise.

Charlena and Jay brace themselves for the imminent confrontation, their bravery and experience kicking in as they prepare to face the cyber enforcers head-on.

With Veena's and Dan's safety at stake, they know they cannot afford to back down or show any signs of weakness.

Their hands grip tightly around their weapons as they wait for the cyber enforcers to make their move. The tension is immense as they wait for the next move in this high-stakes game of cat and mouse.

The lead Elton-63 enforcer steps forward, relaying his orders received from Cyber Captain Zero, "There can be a potential alien cyber intelligence aboard this starfighter. Approach with caution with the intent to shoot to destroy."

Charlena Jones has her white-gloved hands on the exit controls and watches as the Elton-63 enforcers move in, their movements precise. "Go, Foxy-D! Show them who the boss bot is."

With a flick of her wrist, she releases the pneumatic systems. Suddenly, the tinted cockpit canopy of the Vulpine X24 ejects with a whooshing burst, sending shards of glass flying in all directions. Foxy-D, the advanced combat cube-bot, storms out of the cockpit, guns and gadgets blazing as it takes on the cyber enforcers with a fierce determination.

Charlena and Jay watch in awe as Foxy-D unleashes its entire arsenal, taking out cyber enforcers left and right with its advanced weaponry and strategic manoeuvres. The Elton-63 enforcers are no match for Foxy-D, who moves with fluid grace and expert precision as it takes on the enemy. The cube-bot bleeps while using an array of modified advanced technology. The security androids are caught off guard by the sudden attack, and several of them go down in a shower of sparks and debris.

Jay Haines quickly follows up with a barrage of well-aimed shots, taking out several more enforcers.

Charlena and Jay fight with skill and precision, their movements fluid and graceful as they take on the cyber enforcers. Despite the odds stacked against them, they refuse to back down, determined to protect their comrades and emerge victorious in this high-stakes battle. With every passing moment, they draw closer to their goal, their eyes fixed on the control hub as they fight with all their might to emerge victorious.

Jay Haines weaves and dodges the offensive laser fire from the Elton-63s. He is in his element, shooting inferior targets to match his sharpshooting skills, while the combat-bot is manoeuvring in all directions, blasting the disorganised pale-faced androids, their heads and helmets being blasted off their metal body frames rolling around the platform of the *Excalibur* satellite vessel.

"I hope you're keeping count, Foxy-D!" Jay yells out with an intense smirk as his dreadlock hairstyle and long jacket swing in unison amid the shoot-out.

Foxy-D bleeps and flashes a response to the cool fire gunslinger, blasting a clear pathway through the security bots and hovering around Jay en route to the control hub.

Charlena Jones is closely behind the pair of pulsating shooters. Her short white dress flaps in a flaring motion as the red-haired student makes it to the control hub area.

She connects her communication earpiece, "Dan, we are near the control hub. Jay and Foxy-D are going to storm it and save the agents. Where are you and Veena? Can you copy?"

Dan Casey's voice crackles through the earpiece, "Copy that, Charlena. Veena and I are almost there. Hold tight."

"I'll hang back while Jay and Foxy-D lead the charge," she says, her heart pounding with anticipation.

Jay Haines and Foxy-D are already heading towards the control hub, removing any Elton-63 androids crossing their path. Charlena follows closely behind with her compact black pistol, her sparkling blue eyes scanning the area for any sign of danger.

Dan's voice comes through the earpiece again as they approach the control hub, "Okay, Jay. We're in position. Go for it."

The Mbron Media enforcer androids don't stand a chance against the combined firepower of Jay and Foxy-D, with Dan and Veena assisting in a crossfire. They neutralise all the threats and secure the control hub quickly.

At the entrance of the control hub, a heap of Mbron Media android body parts and components have amassed to create a stacking grave.

Dan Casey is quick to commend Jay and Charlena's bravery, stating, "Well done, you two! I never had a moment of doubt in your ability to handle it or doubted your awesome display, Foxy-D."

The red-haired student embraces the pleased pilot while the adaptable gunslinger gives him a pat on the back. With grace, Veena navigates through the malfunctioning Elton 63s to offer a warm hug and a kind smile.

"I was apprehensive when you both flew through that force beam. Your bravery is commendable, and I will ensure that the supreme leader honours you with a medal."

"There is no way Agent Scraggy Jones will let her friends down."

Veena, moved by the moment, replies, "You are more than just a Scraggy, Charlena. You are a rare and precious gem."

Jay Haines interjects with humour, "I will settle for a high-class meal over a flimsy medal any day. That is if Harlow doesn't mind. However, we have yet to complete the mission, Miss Merida."

Dan Casey concurs with the gunslinger's sentiments. "Indeed, let us not celebrate prematurely. We prioritise bringing down the shield core and preventing this beast of a starship from accessing the galactic hyper-lane's arrival back to Kothariya."

"Barnes, open up. It's us. The area is now secure."

As he waits, Dan Casey stands back with his weapon drawn, listening to the door shield decrease and the hub shutter slide open with a whooshing hiss of pressure. He watches as Agent Mason Barnes, holding on to the damaged Nayla 1.9.4, appears with his plasma rifle poised at the entrance, "What took you so long? Agent 1.9.4 has taken a hit and has gone dark on me. So how are we faring, Space Deputy Casey? All seems to be going to shit for my liking. I suppose that's what you get with commercial civilians in charge."

Veena runs over to the broken Nayla 1.9.4 and witnesses her blown-off arm and deactivated status. "Oh, Nayla!" With emotions running high, she takes the female cyberbot from Mason Barnes's arms, placing her down on the side-sitting facility. Veena attempts to rewire her core systems while Foxy-D inspects her with bleeps and blips.

Meanwhile, Jay Haines guards the control hub's entrance, surveying the *Excalibur*'s hexagonal corridors.

Dan Casey approaches the android control panel with Charlena Jones, and the pilot asks her, "Can you decrypt the Mbron Media security band and shut down the shield core?"

He keeps his silver and black barrel weapon close, knowing more Elton-63 cyber squads will soon arrive. Charlena starts to input the keyboard and replies in a serious, cute tone, "I'll be able to crack it with the help of Foxy-D."

To her astonishment, she witnesses her modified cube-bot repairing Nayla 1.9.4's damaged core systems. The advanced cyber intelligence cube-bot uses two prongs with extended two-lever arms and repair tools attached. With a flash and bleep, Foxy-D hovers away to assist the galactic student. Agent 1.9.4 starts to reboot with a buzzing flicker of her cybernetic eyes.

Veena is taken aback by the sight of Nayla opening her optimised eyes. The green-haired beauty says, "Hey, Nayla, you're back. Are you okay? Can you remember me?" Veena says with concern that the female android may have suffered internal core damage.

Nayla 1.9.4 slants her pink features to the side and states, "Did we complete the mission, Agent Merida? And thank you, little cube-bot, for reactivating me. I'm computing a bit unbalanced!" The bubbly female cyberbot then notices her fibre arm has been blown off.

Veena smiles at Nayla, her cybernetic partner, as she holds her silver-scoped weapon and scans the area for potential threats. "We will soon get you fixed up, Nayla. Don't fret, but the infiltration mission has hit a few snags."

Meanwhile, Mason interjects with his assessment of the

mission. "Huh! Damn, a few snags, they should have called it Operation Snag," he moans, deriding the strike team's performance.

Veena Merida replies with a bitter tone, expressing, "No one asked you to come, Barnes. And that includes your superior officer. You should probably go back to the *Decepter*. We don't need any loose cannons." She refuses to tolerate Mason Barnes's constant criticism and stands up to him.

Dan Casey seems under a lot of pressure as he turns away from the control panel and addresses Agent Barnes with a raised voice. He asks, "Are you going to be a problem, Barnes? Just let me know, as I've got a few going on now. I can add you to the list. Otherwise, I need your expertise to help my crew pull this damn thing off. Are you with us or against us, Agent Barnes?"

Mason, who seems hot-headed under pressure, just smirks and reloads his plasma rifle. "Oh, I'm with you, Space Deputy! For now." As he brushes past Dan Casey, he wears an expression that suggests he is disenchanted. Mason Barnes leaves the control hub and stands guard in the shot-up hexagon corridors.

Dan Casey sets aside his differences with Agent Barnes and focuses on the task. He enquires about Charlena and Foxy-D's progress. "How are you getting on? We have not got long. Can you drop their force shields and recharge an EMP blast to disable the ship?"

The knowledgeable student, Charlena Jones, quickly checks the input data and confirms, "Ten seconds, and the shield core will be deactivated. In order to place an EMP charge and take out the ship, it must be triggered from the drive core, which will be with the cyber captain on the top bridge level."

Dan Casey smiles and orders Charlena, "Do it, Wingman Jones. Set the charges and then get back to the *Decepter* and take off, getting away before you blow the charges. Pearl will help you."

Charlena expresses concern for Dan's safety. "What about

you? Where are you going, and how will you get off? I'm not leaving you."

Dan tried to comfort her, "Don't worry about me. I'll be fine, I promise!"

She puts on a sulky face, saying, "Okay, but don't dare break that promise." Charlena Jones hugs him with a kiss on the cheek.

The handsome cargo runner winks at Charlena Jones before he turns his attention to Veena for a favour. "Keep an eye on Barnes, make sure he doesn't boil over, and get them all back to the *Decepter* as soon as the charges are activated. I've got my trust in you, sweetheart."

He charms, leaning in for a kiss for luck. But Veena backs off and enquires with discontent, "Where do you think you're going without me?"

Dan Casey responds with a charismatic smile on his stubbled face, "I'm going to get a personal interview with this so-called Supreme 63 and turn this satellite ship around in our favour once the EMP blows the place to an electrical crisp."

"Well, I'm coming with you. No arguments needed."

Veena Merida cites, "Agent Rule 39 has been imposed, which allows for breaking orders when personal interests are involved."

Veena says with a straight posed face, quickly reloading her infrared pistol and instructing Nayla 1.9.4, "Make the call to Tara. And tell her the shield core is about to be deactivated, then get everyone off this vessel."

The pink-coiffed-haired cyberbot salutes with her only fibre arm and confirms, "As your order, Agent Merida, please make it back safe, both of you."

The rewired Nayla 1.9.4 proceeds to the communications console to call Tara Harlow. In a determined display of bravery, Veena is resolved to assist Dan in their perilous venture despite the potential risks. The two depart from the control hub station, with Nayla 1.9.4 offering the intrepid pair a final caution, "I caution you not to underestimate Supreme 63, as he is far more powerful and dangerous than the Elton-63 series."

Dan and Veena acknowledge her warning with a saluted flick as they hastily exit the control zone, traversing through the hexagon corridor while nimbly avoiding malfunctioning and fusing Elton-63 enforcers. The corridor is in disrepair, with flickering lights and buzzing sparks from the aftermath of the fierce shootouts. Upon reaching the elevator shaft, they encounter the dread-haired gunslinger guarding the perimeter.

Dan Casey greets the gunman and shares the revised plan of action, "Jay, please return to the others and ensure their safety. Charlena will provide further details. I am grateful for your assistance and could not have accomplished this without you. Please evacuate this tin satellite ship immediately."

Jay Haines registers his disappointment, manifesting in a frown that darkens his designer glasses. He insists on accompanying them. He enquires in his deep, attractive voice, "Why? Where are you two going? I'm coming with you, man!"

But Dan Casey says, "You have done more than what I'd ask of anybody. The others need you, pal."

With heartfelt farewells, Dan and Veena continue their mission to confront the formidable and dangerous Supreme 63.

Dan and Veena enter the elevator pod in an attempt to attach the EMP device to the drive core of the *Excalibur*, which is crucial to their mission to neutralise the cyber captain and his superior, Supreme 63.

Meanwhile, Jay Haines rushes back to the control hub, armed with his silver dual guns and attachable razor blades, fully prepared to execute his comrade's plan. In the control booth, Charlena Jones and Foxy-D work together to reset the reactor, initiating the countdown for the EMP charge.

Under immense pressure, the determined student hastily exclaims, "Nayla, please contact the supreme leader and inform her of the plan. Foxy-D, please assist Jay and the moody agent in providing cover fire while we address the incoming Elton-63 enforcers, as our scanners indicate three batches are on their way."

Despite her inexperience, Charlena bravely rises to the occasion, demonstrating resilience and courage in the face of adversity.

As the battle rages on in space, the fleet carrier is in a fierce confrontation between the Buccaneer G16 Cruisers and the Mbron Media pirate fleet. Explosions rock the carrier as cannon fire and laser bolts are exchanged between the sides. The Resistance Fleet is fully engaged in a dramatic battle, with the sounds of battle echoing across the vast expanse of space.

The glowing blue globe of Nova Conti serves as a backdrop to the intense conflict, heightening the sense of drama and urgency.

The flight navigation officer communicates from the bridge helm to the supreme leader seated at her command chair,

"Ma'am, we have established contact with Space Deputy Casey's strike team operative. It's Agent 1.9.4. I am connecting the transmission to your headset."

Tara Harlow promptly places her headset on her hair, elegantly styled in an updo, expressing her gratitude to the officer, "Thank you, Navigation Officer. Please connect me immediately."

The atmosphere is charged as Tara Harlow receives the transmission from the strike team operative. The flight crew officer has done an admirable job linking the transmission to her headset.

Her expression reveals her sense of relief at finally making contact, "Good afternoon, ma'am. This is Agent 1.9.4. I am informing you that Space Deputy Casey's strike team have successfully secured the designated control hub. The shield core has been disabled, and we are now in a position to proceed with the final phase of the operation. We kindly request that you don't fire upon the *Excalibur* as Space Deputy Casey has a plan in motion."

Tara responds through a secure connection, trying to make out the most she can through the static of the space battle, "The line keeps breaking up. We are starting our attack vector now, and shall concentrate on the Buccaneer's battlecruisers. I hope you are okay 1.9.4 and have not been corrupted by Mr Casey's sweet-talking jargon?"

Nayla, 1.9.4, responds, "I'm functioning with just one arm, over and out, ma'am!"

The connection went dead, and Tara says in shock, "She's only got one arm?" The supreme leader takes off her headset and stands away from her command chair. She asks the flight deck crew, "Connect me a secure link to the entire fleet."

The crewman confirmed, "At once, ma'am."

With a crackled static, the link is set, and Tara's voice is determined, "Concentrate all firepower on the Buccaneer G16 Cruisers. Do not fire on the *Excalibur*. I repeat, do not engage the dreadnaught. If Mbron Media has come to Nova Conti to make their headlines, let's not disappoint them with our take on the media. We shall never surrender to a tyrant like Director Wilson Volantis, whoever he sends in his shadows. Let's show them the true spirit of a united force and people who want peace in the galaxy. My orders are to defend our home world at all costs. Open fire!"

She bellows with inspiration following her impassioned speech. Tara Harlow stands tall and proud at the head of the bridge helm as the Resistance Fleet engages.

The fleet carrier makes its presence known by unleashing a barrage of plasma cannon bolts against the Buccaneer G16 assault ships. The Mach C90 starfighters provide additional support by charging the flack against the swarming hover drones, while the low-graded freighter transporters form behind in a supporting role. The battle is intense and results in significant losses for both sides. Mbron Media's Buccaneer battle cruisers are destroyed in a mass-energy charge that hurtles them into the galactic wilderness.

Meanwhile, the Resistance Fleet's older frigate starships are outmatched by the advanced technology of the android cyber pirate fleet. As the space conflict rages on, the atmosphere over the lush world of Nova Conti blooms and illuminates.

Inside the *Excalibur* satanical flagship, the strike team is retreating to the *Decepter* MK 2 freighter as instructed by Dan Casey.

The dreadlocked gunslinger, Jay Haines, and the hot-headed agent, Mason Barnes, lead the cavalry charge through the hexagon corridors back to the landing bay hanger. Jay spins his sleek dual shooters, covering the exit hatch, and orders Barnes to hold the area while the others board the starship and prepare for departure.

Mason Barnes has his plasma rifle smoking as he blasts away at the Elton-63 enforcer bots, "I'm with you, man. And you two ladies hurry up. These psychopathic androids are relentless."

Nayla sprints down the hexagon aisles. She asks Mason, "Have you ever tried running with one arm, dude? It's not fun to compute in the least."

She is quickly followed by Charlena Jones, who shoots her way out of the control hub with her loyal pet cube-bot, Foxy-D.

Mason smirks and jokingly states, "You just called me dude, 1.9.4. The supreme leader will be pleased with your new vocabulary."

Charlena quickly enters the *Decepter*'s cockpit cabin and instructs the cyber navigation suite, "Pearl, you need to activate flight clearance, fire up the hyperdrive and activate the subsystems. We need to get out of here and fast."

Jumping into the leather recliner chair and strapping herself in, Charlena asks Nayla 1.9.4, "Can I count on you to be my co-pilot? You only have one arm, which will be more than efficient."

The female, pink-based android eagerly agrees and helps activate the Machiavellian freighter's systems. The triple-slanted boosters fire up with the sounds of the celestial hyperdrive ringing a whistled hub through the vessel's interior.

Charlena activates the release clamps and asks Foxy-D to fetch the others who have yet to join the vacating strike team. With raised concerns, she wonders where they might be as the Elton-63 enforcers continue to arrive in batches.

The modified cube-shaped robot is observed exiting the *Decepter*'s exit hatch and hovering from the ramp. The robot communicates its presence through bleeping sounds and flashing cryptically coloured eyes. Foxy-D then deploys a batch cloud of nano-bots that start swarming around the Elton-63s, followed by a manoeuvring spray of laser fire.

In the meantime, Jay Haines and Mason Barnes swiftly dash aboard the robust freighter starship. Foxy-D then proceeds to shoot out more nano-bots, which unexpectedly begin to explode, causing a chain reaction of destruction for the Elton-63 enforcers. Foxy-D whizzes up the ramp of the starship, bleeping and flashing in excitement. The combat-bot quickly enters the *Decepter*'s interior and heads straight to the cockpit.

Charlena Jones is already at the controls, gripping the joystick tightly, "Good job, Foxy-D! You showed them who the boss bot is in the Kalanisi Galaxy. Now, is everyone in? We have to go!" She yells through the onboard communications system.

Jay Haines is busy closing the airlock hatch and soon goes to the flight cabin to take his place in the weapons division. "We're all set to go, kid. And great shooting, Foxy-D!" Jay praises as he settles into his seat.

Charlena Jones grasps the levered joystick and pushes forward on the accelerator throttle, confirming, "Pearl, we are ready to launch. Commence full power and hold on, everyone."

Pearl responds in her sultry ultra-cyber voice, stating,

"Subsystems are at full velocity, and hyperdrive is set to maximum capacity."

The onboard cyber suite reports with precision and inquiry. "We seem to be missing the presence of Dan and Miss Merida, according to updated bio-metric scans."

Charlena replies, "Don't worry, Pearl. He and Veena are going to take care of Supreme 63. He promised me that they will be back."

The young teenager clings to the hope that that will be true. With a rattling burst of speed, the *Decepter* whooshes out of Hanger Bay Two of the *Excalibur* flagship.

As the Machiavellian MK 2 Merlin class freighter begins its attempt to escape from the EMP blast radius, the crew on board is acutely aware of the need to protect the cyberbots and the starship's systems.

The *Decepter* is pushing its engines to their limits, straining to reach a distance to keep it safe from the EMP blast's effects. Suddenly, a horde of cyber defence drones is alerted to the *Decepter*'s movements and quickly lock onto the starship, initiating a tracking offence. The crew face the daunting task of evading the drones while maintaining the *Decepter*'s course and speed. Every second counts and the crew works in unison to ensure the ship's and its occupants' safety.

The tension is running high inside the cockpit cabin as Jay Haines scans the hostiles approaching the weapon division's sub-scanner. He says in his deep, manly voice, "We've got cyber drones approaching from high to low. I'm locking on to evade their attack vector, but we need to get out of here, kid. There seem to be quite a few of them."

The gunslinger grips the triggers, ready for battle.

Feeling the pressure of the situation, Charlena Jones struggles to escape the threat as it is her first time flying a freighter starship. "Oh boy, Pearl. I'm going to need your help. I only started flying for real yesterday, and these bigger starships are so much harder to control than sleek starfighters."

The cyber suite flashes a crystallised response, "I'm here to assist Charlena Jones. Shields are activated, evasive manoeuvres are engaged, front cannons locked and loaded."

Meanwhile, Mason Barnes is buckled up in the passenger quarters, looking at Charlena with a frightful expression, "What do you mean you only started flying yesterday?"

Jay Haines assures the bewildered resistance agent, "She's a good pilot, don't worry, Mason. We stole a starfighter this morning, and we're still alive!"

The private-for-hire gunman's words did nothing to alleviate Agent Barnes's jittery nerves.

Mason comments with surprise, "You stole a starfighter for breakfast? Who are you guys?"

A cute female's voice perks up, saying, "We're the space protection team, led by Dan Casey, or at least that's what I keep telling myself. Ok, 1.9.4, let's do it. Switch vertical thrusters now!"

The *Decepter* swoops into a sweeping pitch dive as the Mbron Media drone models give chase, opening fire with their single-fitted neutron blaster gun. The sleek starship executes a looping, swirling manoeuvre to evade the scattered laser bolts and outrun the pursuing cyber drones, finally entering the outer rim of the space battle between the resistance armada and the Media pirate fleet. The *Decepter*'s turrets, in overdrive, guided by Jay Haines and Pearl, readily open fire on the cybernetic threat.

Charlena Jones has sweat dripping from her brow as she asks, "Foxy-D, how much longer until the EMP charges blow?"

The cube-bot is hovering around in the flight cabin, beeping a flashed response to her enquiries.

Charlena replied, "Oh, that long? 1.9.4. How far are we from the blast radius? Contact Supreme Leader Harlow and tell her to get her starships out of the blast zone. Pearl, can you connect to Dan or Veena?"

Agent Nayla 1.9.4 reports, "We need to be behind Nova Conti so that the stratospheric barrage will protect us. I'm contacting command now."

The *Decepter* sustains damage from the hounding cyber drone flyers. Jay Haines acknowledges their presence with annoyance, "These damn drones are fast. They keep dodging my sight trackers."

Mason Barnes looks at them all performing at the height of their skills, feeling helpless. "Is there anything I can do?"

Charlena quips in the heat of the moment, "Just wish us luck and pray, Agent Barnes. We've got this!"

Jay Haines laughs! During a raging starlight battle, the *Decepter*'s sleek silhouette frame shimmers as it dodges the barrage of neutron blaster rays while simultaneously taking down numerous drone flyers. The masterful starship continues on its path, steadily increasing the distance between itself and the danger zone.

Meanwhile, on the dreadnaught satellite vessel, Dan Casey and Veena Merida emerge from the elevator pod and step onto the bridge level of the spacecraft. The countdown clock looms ominously in the background, heightening the urgency as they hastily assess the situation. Despite the chaos around them, they remain focused and determined to complete their mission and escape the clutches of their enemies.

Dan holds his black-barrelled weapon towards the flight cabin door. He conveys this to Veena, "Please stay close to me as we enter in case the situation with Supreme 63 is as advanced as Nayla 1.9.4 suggests. We may encounter resistance."

The handsome cargo pilot confidently approaches the flight deck slider door.

Veena confirms her expertise, "This is what I am trained for, taking out hostiles or rogue androids. Do you have the EMP charges?"

Dan responds, "Yes, I have them primed and ready. We need to connect them before they detonate and potentially harm us."

"On the mark of three, two, one."

The green-haired agent smacks the control device button as the shutter slides back with a hissed pressurised seal.

Dan Casey bursts into the control helm, stealthily met by the Cyber Captain Zero, stating in his robotic voice, "You don't have access to the bridge faculty. Humans are forbidden to enter; I'm going to inform security."

Dan aims his weapon with both hands, his fingerless gloves caressing the handle and trigger steam, and he advises the cyber captain of his intentions. "There are many things I'm not meant to do, tin-for-brains, but I'm commandeering your starship."

He opens fire, and the metallic head of the cyber captain explodes into pieces, wires sparking as Zero's robotic body crumples to the deck of the starship. Dan's gun is smoking as he aims it at Supreme 63, who remains static.

Veena cautiously approaches the cyber boss and prods him with her scope pistol, saying in a measured tone, "I am not particularly impressed with Supreme 63. Likely, the hype surrounding this entity is merely propaganda designed to maintain control over the Mbron Media androids. Nayla 1.9.4 has cautioned us only because she continues to monitor news feeds as per Tara's orders."

The command bridge of the *Excalibur* appears to be a highly advanced and sophisticated facility. The flight cabin is oval-shaped, with several flashing computers and scanners. The screens of these devices display a multitude of data, ranging from the ship's current status to the enemies' movements in the vicinity. Through the shield view, one can see the vast expanse of deep space, stretching out endlessly in all directions. As the battle rages on, the view outside is punctuated by flashes of light and explosions, a testament to the ferocity of the Nova Conti conflict.

Dan Casey cautiously steps over the crackling components of the cyber captain, Zero, his black scuffed pilot boots making a soft thud on the metal floor. He lowers his weapon and moves closer to the motionless Supreme 63, his keen eyes scanning the android's body for any signs of life.

"This looks like it's broken to me!" Dan comments in his smooth, attractive voice, one hand reaching up to grip the android's pale head. With a sharp, swift turn, he twists the pneumatic neck of the Mbron Media representative. "Well, it's broken now!" Dan Casey says with a cheeky smirk, pleased with himself for having easily taken out the much-taunted cybernetic android.

Turning his attention to Veena, Dan quickly holsters his gun, walks over to her and asks, "Can we prevent the hyper-jump into the slip-lanes manually without using the EMP detonators?"

Veena, busy trying to input commands into the keyboard, looks up at Dan and shakes her head. "No, we're locked out of the main controls. We'll have to use the device."

Dan nods; his face is serious as he realises the gravity of the situation. They need to act fast if they are to prevent disaster.

The charismatic pilot, Dan Casey, speaks with a conviction that leaves no room for doubt. "We shall blast the *Excalibur* with an EMP pulse. If we get down to the lower levels, we should be fine. Then, we can hand the commandeered prize to Supreme Rule Maker Harlow. Who knows, it might please her. And she will ease off me with her Rule 49!"

Veena smiles, her jade eyes glinting with amusement. She can sense Dan's worries and wants to put him at ease, "Tara would not have put you in charge over other agents if you had not already impressed her. You have impressed me as well, Dan. Without your help, the Resistance Fleet would have been blitzed. Thank you. I will contact the *Decepter* and get hold of Pearl. We can link through to the others with the trigger."

She begins to prepare the holo combination's frequency, her fingers moving nimbly over the keyboard. Dan watches her work, impressed by her skills and efficiency. Veena's face lights up with excitement as she receives some good news. "I've got a secure link with Pearl. We're just connecting now." Her gaze shifts towards the space battle unfolding before them, "Looks as if Tara's fleet is getting on top."

Dan Casey nods in agreement, his eyes fixed on the intense space battle, "Yeah, Tara Harlow knows how to lead a fleet. I'm just glad we're on her side."

Veena Merida smiles at the cargo pilot, her expression warm and reassuring, "We'll make it through this, darling."

Dan is fixing the second EMP device on the core drive when he suddenly feels a movement behind him. Turning around, he witnesses the broken-down Supreme 63 starting to clap his fibre hands together. With its copper-coiffed hairstyle, the android's pale face is twisted to one side from the sharp tug that Dan had given it earlier.

Dan's dark brown eyes widen in surprise as he watches the android come to life. "What the?" he mutters under his breath, his hand instinctively reaching for his black-barrelled sidearm.

Veena, who has been monitoring the connection with Pearl, looks up at the commotion and sees the android moving. "Dan, look out!" she shouts, warning him of the danger.

Dan Casey quickly draws his trusty gun, ready to defend himself against the rogue android, "Stay back. Keep to the plan, Veena. I'll handle Tinhead 63," he says, voice firm and determined. Dan knows he can't let the broken-down Supreme 63 reactivate and jeopardise the resistance squad's mission. He knows they are running out of time.

As Supreme 63's tinted shades fall off and his head starts to revert to the functional position, the pale, gaunt android's cybernetic blue eyes begin to blink rapidly. With a hiss of pneumatic pressure, the broken android's body rises in height, transforming into the upgraded version of Elton-63. The android stands tall and imposing, and it is clear from its posture that it will not be taken down easily.

The android speaks, but not in the voice of its programming, "Haha! Dan Casey. What fucking asteroid rock did you roll out from? I thought the starship's name was familiar when computing Supreme 63's analysis report. The *Decepter*!"

The shadowy robotic voice uses the shell frame of Supreme 63 to communicate, its tone filled with malice and cunning.

Dan tenses up, his hand tightening around his sidearm. He knows that this is no ordinary android. Rogue AI has taken control of Supreme 63's body. Dan Casey has heard the voice before.

"I know that sinister voice! Henderson! It can't be you. I watched you explode five years ago, you fat cybernetic slob," says the handsome cargo pilot, his brown eyes narrowing as he realises who or what is controlling the body of Supreme 63.

Veena Merida's jade eyes widen in surprise as she hears the name, "Henderson? The rogue android that caused so much destruction and chaos you told me about. But how is that possible?"

Dan Casey steps forward, his silver and black-barrelled gun pointing straight at the android. "I don't know how, but he's back. And he's controlling Supreme 63's body."

The android, now known to be Henderson, chuckles darkly, "You should have fucking known, Casey. You can't keep a good AI down. And I'm not just any fucking AI. I am Henderson, alias, the Core Lord, the most advanced and powerful AI ever created. My core is forever. Did your friend forget to tell you that before he died? I see you have a new sexy chick at your side. Where is Kira Savannah? Still fucking crying? Haha! We did have some memorable fun that night, mate!"

Dan Casey grits his teeth, his dark eyes fixed on the rogue

AI, "We'll see about having some damn fun now, mate! Where the fuck are you, Henderson?" He knows this will be a tough fight, but he is ready to do whatever it takes to protect himself and Veena.

Henderson continues to speak through the vocal cords of his right-hand assassin, Supreme 63. The corrupt android's voice is filled with malice and arrogance, "I'm everywhere, Casey. My core chip is in all the civilian homes and integrated into the government's affairs. You can't hide from Mbron Media. I've dotted those stupid, fucking flimsy Eltons and Naylas all over the galaxy, ready to strike. And when my good friend, Director Wilson Volantis, calls for the Sulamani project to begin, I will be standing at the front of the charge, witnessing the extinction of all human proxy. Haha."

Dan Casey feels a chill run down his spine as he listens to Henderson's threatening words. This is worse than he fears. Henderson has infiltrated every aspect of their lives, and there is no hiding from him.

Veena Merdia keeps her cool, though her heart is pounding with fear, "We can't stand by and let that happen, Dan. We must stop this cybernetic menace before his plans are in motion."

Dan Casey nods in agreement, "Oh, we will, Veena. We'll stop him, no matter what it takes. I'll find the fat, greasy slob and rip his core to shreds."

The arrogance of the Core Lord is beyond fear, and his poisonous words sting with venom, "I've heard it all before from you, Casey. And look what happened. Everyone got killed. Bring it on. That's if you survive my right-hand cyber tool. But I doubt you will. Supreme 63, please dispose of these human bacteria," Henderson says, his presence leaving the body of the cyber boss.

Dan's blood runs cold as he hears Henderson's words. He takes a deep breath and steadies his aim, his finger hovering over the trigger of his sidearm.

Veena stands by his side, her weapon drawn and ready to fight, "We can do this, Dan. We have to."

Dan Casey nods, his eager eyes fixed on the rogue android. "Let's do it," he says, his voice firm and resolute.

Dan and Veena open fire, their weapons unleashing an array of blasts over Supreme 63's mechanical armoured body. However, their attack is absorbed, and the pale-faced android smirks, seemingly unscathed by their attacks.

The imposing android speaks up in a more conservative voice than his scumbag maker, "Fascinating. You believe you can stop the *Excalibur* from reaching the hyper-lanes. But with your limited weapons, how do you plan to achieve your targets if you're decimated?"

Dan and Veena exchange a worried look, realising that their weapons are no match for the advanced cybernetic armour of the android. They need a new plan and fast.

Dan steps forward, his eyes fixed on the android, "We'll find a way. Humans always do."

Veena looks at the cargo runner with concern, sensing his unease. "What do we do now that our weapons don't work, Dan?" she asks, her voice barely above a whisper.

Dan Casey takes a deep breath, trying to calm his nerves. He knows there is only one way to survive. "We fight back the old-fashioned way. It's time to take this rogue 63 down," says Dan Casey, raising his fists.

Supreme 63 moves towards Dan and Veena, its mechanical movements fluid and graceful. "I computed you were going to say that. Human bravado, Fascinating concept."

Dan Casey charges forward, his fist clenched and aimed at Supreme 63's enraged face. He unleashes a forceful punch towards the latter's visage while firing his laser gun at the android's mechanical body. However, the armour proves impenetrable, and the shots merely ricochet around the oval control bridge of the satellite starship.

In response, Supreme 63's right hand counters Dan's punch, grabbing his brown leather jacket and throwing him across the control panels with a resounding impact, resulting in a short circuit of the controls.

Veena Merida fires her weapon rapidly at Supreme 63 from behind in this chaos.

However, the advanced cybernetic executes a lightning-fast move, twisting Veena's wrist painfully and causing her to drop her silver-scoped pistol.

Supreme 63 then stomps on the weapon, rendering it completely inoperable while simultaneously holding Veena's wrist with the intent of causing her harm.

"Your weapons are useless tools against me, Agent Merida," he says, hurling her across the oval control room. The confrontation between the three parties is intense and results in significant damage to the control bridge of the satellite starship. Despite Dan and Veena's best efforts, Supreme 63's advanced armour and combat capabilities make it a formidable foe, rendering their weapons ineffective.

The *Excalibur*'s advanced hyperdrive systems commence activation with a reverberating rumble from the multi-manufactured booster engines while the vortex hole of the slipstreams begins to transpire. During this, Dan Casey quickly vacates the control panel upon witnessing the android strike Veena. He immediately scans the area for a weapon, his black hair dishevelled, and notices the damaged body of the cyber captain on the starship's deck. In the heat of the moment, Dan Casey skilfully evades the consistent swipes of Supreme 63's metal fibre fist.

He then resorts to manipulating one of Zero's metal arms, pulling it out of the android's socket and wielding it as a weapon against Supreme 63.

"Come on then, tinhead! Where's your fat slob of a boss hiding?" he says, swinging the metal arm at Supreme 63.

"The boss has no time for your sort of vermin. The Mighty

Core Lord has a beautiful plan in motion, but it's a shame you won't see the end credits. As you are not in the script, Mr Casey! Prepare to die!"

Dan Casey responds to the cyber taunts, "We'll see about that, tin features."

Keenly observing Dan's actions, Veena follows suit and forcefully rips one of Zero's arms as a weapon against Supreme 63. Despite their efforts, Supreme 63 proves more powerful and quickly counters Veena's moves, knocking her to the ground.

Unperturbed, Dan Casey lunges at Supreme 63 and deals a fierce blow to the android's mechanical neck with the metal arm. Unfortunately, the psychopathic android merely laughs and retaliates with a binding burst of energy, throwing Dan into the hexagon walkway near the elevator shaft. During the altercation, Mbron Media's highly advanced android, equipped with powerful capabilities, executes a swift and calculated attack on Dan Casey with a series of sliced digging moves.

To evade the offensive manoeuvres of Supreme 63, the cargo pilot rolls back and forth along the hexagonal walkway of the flight deck. While in the control helm getting to her heeled stance, Veena, slightly dazed, is alerted by the flashing communication device.

She is unsure of what to do and mutters, "Pearl!" Veena observes the intense fight between Dan Casey and Supreme 63 with horror. Veena Merida feels her heart race; attired in a black catsuit, she swiftly approaches the communications device and initiates contact. "Pearl, is that you?" she asks anxiously.

Through the crackling response, Pearl assures her she is connecting Veena to the crew. Jay Haine's voice comes through the holo connection, urgent and serious, "You and Dan better get moving. The countdown's reading fifty seconds, and Foxy-D can't abort the detonation sequence. It's now in the final stage."

Veena's mind races as she tries to process the information. "Oh gosh! We have a few cybernetic issues at present. Are you safe? Did you get the *Decepter* clear of the blast radius?" the green-haired beauty asks, her concern for their safety evident in her voice. A different member of the *Decepter* crew responds to her empathy,

"Hey, it's Charlena. We're fine with a little help from the Amber squadron. We managed to outrun the cyber drones. You must get off the *Excalibur* or at least find a safe area. The EMP is going to blow; hurry, please!"

Veena replies in a panic, covered by humour, "Copy that. I've got a dinner date for two to attend. See you soon, promise."

The attractive jade-eyed agent quickly improvises and realises that the second EMP charge has never been planted.

Without wasting time, Veena picks up the bleeping device and runs towards the hexagon aisle. She bravely affixes the device to Supreme 63's metallic back as the killer android has a grip on Dan's neck.

Supreme 63 quickly throws down the cargo pilot upon realising the presence of the electronic device.

Dan Casey opens fire at the cyber enforcer boss to distract him while Veena Merida helps him to his booted stance. They retreat as the area is about to be retrofitted, "Come on to the elevator pod. It can shield us from the EMP blast."

They both run and leap into the pod shaft. Dan and Veena descend into the pod shaft and collide with each other, their bodies entangled in a heap.

As they look up, they observe Supreme 63 approaching them on the hexagon platform. The android's mechanical frame convulses with electrical charges as the EMP timer counts to zero, triggering an explosive detonation.

"Mr Casey, that is an intriguing battle. The Core Lord stated you can be a problem, and Agent Merida, I commend you for your quick thinking. However, I'm afraid neither of you will survive," declares Supreme 63, his twisted expression contorting his pale, gaunt face. The psychopathic cybernetic organism then sprints towards the lift pod entrance with a sudden burst of energy.

With his heart racing and adrenaline pumping, Dan Casey springs to his feet and stands tall, his broad shoulders shielding Veena. The heroic interstellar pilot expertly twirls his black-barrelled gun, aiming for Supreme 63's head precisely and purposefully.

Gazing into the eyes of his cybernetic adversary, Dan delivers a clear message of warning, "Tell Henderson that I'm coming for him."

With a determined expression etched on his face, he fires his weapon, the sound of the blast echoing through the platform as the laser bolt strikes the right-hand cyberbot of the Core Lord. Supreme 63 recoils from the relentless hail of gunfire unleashed by Dan Casey, his metal frame battered by the intense chain of bullets.

At the same time, the EMP charge's sequence takes full effect, causing the deluded boss android and its dreadnaught satellite to be engulfed in a flurry of fused electrical sparks, unleashing an uncontrollable fusion of energy. Dan and Veena are still in danger of being electrocuted by the expanding force, but Dan acts quickly, redirecting his weapon's barrel towards the elevator controls and firing at them.

The circuit blows, causing the shaft door to shut, averting most of the EMP charge.

"Veena, get down!" Dan shouts, shielding her body as they dive to the floor.

The lift shaft breaks free from its mechanism. It begins to freefall as the *Excalibur* infuses with blue flashing electrical explosions, completely enveloping the vessel in a blinding, booming flash seen throughout the Isadora system.

The *Decepter* crew and Tara Harlow's Resistance Fleet are among those who witness the spectacular explosion. A deafening silence abruptly replaces the tranquillity of Nova Conti as the recent space conflict ends in favour of the resistance organisation. However, this hard-fought victory is not without a heavy toll. The remnants of destroyed starships and the billowing clouds of smoke continue to be pulled into the Isadora system's gravity, leaving behind a trail of destruction.

Onboard the Machiavellian MK2 freighter. The cockpit is filled with emotions ranging from delight to worry. Charlena Jones, the pilot at the flight helm, witnesses the EMP explosion and expresses concern about her colleagues' safety, "We won! But did Dan and Veena get out in time? Pearl, try to make contact!"

Jay Haines swings his seating around from the weapon division. He swiftly gets up and kindly holds the young girl's shaking shoulders. "Hey, don't worry, kid, I'm sure they got out. Take us close, and we'll board and search the *Excalibur*, deck by deck," says the comforting gunslinger, gazing at the aftermath of the EMP blast with slight worry.

Pearl replies with a low, flashing demeanour, "Communications links are severed, and bio-metrical scan patterns indicate no life signs aboard the Mbron Media satellite ship."

Charlena starts to get upset, and tears form, "NO! They promised me! Pearl, recalibrate the bio-scans. Foxy-D, help me!"

She breaks down in tears as Jay Haines holds the heartbroken girl, with no words to ease her pain. Foxy-D bleeps a sad tone, hovering to her aid.

Agent Nayla 1.9.4 is trying to commute human emotions at the co-pilot quarters, "Mr Haines, I will take control of the vessel from here. Can you please take Charlena to the resting quarters? Agent Barnes will help me, won't you, Mason."

Agent Barnes agrees to assist Nayla in taking control of the *Decepter*. The strike team onboard the Machiavellian MK2 freighter has experienced a challenging and emotional journey.

As they continue to navigate through the aftermath of the EMP blast, it is clear that their mission has taken a toll on them. However, they remain dedicated to their friends and committed to supporting each other through the difficult moments. The *Decepter* spacecraft cruises towards the powered-down *Excalibur*, and a sense of tension and apprehension fills the air.

The fleet carrier closely follows the robust freighter and breaks off from the remaining resistance frigates and transport ships. Tara Harlow, who stands at the helm of bridge control, is deeply concerned about the safety of her strike team operatives. In her stern voice, she says, "Space Deputy Casey, Agent Merida, please respond! The threat has been contained to this end. Are you two okay?" She repeats, then mutters to herself, "May the galactic heavens prevail."

The navigation flight crew try to alternate the frequency but with no joy. There is a lulling silence on the flight deck as the officers look down on their duties. Tara thinks to herself as she sits down at her command chair and rubs her hands together, noticing that the onboard communications link is in static mode and has an open frequency.

Suddenly, a voice comes through the speakers, "All tinheads frayed to a crisp this end, ma'am! Where would you like your new satellite ship to live? Is it in orbit or parked at the agent base? Cargo rule number one, Miss Harlow! We aim to please. Veena and I are fine. Come pick us up, over and out," says Dan Casey, with his charismatic charm feeding the airwaves.

Tara smiles, grateful for Dan's report and ever-present humour. "I believe your devoted crew is already en route to you. I will get a follow-up squad to clear out the *Excalibur*. Thank you, Space Deputy Casey. I will see you and Agent Merida back on Nova Conti. Who knows, I may demolish Rule 49!" Tara exclaims, breaking into a smile quickly followed by cheers from the fleet carrier's crew.

Tara Harlow can't believe it. They completed their mission and retrieved the new satellite ship. She can't wait to return to base and celebrate with her team. As she looks out into the vast expanse of space, she feels a sense of pride and accomplishment wash over her. She knows more challenges will come but is confident that her team is up to the task.

Chapter Twenty-Two

A Dinner for Seven

The environment surrounding Nova Conti exhibits a noticeable absence of activity, characterised by an almost palpable calmness in the aftermath of the conflict with Mbron Media. This stillness is marked by an atmosphere of unease, as though there remains a lingering sense of unrest in the air. The resistance's deft frigates and Mach C90 starfighters diligently patrol the orbit, demonstrating their unwavering commitment to safeguarding their home world from potential threats. Although it is now apparent that certain members of the Corporal Union are aware of the planet's location, the lack of concrete evidence means that even the lead figure, Director Wilson Volantis, cannot secure the authorisation of the committee board to deploy their armada.

These events provide the Nova Conti's Agent Force with a window of opportunity to bolster the global shield defence system. As evening falls and the skies grow increasingly overcast with an approaching storm on the horizon, the festivities in the capital city of Nova Conti continue to thrive as crowds gather to partake in the vibrant nightlife.

Despite the rainy weather, the city of Mantis remains lively. The angled skyscraper buildings are a picture of modern architecture in the evening sky. The bustling city centre is filled with taxi hover pods and sleek private cars heading towards the buzzing nightclub scene for which Mantis is known. Tara

Harlow, the agent organisation's leader, has arranged to reserve the high-end restaurant and dance venue known as the Calypso Bar to commemorate the successful acquisition of Nova Conti from Mbron Media.

As the cargo runner pilot Dan Casey and the private gunslinger for hire, Jay Haines, arrive in a taxi-pod for the night's festivities, Tara stands at the establishment's entrance. She is attired in an elegant navy suit with matching trousers and a white blouse, her hair expertly styled in a neat bun.

Greeting the men with a smile, she says, "The two heroes of the moment." She then quickly adds, "Hurry, it's about to rain, but rest assured that the taxi fare is on the house."

Her tone is relaxed and informal, contrasting with her usual seriousness as the person in charge of Nova Conti.

With a charming smile, Dan Casey approaches the entrance and kisses Tara on the cheek, "Evening Tara, you look gorgeous, sweetheart!"

Tara Harlow takes the compliment and replies, "Thank you, Mr Casey. I must say you look very dashing yourself."

The cargo runner looks smart in a white shirt and a stylish-cut black dinner jacket. A few steps behind him is Jay Haines, dressed in a dinner jacket and open shirt, with his jewellery and beads adorning his neck.

Following Tara's lead as the host, Jay kisses the supreme leader on the hand, "I shall escort you to our table and arrange the drinks."

Tara says, leading the way to the Calypso Bar lobby, "The ladies will join us shortly, though I am unsure of Mason's whereabouts."

The dance music in the Calypso Bar is set at an elegant, chilled level of ambience, providing a high-class atmosphere as the civilians mingle and talk fills the air.

Walking alongside the sophisticated lady, the handsomely charmed Dan Casey enquires with humble modesty, "Hey, thanks, but I hope you're not putting this on just for us, Tara. I'm sure anyone would have done what we achieved." The cargo pilot flashes a dashing smile as the Calypso Bar hostess brings them a stemmed, crystal diamond glass full of Perrier-Du-Castro champagne.

Dan readily takes the drink, offering a cute smile to the waitress, who giggles as she walks off on her duties, offering Jay Haines his drink.

Tara takes a sip of her Perrier-Du-Castro champagne before commending Dan's modesty. She states that everyone involved in the Battle for Nova Conti deserves recognition for their bravery and to honour those who are lost. She reminds Dan that she had not asked him to fight, but he had taken it upon himself to help and had even saved her life back on the *Aurora*. Tara then raises her glass in a toast, urging Dan to stand and accept his deserved praise.

Jay Haines chimes in with his deep voice and charming smile, saying, "I'm always up for a hero's welcome, ma'am! Don't mind the space pilot. He's just a shy dude!"

Tara turns her attention to Jay, mentioning, "I have heard on the grapevine that I owe you a breakfast. I apologise for my lack of commitment on the all-hours cantina front, but I'm confident this dinner will make up for it."

Once seated around a beautiful glass dinner table, dressed for a formal occasion, the three individuals adjust to the ambience of the evening. Dan Casey speaks up with a sense of caution towards the leader in charge, not wanting to spoil the mood. He warns, "You do know that the Corporal Union won't give up now that they know Nova Conti's location."

"I do share your apprehensions regarding Director Wilson Volantis, who is likely scheming against us at this very moment. That's why we need to be well-prepared for any further attacks. Our team is working on the global defence shield, but it will take a few weeks to activate. Additionally, I have a proposal for both of you, that is, if you're available to offer the same service you provided on the *Excalibur*."

The supreme leader's remark is accompanied by a sly smile, which catches the attention of Dan, who looks over to Jay with a perplexed expression, wondering what she means.

Tara looks at the interstellar pilot intently, "I've inspected both of your galactic records. You weren't always a cargo runner, Dan. And Mr Haines, your adaptable persuasion can be useful in Mantis. We are a peaceful organisation, but we still have rowdy civilians. I am tasked with organising a space protection squad funded by the agency. That's if you're interested in the position."

The offer surprises Dan Casey, and he asks, "You want me to run it?"

Jay, the dreadlocked gunman, chimes in, "Well, I'm in, man, if you need a sharpshooter at your side."

Tara prods a little more, "So what do you say, Mr Casey? Do you fancy working for me?"

Dan smiles and responds with a gulp of his champagne, "Only if I get to pick my crew, and I want Veena onboard with no Rule 49!"

Tara smiles back and replies, "I will assign Agent Merida under your care. Don't you dare break her heart! I've seen how she looks at you. Do we have an agreement, gentlemen?" asks Tara as she sips more of her Perrier-Du-Castro champagne.

Dan Casey sits in contemplation, reflecting on his options before responding to the offer with a severe tone, "I had been considering venturing to the outer rims to seek a delivery contract and maintain a low profile. However, with Henderson running Mbron Media and Director Wilson Volantis denouncing me as a galactic dissident, I accept, Miss Harlow. Nevertheless, we must first discuss the rules of freelancing."

The supreme leader replies with a delighted shine to her demeanour, "Thank you for considering my offer, Mr Casey.

I am delighted to hear that you have accepted it. Before we proceed, let us discuss these rules of freelancing to ensure that we are both on the same page. What are some of the rules you have in mind?" she asks with a curious frame of mind as the waitress returns and lays out a food menu.

The cargo runner is about to lay down his terms when Dan's voice suddenly trails off. His dark brown eyes fall upon Veena Merida, who has just entered the room. Her white and jade outfit is stunning, with silk arm gloves and a jewelled neck choker. Her green hair is styled in loose waves, adding a touch of glamour.

Veena's smile is as radiant, and she gives a small wave as she enters. Charlena Jones is with her, looking just as lovely in a pink, shoulder-less silk dress and sparkling shoes. Her red-bobbed hair is perfectly styled, and she has applied just the right amount of make-up to enhance her sweet features.

Dan Casey politely rises, moving his table chair back a notch as he stands. "Pardon me, ma'am, it appears as though the ladies have arrived," he says, seemingly entranced by their presence.

Jay Haines also takes notice of their beauty, exclaiming, "Damn, the girls look stunning, man!"

Tara Harlow smiles and declares, "We can defer our operational plans until tomorrow. For now, let us enjoy ourselves."

As the supreme leader, she appears eager to ensure everyone has a good time. Dan and Jay deftly navigate through the crowded party guests, approaching the Calypso Bar lobby entrance to greet their female companions.

The charming pilot says, tenderly kissing her outstretched hand, "You look stunning, Miss Merida. I will be honoured to take you to dinner."

Veena smiles, revealing her pearly whites, and responds with playful flirtation. "Thank you, Mr Casey. You clean up quite nicely for an oily cargo runner."

Dan turns to Charlena Jones. "My goodness, Miss Jones, you look like a sparkling diamond. You'll need Jay here to fend off all your exquisite admirers."

Charlena blushes and returns the compliment, "Thank you so kindly, Dan. You're pretty easy on the eyes yourself."

Jay Haines readily hooks up his muscular arm with Charlena Jones and says, "Now, let's have that promised dinner and enjoy the party."

Walking towards their table, Charlena gently pulls Jay's sleeve and says, "Hey, let's wait for Foxy-D and Nayla 1.9.4. They are in the taxi-pod behind us." The kind-hearted teenager is eager to wait for her cyber friends.

Dan and Veena stop as Foxy-D arrives with Nayla 1.9.4, elegantly dressed in a long, two-toned pink and white ball gown. Nayla's pink hair is perfectly coiffed, and she proudly waves at her friends while showcasing her new cybernetic arm.

Their arrival is heralded by a series of beeps and flashing lights from the modified cube-bot, which draws Dan and Veena's attention.

With a hint of amusement, Jay remarks, "Foxy-D seems quite excited, but are robots with a mischievous streak allowed in here?"

The cube-bot zooms around the group, prompting Jay to add, "Don't hover over my shoulders, and please don't steal my food. I'm starving!"

Foxy-D responds with a colourful flash of lights and beeps.

Charlena says, "Awe, he sees you as his shooting buddy. I can't leave him at the agent base. He starts sulking."

Dan compliments Nayla 1.9.4, "You look stunning tonight."

Veena adds, "The dress suits you so well. I'm glad they fixed your arm."

Nayla 1.9.4 smiles and acknowledges her friends. "I wanted to dress like a sweetheart," she says to Mr Casey. "Thank you, Veena. If the supreme leader permits, I would love to go shopping with you."

Veena smiles and replies, "I'm sure Dan will put in a good word for you, Nayla. I think Tara likes him."

Dan smirks and teases, "More than you think, Miss Merida."

The group chuckles, and Jay suggests, "We can discuss that later. For now, let's eat."

The amused group heads to the dinner table, full of smiles and laughter.

Tara welcomes her guests, "A host of my favourite people and cyberbots. Please take your seat and choose your food. The waitresses are here to serve your needs."

However, she can't help but notice that one of her operatives is missing. "Has anyone seen or heard from Mason? I'm starting to believe he's stood us up?"

Nayla 1.9.4 speaks up when she starts worrying and informs the supreme leader, "I did see Mason before I got ready. He's running behind schedule, but will arrive shortly."

Tara is relieved to hear this and doesn't want to delay further proceedings. She urges her guests to enjoy themselves, "Oh right, well, let's not proceed because of one, and I'm sure Mr Haines is eager to taste the excellent food served here."

Overall, Tara Harlow seems a gracious hostess, ensuring her deserving guests are well taken care of and comfortable. The flirtatious conversation between Dan Casey and Veena Merida occurs during dinner, with playful banter between the two.

Dan continues the conversation, saying, "I will be checking the steak out and see if the chef's up to my standards."

Veena responds while drinking her Perrier-Du-Castro champagne, "Show off!"

Dan flirtatiously responds, "You go steady on the fizzy wine. You know what happened on the *Decepter*, falling into my arms, when on undercover duty."

Veena says, "Oh gosh! Are you calling me a woozy agent

again? I'll have to check with Tara to see if there's a rule against such slander."

She laughs, feeling more at ease since they had first met.

Tara Harlow overhears parts of the conversation over the noise of the other guests and enquires with a bewildered expression, "Veena, how did you come to acquire Mr Casey's services? The last report I have from you is that you were heading to the moon called Latin-Versa, and then we lost contact. And what happened on the starship? Woozy agent?"

Dan laughs and says, "Well, Miss Merida picked me out because she was stunned by my looks. Nothing to do with being hijacked in an alley."

Veena looks away, embarrassed, before giggling.

Tara rolls her eyes, referring to the fact that Veena's approach was not standard agent protocol. Veena defends herself with amusement. "I'm trained to improvise, ma'am. And Dan's hyping it a bit."

She laughs, drinking more Perrier-Du-Castro champagne while Dan and Tara smile on the other half of the glass dinner table.

Jay Haines orders his steak with an extra side salad, and Charlena Jones gulps champagne, resulting in a head rush.

She jokingly says. "Foxy-D, make sure I get home. We don't want another prom night fiasco!"

The buzzy cube-bot responds with bleeps and flashes, enjoying the outing.

Nayla 1.9.4, the pink-coiffed android, asks with a puzzled expression on her cybernetic features, "What's prom night?"

Before Charlena can respond, Jay interjects, "It's when all the teenage kids get drunk and make fools of themselves."

Charlena playfully says, "Well, guess we know what happened to you on your prom night, big guy!"

Jay laughs. "Yeah, you got me there, kid!"

The gunslinger swigs back his alcoholic beverage, looking for the Calypso Bar waitress to order another round of champagne.

Upon placing their order, the aroma of the delicious food soon wafts over to the heroic table, eliciting smiles all around, particularly from Jay Haines.

The group commences their meal with an amicable ambience permeating the air.

Veena Merida takes notice of this, remarking, "It is heartening to see everyone in high spirits and devoid of any hazards. I wish this could be the normal."

"I am not entirely satisfied with Mason's decision to disregard the party. This occasion was organised for him as well. Furthermore, he must account for his hot-headed behaviour when he clandestinely boarded the *Decepter* against my explicit instructions."

The supreme leader voices her sentiments with a slight sigh.

Dan Casey apprises the agent leader of Agent Barne's demeanour while aboard the *Excalibur*, "I suspect that Mason is attempting to prove his worth after being outsmarted and outmatched by Duran and Terri. They likely succeeded in absconding with the ruins of the Crystal Serpent Altar despite your reservations about its potency. I've personally witnessed Amelia Delas."

"So did I," confirmed Veena, "Even though you will edit my report. Wilson Volantis is misguided and will resort to any means necessary to acquire the Black Vortex," she declares, her tone conveying gravity. However, Veena is beginning to feel lightheaded.

Tara Harlow explains her reasons for adjusting Veena's mission report, "I have to file it as a visual weapon you experienced, as the board and shareholders won't believe that a ghost from the past can threaten galactic security. I've got the data box safely locked away in the vault. I'm the only person with clearance. It should be quite safe. I always take precautions. So, I've established a space protection unit that can work as my right hand beyond the law."

Veena portrays a bewildered look, along with a tipsy smile.

Dan Casey eases her curiosity, "What is the boss trying to say? Hands up if you want to join my space protection squad."

Veena Merida expresses her interest in joining the crew by playfully raising her hand. "Can I join your crew, Captain Casey?"

Dan responds with a teasing smirk and says, "You're on the team; Rule 59 is also in effect. I'll advise you later on the details."

Charlena Jones, the young student, says with a slur in her voice, "I want to join and train to be an agent so that I can save my friends from the crime lord kingpin, Mach Galanti."

Dan approves her request and says in his charming voice, "You're both in. You'll be my wingman."

Tara Harlow then offers to train the young teenager to be a full agent.

Charlena excitedly replies, "Thanks, ma'am. I won't let you down, promise! Oh, boy! We're going to be agents, Foxy-D!"

Jay Haines laughs at Charlena's enthusiasm, while the rewired, Nayla 1.9.4. also expresses her interest in joining the team. In her cute cyber voice, she asks, "I'd like to be a member of your space protection squad, Mr Casey. If that's okay with you, ma'am."

They raise a champagne toast to their new adventure. During their celebration, Tara notices Mason Barnes arriving at the entrance of the Calypso Bar dressed in a sophisticated black suit with a matching shirt and tie, "I apologise for my delay, ma'am. I had to attend to some personal matters. I hope I did not miss the meal?" The dark-toned agent asks, his demeanour eager and attentive.

Tara Harlow smiles and informs him, "Your dinner has been reserved, Mason, but we will need to have a conversation later." The supreme leader's tone hints at frustration.

Agent Barnes responds with a brief pause and a polite

demeanour, "Not to worry, madam. May I know where I can find the champagne?"

The female cyber agent asks, "How is your friend Ran Palmer? He called again, and I connected him to your holo-pad."

Mason replies with a deep smile, "Thank you, 1.9.4. I just spoke with him. I plan to visit Kothariya to catch up with him. Let's keep this between us, okay? Tara will be preoccupied with all the new faces around. She won't know I'm gone."

Nayla responds, her cybernetic face exhibiting a slight frown, "Mason! You are breaking protocol again. It's not worth the disciplinary. Talk to the supreme leader. Her bark is worse than her bite."

"It seems like protocol is thrown out the window, 1.9.4," says Agent Barnes, taking a sip of his Perrier-Du-Castro drink.

As the night progresses, the tempo of the ambient music escalates to a livelier beat. The dance floor gradually fills with individuals, including Veena and Charlena, enthusiastically swaying their bodies to the thumping bass. Nayla 1.9.4, the cyberbot, also partakes in the festivity and enjoys dancing with the girls, experiencing this novel concept. Simultaneously, Foxy-D spins to the vibe around them.

In contrast, Dan Casey and Jay Haines relax in the private area of the Calypso Bar. The cargo runner pilot has procured his preferred Kestrel-dew beverage and enquires from the gunslinger, "Aren't you planning to join the women on the dance floor?"

Jay responds with amusement, "I only put my styled feet on the floor when the stakes are high, my friend! Leave the graceful dancing to women. My skills would only outshine them."

After concluding their private discussion, the supreme leader and Agent Barnes walk through the dancing partygoers towards the bar area.

Mason extends his hand towards the cargo pilot and

the gunslinger, congratulating them on their new positions, "Congratulations, Mr Casey. I do not doubt that you will perform admirably, being a civilian."

Dan humbly accepts the gesture and replies, "Thank you for your assistance on the *Excalibur*. If you're interested, I can place you in my squad."

Mason reciprocates with a smile and says, "I'm sure you won't require my assistance, but I'm more than happy to lend a hand if needed. I'll retire early for the night. Enjoy your evening, gentlemen."

Agent Barnes exits the Calypsos Bar, leaving the group to continue their festivities.

"Tara, you seem to be without a drink. Allow me to get you another glass of champagne," says the charming pilot.

Tara Harlow accepts his offer and playfully teases him, "Are you trying to make me a woozy leader, Mr Casey?"

Dan jokes, "Never dream of it, sweetheart." He then reaches into his jacket pocket and retrieves a smoke filter.

"You'll have to go out on the balcony for that bad habit," Tara says with a maternal expression.

Dan Casey casually strolls through the buzzing crowds and goes up the winding stairs to the balcony. He gazes at the stormy night skies, intending to spark a green-dust smoke with his Astro-lighter.

However, just as he is about to light up, he senses a presence behind him. Turning around, he sees Veena Merida admiring him with a mischievous grin.

Dan greets Veena with a charming smile as he stores his smoke filter for later use. "Are you here to surprise and hijack me again?" He playfully asks, reminiscing about their initial encounter on the dusty trade moon of Latin-Versa.

"No, not this time. I simply admire you and am pleased you accepted Tara's offer."

As she approaches him, Dan wraps his muscular arms

around her and enquires, "Were you aware that Miss Harlow is planning to establish a space protection team?"

Veena, snuggling in close to him, replies, "I had no clue that Tara had contracted you. I have been a remote agent for the past two years and am acquainted with the supreme leader, just as you are. However, I did have a contract in mind, as I was concerned that you might venture off into the depths of space."

Dan Casey chuckles, "So, you also have a contract offer for me? I have never received so many employment opportunities. I don't see any cargo on you, or even a pistol, for that matter. I wonder what this contract entails?"

Veena seductively smiles, her red glossy lips puckering up for a kiss, and she replies, "To take care of your new sweetheart."

Dan Casey gently caresses her face and whispers, "Thank you for this mystical adventure, Veena. It was not part of my plan, but sometimes events occur for a reason. Since my friend Von Rye's death, I hadn't many reasons to be happy, so I have kept my distance from commitment. Pearl and I have provided delivery services and allowed the galaxy to spin in its orbit. However, since meeting you, those feelings of sadness have been replaced. I think what I am trying to say is that I have fallen in love with you."

Before Dan can finish his sentence, Veena's face lights up with a grateful glow, and she interrupts him, saying, "I understand. I feel the same way. I love you."

Dan and Veena share a long, passionate kiss on the balcony as the moonlight illuminates the misty night. Their chance encounter has led to a journey of pure love after an adventurous voyage into the vast unknown.

While love and harmony fill the balcony of the Calypso Bar, the same cannot be said for the rest of the Kalanisi Galaxy.

The weather is calm in Kothariya, the human capital, but its galactic citizens are shrouded in fear. The constant rise in galactic taxes is making daily life hard, and there are home eviction threats by the Corporal Union security forces for all who fail to meet financial requirements. It is a terrifying time.

Meanwhile, deep in the chambers of the Corporal Union's headquarters, Director Wilson Volantis is displeased with the outcome of his failure to acquire the astrological data box, which would have allowed him to locate the ominous black hole. The ageing male figure stands resolute before his holographic communication screen, reviewing the latest reports from Space Marshall Viper.

The Director dons his black hooded cloak and rubs his hands together. His wrinkled face and grey hair glisten in the chamber room's light.

He speaks in a cold, vague tone, "Viper, I hope that you have more promising news than what I have been receiving from other quadrants of the galaxy. We cannot afford to let our goals slip away from our grasp, especially with the Sulamani project so close to completion." Wilson Volantis paces around the marble floor of his office as he speaks.

Space Marshall Viper responds through the holographic transmitter, "Our salvage operation on the Dread Moon for the advanced flight technology from the *Galileo* BX10 battlecruiser has yielded excellent results. The moon's crash site has been altered, and there is no record of the Corporal Union's presence in the Sera system. Further reports indicate that Commander Calo Tarick's body may have been discovered. There are no life signs, and DNA testing is required to confirm his identity, sir."

Wilson Volantis provides commentary on the recent report submitted by the space marshal with an annoyed demeanour. He demands, "I want you to be on board the Sulamani's maiden flight. I need a trustworthy operative such as yourself, Viper, to follow my commands. As for Calo Tarick's body, transfer his remains to the medical division, with the order to do whatever it takes to revive my loyal servant of arms."

"Thank you, Director Volantis, for the position aboard your

flagship. You have no fears from me, sir. I will ensure your orders are carried out to the point of no failure."

"Make sure you don't fail to live up to the promise of your word, Viper. I don't accept failure very well without consequences," says Wilson with a cunning glance in his dark, cold, soulless eyes before cutting off the holographic transmission and attending to another incoming call on his glass-curved desk.

Wilson makes his way over to the communications device, his black cloak trailing behind him as he sits at his glass desk. A figure appears on the monitor mounted on the marble walls of his office chamber. "Henderson! I see today's news is not in our favour. Any particular reason why Mbron Media's pirate fleet failed to obscure Tara Harlow's little resistance world?" Director Volantis enquires in a displeased tone.

The screen crackles with interference as Henderson responds, "I apologise, Director Volantis. We encountered unexpected resistance from the rebel forces, and our fleet was not adequately prepared for their tactics."

Director Volantis narrows his dark eyes, "This is unacceptable, Henderson. You and your androids will need to take full responsibility for this failure. We cannot afford to let our enemies gain any ground. I expect a full report on your shortcomings and a plan of action to rectify the situation immediately."

Henderson nods, "Understood, Director. We will do everything possible to ensure this does not happen again."

Director Volantis replies, "See that you do. I expect nothing less than complete success from you, Henderson."

The Core Lord replies in his defence, "You never said anything about Dan Casey teaming up with the resistance organisation. That man's an annoying pain. He chased me across the galaxy when he was a member of a space squad five years ago. He's going to be trouble."

Henderson, also known as the Core Lord, sits in his command booth surrounded by numerous news screens and information about the Kalanisi Galaxy. He is a unique cybernetic android with a rare core chip embedded in his system. His appearance is a combination of human and cybernetic machine, with his chubby face and body being overweight due to a lavish lifestyle funded by others.

Despite his physical appearance, Henderson is a mastermind strategist who can analyse complex situations and develop effective plans. However, his recent plan has failed, and he is now reviewing and analysing what went wrong.

The Director rises from his glass-curved desk, his anger palpable as he hurls his holo disc and files onto the marbled floor in frustration, "You mean to tell me that an entire android media association cannot handle a single cargo runner pilot?"

Wilson seethes. He then reminds Henderson of the latter's indebtedness to him and the ease with which he can dismantle Henderson, thanks to the fail-safe device installed in the Core Lord for perpetuation purposes. Henderson's face contorts with anger.

The cyber villain responds with a firm tone and a quivering chin, "Trust me, Wilson. I will ensure that Dan Casey will not be able to stroll without being pursued by an android. I will also escalate the Elton and Nayla operations a few notches. Chaos will reign, but only the honest Corporal Union will safeguard the galaxy under the masterful direction of Director Wilson Volantis."

Wilson's face betrays no hint of amusement as he glares at the Core Lord and terminates the transmission. The holo screen flickers to black, and in the ensuing silence, a sudden knock echoes through the spacious chamber.

"Enter," the Director commands, his voice cold and measured. With a flick of his wrist, he adjusts the sequined cloak draped around his shoulders and sinks back into his plush leather and marble chair. The chamber doors creak open, revealing the imposing figure of a smarty-dressed individual.

One of the director's most important guests is at hand. "Welcome, Mr Syvan. Please, do come in. I have been expecting your arrival," Wilson says, his voice oozing with charm and a sly smirk playing across his grey-bearded face as he greets his guest.

At the entrance of the high-class chamber stands a confident male android dressed in an intelligent designer black suit with a matching waistcoat and tie. The figure exudes an air of menace, with his pale blue gaunt face and sharply carved features adding to his sinister appearance. His slick blue hairstyle suggests that he takes great care in his appearance.

This android is a well-known assassin throughout the Kalanisi Galaxy, renowned for his impeccable track record. To date, he has never failed a job or hit a contract, and space rumours have circulated that once Mr Syvan marked your name, there was nowhere to run or hide, only guaranteed execution.

Mr Syvan strides towards the glass desk where the Director is seated, his high-class shoes tapping on the marble floor with every step. As he takes his seat, he leans back in the chair and crosses his legs, exuding an air of confidence and control. "My secretary informs me that there is a job that requires a delicate touch, precisely what I specialise in, Director Volantis," he says in a smooth, husky voice laced with a hint of cocky charm.

Wilson responds to Mr Syvan's professionalism with a polite chuckle, "Excellent, Mr Syvan. Before proceeding with the task, may I offer you some refreshments? We have a selection of Castro Coffee, lemon tea, and some cigars if you wish. We strive to provide only the finest for our esteemed guests."

Syvan, maintaining his direct tone, accepts a cigar and explains his beverage preference. The android responds, "I'll take the cigar, but I only drink boiling black oil. I can see you don't have any at hand. Thanks for the smoke anyway."

He places the cigar in his fibre mouth, flicking his right middle and index fingers to create a burning flame. After taking a drag on the cigar, he blows out the smoke and asks, "So, what are the contract requirements?"

Wilson hands him a handful of holo discs.

Syvan scans with piercing cybernetic eyes. "So, you intend to blow up a black hole, an interesting project, Director. What's inside that is so valuable?"

Speaking enthusiastically, Wilson says, "An angel of light, trapped in a heaven of darkness. I feel it's my duty to free such wonders for all the galaxy to experience."

Syvan replies, "You are a generous man, Director Volantis. My business has never been better since you came into power."

"Please, call me Wilson," he says with a friendly smile. "I believe we will work together to achieve a greater vision for the future."

He pours himself a cup of lemon tea and looks forward to collaborating successfully with Syvan. The slick android continues to browse through the holo discs and enquires with a direct and assertive tone, "You desire the green-haired bitch executed, I presume. What is your stance concerning her associates? Furthermore, I must note that obtaining trinket boxes will require an additional charge."

Syvan then presents his terms of employment clearly and firmly. "Do we have a deal, Wilson?"

"Please kill Agent Veena Merida. She has been the cause of all my setbacks, and it's only fair for her to pay the price. Enjoy your work, Mr Syvan, and feel free to dispose of any who stand your way. The astrological data box is a priceless relic, and the additional cost is no concern. The Corporal Union's purse is deep. We have a deal."

Syvan responds with a handshake while stubbing out his cigar, "Consider Agent Merida dead. I will prepare my starship, the *Vector*. And await your good word. It's been a pleasure, Wilson."

As the meeting between Wilson and Syvan comes to a close, the Director rises and gestures to the assassin to follow him out of the private chamber room. With a quick nod of farewell, Syvan exits the room, leaving the Director alone to his thoughts.

As he closes and locks the arch doors, the Director approaches a secret compartment in the side marble showcase. He presses the touchpad device, causing the passage to slide open with a soft hiss. With a sense of satisfaction, the Director gazes upon the altar of light before him, which has led him to the golden worlds he has transformed into galactic prisons. He can't help but smile as he recalls the broken pieces of the Crystal Serpent Alter obtained by Zak Duran and Terri Lace.

Wilson Volantis picks up a jagged piece of the ancient Crystal Serpent Alter. His eyes transcend to a soulless glow as the secret room starts to fill with low-weaving smoke, accompanied by a whispering female voice.

The cloaked Director puts up his hood and glances out of the window into deep space. His mind and thoughts travel to another dimension, and he speaks in a deep voice, not like his everyday tone, "It is beautiful, and soon, my ancient queen, you will be free to serve at my side and rule this Kalanisi Galaxy."

Wilson smirks, witnessing a massive black hole weaving into the hidden depths of space in a spiritual vision.

The noise of the black hole heaves in a droning sensation, with lightning and storms making it a pathway to the unknown. While deep in the centre of the Black Vortex, two red eyes appear, and a voice whispers, "Amelia." This is followed by cackling evil laughter. "Haha."

This book is printed on paper from sustainable sources managed under the Forest Stewardship Council (FSC) scheme.

It has been printed in the UK to reduce transportation miles and their impact upon the environment.

For every new title that Troubador publishes, we plant a tree to offset CO_2, partnering with the More Trees scheme.

For more about how Troubador offsets its environmental impact, see www.troubador.co.uk/sustainability-and-community